M.C. Scott was a veterinary surgeon and taught at the universities of Cambridge and Dublin before taking up writing as a full-time profession. Now founder and chair of the Historical Writers' Association, her novels have been shortlisted for the Orange Prize, nominated for an Edgar Award and translated into over twenty languages.

For more information on all aspects of the books, visit: www.mcscott.co.uk

For the Historical Writers' Association, see: www.theHWA.co.uk

ROME

THE EMPEROR'S SPY

M.C. Scott

CORGI BOOKS

TRANSWORLD PUBLISHERS
61–63 Uxbridge Road, London W5 5SA
A Random House Group Company
www.transworldbooks.co.uk

ROME: THE EMPEROR'S SPY
A CORGI BOOK: 9780552168007

First published in Great Britain
in 2010 by Bantam Press
an imprint of Transworld Publishers
Bantam edition published 2011
Corgi edition reissued 2012

Addresses for Random House Group Ltd companies outside the UK
can be found at: www.randomhouse.co.uk
The Random House Group Ltd Reg. No. 954009

The Random House Group Limited supports The Forest Stewardship
Council (FSC®), the leading international forest certification organization.
Our books carrying the FSC label are printed on FSC®-certified paper. FSC
is the only forest-certification scheme endorsed by the leading environmental
organizations, including Greenpeace. Our paper-procurement policy
can be found at www.randomhouse.co.uk/environment.

Typeset in 11/13pt Sabon by
Kestrel Data, Exeter, Devon.
Printed in the UK by
CPI Group (UK) Ltd, Croydon, CR0 4YY.

2 4 6 8 10 9 7 5 3 1

For Hannah, Bethany and Naomi, with love

ACKNOWLEDGEMENTS

Thanks, as ever, to the entire team at Transworld, particularly Bill Scott-Kerr for inspired support and for saying in meetings those things an author most wants to hear; to the editorial team, notably Deborah and Nancy; to Gavin for IT; to Patsy for stepping once more into the breach; and especially to my editor Selina Walker, for the skill, sensitivity and unswerving dedication with which she takes the raw ore of a first draft and hones it to the book I was trying to write.

Thanks also to my agent, Jane Judd, for calm, considered unconditional support, always; and to my partner, Faith, for being all that she is and for being there. And last, thanks to Inca, who died as this novel was being put to bed: none of this would have happened without her.

CONTENTS

The Roman Empire in the reign of Nero

Sarmatia

nnonia

Tyras

Oblia

BOSPORUN KINGDOM

Moesia Superior

Moesia Inferior

Pontus Euxinus

atia

Illyricum

Thracia

Bithynia

Pontus

Macedonia

Armenia

Epirus

ASIA

Cappadocia

Galacia

PARTHIAN EMPIRE

Achaea

Lycia

Cilicia

Creta

Cyprus

SYRIA

Assyria

Mesopotamia

Mare Interum

JUDAEA

Alexandria

Cyrenaica

Arabia Petraea

Arabia Magna

Aegyptus

The fact is, that the close of this fourth millennium coincides with a Phoenix Year. As you know, the residue of hours of the solar year that exceed three hundred and sixty-five days add up every 1460 years to an entire year, which in Egypt is called the Phoenix Year . . . for then the Celestial Bird is consumed upon his palm-tree pure at On-Heliopolis and from his ashes rises the new Phoenix.

Robert Graves, *King Jesus*

When the matricide reigns in Rome,
Then ends the race of Aeneas.

Sibylline prophecy current in the reign of Nero

PROLOGUE

Jerusalem in the Reign of the Emperor Tiberius

Sebastos Abdes Pantera was twelve years old and nearly a man on the night he discovered that his father was a traitor.

It was spring, the bright time of flowers, and Passover, the time of celebration, sacrifice and riots. Every year, teams of priests worked without cease from sunrise to sunset, cutting the throats of countless thousands of lambs in the temple.

Every year, the multitudes of the faithful gathered to eat those lambs in memory of the angel of death who passed over their houses, striking down the firstborn of Egypt.

Every year, the Roman prefect cancelled all leave amongst his legions and set guards about the hot, dry city, packed to capacity with the hot, dry pride of a conquered people.

Through the nights of unleavened bread, conquerors and conquered waited alike for a spark bright enough to light the ultimate, uncontainable riot that would see the legions let loose and the streets run rivers of blood. It had not happened yet.

In a private garden beyond the city gates, the sounds

15

of celebration were the muffled roar of a storm not yet broken. The air was heavy with the scent of almond blossom, lilies, crushed camphire and blood. A hot wind rent the trees, raining petals to the earth. It did not move the sullen clouds that marred the sky.

Crouching alone in the dark beneath the nut trees, Sebastos heard the approach and retreat of a watch-guard's feet. He shut out all other noises, and made himself listen only to the soft clash of leather and metal on the path.

Before the second circuit, he knew that the nails of the guard's right sandal had worn thin on the inside heel, and knew thereby that it was his father, best of all men, who strode alone in the leaden dark.

Julius Tiberius Abdes Pantera, decurion of the first wing of the first company of archers stationed in Judaea under the direct command of the prefect, may have got his son as a bastard on a Gaulish slave-woman, but none the less, Sebastos knew himself to be the child of a true soldier.

Since the day he could first walk, his father had taught him the secrets of the archer's craft and had instilled with it, as the food and drink of his son's young life, the twin bedrocks by which a soldier measured his own worth.

First of these was his absolute loyalty to his commander: a true legionary obeyed every order immediately and without question. Second, stemming from the first, was the unblemished virtue of his own honour which required that he always bring respect and dignity to his position.

Honour was everything. Sebastos lived to seem honourable in his father's eyes and by now he knew how to do that. As he had been taught, he made himself explore his surroundings with his fingertips, discovering by touch the nature and size of any obstacles that might hinder or help his progress. In doing so, he kept his mind well away from the terrifying cloud above his head. All night, it had smothered the moon and stars and seemed likely at any moment to fall and smother him.

16

He had mentioned the cloud to his father in the after-noon, before the summons came to guard the tomb. In day's safe light, his father had ruffled his hair and laughed and said that only a true Gaul feared the sky would fall on his head.

There had been a tremor in his voice and Sebastos had hoped that it grew from pride that the only son of an Alexandrian archer should take so truly after the bar-barian tribes of his mother's people, rather than from shame for that same thing.

Later, lying alone in the dark, yearning for the cloud to leave, Sebastos had realized that it had nothing to do with pride, and everything to do with grief – that his father still mourned his mother and Sebastos hadn't thought to comfort him.

What kind of boy forgets the source of his father's pain? Shame at his own stupidity had goaded him from his bed and up the hill, skirting the walls of the city to reach the gated garden on the slope with its many scented flowers and the trail of blood leading up to the tomb. Here, where his father marched alone, he had a chance to undo his mistake.

A thistle grew sharp behind Sebastos' left foot. An ageing pomegranate guarded his right shoulder. To his left, a bed of kitchen herbs spiced the hot air. Beyond that, the path curved snake-like up the hill. Clouds loomed over, threateningly full.

His father reached the first row of almonds. The sound of his tread paused a moment, before beginning the march back up the slope. The watch-fire's red glow caught him as he turned, casting his outline in proud silhouette.

Sebastos grinned. A fierce joy lifted the threat of the falling sky. Swift as the great spotted cat for which he was named, he slid out from under the almonds and ran through the dark towards his father.

'Pantera?'

Sebastos cannoned to a halt, balanced on one foot. The call came from his left, down the path, less than a bow's shot away. The voice was a woman's, like his mother's, but lacking her Gaulish accent.

Sebastos' left hand found a wall of cool rock to lean on. He stood in the darkest of the dark and held his breath. His father, too, had stopped, but – unaccountably – did not challenge the incomer. Instead, he raised his fingers to his lips and gave a short, low whistle.

No answering call came back. Instead, from lower down the path, a whispering flame danced closer, and stronger, until it lit the woman and two men who brought it.

'Julius. Thank you.'

The woman who stepped forward was his mother's age, but under the kind blaze of the torch her face was smooth, her cheeks were clear, and her eyes were bright. Sebastos thought she had been weeping, and was close to it again.

His father was not weeping. His face had softened in a way the boy had not seen in six months.

'Mariamne.'

Stepping into the puddle of light, Pantera spoke the tenderest, dearest form of the name, which a man might use only for his wife, or his daughter, or his sister. He raised a hand as if to touch the woman's face and then dropped it again, his eyes wide with unspoken care.

The man holding the torch moved forward. Its light spilled out beyond the confines of the woman's face and Sebastos saw that she was pregnant. The signs were not obvious yet; she was no more than three months gone. Only a boy trained from infancy to study every detail of those about him would have seen it.

His father knew, that much was clear. He had stepped back, making a sign that she should precede him up the path.

She hesitated, as if afraid to move on. 'Is he still alive?' Her voice was rich and light as a temple chime. The torch set the almond blossom dancing. Moths cast giant, floating shadows into the night.

His father bowed, as he might have done to his commander in the barracks. 'My lady, he was when we brought him here.'

'You have water and linen?'

'Everything you asked for is here.'

'Lead us, then,' said the woman, and Sebastos pressed himself deeper into the dark and watched as his father abandoned twenty years of obedience to his commander and to Rome, and led a woman of the Hebrews and her two companions up the garden to the tomb he was supposed to be guarding.

Men were crucified for less. A dozen had been, through the long day. The body of one of them lay in a tomb cut into the rock at the garden's end.

In a line, the incomers passed Sebastos, so that he saw them, one after the other. The two men walking behind the woman were as different one from the other as lily from desert thorn. The elder was a grey-haired rabbi, marked by the quality and style of his linen robes. He bore himself with an authority that was undercut by fear. He, at least, knew exactly what he risked.

The younger was hewn from rougher rock. The eagle's crag nose and the long, uncut hair said that he hailed from Galilee, where the rule of Rome did not reach, where men thought themselves more righteous than their neighbours in Judaea, who lived in thrall to an emperor who called himself god.

If his hair showed where this man was born, the style of his tunic and the knotted leather labelled him beyond doubt as a zealot of the Sicarioi, the Hebrew assassins named for the curved razor-knives with which they slew the unbelievers and traitors, serving with a fierce fanaticism the word of their master.

True to his calling, the Sicari had killed once already

19

that night; his curved knife was wet with new blood. He padded past, more silent than any leopard, and of the group, he alone knew no fear. His eyes searched the dark, and the light of their look fell on Sebastos so that they stared at one another face to face, or it seemed so.

Sebastos thought he might die then, pierced by that look, or the knife that must surely follow. He screwed up his courage to meet both with honour, but the restless gaze passed on without pause, as if it were normal to see a boy hiding in the dark on this night in this garden.

The small group was almost out of sight when Sebastos dared to breathe again, and slowly to inch his way up the slope behind them.

His night was changed beyond recognition. He had come because he feared the sky might fall on his head and it had done, so that his soul was crushed and the light snuffed out of his heart. His hope now lay in seeing his father set things to rights, as he had done so often in the past.

'He's alive. We will take him now. We owe you more than thanks.'

The woman stepped from the tomb's dark to the light of the coming dawn. She gave her news to the Sicari zealot, to Sebastos' father, to the garden, to the waking birds, to the world. Exhaustion and relief cracked the liquid bronze of her voice.

For a moment, nobody answered. They stood in the part-time between night and day. The cloud had lifted at last, leaving the final stars to blaze at the rising sun. The watch-fire was a crimson haze in the greys of almost-morning. By its light, the Sicari brought from the depths of his tunic a purse of poor hide, with the stitching frayed away at the seams. Silver spilled from it, easy as rain.

From his cramped, cold place of watching, Sebastos saw his father's head snap round in shock. His hand dropped to his knife.

'Do you think money bought him? Truly?'

His voice promised violence, for the cleansing of an insult. The Sicari looked as if he would happily oblige, but before either man could move the woman stepped forward, saying, 'Shimon, that was not called for,' and the man so named shrugged and stooped to gather his insult and when he rose again with the silver clenched in his fist, the moment for fighting had passed.

The woman ducked back into the tomb and returned moments later with the grey-haired rabbi. Between them, they carried a burden that was passed with infinite care through the low opening in the rock face.

The stench of blood was overpowering. Out of respect for his mother, Sebastos turned his face away. Other men took their sons to see the executions, believing fear was the best teacher and that only thus could they keep the hot blood of young men from frothing into open rebellion against the grinding-heel of Rome. When Sebastos' father had prepared to do the same, his mother had stood in the doorway and forbidden it – the only time in his life Sebastos had seen her truly angry.

She was red-haired and taller than his father and while she might once have been his slave, she was free by then, and could speak her mind. At the height of the vicious row that followed, she spat a single word in a language Sebastos did not understand – a name, perhaps. It crashed through their hut like a living bull, leaving shock and silence in its wake.

White-faced, his father had turned on his heel and gone back to the barracks and not returned for nearly a month.

He had not taken his son to the place of execution then or later, but he had made sure Sebastos knew precisely the death inflicted on men who were caught in insurrection against the rule of Rome, the indignity of it, and the appalling duration that could span as much as three days of increasing, unremitting agony.

'If they like you, they'll break your legs,' he had said. 'Death comes more swiftly, but the pain before is greater.' Worst, obviously, was the loss of honour, so much worse than a death in battle.

At the end, in case his son might not believe such a thing could happen to him, Sebastos' father had filled the rest of that evening by reciting aloud the names of the five hundred young Hebrew men who had each been nailed to a cross on a single day after the fall of Sepphoris to the rebel leader known as the Galilean, and his army of zealots.

Whatever his intention, the father had succeeded in terrifying his son. Every night for the two years since that blood-stained evening, Sebastos had woken in the grey early morning sweating for terror of a threat that was as great as his fear of the falling sky.

But his father had failed in so far as Sebastos had not at any time, then or later, ceased to regard the Galilean as his hero, however many young men he might have led to their deaths.

The Galilean was everyone's hero, even if he was the enemy. His growing band of followers drew young men from all quarters of the divided Judaea, uniting them in hatred of Rome and its rule. Sebastos might have considered himself loyal to the emperor, might have held in his heart the dream of Roman citizenship as the ultimate prize, but that did not stop him from idolizing a man who, by force of character, courage and arms, had stayed one step ahead of the legions for nearly four decades.

At a time when the Sadducee high priests kept themselves fat on the prefect's leavings and counselled the proper paying of taxes, the Galilean and his hand-picked groups of Sicari zealots stole the taxes from the Herodian collectors and sent them back whence they came. Like every boy he knew, Sebastos burned to be a hero one day, and the Galilean showed how it could be done, even if he

22

had set his sword against the might of Rome, and was thus destined to failure.

Over the years when mothers used the name to frighten their children into good behaviour, the Galilean had grown in Sebastos' estimation to be a Hercules: courageous, astute and honourable, an indefatigable defender of the poor. Until that morning, when the hero had suffered exactly the death Sebastos' father had so vividly described.

Sebastos was one of the few not to have seen it. As far as he was concerned, he remained under oath to his mother not to view a death by crucifixion unless it were his own, and he did not break his promise to her now, for the Galilean was not dead when the woman and the Pharisee brought him out of the tomb.

That might have been surprising, except that he had not hung for three days as he should have done, but had been cut down on the prefect's orders at the eleventh hour, just before dusk, that his corpse might not profane the Passover Sabbath that began at sunset. In a city so prone to riots, it was a necessary precaution.

Sebastos' father had said aloud at the time that he must have been very sick to have died so quickly, but it was a mercy, and he did not begrudge any man a swift death. That had been a lie to add to betrayal; Sebastos' father had told the woman that he knew the Galilean was alive when they moved him to the tomb.

What kind of man tells lies to his own son?

Cold rage opened Sebastos' eyes as the small cavalcade brought the not-dead man past his hiding place. He saw clearly the bandaged flesh, the ruined skin, the gaunt, un-shaven face and the sunken eyes set deep within it, still clinging to their spark of life.

The Sicari assassin came last of the line, guarding the rear. He did not turn his head, or pause, or give any other sign that he knew they were not alone.

Even so, as he passed Sebastos' hiding place, he stooped

23

to pick up a pebble. Without turning his head, he tossed it high in the air. It bounced precisely on the crown of Sebastos' head.

It took all morning to leave the garden, so slowly did Sebastos move. No man saw him, not even his father, who had trained him to see all things that live, however careful they might be. He was better than his father; he was not sullied by the taint of falsehood and treachery.

Slowness gave him the peace to settle his unsettled heart, and to think. By the time he reached the hut, he had come to a decision. He was twelve years old, and had already made his first kill. He was not as tall as his mother had been; he did not take directly after the great Gaulish warriors who slew Romans in battle with their bare hands, but he was taller than most of his contemporaries, and could pass for a boy at least three years older. He was rich after a fashion; he owned the clothes he stood up in and a new belt he had not yet used, and a worn calfskin pouch that his mother had left him, containing three silver denarii that carried the head of the Emperor Tiberius. He debated taking his bow. There was no doubt that he could steal more food than he could ever shoot, but it mattered that when he presented himself to ask for employment, he should be armed, and so he lifted his bow from its hook, and his hunting knife and his six arrows, three of them fully fletched.

Taking these things – his youth, his height, his training as an almost-archer, and his riches of silver and weapons – he left the house of his treacherous father and set his face to Alexandria where he had once lived.

He had been happy there, but that was not the reason to return. Alexandria was where he had met the pallid Roman philosopher with connections to the emperor.

For two years, the man had come to watch Sebastos often as he practised with his bow, or spun his knife at distant targets. He had seen him fight – and sometimes beat – the other bastard get of soldiers who foraged in the scrap-camp that followed the legions. He had observed Sebastos' solitary nature, his unwillingness to curry favour with those who scorned him, or feared him, or even the few who admired him. Most, the philosopher had seen that his own watching was noticed, and then that he himself was watched in his turn.

It had become an unspoken game between them; the philosopher would go about his business, always watchful, and Sebastos would try covertly to follow him.

Later, when the boy could go a whole day and know all of the philosopher's business and never be spotted once, the man made the game official, and paid him in bronze, or bread, or fletchings, if he could follow a distant man, pointed out in a crowded place, and report on his activities.

Over three more years, the tests had become ever harder, ever more dangerous. Sebastos had excelled at all of them, and grown in his understanding of himself; shadows were his allies, secrecy his life's blood, and the philosopher was a teacher in the truest sense of the word. When his father had been posted to Judaea and the child had been forced to follow, Sebastos found he had lost his first friend without ever having known he had one.

It had been a tearful farewell for both of them. At the last moment of parting, the philosopher had caught Sebastos' chin and tilted his head and promised that if ever a tall, comely boy with skill in knife and bow wanted truly to be a warrior for Rome, he could promise him a wage and a place to live, and perhaps, if he made himself useful, citizenship.

Citizenship: the ultimate prize. Sebastos held the name of his potential sponsor in his heart all the long, dusty journey to Alexandria: Lucius Anaeus Seneca, teacher to a lost mongrel child.

I

Coriallum, Northern Gaul
Late Summer, AD 63

In the Reign of the
Emperor Nero

CHAPTER ONE

The spy made landfall the evening before the chariot races began.

His ship sailed in on a narrow slide of sunlight, splitting the green-grey water from the blue-grey sky. The sails were already unstrung, alive in the snapping breeze. The berthing oars were out. Three pairs swept down either side of the wide beam, making of the *Blue Mackerel* a beetle, stalking into dock. A string of seagulls swayed over her wake.

She could have been any one of the sleek merchant sloops that flitted back and forth across the narrow stretch of sea from Britain to the small, crowded harbour at Coriallum on the northern coast of Gaul, but for the discreet purple pennant flying from the foremast that said she sailed on the emperor's business.

At any other time, that might have been a lie contrived to increase the fares charged for passage, but not when Nero had honoured Coriallum with his presence for the chariot races, and was in temporary residence in the magistrate's villa at the top of the hill.

As ever, the harbour was heaving with men, women, children, dogs and gulls, all watching the *Mackerel* come in. The furled dockside stench of old fish, fresh dog shit, rotting vegetables and seaweed was buried beneath the sweat of a hundred busy bodies.

Stevedores and fishermen leaned in pairs on bollards, picking their teeth, discussing the swell of the sea and the sharp iron taste of the air. Women balanced on either hip baskets of bread and dried figs and dried seaweed that blended their scents with the richer, rounder scent of the fresh wrack that hung from pillars beneath the pier. Old men coiled ropes and mended nets, bare-headed in the blustering wind. Half-naked children played games of tag, dodging round the legs of their elders.

A grubby urchin fishing from the pier's end watched the adults covertly from the shelter of a wide-brimmed straw hat. As he did every day, he assessed the size and weight of their belt-pouches by sound alone, and then checked to see whether those of interest were armed, and what kinds of looks they threw him there at the pier's end, if they chose to notice him at all. The boy-whores of Coriallum were notorious, but not everyone wished to be seen to be looking.

The boy's name was Math, common enough amongst the Gauls. He paid the *Mackerel* no attention at all until the wake from her arrival slewed the mess of flotsam and jetsam floating up against the pier, upsetting the lie of his line. Then, he cursed, loudly enough to be heard, drew up his cord, set fresh collops of mussel on the half-dozen hooks and dropped it back into the water with a splash.

Tying it off, he leaned sideways against a mooring stone. Tilting his hat against the low afternoon sun, he allowed himself a lazy look at the men who had bought, or been given, passage on the emperor's ship.

The first six ashore were Romans, green-faced and swaying on their sea legs, more bookish than bred to the sea. Ink stains on their fingers and the level cut of their hair gave them away as clerks in the governor's retinue, sent with the endless quartermaster's lists, of weapons, corn, hides, horses, men, hounds and slaves, and most particularly of the taxes with which Roman officialdom was obsessed.

Math felt the quality of their glances as they passed. On any other day, he might have considered making a play, but the clerks smelled of vomit and were clearly too ill to think of anything beyond an unswaying bed. None of them threw him a coin to pay for an 'evening meal'.

To make sure they wouldn't think of it, he squirmed his buttocks on the boards of the pier as if his arse itched, and then scratched urgently at his groin.

Ajax the charioteer had taught him that when they had first talked. *There are men who will take you and not pay, however fast you might be with a knife. But if they think you're infected, they'll not come within an arm's reach.*

Ajax wanted him to be a race-driver, or at least to earn an honest living. The advice on simulating the pox had been given reluctantly, but that didn't mean it wasn't good. When Math turned back to look, the green-faced clerks had gone.

A dozen merchants followed them off the ship. They had better sea legs but carried about them the nervous aura of risk-takers, vivid as a whore's scent. Lining up along the dock, they shouted instructions to the gathering stevedores concerning the immense worth of their goods and the disasters that would befall if anything were damaged in the lifting from boat to dock.

There was a long gap then, filled busily by block-and-tackle work with ropes so that the boy thought no one else was coming ashore and that he had lost his fee.

'Fuck.' He said it quietly, but one of the stevedores heard him and reached to snatch the hat from his head. Beneath it, Math's hair hung to his shoulders in a skein of dirty gold, gone to straw in the damp sea air. Set over a slim neck and a thin, interesting face, it shone brightly enough

31

to lift him from the run of the gutter-thieves who worked the docks.

The stevedore whistled an obscenity and mimed the spin of a coin through the air, then sent the hat to follow. Math spat an insult back and retrieved his hat. A ripple of laughter made the unloading work flow faster for a moment. Cursing colourfully, Math began to coil in his line.

His attention had only been gone from the ship for a moment, but it was enough – almost too much.

The man he had been sent to watch stepped lightly ashore between a bale of stinking, uncombed sheep's fleece and a crate of tin ingots so massive that it took four of the laughing men to lift and haul it, and even then it rebounded off the dock and fractured, spreading shards of almost-silver across the stained oak boards. Two ingots slid noiseless into the sea, too heavy to splash. The merchant whose crate it was screamed as if the stevedores had stabbed him.

The slight, slouch-shouldered figure that was the boy's mark sprang sideways as the crate bounced off the side of the dock for a second time. In his bare feet and rough, undyed tunic, he might have been anything from another clerk to a deckhand released early from the boat.

Math knew he was neither. Leaning back on the bollard, he let his hat droop and droop until he was looking through a gap in the brim. A stranger might have thought him asleep, which would have been foolish, but then grown men commonly made foolish assumptions about Math of the Osismi, most common of which was that he was charming, shy, and naturally honest and had never whored himself before.

The scrawny old Roman who had paid him to watch the harbour had not made any such assumptions, which was the first point in his favour. The second was that he'd offered a whole sestertius to Math as payment if he could watch for and then follow a particular passenger stepping ashore from the *Blue Mackerel*. The fee was more than Math earned in a month in his paid work for Ajax, and far more than he would have dared steal.

So that his quarry might not be missed, the scrawny Roman had given detailed physical characteristics of the man he was expecting to sail into Coriallum on the emperor's ship. *He has dark hair, not so striking as the fire-copper of your mad Gaulish countrymen who race their chariots so recklessly for the amusement of the emperor, nor yet the obsidian black of the Greeks, but somewhere between: a deep oak-brown that does not quite catch the eye.*

The man's hair was not catching anyone's eye; a straggling wood-dark nest that had been combed some time not long ago and then uncombed by the sea wind straight after. It lifted again now, jerkily, as he stepped over the fallen ingots to walk down the dock.

He was not a whole man. The old Roman had said so and it was true. Had he been paraded at the autumn horse fair, Ajax would have passed him over, leaving lesser men to bid good silver for a beast that was not overtly lame, yet not perfectly sound.

Ajax had an eye for such things and Math was learning it. So he saw that the man's right shoulder was lower than it should have been and he favoured his left leg as if the hamstring were overly tight. He saw that his features were sharp, as if he had gone hungry through the winter, and summer had not filled the loss, leaving his cheeks too proud to be beautiful and his pressed lips too tight for love.

But nothing changed the core of what this man was – and that was fascinating. There had been just one stride that was not controlled, one stride as he slapped a flat palm to a bollard and sprang up from the gangplank to the dock that had left Math with sweat prickling his armpits in a way nothing had yet done in all his young life.

His name is Pantera, Sebastos Abdes Pantera. It means leopard. You know what that is? One of the great cats that hunt silently through the forests of the hot southern lands. Your mark is a leopard, and he hunts as one such. You will know him first and last by the way he moves. Even now, when he is wounded, and prone to bouts of untrammelled anger, you will know him thus.

And Math did know him thus; however hard he might try to look and act like a deckhand, Sebastos Abdes Pantera, he of the bland hair and the not-bland face, had made one unconscious spring on to the dock with the fluid motion of an athlete, of a man who knows the fine tuning of his body, and cares for it, and can use it as a weapon in any way he pleases.

Watching him take his leave of the merchant, Math felt the nervous itch in his armpits grow hotter. Flustered, he rose and slipped his fishing line over his shoulder, and took one last look at the direction Pantera was taking. Which was a mistake.

His eyes, should you ever see them, are green-brown, like the shimmer of sun on river water. At first glance, he looks through you – unless he wishes to kill you. Then he looks straight at you.

For the barest fraction of a heartbeat, those river-water eyes looked straight at Math, who looked away, and was left shaking as if he had ague. When he dared to look again, Pantera had gone, threading his way through the heaving crowd, stepping lightly over the dog dirt and the coiled ropes, and evading the running children with an unconscious ease. If he had a purse, it did not show. He brushed shoulders with no one.

Math did not run in pursuit, or even watch his quarry closely. The harbour was wide open, from the pier's end to the first row of merchant booths, taverns and brothels a hundred paces in from the sea. There were not many places to go and Math knew the quickest routes to all of

34

them. First, it mattered that no one on the pier should know whom he followed, or why.

Hefting his fishing line, Math turned and looked thoughtfully out at the sliver of sun that was left, at the long, narrow stretch of it on the sea. He wrapped his arms around his thin tunic against the rising wind that was already creaming the wavetops. He shivered and made a show of staring at the incoming clouds and then shrugged to himself and spat into the stinking seaweed below the harbour and picked at the hooks on his fishing line, casting the last few mussels to the gulls.

The birds made a commotion behind him, so that he could walk fast and his steps not be heard. Keeping a careful distance behind, he followed his mark up to the row of merchants' booths. When he reached the end of the pier, Math dropped the borrowed fishing line beside a box full of fish and stooped to rub his bare feet with a hank of dried seaweed, to clear them of fish-slime and filth from the docks.

A short while later, rising, he watched Pantera turning right, up the hill. Rubbing his hands dry on his tunic, Math set off to follow.

CHAPTER TWO

Dusk fell quickly; it always did at this time of year.
In the disappearing light, Math followed his mark swiftly through Coriallum's winding streets by instinct as much as sight. It was his talent, and he used it mercilessly. If the scrawny Roman had not paid him, he would have been at the harbour anyway, and would have followed whichever of the incomers had seemed to have the biggest purse.

He might not have followed Pantera. In the two years since his mother died, he had kept a promise to her memory that he would not put the lure of silver over his own safety. It seemed to Math that Pantera was by far the most dangerous man he had ever tried to follow and he did, after all, have his father to think of: he couldn't afford for them both to be crippled.

He thought of his father as he hugged the wall of a tavern, letting the noise from inside cover the sound of his movement, and then the lack of it as he stopped. Up ahead, Pantera had paused and was asking directions of Cleona, the baker's wife.

The Roan Bull tavern was a large, sprawling affair set at the top edge of the town, with a main room surrounded by sleeping bays and stables and a second storey upstairs, left wide open for feasts and meetings of the town's council. Inside, three men were singing a battle song, sending the notes low and deep in their throbbing, incomprehensible dialect.

The language was foreign. Its words and rhythms caught at Math's guts and tugged him back to long nights of his childhood when his parents, believing him asleep, had talked in this lilting foreign language around the night's fire. Those were the nights when they invited in men and women Math never saw clearly, who spoke softly in their sing-song voices.

The visitors had always left before daylight, bearing with them food and gold and knives and swords that Math was not supposed to know had been hidden in the thatch. Even in winter they took food, leaving none behind, and always they left his parents talking in the heart of the night, speaking riddles in a foreign language.

Then one night a man had come who did not stay long, and in the morning Math's mother had fallen sick with grief and she had stayed sick until the burning fever took her away from him, robbing him of love and his family of its only whole adult.

Math knew that his father had been a warrior once, of the kind whose praises were sung in the taverns; the kind who went to war as a hero and came back as a cripple, unable to earn enough to keep a man and a child fed through the hard days of winter when the woman who had kept them both was gone.

In the Roan Bull, the war-lament ended, dying away to quiet words and the occasional tight sob of a man who had drunk too much. The hanging hide that served as a door was flung back and two men staggered out, arm in arm, still humming.

Less than an arm's reach away from them, Math spat with venom into the gutter and named it for all the heroes of all wars in all countries. They didn't see him. He closed his eyes as they walked past, that they might not be drawn to the contempt in his gaze.

Turning his head back after they had gone, he saw the baker's wife walk past. Of his mark, there was no sign.

'*Shit!*' He said that aloud, pushing himself to his feet. The woman let out a small squeal, then saw it was only Math and flapped her hands at him, hissing annoyance like a goose. He was already away, soft as a shadow, hugging the dark lees of the houses, casting left and right for a sense of where Pantera had gone.

Or a scent. He caught a snatched whiff of the sea and turned left into a dark, stinking, blind-ending alley that was barely wide enough to take a hound, still less a boy or a man. He was running now, ducking low, trying to dodge the puddles of urine and dog turds. He never saw the hand that caught his throat and brought him to a choking halt.

He couldn't breathe. There was no light at all. In perfect darkness, Math felt a knife shave a sliver of skin from under his ear and hot, wet blood ooze after it.

Snoring like a pig, he struck out with both heels, hoping to catch the soft parts of the man's groin. He failed. To prove it, the hand slammed downward, crashing his feet painfully hard into the packed earth.

'Three mistakes,' said a quiet voice in his ear. 'And calling out now would be a fourth. Without doing that, can you list for me what the previous three were?'

He is prone to bouts of untrammelled anger . . . Math felt his bladder squeeze on and off, like a horse taking a piss. He was afraid of Pantera, but more, was terrified that he might soil himself and earn the man's contempt.

He squeaked and hated himself for it. The hand at his throat shifted a fraction. Drinking great gulps of air, Math said, 'Watched . . . men leave . . . tavern. Lost you. Mistake.'

'That was what killed you,' the voice agreed. 'But I had

seen you already by then. Three things drew me to you. What were they?'

In absolute darkness, Math could see the river-brown eyes perfectly, and their promise of death. He said, 'I looked at you. I let your eyes meet mine.'

'Good.' The hand at his throat loosed its grip. 'But I already knew you before then, or our eyes would never have met. So two other mistakes before that.'

Math could breathe normally now, and think more clearly. Screwing shut his eyes, he searched back through his memory to the boat's arrival, to everything that had happened from when it was a speck on the far horizon to the point when Pantera's gaze had met his.

'Something to do with the clerks?' he asked, eventually. 'I shouldn't have looked at them?'

'No, that was neatly done. You looked, you saw nothing you liked, you put them off. I was already watching you, so the mistake was earlier.'

The hand that held him moved from his throat to his shoulder. Hard fingers dug into his collar bone. The knife still rested at his other cheek. With a lesser man, Math might have tried to wriggle free.

He shook his head as far as he dared. 'I don't know.'

'Fish are shade-lovers; they shun direct sunlight,' said the voice. 'You were fishing in the sun's full glare when all you had to do was make half a turn to your right and you could have dropped your line in shadow among the shoals that live there. A genuine fisher-boy would have done that, but it would have meant turning your back on the boat which you didn't want to do. So you weren't a fisher-boy, and then, when the clerks came, you spurned them, so you were also not a whore. That only left two things: a cutpurse, or a spy. You cut no purses on your way through the crowd and so, today at least, you are a spy. Am I right?'

There was no point in denying it. Math said, 'That's only two mistakes. What was the third?'

'This.' Pantera bent his head and sniffed. 'Your hair stinks of horse piss. The wind was coming off-shore to the ship; that's why the master rowed us in. I was already watching you before the boat made dock. Why would a fisher-boy reek of horse piss?'

'Because I sleep in the horse barns!' Too angry to care for the risk, Math threw his arm up and wrenched himself free and did not care about the knife at his cheek. 'Because my father was a *warrior*' – he spat the word with all the pent-up fury of his own failures – 'and now he is old and crippled and can't make harness fast enough or well enough to earn good money and someone has to feed us both and I'm not a good enough cutpurse or whore to do it yet!'

His voice echoed shrill from the walls. There followed a stretching pause, during which the knife disappeared and the hand fell away from his shoulder. The first sharp edge of the moon rose over the wall at the end of the alley. By its light, Math was able to look for the first time into the face of the man who had caught him.

Pantera's nose had been broken and set a fraction off centre, destroying any symmetry his face might have had. He had broad, strong cheekbones, and fine brows that were a shade darker than his hair. A scar notched one of them, giving him a look of wry surprise, barely contained. Lines of wind and sun etched the corners of his eyes. The latter held amusement, Math thought, but under it a storm of passions too powerful and too complex to be let loose without bloodshed.

Math realized he was staring and looked away. Pantera leaned back on the nearest wall and folded his arms. 'You don't like warriors?' he asked mildly.

Math shrugged. 'My mother was a warrior,' he said. 'And my father.'

'I see.' He rubbed the bridge of his nose, where the break was. 'Did your mother die in battle?'

'No. But she would have liked to have done. Like my father. He was wounded in battle and survived when he would rather have died.'

He didn't know what shadows the moon put on his face, or what Pantera might have heard in his voice, but the silence was longer this time, and thicker, and ghosts whispered within it.

'Why do you sleep in the horse barns?' Pantera asked. 'Your father isn't there, surely?'

There were too many answers to that. There was the past, which was his mother, and Math didn't want to speak of her yet, perhaps ever. There was the future, which was Ajax the charioteer and so might never happen; Ajax was a dreamer of wild dreams and had not been around long enough for Math to know if he was the kind of man to make them happen. So he gave the answer that grew from the present, which had the benefit of truth, and didn't hurt.

'I work for Ajax, the charioteer who drives Coriallum's horses. I help to look after the lead colts in the reserve team. My mother bred them, so they know me, which makes them easier to handle. They like it best if their groom sleeps nearby. And it's warm in winter,' he said, which was truest of all.

'Of course. Your father must be proud of you.' A bright thread of pain ran through Pantera's voice, then.

Math looked up, searching for its reason, but Pantera glanced away down the alley, avoiding his eyes.

He said, 'You could try washing your hair in citrus juice. It gets rid of the smell and makes the gold shine better. The clerks will see you all the sooner at the docks, and they'll like you better without the smell.'

'They like me well enough as I am.'

'I'm sure they do.' Abruptly, the warmth left Pantera's voice. His whole attention was directed at the shadows at the end of the alley. 'You should go now,' he said, and took a step back.

Math felt himself released as suddenly as if a key had been turned in a lock. He stole a glance over his shoulder, to where the light of the tavern's torches lit the alley's mouth to amber. The way out was clear. The night had barely started. A world of drunken purses waited to be cut for a boy who knew how to run back down the hill to the richer taverns at the dockside.

Math did not want to run down the hill.

He wanted very badly to do whatever he could to heal the raw hurt he had just heard in Pantera's voice and he knew how he might do it, if only temporarily. He reached forward, confident in his own skill.

'No!'

Math's wrist was snatched away and held. Danger surrounded him again and he did not understand why. He struggled briefly, then fell still. With a visible effort, Pantera loosed his grip.

'Who told you to do that?'

Math felt himself flush. 'No one. I just . . .'

'Whoever paid you should have known better than to send—'

'A whore?' Math spat the word. He had never been ashamed of it before.

He heard Pantera hiss in a breath. The man crouched. His dangerous, fascinating gaze came level with Math's.

'I was going to say a boy as naturally good at following as you. Anyone else would have lost me, and so been safe. You have a gift that grown men would give their last coin in the world to buy. And somebody bought you, obviously.'

It was not a question, but Math nodded anyway.

'Who was it?' Pantera said. 'Who paid you to follow me?'

'I don't know his name,' Math said truthfully. 'I would tell you if I did.'

'You would, wouldn't you?' He saw Pantera soften, saw

42

the planes of his face change, saw him close his eyes, and close off the volcano of his rage until he could smile, and lay his hand on Math's arm, and say, more steadily, 'If you stay a moment, you'll learn something. After that I want you to leave. Will you do that?'

'If you say so.'

'I do.'

Standing, Pantera turned his face to the alley's firelit mouth. Distinctly, he said, 'Are you happy now? Will you come out where you can be seen, or must we come to you, like dogs to a whistle?'

'If you know I'm here, what need is there to stand in the light?' The scrawny Roman, who had offered Math more than he had ever earned for a task that had seemed as if it would be easy, stepped away from the shadow of the alley's wall and stood in the open, cast in hazy silhouette by the torchlight from the tavern behind.

He looked much as he had in daylight, but that his thistledown hair – what was left of it – was cast in gold rather than silver by the flame's kinder light. His head was too big for his body. His neck made the ungainly mismatch between head and body and was ill fitted for both, so that the skin hung in wattles and his larynx stuck out sharp as a stone.

One might laugh at such a man, but for the fact that he had tracked Math for a good part of the afternoon unseen, which was, at the very least, disconcerting.

His attention was all on Pantera now, although he spoke of Math. He said, 'The boy will be as good as you when he's older, if not better. I haven't paid him yet. He earns his coin only if we speak, you and I.'

In a voice that made Math's guts ache, Pantera said, 'Then he has succeeded. You have spoken. I have replied. Pay him.'

'Soon.'

The scrawny Roman was Pantera's senior by at least

a decade, more probably two, he had a bad hip and his hearing was less than perfect, but even so, he carried an authority in his dry, harsh voice that left Math wondering whether he could actually best Pantera in the way he seemed to think.

When he said, 'Will you come with me? I have lodgings not far from here. We could talk properly there,' it seemed inevitable that they should follow.

Pantera ignored him. He opened a purse that Math had neither heard nor seen at any point on the way up from the docks.

'How much did you promise the boy?' he asked.

The scrawny Roman did not answer fast enough. Math said, 'One sestertius.'

He had thought it a fortune. Pantera clearly did not. He swore in a language that was neither Latin nor Gaulish but ripe with the force of his scorn.

'You were Rome's richest man and still you pay pennies to those who would risk their lives for you?'

The old man shrugged. 'I am no longer rich by any measure. Nero has my fortune and I must live on my wits. And Math did not risk his life. You are not yet so damaged that you would kill a boy for following you in the street.'

'Really?' Pantera bent down to Math. 'Have you eaten?'

That was a foolish question. Math stared at him. 'Yes.'

'I mean tonight. Have you eaten since sundown?'

Math shook his head.

'Then take this.' From his purse, Pantera produced a roll of white goat's cheese, thick as his thumb and as long. 'My father taught me this and so now I teach you. Always carry cheese in your purse – it stops the coins from chiming so the cutpurses can't hear it, and it means you have food when you need it; you never know when you might have to stay awake until dawn. A hungry stomach craves sleep in the way a fed one may not.'

Math's experience was otherwise, but he had learned

long since that the man holding the food was always right. With the spit already flooding his mouth, he watched wide-eyed as Pantera led him to the mouth of the alley, and in the full glare of the tavern's torches took the roll of cheese and cut it into four pieces.

He gave the first one to Math. 'Eat it now. Then keep the rest in your purse. Divide the night into four by the arc of the moon. See – it's just up above the houses, so this is the first quarter. When it's high, at midnight, eat the next piece. At half-set eat the third and at dawn, when the moon is down, eat the fourth. That way the night seems less long. Do you understand?'

Not understanding at all, Math said, 'Yes.' He had no purse. He slipped the precious cheese down the front of his tunic until it lay at his waist, above his belt, feeling the warmth of another's body through it. The fragment in his mouth was rich and ripe and exploded on his tongue.

Pantera was already walking away. 'Good. We'll come with you some of the way home. Will you show us which way we go to the horse barns?'

Math hadn't planned to go home yet, but there wasn't the slightest chance he was going to leave Pantera before he had to. He nodded, and walked between the two men away from the light of the tavern and into the dark thread of streets that made the upper part of Coriallum.

They were in full dark, with only the moon to light them, when he heard the footsteps behind them and knew they were no longer alone.

His own steps faltered. Pantera caught him a brief shove in the small of his back and dipped down to breathe in his ear. 'Only one. He's in the shelter of the tannery to our left and behind. Don't stop.'

They walked on, talking together softly, like son to father, with the scrawny Roman trailing behind. The chunks of cheese in Math's tunic began to sweat.

45

They came to the end of the town, at the top of the shallow hill half a mile or so along from the magistrate's residence. Here, the villas and workshops stopped and the great flat grassy plain began, in the middle of which was the wooden hippodrome and the complex of paddocks and horse barns around it.

The moon was high now, flooding the plain with silver ghost-light. Making sure they were in profile to the watcher, Pantera knelt before Math and ruffled his hair, taking his leave as any other man might of the boy he had hired and might wish to see again.

'Seneca was right,' he said. 'You were not risking your life when you followed me this evening, but then you were not paid enough to do that. If I offered you a denarius, would you risk your life for me – really risk it – now?'

Seneca. A denarius.

The two facts collided in Math's mind. A denarius: a silver coin four times the worth of a brass sestertius, sixteen times the worth of the copper that Ajax paid his grooms for a month's work.

And Seneca. The scrawny old Roman was *Seneca*: the man who had ruled Rome in all but name for most of Math's short life. Seneca, who had been deposed, and permitted to retire when all around him had died in a bloodbath of Nero's making. Seneca, who had paid him in brass, when Pantera was offering silver.

A denarius. Math would have risked his soul for Pantera for nothing at all.

Swallowing, he said, 'You want me to follow the man who is following us?'

He said it more loudly than Pantera had done. Hearing him, Seneca's head snapped round.

'Yes,' Pantera said. 'Watch him, find out who he reports to and why, and then come back to Seneca's lodgings with the news – you know where they are? Good. But if you are caught by this man or his master, you'll have to tell them

46

everything you know – my name, Seneca's name, where we met and how, and all that happened this evening. Don't hold anything back. The emperor's men don't ask nicely if they think they're being lied to, but if you tell the truth, they might leave you alone and come after us. Math . . . ?' He caught Math's cheek and turned his head. 'Are you listening? You are following one of Nero's servants and it will serve nobody if you are stubborn and die. You will not be protecting us. Is that clear?'

Math nodded. 'They won't catch me.'

'Good. The man who's following us is currently hiding behind the house with the gold on the roof tiles and the marble lions outside. In a moment, we'll turn away. You will seem to run home. When we have gone out of sight, find him and follow him and hear all that he says and to whom. And eat your cheese sparingly. It might be a long night.'

He gripped Math's shoulder, as men did when they came off the fishing boats after a storm. 'Good luck.'

Pantera turned away and signalled for the scrawny Roman to follow. Math stood under the bright moon a moment and waved at their backs, then shrugged for the sake of the man watching, much as he had done at the docks, and loped off in the direction of the horse barns.

CHAPTER THREE

The night was uncomfortably quiet. Seneca the Younger, stoic philosopher, spymaster and one-time mentor to the Emperor Nero, waited in silence by a table in the dining room of a borrowed villa, and watched Pantera move about in the shadows beyond the candlelight.

Knowing his subject, the philosopher did not ask any of the questions that pressed so urgently for answers. After the disaster of their meeting in the alley, he had no wish to sully the evening further, and he had long ago found that with this man, of all those he had ever taught, patience was his best and most certain weapon.

Patiently, therefore, and in silence, he watched Pantera make a methodical examination of the room exactly as Seneca had taught him long ago, noting the exits and entrances, the points of weakness and of strength, the places where a man might stand hidden, listening to the discourse within.

There were few enough of these. The house was a soldier's, neat and plain, with little by way of luxury.

Two dining couches stood by a table laid with cheese and olives, figs and grapes and small rolls of pickled fish. In one corner, a lit brazier glowed softly red, warding the night's chill from the air. A nine-fold candelabra stuffed with fat candles was set at a careful angle so that it spilled brighter light across the seating, but left in shadow a niche in one wall wherein was set a simple altar. A row of four cages standing against the wall nearby held sleeping doves that might have been for sacrifice, if the god of the altar required such things.

On the floor, subdued mosaics picked scenes from the lives of Achilles and Patroklos, from first meeting through shared war to the final blazing funeral pyre and the frantic chariot race sponsored by the grieving hero in honour of his dead lover. The winning chariot ran ahead of the rest, pointing the way out of the room and through an open archway that, in turn, led on to an unroofed courtyard. Somewhere near the centre of that, a fountain spilled water into a raised pool alive with schools of small fish, while above, scattered stars made a dense and distant ceiling.

On this night of reunion, the moon was not yet full. Its reflection danced lopsidedly on the perfect circle of the fountain's pool. When Pantera walked out under the black sky and stood beside it a while, observing his own reflection, Seneca's patience cracked at last.

'Nero will send for you,' he said.

'He already has.' Pantera hitched one hip on to the fountain's lip and trailed his fingers in the effervescent water. 'I am to meet my lord and emperor in private conversation at the magistrate's residence early tomorrow morning before the chariots line up for the first race. He wishes to thank me for my services in Britain.'

'He wishes to hire you,' Seneca said. 'To bring you into his fold, to use you as he uses all the best that I made for him.' It was his first fear and his deepest. He took pains to keep that fact from his face.

'Perhaps.' Pantera shifted slightly, so that the marble took all of his weight. He balanced, swaying, a breath away from falling into the water. Folding his arms, he turned back towards the light.

'You're thinner than you used to be,' he observed. 'Word has it that you live now on spring water and fresh dates, picked only by your own hand as a means to avoid the emperor's poisoners.'

His voice made it almost a question.

'Partly.' Seneca nodded towards the food arrayed for them both. 'I eat more than dates, as you can see, but no red meat, no wine, nothing cooked. I feel better for it. And yes, I consider it safer. Nero could have me slain at any moment if he chose, but he'd see a particular irony in using poison after all I've done for him. I will avoid that if I can.'

'And so Seneca no longer believes that a man eats to vomit and vomits to eat? The world is changing faster than I knew.'

That was an old barb, slung for a cheap point. Sighing, Seneca pulled a footstool from beneath the table and sat on it. The lower rank of candles in the candelabra guttered above his head. He looked down at his laced fingers, at the clipped and then bitten nails.

'I'm sorry for what happened in Britain,' he said presently. 'I didn't intend it when I sent you.'

'I never believed you did.' As a child might, Pantera ran his fingers through the water, grasping at the stars.

'I'm told you are damaged in mind more than body, and in spirit more than both. Is it true?'

Forgetting one of his own first rules, Seneca spoke to the reflection rather than the man, and did not look up even when that reflection left him, so all that remained on the black water was the moon's truncated circle.

When he did finally raise his eyes, the candles had begun to fail in the dining room, making the shadows darker. In the harlequin light, Seneca could see no sign of Pantera, but heard a snap of leather and a slither of wool on skin. Against all his clamouring instincts, he made himself sit on and on until, unable to hold himself longer, he rose and followed the trail of small sounds.

Forgetting himself, he gasped aloud.

A naked figure stood in the soft spill of the candlelight. It took a moment for Seneca to recognize Pantera, but only because the man he knew had displayed the Hebrew distaste for nudity almost to the point of prudishness. In their three decades of life together he had never willingly shed his clothes in Seneca's company.

They left his face untouched for fear of killing him too quickly, but to the rest . . . they wrote their anger on his body. It's what men do when they have lost their comrades to the enemy and believe they have one alive in their custody. Make yourself ready if you see him.

A legate of the British legions had told Seneca that; Fabius Africanus, in fact, who owned this house.

Now, in the unkind light, Seneca was perfectly placed to observe the truth of what he had said; that the pilus prior of the third century, the second cohort of the Second Augustan legion, and his three junior officers had quite literally written their rage on the body of the man they believed to be a British warrior, as a result of which Sebastos Abdes Pantera, who had once been a boy of wide-eyed, feline beauty, bore for ever branded into his chest and abdomen the mark of the second legion: LEG II AVG.

The stretched leg of the L reached up to meet a knot of hideously scarred tissue at his right shoulder that looked as if a spear had been forced through just above his collar bone and he had been left to hang on it, tearing the tissue. The rest merged with a lacework of less organized burns and scars, where men with knives and hot irons had traced spider's webs and carved their initials and made maps of their home villages, or the hills, or simply counted time on his body.

Hidden behind all that, so that he wouldn't have seen it if he hadn't looked, was an older, flat, scarred oval in the

51

centre of the man's chest that looked as if a fire had been lit there and left to burn.

'Are you weeping?' Pantera asked, with cold astonishment.

'I believe I am.' Seneca moved to the brazier and stood over it, warming his hands. 'It would seem you have the power to hurt me still. Or the men who hurt you have that power. Would you let me arrange for a physician? Nero won't listen to me, but Polyclitus holds the strings to the treasury, and can be prevailed upon. Largus is still the best of the emperor's doctors; he could—'

'Spare me false apothecaries, please!'

Pantera's voice was a whiplash. Seneca flinched. He had not come prepared for this.

Pantera, too, was silent a moment. When he spoke again, it was with the dry humour with which he had always masked his soul.

'Forgive me, but I am a little tired of bonesetters and herbalists. I was under the ministration of the governor's physicians for well over a year. I'm as healed as I'm ever going to be and happy with it. If you think my injuries leave me too compromised to kill a man, or follow one without being seen, then you should have stopped me sending Math out after whoever was following us tonight and sent me instead. I'm sure we'd all have learned something useful.'

'It was never my intent to set you against anyone else, be it in the open or in the dark of an alley. I haven't come to ask you to work again. It has cost you too much.' Seneca sensed a moment's surprise, and allowed himself to believe that the conversation might be moving in the right direction at last.

'What then?' Pantera asked.

'Retirement,' Seneca said smoothly. 'A peaceful step aside. My gold is gone to Nero, but I still own lands at Mentana that grow the best wine in the empire. There's a farm of mine there with your name on it if you wish. Or elsewhere in the empire if you prefer? Dacia is cold in winter but said to be good. Or Britain, obviously. There are whole villages lacking masters now in the lands of the Dumnonii where corn grows thick as moss and they breed cattle, horses and hunting dogs that would shame any other land in the empire. But then you know that; you spent five years among them, so if you want to pick—'

'No.'

The vehemence of that one word, and the pain behind it, were as surprising as anything that had happened in an entirely surprising evening. Pantera sank to sit on the tiled floor. His elbows came to rest on his knees and his hands hung loose. He laid his head on his forearms and turned it sideways to the wall.

For a long time, neither man spoke. At the end, as if in answer to another's call, Pantera said quietly, 'Not Britain. Never that.'

Seneca let out the breath he had held. 'Was it a woman?'

Pantera said nothing, which was answer enough.

'Is she still alive?'

'No.' Pantera still stared at the wall. He shook his head at whatever he saw there. 'I killed her before the legionaries took us. It was her wish. Her name was Aerthen. It means "at the battle's end".'

Seneca said nothing. After a while Pantera went on. 'Her mother was one of their dreamers. She could read the future better than any Etruscan augur. So we knew Aerthen would die at the end of a battle, but not which one. It made the days together more precious, I think.'

'Do you have a child still living amongst the Britons?'

'Not living, no. Her mother and I killed her together when the battle's tide turned. She was three years old.'

The self-hate in that was unbearable. Seneca lowered his own brow to his forearms, hiding his face in his turn.

Presently, Pantera reached for his tunic and drew it on. One of the candles failed. From beneath the lesser light, he said, 'You sent me to Britain to ensure the defeat of the tribes. You had trained me, and I believed that I could do what you wanted. What neither of us expected was that the tribes would change me.'

'Did they?'

'In every way possible. Within months, when I fought with them, I fought for them. By the second year, I was leading their warriors, and at the very end, when Suetonius Paullinus marched his men down from his battle with the Boudica and the men and women I loved were caught between two lines of sword and shield, I fought as I have never fought before, and it was not for Rome.'

'But you lost.'

'Everyone I knew and cared for died.'

Pantera's face was a mask. Seneca railed against that as much as what he had heard. 'You can't take the blame for a battle's loss all on yourself. You are one warrior, one sword, one shield, one—'

'I should have died with them. They were expecting me to do that, to join them with their gods. I had the blade ready. It would have been so easy . . .'

The river-brown eyes came round to meet Seneca's. The pain in them was beyond any man's bearing.

'Why did you not die, Sebastos?'

Sebastos. Seneca had not used that name in the reign of two emperors. It came now from the unexplored depths of his soul, unsettling them both.

Pantera turned. He was holding a small, broad-bladed knife of the kind stabbed into the bull's throat at sacrifice. 'I tried,' he said. 'I killed four men when they came to take us. I didn't think they would let me live after that.'

'And yet, if what I've been told is true, you withstood three days of torture and told them nothing, even when they crucified you.'

The knife spun in the air, sharp as a leopard's tooth. 'And still I didn't die. It's ironic, isn't it? I should have done. I could have done. I wanted to. The god didn't let me.'

Seneca was barely breathing. Pantera lifted a second knife and began to juggle the two, spinning them high from one hand to the other. Iron caught soft gold candle-light and muted it to silver.

Seneca said, 'Was it my name that stopped them killing you?'

'Sadly not.' Pantera smiled. It was not a good thing to see. 'When I told them I was one of yours, they spat at me for a liar and brought in new inquisitors with fresh ideas of how to break a man. It was only at the end, after they had grown tired of their sport and hung me up to die, that one of them passing heard me call on the god to take my soul. No Briton would ever have called on Mithras. The man spoke to his commander, who thought to find the legate and tell him they had one of the faith dressed as an enemy warrior. When he came, they thought I was dead. The physicians proved otherwise.'

Pantera stopped juggling at last. He turned to face Seneca. 'You are going to ask me to work for Rome,' he said. 'And I have just explained why you can never again trust my oath and should not ask for it. In the sight of my god, I tell you now that, for the rest of my life, whatever I do, for whatever pay, the oath of my heart – however and to whomsoever it is given – will carry more weight than the oath of my voice.'

'The oath of your heart was given to Rome, once.'

'It will never be so again.'

Seneca pressed his cupped palms to his eyes. 'Very well. You have told me why and I can believe it. With a wife and child dead at your own hand, it would be impossible for you to come back to us. But, in the sight of your god, whom I respect,' Seneca let his hands fall, 'I will tell you that I am not going to ask of you any more oaths. You weren't listening. I am asking you to retire. It's Nero who'll ask you to work for Rome.'

Seneca had spoken the truth, and it changed the balance between them so that it was possible to lean on the couches, to eat, to drink the cool well water that was laid ready for them. They didn't speak. Once, it had been possible to spend hours in the balm of each other's company in reflective silence, and at last it seemed to Seneca that it might be possible again.

Presently, a scratching at the door led Pantera to cross the foyer and open it, saying, 'Welcome, Math. Have you brought us news?'

The boy scampered in and then slowed at the sight of the room's stark beauty. His slight, angular shadow came to rest on the floor near the philosopher's feet. An outdoor smell of stale urine and tree sap and mud and moss clung about him.

Seneca turned slowly. The boy was filthier than he had been in the alley, which was hard to credit. His tunic had a rent in the hem on the right side and his bare feet and stick-thin legs were coated to the knee in congealing mud so that he left a trail of footprints across the clean marble floor. His hair was no longer gold, but hung in damp dregs to his shoulders. A scrape marred one malnourished cheek, blushing the skin blue in the hollows that hunger had left.

For all of that, his wide grey eyes still commanded all of his face, lighting it with the incendiary mix of insolence, desperation, exhilaration, tenacity and sheer exhaustion that Seneca had seen once before, a long time ago, in the archer's son who had walked to him from Judaea.

That boy, now a scarred and wounded man, followed Math across the room and laid a hand on one thin shoulder. 'Did he catch you?' he asked.

56

Math shook his head. He held himself silent one moment longer, then words spilled out, tumbling over themselves in their hurry.

'He followed you here and stayed a while watching the door, but left when the moon reached its height and went back into town. He met one of the emperor's men at the Striding Heron tavern opposite the docks. He said,' his voice deepened in a good approximation of a man's Latinized Greek speaking Gaulish, '"The Leopard met with the Owl at Africanus's house. The emperor should know before morning." They left together. I followed them some of the way, but they went into the magistrate's residence. I nearly went in after them, but . . .'

'But better to stay alive and come back to tell us,' Pantera said, drily, 'than to face certain death at the emperor's hand. Nero doesn't like to be spied on. Ask Seneca – he was paid to see it didn't happen for the first five years of his reign. Description?'

Math stared, mouth agape.

Pantera said, 'What was he like?'

'He was rich. He had silver and gold in his purse and a green jewel on his dagger's handle. He didn't look at any of the boys, even when they offered. I think he was going to bed the serving—'

'What did he *look* like?'

'Oh.' Math closed his eyes and wrinkled his face. 'Tall. Tall and lean and bitter-faced with no hair on the front half of his head, but straight black hair behind and a high brow and a nose like a hawk's. There was a triangular tear in the left elbow of his tunic and he wears his knife to the right, so that his left hand can draw it. He spoke Greek and Gaulish and Latin.' Math opened his eyes. He looked from Pantera to Seneca and back again. 'That's all I found out.'

There was a weighty pause. Pantera looked past the boy to Seneca. 'Well?'

'Well what? Aren't you going to tell him well done?'

'I might when I know who it was.'

Seneca frowned. 'Tall, bitter-faced with a high brow setting off straight black hair, left-handed, prone to tearing his clothes, speaks eight languages that I know of and kills without a second thought? That would be Akakios. Notionally, he's a tribune in the Praetorian Guard. In practice, he's Nero's unseen hand in the outside world: if someone threatens the emperor, Akakios sees them dead first; quite often they die before they've had a chance to make their threat. He's more dangerous than a nest full of scorpions. If we're all still alive this time tomorrow, then Math did immensely well. I told you he'd be better than you one day.'

'Then he should be paid.' Pantera took a silver denarius from his purse and spun it high, catching the candle's light. 'Thank you, Math. That was well done.'

Math snatched the coin deftly from the air. Aglow with pride, he followed at Pantera's heel while the man found a bowl on the table and filled it with water from the well, then, crouching, used the sleeve of his own tunic to wipe away the filth from Math's face, cleaning the edges of the graze underneath.

He moved slowly, tenderly, as he might with a wounded hound. Finishing, he said, 'You did truly do well, but you know that. And now you have two pieces of cheese to give back to me?'

There was a short, difficult silence.

'You ate it?' Pantera asked.

'I was coming back.'

'And you were sure there was nothing else to be done for the night. In which case—' Pantera stood, dusting his hands. 'You're right, there is nothing else. You may go.'

It was as curt a dismissal as any Seneca had heard. Math's face flashed from white to scarlet and back to white. His eyes became great grey pools, filled to the brink with swimming tears. He opened his mouth to speak and shut it again.

Too fast, he turned on his heel and ran for the doorway, leaving yet another muddy trail across the immaculate floor. A short while later, the outer door was flung open but not shut. A dog snarled in a gateway and fell silent.

Pantera absorbed himself wringing out his soiled sleeve over the bowl. Seneca glared at him, waiting.

'What?' Pantera asked, without raising his head.

'Did you think to stop him loving you?' Seneca threw up his hands. 'You won't do it with harsh words alone.'

Pantera abandoned the effort to clean his sleeve. Wandering over to the table, he picked at a small curl of pickled herring the size of a hazelnut and popped it in his mouth, chewing reflectively.

'He doesn't love me,' he said. 'He's looking for a man he can respect who will take the place of the father he despises. His father was a warrior. When he finds I was the same in Britain, he will despise me too.'

Seneca laughed bluntly. 'If you think that, then five years among the Dumnonii has made you a fool, for you were not one when you left Rome. Take him in, what harm is there? If you treat him well, he'll work for you with all his heart.'

'The spymaster's philosophy?' Pantera's face hardened. 'Take the boy and you can mould the man?'

'I didn't take you,' Seneca said. 'I never touched you, in fact. You'd have killed me if I'd tried.' And still might. That fear was always there.

'I was never a whore.'

'No, but you would have been within a month if I hadn't taken you in. You couldn't have gone on thieving for ever.'

'You may choose to believe so.' Pantera ate an olive, wiping his lips neatly afterwards with the edge of his sleeve. 'But we were talking of Math, who is both a whore and a thief and successful at both. He needs no help from me.'

'You think? For all his bravado, that boy's been plying his trade for less than six months and he'll die a whore's death within the year, as well you know. With a face like that, and the spirit to match, it's only a matter of time before he's taken by someone who finds pleasure in another's pain – and when he fights back, he'll die.'

Seneca stopped. Always before, he had kept his composure while others ranted around him. His final words rang in a leaden silence.

'None the less, I prefer to leave him to his own fortunes,' Pantera said, coldly. 'I have one child's death on my conscience. You'll forgive me if I choose not to add another.'

He was already leaving. 'Wait!' Seneca snatched at his sleeve. 'What do you know of the Phoenix Year?'

Pantera stared down at the offending fingers distastefully. 'Nothing,' he said.

'Nero will ask you of it tomorrow. If he does – when he does – will you find a way to see me that Akakios cannot follow? There's a man you should meet who is asking the same question and has more of the answers.'

'If I'm alive, I'll give it thought.'

Twisting out of Seneca's grip, Pantera followed Math's line of muddy footprints towards the door.

CHAPTER FOUR

'Math? Are you all right?'

Hannah found him; dark-eyed, still-souled Hannah, the healer from Alexandria, who was Ajax's new woman. Not yet so much his woman as he wanted, perhaps; in the month she had been among them, Math had not seen her let Ajax so much as lay a finger on her, but his interest had been clear from the start. In this, she was the due opposite of the other women who hovered on the fringes of the team who would have given themselves to Ajax in a moment, had he but asked.

He had never asked any of them, and Math had thought that women were not his interest until Hannah had arrived, carrying stillness as a gift that gave ease to the driver and his team in a way no one else could do.

It was for this, her gift of tranquillity and the way she lit Ajax's eyes, that the team had loved her first. Soon, though, it became clear that Hannah was a healer of a different stamp from those who customarily served the citizens of Coriallum.

Not ten days before, she had tended one of the younger colts who had gone down with colic, giving him a drench that brought him right within the day. Since then, the entire team had wooed her, not just Ajax, hanging on her every word, running to answer her every need, in the urgent hope that she might cleave to them and not the other teams, that she might keep their horses and their driver in racing fitness at least until the emperor's contest had been won.

They wouldn't win, of course, they all realized that as soon as they saw the magistrate's new horses, but they all knew, also, that a good second would do. It was Math's heart's dream to race a chariot before the emperor – and win – or it had been before he met Pantera. Now, he needed to think about that, to weigh his heart and its dreams, and to do that he needed to be alone.

Hannah was there, close and warm and still, like a forest pool on a summer's river. The barn was lit only by the stars, and those were faint. Math could barely see her; no more than a wave of black hair falling like smoked silk from her high, clear brow, and the straight nose beneath it.

Her face was near his, peering in the dark.

'Math, what's the matter? What happened to your cheek? Did one of your men hit you? Did you cut a purse and someone caught you?'

Hannah was a breath of fresh air in many ways, not least of which was her quiet acceptance of what he did and why. And she was good with the horses, too, nearly as good as his mother had been. Nobody else, except possibly Ajax, could have crouched down now as she was doing, almost between Sweat's two back feet, to look into the warm nest Math had made for himself in the straw. The colt fidgeted, stamping his foot, but he did not try to kick her head to a pulp, or rip her scalp from her skull with his teeth.

She was close to Math now, sharing his huddle of straw. Her forefinger had stroked once down his cheek, feeling the wet, and she had said nothing. His mother would have done such a thing; noting the tears but not having to name them.

Thickly, Math said, 'You shouldn't come in here. Your hair'll smell of horse piss when you go.'

'Really?' She took his hand and squeezed it and he saw the flash of her smile in the warm, damp dark. 'I've probably smelled of nothing else since I first came to look at your colt ten days ago.'

She didn't. She smelled of wood smoke and warm hair, of wool and belt-leather and woman-sweat that was quite different from the sweat of men. The temptation to bury himself in her arms was like a thirst on a hot day. He supposed Ajax felt the same. The thought gave him strength to resist.

She felt the change in him as he edged away, and the clenching of his fist. Tentatively, her two hands wrapped round his one.

'Math, what have you got? Can I see?'

After a moment's hesitation, he uncurled his fingers. She picked up the coin by feel.

'It's a denarius,' he said, but she already knew that. She wasn't rich; she might have hailed from Rome's bread-basket, but if she had brought any of its wealth with her when she left, it was all in her head. Like everyone in the team, she owned the tunic she wore every day and a silver belt buckle. Beyond that, and the linen sack with its bandages and unguents, dried herbs and the five nested copper bowls for washing of wounds, she had come to the race barns with nothing and likely would depart with as little. Anyone who lived hand to mouth as she did knew the feel of a denarius without needing light to look.

Quietly, she gave it back to him, wrapping his fingers closed again. 'Did you steal it? Is that how you scraped your face?'

'I earned it.' He could hear the stubborn pride in his own voice and hated it. 'I didn't steal it, I earned it.'

'Oh, Math . . .' She pulled him close again and this time he let her. 'Please be careful.'

They sat in silence for a bit, breathing in each other's warmth while the horses moved around them.

She was so like his mother. He made himself think of the differences, so that he would never confuse the two: Hannah was dark-haired where his mother had had hair the colour of ripe corn. Hannah's eyes were a deep brown, his mother's had been blue-grey, like a mackerel's back. Hannah was, he thought, maybe ten years younger than his mother, more Ajax's age, ten or fifteen years older than Math. Hannah spoke Greek first and then Latin and a faulty Gaulish while his mother had spoken three different dialects of northern Gaul for preference, Greek when she must and Latin only under sufferance. Hannah was trained in philosophy and medicine; she spoke to Ajax of Isis and Osiris and of Socrates and Plato, Pythagoras and Demetrius as if they were all alive, gods and men alike. Math's mother had told him tales of the heroes of Britain who were dead for the most part, and had taught him the daily rituals by which the gods of oak and river were remembered. He chose, for the most part, to forget those now that she was dead.

But one thing the two women had in common was that their time in his life was short. His mother had already gone and Hannah, he knew, would leave soon, Ajax had said that she wasn't the kind to stay long in one place, or with one man; that it didn't do to fall in love with her. He had been speaking, it seemed to Math, largely for himself.

Hannah moved a little, and Math caught a brief scent of something else in the wood smoke.

'What were you celebrating?' he asked. He felt the searching quality of her look and said, 'I can smell roast lamb.'

'Ajax said you were quick.' She looked down at the straw. 'It wasn't me. Someone was celebrating on my behalf.'

She was less still, suddenly, as if a stone had been thrown

into the pool of her soul, ruffling the surface. Math sat, waiting.

In a while, she said, 'A friend of my father's has searched for me for over half a year. Today his journey ended. He gave a feast to show his gratitude.'

Math said, 'You don't like lamb.' Hannah didn't ever eat meat; it was another way she was different from his mother.

She nodded, 'He doesn't know that. My father died before I was born. My mother returned to Alexandria to give birth to me and see to my childhood. I have never met any of my father's friends until today.'

They were quiet a while, listening to the horses' slow eating. Hannah said, 'His name is Shimon. He wants me to go back with him when he leaves.'

'Will you?'

'I don't want to.'

'But you might?'

He thought this was the first time she had considered that. She reached up and teased a tangle of hair from Sweat's mane. 'I might.'

Math picked a piece of straw and sucked on the end, tasting the flavours of autumn and frost. He thought of how Ajax had changed when Hannah came and would change again if she left.

He said, 'Ajax says everyone who comes to Coriallum is running from something. It's as far away from Rome as a man can get.'

'Or a woman?' Hannah's eyes were sharp in the grey light. 'Might we not be running towards something?'

'He didn't say that.'

They were quiet a long time after that. Math stared up to the dark roof space.

'If we win the race tomorrow, Nero will send us to Alexandria to train,' he said eventually. 'All his horses go there first, then he picks the best to race for him in Rome.

They say it takes two months by sea, or three by road, but that would mean taking the horses over the mountains and they don't want to do that. We'd have to go by the end of next month or the sea-lanes will be closed. If we win,' he added. 'But we won't.'

Hannah's hand moved to his shoulder. Math felt her come back from faraway thoughts. 'Is that what's wrong?' she asked. 'You think you might be stuck in Coriallum all your life? You won't. The emperor will notice your horses, I'm sure of it.'

'Ajax still thinks he can win.' He let his voice show how stupid that was.

Hannah shook her head. Her silk-smoke hair brushed his cheek. He felt her smile. 'No, he doesn't. But he doesn't want the entire team to decide that second place is good enough. "Good enough" is how you lose.'

'Did Ajax say that?'

'Yes, and he's right. You need to keep aiming to win if you want to catch the emperor's eye. It's the fire in you all, the need to win, that'll do it. Ajax said he'll get you to Rome to race for the emperor if it kills him. He promised it on the shade of your mother.'

'I know, I was there, but he can't promise what's not in his gift.' Math shook his head. 'He drew the Green ribbon this afternoon. The gods are against us.'

'Just because you've always been the Red team before doesn't mean—'

'Nero hates Green, he thinks it's unlucky.'

'Then you'll just have to show him it's not.' Hannah took his head in both her hands and kissed his brow. Her lips were cool and dry, as his mother's had been except at the end, when they had been hot. 'And to do that, you need to sleep. You'll never be a race-driver if you spend the night before a race wide awake. You could come and sleep with me in the healer's booth. I've got a straw pallet and hides. It's warmer than here.'

The part of Math that stood apart watching others knew that Ajax would give a month's food for an offer like that. It was almost worth accepting just to see his face in the morning when he found out.

The smell of cheese on his fingers reminded him that he needed to be alone. He shook his head. 'I need to stay with Sweat and Thunder. They get upset the night before a race.'

'But, Math, they're not racing tomorrow. Only the first team goes in the traces.' Her voice was gentle, not to upset him.

'I know that,' he said crossly. 'But they don't. They just smell the axle grease and know there's a race coming. If I leave them now, they'll keep everyone awake kicking the walls. I need to stay here. And I want to. I'm fine, honestly.'

'You're crying, Math. I've never seen you cry before.'

'I was thinking of my mother. She bred Brass and Bronze, who are in the first team. She'd have wanted to see them race.'

'Then I'll leave you with her memory. Thank you for telling me.' Hannah kissed his hair and didn't comment on its smell. Standing, she said, 'My mother's dead, too. She was a healer, far better than me. When I bring a woman to childbirth and both dam and child are healthy, or set a bone and know it will mend, I cry too, out of pride at her memory. It's not a thing to hide.' She squeezed his hand again and began to worm her way back between Sweat and the edge of the stall to the passageway.

At the big open doorway, she paused, a black shadow lit by the starlight behind. Raising her head, she sent her voice back to find him. 'Ajax says you'll be a race-driver one day if you want it enough. Better than him if you put your mind to it.'

'I know. Thank you.' Math made his voice sound true, even if the rest of him knew that Ajax had told Hannah only so that she would pass it on as part of his plan to save Math from himself.

He lay in his straw hollow, listening to her quiet footsteps across the grass, and the splash of urine as she squatted to relieve herself, then the press of straw on straw in her pallet as she lay to sleep.

Her booth was not far from the end of the barn, set at the front of the newly named Green team's huddle of tents and stalls with the white linen rag hung on a pole outside to show her profession. He waited until he could hear the sound of her sleep-breathing before he got up and moved through the warm, horse-filled dark to talk to Sweat first, who was his favourite, and then Thunder.

He was not crying any longer. He wiped his face dry with his hands and let the colts lick the salt from his palms. He told them they were wonderful, and they would win if they raced, but that they must needs be patient in the morning when Brass and Bronze were harnessed to the big quadriga with the two trace horses who ran behind, and were never as important. They nudged him and flicked their tails and returned to the half-doze of sleep from which he had woken them.

My mother bred them, he had said to Pantera, *which makes them easier to handle.*

What he had not said was that his mother had bred all eight of the horses that ran for Ajax, the first and the second team, but that these two she had given to her son, taking him to the field on the day two long-legged bay colts were born, Sweat half a morning before Thunder.

She had let him name them and had kept him with her all the way through their early training, until the year when he was five years old and they were three, when she gave them to him as his gift at the midsummer solstice.

They were too good to be owned by a boy of five, of course, and had been sold, but Math knew that one of the conditions of sale was that he be taken on as apprentice when he came of age.

Gordianus, who owned the team then, had said no boy could be an apprentice before he was ten years old. After his mother's death, nobody expected Math to make ten years, including himself. But Gordianus had broken both his legs the previous year in an accident at the close of the autumn season and it was only by chance that Ajax had been there, just walking in off the last boat before the seas closed for winter, with his shaved head and one ear missing and black, black eyebrows and the scars on his body from races and war and a flogging once. He was jeered for that, early on, before they saw how he could race, and if he had told a dozen different people the story of how he got the scars, he had told a dozen different stories.

To Math, he had said, 'I was young and I hated the legions. I thought I could best them.'

'And they caught you,' Math had asked dutifully.

'They did.' Ajax's quick grin set it on a par with being caught stealing fish from the docks, which happened to everyone. 'And they'd have killed me after they flogged me. But my mother's brother was an officer in the auxiliary and he was able to get me released. If your mother doesn't have a brother in the auxiliary, don't steal from legions, that's my advice.'

Somewhere in all the racing and tale-telling, Ajax had shown Gordianus the weight of his money and the deal had been struck; for an untold amount of gold, the practice chariots, the racing chariot, the eight racehorses, sixteen head of young stock, the wainwright and his three apprentices, the loriner and his son, the various stud hands who had kept the breeding herds going after Math's mother had died, the harness-maker Caradoc of the Osismi – who was Math's father – and Lucius, the existing apprentice, had all changed hands. So too had the promise to make Math the second apprentice when he came of age.

At the midwinter solstice, not long after the fires had been doused and re-lit to honour the death and re-birth of the sun god, Ajax had come to Math and his father bearing a smoked herring and a sprig of mistletoe across his spread palms. His shaved head had shone in the candlelight as if he'd polished it with oil. The hole where his ear had been cut off was blue at the edges from the cold outside and his black eyebrows seemed drawn with charcoal. Even so, he had looked a little like the sun god, brought back from midwinter to give light to the world.

'I am told I should give these to the mother of my future apprentice boy,' he had said in formal tones, 'as payment for the use of her son for the next nine years. But since he has no mother, I would ask Caradoc of the Osismi, father to Math of the Osismi, to do me the honour of accepting.'

Something had already been said, obviously; Math could see it in the way Ajax's eyes met his father's, in the silent communication that took place over his head. It was not the first time; Ajax and Caradoc had got along uncommonly well from the start, which was good, but also meant Math had two of them trying to change who he was.

His father had said, 'Math? Do you still want to be a race-driver? The work will be hard.'

But not harder than working the docks. Math hadn't said that, only thought it, but he saw his father read his face and was sorry for it. He was always sorry for the hurt he caused his father, but then almost everything he had done since his mother's death seemed to bring it on, which was stupid, and made him cross.

And he did not want to be indebted to Ajax. Looking away, he had said, 'I have work. I bring in enough for us both. I don't need more.'

He felt their eyes meet again over his head. His father had wanted to answer. Ajax had forestalled him by standing up, saying, 'Of course. I apologize for insulting you. We don't have to speak of it again.'

He had shaken Caradoc's hand. To Math he had said, 'You have made the horses well. They'll miss you.'

He had gone then, taking the mistletoe, but leaving the herring. Two nights later, Math had been passing the horse barns and found Ajax trying to use a straw wisp to bring out the shine in Brass's coat. The horse had a ticklish stomach; there was a certain way to wisp him that worked and Ajax didn't know it.

Taking the pad of woven straw from his hand, Math had shown him how. Ajax had been leaving when the boy had said, 'I won't stop working the docks.'

Ajax had gone as far as the door at the barn's end before he turned round; far enough for Math to feel real fear that he had lost his chance.

'I won't ask you to,' Ajax had said. 'Just know that work for me comes first, before anything else. If you leave things undone, you'll be out of a job. To save me having to watch you, do you give me your word to put race work before everything else? That's all I ask.'

Nobody had ever asked him for his word. Alarmed and flattered at once, Math had spat on his hand to seal the oath, knowing full well that Ajax planned to work him to exhaustion, so that he wouldn't have time to go down to the docks.

That had been over half a year ago, at the winter solstice, and now it was nearly the equinox and Ajax had become distracted by the need to win the emperor's race. It was not his idea – anyone could tell he would rather have spent another half year getting to know his horses – but he had promised to race, and to win, too, spitting on his palm and swearing by his Greek bear-gods, for Gordianus, and for the shade of Math's mother, just as Hannah had said.

So he had been more than usually busy of late and Math had taken the opportunity to go back to the docks again, and had found himself free there and happy. Until today, when Pantera, the Leopard, had stepped from a boat and Math had followed him up the hill and by the time he came down again his life had changed and he had failed in the eyes of a man he did not even know.

CHAPTER FIVE

Hannah the healer, known in Coriallum for the calm she brought others, lay alone on her straw pallet staring up at the sky, seeking ways to find peace for herself.

The night was warm, not yet sharpened by autumn frosts. The roof of the healer's booth was of sewn goatskin, with gaps at the ends of the ridge poles that let her see through to a blinking triad of stars. At the meadow's end, a wide river ran lazily to the sea, hushing a lullaby for the lost of the world: for herself, for Math, for half of Coriallum if Ajax was right.

Too far from sleep, with her stomach still full from a celebration feast she did not want and the worry of Math crimping the borders of her mind, she let her eyes rest on the brief triangle of stars she could see. Presently, when her heart was less clamorous, she built the full sky around the three visible stars, setting the constellations in their places, naming them as she had been taught. Then, because she was still awake, lying in a tent in Coriallum, as far from Rome as she could get, she tried to remember instead the alien names and shapes of Gaul in place of those she had learned as a child.

The crocodile and the hippopotamus were gone, and she

had no idea what replaced them. Amon, she thought, was still the ram, but Mentu, the bull, sacred to Mithras and Serapis, was named instead as a she-bear and worshipped by the warriors as a pattern on which to mould their own courage.

She had seen bears only in the market at Alexandria, sorry beasts chained through the nose and made to dance, but even in her short time here, the bards of Gaul had woven word-pictures of bears that matched the gods; great-voiced, great-hearted, greatly wise in the ways of beasts and humankind and possessed of a courage and ferocity that no other living thing could match.

She felt it, and then heard it, and then smelled it; richly, warmly dangerous. She was not asleep. In that moment, in fact, she could not have been more sharply awake.

She sat up. The beast padded past a second time.

'Math? Is that you?' She whispered it. The beast, unsurprisingly, did not reply.

In all the turbulence and wonder of her life, in the months of training spent in the desert, facing the demons of the inner and outer worlds, in the complex intrigue among the sisterhood in Alexandria, nobody had ever suggested that Hannah was a coward.

She rose and re-belted her tunic and pushed open the flap to her tent. Outside, a fire sent tendrils of sweet smoke to the clouded sky.

For one heart-stopping moment, she saw a bear crouched there, stirring the embers with a stick. Then she blinked, and there was only Ajax, the chariot driver, sitting with his back to her, staring at the new-wrought flames.

A smell of wetness came from him, of clean, cold river water. His body dripped star-silver dew. His head shone slick where his hair would have been had he not shaved it every morning. The gaping hole that was all that remained of his right ear was starkly black. He had not yet noticed her presence, so lost was he in the fire's red heart.

She sank to a crouch, resting her weight on her heels, watching the lift and fall of his breathing. She saw the moment when he became aware of her presence and the moment after it, when he decided not to move. Some time later, when it was clear he wasn't going to speak, she said quietly, 'Do you never sleep?'

She saw the corner of his mouth twitch. 'As much as you, it seems.' He did move then; a small motion of his hand that invited her to join him at his fire, which had been her fire first.

She took her place at his right hand. 'I thought I heard a bear,' she said, 'but it was you.'

He glanced at her sideways. 'I was blundering more than I thought,' he murmured. 'I apologize.'

He had, in fact, been quite astonishingly quiet. They both knew that.

She said, 'Was it the river caused your clumsiness? Did your gods speak to you there?'

He looked at her directly then, not a thing he did often. In daylight, his eyes were a curious pale amber, entirely at odds with the solid black of his brows. In the firelight, they glowed a rich copper-gold, bright as a hawk's.

'Am I still wet?' he asked.

'That, and you smell of river water.' Hannah nodded to the barn. 'I've been with Math, who has a new friend and has been learning to infer things from scent. Apparently one's hair smells of horse piss if one stays too long in the stables.'

'Good that I have no hair, then.' Ajax laughed softly, and sobered. 'Is Math all right?'

Hannah shrugged. 'He has someone new who pays him in silver. And he's . . . different, less petulant.'

'That would make a pleasant change.'

Ajax smoothed his hand over his naked scalp. Watching him, Hannah realized she had no idea how old he was, only that he was younger than she had first thought, closer

75

to her own age, in fact, and that the scars on his back and shoulders were not, as she had imagined, purely from falls taken racing.

It was a strange mistake to have made. Caught at an angle by the firelight, his scars were quite clearly layered, set years apart, and those at the top, the most recent, carried the savage incoherence of battle.

Beneath them, less chaotically, ran the ripped lines of the flail and beneath those, straighter yet, were splayed the regular cuts of ritual; a warrior ritual in all probability, although she had not heard of such things taking place among the Greeks since before the time of Alexander. She wanted to ask how he had come by them, but didn't know how.

'Did the river tell you about the race tomorrow?' she asked instead.

'Not entirely,' he said. 'I asked for help. Whether the request is granted remains to be seen. One can never fully know.' His eyes returned to the flames a while, listening to the crack of green wood burning. 'Do you have gods?' he asked, presently.

That stole her breath. Such a question wasn't asked of semi-strangers, here on the edges of the world, where Nero proclaimed himself divine and it was a capital offence not to worship him; where the dreamers of Britain, so recently vanquished, were said to visit and men still held to the old gods of moon and water and listened to what they said.

Ajax waited, looking into his fire. His face showed only polite enquiry. Unlike the Gauls, unlike any Greeks she had met, he was not a man to write his thoughts across his face.

'My father had a god,' Hannah said, surprising herself, 'and died for it at Rome's hand. After his death, my mother left her two sons and went to Alexandria. I was born there six months later. In Alexandria, I learned . . .'

On a whim, she looked up. Tents huddled about, but

none too near, and the lines of the horse stalls were silent; nobody was close enough to hear. She made a decision and hoped she would not regret it.

'What do you know of the Sibylline sisters?' she asked.

Ajax bit the edge of his thumb, considering. 'I know they're Egyptian by habit if not by birth and that the Romans are in awe of them as they are of no other women, possibly even afraid of them. Apart from that, I know only that they are respected across the empire as oracles and prophets, that they live in seclusion, keeping themselves unmarried, and— Ah.'

That last a short, violent out-breath. 'So will you never marry?' For all his self-possession, he couldn't hide the broken hope in his eyes.

The fire burned less fiercely than it had done. Hannah leaned forward and busied herself laying on more wood. 'I'm not one of the sisters,' she said. 'My mother was, but she married my father in fulfilment of a prophecy. After his death, she came back. I was raised among them, and trained at their expense. I did—'

'Find love among them?'

She had not thought he might read her as she read him. With a hazel twig, she stirred the fire. Sparks danced amid drifting ash. Memories returned, and were banished, as she always banished them. 'The rashness of youth,' she said reflectively, 'is exceptional only in its self-belief.'

His gaze rested on her face. 'I am at the behest of an oracle of sorts,' he said at last. 'My sister dreamed that I would come here, and perhaps return home in the high summer with a brother I had thought lost.'

'Perhaps?'

'If I find him. If he lives through what is coming. If he chooses to come back with me. It must be his choice, freely made.' Ajax rose smoothly, with the grace of his professions. 'But first, we must win a race, and for that we must sleep. Even you, I think? The team would be sorely pressed without its healer.'

'You go.' Hannah did not stand. 'I'll come later when the fire's less.'

He swept her a salute she didn't recognize and was gone, treading soundless across the grass.

Hannah stared at the space where he had been and thought of choices freely made, of oracles and dreams and the duties they imposed, of family and friends, of past, present and future and knew herself only at a crossroads, with no idea at all of which route to take.

CHAPTER SIX

Between one breath and the next, Sebastos Abdes Pantera woke to the grey stirrings of race day at the Striding Heron tavern.

He lay still with his eyes shut, waiting, as he did every morning and, as every morning, in that finite space between sleeping and waking, Aerthen came to him, alive in the black echoes of his mind, bright-haired, green-eyed and laughing as she raced him on her mouse dun gelding in their first meeting, touched him with her eyes across the fire on a smoky winter's evening not long later, made love to him soon after that, holding him in her long, long legs, in her warrior's arms, against the cushion of her breasts, breathing his name into his ear and that she loved him.

She came to him naked first, and then dressed for war in a stolen legionary shirt with armoured leather wraps on her forearms taken from the tall, bronze-bearded Rhinelander who was the first man she had ever killed in battle.

She stood before him, weapon-ready, as tall as her spear, so that the shine of her eyes and the shine of its blade were as one before the rising sun, and then again, before the setting sun, when blade and face and body were rusted with others' blood, and her smile was savage, lit with the hope of victory.

In the thick of battle she came to him, fighting to be at his side, to keep him safe, trusting him to keep her safe, and they fought together until that moment in the evening of the battle's second day, when it was lost and all were dead, or soon to be so.

Then, she came to him still smiling her love and her courage, holding Gunovar, their golden-haired, ocean-eyed daughter, who was named for a hero of the Dumnonii who had fought in the Boudica's rebel army against the legions. Aerthen's loathing of Rome was legendary and so her child must feel it too, when she grew; how could she not with two such brave, proud parents? She slept in her mother's arms, her peace perfect in all the din and chaos of battle.

Except not asleep, because now, in this last part of the visiting, there is bright, wet blood scarfing Aerthen's stolen shirt, gathering in pools at her feet, and the smile on the child's face is matched by the broader, red-lipped smile in her throat, where her mother's blade has sliced it, so fast and so sharp that the child has never woken from the tea-drugged sleep.

And as he feels her spirit leave her to make the last walk to the gods, the man known as Hywell, the hunter, feels his wife reach for his hand, and press the blade into the sweaty wetness of his palm.

She has more courage than he. She caresses each part of him with her turbulent gaze and she smiles and tells him she loves him and asks this last gift of him and he gives it, he who has killed before in pity, in anger, in detachment, in scorn, but has never yet killed in love.

He kills in love now, holding her head in his one hand, finding the place with his fingers, in the ninth rib space, a little to the left of the breast bone, trying not to think of how often he has kissed here, how precious the skin, how strong, how fragile.

He finds the space and steadies it and she says his name,

'Hywell,' as a prayer and then, smiling, in love, 'I will know all of you in a moment, all those places I could not find,' because this has been a joke between them, that he had no past before he came to her, and he knows all of her but she knows so little of him.

And in this last moment, he smiles for her and says, 'You will, and gladly so. I give you all of myself, in love, for now and ever. Wait for me.'

Before he can fail her, he slides the knife forward and up, through skin, through muscle, past the grate of her bone, through the sudden give of her lungs and up to the beat of her heart that makes the blade twitch like a live thing in his hand.

He almost stops there, but her eyes draw him in, and her voice, whispering, because she cannot speak. But she has not cried out, and will not, and so he slides the blade on, and tilts the point upwards, cutting the great muscle of her heart, and she bleeds, as their daughter Gunovar bled, but inwardly, so that she lives and lives and only leaves him when her eyes can no longer hold his face, and her mouth can no longer speak his name.

In his mind, he lowers her to the floor, as he has done every waking morning since. As every morning, he hears her voice, echoing in the sea's rush of her eyes, *I will know all of you in a moment, all those places I could not find*, and his own voice, rich with his love for her, poisoned for ever by his own cowardice, *You will, and gladly so. Wait for me*.

Wait for me.

He had meant it, and would have joined her then but that, in wanting to leave both mother and child untainted by Rome, he had taken time to build a pyre for them, laying down his weapons for the first time in days. He had fought like a cornered rat against the men who came for him and four had died, but not him. Later, he came to understand that a part of him had wanted the kind of death they offered by taking him alive, in all its lingering pain.

They gave him his wish. With a skill born of fury, they had slowed the passage of his days until each hour became an eternity spent in agony. The pain surpassed anything he had ever known and his life had not been one of overwhelming comfort. But even then, he did not go to join Aerthen, however close to the brink they might have driven him.

In the end, that, too, was his fault. In a moment's weakness he had lost the sense of her presence and called instead on the god that Rome had given him, and that god had answered, granting the blessing, or perhaps the curse, of life.

Wait for me.

Every waking moment, Pantera could feel her there, waiting on the other side of the silk-fine divide between living and dying. He had only to reach for her and she came.

Thus it was that in the attic room of the Striding Heron, on the morning of the day he was due to meet his emperor, Sebastos Abdes Pantera, who had also been Hywell the Hunter, gave his customary morning greeting to the woman who had been his wife and then, forcing himself to look beyond her ocean-green gaze, opened his own eyes and began to take stock of the day.

He started with his own body, documenting the pain, beginning with his ankles, working up through his spine and chest to his arms and last to his face. After the sea ride, his shoulders were on fire where the muscles had torn and never fully healed, and a nagging ache in his left ankle where the legionaries had seared the tendon had become sharper.

None of it was new or unexpected, only to be noted for how it might affect his movement in the day.

Rolling over on his side, he turned his attention to his

immediate surroundings, to the straw in the mattress beneath him, to the rat urine recently voided near the foot of the bed, upward to the first grey light of dawn outlining the shutters, to the door a few feet away, which remained closed and had not been opened in the night; and finally, when he was sure he was alone in a room that had not been disturbed while he slept, Pantera directed his attention out to the coughs and curses of the waking guests in the tavern rooms on either side and below.

Listening with half an ear to bets offered and laid, and lengthy morning commentaries on the health of the horses and their drivers, Pantera rose at last, dragged his hand through his hair and crossed the room stiffly to the window, where he pushed himself through morning exercises that would have shamed Leonides and his Spartan martyrs at Thermopylae.

Feeling looser in spine and limb, he dashed water on his face from the ewer in the corner, rearranged his hair again, and lifted from his travelling chest the fine linen tunic that had been the legate's gift on leaving, and the leather belt with the silver buckle fashioned to show the running deer of the Dumnonii that had been Aerthen's and had by some miracle survived the inferno of the battle's end.

His sandals had been made to his own design by the cobbler in Lugdunum. Their chief asset was that he could shed them easily and go barefoot if he needed to be silent.

His four knives lay on top of his second tunic in separate sheaths of walnut-dyed doe hide. Two together were ready to be strapped to the inside of one forearm, one other for his leg, and the last for his waist if he wanted it for show.

They were plain, but finely balanced, with only the single mark of Mithras branded into the pale beechwood hilts – and entirely inappropriate for his morning's task. With regret, he placed them back in the chest, closed the lid and padlocked it.

On leaving, he took a pinch of fine, white flour from a

pouch at his belt and blew a drift of it across the floor just inside the door. Thus protected, or at least forewarned, Sebastos Abdes Pantera readied himself for his meeting with his emperor.

In the lushly tended garden, in the heart of the magistrate's residence, a eunuch of moderate provincial talent sang the Lament of Daedalus to greet the dawn.

Pantera stood under a sun-pinked marble archway and listened to the first notes waver up to a scratchy peak as four Germanic gate-guards searched him for weapons. They found none because he had left them locked in his chest for precisely this reason. When he said as much, stretching the limits of his German, they laughed at him and spoke fast amongst themselves in a dialect he could not follow.

They were Ubians, big, red-haired, over-armed barbarians from one of the tribes that lived along the swampbanks of the Rhine, a hangover from Caligula's time, when they had fought one another in single combat for the privilege of providing the emperor's bodyguard. In Nero's retinue, they outranked the praetorians, and were known from one side of the empire to the other for the blind ferocity of their loyalty. Astoundingly, given their reputation, these four were sober.

Ahead of him, on the far side of the atrium, the singer dragged Icarus to new heights.

The guards were immune to the song's missed notes. Forming a small column fore and aft, they marched Pantera in through the gates and down a wide, echoing marble vestibule where the floor was a chequerboard of black on white mosaics and the walls were alive with a gilded, many-coloured frieze of Apollo Kitharoedus that showed the god holding forth with his lyre to four listening nymphs of striking, if androgynous, beauty. The high roof was laid with gold leaf, angled so that it caught the sun's first rays and cast them ahead into the garden, blindingly. For the first time in many years, Pantera knew himself to be in the presence of truly effortless wealth.

The guards clashed to a halt. Pantera was ushered across the atrium to the edge of the greenly forested space that was the magistrate's colonnaded garden.

The magistrate's guests were at breakfast, or perhaps had not slept at all and were simply on the latest course of a many-layered dinner with suitable entertainment. Somewhere in all that foliage, screened behind the mulberry trees and cultivated citrus, the twining ivies and honeysuckles, the lament paused on a long, aching note. Small songbirds fluttered brightly in cages hanging from the pillars. A tame jay swooped down from left to right, and rose again, carrying a grape. Grey carp kissed the surface of an oval pool, reaching up to the endlessly still fingers of a naked stone Narcissus who leaned over the water, absorbed in his own reflection. The largest carp, when it rose, had a gold ring embedded in its dorsal fin.

In a garden of such beauty, the inhabitants could not be less so. An unclothed Nubian girl-slave passed by, who could have modelled for one of the nymphs on Apollo's wall frieze. Two more girls and a boy followed, all naked, long-limbed as herons, graceful as swallows. Their bare feet made no sound on the marble floor.

The members of the emperor's retinue were at least partially dressed; it was the easiest way to tell them apart from the slaves. For the most part, they were equally beautiful. The magistrate was one of the exceptions. Older than the others, his hair was silver and his features bore the stresses of political life. Even so, he had an air of grace that bound him to the group as a man of like kind.

One man there was not beautiful, neither did he drift between the columns talking to the other guests, but stood in the citrus grove to the magistrate's right, staring at Pantera with undisguised loathing.

He was tall and bitter-faced, with a high brow and straight black hair pressed back by a receding hairline. He bore no obvious weapon, but a disturbance to the outline of the sleeve on his right arm spoke of a knife strapped there.

Inwardly, Pantera thanked Math for his night's work. Affecting an interest in the carp, he edged round the pool, gauging the distance between them, all the while surveying the rest of the garden, and seeking his emperor.

He failed to find him, although the meal was clearly in Nero's honour. The table laid at the garden's far end was piled with such a magnitude of food that it could only have been for the imperial party. Set in the centre was an ice statue carved in the shape of a lyre, the emperor's favoured signature for this year.

The Empress Poppaea walked out from behind the mulberries, Nero's amber-haired second wife, who had been the wife of his friend. Her mother, they said, had been the loveliest woman of her day.

They, the chattering classes of Rome, Gaul and Britain, said very little about Poppaea herself and most of it recorded her earlier marriages as calculated stepping stones to her position as empress. They said also that she had made Nero kill his own mother because the old woman had disapproved of the wedding.

Given the long gap between one and the other, sane heads deemed that tale untrue and the empress, if she heard, didn't show it. She took her role and built it around her with beauty and not a little grace.

Now, she glanced at Pantera and turned slowly as if she had not known he was there. Her eyes drifted across his face, as Aerthen's had once done. He had not been scarred then. More recently, he had become used to the way eyes found him, then flinched away. The empress did not flinch, but let herself see all of him and him all of her.

She was taller than most Romans, with long hair

arranged in coils to her shoulders. Outwardly, her chiton was modestly cut, of pale yellow linen, belted with silver rope and extending down to her ankles, but the modesty was overcome somewhat by the translucent nature of the silk from which it was fashioned, which served admirably to enhance the curve of her hips, belly and breasts. Her neck was slim and fine as a swan's, held with the internal grace of the astoundingly beautiful. The skin of her face was fine as new-fired clay and her features carried the almost-Greek symmetry of the true Roman aristocrat. Her toenails were dyed a deep orange. Threads and chains of gold, silver and diamonds adorned ankle, wrist, neck and hair. On a lesser woman, they would have seemed vulgar.

Pantera bowed, but did not meet her eye. So far, he had counted thirteen among the emperor's retinue. There was still no sign of Nero, even in disguise.

From behind Pantera's back, one of the guards rang a small bell. Silver chimes wove through the garden, resting here and there on the spring blossom.

Beyond the mulberries the eunuch sent Icarus crashing mournfully to earth. There was a moment's pause before the garden rang to enthusiastic applause, such as might have been offered to Rhemaxos, the Thracian singer currently wooing Rome with his exquisite songs.

But it had not been Rhemaxos who had sung, not even close, and thus the applause gave its own warning even as the high, thin voice reached out to Pantera.

'You are early; good. We like that in a man. You may present yourself to us. It is long past due.'

Schooling his face to mild astonishment, Pantera stepped through the screening flowers and saluted, as if he were still attached to the legions, and thus owed this man his allegiance as his supreme commander.

'You enjoyed my singing?' asked Nero, emperor of Rome and all her provinces.

87

'It was singularly exceptional, my lord.'

Nero might have sung like a eunuch, but he was older than the coin images made him out to be, less portly, more lightly graceful on his feet. His face was round, but still built on the strong bones of his ancestors, so that it wasn't impossible to imagine him a scion of Augustus' line.

Like the bodyguards, he was fully dressed, although not overly so, given that he was to grace the races later in the day. His toga was of linen, brilliantly white, with porphyry deep around the hem. A diadem of artfully cut diamonds lay on his thick, unbrushed curls, which took some courage: in Rome only women wore such gems in their hair. His body was freshly oiled, scented with mint and citrus and something else that Pantera recognized but could not name. The mix blended pleasingly with the camomile and lavender of the garden.

His eyes were sloe-dark, hidden by half-lowered lids dusted in blue powder. He pursed his lips. 'Sebastos Abdes Pantera,' he said. 'Named for Augustus, my honoured forebear, and for the leopard, for which you are famed. They say you are broken and will never mend; that you are prone to bouts of unruled anger during which you might kill a man out of hand. Is it true?'

He tested men, of course; it was his nature. And he was an actor, who could sense acting in others as a serpent senses blood.

For both of those reasons, Pantera, bowing, spoke the truth. 'I would like to believe it not true, lord, although I may yet be proved wrong. Did Fabius Africanus tell you that?'

Surprise purred among the courtiers. To Pantera's left, a woman gave a short, astonished gasp.

The emperor laughed, lightly, not unlike the silver chimes of the bell. 'How refreshing. Few people have the courage to ask questions of their emperor. It was Akakios who said it, actually. He had it from Suetonius Paullinus, who used to be governor in Britain. The legate, Africanus, told us that you called on your god when you were dying, and that you are given to Mithras.' That, too, was a question.

'Each of these is true, lord.'

'We are a god also. We, too, can save lives.'

'I am sure of it, lord.'

'We could make you worship us, calling on us as you did on Mithras.'

'Of course.'

All humour had gone. Slow death hung a hand's clap away. In Britain, they had crucified him, using ropes instead of nails because the death took longer. If Pantera let himself think about that, ever, at any point of the day or night, he broke into the kind of sweat that covered horses after a race.

Not thinking of it now was hard, but necessary. Aerthen stood exceptionally close.

From the citrus grove, the Empress Poppaea said, as if to her slave, 'For myself, I have always found love to be sweeter when it is freely given.'

'How immensely wise.' Nero smiled at his empress. The threat of death moved away. Released from a diverting tension, the ladies and gentlemen of the emperor's retinue murmured to each other in low voices. In the citrus grove to Pantera's left, the tall, bitter-faced man moved, subtly, using the sound as cover.

Nero saw it. The black eyes flickered there and back to Pantera. Thoughtfully, the emperor said, 'We hear you had a different name when you lived amongst the tribes in Britain.'

He should not have known that. Nobody should, except the men and women of the Dumnonii who were safely dead. Pantera bowed again, hiding more than just his eyes. 'Among the Dumnonii, I was Hywell, lord. It means hunter.'

'A leopard who is also a hunter. Very good. You were their hunter, and yet you hunted them on our behalf, striving to bring us Britain as your prize, just as, six years ago, you gave us first blood against Parthia at great risk to yourself. We commend you and would find ways to repay the debt we owe. To that end, we wish to visit the chariot yards before the races and require that you be our bodyguard. Are you armed?'

'Lord, no. I would not so profane your presence.'

'Then that must be rectified.' Nero clapped his hands. By a miracle of training, or of chance, the songbirds fell silent.

The tall figure moving to Pantera's left also fell still. Without turning, Nero said, 'Akakios, fetch for our leopard weapons to suit his needs. A knife, I believe, balanced to throw? And perhaps a second, longer blade?'

With palpable courage, the bitter-faced man stepped forward, saying, 'Lord, may I ask . . . With greatest respect, is this safe? I do not question your wisdom, only desire to protect your hallowed person.'

'Yes?' Nero put his index finger to his cheek and tilted his head in an actor's parody of contemplation. His gaze switched to Pantera.

'Will you kill us, Leopard-who-is-hunter? Or assault our person?' His voice was deeper than it had been; more like a woman's, less like a boy's.

'No, lord, I will not. I give you my word.' Pantera did not bow now. It mattered that his eyes be seen.

'Your word, sworn on the slain bull of Mithras?'

'If you request it, lord.'

'Not yet. The offer is enough.' With a wordless wave, Akakios was sent for weapons.

Summoning a slave to remove the diamonds from his hair, Nero began to walk towards the vestibule. The four Ubian guards jumped to present arms, two either side. What they lacked in legionary crispness, they made up for in their sheer bulk, and the ease with which they swung their long cavalry swords. They smiled for their emperor, showing corded necks, thick as bulls'.

'Come,' said Nero. 'We would have you walk in our company.'

Pantera moved swiftly to catch up. Together he and his emperor passed over the black and white chequered mosaics, between the multicoloured visions of Apollo on his lyre. The god, he noticed now, had a thatch of thick black curls amongst which diamonds nestled.

The naked Nubian girl-slave came with a steaming cloth to wipe the paint from the emperor's face. Standing for her in the vestibule, Nero said, 'Akakios hates you. Why is that?'

'I was trained by Seneca, lord, and he was not.'

'That is reason enough?'

'For a spy it is, yes. He trained with us for three years before he was turned away. Rejection makes a man bitter and such a thing can turn to hate if it festers long enough.'

'Why was he rejected?'

Pantera shrugged. 'He was impetuous. He didn't listen. He thought he knew best one time too many. You, of all people, know exactly the standard Seneca requires of his pupils. Akakios had not the intellect or the self-restraint under pressure that was necessary. You will have seen that, I think, by now.'

'But an impetuous man can kill as easily as one trained by Seneca. Watch him, he's there now.'

Akakios was waiting for them at the entrance to the vestibule, bearing two knives and a sheathed blade. He was of Assyrian descent, which gave him the height and the angular hawk's nose and the sharp-arrow eyebrows that pointed up in perpetual surprise. Always bitter, his face was scored now with a freshly kindled hatred.

'Where were you last night?' he asked, as Pantera and Nero emerged into the sunlit morning.

That he could speak so abruptly in the presence of his emperor spoke greatly of his power in the court. That the Ubians stepped away to give him privacy said even more.

With a further prayer of thanks to the half-starved urchin from the docks, Pantera said, 'I spent the evening with my foster-father, Seneca, who once had the honour of serving his excellency. He has borrowed the lodgings of Fabius Africanus, legate to the Fourteenth legion. Afterwards, I took a room at the Striding Heron. It's a rude place, but clean enough, and—'

'At the docks?' Nero said. 'Full of fishermen and boys? We know it. Rude, as you say, but the fare is wholesome. Now you are here and I see Akakios has brought you a pair of throwing knives to use in our defence. You are expert in these, I believe?'

'I have some small skill, lord.'

The knives were a matched pair, one balanced for a right-handed throw, one for left, with the weighting set subtly off centre for each. They had sanded beech handles, and plain iron blades. They were, in fact, the very image of the ones Pantera had left in his trunk in the inn, except that these did not have the mark of Mithras on the hilt. Pantera rubbed his thumb over the place, to see if it had been sanded away, and decided not.

'They are perfect, lord. With these and the third at my belt, I believe I can keep you safe from any two or three men who may come against you. If there are more, we may have to fight together.'

'Back to back, as the Gauls do?'

'Exactly so.'

It had been a jest, offered as a foil on which the emperor could claim his battle skills.

Instead, smiling to show he had seen the joke, Nero said, 'Then we had better hope our other defenders are prepared to give their lives in our defence, for we have not mastered the skills of battle. Our energies have all been on the chariots. You don't race? A pity. We need someone of mettle who can . . . Wait!'

They were still within the line of the Ubian guards. Nero reached for a blade from the nearest. Without hesitation, it was given. The emperor was not deft, but he was not as clumsy as he allowed others to think. He swung round, setting the blade's edge on Pantera's bare skin at the place where his neck met his shoulder above his new court tunic. The scar was there, that had been made by a spear's head and continued into a burn.

'Kneel.'

Pantera knelt. The stone pathway was cold beneath his shins. Fragments of grit pressed into his knees. His left ankle ached suddenly. For a man who thought he wanted to die, he felt an uncommon desire not to do so now, with Akakios' toxic shadow sliding between him and Aerthen's presence. He licked his lips and found his mouth dry as a summer river, and sharply metallic, as if he had licked his own knife blade.

Nero moved the sword on to his collar bone and let it rest there. 'You are not a citizen of Rome, is that correct?'

'It is, lord.'

'Which is why the legionaries in Britain were able to do to you what they did. If you had been a citizen, they could not have acted thus.' The blade stroked across the scars on his shoulder. 'We wish to rectify that. In any case, we cannot be seen to be guarded by a man who lacks the necessary status. What ever would the senate say?'

Nero laughed. Belatedly, the men around him laughed too, except Pantera, who studied the black eyes and saw no mirth in them. The blade drew a sliver of blood, much as his own had from Math in the alley's dark.

'What would you have of me, lord?'

'That you swear to uphold the laws and honour of Rome. That you swear to defend my life and that of my family before all other lives, including your own. That you

93

acknowledge the genius of your emperor as your guiding light. Do you so swear?'

Pantera swayed in the morning light. Voices from his childhood murmured in his head, bypassing the echoes of his more recent past; his mother was there, and his father, and Seneca. *What do you live for but to earn your citizenship?*

They were all wrong; Pantera had never lived for it, only used it as the mark by which he might have measured his own success. Britain had taken that from him. He had no concept of success since Aerthen's death.

He said, 'I do so swear.'

'Rise,' said Nero. 'You are Roman, and so the fullest of humans. Now, Sebastos Julius Abdes Pantera, you will escort us to the chariot grounds and guard us as we inspect the teams. If you can pick for us the winner, we shall be well pleased.'

CHAPTER SEVEN

It was said of Nero Claudius Caesar Augustus Germanicus that he would often pass incognito through the slums of Rome at night, listening to the talk in the taverns and the baths to assure himself of his people's care for him. It was further said that he knew chariots, horses and racing as if they were his profession, and could pick a good team by sight at a hundred paces.

Walking with him through the bright, blustery morning, beside the oval sawdust-lined training track, stopping among the great sea of traders' booths before the four long barns that housed the race teams, watching the ease with which he caught an eye and drew a man to him, to talk of horses, of chariots, of the drivers, of the odds on one team or the other, of the training to win a race, Pantera could imagine both of these tales to be true.

Nero no longer wore gems in his hair or paint on his eyelids. Were it not for the unusually wide band of porphyry at the hem of his toga, and the fact that his face was on every coin in the empire, the crowd around them would not have known that their emperor passed among them, pausing here at a booth to examine the craftsmanship, or slowing there by the ropes at the head of the training track, wreathed in the rich, ripe fog of resin and horse manure, to watch the first of the quadrigas begin the slow warm-up before the race.

As it was, men, women and – belatedly – children bent their knees as soon as they realized who was among them, but it was all behind, after he had passed, so that Nero's progress was that of a scythe through corn, leaving untidy rows felled in his wake.

None of it made life easier for Pantera in his role as bodyguard. Unlike any of his immediate predecessors, Nero had not taken a full company of praetorians to protect him in this sortie among his people, but only a small retinue of four companions amongst whom were Akakios and a pair of nervously alert Ubians, who had instructions to keep their weapons sheathed except in extremity. Pantera therefore gave only as much attention to the horses as Nero required at any given moment, and kept watch in turn on the wide plain in front, the training track to his right, and the booths and wooden horse barns lined up to his left.

The promised storm from the day before had not yet come; the morning was set fair, with white goosedown clouds flying before a brisk wind. Ahead, the sky met the earth in a long, smooth arc that left Pantera slightly giddy. After the mountains of Britain, it was strange to be in a place with no hills to carve open the perfect spread of the horizon.

The grassy plain that stretched from the magistrate's residence to the hippodrome was open and flat. If a man was intent on exposing himself to danger, it was not a bad place to choose. No hills broke the perfect hemisphere of the horizon, no spinneys hid the horses of a mounted ambush, no rocky outcrops served to hide a company of archers, or spearmen, or armoured infantry. But the traders' stalls, healers' booths and cooking fires that lay sprawled in a veritable village to the left of the sawdust pathway were a nightmare of open possibilities and the horse barns beyond were worse: four long, low buildings with shadowed doorways along their lengths and narrow grassed alleyways between.

At the nearest end, almost blocking the path between the barns, clusters of tents marked the professions that kept each team running: the wainwrights, the harness-makers, the loriners, the boys who boiled the axle grease, the weavers who made the banners. Above each flew the colours allocated for this race: Red at the front for the magistrate, then Blue, then White and finally the Green of the home team.

'The Red team will win, of course,' Nero said. 'The horses were a gift to the magistrate from the king of Parthia, who wishes to buy our favour and does it by flattering our friends. That team we cannot buy, and so our task for today is to decide which of the other three teams is worthy of our attentions and our gold. They are the best in Gaul. One of them must be good enough.'

Following the emperor's gaze, Pantera saw a team of four grey colts grazing at the side of the track further down near the hippodrome. As yet they bore no ribbons in their manes to identify them, but even at this distance, with the high walls of the wooden hippodrome behind, it was clear these four were of a different stamp to their thicker, heavier brethren who ran for the other teams.

Pantera had lived five years in Britain where the tribes prided themselves on breeding horses to beat the world. The women of those horse runs would have given an entire year's crop of colts for even the least of these.

Pointing, he said, 'That'll be the Red team there? The four matched greys? They look fit to beat anything Gaul could produce. Are they the magistrate's gift?'

'They must be. Come.' Nero's cheeks dimpled with the pleasure of finally finding a man who understood his passion. Together, he and Pantera turned back towards the training track.

The magistrate's team of gift-horses was momentarily blocked from sight by the passing of two other beribboned teams – chestnut colts sporting Blue and a team of blacks spectacular in White – already hitched and warming up ostentatiously before groups of watchful gamblers who changed the odds with each slow circuit. Knowing they were watched, the drivers trotted sunwise on the thick layer of sawdust, showing off their paces, but not tiring their horses. In the race, they travelled in the opposite direction; knowing this made the difference.

The colts in both teams were snappy and moody, snaking bites at their teammates and opponents. Their drivers called to them, cajoling and threatening in turn. Other men ran alongside, shouting instructions and encouragement, or calling for a stop to change the set of the harness. Only the local Coriallum team was not out yet, and still last in the betting.

The grey colts grazing at the track's end had not even been harnessed, which said a lot for the confidence of their driver, but even as the emperor's party turned to watch, two boys in the magistrate's livery began to weave ribbons of brightest scarlet into their manes, leaving the ends hanging loose to fly back as banners with their speed.

Appreciatively, Nero said, 'They're built of the wind, with desert storms in their blood and stars lighting their feet. They'll win today unless each of them breaks a leg; they outmatch the others by more than a track's length without trying.'

'If you wanted to buy a team to race in Rome, surely these are they?' Pantera asked.

'But Cornelius Proculus, the magistrate, has long been our friend, and these are his heart's joy; it would be theft for us to buy them from him. In any case, they may be fast as the wind now, but they won't stay that way for long.'

To Pantera's frustration and the evident consternation of the Ubian guards, Nero turned away from the peeled hazel barrier at the edge of the training track and turned left towards a leather-worker's stand set back amongst half a dozen others, where he fingered a tooled woman's belt with images of storks and cranes set about it, the better to bring on a child.

To Pantera, he said, 'Parthian horses are weak in the hocks and can't manage the constant tight turns of a chariot track for more than half a season. We need horses that will last all year, if not longer. There will be another team here today that will be the one to take with us to Rome. We will buy it, and its driver, and all who come with it, and make it our own. In time, if the horses prove suitable, we will race them ourselves.'

A wave of a finger saw one of the Ubians reach into his purse to buy the belt.

The stall-tender, crimson with shock, or pleasure, or terror, fell to his knees, protesting in halting Latin that it must be a gift, that he could not possibly accept money from his emperor whom he adored and who was doing him the most exceptional honour of attending his unworthy stall.

He was given a gold coin in any case, which was a hundred times the worth of what he might have dared ask for the belt. The air rang with the emperor's praises as they passed on.

Notoriously, Nero said of himself that he was the most popular emperor Rome had ever seen. In Coriallum in northern Gaul, if only on that day, it was true.

The imperial group moved deeper into the sprawl of booths and stalls. Pie-vendors bawled their wares. Bolts of woollen cloth, plain or dyed, lay in neat rows on wooden planks, to be untidied by a thousand feeling fingers by the day's end. A healer's booth was marked by a rag of torn white linen showing that the occupant was a woman and would undertake a childbirth. Closer to the horses, harness-makers plied their wares. Nero stopped at several to feel the quality of the leather, but, to the chagrin of the vendors, did not buy.

Keeping abreast of his emperor, watching ahead on both sides for signs of ill intent, Pantera said, 'Talk in the tavern this morning was that the team of black colts from Gallia Lugdunensis running under the White banner might win the race if the magistrate's horses all died in the traces. Blue and Green were not words on the lips of anyone sober enough to think.'

'Truly?' Nero raised a delicately plucked brow. 'The magistrate seemed to think the local team was good. But they drew Green in the lottery for colour, and while it may be for Ceres and the vernal season, in our experience it is always unlucky. Perhaps we make it so by believing it; we are emperor and such things are not unknown, but it cannot be changed. Come, we shall go to the horse barns and view the second teams. Sometimes the ones that do not race are better than those that do.'

Pantera spun in alarm. 'My lord, as your bodyguard, I must protest—'

He fell silent as Nero caught his arm. Men around them looked away, too quickly. The Ubians raced forward, laying hands to their sword hilts, but not yet drawing. Akakios was already there. His knife blade glanced in the blustery sun. Its tip was dulled with a brown, waxy resin.

Nero dismissed them all with a wave of one finger, as an infant might wave away a wasp.

'Walk with us alone, Leopard,' he said. 'We would speak to you in private.'

Given no option, Pantera followed where his emperor led, leaving Akakios and his poison behind. To their left and in front, stall-tenders fell silent and bowed. Word of their coming was spreading even as they walked.

Ahead were the four horse barns, with their thin oak-planked sides and roofs thatched with reed from the river's edge. Grassy avenues the width of a chariot's length kept them apart. Manure heaps smouldered at the end of each, ripening the air.

The colours flew above them, snapping in the wind: Red for Mars, battle and summer, which had been taken by the magistrate and not entered in the colour lottery the day before when the other three teams drew their ribbon. In that lottery, Lugdunum, capital of Gallia Lugdunensis to the south, had won White for winter. Blue was for autumn, the colour drawn by Noviomagus across the easterly border, who fielded the best team from Gallia Belgica. Green, as Nero had said, was for spring and Ajax had drawn it for Coriallum. Thus all three parts of Gaul were represented, plus the magistrate's team, racing for him alone.

Nero and Pantera turned down the barn side, passing the Red-bannered barns of the magistrate on the way to the White of Lugdunensis. Here, boys were still mucking out, heaving straw on to the manure heaps with a demented speed, desperate to get their task done before the race began. At the barn itself, four black heads peered at the incomers from open-fronted stalls; the second-string horses, left behind and unhappy for it.

Nero walked up and fussed the first, looking behind to check that his retinue had not strayed too close. Satisfied, he planted himself near a barn and set both fists on his hips. It was a practised pose: old statues had shown his ancestor Julius Caesar thus.

He said, 'Pantera, the Leopard, we wish you to work for us. Akakios' loyalty is beyond question, but he has shown himself to be reckless in his execution of orders. And as you have confirmed, he was not of the status that Seneca required. We believe you are his superior in the field of espionage.'

Pantera let a horse nudge his elbow, and teased a tangle from its mane. He kept his face studiously still. 'I am flattered, lord, and what you say might once have been

101

true, but I am not the man I was. As you have been told, I am damaged, possibly beyond repair. Akakios is whole, which is worth more than it may seem. He is reckless because he feels it necessary. Like an unruly race colt, it may be that he could be calmed by a judicious hand on the reins.'

Crowds were growing at the far end of the barn. Pantera began to walk away from the horses, leading the dance for the first time. Nero followed, twining together three strands of black mane hair that he had pulled loose.

'We could compel you,' he said.

'Undoubtedly. But a man does not spy well who has been broken to another's will. I believe we touched on that this morning in the magistrate's garden.'

They passed beyond the boys mucking out and came away with the mellow ripeness of manure scenting their clothes.

Feeling his way to the truth, Pantera said, 'To be a good spy, a man must immerse himself in the identity of another, and I have done that for too long in Britain to be able to do it again successfully now. I must be myself again, and find what that is, before I can ever take another's place. I can't believe there is such peril to Rome that it would not be better served by Akakios, however much it pains me to say so.'

'Gods alive, why are we ever surrounded by arrogance!' Nero bounced his balled fist off the oak plank of the barn. White-lipped, he said, 'There *is* such peril. Would we ask you else?'

It was necessary to resist a matching anger. With fragile calm, Pantera said, 'What nature of peril, lord?'

'The Phoenix Year; what do you know of it?'

'Nothing.' He had said the same to Seneca. 'Should I?'

'If you love Rome and would save it from burning, you should, yes.'

They turned together into the next avenue between the

barns. Green banners flew from the roof of the barn to their right, bright as spring grass. On the turf in front, the quadriga stood almost ready to race: a marvel of woven wicker, with fine larch spars bound in oiled bull's hide and sinew, made to be light and flexible and yet strong enough to last the full seven laps, if not necessarily any further.

Two geldings waited ready in the traces, bright chestnuts, red as gold, with the grass-green ribbons of the corn goddess already woven into their manes and tails. A lanky youth came out of the barn, glanced left and right, and, satisfied, knelt at the back of the chariot, working on the harness. If he had noticed Pantera and the emperor, he did not recognize either man. From within the horse barns, a younger voice murmured the tones that every horseman uses to calm a fractious horse. Impatient hooves slammed on hard earth soon after.

Nero stood in the shadow of the reed roof's overhang, watching.

With a prickle of premonition, Pantera said, 'You said Rome would burn. What has that to do with the Phoenix Year?'

'If we knew that, we would not need to ask you!' Nero made a visible grasp for calm. 'A prophecy is in circulation of which we have secured a part. It says that if Rome burns in the Phoenix Year, it will bring about a miracle.'

'And the Phoenix Year is . . . ?'

'A thing of Alexandrian making, and perhaps of the pyramid-priests before them. As you know, a year is not exactly three hundred and sixty-five days long, but exceeds that number by a small amount. Those who know of such things measure the leftover hours in each year beyond the three hundred and sixty-five days and gather them together.'

The emperor was pacing now, watching the horses and Pantera equally. 'Once every fourteen hundred and sixty years, the sum of those hours adds up to an entire year which they name for the Phoenix, believing that at midsummer of that year, after three days of death, the flamebird arises from the ashes of its own destruction and soars up to perch in the upper branches of a date palm.'

'And we are nearing such a year, or you would not speak of it.'

'We are in it. The year began on the ides of August.'

The crowds were coming nearer again. It did not do to stand still. Pantera moved off into a bright place of safety, where all directions could easily be seen. Akakios came into view behind, but did not approach too closely.

Out on the training track, the four grey colts belonging to the magistrate were safely harnessed. A driver in the long grey battle-cloak of the Parthians, bordered in red with inlaid threads of gold, was trotting them round the track.

Nero was not watching. He said, 'Can you read Greek?' and at Pantera's nod, pressed into his hand a piece of folded papyrus, thin as a leaf, such as the Alexandrians use for their writing.

Unfolded, the surface was clean, the writing neat and professionally done, with lines of even size and spacing, straight as a rule. Pantera read it once to himself, and then again out loud, to prove that he could.

'. . . *and thus will it come about in the Year of the Phoenix, on the night when the* . . . there is a gap here . . . *when the – something unknown – shall gaze down in wrath from beyond the knife-edge of the world, that in his sight shall the Great Whore be wreathed in fire, and burned to the utmost ashes, seared to nought in the pits of her depravity. Only when this has come to pass shall the Kingdom of Heaven be manifest as has been promised. Then shall* . . . here's another gap . . . *be rent, never to be repaired, and all that was whole shall be broken and the covenant that was made shall be completed in accord with all that is written.*'

In the gusting morning, with the sharp colours of the banners crisp against the late morning sky, with the chatter of children and the crying seagulls at the harbour, Pantera felt the world grow still and quiet.

Nero said, 'Pantera?'

'My lord, forgive me, this is . . . a deeper thing than I had imagined.'

'So you understand it?'

'Some of it, I think. Not all.'

Animated, Nero said, 'It is the Hebrews, isn't it? They believe in the Kingdom of Heaven, a time when their god will rule over all others, when their laws will be the only laws, when all men must be circumcized and refuse the meat of idols. Our uncle Claudius had them banned from our seat of rule seventeen years ago. We could do the same thing again.'

'It is Hebrew in concept,' Pantera agreed. 'But only a fanatical few desire it and even they know that you would raze Jerusalem to the ground if they so much as contemplated burning Rome. If there's a fire, it will not be lit by any man who cares for Judaea.'

He folded the note squarely, and handed it back to the emperor. 'This is a copy,' he said. 'The gaps are deliberately made to leave the full meaning unknowable, particularly the date of the burning. May I see the full script?'

Nero shrugged. 'We don't have the original. Akakios . . . retrieved this from a Syrian messenger who was endeavouring to sell it. For a further sum of gold – a quite extortionate sum – the highest bidder was to be given the prophecy in full, which would give the date when the fire must occur and also a greater insight into what might be rent thereafter.'

'The Syrian, then, can tell you where to find what you seek.'

'Regrettably not.'

'He died under questioning?'

105

Nero pulled a face. 'As you have noted, Akakios is reckless. But the Syrian knew nothing of the prophecy or where it was kept. He hadn't seen it or read it and knew nothing beyond that a white-haired, hoarse-voiced man had given him the copies and charged him with getting the best price for each. That much, I believe.'

'Where did this take place? Where was he given the copies?'

'In an inn named for the Black Chrysanthemum which is on the Street of the Lame Lion in Alexandria.' Nero spoke the place names as if they were sacred text. 'He believed the vendor to have been a local astrologer, but could not be sure. The man spoke Greek with a local Alexandrian accent, and had ink stains on his fingers.'

Pantera laughed, and only late remembered that to do so in front of one's emperor was not wise. 'Astrologers in Alexandria are like fishermen in Coriallum: every second man makes it his profession and those in between believe they know more but simply don't choose to make money thereby.'

'And to say he was old, white-haired and greedy is merely stating a fact of all astrologers. We know this.'

The emperor leaned back against the stables, chewing his lip. Pantera moved to get the best view of both ends of the row. Around them, the barn was coming to life as, at last, the Green team began to make ready. The lanky youth at the chariot moved round and began to work on the harness on the offside. He gave every appearance of not yet having noticed the presence of his emperor.

Beyond him, a smaller, thinner boy with grubby blond hair and a tear in the hem of his tunic brought two fresh colts out of the barn, one rope held in either hand. His charges danced and spun irritably beside him. They were not of the calibre of the magistrate's team, but Pantera would happily have bet the contents of his purse on their coming second.

Nero, too, was watching them. Absently, he said, 'I was there when the Syrian spoke to us, so that I could hear the truth of it. At the end, he said something that was true, out of his love for me, not because it was wrenched from him by pain.' He frowned, remembering. 'He said that the prophecy is harmless to me and to Rome unless someone wishes so badly to bring about the Kingdom of God that they count it as nothing to murder thousands of men, women and children. What kind of man does that?'

'The kind who hates Rome and Jerusalem equally,' Pantera said, carefully. He, too, was watching the horses. 'Men like that are few, and there are ways to find those with whom they conspire, although I doubt if they're in Gaul, or even . . . my lord, forgive me, this is a subject of great weight, but I think we must speak of it later if we are not to see bloodshed. Those two chestnut colts are going to fight.'

CHAPTER EIGHT

Math saw Pantera at the moment before Brass bit his arm hard enough to draw blood, and then lunged for Bronze.

In a morning filled with bad omens, it was the worst. First, Ajax had been called away by the magistrate's steward to a meeting of the four race-drivers and had not yet returned. Then Lucius, the motherless son of a mange-ridden street dog who was the elder of Ajax's two apprentices, had taken to fiddling with the traces and refused to help harness the two lead colts.

Lucius was sixteen years old, lanky and callow with bad skin and crooked teeth, and he was scared of horses. Gordianus had been his uncle, which was the only reason he had been given the apprenticeship, and Ajax, who could be breathtakingly soft at times, had promised to let him finish.

He and Math hated each other, and Lucius had taken to spending the nights in town with one of the newly arrived harness-makers, coming back with stories of work that far exceeded anything Math's father could do. Ajax had neither listened to him nor beaten him into silence. Math was waiting for the day either might happen.

True to form, Lucius had spent the night before race-day

in town and come back looking ragged and tired. He had been more than usually afraid of the colts all morning, and had not denied it when Math shouted the accusation, just put his head down by the back wheel and made a show of fixing the harness. Left alone, knowing that the other three teams were already out on the training track, Math had done what seemed best and brought the two colts out together.

His mother had always taught him, and from the first days of his apprenticeship Ajax had agreed, that if he were ever to harness the quadriga on his own, Math should always lead out the colts as a pair. Brought out singly, whichever of the two was put first in the traces was likely to fight the new one coming in and, as Ajax said at least once every morning and often in the afternoons and evenings as well, the colts were built of meat and bone and fury, while the chariots were of fragile wood and wicker. 'Better to lose a bit of skin off a colt than the entire racing chariot.'

Ajax had never, Math thought, owned his own race-chariot before, while everyone in the world had owned a colt or two by the time they were twenty.

So he did as he was told and brought out Brass and Bronze together, the two chestnut colts, seven years old, in the primes of their lives, race-fit and lethal and, as Ajax had said, filled with fury.

They hated each other; it was what made them so exceptionally good, and so exceptionally difficult to handle. For the right driver, who could take all that rage and turn it into speed, they would run their hearts out to best each other, and so win the race. With the wrong driver, a man who lost his concentration, or did not have the beasts' respect, they could run themselves to a halt and fight in the traces, wreaking havoc on the track. Math had seen that happen once, and never wished to again.

Getting them into the traces in the first place was his

109

responsibility and, on the morning of the emperor's race, it had seemed for a while as if he might succeed.

He had prayed to Nemain of the moon and to Manannan of the seas, who had become something of a favourite with the boys who plied the docks, and to his mother, who was his patron god and had bred the colts. With all that divine help, he had backed Brass and Bronze nearly up to the bar, with the two rearmost geldings standing peacefully enough.

And then Math saw two men standing in the avenue between the horse barns, and while the wealthier of the two was a stranger the other was Pantera, who was looking at him with exactly the same look he had given when Math had not returned the cheese the night before. For a fleeting moment, Math lost his focus on the colts, and the sky fell on his head.

'*Keep them away from the chariot!*'

He had time to scream that, and haul both the lead ropes forward, before the world blurred to sky and turf and hooves and pain and his shoulder was wrenched from its socket and the colts were screaming and Lucius was screaming louder and higher, like a pig at slaughter, and other voices were shouting . . .

'*Math!* Lord, stay back! *Math, let go!* Lord, you must not be injured, please stay back. Math, will you *let go*, I've got him.'

Math let go of Bronze and held on to Brass and hoped he had them in the right order. Not that he had any choice: Brass's rope had become wrapped round his arm and he couldn't have got free if he'd wanted to. With the hated enemy taken out of reach, the big chestnut colt reared one more time and came down, shaking and blowing and stamping, but no longer fighting.

Panting, bleeding, too shocked to speak, Math stood in a bubble of calm, with Pantera close by holding Bronze and looking, briefly, equally shaken.

They were not alone, although for a moment it had seemed so. A great many people stood around. A glance at either end of the barn showed a massive, flame-haired warrior-guard standing with his weapon bared, blocking entry. People crowded beyond, trying to see in, to find gossip to spread, but dared not pass. In the quiet avenue, Lucius sobbed piteously and was rightly being ignored. A number of young men in immensely expensive tunics, with silver and gold at their belts and fatly jingling purses, stood around, looking interested and amused in equal proportion.

The youngest of them, and the most expensively dressed – in a toga, actually, not a tunic, and with purple around the hem – was leaning down, examining Bronze's off fore as if he knew what he was doing, ignoring, as he did so, Pantera's strident protest.

So there was one man in the world who could ignore Pantera with impunity. In his dazed state, Math found that as interesting as what the young man was saying.

'He's bleeding. Is there a healer?'

'Me,' cawed a woman's voice, in Gaulish, and Math spun round to see Hannah, looking uncommonly shabby, as if she had paused to wipe muck on her bare arms and scruff her hair and taken pains to coarsen her voice.

It was hard to believe someone so unclean could be a healer. Certainly the young man looked as if he were about to dismiss her, when a commotion at the end of the stands told of Ajax confronting the big flame-haired guard who was blocking his way to his horses.

Bronze and Brass heard him, and perhaps saved his life, for the warrior-guard had raised his sword and, far from backing off, Ajax's face had grown very still the way it did before a race. Math heard Pantera say, 'Mithras, no!' very quietly, under his breath, and then Brass and Bronze spun and reared and threw their heads back and screamed a clarion call for their master.

The sound carried all over the barns and the training track and the hippodrome, and made everyone else fall silent.

'Lord, that's the driver. The guard would do well to let him past.' Pantera was diffident. That was new, too; he had been a great deal less than diffident with Seneca. But the wealthy youth in the toga listened and called an order, and the guard-giant lowered his sword and stood back just enough to let a single man step through.

Ajax was in driving mood. Even Hannah knew better than to go near him when he first stepped down from a chariot after a race, and he looked the same now: white-faced and grim, fit to kill anyone who came against him, not out of anger, but just because the need to win was so profound that he would clear anyone from his path to do it.

Pantera was in his path. In fact, to Math it seemed as if Pantera had put himself in his path, directly in front of the youth with the toga.

For a moment, Pantera, too, looked as if he had stepped off a chariot, tense and relaxed at the same time and with that careful, still look to his face that took in everything equally. He angled his head so that his eyes met Ajax's and the world held its breath a moment, as each took the measure of the other.

Then Pantera shook his head, to himself or to Ajax or both, and turned to the youth and said smoothly, 'Lord, I believe this is Ajax of Athens, driver of the Green chariot that will race today for your entertainment. Ajax, you are in the presence of Nero Claudius Germanicus, emperor of Rome.'

Emperor of Rome. Nero. The young man with the purple-edged toga who had stooped to examine an injured colt and had its blood even now on his hands.

In bowel-watering consternation, Math saw Ajax turn on the emperor a heartbeat's savage hatred that went far

112

beyond the ice-cold, driven rage of racing, but that moment, too, was gone almost before he saw it, and then Math watched a small and unpleasant miracle, as Ajax folded into himself, in the opposite of what he did to race. He curved his shoulders, making himself smaller, and wrung his hands together and simpered – *simpered!* – in the way craven stall-holders did to rich men.

He fell to one knee. 'Lord, please accept my apologies. Our horses are raw and not fully trained. The boy—'

'Get up, man! The boy did well to hold the colts as far as he did. He should never have been left alone. He is to be commended.' Nero turned commending eyes on Math.

Pantera was moving. Ajax was moving. Because they were both moving towards Math, they collided before they reached him. And so it was that they left the way clear for Math to look squarely at his emperor and for Nero to favour Math with a fond and certain smile.

Math blushed and looked down. Not because the look was new, although he didn't especially want Hannah to see him working, but because it was what he did when a man of great wealth looked at him like that.

And even then, glancing down at his own bare feet, which were filthy from the unshovelled horse muck, a part of him was singing bright, sparkling praises to Nemain, god of moon and water, favourite of his mother, to Manannan, to Hannah's Egyptian Isis and her philosopher-gods, to whoever had brought him to this glorious possibility to earn himself a gold piece, and maybe more than that.

The emperor was known to buy chariot teams for all kinds of reasons, and some of those reasons had nothing to do with the horses.

There was a short, hard silence, when everyone knew what had happened, and nobody knew what to say.

The emperor broke it; he was the only one who could. 'This colt has injured his tendon,' he said. 'He should be trotted up, to see the damage.'

'I'll do it,' Ajax said.

With a surprisingly regal bow, he took Bronze from Pantera and trotted him out, away from the small group and back towards them. The colt was brave and fired up and ready to race, but the emperor was right, he was definitely lame. It took a good horseman to see it, but Math was a good horseman, and surrounded by the same.

'He will heal, given time,' Nero said. 'But he will need to be replaced for the race. Have you another horse?'

'There's Sweat,' said Ajax doubtfully, 'but—'

'He won't run with Brass,' blurted Math, forgetting his place. 'He'll fight and not run. Really. They'll kill each other before they get to the track. It'll be worse than war.'

'Is it so?' The emperor smiled as if this were a great insight. Math looked down at his feet again.

'It is so, lord,' Ajax said tightly. 'If you wish a true contest, it would perhaps be better to run the two second-string colts together, although they are not yet fully racing fit. Lucius, go and fetch—'

'No. He's the reason the accident happened in the first place. Send this one. What's your name, child?'

'Math,' said Math, 'Math of the Osismi.' A thought struck him, displacing the near promise of gold. 'But Sweat and Thunder aren't groomed. They have no ribbons. We'll be late for the race if we take the time to do it properly now—'

Nero laughed, lightly, with a new intimacy. 'The race cannot start before we start it. Therefore, if we were to help you, Math, you could not be late. Get the horses. Fly. We shall do it together.'

They did it together, Math of the Osismi and Nero Claudius Augustus Germanicus, emperor of Rome, who had deft fingers and a surprisingly good way with a horse so that Thunder stood for him who sometimes would barely stand

114

for Ajax, and Sweat let Math vault on to his bare back so that he could plait the mane from the withers, standing up, with the horse raising his head high to let him reach the ones round his ears.

It was a recently developed trick; he had done it once to amuse Hannah. He did it now quite differently, blushing as if it were foolish but necessary, looking down and making shy as the emperor asked him questions and drew out of him the small facts of his life: his mother's death, his father's near-fatal wounding in a trivial bar brawl, his own miraculously early apprenticeship, his burning desire to be a race-driver and to take his mother's horses to Rome, to race against the best the world could offer.

Math was honest to a fault. If he said nothing of theft and working the docks, it was because the emperor did not think to ask him.

Grown men commonly made foolish assumptions about Math of the Osismi. On this day of the races, with all to run for and success newly dangled in reach, Nero, emperor of Rome, seemed to be making most of them.

CHAPTER NINE

'*Go Thunder! Go Sweat! Go!*'

Math was hoarse. His ears overflowed with the noise of his own voice lost in ten thousand others. His eyes watered from shouting. His bones rocked and his teeth rattled with the pounding thunder of four white-eyed, sweating chariot teams as they strove for the last ounce of speed.

There was sand on his face, in his mouth, in his eyes. His body poured sweat, crushed on all sides by other apprentices in their place down by the track, where they could run to the teams and help if needed. They paid nothing for this place, and it was the best in the whole hippodrome.

Math was young and therefore near the back, but if he pushed in the right places at the right times he could see through the tangle of waving arms in front of him and catch flashes of the teams: a gobbet of spit on a horse's mouth, a spinning wheel, part of a raised whip, Ajax's shaven head shining under the glancing sun . . .

He could taste the creaming sweat. Almost, he could smell the scent of winning. The Parthian team were not as fast as he had thought. They had two lengths on the other three; hardly anything.

'*Ajax! Go!*'

Ajax was going like the wind. He had promised the emperor he would. The dream-like start to the race that had begun with Nero helping Math to plait the Green ribbons into the manes of the colts had continued with the emperor and his retinue – there had been sixteen of the giant flame-haired warriors by then – walking with Math and the Green team up to the mouth of the tunnel that led into the hippodrome.

Ajax had stripped off his jerkin and wound the four sets of reins round his waist, with the soft goatskin belt beneath so that they didn't cut into him as he angled his body round the track.

The scars on his back and shoulders had gleamed under a layer of goose-grease, laid on to stop him losing his skin if he fell on to the sand of the track. Math watched the emperor study the scars of the flogging. Nero raised his brows once but said nothing. It was a day for not speaking the things that were thought.

The greatest of the not-spoken things was Math's. He raged silently all the way to the hippodrome, and everyone with him knew it, if not why.

For the first time in his life, he had been allowed to lead the horses to the start. Ajax had promised that he could do it 'some day': a gift for when Math was ready; for when Lucius had gone; for when there was a good, well-earned reason to give a wayward child a reward for good behaviour.

Today had not been a reward for anything but an obvious attempt to break the growing connection between Math and the emperor, and it had failed for the simple reason that, in a blatant act of favouritism that had earned Ajax thunderous looks from the drivers of the other three chariots, Nero had chosen to walk alongside Math and the Greens to the mouth of the tunnel.

For Math, Nero's presence had made the event a heart-crushing anticlimax. There were few things in his life he truly craved and the chance to lead Sweat and Thunder to a race had been one of them. But he had dreamed of it done with ceremony, and on his own merits, not as a means to keep him from an end.

All the way to the hippodrome, therefore, Math had been crabbily sullen and Nero had misread it, thinking him overawed, and had chatted pleasantly about nothing.

Ajax had been desperate and barely hiding it. He had swept his hand over and over across his shaved skull in the way he did only when he was most worried about the horses. Hannah had walked on the other side of the chariot, still looking like a tavern drudge. It had been impossible to tell what she thought, except that she was particularly wary of Nero. Whether the emperor had noticed or not was equally a mystery; he had been charming to everyone.

At the entrance to the tunnel, when it was truly impossible for him to walk any further without causing an irretrievable scandal, Nero had reached out a hand and brought the small procession to a halt.

He had not spoken to Math, only favoured him with the smile that said more than words. Almost as an afterthought, as he was turning to leave, he had turned back and looked up at Ajax.

'Losing will change nothing,' he had said. 'We may buy the team, but not the driver. It would be best for everyone if you did your best to win, do you understand?'

Ajax was race-ready, pale-lipped, wet with sweat and smelling of the pine resin that swathed his hands to keep the reins from slipping, and coated the pale skin of his head simply because he had rubbed it so often. Already he was looking inward, beginning to weave himself into the minds of all four horses, so that they and he became one.

Too curtly for true politeness, he said, 'I understand perfectly, lord. I always drive to win.'

'See that you succeed.'

The flame-haired guards had formed a double line of

eight on either side of the tunnel's mouth. They saluted, as one, making the moment a ceremony in itself.

With a final nod to Math, the emperor had turned away and begun to mount the steps to his dais. The magistrate was already there with his wife and three daughters, dressed in such finery as Coriallum had never seen before.

The tunnel had beckoned: a short stripe of dark before the bright, wide swathe of the track, gleaming with new gold sand, and the central oak spina around which the track was built newly carved in the likeness of dark-haired Apollo, with his lyres and chariots. The smells of fresh sand and horse-sweat, of axle grease and pine resin, mingled to produce the unmistakable scent of a chariot race.

Sweat and Thunder knew and loved it; they grew half a hand taller just breathing it in, and strained forward in the traces, desperate to go.

Math had felt himself grow as they grew, had felt the faster beat of his heart, already racing. From the sand, three trumpets sounded, calling in the Red team. The line of chariots shuffled forward, leaving the Whites next to go. Green was last, because of Nero. Math had taken the first step to lead his colts into the tunnel when a hand fell on his shoulder.

'I'll lead them in,' Pantera had said. 'There is a thing your driver must know.'

Math had gaped at him, horrified, then looked to Ajax for permission to carry on into the tunnel. But, once again, Pantera's green-brown eyes had met Ajax's amber ones over Math's head, and once again a decision had been made without him.

'Math, go to the apprentices' enclosure,' Ajax had said. 'The horses will be safe with the emperor's bodyguard.'

It was the last in a series of mortal insults. Always, every single time, in every race in the history of racing, the boy who led the racehorses to the tunnel led them also through it to the start line.

Math had relinquished the lead ropes as if they were his life, swearing inwardly to all the gods he could think of that if the Green team lost he would know it was Pantera's fault, or Ajax's, or both.

He spun away, kicking at the chariot wheel in passing, kicking again at the wall of the hippodrome, kicking at the shin of the last boy in the queue lining up to go into the apprentices' enclosure, which was suicidally stupid when Math had just been marked for the kind of special attention that saw boys scarred for life, if not dead.

Murder happened often enough in the apprentices' enclosure and was never of great concern; the strongest lived and the weakest died and sometimes a silver coin changed hands afterwards to soften the blow to the driver who must find a new boy.

The offended youth had turned, slowly. He was as tall as Ajax, and as broad, but with a head full of hair and lacking the scars. His nose was flat from many fights, his eyes small and violent as a boar's.

A White band at his brow identified his team as the matched blacks that ran for Gallia Lugdunensis. White ribbons danced and dangled from his wrists, light as a flight of moths settled by chance on a rutting bull.

He had two companions, equally big, equally be-ribboned. All three were armed with short, vicious eating knives, honed on both edges and curved at the tip. They had flashed forward, close enough to lift Math's hair with the wind of their passing.

Math did not carry a knife; he had always relied on his speed and a greater knowledge of the streets to protect him. Here, in the open, the three youths were too close and the crowd pressed too tight to make running an option. He had stood his ground obstinately and thought what Ajax and Pantera might say when they found him dead. The idea held a certain bleak satisfaction.

'Math?'

Hannah had caught his shoulder, spinning him round, away from the danger. In the few moments since he had left the tunnel's mouth, she had become cleaner, and ceased to stoop. Green ribbons were bound about her wrists. On her, they were bright as new leaves.

'Look.' She had spoken in Greek, which lifted them apart from the mob. When Math had looked up at her, she had pointed back to the tunnel's mouth. 'It was for a reason you were sent away.'

She was a woman and a healer and she had held him in the crook of her arm as if the knives did not exist, nor the youths wielding them. For all of these reasons, but more for her courage, the White youths had left them alone.

Math had felt death brush him close and then leave. The knots in his bowels had loosed themselves, and he had passed wind noisily.

Hannah had said only, 'Do you see? There's something wrong with the chariot. The emperor's scarred man saw it.'

'Pantera,' said Math, laying claim to the man by virtue of his name. 'His name is Sebastos Abdes Pantera. He's not the emperor's man. He's the one who paid me the denarius last night.'

Even as he was speaking, Math had watched Pantera say something and gesture towards the offside wheel of the chariot, and Ajax had turned in consternation, peering down at the chariot, or the harness, or the wheels.

He might have jumped down to look at whatever was wrong, but the three horns sounded for the fourth time, summoning the Green team to the start.

With an oath that Math barely heard, in a language that was not Greek, Latin or Gaulish, Ajax had clucked his tongue and flicked the horses forward and let Pantera lead him into the tunnel.

Math did not see the race start – the apprentices' stands were good for the end of the race, not the beginning – but

121

the roar of the crowd told him the Greens got off to a good start, and when they came into view it was clear Ajax held a good position, not quite in the lead – the Reds were truly unassailable – but good enough, and with no signs of a crisis.

For the first three laps of the seven, Math learned the details of the race from the cheers of those around him. Confused, unhappy and terrified at what Pantera might have seen that he had not, he had made the effort to jump to see past the boys in front.

The rest of the Green team had filtered in afterwards but kept their distance, ashamed to be with him. The wainwright's apprentices were there, and the loriner's half-blind son, plus one or two others who could lay claim to a Green ribbon and a place in the enclosure. None of them had spoken to him.

Even Hannah had not stayed with him. Seeing him safe from attack, she wormed her way out to the oak rails at the sides of the enclosure and hoisted herself up to perch on the top rail, the better to see the race.

Math joined her halfway through the fourth lap when the hammer of the race had moved his blood so that it wasn't possible to stay silent any longer. There was no room for him on the rails, but he stood at her side jumping whenever he could to see the flashes of coloured ribbons from the horses' manes and screaming when Hannah screamed.

Sometime in the progress of the laps, Lucius arrived, sullen and stupid and barely carrying a Green ribbon, but even that had not taken the shine off the morning. Math screamed louder, to make up for the older boy's silence.

'*Ajax! Go! Go Green! Go Sweat! Go Thunder!*'

'May I help you?'

The yellow-haired Gaul sat at a bench in front of the harness-maker's booth at the end of the Green barn. He was almost alone; every other man, woman and child of Coriallum was in the hippodrome watching the races. The laps could be counted by the volume of the screams; a notch higher with each dipping dolphin on the central spina. They were on the third as the man asked his question.

Pantera did not answer immediately, but leaned his shoulder against a pole of a nearby booth and watched a man of perhaps fifty years, made old early by battle, pain and loss, deftly turn the end of a breastpiece, stitching together two flaps of leather with padding between to make it softer. He used two needles, one above and one below, making a row of neat double stitches, perfectly spaced.

Behind him, the booth was clean and uncluttered. His tunic was old and worn thin at the elbows, but fastidiously clean. He smelled of new grass and neatsfoot oil and, beneath that, of the rubbing stones the warriors of Britain – and likely of Gaul – had used daily on their blades to keep the soul-spirit of the iron fresh and fed.

It was a combination Pantera had not encountered in nearly two years. It caused his mouth to water and his chest to ache with remembered loss. He pushed himself away from the tent pole and squatted on his heels in the way the elders had done among the Dumnonii.

'I am told you are Caradoc of the Osismi,' he said, 'father of Math of that tribe. I had hoped to find you here, but I confess to surprise that you are not watching the race.'

'My son prefers it thus. He fears I bring ill luck to him and his horses. On a day such as today when his team may be victorious, I would not blight his joy by my presence.'

'And the team's progress is as easily gauged from here as the stadium,' Pantera said, cocking his head to the roar of a half-lap from the hippodrome.

'Indeed.' The rhythm of the stitching paused only a moment. 'And you are?' The man's voice was perfectly neutral. A sheathed sword lay under his seat. His right foot had moved to rest on the hilt.

'A friend,' Pantera said. 'One who cares for Math and his future. Not in the way you might think. I have just watched him encounter the Emperor Nero. It was . . . unfortunate.'

'I imagine Math did not find it so.'

'He told the emperor that his mother was dead and his father had been crippled in a tavern brawl. He told me, on the other hand, that you had been a warrior and were injured in battle. Either way, I am surprised to find you so active.'

'It suits Math that others believe what he wishes. And he believes it to be true that I am injured beyond all use.'

'Perhaps he is also protecting you with the story of the tavern brawl? It would not do to tell the emperor that his father had been wounded in battle against the legions.'

'Did he tell you that?'

'No. He told me you and his mother had been warriors. It may be that in our ancestors' time the men and women of Gaul fought shoulder to shoulder. But in my experience, only in Britain has such a thing happened in our lifetime.'

'Then your experience is wide indeed.'

Caradoc of the Osismi did not stop stitching, but he did lift his foot from his blade. Something altered in the angle of his shoulders and, for the first time, he looked up from his work.

His eyes were a clear, rain-washed grey, exactly like Math's. His hair was the colour of old thatch, streaked through with grey, older by three decades than Math's grubby gold but easily imagined as once the same, only cleaner, and so brighter. Manifestly, he was the father of his son.

He was also a reader of men. Pantera stood still under a scrutiny such as he had not borne since his first meeting with Aerthen's mother.

'Will you sit?' Caradoc said at last. 'I have no wine, but could offer ale.'

It sounded a simple offer. Pantera, who knew it was not, found he was offered both an answer and another, more difficult question.

The past days had been full of such. In each, he had made a choice that did not fit with his idea of the man he had become since leaving Britain: the choice to answer the emperor's summons when it would have been as easy to walk up the long road from the Roman camp in Lugdunum and lose himself eventually in the wild tribes north of the Brigantes; the choice to let a grubby urchin follow him from the docks, and then not to kill him; the choice to let Seneca find them, and then not to kill him either, but to eat with him, and listen; the choice to speak to a race-driver who claimed falsely to be Greek about what had been done to his harness; and now, last, the choice to find the urchin's crippled father, who was not, after all, anywhere near so crippled that his son must ply the docks to feed both of them.

At any point, Pantera could have walked away. He did not yet know why he had not.

'Thank you.' He sat on the iron-bound chest at the tent's entrance that served both as a lock-box and a seat, waiting while Caradoc set down his harness and went to fetch ale from the back of his tent.

The former warrior moved slowly, using a stick for balance. His left leg had evidently been broken at some time and set at an awkward angle, so that his knee and foot turned outward.

Cautiously, Pantera said, 'I have seen others who were fallen on by a horse. Few of them escaped with only lameness.'

'But many more are able to throw themselves clear and walk away unhurt.' Caradoc spoke with his back still turned. 'I was holding Math. He was less than a month old. I had to keep him safe from more than a dying horse.'

Only in war were horses killed beneath their riders, and newborn infants threatened with danger so that their fathers must accept injury to keep them alive. 'Does he know?' Pantera asked.

'No.'

Caradoc poured the ale and, halting, brought it back. In the hippodrome, the fourth lap came near its conclusion. At the tents, Pantera accepted the small beaker of boiled leather and the foaming ale within it. A further decision settled in his mind.

Raising his mug to the sun, he spoke aloud the first line of the invocation to Briga, mother of Nemain, keeper of life and death, of war and poetry, patron of leatherworkers and of the chariot drivers' death-dance. Into the still silence after it, he said, 'When I lived among the warriors of the Dumnonii, it was considered an insult to offer a man wine, it being of Rome. Ale, by contrast, was an honour.' He spoke it all in the language of south-western Britain, enemy of Rome.

The clear grey eyes regarded him a while. 'There are places in Britain still not under the heel of Rome,' Caradoc said eventually. 'The dreamers are gathered again on Mona, the island off the west coast, led by the Boudica's brother, with her daughters at his side. Graine, for all her youth, is said to be amongst the foremost dreamers there. She has said already that Rome will take Mona in her life-time, but that Hibernia, further west, will be safe and can be reached in time. Those who will set themselves against Rome believe her and gather under her uncle's banner.'

He spoke the forbidden language with an ease and fluency that told of a lifetime's daily use.

Pantera held the leather mug between his knees and stared down at the slow-moving islands of thin foam on the top. As Caradoc had done, he, too, answered the question that had so carefully not been asked. 'I lost too much in Britain to go back there now. You, though, could return at any time.'

'And take Math?' The grey eyes flashed even as they looked past him to the hippodrome. 'The boy who tells the emperor that his father was injured in a bar-room brawl? If you know my son at all, you will know that he despises warriors and all they stand for. How could I take him into a culture where warriors are honoured above all else?'

'They're not honoured above the dreamers,' Pantera said softly.

'My son is not a dreamer,' Caradoc said. 'Nor is he a leatherworker, a hunter, a weaver, a builder of round-houses, or one who can find water, who can sense shoals of fish and draw them to his nets, who can charm a hare from the hill. He is a thief and a seller of himself and neither of these has a place in the tribes. In the pitiful port-sprawl that is Coriallum, Math has learned to be an urban creature. What would he be if I wrenched him from that?'

'He would be safe from Nero. No one here can give him that protection now.' Pantera set his ale on the grass. He had drunk a mouthful, which was more than Math's father had done. 'You are not of the Osismi,' he said. 'Ajax who drives for the Greens is not of Athens. Might he not help you to take Math to safety?'

Caradoc shook his head. 'Not if Ajax wins the race. Or even if he comes a good second behind the magistrate's wing-footed Parthian colts. He made an oath on the shade of Math's mother he would do whatever was in his power to get the team – and so Math – to Rome if he could. And no' – Caradoc held up his hand against Pantera's almost-question – 'I did not think it wise to give such an oath, but it was Math's greatest wish and it seemed safer that he go with Ajax than that he try to get there alone.' The old man smiled thinly. 'He thinks Rome will be Coriallum wrought larger, and he will be the greatest dock thief of them all.'

Pantera said, 'When I was a child, I thought the greatest gift I could have was Roman citizenship and that I would do whatever was in my power to earn it. We all make mistakes that in later adulthood we look back on with dismay.'

'If we survive them,' Caradoc said, and Pantera found it politic not to answer, but paused, listening to the sound of another lap finishing. The roar was the longest it had been, as the teams began their final lap.

He turned to face Caradoc for the first time. 'If Ajax were to lose the race,' he asked thoughtfully, 'and Nero were not to require him to come to Rome, would Ajax help you get Math to safety then, do you think?'

Caradoc looked at him in alarm. 'Tell me why Ajax might not win,' he said sharply.

'A youth of the Green team cut partway through the harness of the offside traces just before the horses left the barns. It was carefully done: the harness will stand for the greater part of the race, but it is my belief that if the team is made to angle hard to the outside, the strain will break at least one of the straps.'

'Does Ajax know of this?' They were both standing now, staring out towards the hippodrome. The thunder of the crowd was deafening.

'I told him before he entered the arena,' Pantera said. 'I wouldn't have come here to tell you otherwise. He will need help later. I thought you would be in a position to give it.'

In the hippodrome, the crowd sucked in a collective gasp. The noise was exactly that of the moment in battle when a champion has been downed in single combat.

Caradoc gripped Pantera's shoulder. 'If Ajax is injured, tell Math and Hannah to bring him to the upper room of the Roan Bull tavern; it's closest to the hippodrome. Go now!'

CHAPTER TEN

'**G**o Sweat! Go Thunder!'
The fifth lap marker fell – another tumbling dolphin that spun and arced down a water slide on the spina to bob in the pool at the base. By the time it settled in its place, the teams were halfway down the far straight, running against the sun, with the Green ribbons lying in third place of four. The Parthians were in the lead for Red, but not as far as they might have been if they had really raced. The magistrate's four matched grey colts had barely broken sweat and were not being pushed by their driver.

Behind them, Blue, Green and White, in that order, were straining in a tight pack, bunched together, the drivers leaning steeply into the turns, each vying for the place on the rail that gave them the best chance into the bend. Ajax's bald head was a beacon in the middle, with the coloured ribbons flowing past his ears. Sweat and Thunder were running their hearts out, low to the ground, stretched flat and hard with every stride.

Through the sweating gap under another boy's elbow, Math watched a space appear between the rail and the inner wheel of Blue's chariot. Ajax had seen it before him. He always did.

Math watched Ajax shift his weight to his inside foot,

felt in his own body the pull of the traces shift a fraction inside, saw the crack of the whip high above Sweat, but not Thunder, pulling him just a step to his left, and then – wait, wait, wait another stride . . . *on!* – aiming for a space that was barely wide enough for a single horse, never mind two and a chariot behind.

Math thought his heart might stop with excitement. Ajax was his hero, Pantera forgotten. He grabbed Lucius' shoulder and jumped high in the air, fighting to see.

What he saw was near-disaster. Thunder broke stride, a thing that never happened.

'*Nooooo!*'

Ten thousand men, women and children groaned as one. Math jumped again, but Lucius jumped in front, blocking the view, and by the time he could leap a third time and look, the disaster had been averted. There was no crash, but Ajax was still caught in behind the Blues and now the Whites were coming up on the outside, four sweat-streaked black colts, stretched flat to the floor with a thread-fine whip above, moving smoothly into place to box Ajax in.

The boys of the Blues and Whites jumped in unison, cheering. '*Go! Go! Go!*'

'*Unfair! Foul!*'

Math was screaming himself hoarse. So unfair! Everyone knew the Reds were going to win, but it mattered to come second. It had not occurred to him as he walked with Nero that the other drivers would see it, and mark the Green team as the one to beat.

'Foul! Unfair! They can't combine, it's not legal! Foul! Fou— *oof!*'

A boy from the Blue team slammed his elbow in Math's gut. He sank to his knees, retching. Hannah jumped down from the rails and pulled him up before he was trampled.

'One of the other drivers made Thunder break stride.

They must have done!' Math shouted over the havoc around them.

Hannah cupped her palm to his ear and shouted back. 'The White driver spun his whip at Thunder's eye. Ajax saw it and pulled him back in time. In Alexandria, even in Rome, the driver would have gone for the gap, and risked a blind horse. Ajax is better than that.'

Math heard the thread of pride in Hannah's voice, and jumped again. The teams were nearing the bend. The track began its smooth angle to the left and the Blues' driver lost control of his outer lead stallion, and so lost his tight line to the rail. The chariot swayed out again, leaving the same gap as before. This time, Ajax leaned in over his four, bald head flashing, using voice and whip and reins to ask more speed of them.

Math's heart hurt; he had never seen the horses strain so hard, or so valiantly. Still, when asked, they dug deep and gave more. Ajax pushed forward and slid neatly through.

'*Go! Go! GO GREEN!*'

The roar of the crowd became a constant, deafening scream. The last of the leaping dolphins tipped and fell at the end of the track. Math pushed on Lucius' elbow and saw the grey Parthian team flash past, way ahead of the rest. They had three lengths on the others by now, if not four; an almost unassailable lead.

There was no point in jumping; a dozen of the older boys had gone to stand on the low rails at the front of the enclosure, blocking the view. Math had to duck down and squint under Lucius' elbow to stand a chance of seeing anything at all.

Through the sodden angle of the boy's armpit, he saw a smear of white hides and black harness, of red, flared nostrils, of pitted eyes and the white rims around them, then the nearest chariot wheel, so close he could have reached out to touch it. The whine of the wheel-rims on the sand was the sing of angry wasps in summer. The crack of the whip was a lazy breaking branch, no urgency in it at all. They had no need to hug the inside rail, these horses, they could afford to take the corners wide and still win. Their charioteer was relaxed, braced easily against the leathers that held him. The reins were wound round his waist and he barely bothered to touch them with his hand. He, too, was Parthian. He might have known all the legal and illegal manoeuvres ever raced, but he needed none of them.

They were gone, red-ribboned tails flagging the wind. The group of three struggling for second place were not yet at the bend. Math counted four thundering strides, then executed his own manoeuvre, planned in the night.

The mass of boys around him swayed forward, straining their necks hard left to see. When they were at their most precarious, leaning forward on tiptoe, he stuck out his arm, levered up Lucius' elbow and squirmed in through the gap before the older boy noticed. In a swift, wriggling move, he made it through to the rail and stood up. Nobody tried to knife him.

He and Hannah stood crushed together, in an intimacy of shared excitement that went beyond anything Math had found in his dockside encounters. He grinned for her, shouting, 'They'll do it! They'll come second!'

Then he saw her face.

'*What?*'

'Lucius has gone.' She was white, strained, worried. 'And the emperor's man has left the imperial box. Pantera. The one who gave you the denarius.'

'He finds it more pleasant down here amidst the sweat of the apprentices,' said Pantera's quiet voice from his other side. 'If I were you, I'd watch the harness. If Ajax pushes them hard round one more bend like that, it'll break.'

Math twisted round. Where a moment before had been a heaving pack of boys, now Pantera leaned on the rough-

132

sawn rail. And there was space on either side of him. Space. At the rails.

Math gaped at him, caught in a turmoil of joy and resentment. Then the meaning of what he had said sank home. 'My father makes the harness!' He had to scream it over the crowd. 'It never breaks!'

Pantera pulled a face. 'I know, but it will this time. Your lanky friend shaved the traces with a knife as you were tacking up. They've held this long, but they won't stand up to the stress of another hard turn.'

In all the noise, they stood then in a bubble of bewildered silence. 'Ajax will kill Lucius,' Math said, with utter confidence.

'He has to live long enough,' Hannah said softly. 'The Blue driver knows about the harness. Look.'

Not wanting to look, unable to look away, Math tore his gaze round in time to see the team of roan colts that ran for the Blues sweep past Sweat and Thunder and cut in hard across the track, slewing their chariot sideways so sharply it nearly tipped over.

It was a dangerous move for both teams, and nearly illegal. In Rome, such things happened all the time. In Gaul, Math had never seen anything like it. A great aching groan rolled across the spectators, deepest among the Whites, who were cut to the back. Even the Blues gasped.

Amongst the small group of Greens around Hannah, there was silence. Very quietly, Pantera began to curse.

Ajax was left with no choice. Math saw the flash of the sun on his shaved and sweating head as he threw himself sideways, wrenching his own team out of the way, spinning all four on their hocks in a turn as sharp, as hard and as desperate as any ever executed.

They almost made it. Sweat and Thunder reared high, screaming anger and defiance. The two geldings behind took the brunt of the quadriga's weight and turned it bravely to the outside, arcing out beyond the Blue's team.

Then Ajax howled a new order, throwing himself and his whip forward, as if, by his own two hands, by the power of his command, by sheer force of will, he could move his four horses out of the way of the White team.

He came so very close to succeeding.

For months afterwards, taverns across Gaul were packed with men who had never driven a team of four in their lives describing in detail how they would have wrenched the four White colts to a halt in time to stop them surging at full speed into the back of Ajax's chariot.

Because the White driver was only human, he tried to do exactly that – and failed. His horses slowed, but not enough. Ajax's team strove with all their strength to cut outwards and away to safety, but not enough.

The crash happened slowly, with too little noise, tumbling out along the track like a mosaic spread by the gods.

Fragile wicker and wood, bone and flesh and fury – and a man caught between, who was all three.

Math was over the rails at the front of the enclosure before the first of the colts had crashed, screaming, to his knees. Hannah was with him.

Pantera caught his shoulder and pressed a gold coin into his palm. Pantera's voice said in his ear, 'Get Ajax to the Roan Bull tavern and pay the keeper for the upper room. Leave quickly, before the riot starts. The Reds have won, but nobody will care. The local team has been damaged and tempers are running high; they'll be fighting as soon as the emperor leaves the stadium.'

In the gathering, clamouring crowd, he was gone.

Chapter Eleven

In all the chaos at the race-side, Lucius was easy to follow: the only boy pushing away from the rails.

Pantera tailed him effortlessly away from the apprentice boys' enclosure, across the grassy plain past the stables and down the long hill into town and along the harbour front until he arrived at the green door of the last and least of the whorehouses ranged in a row at the dock front on either side of the Striding Heron tavern.

It was harder to manufacture a reason to wait outside, but presently Pantera was seated in moderate comfort on an upturned half-barrel, mending a net. He wasn't entirely alone; three older men, too deaf to care about the races, were doing the same further down the dock and half a dozen filthy boys gathered soon from nowhere, recognizing him as a stranger, and therefore a potential victim.

The leader was Math's age, but taller and with ginger hair. Pantera slipped a pair of silver coins from his belt pouch and, as the boy edged forward, explained the three things he wanted done, each more difficult than its predecessor.

The boy's name was Goro. With a lopsided grin, he accepted the first coin as a down payment, and took promise on the second, issuing a stream of orders in a local patois that no one older than fifteen, or from further away than ten miles, could ever hope to understand.

The boys broke into three groups and went their separate ways. Pantera watched until they were out of sight, then settled back in the afternoon sun to mend a net that wasn't broken, and to wait.

The shadows had stretched by half a hand's length before Goro returned to the alley that ran between the tavern and one of the more salubrious whorehouses.

Pantera set his net on the ground, stretched his arms, yawned, and sauntered to the alley to relieve himself. Goro leaned on the wall further back, too far in to be seen from the dockside.

'The men are on their way.' The boy flicked a glance to the alley's end. 'And no one's come out of the back window of the whorehouse. Your friend's still in there.'

'A lusty youth,' Pantera observed drily. 'If he leaves, let me know where he goes and with whom.'

The second silver coin slipped from palm to palm and Goro was gone, fast as a slipped fish, whistling a long looping call, like the cry of a seagull, to summon his small group of followers.

Pantera finished his business and walked down to the alley's far end, beyond which both the tavern and the brothel were graced by south-facing, low-walled courtyards.

Olives and lemon trees grew in the corners of the brothel's yard with benches set in the shade below. Behind the tavern, the same space was occupied by a goat pen. Leaning over, scratching the wiry neck of the milk-goat within, was Seneca the Younger, former spymaster to the emperor.

Pantera vaulted on to the courtyard wall and sat astride it in the sun. 'This morning, Nero asked me to work for him,' he said conversationally. 'I turned him down.'

'Then why are you here?' Seneca ran his thumb along the goat's arched neck. 'Why am I?'

'You're here because Goro spoke a pass code you haven't heard in twenty years and your curiosity is insatiable.' Pantera picked a sprig of olive leaves from the neighbouring garden and offered them to the goat. 'I'm here because Nero spoke to me of the Phoenix Year. You said that if he did so, there was a man I should meet – in privacy and without Akakios' knowledge.'

'And Akakios is currently occupied trying to prevent a riot at the hippodrome,' Seneca observed drily. 'I gather he may have some trouble preventing the Green supporters from killing the Whites and both from slaughtering the Blues, but even so, he has agents who are less easily deflected. Goro and I were followed at least for the first third of our walk here.'

'Of course you were; after last night, they're hardly going to let you wander the town with impunity. We should go on down the row. Goro will provide us with a diversion.'

Pantera slid off the wall, took Seneca by the arm and steered him through the courtyard's gate to the small alley behind that served the entire row. Walking briskly towards the brothels at the row's end, he said, 'I took the liberty of sending another of Goro's friends to request the presence of Shimon the zealot, formerly aide to the Galilean, currently guest in the home of the deputy governor.'

Seneca shot him a startled glance. 'How did you know?'

'The Phoenix Year is Alexandrian, not Gaulish. In the entirety of Coriallum, only half a dozen people at most hail from the east and of those only two have the initiative and courage to speak to you. One is Hannah, physician to the Green team. On balance, I thought it unlikely to be her.'

'Nevertheless, she's an exceptional woman,' Seneca murmured. 'Sorely wasted on the Gauls.'

'I doubt if they see it that way,' said Pantera. 'Turn right through the gate here. I've paid for a room and unlocked the shutters . . . the green ones on the left.'

The shutters were palely painted, new and neat. They opened smoothly, and clipped back against the white wall. Seneca leaned inside to take stock of the small room.

'You know Shimon led the Sicarioi after the Galilean's death?' he said. 'He'll cut our throats and leave us dead if he thinks this is a trap.'

'Then perhaps it's as well that I sent for him in your name, with promises of safe-keeping,' Pantera answered. 'Is he tall, with a thin face and white hair?'

'You've seen him?'

'He was making his way along the harbour front when I left. If Goro's boys are good enough, he'll be here to meet us soon. I suggest we go in through the window; there's less chance of being seen that way.'

One after the other, they climbed in through the open window. The room was clean and sparse, scented with thrown thyme and fresh straw, with a bucket in one corner and shuttered windows to both front and back. The bed was low and narrow, its straw pallet big enough only for two adults if they lay on their sides, or one atop the other. Seneca sat on it, rubbing his hands free of the faint aroma of goat.

Pantera positioned himself with his eye to the shutter at the front, watching a flock of gulls mob a boat coming into dock. Along the harbour front, four of Goro's boys similarly circled a merchant waiting at the dockside who had made the mistake of letting his wealth show. Shimon the zealot, tall, barefoot and considerably less foolish, passed through them like a blade through cheese, and came away unscathed. Moments later, he tapped on the door of the room, and was admitted.

Seen close up, he was as old as Seneca, but the pressures of life had worn him more thoroughly. His hair, though plentiful, was the white of old snow as it rots in spring, flat and greyly stained in places with the colours of his earlier life.

He was dressed in a much-travelled linen robe, undyed and tied at the waist with a cord of the same material. His bare feet were hard as hooves from a lifetime's unshod wanderings. The olivewood staff on which he leaned was old and notched where it had been used to effect against blades that might have sought its owner's life. If he carried up his sleeve the infamous Sicari blade with which to cut the throats of apostates, Pantera could not see it.

Shimon leaned back against the closed door and took out a battered cloth from his belt to wipe the sweat from his face. From behind it, only a little muffled, he said, 'My lord Seneca I know. You . . . I could not name?'

He asked his question in Greek, language of all civility. In Aramaic, language of his youth, Pantera answered, 'I am Sebastos Abdes Pantera, Lion of Mithras, honoured to meet you, although it is not the first time.'

He had not intended to mention it, but the memory of a pebble thrown in a dawn-lit garden was so vivid that it occupied the whole of the small room, and could not be ignored.

Shimon let his kerchief fall. 'Your father,' he said slowly, 'would be proud of his son who has become a friend of Seneca's. And perhaps more?'

Seneca was looking out of the back window. Without turning, he said, 'He is my foster-son. Best of all the men I trained. And was made a citizen of Rome by the emperor yesterday morning.'

'My lord has ears in the most unlikely of places,' said Pantera. 'And he is overly kind. I am an agent of limited means and I doubt very much if my father would have been proud of what I have become.'

Shimon eyed him with wry amusement. 'I'm sure your father was a good man,' he said. 'He will know your heart and see it good. In his honour, then, we meet. You should know that I was followed on my way here. It will surprise them that I have come to a whorehouse, but it may not prevent them from coming inside.'

He joined Seneca at the window. 'This courtyard is not easily overlooked. If we were to leave the way you came in – I am correct, yes? – then we could avail ourselves of the warren of small lanes behind here. I am the eldest among us. If I undertake not to slow down our party, perhaps we could leave behind the slothful idiots who think to set themselves against us?'

It was a challenge, however diffidently made. Pantera let Seneca catch his eye. The philosopher was already kilting up his tunic, tucking the long ends into his belt.

'By all means,' he said. 'If we three can't outfox Akakios' agents, we deserve all that he can visit on us. Shall we go?'

Shimon might have been the oldest, but he did not need his staff to climb out of the small window, nor, afterwards, to follow soundlessly as Pantera led them down the alley that ran behind the inn and thence, via a potter's shed, a baker's courtyard with an uncovered well and long pans of dough souring in the afternoon sun, and a weaver's shop displaying vats of green and yellow dye, to the western edge of town where the magistrate, his two brothers and his many cousins had their houses.

A little breathless, they paused in the angle between two high walls, with three streets leading away and an orchard behind. Apples and pears drooped and swayed above them, and wild doves called. The hubbub of the dock was no louder than the sea, the sound smothered by fountains and distant, well-bred laughter.

Seneca was enjoying himself, hopping from one foot to the other, his head flicking three ways at once, checking each of the streets at whose intersecting corner they had paused. Shimon kept in the shadows with the smallest of

140

the walls at his back, and his olive staff angled so that he could use it equally as a weapon or as a means of pushing himself over the wall. When nobody appeared to be following, he turned to Pantera.

'My host owns this house,' he said. 'I came from here less than an hour ago.'

'I know. And so the last thing they'll expect is that we'll come back, which may buy us some time. We won't stay long, but I think we all three need to look at this.'

Watching both men, Pantera drew from within the fold of his belt the slip of papyrus Nero had given him in the morning and spread it flat against the wall in a leaf-dappled band of afternoon sun.

Shimon sighed a long-held breath. Squinting a little, he leaned forward. 'Where did you come by this?'

'Nero gave it to me,' Pantera said. 'It's a copy of a copy that was taken from a Syrian who had it in turn from an apothecary-astrologer with ink-stained fingers who works out of the Black Chrysanthemum tavern in the Street of the Lame Lion in Alexandria. You now know as much as any of us does, although it may be that other copies were sold before our hapless Syrian made the mistake of trying to sell one to Akakios. Have you seen it before?'

'No. I have hunted across nine nations for this and had given up hope of finding it.' He held out his hand. 'May I?'

'Of course.'

Shimon held the note at arm's length, the better to see it with his ageing eyes. He became a harder man as he read. His fingers whitened on the text, his breathing slowed. At the end, he laced his fingers together, and said softly, furiously, '"*Then shall* the veil *be rent, never to be repaired.*"' He spoke in Hebrew. The papyrus was written in Greek. The new language was itself an answer to one of their questions.

From his place at the junction of the three walls, Seneca said, 'It refers to the veil in the Temple of Jerusalem?'

'Where else?' In his agitation, Shimon strode to the corner and back. Doves erupted from the apple trees above. 'Even now, he wishes to destroy us.'

'Who does?' Pantera asked.

'An apostate. One who hates us, who despises us, who wishes us removed from the earth.'

'Why?'

'Because we would not let him train to be a teacher. He thought himself the best of our scholars, when in fact he never had the sharpness of mind and hid behind vehemence and passion, thinking them enough to win arguments. We dismissed him, but did not kill him. That was our first mistake.'

'He would do exceedingly well in Rome,' Seneca said sourly.

'He has done exactly that, and in the Greek cities on the eastern shore of the Mother Sea. With his self-taught rhetoric and his passions, with his half-knowledge and his reading of un-truths, he has taken the law and broken it, has turned men to the drinking of blood and the eating of flesh, has claimed for himself a death that never was and made of it one of his Greek sacrifices. He is an apostate, a liar and a thief, and now he would destroy us by—'

The old man stopped suddenly, his face a rough terrain of warring passions.

Pantera had held up his hand. 'Listen.'

Coriallum was quieter than it had been. At the hippodrome, order was being restored. At the docks, Goro's boys were silent in their work. In the house behind the orchard wall, a woman spoke to her lover, and was answered.

None the less, someone hid in the small sounds that remained, and was coming closer. Pantera eased his sleeve-knife in its sheath. To his left, Shimon held up three fingers. 'Three men,' he whispered. 'Perhaps one followed each of

142

us and now they are joined? They come from the direction of the whorehouses.'

'Then we should go where they least expect us.' Pantera set his back to the wall and linked his hands to make a foot rest. 'Will you accept my aid to mount the walls? And you, my lord Seneca?'

'We'll be seen,' Seneca said.

'Not if we go north and drop down. Trust me. I have been in this town for nearly a day and have explored it. I know where we can go. But only if you can climb.'

'I can climb,' Shimon said.

'And I,' added Seneca.

'Good,' said Pantera. 'If you go up from my hands, there's a niche for a foot and a handhold higher up.'

'Then you may grasp my staff to make your ascent,' Shimon said.

Pantera grinned. 'Thank you.'

The wall was eight feet high. The top was capped with curved stones, firmly mortared in place. The two old men swarmed up it like lizards, to crouch on top.

Pantera joined them, and led them away, crouching, grasping the capstones with both hands. Behind, Shimon came delicately with his staff held horizontal, giving him balance. Seneca skipped sprightly after. The eyes of both were alive with the joy of young boys stealing apples.

Pantera felt his own blood fizz through his marrow. Every sense was sharpened so that he could smell the different layers of the sea from the weed-rimed depths to the cresting swell to the prickling air of an incoming storm. He could feel each stone of the wall. In the afternoon light he could see the edges of the streets and the houses beyond.

And in all of that was the sense of a razor's edge drawn slowly down his skin, the beginning needles of fear that were the food on which his soul fed.

For the first time since Britain, Pantera felt alive, and

Seneca knew it. He glanced at him and raised one brow in a question that was its own answer.

Standing, Pantera turned on the balls of his feet. 'Can you jump?'

Two old men nodded.

He asked, 'My lord Shimon, will your faith allow you to hide atop a pig pen?'

'It will allow me to do whatever I might in order to live.'

'Come then.' The pig pen across the street held a lazy sow and her near-grown young. Pantera measured the gap by eye, swung back his arms and leapt.

He caught the edge with his foot, swayed back and then forward and was on. Seneca followed, not as clumsily as he might have expected. Shimon jerked back his arm and hurled his staff like a spear so that only three years of battle training amongst the Dumnonii let Pantera catch it and swing it out of the way as the old man launched himself across after it.

The sow grunted and opened one eye, flounder-like, to view them. The piglets squealed and played, but no louder than they had done. Pantera made a sign, flattening his palms, and then lay down, pressing his face, his chest, his whole body tight to the clay tiles of the sow's stall.

As he did so, three men rounded the building's end cautiously, heads high like hounds on an air-scent, all shabbily dressed to merge with the dockhands, and armed with knives that caught the afternoon sun.

Pantera kept his eyes half closed and his breathing shallow. His own knife was in his hand. Shimon was likewise armed, his knife slender and curved along its length.

The men padded past in the alley below, leaving a scent of anxious sweat and wine and iron that wove upwards briefly to swamp the smell of pigs.

Pantera, Shimon and Seneca lay a long while afterwards.

The wind rose and a thin rain stuttered, so the pearl sky became steadily pewter with streaks of sulphured yellow over the ocean where the clouds were most dense.

At last, Pantera rose to a crouch and dusted off his tunic. 'All three were at the races earlier this morning.' He turned to his left and bowed. 'My lord Shimon, are you well?'

The old zealot grinned. 'Apart from the smell of pig, I am exceedingly well. It's been far too long since I hid on a rooftop. They are gone and will spend a happy afternoon searching where we have been. But I think they won't go back to the room where we first started. Shall we return?'

They were stiff, and the jump down to the lower wall was not without mishap and swearing, but soon enough another wall-run and a jump down brought them back at the rear of the whorehouse with its clean, spare room already paid for.

Shimon went first, kicking his bare feet into the gap where the shutter slid back, tucking his tunic close to his buttocks so that he might not show his nakedness. Seneca followed less elegantly but with as much decorum. Pantera slid in like a fish and found himself between the other two. They stood all three, breathless as children with laughter and fear.

'That was neatly done,' Shimon said. 'How long have we here?'

Pantera pulled the shutter across. In one corner, a shelf stood host to a small oil lamp with flint and tinder beside. He lit it and trimmed the wick until the light feathered the room, then set it beside the bed.

'The room has been paid for until dusk,' he said. 'We'll be gone long before then. What we have to do won't take long.'

He sat with his back to the wall, looping his hands behind his head. 'If I may reprise,' he said, 'you wish to prevent the destruction of Jerusalem while my lord Seneca wishes to prevent the burning of Rome, as does Nero. The man you call the Apostate wishes to bring about the Kingdom of Heaven and so will do his best to destroy Rome and then Jerusalem. It seems to me that the first may be easy – Rome is a tinder box and fires run through it like mould through cheese – but Jerusalem is not for the taking.'

'If the young men rebel, Nero will send in the legions,' Shimon said. 'He has promised it. They'll raze Jerusalem to the ground.'

'And will the young men rebel?' Pantera asked.

The old zealot nodded sadly. 'Jerusalem, like Rome, is a tinder box waiting for the match. Every day I wake fearing I will hear news that riots have already begun.'

'Then why are you not there, stopping them?' It was Seneca who asked that, from his place by the door.

'Because I used to be of the war party.' Shimon's gaze sought Pantera's and held it. 'In the days when the Galilean led us in constant battle against Rome, I was known as his lieutenant. I am old now, and I have seen what Rome can do. I will do what I can to work for peace, but I can't speak for it with any credibility.' He looked down at his hands. 'I am here in Gaul for two reasons. First was to seek out the prophecy – we had heard that it was circulating and that it would be where Nero was. But I would have been here anyway, to speak with the Galilean's daughter, to ask if she would come back with me to speak against her brothers in the name of peace.'

'And will she?'

'No. She has not said as much, but I fear not. Her life is here. Her troubles are not ours. Which leaves me with a question.'

He raised his old, tired eyes. The exhilaration of earlier had gone, but not the unbending pride. In formal Aramaic, he said, 'Through you, I have found the prophecy – and yet it remains incomplete. To keep my people safe, I must find the prophet, and thereby discover the date on which

Rome is set to burn, that I may prevent it. All other things lead from that. May I ask if Pantera, foster-son to my lord Seneca, would undertake to find this for those who used to be his people?'

There was time, in the pause before Pantera spoke, to hear the sow grunt again up the street, to hear a merchant on the dock discover that his purse had been cut, to hear the race crowds begin to leave the hippodrome and flow down the hill.

In the small, thyme-scented room, Pantera said, 'I regret not,' and meant it. 'My emperor asked for my aid today in preventing Rome's destruction and I refused him. With far greater sorrow, I fear I must also refuse you. I am not who I was and other things require my attention. I wish you luck, with my fullest apologies. And my earnest suggestion that we leave, and are not seen together again.'

They separated in the alley, Shimon to walk west towards his lodgings, Pantera and Seneca east to the tavern. Seneca waited until the pad of the old zealot's footsteps could no longer be heard and then turned to Pantera.

'*Other things require my attention.*' He gave an effete lift to the words. 'He'll think you're working for me.'

'And he will be wrong.'

Pantera felt drained, as if he had marched his twenty miles and still had a way to go before he could rest. He said, 'Nero saw Math at the races this morning. They walked the horses to the hippodrome together. The good citizens of Coriallum nearly died at the scandal.'

'Ah.' Seneca's gaze was sharply amused. 'How immensely fortunate that you don't love the boy, nor he you.'

'Will Nero kill him?'

'He didn't do such things when I ruled him, nor would he here, under the gaze of the magistrate. But in Rome, with the likes of Akakios and Rufus goading him to ever greater excesses? Yes. He'll use Math, and then kill him.

He won't be able to help himself.' Seneca turned and began to walk back towards the tavern. 'If you would have the boy live,' he said, 'you will need to find something Nero values more highly and offer it in exchange. He understands that kind of bargaining. But it must be something he cannot get by other means.'

'All I have to offer is myself.'

Seneca pursed his lips as if the idea were a novel one. Pantera caught his wrist and turned him round. 'You said you didn't want me to work for Nero.'

'I don't. I want you to work for me. But if, in doing so, you were to *appear* to take a commission for Nero, that would be different.' Seneca was held in a patch of sunlight. His skin had the transparency of the old, but his eyes were sharp with plans laid and threads aweaving. 'I love Rome. I have given my life to her and I don't want to see her burn. Very few people have what it takes to stop this, perhaps only one.' Seneca's blue-veined hand caught Pantera's chin and tilted it as it had when he was a child. 'Will you do this for me?' he asked. 'Please?'

In all their time together, Pantera had never known the old philosopher beg. The hope in his eyes was hard to bear, and harder to crush.

'I can't,' Pantera said, and heard genuine anguish in his own voice. 'You are Roman.'

Seneca departed as Shimon had; despondent, but still able to keep to the shadows and, once in the open, to affect the dejection of poverty that makes a man invisible.

From the darkness of the alley, Pantera watched him leave, then turned and made his way back along to the endmost house of the row. One of Goro's younger boys sat in the shade of a bay tree not far away chewing a leaf and playing knucklebones, right hand against left. He did not look up as Pantera passed, but shook his head.

Pantera bent to retrieve a coin he had not yet dropped.

'The shutter's open,' he said to the dust at his feet. 'Was it so when you came?'

By way of answer, the boy attempted to toss five small bones from a sheep's knee from the back of his left hand to his right. As they landed, wobbling, he nodded, as if in satisfaction at his own skill.

'You're sure nobody's been?'

With a huff of irritation the boy looked up and met his eye. 'You paid silver. I'm sure.'

Pantera cursed. It had been closed when he had first checked it, when Lucius had newly entered. He let a copper coin slide to the dust, checked both ways along the alley and, seeing no one, hopped the low stone wall of the brothel's courtyard. Then, stepping over a small but noxious midden, he hooked a leg over the sill and eased himself into the room the boy had been watching.

It was late afternoon. By the sun's grim light alone, Pantera saw the narrow wound in Lucius' throat and the black blood that spilled from it.

The body was cold to touch, but still pliable. The hands held no last record of hair clutched or a face scratched. If he had known death was coming, Lucius had faced it bravely; his face was at peace. His purse held half a dozen coins, none of them silver. Pantera emptied it and passed the contents to Goro's boy, who was leaning in through the window.

'Go,' he said. 'Tell Goro there's no need to watch the front any longer.'

CHAPTER TWELVE

A red roan bull lowed in the courtyard of the Roan Bull inn.

Leaning over her patient in the long upper room, Hannah wiped sweat from her forehead with a hand that was still wet with blood. Her hair stuck to her temple. Wearily, she rubbed at the place. The bull lowed again, more urgently.

'It needs water,' Hannah said. 'Can someone take it some?'

As a living sign of the inn's name, the bull had been penned for the day next to the road in the hope that the emperor might see it and be enticed inside by the novelty. It was known, however, that the emperor disdained filth, and so a boy had been paid to keep the beast's hide curried to shining copper, its manger full of dry hay, its pen freshly swept of every outpouring of shit and piss, and its water trough full. Doubtless it had been done assiduously before the race.

The emperor had not yet chanced to visit, and hence the inn was not only largely empty but clean, with new, sweet rushes on the floor. The miracle of Math's gold coin had persuaded the gap-toothed tavern-keeper to open his doors to the healer, her patient and the crowding members of the Green team who insisted on being allowed to follow them inside and up the unstable ladder to the big, broad upper room that took up the inn's full length.

The gold bought also the innkeeper's solicitude, if not his speed. With aching slowness, he had arranged a winch and ropes and a long table had been hauled up through the trapdoor and set in the centre of the room and Ajax laid on it.

Early in the chaos that followed, Hannah had recruited the bull boy to fetch water and then linen; Math's gold had bought speed from him. She was aware that at some point she needed to find out where the gold had come from – he swore it was not stolen and she wanted to believe him – but for now Ajax was her most pressing concern.

The bull lowed again, less loudly. She heard a splash of water and the slobbering of bovine drinking and was glad of the quiet. Turning back to Ajax, she found that the gush of scarlet blood flooding from where a shard of wheel had pierced the top of his left leg had slowed to an oozing dribble, although that was not always a good sign; in Hannah's experience, men who ran dry of blood often died soon after.

She examined again the lengths of blood-soaked linen for the volume they might hold and allowed herself to believe that her first frantic efforts to stem the tide had been successful and his body was working with her now, not against her. More worrying was the blow to the left side of his head that had left the whites of his eyes red, and might yet kill him. She could do nothing for that while he remained unconscious, hovering on the borders of death.

Her visitor of yesterday, the friend of her father, would have said Ajax was visiting the judge-god of the Hebrews, whose name must not be spoken. The Gauls in the Roan Bull tavern believed he was flying to the heights of the sky with Taranis, god of lightning, and might choose to stay in the heavens. The few Romans in the party – at least one of whom Hannah recognized as an agent of the emperor – insisted he was sailing with Charon halfway across the Styx and might yet persuade the ferryman to turn about and bring him back.

All of these, in their own ways, feared the grim dark of death and tried to fight it. In Alexandria, the men and women amongst whom Hannah had trained, and for whom she had the deepest respect, loved death as a gift, a place of colour and light and all-seeing, a journey to be undertaken joyously, as a homecoming.

Kneeling on the floor in the upper room of the Roan Bull tavern, Hannah of Alexandria acknowledged the truth of her own heart: that she desperately wanted Ajax to come back to the living and to her; she yearned for it, in fact.

That realization, the unexpected power of it, was her own surprise in a day of difficult surprises, and her secret. It had crept up on her, much as her care for Math had done, but more quietly so that she only faced it fully at the point when, examining his head, she had found that the hair growing through on Ajax's scalp was gold and not black.

His eyebrows were black, the hair of his armpits was black; even, she had observed with the detachment of a physician, the hair about his groin was black. But the hair on his head was growing through gold as summer's corn.

She had bound his crown with linen then, not because she imagined it would change the outcome of his conversations with death, but in order that nobody else might see what she had seen. Briefly, she found herself wondering what dye he used that was proof against sweat and rain. Then she had rolled him over and discovered what had happened to his ribs and all thoughts of hair and dye and rain had burned away in the need to heal him.

The damage was on his left side, halfway down, near

the strongest beat of his heart. A crescent of bruised and broken flesh showed where a hoof had struck with the full force of a galloping colt. Hannah thought it the pair to the one that had struck his head, if only because, when she closed her eyes, she could see the moment when the outside lead colt of the White team, racing out of control, had run across the top of him. She thought she had screamed then, but in the noise of the hippodrome she had not heard it, and even now was not sure.

The ruined flesh under her fingers was warm but not hot; that much was good. The skin had peeled back, with a sand rash all round it. She winced at the imagined pain, and thought ahead to the salves that would help it, but it, too, was not lethal. A strip of bone glinted white at the deepest arc of the hoofprint and there, along its length, was a fine, linear bubble of air growing through the blood. It was no bigger than the nail on her small finger, but it grew and grew as he breathed, then popped and fell back, leaving her awaiting the next small eructation.

Her mother had taught her that there were times when listening was better than looking, and this was one of them. Pushing back her hair, she bent her head until her ear was tight on her patient's sternum.

Ajax breathed in. Hannah closed her eyes and tracked the breath as it came down past her ear, then split into two parts. Her mother had showed her the path it took, opening the body of a dead coney and blowing down its nose, inflating first one side of the chest and then the other. Men, she had said, were the same inside, at least within the confines of the ribs.

Now, Hannah followed the right part of Ajax's life-air. It sang as it passed, bubbling only slightly with the blood in his mouth where he had bitten his tongue. Night after night in her childhood, she had lain thus with her ear on her mother's chest, listening to the flow of breath back and forth. Her mother's death was a knife's pain at each remembering. Hannah felt it now, and held her own breath, waiting for the moment to pass.

On the next inhalation, she followed the left life-path as it moved on down to the bruise. It didn't so much sing as whisper and crackle; the creep of a spider through leaves. She moved her head a fraction and listened again as the air came close to the damaged tissues around the injury.

It crept, it crackled, it seeped out slowly at the place where the rib was cracked and the bubbles had formed, but even when she tapped her forefinger on the bridged arc of a rib, Ajax's chest did not make the too-resonant drumbeat that foretold death, nor did she hear the hiss of air escaping in great quantities that often spelled the same.

When she lifted her head it seemed that already the bubbles were forming more slowly, and that his breathing was better with each breath. The pulses at his throat and wrists, too, were stronger. His tongue was bleeding less than it had.

Hannah straightened, pushing her hair from her face with the back of her wrist. A circle of men and boys watched her, making a ring of waiting eyes. Math was in the centre, of course, flanked by the wainwright and his four apprentices. Beyond them she recognized among the others the loriner's wall-eyed son, the widower who brought the hay and corn and had, apparently, helped with the foalings since Math's mother had died, the German twins who had built the barns near the hippodrome and the old man with the bent, arthritic fingers who was still best at breaking the young stock.

She found a smile for all of them, and did not know how tired she looked.

'Ajax's rib may be cracked,' she said, 'but he is not yet suffocating on the air he breathes. His bleeding has stopped. If his spirit chooses to return from the place it has gone, wherever that may be' – she saw the wainwright's boys make the sign for Tanaris where they thought she wasn't watching – 'he will live.'

Someone passed her a mug of clear water. She drank and said, 'He won't heal faster for being watched. If one of you stays, the rest could eat and drink. If Math's gold will allow it?'

'My gold will allow it,' said a man's voice to her left.

She turned, slowly, not knowing the voice, but recognizing its arrogance and fearing the damage it could do.

He stood with his back to a window, framed by the sun's last light, a tall man, with a hawk's nose and a high brow and black hair that fell straight as a rod to his shoulders. His bitter eyes raked across each of them.

Hannah found that she knew him after all. Akakios. In the nightmare of the walk to the hippodrome, with Nero's presence scorching her skin, she had heard the name spoken. Thinking back, she believed Pantera had said it, so that she and Ajax would know.

Akakios flipped a coin high in the air, a small, spinning sun that held everyone's gaze. By chance or design, Math caught it.

Softly, Akakios said, 'His excellency wishes you all to dine in his honour. Red may have won the day, but he feels the Green team has proved at last that Ceres may grace a worthy team. He will address you in the morning, with an invitation to join his teams in Alexandria, where they train away from the gaze of the empire. I will lead you there and look over you until the race season begins in Rome at the ides of July.' He let his gaze drift across them all, to end on Ajax's supine form. 'In the continued incapacity of your driver, who leads the team?'

'I do. I am Caradoc of the Osismi. In Ajax's absence, I own the Green team. On his behalf, I offer our profound thanks to his excellency, and of course will attend him at his earliest request.'

Math's father spoke better Latin than the emperor's

155

man. His voice filled the tavern's upper room with a quiet certainty that left everyone silent, even while it calmed their fears. Hannah had heard that before only from her mother.

Math alone was not soothed, nor did he view his father with the respect accorded him by the others. Hannah saw him flush, as he had done for Nero, but angrily this time. Setting his jaw, he took the moment of the others' inattention to search the group, checking the size and weight of the purses around him: a reflex reaction to his father's presence.

He was reaching sideways towards the belt of the wainwright's son when Hannah interrupted.

'Math.' She whispered it, that the others might not hear. His hand stopped, then withdrew. He looked up at her across Ajax's body, his eyes hot and hurt and angry. Raising her brows, Hannah turned her head a fraction to where his father stood.

Caradoc had emerged now from the dark corner in which he had been standing. Hannah had no idea how he had got there. She had thought his old injuries too great for him to climb the three stone steps from the courtyard into the inn's main bar below, let alone the tilting ladder to the upper room. And yet he had not only done it, but done it so silently and carefully that the men and boys of the Green team had not seen, heard or sensed him.

He stood in front of them now a figure of perfect, un-bent pride, not hiding the damage to his arms, shoulders and knee that left him lame and fighting pain daily simply to have the use of his hands.

He was Math made old, everyone could see it; his hair was greying at the edges, but the difference in their colour-ings only served to make him more like his son, not less.

Hannah stepped away from the table. In the same formal Latin that Caradoc had used, she said, 'Ajax may wake at any time. But meanwhile, he would be honoured that you

156

are acting in his stead. If the emperor's agent is serious in his offer, perhaps the other members of the Green team could eat? It has been a long day.'

'And the horses have not yet been seen to,' Caradoc said.

Almost to a one, the apprentices of the Green team studied their feet. Math alone glared wordless defiance at his father. The air between them crackled back and forth with disappointment and resentment, sharp as lightning, and as hurtful.

From the door, Akakios said, 'His excellency understood your need to see to the injured man. He has set four of his own men to see to your horses. I am sure they will be settled by now, and perhaps best not further disturbed.'

Caradoc bowed. Crisply, he said, 'On behalf of Ajax and all the Green team, we extend our grateful thanks to his excellency. We are desolate that he has had to undertake our work in our absence, but are confident that the horses are receiving the best possible care. And we thank you for the offer of gold, but will not need it. Math, if you will return the gentleman's coin?'

Math flushed from the neck of his tunic to the burning red tips of his ears. With insolent slowness, he fumbled in his tunic for the coin, examined it, then tossed it high in the air for Akakios to catch. It glittered no less than it had done before, for all that it so clearly carried the taint of shame.

Hannah wanted to hug Math, and could not. Nor could she help his father, who possibly needed it more. With a healer's eye, she saw the effort it took for Caradoc to hold himself upright, and because she was looking, she witnessed the brief, private moment when his gaze fell on Ajax's face weighted with a depth of love and grief that easily matched his desperate, unrequited care for Math.

*　　*　　*

As with all rumours, news travelled fast that the emperor favoured the Green team, and would send them to Alexandria to match with his best and perhaps thence to Rome.

Finding he had heroes in his inn, the gap-toothed tavernmaster sent up a second table, and a third, and followed the stews of pork and wild garlic with bread and ale and wine for those who wanted it.

Sated, drunk for the most part, elated as much by their belief in Ajax's recovery as by the prospect of their promised journey, the family that was the Green team slept in the upper room, all twenty-three of them, laid out on straw pallets, with their cloaks rolled as pillows. Even Math was persuaded not to leave them in favour of the horses. In a gesture as close to conciliation as she had seen from him, he brought pallets from the pile for Hannah, his father and himself.

Hannah settled herself by the still-sleeping Ajax and nobody offered any ribald comments. Caradoc took the wounded man's other side. She felt him lie awake for a while, staring at the thatch and the flittering bats and the sprinkling of starlight squeezing through the eaves. Later, she heard the steadiness of a breath that moves to sleep.

Math was on her other side. He lay awake longer. She thought he might get up and go down into the town as he had done so often before. She felt him tense once, and slid her arm across, so that the back of her hand touched his.

'Please stay?' she said, and waited until she felt him subside. She rolled on her side. He was a shape barely seen in the dark. She stroked a finger down his face. 'You did it,' she whispered. 'Your horses were the best. They'll be the best in Egypt too. You'll go to Rome.'

'Will we?' He was too solemn for a boy of nearly ten, too aware of all that might go wrong, or that might go right, which could be worse.

'All of you. Even your father.'

He pulled a face. She picked up his fingers and kissed them, and then his brow. After a while, he took her hand, too, and pressed hot, dry lips to the knuckle of her thumb before he rolled away to face the night. She thought he sank into sleep soon after.

Hannah lay awake longest, but even she slept in the end, on the well-tested basis that she could do her patient no further good by staying awake through the night, and that worrying changed nothing for the morning.

CHAPTER THIRTEEN

In her dream, Hannah lay on a river's bank. Three men lay around her. Ajax was closest, sleeping, but whole. His hair had grown back gold as corn, but only in a ridge along the length of his scalp from brow to spine, so that it stuck up like the crest on a cockerel. His missing ear showed more clearly because of it. His face was peaceful. She loved him; in the dream, it was possible to acknowledge that.

Pantera lay on her other side, bleeding from wounds to his arms and legs. She knew those; they came from her earliest dreams of childhood. Because of them, she thought the third man, whom she could not properly see, might be her father although it could as easily have been Caradoc, who was the kind of man she would have liked as a father. She wanted to tell Math, but he was gone and she could not find him.

A frond of grass tickled her nose, making her sneeze. She pushed it away and it became instead a veil of long black hair, shimmering in the river light. Two women in her life had had hair like that. One of them was dead. Hannah sat up slowly.

Her mother knelt at her side, young and beautiful, as in her earliest memories. Her mother's hair made her sneeze a second time. Her mother's voice said, 'Wake. Hannah, you must wake. It is not for this you were born. Your world is afire.'

'Three men,' Hannah said, smiling, 'do not constitute a fire. Perhaps a small conflagration, but nothing I cannot walk away from.'

'It's a fire,' her mother insisted. 'You must not walk now, you must run, and the men with you. Two of them only, not the third.'

Once before, Hannah had dreamed of a death, and had not acted in time. The weight of it pressed her days. To repeat that mistake was unthinkable. Urgently, she caught her mother's wrist. 'Which one dies?'

But her hand closed on river air; her mother was already gone. Only the warmth of her voice remained, becoming warmer, even as she departed. 'Wake, Hannah. Wake and run.'

'*Hannah!*'

Math tugged at her wrist. His face hovered over her, his eyes wide as owls'. 'Hannah, wake up. Please wake up. Hannah!'

In the middle of the night, she could see the shine of his hair as if it were noon. That fact alone brought her sharply awake. Smoke streamed around her, like morning fog, stinging her eyes. She sneezed again, the third time, and heard the predatory roar of a young fire, stretching itself.

Math shook her again. 'There was a man,' he hissed urgently. 'I saw him! Quiet, like Pantera. He's just gone.'

'Who?'

'I don't know. I've never seen him before. But he's made a fire!'

Hannah sat up. Blistering orange flames lit Math and then Ajax, and beyond them both a room of sleeping men.

'We have to get Ajax out,' she said, rising. 'Wake your father.'

161

Caradoc lay on Ajax's other side, nearer the smoke. Math leaned over and shook his father, stiffly, as if it were a thing he had never done.

Hannah saw the heartbeat of wary unknowing as Caradoc opened his eyes, the shock of understanding and the need to move. Then she saw him reach for his son's hand and briefly clasp it. 'Thank you.'

Math flashed a shy grin and helped his father up. Caradoc turned an uneven circle on his heel, taking in the room, the smoke, the flames, the single exit. As he came full circle back to Hannah, she felt him lift the weight of responsibility from her to him. 'Take what help you need to get Ajax down the ladder,' he said. 'Math and I will wake the rest.'

Math needed no second word. Through the haze, Hannah saw him dodge nimbly among the pallets, shaking awake men and boys who had taken wine with their meal and so were slow to wake, and fuddled when they did so.

With a thief's quick wits, he began to sift those who could help from those whose panic made them a liability. The former he sent to Hannah, to help her move Ajax. The latter he herded instead towards the ladder, with orders to wake the landlord and the town's foremen, who might come with water to help.

Caradoc gripped Hannah's shoulder. 'Get Ajax out as soon as you can,' he said. 'I'll help Math.'

Her mother's warning sang in her mind. Two of them, not three. She took Caradoc's hand and held it. 'Keep safe.'

He smiled for her through the fire and smoke and was gone.

Flames skirted her head, singeing her hair. She knelt at Ajax's side and laid her fingers on his neck, to feel his pulse. At her touch, he opened his eyes, foggily.

She said, 'Fire.'

'Deliberate?' Even wounded, he thought faster than any man she knew.

'Math said he saw someone.'

'The Blues,' Ajax said caustically. 'Come to finish what they started in the race.'

Men and boys pushed past her, heading for the hatch and freedom. She heard the hollow clatter of their boots on the ladder. Already, the smoke was too thick to see who went down.

At Math's instruction, three had stayed back from the rush to escape: the German twins who were from the Rhine banks and so feared nothing but the river of their birth, plus the loriner's son, who was blind in one eye and not great in the other and had long ago learned to move by feel, and not to panic in the dark.

A clod of burning thatch fell near the trapdoor and the ladder. Holding her breath, Hannah rolled Ajax on to his undamaged side. His nose was streaming; she felt the mucus smear up her forearm.

She said, 'Do you hurt?'

'Everywhere.' Remarkably, his smile was real. 'I don't think I can walk. I'm sorry.'

'I don't want you to. You've cracked a rib.'

She turned to the shapes half seen in the smoke. 'Get the table! We need to carry him flat.'

The German twins broke the table in half along its length and dragged the slimmer part to her. The effort brought them all to coughing. In the short time of her inattention, the smoke had filled the room. She looked down. All she could see of Ajax was his eyes and the pale bandage at his head.

Caradoc came to her, a figure in the dark. His tunic was gone. He felt for Hannah's hand. 'Take this.' He pressed into her palm a scrap of torn wool, hotly wet.

'What?' She, too, was coughing now.

'Tunic . . . pee,' he said, and then, more clearly, with his mouth near her ear, 'Wool soaked in urine. Press it to your nose and breathe. It keeps off the smoke.'

He was right. Her mother had given her the same advice once, in life, not in a dream. Her mother had not had Caradoc of the Osismi to tear up his tunic and piss on it for her.

Hannah pressed the square of wool to her nose and breathed in. Above the howl of the fire, she shouted, 'It works. Do it,' and saw the German twins shrug at each other and take what Caradoc gave them.

With their help, she rolled Ajax on to the table. He winced, but offered no complaint. The Germans took one end, a corner each. The loriner's son took the other. She felt Caradoc push forward for the fourth.

She caught his shoulder. 'Where's Math?'

'Gone down the ladder.'

'I didn't see him.' She looked about her.

The Germans shook their heads. 'Not here,' they said together.

Caradoc spun about. She heard him breathe in through the pissed wool, then lift it away.

'Math?' His voice echoed damply from the rafters, and again, louder. '*Math!*'

The fire answered, roaring. Somewhere in the middle of the room, an oak beam cracked and fell with sickening force.

Above the noise, Hannah shouted, 'He must have gone downstairs.'

'I'll make sure,' Caradoc yelled back. 'Get Ajax out. The four of you can do that.'

They could. Slow as slugs, they crossed the floor, kicking burning pallets out of the way, swimming through a fog of smoke to the bright light that was the flame-arched trapdoor and the ladder to safety.

Or not to safety. Reaching it, Hannah found the ladder led to more fire; the downstairs was on fire now as well. A gout of flame shot up from the trapdoor to greet her.

From the table's end, one of the German twins shouted, 'The table will not fit in the trapdoor. Go down, you and the blind one. We will pass you the driver.'

Hannah hesitated, feeling the fire's heat. The loriner's son shouted close to her ear. 'We may as well die in the fire down there as up here. If they lower him to us, I can run with him.'

The climb down the ladder was a nightmare of burning oak that ate the skin of her hands, but they came to the beaten earth of the tavern's floor alive. Shouting a warning, the twins sent Ajax slithering feet first down the ladder.

He came to her only barely conscious. She caught him round his waist so that his head fell on her shoulder. Flames washed them both. Every breath scorched her lungs.

'Let me.'

The loriner's son was thin and wiry and had a persistently bad chest. If she'd been asked, Hannah would not have thought he had the strength to carry a lamb fresh from birthing, but, true to his word, he slung Ajax over his shoulder and ran with him. She could not see where he went.

The German twins slid down the ladder's edges, stripping the skin from their palms as she had. They landed on either side of her, shielding her from the flames with their bodies. Another beam crashed down upstairs, rocking the oak above their heads. Somewhere in the conflagration of the ground floor, a wall collapsed.

To the twins, Hannah shouted, '*Caradoc? Math?*'

'Coming,' said one.

'Behind us,' said the other.

'Both?'

'Yes.'

They tried to make her leave, one on either side, taking her elbows. She dug in her heels and held the ladder and

165

fought them to let her go. Her hands were burning, she felt the skin part on her knuckles.

'Hannah, don't.' A new hand grasped her shoulder firmly. In the searing, stinging, flame-bright dark was a new shape. Smoke-tears blurred everything.

'Pantera?' she said hesitantly, and then, with a surge of hope, 'Math's still up there.'

Pantera was drenched; steam rose from his tunic, making an arc of blessed cool. He shielded her with his body, drawing her fast away towards what was left of the door. 'There's nothing we can do.'

She might have fought against him, too, but Math was in front of them suddenly; a small and ragged shape struggling down the ladder with a reluctance that made her heart ache.

Turning back, Pantera caught him before he reached the bottom, lifted him bodily off and set him at her side. His arms swept both of them. 'Let's go.'

'Father's there. He can't walk.' Math was weeping, not only from the smoke. He was blue from holding his breath and could barely speak. 'At the top of the stairs. I couldn't carry him. He—' He fell into paroxysms of choking.

'Go with Hannah.' Pantera pushed them both together and propelled them towards the door. 'I'll bring him down.'

Chapter Fourteen

The burns on Math's hands were already seeping yellowing fluid, like rope burns, but flatter and spread further across his palms, stretching up beyond his wrists on to his arms and shoulders. Smoke and ash made cooling crusts across his face, but he was not scarred there; his father had protected him from that.

His father was still trapped inside the burning tavern while Math sat out in the meadow and watched the building collapse. It fell slowly, beginning at one end and sagging down its length, like the capsizing of a long and stately boat caught by the stern on a reef.

Sails of flame billowed in the wind, lighting the surrounding land. Sparks tied twisted ropes to the smoke-blued moon, outshining the stars. Falling ash tainted everything.

The entire population of Coriallum was watching by then, standing, sitting or lying on the wide grass paddock where the cattle had grazed with their bull until the tavern-keeper had moved them out of reach of the fire. It had been his first move on escaping from his inn. Now he sat on an upturned pail, watching disconsolately as the last of his livelihood sagged into the gorging flames.

Around him, the burned and smoke-strangled survivors

of his clientele lay on the grass, tended by Coriallum's healing women, who put their pitch torches down unlit, finding they could work by light of the tavern's blaze.

Math was sitting a little apart, with Hannah and Ajax and the rest of the Green team. He saw Hannah walk over to speak with the healing women. She came back with some salve in a small wooden pot.

'It's for burns,' she said. 'If you put it on your arms and hands now, they'll heal faster.'

The salve stank of goose fat and seagull oil with a lift of rosemary. It rolled under Math's fingers and stung the sore places so that he had to hold his breath as he rubbed it in. He did it anyway, feeling Hannah's eyes on him. The warmth of her presence did nothing to shut out the cold from the place where his father should have been.

That one fact turned his world on its head, removing all the certainties by which he had lived. He gave back the pot and sat hugging his knees to his chest, half watching as Hannah knelt by Ajax and smeared the salve on his shoulders and arms.

This once, Hannah and Ajax were not what mattered most, and so not what he saw. Against his half-closed lids, Math watched again the shadow-figure pacing soft as a fox from the far corner of the inn's upper room to the stairs, leaving a moth's wing of flame and smoke behind him.

Math had only ever met one man who could walk that quietly: the man who had shaken his nights twice in a row; the man who had brought Nero to him and then kept him apart; the man who had taken the horses from him to walk into the hippodrome, having seen what no one else had seen, so that he could warn Ajax; the man who had given Math a gold coin – *gold* – and sent him to safety; the man who was, even now, struggling to bring his father out alive.

Pantera still made his armpits sweat as he had on the docks when first they met. Math didn't believe for one moment that he had set light to the inn, but he knew that he was the one man who could find, and then kill, whoever had done. First, though, and far more important, he had to bring Math's father out of the inn alive.

And in that was the turning of his life. Because what he saw in the dark of his half-closed eyes was his father, or rather the care that had leapt to his father's eyes when Math had woken him with the smoke already filling the room.

His father had never looked at him like that before. Or perhaps he had, and Math had not seen it. Whichever was true, that single look had pierced his chest and set itself in his heart, so that when all the team had been woken and sent to the ladder and Math could have run to safety he had turned back, searching for a thing he knew his father had forgotten.

Sitting on the cold grass with the sour-sea stench of the seagull salve thick in his nostrils, he smelled again the smoke and the burned-hair smell of his father, and saw again the shifting thickness in the air that was Caradoc's crippled progress as he came to find him.

'We need to go,' Caradoc had said. He was a warrior. Every part of him showed it.

Math felt a pride he had never thought possible. Under his father's gaze, he lifted the leather coin pouch he had found in the nook of the inn's corner, not far from where they had slept. Four gold coins and three silver jingled inside.

'I got this for you,' he had said, holding it up to be clear he had not meant to steal it. The confrontation over Akakios' coin still lay between them and he wanted it gone. 'I saw where you hid it.'

'I thought you might have done,' his father had said. 'That was well done.'

Caradoc had said that so often, in exactly that voice. Never before had Math felt it touch him. There, in all the smoke and the flame, his father reached out and raised him to his feet. The smoke hung like a curtain between them. Only now, looking back, did Math see his father properly.

'Hannah's taken Ajax to the ladder,' Caradoc had said hoarsely. 'Nobody else is left to get out.' And then, as Math turned back to where the ladder had been, 'Not that way. A beam's falling there. We need to go round by the other wall.'

His father set the pace. Through the thickening smoke, they felt their way round the seating benches and the smouldering remains of the pallets to the safety of the far wall.

Even that was burning. Flames lanced without warning through the smoke, spearing at their eyes. Sparks flew and lodged in their hair.

'Math!' Caradoc caught Math and drew him into the hollow of his body, hunching his shoulders round to keep him safe. They began a strange, shuffling run, dodging the falling debris, feeling forward with four hands, like a creature from the winter tales. The building goaded them, groaning and grinding, threatening to break apart under them, or over them, to carry them to death in fire and rubble.

Math had felt the floor lurch under his feet. Jumping sideways, he had felt his father follow, then brace and, with a lightness that defied his injuries, spin in mid-air, grabbing him by the waist and throwing him forward, and sideways, back the way he had come.

The beam had fallen to the place Math had been; the place his father now was. With sickening slowness, he heard unfragile wood smash into fragile bone and flesh.

'Father!' He groped outward, grabbing at wood and skin equally.

170

'*Go!*' The power in his father's voice would have moved a tree from its rooting.

Math was not a tree. He was a son with an injured father. He crept forward. 'Father, come with me.'

'Math. Go to the ladder. I'll follow.'

'You can't.' Math was weeping. 'I won't leave you. We can go to Mother and the others together.'

There had been others, nameless brothers and sisters, he was sure. He had never spoken of them, nor heard them mentioned in his presence, but they had been the missing parts of his family, gaps that should have been filled, for as long as he could remember.

More than anything in the world, more than racing in Rome or being cherished by Nero, more than stealing gold or being with the horses, more than winning Pantera's approval, in that moment Math wanted his family to be whole again.

'Math, please, will you . . .' His father's voice had fallen away. Math turned his head, listening, and then he, too, had heard the miracle.

'Pantera!' He squirmed back towards the ladder. 'He'll help you. I'll make him come up.'

'Math, no—'

But he was already gone, and Pantera had done as he was bid, and gone up the ladder back into the fire to get his father, and all there was to do now, out on the cold meadow, with the blaze of the tavern lighting the whole sky, was to sit and wait and watch and listen to Ajax speaking to Hannah and pray with every part of his soul to the gods of sea and land and wind and forest that Pantera could bring out his father alive.

Hannah sat on the scorched grass and watched Math come back into himself from the place he had been. He was white and cold, so that the skin around the burns' edges was blue.

171

She reached for him and found him stiff as wood. 'You did well,' she said. 'He'll be proud of you.' She did not have to say who.

'You're peaceful,' he said, as if that followed from what she had said. 'But you're alive.' His face crumpled in a frown. 'Father told Ajax that my mother found peace when she died. I heard him.'

'Math . . .' Hannah laid his hand down. Hesitantly, she leaned over and kissed his forehead. It tasted of soot and smoke and boyish sweat. She said, 'When you live with peace, death seems not such a great thing, and not so far away. Like a leaf seen through thin ice, you could reach for it and take it easily.'

'It's not a bad thing?'

'I don't think so, no. Sometimes . . .' She searched for words that she would not regret later. 'Sometimes, it can seem like a gift. But it doesn't do to seek it too early.'

He toyed with a tugged blade of grass, his eyes seeing something else. 'But a warrior gives his life for his friend's, so that his friend might not die.'

'A warrior does that for honour,' Ajax said, thinly, from Hannah's other side. 'Not because death is bad. Pantera's been a warrior. He'll bring Caradoc out alive if he can, even at the cost of his own life.'

'Ajax!' Hannah spun from the boy to the injured man. With consciousness had come pain. His face was grey, tinged to a bilious yellow around his eyes and mouth. She pulled back her hair and laid her ear to his sternum. His skin was warm, but not hot. She could hear the drum of his heart, stronger and more regular than it had been.

When she sat back, his eyes rested lightly on hers, questioning. He managed the ghost of a smile. 'Will I live to see dawn?'

'You should do. Whether you'll drive or not remains to be seen.' She lifted his left hand. 'See if you can hold my

finger with this hand . . . and this one . . . and then tell me
if you can feel it when I pinch the finger ends . . .'

She tested the fingers of each hand to make sure he was
able to feel and flex all of them. Across her head, to Math,
Ajax said, 'Drivers are indestructible.'

Math's whole being was fixed on the fire. Hannah shook
her head slowly. With a feigned lightness, she said, 'That I
doubt, but you'll at least be able to hold the reins.' She laid
Ajax's hands down on his lap. 'I need to test the health of
your mind. Can you tell me your name?'

She asked it without thinking: the question she always
asked of men who had crossed the Lethe and returned
again.

She saw him take a breath and let it out. 'For tonight,'
he said, 'I am Ajax, son of Demetrios of Athens.'

She felt her face freeze. 'Will you name for me your
parents? The ones for tonight?'

'Hannah—'

He caught at her hand. She pulled it free. 'Any names
will do, as long as they're consistent with who you claim
to be.'

He closed his eyes. 'Demetrios, my father, was a potter.
My mother was the daughter of a horse trainer. Her name
was Eurydike. She died two years ago.'

He forced open his eyes. He was angry, which was a new
thing to see. 'Must I speak of my cousins and uncles, or is
that enough for you to believe my mind isn't curdled?'

'It's enough.'

She had never been curt to him before. He grasped for
her hand again, catching her one finger in the clumsiness
of his burned palm. 'Hannah . . .'

'Don't.' She shook herself free. 'I have never pried where
my patients did not wish me to go.'

'Am I only a patient? Still? You saw the bear last night.'
He was beyond tired and in a kind of pain she couldn't begin to imagine, or he would never have said such a thing.

173

She laid a hand on his shoulder, where she thought it would hurt least. 'You've cracked two ribs. You won't drive a chariot for at least two months, but that should get you on board the ship for Alexandria. Once you get there, ask whoever you retain as the team's physician to let you know when you're fit.'

His eyes, which had drifted shut, flashed open. 'I thought you'd come with us?'

'Then you were wrong.'

'But—' He made himself sit upright. 'If I lie, it's for your safety.'

'I know. I meant what I said. Your life is your own. I don't want to know a name that will harm us both. It isn't that.'

'But you don't want to return to Alexandria? Is the pain of old loss too great?'

'It's not that, either. I could return tomorrow if that were all that was keeping me away. The grief is old and long since ceased to hurt.' That was a lie, but she spoke with a conviction that made it possible to believe otherwise.

'Then why . . . ?' He started to reach for her a third time but let his hand fall. 'Hannah, you're a part of our team. We're going to race for the emperor. We need you if we're going to win.'

Hannah stared down at her hands, at the smears of old blood and new, at the burns and the cuts, at the miracle of their being whole, and not burned to raw stumps.

'I can't.'

'Hannah!'

'The fire was deliberate,' she said. 'It may be, as you said, that the Blues came to finish what they began this morning, but if they did so it was too late: for good or for ill, for your skill or' – she glanced at Math and away – 'for other reasons, Nero had already chosen the Greens. Akakios came to tell us in the inn before we ate and the whole of Coriallum knew it long before the fire started.'

'So if the Blues lit it, they did so out of revenge rather than hope of success?' Ajax eyed her thoughtfully. 'Men have killed for lesser reasons. And if they had wiped out the entire Green team, they might yet have been chosen.' Tentatively, he reached up and smoothed a hand across his scalp, feeling the bandage she had put there. 'But none of that is a reason for you not to come with us to Alexandria or on to Rome. Do you think it was someone else?'

She looked down at her hands. 'A friend of my father's came to talk to me yesterday. He asked me to go with him to Judaea, to help calm the hotheads who are voting for war against Rome.'

'Will you go?' Math had asked it, in the same tone.

'I don't know. I told him I'd think about it. I am still—'

'Hannah, they're there!' Math caught her burned shoulder. 'They're coming!' His face shone.

She turned where he pointed, back in the direction of the burning inn. Through the dazzlement of flame, she made out the emerging figure of a man, and the burden he carried.

'It's Pantera,' she said. 'And he's carrying your father.'

CHAPTER FIFTEEN

Pantera had been asleep in the Striding Heron tavern when Goro knocked on his door.

He woke sharply from dreams of dead youths and poorly mended nets. The first hint of smoke filtered through the shutters to his room even as the boy stuttered his news. Outside, the cries of a few voices multiplied in the brief time it took to rise and throw on some clothes. He felt Goro staring at his scars and passed him another denarius, destroying even further the economy of the dockside where far greater intimacies were bought and sold for copper.

Outside, the fire lit the sky. Men were forming half-built chains, trying to commandeer buckets, to shout orders at one another. All along the row of whorehouses, fishers' hovels and taverns, men and women in various stages of undress began to spill out on to the dockside.

Goro was watching them, alert for a loose purse. Pantera caught his shoulder, 'Get word to the emperor,' he said. 'The Ubians will tell him.'

'Tell him what?'

'That someone has tried to burn his new race team to death,' Pantera said grimly.

He waited to see the boy forge his way through the

swelling crowd, then elbowed his own way to the front and ran.

He reached the tavern as the first trickle of men and boys was dragged out from under the smouldering thatch. He looked for Hannah, or Math, and saw only the wainwright, who stumbled close enough to be caught and hauled clear of the morass.

'Who of the Greens is still inside?' Pantera asked.

'All . . . they're all upstairs.' The man stared wildly about, as if they might appear at any moment as ghosts.

Pantera shook his shoulders. 'Not all. Your apprentices are out. And some of the others.' They were crouched not far away, with their heads between their knees, choking. 'Who's left? Is Hannah in there? Or Math?'

'Math.' The man snatched at the word. 'And his father.'

'And Ajax?'

'I think so.'

Letting the wainwright go, Pantera had pushed through the gathering throng, counting heads of those who had soot-smeared faces and singed eyebrows. Math was not among them, nor his father, Caradoc.

A white-haired Gaul with soft eyes caught his arm. 'You're the emperor's man? The boy's still in there. Best get him out.'

He had no idea how he might do that. The door in front of him was no longer a door, but the searing mouth of a furnace. On either side, the once shuttered windows belched flame.

Three more men barrelled out, falling over each other in their haste to escape. A lone youth staggered after with a weight over his shoulder, calling aloud that he had Ajax, the Green driver, and needed help. Others rushed forward with water and rags to beat out the fires on his hair and clothes.

Pantera pushed his way to the threshold and stood

there in the wash of flame and smoke, staring in.

Hannah was there, crushed between two Germanic warriors, as big as any of the emperor's guards, trying to get back up the ladder.

'Hannah!'

She couldn't hear him. At that distance, she couldn't hear anything but the fire. Even from the doorway, the heat was driving him back. Turning, Pantera grabbed a bucket of water from a man in the useless chain and upended it over his head, soaking his tunic, his hair, his shoes.

'Hannah . . .' She was trying to get up the ladder. 'Hannah, no.'

He caught her shoulder and held her back and was about to speak when Math tumbled down the ladder sobbing that his father was upstairs, trapped under a fallen beam.

And so, against all reason, for a child, for a man, for the memory of a woman, or for the woman herself, Pantera hauled himself up into an inferno that was eating the ladder even as he climbed.

Caradoc was at the top, lying where he had fallen, with his head near the trapdoor in a slipstream of smoke-free air. Flames lit up a blooded burn across his forehead and the same ash-smeared features as everyone else. Smoke shadowed the rest of him. There might have been a roof beam near his legs, but in the gloom nothing was certain.

Pantera came up through the trapdoor so that their heads were level. Gratefully, he breathed the small pocket of smoke-free air that allowed him to speak. 'Let me take you down.'

'No.' Caradoc caught Pantera's wrist. 'My back's broken. There's . . . bleeding inside. I've seen men die; I know the signs. This is my time. Not too soon.'

It did him no honour to argue with the truth. Pantera said, 'I can still take you down. You can be with Math at the end.'

178

'No. There's not time. And there's a thing you must know. Only you.'

His drenched tunic was steaming hotter than Rome's hottest baths. Even so, the small hairs came erect on the back of Pantera's neck.

'Why me?'

'You have been a warrior. There are few others in Coriallum.'

'Ajax is one, I think?'

Caradoc gave the ghost of a smile. His hair was lit to gold by the fire. They could have been at a riverside, or in a roundhouse on a winter's evening, waiting for the children to sleep. 'Who were you?' he asked.

The question caught at Pantera's throat. Hoarsely, he said, 'I was—' He shook his head. 'I *am* Hywell the hunter, heart of Aerthen, father of Gunovar. Both of these are dead. I fought with the Dumnonii at the end-battle. We had defeated the Second legion, but Paullinus came on us and we were trapped.'

In the swirling fire, Aerthen and Gunovar were beside him. They were real here, in all the smoke.

Caradoc's gaze searched his scars. 'The legions caught you,' he said. 'But you escaped?'

In the face of death, Pantera could not avoid the truth. 'Not escaped,' he said. 'Let go. I was Roman first.'

The dying man nodded, and closed his eyes against the pain of the movement. 'So you have lived a lie also. Not an ... easy thing.' His eyes opened. They fixed on Pantera with the same intensity as had his son's. Only the question they asked was different. 'And now you have a debt to pay?'

Their gods breathed on Pantera then. 'I have a debt to pay,' he agreed, and felt the same sense of hope he had felt on the rooftops with Seneca and Shimon. 'I would gladly give my life for yours now in the warriors' way to pay it, but we both know that hope is gone. Is there another way I might pay?'

Caradoc's cold hand squeezed his wrist, briefly, and let go. With an effort, he reached round and brought a knife from the sheath at his belt.

'Swear,' he said. 'And then take it for Math.'

Pantera laid his hands on hilt and blade. 'I swear to the ends of my life and the four winds to do your bidding.' He took the knife. 'What must I do?'

'Tell Math . . .'

The voice was almost gone. Pantera had seen men die and knew how fast it came at the end. He brought his face closer. 'To know himself truly, Math must truly know who his father was. I'll tell him if you tell me. Quickly. It matters.'

Pride warred with pain on the dying man's face. 'I am Caradoc, son of Cunobelin, scourge of Rome, heart of the Boudica, father to Cygfa, Cunomar, Graine – and Math. Cartimandua betrayed me to Rome. Claudius pardoned me. Nero ordered me slain.'

'And you have lived, and under his nose this last half-month.' The sheer audacity of it was breathtaking. Pantera exulted that such things could still happen. He had thought them all gone when Britain was crushed.

Caradoc grinned tightly. 'Nero believes me dead. Men attested to it, swearing that they had seen my body; good men. So Math has been . . .' His words dried. His eyes fell shut.

Pantera said, 'Math has been kept safe. You did that for him. I'll see he understands.'

Caradoc coughed. Bright blood spewed on to the oak beneath him. His grip on Pantera's wrist tightened at the closeness of death. 'Keep him safe. You were right this morning. Math is safest . . . with his family.'

'Then hear my oath,' Pantera said.

In the smoke and the searing heat, he found the formal ceremonial language of the tribes. Laying his hands on the blade that had been offered, he said, 'In the name of

Aerthen and of Gunovar, my daughter, I will keep Math safe and see him joined to his family. I swear it by my heart and my soul. While I live, my life is given for his.'

It was enough, and in time. Caradoc of Britain, scourge of Rome, smiled his relief. With a last, long-hoarded breath, he said, 'My . . . son. Proud. Tell him I am . . . very proud.'

CHAPTER SIXTEEN

Scorched and hoarse, with his tunic abandoned to the conflagration, with every muscle in his body aching, Pantera carried Caradoc's body from the blazing inn towards the huddle that was the dead man's friends and family.

'Does any of you know the rites that may be sung to usher a dead warrior to his place with the gods?'

A light breeze lifted the grass and the leaves and caressed his skin, seeking out the burns and soothing them. His question hung in the air. One man levered himself up from the ground. 'I know the rites of a warrior's passing,' said Ajax of Athens.

He was naked, but for bandages at crown and thorax made from strips of torn linen, not of imperial quality, yet wound by a professional hand. He stood with the moon at his head and the fire bronzing his skin so that it shone as if greased with bear fat. His one ear poked out from under the linen at his crown, highlighting the loss of the other. If his head beneath had not been shaved, but instead had been crowned by the single line of hair that was the mark of . . .

In that moment, Pantera knew with certainty who the

other man was, and could not think why he had taken so long to see it.

He was gaping, foolishly. He closed his mouth. 'What should we do?'

'Caradoc must be laid beneath a tree,' Ajax said. 'There's an oak by the stream beyond the cattle. I can walk. I can't carry him.'

'I can do that.' Pantera looked beyond the driver. 'Math?'

Math stared up. His red-rimmed eyes, wide as an owl's, searched the length of Pantera's body and came to rest on his face.

He looked exactly like his father in the moments before dying, save that Caradoc had not been weeping and Math couldn't stop. His face was awash with tears.

Balancing the dead man on his arms, Pantera eased himself into a crouch. 'Math, your father was proud of you. Those were his last words. Would you come and see his soul set free?'

He did his best to ask it cleanly, but the weight of his oath pressed newly on him and he heard a hint of desperation in his plea.

Math heard it too. He turned away, his face a landscape of sorrow and scorn. 'He was a warrior,' he said thickly. 'I don't know the rites.'

'Math, you can still—'

'No!' The boy wrenched away, running past Hannah, past Ajax, past the others of the Green team to the anonymity of the crowd.

'Let him be,' Ajax said. 'Now is not the time. Hannah will care for him. For Caradoc's sake, we need to act quickly. Come with me.'

The oak was old and vast with branches thick as a man's two thighs. It stood alone in a quieter part of the meadow, where the blaze of the burning tavern barely outshone the stars. A stream ran nearby, murmuring songs to the moon. The grass was longer here, enough to shroud the dead man's face when they laid him under the tree's dappling branches. They knelt together. Ajax began to sing.

Pantera remembered the words and melody of the rite only slowly, joining in with Ajax's resonant rendering halfway through. At the close, when the stream had carried the last notes away, Pantera stood. As the last one to see the dead man alive, he spoke the ending.

Softly, to be heard only by two men, the stream and the gods, he said, 'He was Caradoc, lover of Breaca, father to Cygfa, Cunomar, Graine and Math. He was the greatest warrior his people have ever known. May he be remembered as such, by his sons and his daughters. May he return now with joy to those who have loved him.'

He made the sign over the man's brow, releasing his spirit to the care of his god. In the still night, a subtle wind soughed briefly through the grass and then through the leaves of the oak. Pantera did not look at Ajax; he did not need to. Nothing that he had just said was news to this man.

Presently, Ajax pushed himself to his feet, taking care for his injuries, and slowly unwound the bandage from his crown. The moon shone on his shaved head, casting warped patches around the place where his ear had been cut away. His face was as unreadable as ever.

'Shall we walk?' he asked quietly. 'Caradoc has no need of us now, and I would be further from the tavern fires.' And from the small cluster of townsfolk who had gathered and listened to the rites as they sang: that did not need to be spoken aloud.

They walked together down the side of the stream, keeping by instinct to the darker places beneath the trees, not the light.

The river grew wider and then narrowed to tumble over a rocky lip in a shallow falls twice the height of a man. Above the cresting white rim, a single fallen dolmen hung out across the falls and the pool below, narrower at the neck, broad as a horse's back as it approached midstream. It was the kind of place boys might come to fish in the summer, and cast their lines in the river behind; the kind of place where, later, they might test their courage on a moonlit night, seeing if they could walk barefoot along the ridge in the dark; the kind of place from which they might dive into the pool of unknown depth below, to show they had no fear of death. A boy could easily die, diving like that.

In Britain, Pantera had seen the warriors set each other such tests in the winter, to keep them sharp for the battles of spring. It was autumn now, with no battles in sight, but still the water's promise drew him. Feeling the kiss of flying water on his naked back, he stepped out along the narrow stone to sit at the rounded end with his bare feet dangling over the water, and was not surprised when Ajax joined him and began to unwind the bandage Hannah had so carefully set about his chest.

A red-black bruise in the shape of a horse's foot showed under the driver's left armpit. Across the rest of his chest, other, more linear bruises showed where he had been dragged in the sand.

Slowly, Pantera said, 'When I was in Britain, it was said that the bear-warriors of the Eceni were most feared by the legions of all those who fought against Rome.'

There was quiet, with the rush of the river beneath their feet to take the words safely away. Ajax was naked now, his flesh starkly white between the bruising. He came to sit on the stone, close enough for Pantera to feel his body's warmth.

'Do you think Nero recognized the bear-scars this morning?' He made no effort to deny what he was.

'If he had done,' Pantera said, 'you would be dying by now.'

The night was quiet, waiting for what more he might say. The pool beneath their feet was a cauldron of busyness, except at one corner, where the surface was still, mirroring the stars. In such places, the gods or the beloved dead were known to show their faces.

Pantera found himself looking only there. The water was smooth as poured silver, and perfectly black. He could not see Aerthen anywhere in it, only the clear reflection of Ajax, who had pushed himself to his feet and stood at the dolmen's edge, looking down.

'How deep do you think the water is in the pool?' he asked. 'Deep enough to dive into?'

Pantera felt a tug in the pit of his guts. 'I think the gods intend us to believe so,' he said.

'Good. Then we can continue this conversation in the water, where the gods will heal us best. I have need of a cleansing.'

Ajax's dive was neat and straight; he entered the water sweetly, as a cormorant might, with little noise.

In the wait before he surfaced, Pantera stood and readied himself to dive, an act he had last performed in Britain, in the sweet time of peace when his love had consumed him. Before that, he had never been confident in water. In Aerthen's company, he had learned to swim, if not to enjoy the experience.

He counted slowly to ten and Ajax did not reappear. Holding his breath, Pantera pushed off the balls of his feet.

The water was so cold, it burned his scorched skin. The pool was deeper than he had imagined, but not so deep that he did not feel rocks graze the skin of his forearms as he came to the limits of his dive.

Because Ajax had done it, he swept his arms against the current to keep himself under. Opening his eyes in the fierce black water, he found Ajax in front of him, alive: a face, a pair of wide, coppery eyes, a hand that reached out to take his forearm in the grip of one warrior to another. To take that grip and return it, even on dry land, implied an oath manifestly more binding than the one Pantera had refused to give Seneca in the afternoon and matched exactly the one he had freely given Caradoc.

Ajax gripped his arm again. His face came closer. The coppery eyes held Pantera's, hard as stone, giving nothing, taking nothing, only offering in their depths, perhaps, a glimmer of friendship such as Pantera had long forgotten.

They had been underwater too long. Pantera's lungs burned, and a reddening blackness made tunnels before his eyes. Hazily, it came to him that what was offered did not interfere with his oath to Caradoc. Blinded by lack of air, he felt the hand leave his arm and return again, urgently.

As urgently, he took it.

They breached the surface together like porpoises, coughing, and sucking in air. Together, they climbed up the side of the falls, and sat face to face on the harsh, prickling grasses, so close that each could see the goose-flesh rising cold on the other, that each could see the time the other took to come back to himself, and so find in the other a mettle worthy of respect.

In time, Ajax rose and crossed unsteadily to the stone that had been their diving platform. For a shocked moment, Pantera thought he might be about to jump again, but he stooped to pick up the bandages and brought them back so that Pantera could rewind them for him.

'I gave an oath to Caradoc before he died,' Pantera said, tying the first knot. 'I swore to keep Math safe, my life for his, and to join him with his family. You, on the other hand, have already sworn to help Math get to Rome. It is in my mind that these two may not be as different as I had thought.'

The fire behind them was less now. In its place, other, smaller campfires had been lit across the paddock. The oak tree had been left, and the dark shape of a man's body at its foot. Ajax stared at it a while. 'If I can keep Math safe, if I can fulfil my oath to his mother and yet get him safely home to the rest of his father's family . . . that would be a very good thing.'

'Then we have a common goal. All we need to do is find a means to attain it.' Pantera tied the last knot of the linen and stood. Together, they walked along the river's bank to where the refugees were gathering, with fires and food and ale. Before they reached the greater light, Ajax paused and stooped to pick up a pebble and send it skipping across the water. It bounced three times, number of luck.

'We have need of a leatherworker,' he said. 'You have lived among the Dumnonii. You could join us, perhaps, in that capacity?'

'You flatter me.' Pantera, too, chose a pebble from the river's edge. His was a good one, flat and sharp around its edge; it went further, skipping seven times along the river's length. In the good omen of that, he made the day's last and greatest decision.

'Yesterday, the emperor asked a service of me,' he said slowly. 'I refused. Now . . . it may be that the best way to protect Math is to accept. Whatever is said of him, Nero is not without honour. If I can do as he wants, it may serve us later.'

'So you won't come to Alexandria with us?' There was disappointment in Ajax's voice.

'I will go, but on the emperor's business, not as part of the Green team. You will be left to take care of Math. I'll do what I can from outside the training compound.'

They were near the fires. Pantera stopped before the light caught them. 'Caradoc gifted his knife to Math,' he said. 'But with his last breath, he said I was to tell his son

188

that he was proud of him. It is in my mind that I told the wrong son of his father's pride.'

'He may have meant both.' Ajax's face was caught in shadows, unreadable. 'We could be glad if it were so. A father should feel pride in all his children.'

CHAPTER SEVENTEEN

The next day's dawn saw Coriallum veiled in white ash, pure as virgin snow.

Hannah rose with the cock's crow and found Math already up, with the fire lit outside her tent and a pot of water warming on it.

'Did you sleep at all?' she asked.

'Of course.' He eyed her askance, as if there were something improper in the question. 'But Pantera came by earlier and woke me. He says the emperor will send clothes for us, so we can be decently dressed for our audience. He thought perhaps we should . . .' He drifted to silence, his eyes flickering from the heating water to Hannah and back.

'He thinks we should wash?' She was laughing and scandalized at once. 'Did he say that?'

'He said that Nero would send Akakios to say it and it might be better if we were ready.' Math was brittle in defence of his hero, but not as withdrawn as he had been. His face was filthy with ash, but there was colour beneath.

He had baked oat cakes. Now, he used a stick to ease one from the embers, spat on his fingers against the heat and passed it to her.

'We went together to see my father's body,' he said. 'Pantera thinks we could build a high frame later today and lay my father on it, so that the crows and ravens might take his body, piece by piece. It's how the warriors were given their sky burial in the days of our grandfathers.'

'Pantera said that?'

'Ajax agreed. He was awake when we came back.'

Hannah had slept badly and was sluggish with exhaustion. Nevertheless, it seemed everyone else was ahead of her. She looked for Ajax where she had left him and saw only a ruck of folded bedding.

'He's with the horses,' Math said. 'I'm to tell you he'll be back in time to wash his face for Nero.'

Slowly, she sat down on a stone set by the fire.

'Then by all means let us wash,' she said. 'I have some ash soap in my tent, in the box with the acorn carved on the lid, under the nest of copper bowls. If you can find it, we might even get ourselves clean.'

As Pantera had predicted, Akakios arrived to collect the team just as the sun nudged over the horizon.

He required that they be cleansed of ash and the remnants of fire and when he found that they were already as clean as water could make them, he provided tunics of fresh new linen, bound at hem and sleeves with green. They were given each a leather belt buckled in silver, with the shape of a lyre emblazoned thereon. Math's hair, which Hannah had washed and combed, was bound back with a fillet of silver. Ajax was brought a litter carried by four Dacian slaves and was not allowed to refuse, even when he showed he could walk.

And so, as his physician, Hannah had to go with him, and did not have time to inform Akakios that she was not committed to the Green team, and might yet follow her father's friend to Judaea, nor, when they were ushered into the magistrate's empty garden, with the fountains

191

silenced and the gilded birdcages covered out of respect for the dead, did she find an opportunity to say the same to Nero.

The emperor entered, dressed in white for mourning, with few rings. He walked with the slow rhythm of the stage, used to denote a death. At the couch he reclined, gracefully. Through Akakios, he invited his guests to sit, and had them given food and watered wine. Out of sight, a single lyre played in perfect pitch.

Pantera did not take food with them, but was ushered in by three vast Germanic guards a short while later. He, too, had washed since the night. Like Math's, his hair was flat from water and the comb. Like Ajax, he walked stiffly; worse, Hannah thought, on his left leg. His new tunic of snowy linen was belted with silver, not leather, its buckle inlaid with lapis and ivory.

He did not acknowledge Hannah, Math or Ajax. Walking between two of the guards, he came directly to the emperor and, kneeling at his feet, kissed his ringed hand. What oath he took they could not hear, but it pleased Nero and displeased Akakios equally. Nero slipped one of the rings from his thumb and gave it to Pantera, who accepted it with gravity and every outward appearance of humble gratitude.

He was dismissed soon after and it was the Green team's turn to be led forward one by one to swear fealty to their emperor, to accept his nomination as the third of his three teams in training in Alexandria and to listen to the details of their journey: a ship to be made ready before the first of October, a bare month away; the horses to be ready and fit to travel, having been on and off a ship daily for the intervening time; both training and racing chariots to be dismantled for transport; the loriners, wheelwrights and grooms to be fit to serve; a new leatherworker to be found, although the emperor, in his wisdom, had found one, a nervous individual of late middle years, so profoundly unremarkable in dress, hair and features as to be almost invisible.

The new man's nose ran with nerves. He cleared his throat with every second breath and wrung his hands throughout an unpromising introduction in which Akakios named him as Saulos, an Idumaean of good breeding fallen on hard times who was competent in leather working and desired to return to Alexandria, the city of his youth. Left to speak for himself, the man stammered his way through a salutation to the emperor, his hands twitching with terror.

Gravely, Nero welcomed him to the team, although of course there could never be any as good as the sadly deceased Caradoc. The emperor had given his approval for the sky burial that had been proposed. It was fitting, he said, for so honest a man, whose son now carried the family's honour.

At last, Nero let his gaze drift to Math for the first time that morning. He nodded but refrained from anything more intimate. Math nodded solemnly in return and did not simper and Hannah breathed freely for the first time since rising.

Soon enough, the team found themselves dismissed, free to return to the tents and the stares of their former compatriots. Ajax, who had climbed down from the litter as they passed out through the gates to the magistrate's house and made himself walk from there to the tents, allowed Hannah to lead him into the shade and took the drink she made for him of mugwort and valerian and the barest sprinkling of poppy, designed to bring sleep and ease the pain. She mixed something similar for herself, without the poppy, in the hope that it might damp down the worst of the headache that had grown through the morning and now held her skull in its vice.

*　　*　　*

Pantera came later in the afternoon, when Ajax was still asleep and Hannah had persuaded even Math to cease tending the horses and lie down away from the sun's worst heat.

He squatted on the ground by the reddening ash of the fire and accepted an oat bannock with a smear of the soft white honey that had been a gift from the White team, delivered while they were away. After Caradoc's death, no one begrudged them the win, it seemed. Even the Blues had sent a jug of ale and a set of racing bits as a gift.

Hannah sat on a stone, nursing her headache, fretfully. 'We washed,' she said, 'as you told us to.'

He pulled a wry smile. 'I'm sorry I couldn't stay to see you take your oaths. Was it bad?'

'It was . . . decorous. The emperor understands how to mourn.'

'He's experienced enough of death to know how to behave. And he wishes to be seen above all as a ruler who cares for his people.' He nibbled the edge of the oatcake, looking at her. 'I heard a rumour you had been approached by a Hebrew. It is said you might yet go to Jerusalem.'

The headache knifed at the back of her eyes. She squinted at him, shading her brow against the enemy sun with the edge of her hand. 'Did Ajax tell you that?'

'No.' Pantera shook his head. 'I've had time to ask some questions. It's what I do.'

He was looking at her, weighing her intelligence, or her awareness. Hannah thought of what she knew of him; a half-dozen meetings. Less. Flashes of wit and thoughtfulness and a striking ability to be in the right place at the right time. A realization came to her slowly, through the fogged pain in her head.

'You're a spy!'

'I'm a *good* spy.' His inflection robbed the word of its insult. 'Better than Akakios. That's why Nero wants me. That's why I have to go to Alexandria. But if you

194

choose to go to Judaea, Ajax will be left to care for Math alone.'

'You think the rest of the Green team doesn't love him like their own sons?'

'I'm sure they do. But the rest of the Green team are provincial Gauls. They weren't born and brought up in Egypt. They'll be felled by the heat before they ever get off the boat. They'll go mad at the sight of the first scorpions and faint at the snakes. And they'll be too busy getting to grips with the rivalries in the compound to care for a boy who must break the rules or die of boredom.'

'He might be different in Alexandria,' Hannah said faintly. 'The compound is locked against incomers and outgoers alike. He'll be penned in with nothing to steal, and nowhere to go. He might take to racing and forget who he has been here.'

'And snow might lie thick across the deserts in July.' Pantera laid down his half-eaten bannock and leaned on one elbow on the dusty grass. 'I came to make an offer, to you and to Math. I can't travel with you, but I can stretch out my time here for a month. If nothing else, I can be looking for whoever tried to kill you all. In a month of nights, I can also offer to teach Math all that I can of spying, to build on that grounding so that he'll have a chance to survive if he finds himself cast out alone. Thereafter, I'll have to go to Alexandria and we may not meet until you're well settled in. Will you go with him, at least that far, and stay that long? Or are you committed to go to Judaea with Shimon?'

Far behind him, a man was teaching a boy the use of sword against shield. The sun glanced off the polished bronze boss into Hannah's eyes. Blinded, with a knifing pain in her head, she put her palms over her face and stared into darkness, seeking a clear path forward.

Thickly, she said, 'In the night, I told Ajax I wasn't part of the Green team.'

Pantera said nothing. She took her hands from her eyes and found him looking at her with patient curiosity.

'And this morning?' he asked. 'Must the chaos of the night set the future's path? Do you want to go to Jerusalem, to meet your cousins and persuade them that peace in servitude is preferable to war?'

'No.' With the saying of it, her headache began to ease. 'I've never met them and they've never met me. My father died before I was born and my mother brought me up among the Sibyls. We would have nothing to say to each other that would not be better left unsaid.'

'Then you could spare half a year at least.' Pantera spread his hands. He was smiling, crookedly, with real humour. 'Alexandria would be a very dull place without you.'

II

ALEXANDRIA, LATE SPRING, AD 64

IN THE REIGN OF THE EMPEROR NERO

CHAPTER EIGHTEEN

In the still night, a single drop of water rolled the full length of a tin sluice and splashed into the lower of two bronze vessels. Somewhere deep within the surrounding globe of brass and silver, the added weight caused a pan to tip, a lever to edge forward, a sprung arm to ease back. Elsewhere, a ratchet shuddered towards the end of its hourly cycle.

Math lay on his side on the sand beneath Nero's great mechanical water clock, listening to the rumble of the falling water. If he held his breath and pressed his upper ear to the cold metal, he could hear each of the individual tubes and whistles making ready to strike the hour.

Know your friends, the spy, Pantera, had said at the beginning of Math's month of secret nocturnal tuition in Gaul. *A bull pen is your friend, a dog kept kennelled through the night, the uneven line of a roof ridge. Each one of these will hide you if you let it. Come to know them intimately.*

The water clock was Math's closest friend for the night and it told him the hour was nearly up. Covering his ears with his hands, he risked the last wriggle forward to where he could make out the outline of Nero's geometric compound. The clock was its centrepiece, antique apple of the emperor's eye, a gift from Alexandria's elders to honour their Lord's ambitions of Platonic perfection.

Laid out in a triangle around the clock's sphere were the three dormitories within which slept the members of Nero's three chosen teams, Green, White and Blue, marked out by the roof tiles of verdigrised copper, limed shingles and deep blue clay pans respectively.

At the end of the Blues' line was a single chamber for Akakios in his role as overseer. A flag was bound to a mast there, as a sign that the emperor's spymaster was not currently in residence, and that, instead, Poros of the Blues was in notional charge of the compound. It served as a timely warning; men – and boys – were flogged more often when Akakios was in residence and Math had promised the ghost of his father that if he saw the flag fluttering free he would turn round and go back to bed.

Tonight, it wasn't. Safe, at least from that quarter, Math looked out beyond the triangle of the dormitories towards the square made by the horse stalls, the kitchens and the dining area and then on to the oval training track to the north and finally to the wide circular palisade that enclosed the whole compound, keeping the teams in and the curious onlookers of Alexandria out. Thus were all the philosophers' shapes fulfilled in Nero's creation, that their wisdom might infuse the drivers and their teams with all the skills necessary to outmatch the best of Rome, while at the same time keeping them well clear of the betting syndicates that would have paid in gold for news of their form.

That didn't stop the team members from gambling amongst themselves. It didn't, actually, stop them from laying bets outside the compound, just ensured that they were conducted secretly, and Math had only recently heard about it. The baker, apparently, was the conduit. His donkey cart drove in at dawn every morning laden with the day's bread, and lately two or three of the loaves had contained gold in their heart, sent from the outside by men whose job it was to feed the betting circles of Rome with the information they needed to lay odds in the coming season. One of the Blues' middle-ranking apprentices was said to be richer by three denarii as a result.

Doubtless, he had laid most of his money on his own team. Of the three teams, the Blues from Galatia were far and away the best; everyone had at least one wager on their winning the trial.

The Whites were from Cappadocia, which meant in their own tongue 'Land of the White Horses', which romantic fact, according to the guards, was the sole reason Nero had bought them here. Certainly it wasn't for their skill.

They were widely acclaimed as the pacemakers. Everyone who wasn't actually a member of the Whites expected them to be sent home as soon as another team came along that stood a hope of thrashing the Blues.

The Greens from Gaul were that team. All winter Ajax had trained under the eyes of the guards and the sensible money had been moving quietly in his direction for the past month. The fear amongst them all was that Ajax might fall ill or succumb to injury, for they lacked a credible second driver. Everyone agreed that Math had the talent, but he lacked the skill and experience to drive a winning team.

In Gaul, his dream of driving had been a pale, bloodless fantasy besides the excitement of the dockside thieving. But Ajax was a good tutor, possibly the best, and here in the compound, where every man and boy lived and breathed racing, Math had found that he wanted to drive a racing team more with each passing day.

Biting his lip, he dragged his mind back to the clock and the night; thoughts of racing ruined his concentration and tonight it mattered that he not make the same mistakes he had six months before.

Then, he had been caught by the Egyptian guards as he tried to climb the palisade, and had paid the price. The penalty for boys caught trying to leave the compound was precise and, as his team leader, Ajax had been woken and dragged, yawning and cursing, from his bed to administer the flogging.

The surprise of that had lasted at least for the start of what came after – because it was Ajax that Math had been following, and Ajax whom he had last seen very much awake and opening the small postern door with his key just before he had been caught.

The surprise had not lasted long; very soon it was impossible to think, or to breathe, or to do anything but hold the image of his father in the forefront of his mind and not let it go. At the end, he remembered Hannah coming to carry him back to her cell, and the bitter taste of the drink she had given him, and how it had shrivelled his tongue even as it stole the pain and let him sleep.

Afterwards, when Math was well enough to begin driving the horses again, he thought Ajax had treated him with more respect. Certainly he had pushed him harder, which was probably a good thing, even if the falls came more frequently and the bruises were worse.

Even so, Ajax had not told Math that he was going to meet Pantera. Math found out only because he had smiled his particular smile for the melon-seller's assistant every day through the entire winter and it had finally paid its dividend that morning, when the melon-seller had delivered to Ajax a gift of a bear standing with its claws outstretched towards half of a moon disc. Math, who had been given a secret glimpse beforehand, had read in it a message that he thought he understood.

Which was why he was hiding under the water clock within sight of the palisade for a second time, six months older and wiser, with greater respect for the Egyptian soldiers who stood night-guard along the heights, and an absolute terror of Akakios, the emperor's spymaster, and de facto overseer of the compound.

The last drop of water rolled from flute to vessel. A pan tipped, a lever moved, a ratchet clicked suddenly off the end of its cycle. The entire clock shivered like a hound shedding water. Three hammers snapped forward, hard.

In the silence of the compound, the great mother bell rang not quite loudly enough to wake those who slept. A flute whistled twice. A chime pierced the air with teeth-aching insistence.

On its second ring, Math threw himself across the sand on his hands and knees to the foot of the palisade.

Pressing up against the postern, he eased a key from within his tunic. Apart from Akakios' master key, there were four other keys in the compound: one each for the three team drivers and the last given to the chief cook, who was trusted to go out to the markets. The cook had a fondness for wine and a particular boy of the White team and Math was betting the skin of his back that the key wouldn't be missed before morning.

His hands were shaking. Under the fading chimes of the water clock, the key hushed in the lock. The well-oiled door opened without a sound.

Never go through any opening – a gate, a door, a curtain to a room, the entrance to a cave – if you are not certain what's on the other side. One day, it will be your death.

With Pantera's instruction ringing in his head, he pressed his face to the opening and let his eyes find the shapes and the unshapes of the world beyond the compound: the outlines of the city, half a mile distant, with its tall silhouetted palaces and the taller beacon of the lighthouse behind; the closer bulk of the city's hippodrome; the canal that led to the Nile and the shuffle of boats thereon.

Tilting his head, Math listened for the rhythmic breathing of the guard directly above, the grunts of night beasts in the desert, the sea's distant serenade, so much like home. Last, he sifted the scents of the desert, of cold sand and wood and men, from the more distant sea-smells of the harbour. He smelled the garlic that the guards had eaten at the last meal, and the wine, and the old, stale flatulence. He didn't smell either Ajax or Pantera, which meant that neither of them was there yet. Ahead, an unbroken expanse of sand reached out fifty paces to the emperor's horse trough with the bent arm of the pump over it like a standing heron. Math slid through the postern gate and locked it behind him, then set out to crawl across the open desert.

It was further than it seemed in daylight. Desiccated grit pushed itself up his nose, into his mouth and eyes. Twice, he had to stop and press his nose to stop himself from sneezing and when he finally lay prone in the cold, safe dark beneath the trough, sharp-footed insects bigger than mice began to scrabble over his arms, exploring routes into his tunic and out again so that lying still was a torture in itself.

He chose to believe that none of the insects was a scorpion. According to Saulos, the stammering Idumaean who had taken Caradoc's place as the Green team's harness-maker, the emperor had ordered his compound kept clear of venomous things and Akakios would have been required to fall on his own sword if so much as one brown snake had been found within the palisade.

Away from Nero's malign influence, Saulos had proved to be a fluent communicator, possessed of an encyclopaedic knowledge of Alexandria which was second only to Hannah's in its depth and breadth. He seemed also to be the only man in the compound who chose to spend friendly time with Akakios, which was little short of amazing, but meant that the story about the snakes might actually be true.

The night passed and no scorpions came. Math lay still and practised the ways Pantera had taught him to keep his mind awake without succumbing to a boredom that could kill him. After a while, for the fun of it, he imagined seeing Pantera, gliding ghost-like towards the palisade.

It worked. Between one blink and the next, Pantera was there – *there!* – a knife-blade shadow sliding over the sand with the same halting fluidity that Math had seen when first he had stepped off the boat on to Coriallum's dock half a year before.

The spy might have been lame, his shoulder might have been scarred beyond repair, but Math had not yet seen anyone else who could move like that. Even Ajax, who had once seemed to be the best of the best, was not that good, which was one reason, Math supposed, why Ajax felt the way he did.

Pantera stopped halfway to the palisade and turned on his heel, scanning the land around. Math's palms sprang suddenly sweaty. He half-closed his eyes and tried to press himself deeper into the sand.

In the desert night, an owl called softly twice and was answered. There were no owls near the emperor's training compound, but the sounds merged so completely with the waking coughs and cries of desert and city that only a boy who would make of himself a spy might have noticed them.

Because he was looking in the right direction, Math saw a man's shape peel away from the palisade and walk towards Pantera. At the last moment, dusty starlight reflected from Ajax's shaven head, leaving no doubt who met whom in the shadow of the palisade.

Singing to himself inside, Math watched the two men reach for each other in the warrior's grasp he had once so despised, then move together back into the shadows, to a place he had no hope of seeing or hearing.

He felt rather than heard the murmur of quiet speech. Words rolled together and even their timbre was not clear. Math frowned into the dark, begging the half-moon to give him more light.

It didn't; instead, a billowing cloud drew its veil across what little light there was, and a sudden breeze tossed handfuls of sand about the open space, making a noise that covered any other sounds. The two men could have coupled there, standing upright against the oak planking, and Math wasn't even sure he would hear it.

Certainly, he wouldn't have seen it, just as he had seen nothing when Ajax and Pantera had walked together down the riverbank on the night of his father's death. They hadn't been out of sight for long, but Math knew – who better? – how little time it took to consummate desire if both parties were eager. And he knew enough of such things to name for himself the change he had seen in Pantera and Ajax afterwards: two men who had departed the inn fire as strangers had come back close as brothers, with the shine of new discovery bright on their skin.

Things had passed between those two that night that no other heard or knew, but Math had seen Pantera grip Ajax's arm as he left them to return to his solitary bed in a distant tavern and had seen him the next day giving his oath to the emperor; an oath that had kept him apart from the Green team, so that, in the busy month of preparation that followed, his absence had hung over them as certainly as Math's father's had done.

None of which explained why Pantera was meeting Ajax in secret when, as the emperor's oath-sworn man, he could have walked in through the gate and demanded an audience. Akakios seemed the likely answer. Akakios was the answer to most of Math's problems, including the interesting question of how to get back into the compound unseen. He had an idea about that, if he managed to stay hidden until dawn.

Too late, the clouds unveiled the moon. Math moved his head a fraction, the better to stare at the place where a single shadow moved away from the palisade, and, splitting down its own length, became two men.

Morning was close. The baker was late again – the man was an unreliable harbinger of dawn – but beyond the palisade the first lick of light coloured the flat horizon. In the newly sharp shadows, Ajax and Pantera stepped apart with lingering slowness. Math heard his own name spoken softly as a question and a hushed reply.

Straining to hear, he closed his eyes. When he opened them bare moments later, the silence was so complete he could hear the crimp of sand under his own fist, but Pantera and Ajax were gone. He had heard neither the turn of the key nor the sound of a lame man's walking, but clearly he was alone.

There was no point in trying to follow Pantera; Math knew his own limits. It was also pointless, not to say dangerous, to try to get back into the compound now when the dark was in retreat.

He relaxed, therefore, under the shadow of the horse trough, and looked out across the sea towards the great lighthouse of Pharos with its bronze mirror and indefatigable flame that sent its signal, so said the guards, five hundred miles out to sea, guiding sailors past the man-eating shoals at the mouths of the two harbours.

The flame shimmered to new life, even as Math watched, its pitch fire overtaken by the greater flame of the sun. Brought early to morning, cocks crowed and the gulls began to keen and wheel as, out on the eastern edge of the training grounds, the first savage edge of the sun lifted over the horizon, signalling the start of the working day.

Precisely on time, the melon-seller arrived, leading an ass-drawn cart and accompanied by the man who came three times a month with dates and almonds. A message-runner from Akakios stood apart, not wishing to sully the authority of his station. The baker had still not arrived, which meant they'd be eating yesterday's bread at least until the noon meal. The chief cook hadn't risen, and so hadn't missed his key.

From inside the compound came the slow beginnings of the morning: cooking fires flared through their kindling, sending thin smoke to pepper the air; horses whinnied as stalls were opened; a gaggle of groom-boys flooded out of the gates, heading for the troughs with their buckets.

Elsewhere in Alexandria, the houses of the rich had their own cisterns, so that even the slaves need only turn a tap. In designing his compound, Nero could have diverted a branch of the Nile had he chosen. Instead, he had decided that it was healthier for the boys to carry water in from the pumps for the horses, for the small army of cooks who fed the greater army of drivers, grooms, stable-boys and slaves, and, first, for the great brass and silver clock that was the centrepiece of his compound. There were thirty boys, ten to each team. It took three trips each with two buckets to provide the necessary water.

They flooded out, muzzily sleepy and caught up in the squabbles of the day before. As the first of them gathered, Math stood, ducked his head into the trough and sluiced himself free of the night's dust, then lifted the two buckets he had hidden here the day before for exactly this purpose, and filled them to the brim with the night-cold water.

The boys moved in a pack, not wanting to be either first or last, and it was easy to slide into the middle. Just inside the gates, Math let fall the stolen key and kicked sand over it, but not so much that it might not be found by another boy, more sharp-eyed than he, and returned in safety to the chief cook when he came to look for it.

Humming to himself, he set in motion his plan for the rest of the day.

CHAPTER NINETEEN

'Did you see Math go out to get the water?' Ajax asked.

The morning was still young enough to be cool. He sat opposite Hannah at the weathered wooden dining trestles under an awning of shaved goatskin so thin the sun's disc shone clearly through. It served to keep the worst of the glare from their breakfast, but not the flies. Nothing kept the flies off for long, although a gaunt slave squatting nearby pulled rhythmically on an overhead fan that kept them away from the fruit, bread and honeyed barley porridge with which the emperor's chariot teams so richly broke their fasts.

In her time away from Alexandria, Hannah had forgotten the flies, and how summer multiplied them. They were bad enough now, in spring. Sighing, she batted the edge of her hand across a melon rind. 'I didn't see him go out with his bucket,' she said, 'but then I wasn't really paying attention until Lentus of the Whites found the cook's key in the sand at the gates.'

'He depends on that, I think. None of us pays sufficient attention to the things we see every day. In some ways, Pantera taught him too well.' Ajax kept his gaze averted as he spoke, which told Hannah more than he meant it to.

'He's been outside the compound without permission?' She stared at him, disbelieving. 'You've been out too, or he wouldn't have dared! Why didn't you tell me?'

'I'm sorry.' Ajax shrugged awkwardly, 'I thought I'd rely on you to heal my back afterwards if they caught me.'

'It wouldn't have been your back. For talking to some-one from the city, they would skin you alive and peg you out on the sands to be food for the flies!'

Hannah wanted to scream at him, and could not. Already the boys were milling about the training area harnessing the horses, close enough to hear. In any case, Ajax was looking at her at last, his gaze aggrieved.

'I may not be Pantera,' he said, 'but you have to trust that I can get out of the compound and back in again with-out being caught.'

'And that Math can do the same?'

'He can. He did. Look at him. Does he look like a boy who might let himself be caught a second time?'

Math was leading out Brass and Bronze, his two wild-mad colts, ready for the morning's run. Already they were creamed with sweat.

Hannah watched as he bridled them and set their har-ness on to the training chariot. He was fast and nimble, and the colts didn't lunge at him with quite the savagery they reserved for everyone else. Then he was finished, and dived back into the crowd and would have been lost but that, amongst a horde of dark-haired, dark-skinned boys and their sweat-sheened colts, he stood out like a shooting star fallen to earth.

His hair had always been gold, but dustily so. Since Gaul, he had taken to rinsing it in citrus juice and that, combined with the Alexandrian sun, had spun it to finest gold. Then, too, he was smaller than the rest, and his skin less brown, and these three together made him a golden bounty-cock in a flock of black-brown hens. For these reasons alone, he could have been bullied without cease, but the other boys liked him, and revelled in his difference, and he was learning to play and take joy in others' levity as he had not done in Gaul. Hannah wasn't sure who had taught him that.

A slave hovered close by, ready to clear the table. Ajax selected a peach and began to rub it between his palms until it glistened.

Hannah said, 'You met Pantera.' If she closed her eyes, she could see the spy sitting on a stone by a fire eating an oat bannock smeared with honey, and hiding from her the sharpness of his mind. 'And not for the first time?'

Ajax balanced the peach in the centre of his palm. 'I was going to meet him six months ago, on the night Math was caught trying to leave the compound. Clearly, I missed my appointment. Last night was the first time since then. We didn't intend it so, but we had to wait for the right circumstances.'

'Like Akakios being away from the compound for the night?'

'And the moon giving favourable light and the right guards on the palisades. Indeed.'

Behind Ajax, a flash of gold caught Hannah's eye. Out on the sands of the training track, the teams of each colour were harnessed and ready to begin their warm-up. This once, Math was ready first, with the resin wiped on his hands and the harness wound round his waist exactly as the first drivers did it.

With Hannah and Ajax watching, he took Bronze and Brass for what should have been an easy, lazy circuit of the track, except that nothing with these horses was ever lazy or easy and Math would not have wanted them if it was. He took them round one full circuit steadily enough; then, at the next corner, leaned into the turn as if it were a real race, and very nearly succeeded in lifting the heavy training rig on to two wheels, as if it were a racing chariot in full flight.

211

It was an impressive attempt. Other boys would have punched the air and checked to see who was watching. Math frowned and spoke to the colts and then rebalanced himself and took the next corner faster. This time he managed to lift the chariot up on to the two inside wheels for three paces, and set it neatly back down again. It wobbled a little as it settled.

On the sidelines, some of the younger apprentices applauded. Math didn't look up. Hannah saw him bite his lower lip, frowning. The colts felt something from him, and extended their paces, so that for a while they flew with racing speed, until even the guards were cheering.

At Hannah's side, Ajax cursed quietly. 'I should thrash him senseless. He knows better than to push the horses before they're properly warmed up.'

Hannah glanced sideways, expecting to see in him an undercurrent of pride. Instead, she saw that rare thing: Ajax truly angry. She took a moment to uncramp her hands. 'We forget he's only ten,' she said. 'You should let him race. He won't stop trying to impress you until you do.'

'*He* forgets he's only ten,' Ajax said. 'We don't. And there's no point in his racing until he can control the horses at speed, which he isn't close to doing yet. In any case, the only race in sight is the trial against Poros and Math won't be ready for that.'

Hannah was struggling to marshal a response when Ajax leaned both forearms on the table and said, 'Pantera brought news this morning.'

'He's found the ink-stained apothecary who held a seat at the Black Chrysanthemum?' Hannah felt her eyes flare wide.

Ajax grinned tightly. 'After six months of searching and a great deal of Seneca's gold surreptitiously spent, yes, Pantera has tracked down a particular man who sometimes dines at the inn of the Black Chrysanthemum on the Street of the Lame Lion and once asked a Syrian to sell copies of a certain prophecy to the highest bidder. The Syrian, it is said, sold precisely one: to a thin man with dark hair, shortly before he fell in with the emperor's messenger, who is rumoured to have stolen another and killed the seller. If the man Pantera has found knows the date by which Rome may burn, then we have the first part of the riddle.'

'But not the answer to who is trying to light the fire.'

'We might have that, too.'

A slave-boy had come to hover nearby, sent by the chief cook, who, against all recent form, favoured the Whites. Ajax finished his peach and tossed the stone back into the bowl. Lacking any reason to stay, the boy picked it up and returned to the chief cook.

When he was out of earshot, Ajax said, 'Akakios' agents have been following Pantera for the past month. It may be that they simply want to know what he's doing, but it may also be that Akakios is trying to discover the date of the fire.'

'That doesn't mean he's necessarily trying to light it. Akakios won't want Pantera to succeed where he has failed. He'd lose Nero's favour.'

'Which in this court is likely to be fatal.' Ajax chewed on his lip. 'At any rate, if Pantera can dispose of whoever's following him – and I would bet on that man against anyone in Alexandria – then he'll visit the ink-stained apothecary later today and return here tomorrow morning with news of what he's found.'

'And what makes you think Math won't try to leave the compound again to watch you?'

'Unless he's got the hearing of a hawk, he won't be there. He hid under the water troughs too far away to hear what we said.'

'*Ajax!*' Heads turned. More quietly, Hannah said, 'If you saw him, then there's no saying who else might have done. What will you do if—'

'I didn't see him. Pantera pointed him out or I wouldn't have known he was there. I told you, he's learned too well, just not yet perfectly, for which we should all be grateful.' Grim-faced, Ajax stood, pushing the bench away from the table. Like all the drivers, he wore only a loincloth, so that when he raised his arms to ease his shoulders a stray finger of sunlight feathered the side of his ribs, filling the indentation where the hoof had crushed his chest.

In Gaul, the edges had flared scarlet, with fierce lancing scorch marks stretching out across the whole of his chest. But he was young and as fit as any man of his age and the scars of this accident had grown white, joining the mess of others on his back. Hannah had no idea where those others had come from. She traced them sometimes in her mind. He had been flogged once, clearly, but beneath that were marks she could not begin to name, and—

'Hannah?' Ajax tapped lightly on the trestle. 'Your admirer is here.'

'Saulos?' She snatched her mind back to the present. The team's newest member had a wound on his back that she had been treating since before they left Gaul.

'Saulos of the talking hands. The Idumaean harness-maker with a Greek education. Who else?' Ajax spat succinctly into the dust. As everyone else had come to know and like Saulos, Ajax had come to loathe him, and made no effort to hide it. Saulos, for his part, was unfailingly civil. 'He'll offer you marriage soon, if you keep on encouraging him.'

Hannah laughed aloud. Against all her foreboding, it was a good morning, with kindness in the air.

'I'm not encouraging him,' she said, shooing Ajax away with her hands. 'I'm his physician and he's my patient. But if he offers anything more substantial than a copper coin in payment for his treatment, you can be sure I'll tell you before anyone else.'

*   *   *

214

'Good day.'

Saulos stood diffidently at the edge of the dining area. His expressive hands made a fluid, apologetic movement that conveyed both his regret at disturbing her, and his joy in her presence. 'May I sit?'

'Of course.' Hannah motioned him forward. He stepped neatly past her, to take the bench Ajax had so recently vacated.

He was a neat man. Early on in their acquaintanceship, in her effort to find something remarkable about Saulos that might make him more visible than the invisible slaves, his fastidious neatness was the first thing she had noticed; he carried a rag of linen in his sleeve and wiped his lips with it after eating, which was curious enough to be memorable.

Later, she had come to enjoy the landscape of his mind; he was articulate, intelligent, thoughtful and funny, but shyly so, and it had taken work on her part to bring him out of himself.

It had been worth the effort. Through the winter, she had found that he was schooled in Greek, Latin and Hebrew literature, that he could recite the poetry of Homer and Nicander for an hour without pause, that he understood philosophy and could conduct reasoned discourse on the nature of thought and had been known to hold forth at length on the differing philosophies of Socrates, Plato and Epicurus, as if he had known each one personally.

He didn't stammer, either; that came only when he was afraid. In Hannah's presence, he was fluent and engaging and therein lay the heart of her conflict.

She loved Ajax; six months in his daily company had made that certain. She loved him for his courage, for his wisdom, for the scars on his back and the history she might never know. She loved the tone of his voice and his wildness, the sense of danger in his presence that left her

215

so very safe. She loved his cautious, overwhelming care of Math, and his honouring of the oaths that bound him. She loved his eyes and the curve of his mouth. She loved his scent, after the end of a day's riding.

But Saulos . . . Too often, the face that held her mind when she lay down to sleep was Saulos'. Too often, the voice that continued unbroken the discussions of the day was Saulos', engaging her in conversation as if she were an equal, setting him far apart from the Greek-schooled sophists of Hannah's acquaintance, all of whom treated women like cattle.

Unexpectedly, she remembered her mother, who had taught her of Pythagoras, who, almost uniquely amongst the philosophers of old, had schooled women alongside men. Blinking fiercely, she reached for the bag of linen, knives and salves and the nested copper pots that were her constant company.

'I make you unhappy?' Saulos asked.

Hannah shook her head. 'I was thinking of my mother,' she said. 'She instructed me in the treatment of festering wounds.'

She spoke Greek with him, where Ajax and Math still spoke Gaulish. It felt fresh and sharp on her tongue, the language of poets and medicine. She said, 'You wish me to change your dressing?'

'I'm afraid I do. It's the heat, I think. The wound festers more in summer than in winter, and here more than in Gaul. In the past day, it has become exceptionally fluid. I wouldn't bother you otherwise.'

He leaned forward, resting his arms on the trestle in front of him, that she might see for herself. Unlike the drivers, he wore a thin linen tunic which meant that when flies came to investigate his wound, they settled on the fine weave and left spots behind. Hannah noted the speckled dirt of their passing just before a chance shift in the breeze brought her the smell. Saulos saw her wrinkle her nose.

216

'I'm sorry.' His hands spoke it better.

'Should a patient apologize to his physician for needing care? I don't think so.'

Hannah busied herself with the routine of preparations, the same each time so that she might not forget anything; first the linen strips laid out, and then the cotton dressings. Near to them, the salves in their order, and beyond them the nest of five hand-beaten copper pots that held each half the volume of the one above, down to the smallest that held a mouthful and was only for the very sweet or very bitter drenches. Last were the knives, forceps and the lead vessel topped with wax that held her scouring paste for the debridement of wounds.

No man ever liked to watch her lay out cold iron. Saulos sat in profile, looking past her to where Ajax had walked on to the track and was explaining to Math exactly why he should not have tried to show off earlier. Ajax was not speaking especially loudly, but his voice carried from one side of the compound to the other and every other apprentice boy heard it.

Math was scarlet; every part of him burned with shame. Hannah winced inside. On the far side of the table, Saulos pinched the bridge of his nose and clicked his tongue. 'Math should ride a race soon,' he said conversationally. 'He'll only learn properly if he's put under pressure.'

'We were just speaking of that,' Hannah said. 'Ajax pointed out that the only race coming up is the trial to see who will go to Rome. Too much hinges on it and, in any case, Math's not ready.'

'With respect,' Saulos said, 'I think he's as ready as he's ever going to be. He won't improve without the added pressure. That boy is brilliant but lazy. He learns best when he must. What more could he ask for than a trial to prove himself?'

Hannah blew out her cheeks. 'He's not good enough yet,' she said, and in the saying, knew it was true. 'He was brought up riding horses, not driving them. It's a different skill.'

'But one he's desperate to acquire. The need shines from him throughout the day. Only by being given the chance will he begin to learn what he needs. You wish me to remove my tunic?'

'If you would.'

With a self-conscious modesty that only a Hebrew could achieve, Saulos turned fully away, stripped off his belt and pulled his tunic over his head, and with that she had to tear her mind away from Math and Ajax and turn it instead to her profession.

The bandage that encircled Saulos' chest and reached over his right shoulder was soiled with only the usual dust and sweat, except at the place where the ulcer had oozed its foulness on to it. There, it was evilly crusted and glued to his body.

With clinical care, Hannah cut the linen, letting fall those parts that could do so. The skin beneath was the pale white of a Gaulish winter, untouched by the Alexandrian sun. The ulcer lay just medial to his scapula, and was a circular hand's breadth in diameter. Here, in spite of the grease and ointments she had applied not five days before, and the lace of thin cotton gauze after, the dressing stuck firmly to the wound and surrounding skin.

She held her breath as she eased the stiff, foul cloth inwards from its margins. Saulos gasped, tightly. The excess flesh of his belly quivered and rolled. For both their sakes, she tugged the last bit sharply away.

'Done.'

'Thank you.' His voice was a thread, whispering.

He had been right about the wound's new fecundity. Damp humours, ripe and yellow as custard, covered its surface, with the wound edges palely friable beneath. The smell was of old death and liquefaction, sweetly rotting. Breathing only through her mouth against the stench,

Hannah dropped the fetid bandage to the floor. An avalanche of flies fell on it, feasting.

She kicked the mess away and began to clean the wound, examining the ripe flesh at the edges and the bed of healing tissue beneath. A slave had brought warm water without her asking; after a winter in which she had cared for them as if they were freeborn, the slaves watched her as if she were the empress, whose will must be anticipated at every step. She reached for her gauze and began to swab at the edges.

'It's deeper and more extensive than it was,' she said, when she had cleaned it fully, 'but it hasn't begun to under-run the skin again as it had done in Gaul.'

Saulos grimaced. 'Forty lashes less one. You'd think that by now I had paid enough.'

Hannah raised a brow. She had been treating him for over six months and not once in all that time had he admitted that the wound was the result of an unhealed flogging. Now, she thought she heard regret in his voice, or shame.

Carefully, she said, 'Ajax has been flogged. The scars are clear on his back. It didn't make him a lesser man.'

He had no time to say he was less than Ajax, or that his flogging was for a lesser offence – both of which would have been his style – because by then she was applying the scouring paste and Saulos couldn't have answered even if he had wanted to. He folded his forearms on the trestle ahead of him and leaned his brow on them, blanching the skin with the pressure. Over the space of the next while, the sweat grew slick at his temples and his fingers pressed on to the boards until they took on the same colour as the pale, sunned wood.

Hannah dropped the fouled spatula into a bucket of sand and used another the same to scrape the paste off, bringing with it the dead and dying matter of his wound. Slaves took the foul ones away and burned them.

When she had a bed of clean tissue, only bleeding a little, she layered on a fresh mix of honey wax and goose-grease as the base and set the herbs in it before she laid on the gauze and then wound the bandages.

At the end, as she knotted the bandage under his shoulder, Saulos lifted his head from his arms and asked, thinly, 'Will it get worse?'

'Yes, but you knew that. The heat has made the wound weep far more than it has done before now. To my shame, I haven't healed you yet. I am a disgrace to my profession and my tutors.'

'You are neither of those.' Saulos pressed his hands to his face. 'You've done your best, which is all anyone, god or man, can ask of you.' He lifted his arm experimentally. 'It feels better. It always does when you do it. My thanks.'

He drew on his tunic, sparing her the need to reply. The sun lit them both, angling in past the date palms that hedged the southern wall of the compound and the row of hay forks carefully lined along it.

Hannah took another bucket of sand and began to scour out the copper pots. It offended the slaves that she cleaned them herself, but she had always done so and saw no reason to change.

'I've applied the yarrow and oil of almond as before,' she said. 'If you can find oil of spikenard, made from the crushed roots dug under a waxing moon, I think it might be better proof against the heat.'

'Spikenard ensures sexual fidelity, does it not?' Saulos' glance flicked to her face and away. He was making fun of her, clumsily, as if he wasn't sure how it was done.

'It may do, I don't know.' Hannah washed her hands briskly in a fresh basin of warm water. The slaves carried the soiled bandage to a fire on the edge of the compound, where the smell would not infest the cooking. 'If the spikenard is combined with a soured butter boiled with fennel, it may aid the closing of long-open wounds. You have Akakios' trust – you can leave the compound any time you choose. If you were to go to the market, you might find someone to make you the ointment. Or at the very least find the base ingredients and bring them here for me to do it.'

'After which, whether my wound heals or not, I will smell fit to send the dogs fleeing with their tails curled under their bellies.' Saulos grinned. His hands opened a path in the air. 'As you say, I have Akakios' permission to leave the compound when I choose. I have also permission to take with me whomever I wish, as long as I provide surety for their behaviour and their safe return. Perhaps you might join me in visiting the city?'

If Hannah had one wish, it was to leave the compound and walk freely through Alexandria for an afternoon, to see how it had changed in the years since she had last been there, perhaps to call on old friends. But there were reasons why she had not yet asked Akakios for permission.

'Thank you,' she said, 'but I need to be on hand while the teams train. If someone's hurt, the compound has no other physician.'

'Hannah, I think you forget that there was no physician in the compound before you came and they managed well enough. Poros of the Blues is skilled in basic physic and I have no doubt Ajax would prove competent in your absence. Math, of course, is prone to taking risks. But if we were to take him with us . . . ?'

Saulos caught sight of Hannah's face. Laughter danced in his eyes as his so-expressive hands opened a door and ushered her through. 'So that's settled. All you have to do is get Ajax to agree and we can leave as soon as Math can be spared from his duties.'

Chapter Twenty

In the rising heat of the day, Sebastos Abdes Pantera walked fast along the Avenue of the Sphinx.

He wore a slave's cheap long-sleeved tunic tied with hemp rope, frayed at both ends. He went barefoot, wearing neither sandals nor any ornament, and if he was armed, none of the passing merchants, fish-sellers, rope-makers, water-carriers, charcoal-makers, merchants, artisans, slaves or prostitutes of both genders saw it.

The Avenue of the Sphinx was one of the linear pulsing arteries of Alexandria. It stretched from the waterfront past the gold-roofed, white-walled palaces and on to the less gilded, better protected barracks of the legions permanently stationed in this, the gateway to Rome's granary.

From these, it passed the houses of the tax collectors and the well-connected merchants with their gilded rooftops and saffron-painted shutters, and cut straight through the tentacled cobweb of the Hebrew quarter where the rich mixed with the less rich and no house was truly poor, to the slums, where a man's god was as nothing compared to his ability to scrape a meal from the stinking gutter and defend it against all comers.

Somewhere near the indistinct boundary between these

two last, on the Street of the Lame Lion, which ran at right angles to the Avenue of the Sphinx, the inn of the Black Chrysanthemum lay squeezed between a fishmonger and a tannery, in the forecourt of which a dozen clay pots of fermented human urine and dog faeces gave off a fog of unspeakable odour.

For six months Pantera had been engaged in careful idleness. He had gone sightseeing at the lighthouse, and visited the museum and the library, where a man versed in Greek and clothed in calfskin, tissue-of-gold and silk might yet converse with some of the sharpest minds of the age.

Changed into lesser clothing, he had drunk in taverns, caroused – sober – through whorehouses and haggled at the market. All of which, piecemeal, had yielded the location of the Black Chrysanthemum and, a long time later, the name and details of a particular alchemist-astrologer with white hair and ink stains on his fingers who ate and drank there.

Pantera's past nine days had been devoted predominantly to watching the inn's two entrances; the one on the street, and the lesser-used, more circumspect one that led out into the courtyard behind. In so doing, he had identified and then followed the astrologer to a house in a narrower, marginally less grim alleyway abutting the Street of the Lame Lion some distance down from the inn. The fact that this house had a rear door and that the tiny alley on to which it opened led directly through a particularly narrow passage to the inn was a useful feature that he had only recently discovered.

The inn was open, as it always was, but business was never brisk in the forenoon. In any case, the carrying of one of the foul tanner's pots was sufficient to render any man invisible, slave or not, with the added advantage of a boundary at least ten feet in diameter within which no one sane dared step.

Knowing this, Pantera stooped to collect a black-lidded

pot from the place he had left it the night before. The body was bulbous, flaring out to the base with a subtle inward curve that allowed it to sit on his shoulder without undue discomfort. It did not contain either men's urine or fermenting dog excrement, but fluid slopped in it audibly and nobody came near enough to discover how bad it might smell.

Thus burdened, he adjusted his route more to the edge of the road as he continued on down past the inn of the Black Chrysanthemum, with its surprisingly smart red-tiled roof and the thousand-petalled flowers done in charcoal on the side boards, into the narrowing street where slaves and freemen mingled with little to distinguish them but that the former were, on the whole, better fed than the latter.

A gaunt prostitute standing in a doorway shouted an offer of exact anatomical precision. She was dressed in loose black, to hide her shape. Her lips had been painted with honey glaze and red dye, but not recently, and she wore bangles of copper about her bird-thin wrists and more at her ankles. She looked Hebrew, which set her apart from the bulk of her sisters who were Greek, or Egyptian, or, more rarely, black-skinned Nubians, who commanded a premium for their colour. She called to Pantera again, disparaging his manhood.

Grunting, red-faced, he gestured obscenely back, informing her in the local Greek patois that he was a slave with no money. He added a curse inventive in its ugliness.

Ten paces on, he hefted the pot down from his shoulder and set it on the ground near the whore before turning right, into the dark of an alley the sun had long ago abandoned all efforts to reach.

From the dark, he watched the woman retrieve the bronze coin he had left her beneath the pot. Some brief time later, he saw her take as a client a round-faced man wearing the short tunic and belted trews of a ship-hand, ˜

who turned her face to the wall and accepted her offer in all its exactitude.

Her new client was not a stranger to the street, but drank each night at the Black Chrysanthemum where he shouted tales of seafaring and piracy, all saved by the wonder of the lighthouse. Pantera had watched as, drunk and friendly, he had swayed with his companions from the tavern in the small hours of the night. Only when he had parted from them, never quite going where they went, did he become miraculously sober and return to the pleasanter surround of the legions' barracks. There, he exchanged his sailor's trousers for a tunic of quality linen and changed the nature of his dialect from that of a dockhand to the equally rough, but distinctly different patois of a legionary.

For five days, this particular individual had followed Pantera, and Pantera had gone about his business as if he had not seen him. Now, as the man released the whore without payment, looked left and right, belted his trews and stepped silently into the blackness of the minor alley, Pantera flicked out the edge of his palm much as he had trained Math to do in their nights together, aiming at throat height. The impact hurt, satisfyingly.

It hurt the man he had hit far more. Pantera caught the front of the sailor's smock and twisted it tight on his neck, choking him. 'I will say a name,' he said, softly. 'You will answer with a nod if you know it.'

The choking increased. The man flailed his feet, battering at his assailant's calves. As he had done with Math, but with considerably more force, Pantera kicked his heels from under him and drove him into the ground. Bones shattered under the impact. The choking became an abortive attempt to shout.

Pulling the head into the crook of his arm, Pantera brought his mouth close to one cauliflower ear. 'Akakios of Rhodes,' he said.

The head jerked once.

'Thank you.'

Pantera moved his elbow up and up and used his free hand to make the twist until he felt the vertebrae of the man's neck begin to grind against each other. A final abrupt movement brought a short, hard snap. The ship-hand who had never manned a ship jerked once and fell still. Pantera lowered his body to the ground. It smelled suddenly of urine, and the first ripeness of faeces.

'And me?' asked a harsh voice made soft. 'I told him where you had gone.' The prostitute stood in the alley's mouth, her face scarved by the shadows.

'But first you told me that the man I seek is at home, for which I am grateful.' Pantera opened his purse, and pulled from the hank of soft wool he kept therein – cheese became rancid too soon in this weather – a copper coin. She caught it without turning her head.

'I don't kill women unless they threaten me. Will you do so? Or your unborn child?'

He heard her hesitation. She was, he thought, pregnant by no more than four months and had believed her cloth-ing covered it. 'No.'

'Then go. If someone asks what happened, tell them what you have seen. If nobody asks, I would advise you not to volunteer. Our late friend's employers don't stop at taking favours without payment.'

'I saw a man kill another man,' she said, turning away. 'He paid me when he could have killed me. I will tell no one unless they ask.'

He reached for her wrist and held it. The bones were sharp. 'My name is Abdes Pantera. I seek a man named Ptolemy Asul. If they ask, tell them I told you to say it.'

'Such names would buy my life?'

'One of them may do. I don't know which one.'

The sun scooped her up and returned her to the door-way. Pantera waited in the dark for long enough to be sure no one else followed, then walked on, away from the light.

A door of iron-bound oak blocked the end of the alleyway, its very thickness setting it apart from the others in the Street of the Lame Lion.

Pantera stared at it, then slid a knife from his left forearm, and, holding the blade between thumb and fingers, rapped the hilt five times on the door in an offset rhythm. He heard light feet on the far side and sheathed the knife, stepping back out of sword's reach.

What came was not a sword, but fire: a pitch-soaked torch, thrust out at chest height. Pantera stepped in, ducking under the flame, and came up hard, grabbing the wrist that held the torch and slamming it back against the door jamb so that the brand spun loose. His other hand brought his knife up to eye height.

Flames flared across the alley's floor, stuttered and died. In the subsequent dark, two white-rimmed eyes gazed at him without fear. The hand he held did not move, either to pull away or to fight. He caught a faint scent of wild flowers, bright as spring.

He drew the knife back, ready to use it. 'I thought you did not kill women?' a woman's voice said, lightly.

'Stop this nonsense, both of you!' That was a man, aged, but clear as struck bronze. 'Pantera, if you are he, you would be made more welcome if you came to the front door and announced yourself properly.'

'To whom should I make my address?' Pantera did not relax his grip on the woman's hand, or lower the knife. 'An agent of Akakios?'

'Hardly.'

The man spoke Greek with an accent too subtle to place. It sounded, in fact, exactly as Seneca had sounded at the height of his power, when the fate of the empire was his to command.

A single candle was lifted and brought forward down a dimly ambered corridor. By its light, Pantera saw a balding head fringed with white hair and, beneath, a long, lean face. He could not yet see the woman whose wrist he still held, but could only feel her breath stir the hairs on his cheek and the slow, steady lift of her breast against his arm. She had no fear of him, which was as unsettling as it was surprising. He thought she laughed at him, but could not be sure.

From the corridor, the dry Greek voice said, 'If you will consent to follow her, Hypatia will lead you to an inner room, better hidden from prying eyes. There, you may make your address in the proper form to the man you seek. You are searching for Ptolemy Asul, are you not? I am he.'

CHAPTER TWENTY-ONE

Ptolemy Asul, it became evident, lived a life of contradictions.

His house was as hidden as it was possible to be in Alexandria. Surrounded by stinking shadows, another iron-bound door at the end of the corridor contrived to open on to a peristyled garden, where a fountain played into a marble bowl and small birds pecked in dusty sunlight. The rooms off were open and airy, scented with dried roses and peppery hyacinth, the floors done in mosaics of the old type, depicting Ptah and Sekhmet, Hathor and Horus in pastel shades of blues, citrons and golds with an artistry that had been lost three generations before. Sunlight angled in through painted screens so that Pantera walked on a carpet of subtly shaded teardrops in honey, amber, lavender and lime.

At length, he was brought to a dusty library. Shutters closed the windows incompletely, allowing light to leak around their edges. Shelves lined all the walls, piled high with papyrus scrolls and sheaves of parchment, with jars and vessels and bottles marked illegibly with the signs of the apothecary's trade and all covered with the dust that thickened the air and layered every surface.

'Will you be seated?'

Hypatia's voice was laced with scorn, but there was a richness beneath that roused hidden memories from Pantera's childhood. Tall and Greek-boned, she had a fine, long nose and high eyebrows plucked in the old fashion of Cleopatra and Octavia. Only her arrogance prevented her from being breathtakingly beautiful.

'Thank you.' He sat where he was shown, on an ebony stool carved in the likeness of an elephant, bearing in its coiled trunk the gift-sheaf of corn. Hypatia towered over him. Her black eyes burned. 'You're not here at my invitation. If I could make it so, you would never have lived the length of the alley.' She backed away out of the room, leaving him to explore his surroundings alone.

On the shelf beside him, a lone candle sat atop a volcanic mound of old wax that yet failed to hide the curved limbs and lithe form of the candlestick beneath, which was shaped as a woman, barely dressed, and raising her arms above her head.

Curious, Pantera picked it up and, turning it aslant, tested the yellow metal of one graceful female foot with his fingernail.

'It's gold,' said a quiet, grey voice behind him.

'From west Britain,' Pantera agreed, without turning. 'Cut with a little silver to brighten the hue. Caesar had such things made as fancies to present to his friends. I saw one once, in the shape of Isis, said to be modelled on Cleopatra. It had feet such as this, spread wide in a dancer's pose, balanced on the toes, with the arch taut as a bow and ankles fine as a gazelle's. That such an ornament could stand upright was considered a wonder of the craftsman's art.'

'Then you are, I think, the only man still living who has seen both of them. The other was given to Mark Antony, whence it passed to Octavian and then ultimately to the tyrant Caligula, who rendered it into bullion to pay for his failed venture in Britain. Will you join me in a drink?'

Ptolemy Asul was of middling height. His lean, ascetic face was built around the strong bones of the true patrician, blurred only a little by age. He stood in the middle of the room holding out a clay beaker, filled to the frothing brim with a drink whose scent pervaded the room.

'Please,' he said. 'I can offer little of great worth, but the keeper of the Black Chrysanthemum is a native of Heliopolis where they retain skills lost to us since the time the gods walked the earth. They named the inn for this, his drink, and he has not yet been induced to give up the recipe. Rich men venture deeper than is prudent down the street just to taste it.'

Pantera felt himself sucked into a rusted courtesy. Gravely, he raised the beaker in a toast. 'I am honoured by both your trust and your gift.'

The mug foamed with the lightness of sherbet and was cold to touch in the sweating heat of the morning. Over the sweet spice of the incense, Pantera caught the lighter scents of citron, marigold and chrysanthemum oil.

He drank and the taste crashed along his tongue, surging simultaneously up to his head and down to his stomach, sweetening both. After the shock of the cold, his first thought was that Hannah would like it, and that he would like to share it with her, soon. His second, longer, less happy thought was that he should have thought of Aerthen first.

He looked up. Ptolemy Asul regarded him owl-like over the rim of his own mug. 'The living deserve more of our consideration than the dead,' he said, as if that last thought lay in common between them. 'The living know pain and hurt and heartbreak and wish only to escape them, while the dead remember these things with nostalgia.'

Pantera tasted ginger, honey and wild sweet-sharp berries beneath the shock of the first flowers. It still left him thinking of Hannah.

231

Shreds of marigold sparked the surface. He picked one up and tasted the tip between his teeth.

'I killed Akakios' man on the way in,' he said. 'I may have led him here, although I believe not. Either way, if Akakios is on the same quest as I am, you would do well either to give him what he wants or to leave before he can ask.'

'So soon the pleasantries are gone.' Ptolemy smiled sadly. 'What is your quest?'

'Do you not know?'

'I would hear it from you. What is it that you and Nero's spymaster both seek?'

'The missing words in the Sibyl's prophecy, that will tell us the date on which Rome must burn in order to bring about the Kingdom of Heaven.' Pantera drew from his tunic a piece of folded papyrus and laid it out on the desk.

At the sight of it, Ptolemy Asul reached behind him for a candelabra and, with swift economy, lit all nine stubs of wax. Numinous golds swarmed across the marble desk, across the inlaid sigils thereon, across the old man's white hair, as he sat to read the neat writing with its purposeful gaps.

He read aloud, as Pantera had done.

'. . . *and thus will it come about in the Year of the Phoenix, on the night when* – that which is unknown – *shall gaze down in wrath from beyond the knife-edge of the world, that in his sight shall the Great Whore be wreathed in fire, and burned to the utmost ashes, seared to nought in the pits of her depravity. Only when this has come to pass shall the Kingdom of Heaven be manifest as has been promised. Then shall* – the second unknown – *be rent, never to be repaired, and all that was whole shall be broken and the covenant that was made shall be completed in accord with all that is written.*'

Ptolemy Asul lifted his head. In the wavering light, his

eyes were dark. 'Rome, of course, is the Great Whore, and the veil is in Jerusalem's temple, but you know that. As does your enemy, I'm sure. In your opinion, why is Akakios hunting the prophecy?'

'He must know that Nero has commissioned me to find both the date when Rome must burn and the identity of the thin man with the dark hair who bought the other copy. He won't want me to succeed in my endeavour. His status with Nero would be . . . tenuous, if I did so.'

Ptolemy traced his forefinger in the dust on the desk. 'And, again in your opinion, he has no interest in facilitating Rome's destruction?'

Pantera hesitated. 'I don't know. You're not the first to suggest that he might have. Rumours say Nero wishes to build a palace that will outshine even the Forum Augusta, a place greater than any temple, more spectacular than the pyramids of Egypt. That's hardly unusual – unless someone has convinced him to build it in Rome, not outside. To do so, he would have to clear the ghettos around the forum.'

'So it may be to Akakios' advantage to burn the city – but selectively, so that the slums are cleared and the greatness preserved?'

'If he is to be the architect of the new colossus, then it would be very much to his advantage. Nero, however, may not be party to this. He is, after all, paying me to stop the fire, whoever is trying to light it. If I can find out the date the prophecy implies, I'll be a step closer to doing that. Will you tell me?'

'I would if I could, but the gaps in the manuscript were there in the original. I was required to copy it, nothing more. I neither made the prophecy, nor heard it spoken.' Ptolemy Asul held the papyrus towards the light, the better to study the script. 'This is not in my hand,' he said. 'Do you have the original somewhere safe?'

233

'I have the original, and three copies made by me, all hidden in different locations.'

'In that case . . .' Ptolemy Asul held a corner of the papyrus over a candle. Flames blossomed bright, and swept up its length, dying back as soon as they had come. The last scorched his fingers, but he did not let go, only turned his hand over and caught the black ash, crushing it in his closing palm.

'Jerusalem will fall,' he said absently. 'No one can stop that now. Some things must run their course.'

Pantera snuffed the candle before it burned Asul's hand. 'But if Rome can be kept from burning, then surely the prophecy is broken? If I can find the date on which Rome must burn, then I can stop it.'

'He can't tell you what he doesn't know, however you plead.' Hypatia's voice came sharp as a sting. Pantera had not known she was there. 'To find the truth, you must go to the source.'

'I thought I had done so, lady, in so far as I am able. I was under the impression that it came from the Sibyls, whom no man might approach.'

'And yet you must approach them.' Asul moved the candlestick across his desk. 'To find what you lack, you must ask a boon of the Oracle at the Temple of Truth, who resides in Hades.'

There was a long silence, when Pantera expected someone to laugh. 'I thought the underworld a child's tale, spawned of the dark nights,' he said at last.

'You thought wrongly.' Hypatia stepped up to the desk and lifted the gold dancer. 'Every tale has its seed. This is no different. Did you think Alexander built his city here just for the harbour? Because it was a good place to set a lighthouse? No: he met the Sibyls and made his own pact with them. Had he listened to their advice, he would have lived to see his vision made real in bricks and mortar. Men never listen.'

234

'Some do,' Ptolemy Asul said mildly. His slow gaze came to rest on Pantera's face. 'Only a woman can take you; one who was raised by the Sibyls, is gifted in their laws and familiar with their ways. My father, for instance, was escorted by the woman who became my mother. She's dead now, of course.'

Pantera's heart missed a beat. A number of things became clear, suddenly. He felt very stupid. 'Hannah could guide me?' he said.

'If she's willing, yes. Be sure you are clear beforehand why you go. The truth is not always easy to hear, but the Oracle can give nothing else.'

'And before that,' said Hypatia, 'you should speak to Shimon the zealot. He has some questions that only you can answer.'

'He's here?' Pantera stared out at the pale garden beyond the doorway. 'Where?'

'In the library on the eastern side of the town. He's conversing with men whose philosophy he abhors, waiting for you to join him. I told him you would be with him before noon. If you leave now, you will reach him just in time.'

'Go.' Ptolemy Asul bowed over his clasped hands. His speech had settled back into the old archaic cadences of the past. 'Go with our good grace. You will not return here in my lifetime. Know that I have found joy in your presence, and need nothing from you but peace.'

CHAPTER TWENTY-TWO

Alexandria in spring: a youthful place, caught in self-delight, dancing between the bright ocean and the gilded mirror of Lake Mareotis. Intoxicated by its nearness, Hannah left the emperor's training compound in the relative cool of the morning's third hour with Saulos on one arm and Math at the other, and felt as if she were coming home and nothing could assail her.

Math was the song of her heart. He had left Brass and Bronze in Ajax's care as if no mention had been made of his fitness to race, and walked out through the postern gate with his hand happily in hers. Out on the paved granite track that led to Alexandria, with the city itself still lost in the morning's haze, he tugged a little against her, like a hound at the leash. She let him loose to run across the sand. He ran away and came back to her, laughing.

On her other side, Saulos, at his most charmingly accommodating, took on the role of tutor, declaiming Alexandria's history to the high circling hawks as much as to Hannah, who had been born there and knew its past as well as any man, or Math, who did not yet know why he should care for the pasts of other places.

'This was a swamp stuck behind an island when Alexander saw it could be great,' Saulos said, and his fast,

236

clever hands sketched out the birth of the city. 'He had his men lay out the grid lines of the streets with bread flour for want of chalk. Flocks of birds feasted here for days after, but the lines were not lost, so that even when Alexander had died, Ptolemy Soter, best of his generals, was able to return and give life to the vision. Men say that Alexander was the greater of the two because he became a god, but I would ask, who worships him now?'

'Alexander was known from one end of the empire to the other even while he was alive,' Hannah answered. She was watching Math, who was a speck in the distance running out across the sands with his arms spread wide in the wind and his gold hair bannered behind. He had no idea who Alexander was, nor cared if the man was a god. He ran towards the hippodrome, so much bigger than the one in Coriallum. It had been closed for winter, dusted by the late season's storms so that it hunched down into the desert like some sleeping sphinx, waiting for a new prey.

One gate hung open. Inside, teams of slaves were beginning to clean the stands and their gilded handrails, to brush dust from the marble dolphins atop the central spina, to sweep and rake and level the track, wide enough for ten teams abreast.

Hannah saw Math plough to a halt as he caught sight of the wonders inside. He spun round, pointing and laughing. She waved for him and he sprinted back, a blaze of life burning across the sands to hurtle, chattering, into her arms.

'Did you see it? Did you see the colt cut from bronze? Did you see the way its mane flies? And the white dolphins at the ends? There are three! Did you see them?'

'I saw, I saw . . . Aren't they a wonder?'

He was joy made manifest; hers. His arms were clasped round her neck and his ankles at her hips and she could feel his pounding heart and the sweat of his palms and

237

smell horses and sand and excitement billow from him in a mix as headily exhilarating as any bazaar-sold drug.

She grinned at him, carefree, and he beamed back and dipped his head down and planted a cheerful kiss on her forehead, then tumbled backwards like a gymnast, using her abdomen as his board, arcing out to spring off his hands on the sand.

It was a new trick, and not one Hannah had seen before. She applauded, loudly. He flashed her another grin and was gone again to examine the bleached bones of a camel cluttering the side of the track.

'He does that to men,' Saulos said conversationally.

'I'm sorry?' She had forgotten he was there.

'Math. He steals men's hearts with that smile and that kiss. And women's too, now, it seems.'

'One day he'll know what he does.' She smiled ruefully. 'You were talking of Ptolemy and Alexander, asking which was the greater. I would say the man who first had the vision soars over the one who came after. Even now, Alexander's name is a watchword for courage and honour. Few of us will have that kind of fame when we die.'

'But what worth is fame?' Saulos asked. 'Who worships Alexander now?'

Every boy over the age of five worshipped him, but for his skills as a general, not as a god. Hannah shrugged. 'Nobody worships Ptolemy Soter, either.'

'But they gather daily to give thanks, to raise their prayers, to present their offerings, at the temples of the god he made.'

'That was his genius? To make Serapis?' It was Hannah's turn to break stride, to turn sideways in the sand, to walk backwards, staring at the man at her side. She was caught again, drawn into the web of his philosophy.

Saulos spread his hands. 'What better thing could a man do than make a god? Ptolemy Soter melded the best of Greece and Egypt, took all that people loved of the all-father, Zeus, and welded it to Osiris, who died and was raised on the third day. And to take the sting from death, the god-maker wove in the life-joy of Dionysius, and Aesculapius, both healers in their way.'

Out in the desert, Math had abandoned the camel bones and was practising handsprings across the sand. 'But in Egypt,' Hannah said absently, 'death has no sting. Even the untutored know that death is another doorway that leads to the journey they left at birth. Ptolemy knew that; he wanted his new god to— There's something ahead. Can you see it?'

Math had stopped his handsprings, and was standing absolutely still. Ahead, near the Canopic Gate with its carved eagle and the Eye of Horus above the keystone, a vulture erupted from the sands, and another. Three others wheeled in the sky.

Five vultures. Uneasily, Hannah glanced at the shadows to see if it was noon yet; one of her tutors had taught her the Etruscan augurs by which bird-flight might be read. Finding it still morning, she strove to remember the lines as she had been taught them.

If five are they who circle 'neath the fore-day sun
Bring forth the witness who with clearest heart may—

Saulos caught her arm. 'There were five,' he said. 'Now there are nine. That changes the meaning.' Always, he surprised her with the things he knew.

'Nine. Number of ill-omen.' Hannah's head snapped round to count. Nine. In three groups of three, circling sunwise. She knew the meaning of that without needing the couplet; some things are never forgotten. She said, 'Someone will die this afternoon, before sundown.'

'We could turn back now if you're worried,' Saulos offered.

'The danger's not for me,' Hannah said, 'or for Math. Nine signals death for a grown man. If you like, certainly we could return to the compound.'

Saulos looked up at the dense blue sky, as if instruction came from it. 'There are many grown men in Alexandria,' he said presently. 'If I am to die, turning back will make no difference. And each of us can only do his best in the eyes of his god. The best I can do, I think, is to go on in, although—' He turned a frank, clear gaze on Hannah. 'The gate takes us through the Hebrew quarter. You're an unmarried woman and Math is neither your son nor mine.'

'We will meet with disapproval?'

He grinned. 'At the very least. And if we're unlucky, disapproval might lead to stones being thrown. I love this place, but the people are hotheads, prone to over-zealous action. I hesitate to say this, but I think we might attract less notice – less opprobrium – if we were temporarily family: you as my wife, and Math as my son.'

Despite the vultures, Hannah laughed. She let her gaze rest on Saulos' lank hair and unremarkable eyes. 'I might reasonably be taken for your wife,' she said, 'but only a blind man would think Math was your son.'

'Of course.' Saulos shrugged. 'But then it will seem as if I have been told by my unfaithful wife that he is my son, and that I have not had the courage to confront her. Men see what they want to see, and they delight most in feeling scorn for others. It renders them blind to many things, which can be a boon at times. They will not, for instance, question why a woman of your beauty would choose to marry a man of such little distinction.' He cocked his head to one side. 'If you will let it, we can make this happen. I believe it will be safer.'

'I'm sure it will, as long as we— what is *that*?'

Something bloody lay on the sand. Math had stopped and was backing away. The hesitant breeze brought a

240

first scent of blood, and pain and terror. Hannah said, 'Somebody's dying.'

'Ah.' Saulos bit his lip. 'We are under Roman justice, after all. Will you wait here while I look? For Math's sake?'

For Math, Hannah waited, and for Math's pride, she didn't go out and gather him from the desert, but stood and watched him, and he her, so that they seemed each stranded on a spit of sand, unreachable.

Saulos returned faster than he had gone, with the news she expected. 'The baker,' he said quietly. 'Flayed and pegged out. And the boy of the Blue team who sold him the information on Poros' third colt that has strained its tendon.'

Hannah quelled a surge of bile. 'Dead?'

'The boy is. His throat is cut. The baker . . . may not be dead yet. A man can't live long under the sun without his skin, but I think he's breathing still. The guards are watching, so we can't go close, but we must go past to enter the city. If you don't want Math to see it, I suggest we walk past swiftly and he doesn't look to his right.'

They passed subdued, averting their eyes. The baker was not yet dead, but there was no way to hasten his passing. Eight legionaries watched from the city walls, to be sure nobody interfered with the emperor's justice.

Math was sick before they reached the gates. Hannah held his shoulders while he fell to his knees and vomited thin bile and the remains of the morning's bread. She had no cloth to wipe his mouth and would have given him her sleeve, but he used desert dust and smeared it, so that his whole mouth was darkened.

After, she picked him up and carried him for a few paces, but he wanted to walk and she set him down, and kept hold of his hand as they entered Alexandria.

The Canopic Gate loomed ahead, the height of four men and three across. The Eye of Horus gazed down at them, and an eagle hovered over with outstretched wings, mirror to the wheeling vultures.

'Math?' Hannah pulled him to a stop. 'As we pass through the Hebrew quarter, you're our son, mine and Saulos'. Can you be that?'

His quick, scornful glance said that he was a spy, trained by a spy, and he could do anything. She watched him shrug on the new mantle, and the change it brought to his eyes.

'I can try,' he said, with a child's solemnity, so that she and Saulos laughed a little and then more, and like that, laughing, their small family left behind the heat of the desert and passed under the Canopic Gate with its welcome in three languages carved across the keystone.

CHAPTER TWENTY-THREE

Math spat, to clear his mouth of the sick. Hannah had asked him not to look as they passed the baker, but it was too late; he had already seen. The image of a man he had known, skinless, pegged out on the sand with his mouth full of flies and his muscles laid bare to the feasting vultures was printed on the back of his eyes so that he thought he might never see anything else.

At least it washed away the humiliation of Ajax's fury. Math should have known, of course, that tipping the chariot on two wheels risked destroying not only the rig, but his horses' legs with it; he should have known that it was necessary to bring the colts into matching stride on the long straight, and that, by failing to do so, he had put an inexcusable amount of pressure on Bronze, who had to hold the inside of a badly executed corner. Most, he should have known that nothing he could do would impress Ajax or make him any more likely to let him ride the racing rig before he was ready.

He *had* known that. He had just thought . . . he wasn't sure what he had thought and whatever it might have been was washed away in the tidal wave of Ajax's rage so that Saulos' offer of a day outside in the city had been a gift straight from the gods.

Until he saw the baker, Math's day had been almost made right again. Striving to set it back on course, he applied himself to spying, at which he was at least good enough to pass in the way Hannah wanted.

Pantera's voice echoed in his mind's ear.

Hide when you can; it's always better not to be seen. But most of the time you can't hide, and that's when you need to know the spectrum of all that you could be and then choose one identity out of all the others and be *it, in every part of your heart and mind and soul.*

Of all the possibilities open to him, from apprentice driver to thief to whore, Math felt most comfortable in a wide-eyed curiosity that applied equally to any of these. It was a mask he had worn so often on Coriallum's docks that he could don it now without effort.

And so, as they emerged again into the sun, and the noisy, cheerful chaos of the Hebrew quarter, he held fast to Hannah's hand and sauntered at her side, staring at everything as if it were new, which it was.

He stared at the men in their multicoloured robes, at the women with dark skins and hidden hair, at the small signs of wealth displayed increasingly about the houses as they walked ever closer to the city centre; at the painted window shutters that took over from those simply carved, and the iron door fittings that replaced the leathern hinges and became in their turn gaudily gilded. He revelled in the feel of paved streets underfoot and breathed in the scents of spices he had never encountered in Coriallum or even in the compound.

Hannah was his mother in look and deed. She laughed and scolded and joined him in looking at the curiosities. To his delight, on this day of delights – he wasn't forgetting the baker, only walling him off in a part of his mind that he didn't have to look at – she, too, was good at *being* other than she was. She walked taller and smiled broadly at people she could not possibly know.

Smiling back, they did indeed take her to be Saulos' wife and Math's mother, and it seemed to him that she didn't resent it, but rather gloried in the deception.

Saulos did not walk tall. Math wasn't sure what he made of Saulos. Ajax loathed him, and Ajax was Math's touchstone for almost everything, but Hannah seemed to like him, or at least to value his conversation, and now, it seemed, Saulos had a natural talent for deception.

With something close to awe, Math watched how, without altering his dress or his ornament – he had none – without so much as running a hand through his mouse-brown hair, Saulos became a shame-ridden cuckold, almost invisible beside his golden-haired son and radiant wife. Passing Hebrew men eyed him with pity, seeing one of their kind providing for a child so clearly not his own.

The houses became richer than any they had seen and the street broader, paved with granite and marble. Ahead, the road broadened, coming to a bridge over the Canopic Canal. A donkey cart piled high with bushels of onions and string upon string of garlic blocked the way on to it.

They were at the limits of the Hebrew quarter. With interest, Math watched to see if Saulos might abandon his guise and revert to the man of letters he was with Hannah, or the stuttering leatherworker who serviced the Green team's harness, either of whom could plausibly have ordered the donkey's youthful driver out of the way.

He did neither. Seeing the cart, Saulos sighed and ducked his head and turned right, and, still weighed down by the iniquities of his life, led his dissolute family upstream along the canalside to a second, unblocked bridge, and over it, towards the harbour.

'Hannah, look!' Math tugged at her arm, pulling her to the edge of the bridge to look over. Boats were below, laden with goods. He flagged his free hand, chattering, pointing out the colours and the goods as if he were perhaps a tall boy of six, not a small apprentice driver aged ten.

It was not hard to feign enthusiasm; Math had never seen the like. In Coriallum, bridges had been small things, often of wood, and the rivers beneath had not held boats. Here, within spitting distance of Alexandria's royal quarter, the bridge was a wonder of engineering, with marble and granite facings and images of the gods worked within. It was wide enough for two donkey carts and the pedestrians who might accompany them.

The water in the canal was clear and utterly blue. Small fish flashed in shoals, clouds driven by an unseen wind. River birds paddled, twinned by the water's mirror.

Floating as if on air, small flat-bottomed boats painted gaily in golds, blues and greens and garlanded with flowers drew dates and figs, dried and fresh fish, baskets of marigolds and bundles of sweet hay for the feeding of cattle and donkeys up to the inland harbour that lay to their north, and thence to the bazaar.

On the canal's far banks a bustle of boys called up, offering small baubles to Hannah. One of them shouted something at Math in a language he did not understand. It sounded like the groom-boys at the stables, though, who managed to combine an insult, a question and an offer all in one. He grinned and made a gesture that was at once a greeting and a deadly insult. They laughed and ran away. He thought about running after them and remembered that he was *being* a street urchin, but was not one.

Hannah had felt it. She squeezed his hand in hers. Still looking down at the water, she said, 'Math?'

He looked up happily.

'Will you promise that you won't leave us while we're here? If we lose you, Saulos will be punished for it. And they might not let me come out again.'

'I promise,' Math said effortlessly. Promises were easy.

'On your father's shade?'

That was harder. He had to think past all the acting to the sacred core that was his father's memory. He saw brief

246

panic cross Hannah's face before he said, 'On my father's shade.'

Saulos was at the far end of the bridge. Behind him was the massive central bazaar of Alexandria, long and low and flat, ringed about by the raised and gilded roofs of the palaces and the blazing lighthouse to the north and the temples, museums and libraries to the west and south.

'We should keep moving,' he said. 'We might lose our son to the market boys else.'

'And you?' Hannah asked. 'Have I lost you or are you a man again?'

Saulos spread his palms, as merchants did at the end of a hard bargain.

'I am what you see,' he said. 'What others see, I am also. A Hebrew amongst the Hebrews, a Greek amongst Greeks, a merchant in the marketplace and a harness-maker to the winning team in the compound.'

'And with us?' Hannah asked. 'What are you when you're with us?'

Saulos' smile encompassed them both. 'In the company of a woman physician and a boy thief, what could I be but a simple man, purchaser of spikenard and retriever of honest men's purses? Shall we go?'

Hannah offered thanks to whatever gods of sand and sun might be listening as she and her small family left the bridge together and, still together, entered the bazaar with its confusion of colour and noise and scent, with its proliferation of merchants and travellers, each with a purse inadequately hidden.

She held Math firmly, and felt the pulses of his intent come and go as he thought about leaving her, and re-membered his oath and stayed at her side as they walked down the aisles and alleyways, as they examined silks for the quality of their weave and colour, linens for use as bandages – Hannah bought some of those; they were better than anything the guards had brought her – ate melon slices and dates, watched a black-skinned woman juggling firebrands and knives near a fountain, and saw a man selling mule foals with great sores on their backs so that they had to wait while Hannah found and bought salves and instructed him in their use.

It was some time soon after that she realized she was walking alone, hedged on either side by a man and a boy whose attention was all outward, however much they might try to disguise it.

She noticed it in Saulos first. He offered observations, picked at fabrics and tasted honeyed almonds as if he might seriously be thinking of making a purchase, but there was a subtle change in the quality of his looking, in the way his gaze lingered on the shadows rather than the light, that set him apart from the average stall-stroller.

Math was still a boy thief. She had no doubt he would cut any purse that lent itself to the cutting, but behind that mask he, too, was sifting the cross-current breezes that joined the lake in the south to the sea in the north and the information they carried of the hiding places and the watching places that might one day be useful and the people who had already found them so.

Forging her way through a thinning crowd, Hannah inhaled deeply, with something approaching joy. In the sun-baked air, freshly picked coriander vied with olive and almond blossom, rose oil with citrus fruits, and yes, in the midst of it all, the scent she had half followed, the earthy musk of spikenard, oil of nard, most expensive of unguents, prized for the anointing of royalty and for incense to favour the gods. She turned again down a new aisle, following the thread of its aroma as fast as she was able.

Three paces in, a hand grasped her elbow. 'Are we playing a game?' Saulos was panting as if he'd run a race. She had not known she was moving so fast, nor that he was having such trouble keeping up.

'We're finding your spikenard,' Hannah said, with grace. 'For the wound on your back. And also, should you need it, for the assurance of sexual fidelity.' She favoured him with her best smile. 'Do you find you need it, here in the bazaar that feeds the world? You have money. You could buy whomsoever you desired with that.'

She was fishing, which was unfair. He eyed her with sudden seriousness. 'Whom I desire is not for sale.'

She turned up the aisle of the animals, past a chicken-seller, with his white-grizzled birds hung up by the ankles, still alive, past a basket of snakes, rustling, past parrots and finches, jewel-bright in their cages, past calves and lambs that panted, drooling, in the heat.

Math was a butterfly resting on her palm, light and dry, neither dragging behind nor leading ahead, but not fully present.

'Come on, there are nightingales in cages at the bottom of the aisle. If Saulos lets you buy one and we let it go and it flies in the right direction, Osiris will grant you a wish and Isis will give us our luck back.'

Tugging him with her, she half ran to the stall of the nightingale-vendor who, by a miracle, was still where she remembered him to have been when so much else had changed.

Saulos offered to give them the necessary silver coin although it transpired that Math had some of his own. Hannah knew for a fact that when they had left the compound he had had no money, but his liquid eyes did not offer her lies and she let him pay for, and then release, the small brown bird.

A small crowd formed about them; for such things, men and women always stopped, ready to divine their own luck from the flight path.

This bird circled three times in the direction of the sun

before straightening briefly northwards across the tomb of Alexander, heading straight towards the lighthouse, then turned left and flew with perfect purpose west towards the towering white marble edifice of the Serapeum and its attendant libraries.

Three sets of eyes in particular watched it fly – and then did not, for after a moment's attention given to the divining of its path, Hannah felt first Math's and then Saulos' attention waver.

Both turned their awareness to the same place, but she looked later than they, and couldn't find a face she recognized in the loosely gathered crowd.

Math glanced up at her. His mouth framed the question his eyes had already asked. Hannah looked round one more time. She could think of no one who would make him break his oath but Pantera.

At her side, Saulos was shading his face with his hand, staring up at the sky. He wished her to believe he was still watching the nightingale, but he, too, was scouring the crowd. For reasons she could not precisely divine, Hannah gave a small squeeze and opened her hand as if she were releasing a sacred soul to the fates. Light as a feather, Math slid away from her and was swallowed by the mass of people.

Saulos didn't see him go. A crease knifed his brow, as when he was disconcerted in some point of argument. Still apparently watching the nightingale, he said, 'Is the spike-nard essential? Might you humour me and follow the bird to the temple of Ptolemy's manufactured god?'

'I'm your physician. I follow where you lead.'

She had said it in jest, but he took it as an order and swept forward, scything a path through the crowd to-wards the Serapeum.

The crowds lessened as they turned down the Serapic Way. Columns and temples to smaller gods lined both sides of the broad granite avenue. Here the prayerful could deposit a coin in a machine not unlike the water clock in the compound, only this dispensed holy water instead of chimes; or, with a different machine and a different coin, the faithful could pose a question and be given the answer, provided it was either yes or no.

The Serapeum dwarfed them all, the vast, overwhelming temple built by Ptolemy Soter for the god he had made.

She had been here before, many times, but always, when she came so close, Hannah was breathless for a moment, dazzled by the sun's glance on the perfectly cut white marble.

That was its purpose, of course; the engineers of old knew every angle of the sun's inclination and used them to further the glory of their god, drawing worshippers and casual visitors alike from the blistering white of the exterior in and ever in to the great, blue-robed god inside, vaster than anything in Alexandria or beyond, stretching his fingertips from wall to distant wall, taller, more sumptuously dressed, more peaceful in his stance at the gateway between life and death than any other counterfeit of man she had ever seen or hoped to see.

He stood, they said, on progressive layers of gold and silver, bronze and glass, Nile-mud and pottery, so that he might intimately know all parts of his earth as they lay beneath his feet. Standing in the doorway with blazing white marble at either side and the majesty of his image in front of her, Hannah believed it.

'There are seats at the margins, where the prayerful might sit,' Saulos said, making her jump. 'If I were to ask you and Math to sit on them for a moment while I undertake some private business, would you do so?'

Which was when, with all semblance of surprise, Hannah discovered that Math was no longer with them.

CHAPTER TWENTY-FOUR

'He can't read Hebrew, did you know that?'
'I'm sorry?' They were in the library, speaking softly. Pantera bowed, as befitted a pupil who has recently found his master.

Shimon favoured him with an imperious gaze. 'The Apostate. The one who wishes to destroy Rome and then Jerusalem. The man I have been hunting since we last met. He preaches the word of our god but he can't read it in the language in which it was written. He relies instead on this—' He jerked a disparaging thumb at the open scroll before him. 'The Greeks have never understood our language. Why they thought they could render holy scripture into their godless tongue is beyond me. He uses it in his ministries, and so his lies are based on a falsehood at their start.'

Shimon of Galilee, zealot in the service of his god, leaned his elbows on a table in the library of the Serapeum and glared at Pantera, daring him to answer.

He had aged since Pantera had seen him in Gaul. Soft, slanting light angled kindly down from the tall, narrow windows and domed roof of the library, but even so, the lines about his eyes and mouth were more deeply scored and his eyes did not hold the humour they had once done.

His voice, when not livened with anger, was flat.

In his guise as a junior scholar, Pantera picked up a scroll from the pile lying on the table at the old man's elbow and began to untie the thongs. Around him, oak shelves lined every part of the interior, with sections for the scrolls and papyri that were the library's gold. The benches and tables were of cedar inlaid with ebony, amber and silver. The smell of resin mixed with the dusts of ink and learning and the sweat of many men, reading.

He smoothed open the scroll and weighted down the corners with small stubs of lead. 'Why are you telling me this,' he asked, 'when we are hunting Akakios?'

'*You* are hunting Akakios. I told you in Gaul that the only man who would light your fire was the Apostate. No one else loathes Rome and Jerusalem equally.'

'Akakios doesn't loathe Rome, but he might conceivably want to rebuild parts of the ghettos to the greater glory of the emperor. Currently, people are living on the land he wants to use. The fire will clear it for his architects, in the way it clears a forest for the plough.'

'You have proof of this?'

Pantera pinched his lip. 'No, but I have heard it often enough now, from sufficiently reliable sources, to begin to believe it.'

'Does Nero know?'

'I hope not.'

A short-sighted scholar walked past, reading from a parchment held close to his face. Pantera cocked his head towards Shimon and ran his finger along a line on the scroll, as if underlining a particularly difficult passage. 'Akakios is seeking the prophecy,' he said. 'There's no doubt about that. Have you proof that your Apostate is doing the same? Is he even in Alexandria?'

Shimon bent low over the scroll. 'He's here. I haven't found him, but I can feel him the way you can feel another spy in the room.'

'Is he preaching?'

'No. He'd be easier to find if he were. He hasn't preached since he was excommunicated two years ago and the synagogues won't let him through the door. Any honest Hebrew has a duty to kill him if he reveals himself. He's keeping himself hidden somewhere. I have no idea where.'

'So to achieve anything, he'll have to work through others? That should slow him down.'

'Not noticeably.' Shimon pulled a face. 'He has no shortage of followers. Even now, there are men who prefer his imaginary covenant to the one given by God. Poros of the Blues, for instance.'

'*What?*' Heads jerked in their direction. The parblind scholar half turned on his heel. Pantera hissed, 'Poros barely leaves the compound and then only to source fodder for the horses. How can he have turned into a follower on the basis of one meeting a month, if that?'

'The Blue team are from Galatia. The Apostate has preached often in the synagogues of the eastern sea coast. Poros was suborned long before he came to Alexandria, and to good effect. Until Ajax arrived, the Blue team was going to Rome with nothing in its way.'

'And Akakios with them. Are they working together?'

'Poros and Akakios? I don't know. I don't have access to the compound.'

'Whereas I do.'

'Exactly.' Shimon tapped the table for emphasis. 'Which is one of the reasons I thought we should meet.'

Thoughtfully, Pantera re-rolled the scroll, tied the calfhide thong about it and set it with the others. He took a moment to make the stack neat, like a pyramid with even sides. The morning's amber light slid along each one, setting them in honeyed sun against the rich wood.

He said, 'I was sent here by Hypatia, from the home of Ptolemy Asul. You have found him also, evidently.'

'I received your letter. Of course I found him. The question is whether Akakios, too, has done so.'

'I killed one of his men in the alleyway outside Ptolemy Asul's house, so we can safely say that he has. He's here, did you know?'

'How could I not? The entire Roman world knows that the emperor's spymaster is in a compound in the desert taking care of the emperor's racehorses – and the golden-haired boy who may one day drive them.'

'No, *here*,' Pantera said. 'In the temple of Serapis, less than a hundred paces from where we stand.'

'*Why?*'

'I have no idea. He didn't follow me. And I assume you didn't let anyone follow you. I imagine he's here to meet someone although, as far as I know, Poros is still in the compound. It may be one of his agents?'

'Or the Apostate?'

'If he dares show himself.' Pantera's left arm lay on the lectern in front of them. He eased back his sleeve a fraction; enough to show the tip of the knife he kept there. He said, 'Akakios has at least four men who guard his life wherever he goes. When I lived amongst the Dumnonii, we spoke an oath to our shield-mates as we prepared for battle: *My life for yours in the face of the enemy*. If I were to offer that oath to you for today, for the duration of whatever we find when we track Akakios, would you take it?'

'Your life for mine?' Shimon eyed him thoughtfully. 'And so mine for yours?' He had already wrapped the last of his scrolls. He took a moment to hang it correctly, tags out, in its ordained position on the shelves.

When he turned, the colour had returned to his face. 'My life for yours,' he said. 'I accept.'

The dome of Serapis' temple was the highest in Alexandria, and still the god's head nearly touched the top. Sunlight came in from all sides, glancing off polished marble, off silver, off gold. Mosaics of sapphire, topaz and lapis gave colour to the light, casting a blue glow about the god's head that then danced in reflected glory down his raiment to his feet.

His feet were human feet, rooted in the earth. His hands were human hands, pulling down the light of heaven and directing it in brilliant shafts from each of his fingers to enlighten his worshippers below.

Around his feet, set far enough back for those within to see up to the god's crown without doing themselves undue harm, were open-fronted cubicles, with seats running round the three edges and, in some, a bed whereon the petitioner might lie the better to incubate a dream. A wealth of incense fogged the air, so that men and women sneezed in the silence.

'There.' Pantera's voice was barely a whisper. 'Waiting to go into the second booth from the end. He carries his knife in the right breast of his tunic.'

'The one haggling with the incense-seller? There are three others similarly armed in neighbouring booths. And to the left of the bronze door to the library, affecting an interest in the soothsayer, is the Galilean's daughter. It would do us both a service if you stopped pretending not to have noticed her.'

As befitted petitioners in the presence of their god, they approached Serapis' right foot. Each reached for it, as if in pious awe. Shimon's fingers brushed the air just above, not quite touching.

Pantera said, 'I'm not the reason Hannah didn't go with you to Judaea.'

'Not entirely, no. Ajax was an equal reason. And the boy, Math, of course, who is a child in need of a mother while Hannah is a grown woman who has never conceived a child. Among our people, she would be considered an abomination. Did you know that Hannah's mother was a Sibyl and she herself was raised by them?'

256

Pantera said warily, 'Ptolemy Asul was raised by the sisters, too, I think. His mother was one of them.'

'Indeed. He and Hannah will have known one another from the moment of her birth.' Shimon nodded to a priest in a far alcove. He clasped his hands and his lips moved as if in prayer. 'Akakios has given his incense. He is speaking to someone on the far side of the screen. I can't tell who, but he'll leave soon. If you wish to speak to Hannah, you should do so swiftly.'

'I can't leave you.'

'Ha!' Shimon laughed, quietly, then knelt and placed a fragment of incense on the god's foot. He spoke the name of his own god as he did so, that he might not be guilty of idolatry. 'Go. Speak with her to the ease of your soul. I will leave marks so that you will know which way we go.'

Pantera gripped his shoulder, briefly. 'Keep safe. If Akakios is going to Ptolemy Asul's house, don't go in without me. I'll catch you up soon.'

CHAPTER TWENTY-FIVE

Hannah knew Pantera was nearby almost before he came through the door, certainly before he saw her. He was with Shimon, who dared to nod to her. She stood by a stall selling silver images of the god, weighing two as if deciding which to buy. When she looked up again, both men had gone.

She was searching the crowds for them when Saulos caught up with her. He thought she had been looking for him, and was briefly cheerful so that she had not the heart to tell him she hadn't noticed he'd gone from her side.

'I'm afraid I have to leave you for a while.' He sketched a bow. 'What I have to do shouldn't take long, and then I'll help you find Math, I promise.'

'There's no need for that,' Hannah said. 'Math won't be far. We'll go back to the marketplace and wait near the nightingale-seller until you come back. If it comes to the eighth hour and you haven't returned, I'll take Math back to the compound.'

'Thank you.' Unbidden, Saulos gripped her hand and then dropped it again. 'Thank you. I will make it up to you one day.'

'Go. This is my home. I'll be safe here.'

She watched him weave his way through the crowds

and then made her own, more circumspect route towards the exit, looking around haphazardly as if searching for a small boy thief who might have decided that he could put the god's gold to better use if he liberated it from the supplicants.

'Math?' He was nowhere close, but she called anyway, pushing past the stall of silver idols and out on to the steps that led down to the Serapic Way.

After the temple's shadow, the day was blindingly bright. She shaded her eyes with her palm and scanned the crowds. Even in the short time she had been in the temple, they had multiplied tenfold; she couldn't have seen Saulos even if she wanted, but she did glimpse a shadow heading out towards the Temple of Apis, down the street on the left.

'Excuse me. Excuse me, please. I'm so sorry, I've lost my son.' She swept through the centre of a Syrian delegation, scattering men left and right. Those ahead had the sense to step aside, letting her through.

The temple itself was empty, or seemed so. She stepped into the dark, calling in a false whisper, '*Math!* Whatever else you do, you can't rob a god of his silver.'

The temple's only room was too dark for her to see anything. She stood still.

'That was well done,' said a voice that was not the god's.

To the dark, she said, 'Math's been teaching me.'

Her eyes were lost after the blazing day. Blindly, she turned to where she thought the voice had come from. 'Have you found what you sought?'

'Not yet,' Pantera said, 'but I have Shimon to help me. One of us will.'

He moved as he spoke. His voice came from three places at once. She remembered the sound of it from Gaul, rich as a river over stones, but dry, giving nothing away of heart or mind. It echoed in the small chamber.

She began to see things: the outline of the bull, solid in its overwhelming power; to its left, a closed door; at her side, the brass and bronze water-powered machine into which supplicants could slide a coin to find the answer to their question.

Still, she couldn't see Pantera. 'Math saw someone in the marketplace today,' she said. 'He left me to follow whoever it was. I assumed it must be you?'

She felt him smile in the dark. 'I hope not, unless the pupil has already overtaken the master. I believe he was following Akakios. It is a thing he did for me with some success in Gaul.'

'You set him to follow Akakios?' Hannah slammed her balled fist on the side of the coin machine. 'You're as bad as Ajax! You must have known he'd try to get out of the compound to see you two meet this morning.'

She heard him pause, and think, and then, hesitantly, say, 'Math's good. He has the capacity to be very good. We either help him, or we leave him to find out for himself where his mistakes are made. I judged it better to help him. If I'm proved wrong, I'll do whatever I can to make sure he doesn't come to harm. There's nothing more I can do. Will you accept an apology, sincerely given?' Pantera took perhaps two steps forward. He had been standing between the bull's forelegs. It was so tall that he could stay upright there and not have to crouch.

He was different from when she had last seen him. Then, he had worn Nero's snowy tunic belted with silver. Now he was dressed in cheap linen with his hair crammed into a ridiculous cap. His bare feet and legs were covered with a week's worth of dust and mud. She couldn't see his scars and nor, therefore, could anyone else.

His face had seen Alexandrian sun for a winter and on into spring. The lines were cut deeper around his eyes and mouth, but the whole was as she remembered it from the first moment's meeting when she had made herself filthy in Nero's presence.

Her throat was filled with sand. She said, 'You're too like Ajax.'

'Not in all ways. I think, in fact, not in many ways.' He leaned on one of the bull's forelegs. She could smell Nile mud and frankincense and the wildness of a barren mountain in spring. 'But I do care for Math. I'll find him and bring him back. Where will I find you?'

'Near the nightingale-seller. Ask for Hannah the apothecary. Everyone knows me.'

She stood a long time alone in the shadow of the bull after he had gone. Presently, she searched for and found a coin of the right size and dropped it into the oracle machine.

As a child, it had fascinated her; she had come here often to ask questions that never needed answers, just to hear the mechanical swing of the gears, and watch the levers work. Now she found that, as so often with her childhood, memory dwarfed the reality; the water clock in the compound was a far greater feat of engineering than the one in front of her and she could too easily see how the god's machine reached its conclusion.

The answer, when it arrived, was in the affirmative, but since she had not clearly set a question, it did not help at all in the matter of her choices. She left the machine to its deliberations and went back out into the hot and dusty day.

The Serapic Way was a tide of petitioners, sweeping back and forth to the great temple to her south. As she stepped out into the stream, it came to Hannah that she was alone, and likely to be so for some time, and that, given this unexpected freedom, there was one man in the whole of Alexandria whose company would soothe her soul and whose wisdom she cherished. And he would no doubt have spikenard, and could make the unguent she needed for Saulos.

As a native of the city, she knew all the best short cuts. Leaving the crowds, she passed south of the temple to a small bridge. Crossing it, she entered the friendly clutter of the streets she had known in her youth. For the first time in a decade, she felt herself truly at home.

CHAPTER TWENTY-SIX

Math caught the eye of the small dark-haired boy with the scarlet silk thread tied at his throat. He was young and very thin with bright, sharp eyes. He flashed Math a wary look but edged sideways under the fruit-vendor's stall and past the man selling carobwood jewellery boxes until he crouched nearby under the shelter of an empty donkey cart.

Math took off the cap he had stolen, which was covering his hair. 'I want the one with the nose like a knife and no hair on his brow,' he said to the silk-boy. 'Only him. I won't look at any of the others, I swear.'

A boy's oath was worth nothing, they both knew that, but the law of the street – of any street in any city in any province or nation of the empire – said that promise must be given and taken, as if it had true value.

The silk-boy looked where Math pointed. Akakios was not overly fast, but he brooked no delay and even merchants about to seal a bargain stepped briskly aside to let him pass.

The boy twirled his red cord, thinking. 'He's going to the Hebrew quarter,' he observed. 'Men like him cross at the jewelled bridge on the main way where everyone can see them.' Implicit was the assumption that Math would not want to be seen. 'You could get there as fast if you go by the north bridge. It's old and uncertain, but boys can cross it easily.'

Math nodded, looking around. 'Where is it?'

'Follow him until you reach the ivory-seller, then turn lakewards and go past the fish-women. Follow the fisher trail until you reach the soldier with one arm who begs. He'll try to grab at you. The bridge is ahead of him. Go over it and you'll be on the Street of the Three Palms. You'll get there ahead of your man if you run.'

'Thank you.' Math ducked a nod. He could have paid, but he knew better than to open his own purse and reveal that he had silver in there. A wad of rancid cheese kept it silent.

He was nearly gone when the silk-boy caught his elbow. 'What about the old Hebrew? I could slow him down.'

Math had seen the old Hebrew, but didn't know the boy had seen him too. The old man was clearly a spy, that much was plain from his behaviour; he slid through the shadows like an eel through weed and neither bought goods nor examined them.

Math had noticed him first in the temple, when the old man had come out of the library. He was with Pantera and, it seemed, he knew Hannah and she him, both of which combined meant he was not a stranger, and might be a friend.

Most important of all, the old man didn't want Akakios to see him and seemed to be succeeding in that, which made him very good indeed, because the emperor's spymaster had eyes on all sides of his head that saw everything, almost.

'No,' Math said. 'Let him alone.'

'He hasn't got any money anyway.' The boy grinned and spat on his hand and held it out in a universal gesture as common on the docks of Gaul as the streets of Alexandria. 'If you need help . . .'

'I'll whistle,' Math said, and slipped away.

The boy's directions were good. Keeping Akakios in sight, keeping his face mostly averted and his cap always on, ducking under stalls where he could do it without causing havoc and making use of all the available cover when he couldn't, Math tracked Akakios – and by extension the nameless old Hebrew – until he came to a stall ripe with elephant tusks, lying in bundles, tied together with twine. To its left was a profusion of women selling dried fish, flat and black from the sun.

There was no room between them, but he flashed a grin at the three nearest women and slid into the stinking space under the counter, pushed his way past three sacks of stiff fish and emerged at the back of the stall.

Right, then left, and he saw a crippled legionary sitting in the noonday shadows with his cap on the ground. Some coins flashed in it, which was, frankly, reckless. Out of sheer habit, Math estimated the sum, the distance from here to there, and three distinct routes of escape – and abandoned them all in the sad understanding that the last thing he needed was a hue and cry.

Regretfully, he slipped past the old soldier – and only a month of Pantera's uncompromising tuition stopped him from crying aloud as a hand grabbed at his ankle.

He stood very still. The hand was far stronger than any crippled beggar's had a right to be. 'Pantera?' He whispered it, barely a sound.

'If not, you'd be dead. Don't walk so close to men you don't know. I thought I'd taught you that.'

Abruptly, his ankle was released. Math managed not to gape with joy. He forgot all about Akakios. To be here, to *be* in Pantera's presence, to have got this far himself . . .

He became aware that he was grinning foolishly, while Pantera was squinting up at him, grunting vague threats, because that was what the old soldier would have done. The threat in his eyes was not vague at all.

Coming to himself, Math let rip a stream of dockside obscenities and kicked out at Pantera's ribs, striking the sand behind.

Pantera spewed an oath in return of anatomical invention that left Math's ears burning. Then, quietly, so that nobody else could hear, he murmured, 'Akakios is going to a particular house in the Hebrew quarter. I know which one, so there's no need to follow him too closely. If you go over the bridge just there, I'll go the other way and meet you on the Street of the Lame Lion when I've caught up with Shimon. Follow the sign of the bull or the star and wait when you see both together for the second time. The cap is very good, by the way. Well done.'

Well done. Well *done. Well done.* Glowing, Math made his way with exemplary care to and across the old, unstable wooden bridge that was suitable only for boys, women and reckless men.

On the far side, a six-pointed star was chalked on the wood, and beside it a very rapid sketch of a bull. With an excitement that made his blood fizz and his heart skip, Math sauntered down the road, turned left at the mark of a star on a gatepost and then left again when he saw it on a water pump.

He was turning into a narrow alley when he saw Hannah. She was walking openly down one of the more brightly lit streets, with the river on her right and a kaleidoscope of brightly painted shops, houses and taverns on her left. She made no effort to hide herself, but stopped here and there to greet men and women who clearly knew her of old and had time to share pleasantries.

He followed at a distance, never showing himself to her, until she stopped outside a tavern full of Gauls. That surprised him; he had never seen her take either wine or ale and in Coriallum she had never shown a liking for the mournful battle dirges of the kind currently emanating from the tavern's interior.

To his relief, she didn't go inside, but instead examined a bronze statue of a cow set at the edge of the tavern wall. Flowers hung in garlands about its neck. Hannah touched them, and then the beast's ear, with an intimacy that left Math wishing he hadn't watched.

He looked away, and when he looked back she had vanished as completely as if the sky gods had reached down to pluck her away.

Sprinting to the place he had last seen her, with his mind creating horrors of her lying in an alley with her throat cut, of her dragged into the tavern, of her curled in a back street half dead with her hands bound and her purse cut, dying of wounds untended because Math hadn't run fast enough, he reached the alley that the cow statue was guarding. There were no bodies or blood, but it was so narrow Math had to turn sideways to squeeze in, shuffling his feet like a crab.

She was there, though. He couldn't see her because the alley was too dark and he couldn't hear her because the Gauls were still singing, but he felt her presence as a shiver in his guts. With his eyes adjusting slowly to the poor light, he felt his way forward, running his hand along a single line of smooth tiles set into the wall as if for that very purpose: to guide the incoming traveller.

He couldn't smell her at first; old, stale urine overwhelmed the scents of flowers from the entrance. Soon, though, he caught the faintest scent of Hannah, of her womanliness, and the ashwood soap she used.

Slowing, he heard her open a door, cautiously, and then her light tread on tiles that were harder than the beaten earth of the alley's floor. Last, he heard her knock on another door.

Her voice reached him, lightly amused, saying, 'Ptolemy? Ptolemy Asul? Might a poor physician enter your home and avail herself of your pharmacy? I have a patient in

267

need of spikenard for a wound and no one else in the city can—'

A blast of fetid, charnelhouse air swept over Math, ripe with the terror and stink of the slaughter fields. He smelled blood, singed hair and burned flesh, just as he had in the fire that killed his father, so that he doubled over in remembered pain, spewing bile, and even as he did it he heard Hannah's voice say, 'Ptolemy, whatever are you— My apologies, my lord, I had no idea you were— *What are you doing to Ptolemy Asul?*'

The door began to swing shut. Abandoning caution, Math dashed down the alleyway, slowing only at the end. Peering round the wall's end, he saw a short corridor with an open door at the far end which seemed to lead to an open courtyard. He couldn't see Hannah at all.

For a paralysing moment, Math thought he would have to go in and try to bring her out, and knew he would die. Then he remembered the chalked stars.

Sick with nerves, he slid back to the alley's end and there became a lost boy in search of his father, running headlong down the streets, staring in distress at strangers who threw him sympathetic glances and didn't recognize him as the whore they had shunned less than half an hour before.

He found the last of the chalk marks he had followed and turned right, then right again at the next, still running.

'*Math.*'

He careered sideways into another alley, bigger than the one that had swallowed Hannah, with more light, and taller houses on either side that had carvings of grapes on the shutters.

Pantera was there, and the old Hebrew, leaning against a wall for all the world like a pair of merchants conducting deals they might not wish seen in public.

Math crashed to a halt. 'Hannah,' he said, breathlessly. 'Akakios has her. They're hurting her friend.'

CHAPTER TWENTY-SEVEN

Out of habit, Hannah had touched the ear of the bronze Hathor at the alley's mouth. The statue was worn there with a lifetime of her touches. Taking a breath against the stale stench inside, she stepped out of the sunlight and into the alley.

The gap between the god and the wall had seemed impossibly narrow when Hannah was younger, but she had not been on a boat then, where everything was small. Now, it seemed an obvious thoroughfare, for all that it was dark and stank of old urine.

She edged into it as she had always done, with the Gaulish songs reverberating through her chest as she walked. So much sorrow, so much loss, so much despair that Rome, a race of such small men, could overwhelm such great golden warriors.

Within three paces, she had lost sight of the sun. Soon, it was too dark to see and she felt her way forward with a finger running along a row of tiles set in the wall for that purpose.

The alley angled sharply left along the back of the Gauls' tavern. Her fingers edged out, seeking the handle of the iron-banded oak door she knew blocked the end. From the time of Cleopatra and her two lovers, the handle had been cleaned daily by those who used it. Even now, ancient grease kept the hinges silent as it let her through into the corridor of Ptolemy Asul's house.

She was about to knock on the door at the other end when she breathed in again, and caught, as if in a dream, the iron-honey smell of blood and burned flesh and the sound of a man's wet-hard breathing.

She knocked sharply, to help her own courage, and called out, 'Ptolemy? Ptolemy Asul? Might a poor physician enter your home and avail herself of your pharmacy? I have a patient in need of spikenard for a wound and no one else in the city can—'

There was a pause, a muffled order spoken in a voice she knew, a panicked clattering of feet back and forth until eventually the door swung open, releasing the full horror of what was on the other side. It surged over her: the stench of pain and blood and fire.

Tight with fear, Hannah stepped over the threshold. 'Ptolemy, whatever are you— My apologies, my lord, I had no idea you were— *What are you doing to Ptolemy Asul?*'

In his own home, under the blazing sun in his own courtyard, they had stripped him naked and crucified him, crudely, fixing his blue-white old man's arms to a plank tied between two columns, and that was the least of it – a convenience designed to hold him still while they destroyed his body with knives and hot irons.

His right ear had been cut away early in all they had done; the blood crusting the side of his head was older than the blooded stump of his right wrist where they had taken off his hand, his writing hand, his lamp-lighting hand, the hand he mixed his unguents with. The bone ends and pumping vessels had been cauterized to keep his blood in his body.

A brazier burned red near his feet, scalding his thigh. A selection of irons lay in it still, shimmering white. The

270

smell of scalded metal was as great as that of hair and blood and bone. She made herself look at his face.

Both of his eyes had been burned out. Blisters around the sockets showed that his head had not been still as they approached. Crusting yellow fluid marred his cheeks, streaked with tears.

His torso hung full-bellied down. His feet twitched, seeking the floor, but at a bad angle; she thought they had broken both his knees. Higher up, liquid dung and urine stained him. She remembered how that shamed men when pain first came, and how soon they ceased to care.

'Where did you come from?' Akakios stood behind her, so close that she could smell garlic and wine on his breath. She turned to face him, slowly, so that she might not seem afraid. He looked just as he did in the compound, only that his bitter face and high brow reddened a little in the firelight, and here he smiled more readily than usual.

'I walked in through the alley that leads to this man's door.' She spoke as if the door were the obvious entrance and they should know of it. Evidently, they did not.

At Akakios' furious signal, two of his five guards sprinted down the corridor and into the alley, dragging their weapons free as they ran. They were all dressed as slaves or minor merchants, but they were Romans: wiry, dark-haired men with the arrogance of the conqueror in their every step.

A limed oak bench stood nearby. In other times, Hannah had sat on it and listened to the music of the fountains, of the stars, of her lover's heartbeat.

Now, one of the remaining guards sat on it, tending the brazier. Shoving him off, she hauled the bench across the marble floor to give respite to Ptolemy Asul's feet. The wave of relief that swept his body and as the weight was taken from his nail-bound arms was heart-breaking. Blood slid down on to the pale wood.

'What is it you want?' Hannah spoke without turning,

her voice acid with scorn. 'I'll tell you, and then we can set about healing him.'

'*Not heal . . .*' That from Asul, a whisper.

'Oh, my dear man . . .' Reaching up, she touched Ptolemy's forehead, high up, near the line of his hair where there was no damage. He flinched. She said, 'Why don't you tell them? Nothing is worth this, surely?'

'*He seeks . . . the date for . . . Rome to burn. I was the copyist. Never . . . knew the date.*'

He could barely speak. He must have screamed a great deal, here in this hidden house with its so-quiet walls that let loose no sound. He had been her almost-brother, the older voice in her childhood that had offered friendship when she had none, and later, when she had found more than friendship, he had given her a trysting place to meet her lover when others wanted them kept apart, to follow other paths.

'*Han . . . ?*'

That was a whisper, barely a breath. She could feel the silent plea from the spaces where his eyes had been.

Hannah carried a knife. Even Ajax did not know that, but Ptolemy Asul had always known, and wanted her to use it.

She used her body to shield the movement of her hand. 'Go well, my love.'

She spoke in the language of the past, that only the Sibyls knew. On the last word, she sliced fast at his throat.

But not fast enough.

'I think *not!*'

Akakios snatched at her hand, wrenched and twisted. The knife clattered to the floor and Hannah was thrown after it, crushing her cheek to the marble. A shod foot pressed on her neck, holding her down.

Akakios stood over her. 'For wielding a weapon in the presence of the emperor's envoy, you are sentenced to death,' he said pleasantly. 'In the emperor's absence, the manner of execution is mine to decide. Take her.'

There were no more planks and they could not nail her on to marble, but used rope and bound her to the pillar alongside Ptolemy Asul, with its carvings of lotus flowers and irises. Pain racked her shoulders. Her own pulse crashed in her ears. Her bowels loosened but did not yet leak. She found she did still care about humiliation.

Akakios came to study her face, feeding on the signs of fear. She did not know how to erase them. The fire etched fresh lines about his own mouth, accentuating the beak of his nose so that he became a vulture, added to those of the morning; a tenth, sign of treachery in business.

'Perhaps now he'll think differently.' Stepping back to the brazier, he lifted a padded leather glove from a rack beneath and slid it on to his left hand. In the glowing coals, an array of knives and pokers lay white with heat.

'Were you his lover?' he asked.

'Ptolemy Asul's?' By a miracle, she was able to laugh. 'Hardly. He's my friend.'

'But he loves you,' Akakios observed. 'Always a useful trait in a man. What will he do, do you think, to keep you unblemished?'

With a sudden movement, he kicked the pale oak bench away from under Ptolemy's feet. The man dropped, sickeningly, on to his riveted arms. The noise he made then was not one Hannah had heard from any living thing. She found she was weeping, and could not stop.

When, at last, he could be heard, Akakios said, 'Ptolemy, listen to me. I will take her nose first, and then her tongue. If she lives, she will walk out of here condemned to a life of silent, disfigured harlotry. You know I will do as I say. To stop it, give me what I need by the count of three. One . . .'

White iron crisped the air in front of Hannah's face. Her hair burned. She felt her skin already blister.

'Two . . .'

She fought to keep her head away. One of the guards caught the back and forced it forward.

'Three . . . Hold her . . .' White-hot iron jabbed at her, smoking. Shamefully, she screamed. It was impossible not to.

'*No! I can tell you*—' The iron stopped moving. Hannah stared at it, petrified.

'Go on.'

Afterwards, when she dreamed, as she did many times, of that afternoon, it was the mild curiosity in Akakios' voice that woke her, sweating, to stare into the dark.

Ptolemy was straining round, trying to make his blind eyes see her. '*In Hades. You will find the date only in Hades.*'

'Hades? Are we children, afraid of the dark? You'll have to do better than that.'

The iron moved again. Hannah felt her skin blister. Somewhere, she heard Ptolemy cry out, and then a woman's voice, her own.

'*Stop!* He's telling the truth!' Words spilled from her, disorderly. 'The Sibyls tend the Oracle of Hades in the heart of the city. It was here long before Alexander and Ptolemy. For a thousand generations the Oracle has spoken there. Only now, under Rome, is it silent.'

The iron went away far enough to stop the scorching. Mesmerized, Hannah watched the white-hot metal cool to straw, to amber, to the darker colour of autumn Nile honey. Tears burned her cheeks where the skin was broken. She had not soiled herself yet. She didn't care.

Akakios looked from her to Ptolemy Asul and back. 'Am I to understand that the Sibyls wrote the prophecy?'

'Yes.' Ptolemy had found his voice. More strongly than before, he said, 'The Oracle can tell you the date on which Rome must burn. I don't know it. I never have.'

'But you can gain me access to the Sibyls?'

'No.' Ptolemy Asul shook his head.

Sighing theatrically, Akakios laid his cooling iron on the charcoal and selected another, hotter. 'Truly, if you think there are limits to what—'

'There are,' Hannah said, desperately. 'There are limits that will not change whatever you do to either of us. Only a woman can lead a petitioner to the Oracle.'

Ptolemy Asul said, 'Only Hannah.'

'Ah.' Akakios stepped close. His eyes fed on her face. The heat of the iron blistered her hand and neither of them noticed it. 'Is this true?'

Hannah dared not look across at the hanged man opposite. 'I know where to go, yes.'

'And you will take me.'

'I—'

'You will take me because I hold the lives of those you love in the palm of my hand.' Akakios dropped the iron. It lay dully hot near her feet. With a sweep of his knife, he cut away the cords that bound her. His smile was terrifying in its triumph. 'You will guide me in and guide me out and if I get what I want it may be that I will allow—'

A guard coughed, suddenly, as if in warning. Akakios swung round in time to catch the man as he fell backwards, vomiting blood. He died at Hannah's feet.

Two figures loomed in the doorway. Akakios shouted an order Hannah did not hear, but the sun was in her eyes so the last thing she saw was two figures hammering in through the ruin of the door, and then there was nothing but the after-image of Ptolemy Asul's hanging body – and Akakios, who stood in front of her with the point of his knife resting on the bone beneath her eye.

CHAPTER TWENTY-EIGHT

They had caught the stink of pain and burned flesh even before Shimon eased open the door. Pantera stepped ahead of him into a hot, bright courtyard full of men and threw both knives. The first missed. The second struck a guard in the chest, catching him on the angle as he spun round, and he fell backwards. The space where he had been revealed a tableau from Pantera's worst nightmare: a crucified man and Hannah tied to a pillar and Akakios standing between them, ready to kill.

'Hannah!' he shouted.

Akakios grinned at him. His knife shone at her cheek.

'Math needs us first.' Shimon caught Pantera's arm, wrenching him round. 'By the far pillar. The guard has him.'

The guard held Math in front, like a shield, twisting the boy's arm up behind his back with his sword blade under his chin. He was backing towards a door on the far side of the courtyard. Math was limp as a kitten, staring down at the sword with the numbed terror of the condemned.

Shimon had spoken in Aramaic, which none of the guards understood. There was a moment's confused hesitation, then Pantera, who did understand, dived forward, rolling, and scooped up the first knife that had missed and lay now on the floor.

Coming upright again, he hurled the blade before his mind had time to tell him it was an impossible throw, that he might as easily hit Math as the guard, that the man was a war-scarred legionary and could duck a blade in his sleep, that—

His knife hit the guard's left eye, striking so hard the tip pierced his skull at the back. He crumpled where he stood, dead too fast to cry out. Even as he fell, Pantera was tumbling across the floor like a circus acrobat to sweep Math out and away from the killing blade that shaved the skin on his throat.

They rolled together, Math held close in Pantera's arms, spinning and spinning, close as lovers, as father and son, heartbeat to heartbeat, both of them afraid. Blades passed them close. None of them hit.

A fourth guard fell nearby, his throat a bright fountain. His blood glued them tighter together.

One left, then, and Akakios. And Hannah.

In his measured Aramaic, Shimon said, 'Akakios has gone. Hannah is alive. We have one man left to kill.'

A shadow passed over Pantera. He stopped rolling, released Math and stood up. The last living guard was caught between him and Shimon, his head swinging back and forth like a cornered lion's. He had a sword in one hand and a knife in the other. Neither Pantera nor Shimon was armed any longer; their knives were lost in the bodies of dead men.

Pantera put Math behind him. The blade dropped by the guard who had held Math was an arm's length from his right foot. In his own rusty Aramaic he said, 'If you claim his attention, I'll get the blade.'

'He's wearing a mail shirt, you'll have to take his legs or his throat. Are you ready? Go – *now!*'

Pantera felt the bruises as he rolled this time, but he

277

came up with the sword's bloody hilt clutched in both fists. The guard was doing his best to kill Shimon, stabbing at him alternately with his left and right hand, so that when Pantera, sliding sideways, hacked at the backs of his knees he didn't jump as he might have done, but only twisted away, so that the blade bit deep into one calf, cutting the muscle through to the bone, taking that leg from under him.

Pantera lost the sword again; the hilt was too slick to hold. The guard's knife slashed at his face, seeking his eyes. Screaming the war cry of the Dumnonii, Pantera leapt forward, grasped the man's head under the chin and behind the crown and, using his own body as a lever, broke his neck.

Pantera stood slowly, lowering the body to the ground. The courtyard swayed around him, the shimmering colours nauseatingly bright. The sweet-iron smell of blood clogged his gorge.

'My life for yours. I had not thought to have another fight like that, so late in life.' Shimon was standing an arm's reach away, looking drawn and satisfied in equal measure. He offered Pantera his hand and they grasped, fist to elbow, in a grip that spanned continents and cultures, and spoke of the brotherhood of slaughter.

It helped to make the world still, and to steady Pantera's stomach, so that the clarity of battle went away, and he was left slow again, and able to think.

Hannah was on the floor, sitting with her back to the pillar, regarding him with glazed eyes as if he were as monstrous as the men he had killed. Ptolemy Asul hung dead from his makeshift crucifix. A neat wound less than a finger's width across to the left of his sternum showed how he died.

Pantera said, 'I had not thought Akakios had any mercy in him.'

'He doesn't,' Shimon said. 'Look what she's holding.'

Hannah's hand was wrapped around a small-bladed woman's knife. Her knuckles were white and shaking.

'Hannah . . .'

Pantera walked the ten feet between them slowly, no longer certain what he read in her eyes, afraid that she might turn the knife inward on her own breast before he could reach her.

'I'm sorry we were too late to save him. But Math's unhurt, and you . . .' He didn't know what they had done to her. He crouched at her side, not too close. 'Can you give me the knife?'

She shook her head, but let it slide into his palm. Tentatively, he took her hand. She was shaking lightly all over, like a horse in a thunderstorm. Her eyes were on Math.

Shimon was with him, talking to him as an equal, explaining how well he had acted, how he had the capacity to be a fighter one day if he chose, but that there were better ways to live if he didn't. The colour was returning to his cheeks. Hannah's glance skipped across Math's face, as if seeing him whole was as much as she could bear.

She said, 'Will you take him down, please? He should have dignity now.' She didn't look round at the man whose life she had ended. Pantera thought perhaps she couldn't.

'Of course.' He had already selected which irons from the brazier would best lever the nails from the dead man's arms.

Shimon, who had more experience of taking down the bodies of crucified men, came to help. They laid Ptolemy Asul on the bench at his feet, with his arms crossed on his breast in the Egyptian way. Pantera found a dagger and cut away the tunic from a dead guard to lay over and cover the worst of his wounds, and took pennies from his own purse to lay on the still-open eyelids.

When he was done, he turned back to Hannah. 'Can

279

you tell us why they did this? What question was it that so badly needed an answer?'

Hannah stared past him. 'Can't you guess? They asked for the date on which Rome must burn to fulfil the prophecy. Ptolemy told them he didn't know it, that he was the copyist, not the maker of the prophecy. He told them that the Oracle of Hades, which lies in the Temple of Truth beneath the Serapeum, could tell them what they need to know.' She drew a hoarse breath. 'I said I would take Akakios there.'

'You can't do that,' Shimon said. 'With what he has done even here, he would die before he ever reached the Oracle. And you with him.'

But Pantera had seen where her gaze was resting. Math was standing between two columns with the wreckage of a broken brazier at his feet and his wide, grey eyes fixed on Hannah's, as hers were on his.

'She has no choice. Akakios holds Math and Ajax as hostages to her good behaviour. Am I right?'

'Yes. He'll kill them if I don't take him in. At least if we both die, they will be free.'

Saying it broke something, so that Hannah could stand up at last, and, slowly, turn round to look where she had not. She said, 'He died to protect us, even as he lived.'

'No.' Pantera caught her hand. 'Ptolemy Asul died because of a prophecy he was made to copy. Akakios' men were hunting it, and so found this place. I knew of the danger, but came to late to save him. If there's a blame, it's mine.'

'Ptolemy knew they were coming. I think he's always known it would end here, even when we were young.' Her eyes were closed. 'He opened his house to us when we wanted to be alone. He made us his sisters. He would have done anything, I think, that we asked of him.'

Pantera lowered her hand. 'We?'

'Hypatia and me. We came here together. We were

280

lovers.' Hannah opened her eyes. 'He lied,' she said, in wonder. 'Even after all they'd done to him, all they were doing, Ptolemy Asul lied to Akakios.'

'What was the nature of his lie?' Shimon was the one to ask it. Pantera could not.

'He told them I was the only one who could petition the Oracle. That I alone could lead a man to the Styx.' She smiled, thinly. 'They don't know that Hypatia exists. She can do more than I ever could, but Ptolemy didn't tell them.'

'Why?' Pantera had found his voice, and wished he had not. A cold weight was settling on him, becoming more solid by the moment.

'They wanted you to go to the Oracle, too. He and Hypatia.'

'Why should I have any greater chance than Akakios of crossing the Styx alive?'

'Your soul is . . . less damaged than his.'

Pantera closed his eyes. 'How will I find Hypatia?'

'Put a garland of wild irises on the idol of Hathor at the alley's entrance. She'll find you.' Hannah spoke to Pantera, but her eyes still rested on Ptolemy's blue-grey body. 'We should burn him. It would have been his choice.'

There was very little wood in the garden. Pantera looked about. 'We could break up the bench he's lying on, but—'

'Math and I will find wood and things to burn if you and Shimon get the brazier ready. There's more charcoal in an iron bucket by the outer door.'

With a kiss and a gentle shepherding, Hannah gathered Math into the house while Pantera and Shimon built up the brazier again to an orange heat. Hannah returned presently, bearing linens to make a shroud. Math followed, bearing wood for a pyre.

'We'll burn him here, near the pool, so that the house is not destroyed,' Hannah said. 'You two should go to the library and read the note on his desk. He has left you each a gift: to Pantera, the dancing Cleopatra in gold, and to Shimon the Scroll of Life. You each know how to find what is yours.'

They did. In the face of her authority, they went without speaking and took the things they had each noted before. If Shimon was pleased with his gift, it did not show.

Pantera found the candlestick that had once belonged to Julius Caesar. It was, indeed, a thing of astonishing beauty. He brought it back to Hannah. 'I can't keep this. In Alexandria, I'm a labourer. It'll be found and taken and I'll be hanged as a thief.'

She had built the pyre so that it covered all of Ptolemy Asul's body. Too many old things were on it that should have been saved, but she was working automatically, as if under orders that couldn't be questioned.

She paused, frowning. 'Lift the elephant in the library. Under it, a tile is loose, and beneath that is a locked box. If you can open it, the candlestick will be safe in there. It has protections that will keep any others away. Take nothing else when you come to retrieve it, unless you wish the Sibyls to mark your name on their scrolls.'

He could think of little he would like less. In the library, beneath the stool carved in the shape of an elephant, he found an oak box banded in iron. The lock was easy to pick. Inside were treasures he could not name and did not have time to explore. Not gold, but scrolls and icons and amulets that sang their power. He nested the dancing woman in their centre and locked the lid.

Coming back, he found that Hannah had lifted Math and was holding him close. 'I know you hate Gaulish singing,' she said. 'But will you go with Pantera and Shimon back through the back rooms of the Gaulish inn? I'll change clothes here and follow you when the pyre is burning well. We can meet in the market, near the nightingale-seller. Then we have to find Saulos and pretend that none of this

282

has happened. It'll take every part of your learning, but I know you can do it.'

Math hadn't spoken since the mouth of the alley. Hannah waited until he had nodded, then kissed his brow and sent him gently to Pantera.

'The Oracle will speak on the day of the new moon,' she said, 'which is nine days from now. We have a lot to do between now and then.'

CHAPTER TWENTY-NINE

Nero's ship, the *Hera*, made harbour at dawn two days after Ptolemy Asul's death.

On his arrival, the great lighthouse of Pharos burned multicoloured fires through the night in celebration. The following night, at the emperor's command, the fire shone through a tinted lens, splashing a pale green light across the entire city of Alexandria to honour the spring.

Under that unworldly cast, Pantera contrived to deliver a message to his emperor, and received a response. Shortly before midnight, after several hours spent watching one of the two doors, and with Shimon watching the other, he entered the comfortable, intimately lit bar of the Black Chrysanthemum tavern.

The light came from reed candles set at careful intervals along the walls. Mottled shade spilled over the spaces between, so that it was possible to navigate round the small round tables or the three-legged stools that stood around them without intruding on the commerce that took place there. The clients may have come for their host's miraculous drink, but they stayed for the chance to conduct their business in discreet company, away from the city's rumour mill.

To protect their anonymity and their purses, the windows were shuttered and the two doors were protected by Germanic tribesmen hewn from the same rock as the emperor's Ubian guard, but taller and broader, with arm rings fashioned from human knuckle bones and hanks of red-dyed, tallow-dipped horse hair fixed at their temples as visible proof of their killing power.

The guards had removed Pantera's two most obvious knives at the door. In a brief exchange of glances, it was made clear that they knew about the third, and that any attempt to use it that did not have their agreement would be unfortunate.

Pantera avoided catching anyone's eye while he ordered two mugs of foaming iced sherbet water and carried them to a corner where a cluster of stools embraced a low table. A charcoal fire glowed dully behind him and a wall kept his left flank safe. Three tables of busy merchants filled the space between him and the nearer door-guard. Even so, when he looked up, the guard was watching him.

He turned his back to the wall and let the shape of the room order itself in his mind: the men who might fight if pushed to it, those who would try to run and so block the exits; those who were engaged in matters that might lead to arrest or death if they were overheard; those who were simply there for peace and a particular drink that could not be had anywhere else in Egypt, and so the world.

Nero entered as the Watch called the hour. The guards showed him no deference, but searched him as they did everyone else – and found nothing. Pantera could not tell if they knew who he was.

The emperor was dressed as a merchant; not flashy, but wealthy enough for nobody to question the manicured nails, the oiled hair or the scent of rosewater that followed where he walked. Two groups of three men trailed in behind him, not obviously bodyguards, except perhaps to the Germans, who searched them with particular thoroughness. They bought small beer and took up stations near both doors while their master pushed his way through to the fire and warmed his hands against the night's chill.

It was surprisingly well done. Nobody looked up, no man nudged a neighbour, or nodded and turned away. The six bodyguards were close enough to be useful, but not suffocating, and nobody had linked them to their master.

'Welcome.' Pantera raised his mug in greeting and kicked a stool into place. The emperor sat down, leaning his arms on the table. Like Shimon, he, too, had lost weight over winter. The skin around his eyes was pulled taut as a drumskin and the ink wells beneath were filled with lack of sleep. Even so, he looked briskly alive, out here, away from the court.

'Rome is a place of much intrigue,' Pantera said, by way of greeting. 'Has it been hard leaving Akakios in Alexandria over winter?'

'Harder than I had imagined.' Nero gave a tired smile. 'The senate hates me, and yet must appear to love me. Without Akakios at my side, the veneer of their care wears thin.'

'Do you hate the senators?'

'Most assuredly I do.'

'Enough to burn Rome to be rid of them?'

The emperor's face lost all its life. His wearied eyes regarded Pantera flatly. 'That is treason. You will apologize.'

Pantera said, 'My lord, I apologize. An emperor never desires the harm of his subjects.'

'On the contrary.' Nero leaned his shoulder against the wooden wall. 'As we both know, an emperor frequently desires the harm of his subjects. We have arranged the deaths of several ourself. What we do not – and never shall – desire is that those who love us should die. And while the senate plots our downfall, the men and women of the suburra and the ghettos still love us as their father and protector. Answer me this: if a fire was lit in Rome tonight, where would suffer first and most?'

'The ghettos and the suburra, as you just said.' Pantera stared into his mug. A froth of sherbet still laced the top. He dipped his finger into it and drew a rough circle on the barrel top. 'This is Rome. The hills are set around. The forum is in the centre. The devastation would depend on where the fire was started and how the wind hurried it, but the ghettos of the palatine, the Circus Maximus, the suburra, are all dry as tinder. The dwellings are made of wood and muddy straw and are too close together. They'd burn like pitch torches.'

'While the granite and marble of the senate houses up the hill will survive with ease.' Nero leaned forward, his mug held between both hands. Bands of white skin showed on his fingers and thumbs where rings had been removed for this foray into Alexandria's underworld. He said, 'Know this: if Rome burns, it will be without my blessing.'

'But there are men who work for you who may think they know what is best for your future, even for the future of Rome.'

'They are mistaken. I expect you to stop them.'

A name hung between them. 'There may come a time,' Pantera said cautiously, 'when I need to use your authority to gain control of men notionally sworn to you. I have your turquoise ring, but it may not be enough.'

'We had considered this.' Nero pulled a belt pouch from his waist and slid it across the table. His every move telegraphed a merchant making an underhand deal. Men at neighbouring tables turned away out of instinct, that they might be able to say they had not witnessed anything.

As Pantera took the purse, it fell open, spilling on to

his palm a reproduction of the royal seal. He hoped it was a reproduction. To hold the real thing was not given to ordinary men. Even to hold a facsimile without Nero's express consent was a capital offence.

Nero raised a brow. 'With that, you have absolute authority,' he said. 'There is not a man in Rome or the provinces who can stand against it.'

'Save yourself.'

'Of course. And so there will be an accounting if you use this. We will require to know the detail of what was plotted against us.'

'I have nothing to give you yet, but on the night of the new moon I hope to learn the date on which Rome must burn. If I don't die in the attempt, I will also know who else is trying to find that out. Besides Akakios.'

'He may seek it to save us.'

'Indeed.' Pantera finished his drink, slapped the mug on the table and rose. He grasped Nero's hand, one merchant taking his leave of another.

Nero's fingers closed on his, holding tight, so that he could not easily slide free. A new passion haunted the bleak eyes.

'You care for us,' he said. It was not inflected as a question, but was one none the less.

'I care for a boy called Math,' Pantera said, truthfully, and then, surprising himself, 'but yes, I care, too, for my emperor.'

Nero's lip curled. 'Out of pity, or duty?'

'Neither, my lord. Out of understanding for one forced to act against his better instincts by petty men who would bring him down. Out of respect for his courage and his care for his people.' Pantera could have lifted his hand free now, but did not. The fingers that held it trembled. 'Seneca told me you could scent a lie in a man from a hundred paces. I will not lie to you. You must know that.'

'I do. You would not be alive were it not so. But I know, too, that you do not tell me all of the truth.' Nero lifted his own mug for the first time. His eyes closed as the first explosive taste hit his palate. 'Leave us now. We would enjoy our evening in peace.'

Chapter Thirty

For Nero's visit to the training compound, Akakios demanded that the three teams demonstrate the quality of their improvement since the emperor had last seen them.

To that end, three heavy parade chariots had been brought out of storage, stripped of their cobwebs, polished and garlanded with ribbons. They were larger than the practice rigs, made of oak and iron inlaid with ebony, ivory and copper, and were so heavy that a full team of eight horses was needed to pull them.

And because there were eight horses, pulling a chariot of three times the weight and twice the size of the practice rigs, the driver required a second man on board to help keep the balance on the corners.

For the Green team, Math was that second man and, standing on the thin planking high above the start line with the four pairs of horses strung out ahead, he knew without doubt that he was staring death in the face. The air was wet with rank, sour horse-sweat and heavy with the threat of a dust storm.

From outside the compound, a single brass trumpet sounded. At its signal, the gates eased open. Bronze stamped at the sand, sending a judder back through the team and up into the chariot.

Math felt it faintly through the soles of his feet. A brief swirl of wind sifted desert sand into his mouth. He hawked and spat without ever taking his eyes from Akakios, who stood ten paces away at the trackside with his arm raised.

At his side, Ajax murmured, 'A hundred heartbeats till we start.' Math swallowed the rest of the grit.

The air became less heavy. A slow, hot wind raised the sand in sluggish dust demons. Brass bit the air as if he hated it. His every muscle twitched.

Ajax said, 'Fifty heartbeats. Less. It will only seem like a lifetime, but— Gods alive! Close your eyes, *now*!'

Math clamped his eyes tight shut. The chariot's floor bucked twice beneath him as a blinding spray of sand scoured his face.

More followed, driven by a withering wind that destroyed in its first careless flurry the five days of washing, polishing, oiling and grooming that had stripped away the shabbiness of winter and transformed the compound into a place fit to greet an emperor.

Out beyond the gates, the lone trumpet was joined by others and others until the wind's howl was drowned under the raging brass and even the horses were still. It was deafening. Math clamped his teeth and kept his eyes shut and dug his nails into his palms and knew that around him men and boys were doing the same, or more; whatever it took not to scream against the murderous noise and so bring disgrace on the team.

The horns stopped all at once, with the finality of a fallen blade. As if by imperial order, the wind, too, fell away, taking the dust devils with it. In the crushing silence after, a boy coughed and was hushed.

Math opened his eyes. Ajax's hand on his shoulder kept him still which was as well because Nero was nearly on them, hovering ten feet above the ground, a god floating on a cloud of gold with white-robed boys parting before

291

him, strewing pink and gold flower petals in his path. The tamed wind tossed them lightly skywards, mixing them with the sand.

'Look again,' Ajax said. 'He's on a cart taller than ours. And not as close as he looks.'

Math blinked and peered through the settling dust and found that the emperor was not possessed of magic, but instead stood on the platform of a parade chariot filmed in gold leaf and laced about by foamy cloth of gold, and that he was not within reach, but stood framed between the pillars of the gate.

Two dozen chestnut horses drew him forward, each with a fountain of gilded ostrich feathers fanning high above its head so that they were no longer mere horses, but the fable-beasts of childhood tales.

'This is it,' Ajax said.

He lifted the reins. In front of him, four pairs of horses tensed. On either side, the Blue and White teams did the same. Eight horses in each team. Eight. It was madness.

It became hard to breathe, to think, to swallow. Math clamped his hands on the hard oak edge of the chariot rail. Hannah was somewhere in the crowd, with Saulos. Her burns were healing quickly and the haunted look in her eyes was less wild than it had been at Ptolemy Asul's house. Best not to think of that. Math stopped trying to see where she was.

Ajax whistled a long low note. Brass and Bronze pushed forward to take up the slack in the harness. Ajax flipped back his whip. From his place inside the gates, Akakios' arm fell.

'Go!'

'Go!'

'*Go!*'

Three drivers shouted together. Three long whips flicked far, far out over the waiting teams to the powerful colts in the lead. Twenty-four horses erupted from the starting line. Three big, beribboned show chariots sped flat out down the full length of the track.

Math was placed behind Ajax at the point of balance from where he must lean his weight either way on the corners to keep the whole rig from tipping over.

They had practised exactly three times, once on each of the past three days, and each time had been a catastrophe of bruises and broken wood. For all his practice in falling through the winter, Math had been lucky to walk away with his bones intact.

He wasn't alone in that. The chaos in practice had been bloodily painful and there had not been time to get it right. Even so, Akakios had been explicit that their lives depended on a perfect display and nobody doubted him. News of the baker's fate had spread through the compound faster than a dose of flux. If nothing else, it had brought the teams to a level of cooperation that had been unthinkable through the winter.

But this wasn't a race. Racing would have meant only one man driving only four horses and a light chariot. Racing would have been easy. This was a contrivance designed to show the emperor how inspired had been his choice of teams, how perfectly trained they were, and, contrary to the reality, how closely matched.

Thus, setting aside all they had worked for through the winter and knew to be true, Blue, White and Green had to leave the start line in foot-perfect synchrony and reach the finish in line abreast, keeping together all the way.

In a steam of horse-sweat and hammering feet, they thundered down the long straight with their wheels in perfect line. The speed was terrifying, far faster than they had dared risk in practice. Ajax, Poros and Lentus of the Whites seemed consumed by gods, or demons, determined to show their best speed, even if it saw them all dead.

Math clung to the back rail of the chariot with his teeth loosening in his head and his palms cut in ridges by his nails and knew that the second man in the Blues to his outside and the Whites to his inside were doing the same.

Too fast, the first bend came.

'*Math!*'

Ajax's shout cut through the roar and fury of the race. Math prised his grip from the rail and leaned away from the tilt, pressing ever more of his weight over the outside rear wheel, leaning out and out, balanced on one foot, until he was flying, precariously suspended in space over the packed sand with the crown of his head a hand's breadth from the spinning, hissing, burning wheels of the Blue chariot and his hair brushing the spokes.

For a moment, he thought he might be sick with terror, but then it was over, the apex of the corner was passed and the pressure of the rails on his ribs meant he could bring himself back on to the platform again, and balance with the balls of both feet over the rear axle directly behind Ajax as they pounded along the short straight at the top of the track.

His mouth was dry, and his heart smashed itself sore against his ribs. His hands were wet and cramped and he had to focus on each finger to move it. He stared at the back of Ajax's neck as a snake stares at its prey, watching the bunched muscles cording the naked shoulders, trying to gauge how far and steeply they were going to lean.

Unconsciously, he counted the horses' strides. Four, and the short side was over. He saw Ajax widen his stance, saw his left arm swing a little out, and almost by instinct began to lean himself ever further to the right, to balance the turn.

This time it was not so terrifying. Math flew for a moment and returned to stand square behind Ajax. He didn't feel sick.

Twice more, and they were done with the first circuit. Four more to go, and then three, and then two. The corners became easier each time. Nobody made any mistakes and the rhythm of the hooves fed the rhythms of the race so that it became a dance between men and boys and horses, beautiful and lethal.

A lap and a half to go. Math found he could take his hand from the rail down the long straight and smear the sweat from his forehead. He risked a brief look for Hannah and found her standing at the rails. She waved, and Math returned it.

Behind her, Nero stood atop his gold-layered platform, legs spread, arms folded across his naked chest. He was wearing only a driver's loincloth made of white silk, an already strange effect that was further confused by the slaves standing to his either side who kept him cool with ostrich-wing fans.

'*Math!*'

A corner again. Math wrenched his attention back to the track. Two strides. One. Math watched Ajax's neck and leaned out and out and out, his fingers relaxed on the rail, so that he could lean ever further out over the speeding sand, so that he was flying, weightless, perfect, with his hair streaming behind and the hiss of the wheels in his ears and the bounce and sway so like the ship from Gaul that he—

'*Lentus!* Move over!'

Ajax called too late to the Whites' driver. Twice, in practice, the boy in the White chariot had leaned too far so that his chariot had swooned out on the apex of the turn, touching wheels with whoever was next to him. Once it had been Ajax and once Poros and each time it had thrown them into a rig-destroying crash.

Akakios had promised a slow death for them all if they did it in front of the emperor.

Math felt the subtle judder of wood on wood. He felt the wind of the Blue wheels cut the air a hand's breadth from his head and thought that if he leaned out just a little further it was possible he might buy himself a swift death.

'Math, lean out more. Lean *out*!'

The shout came from his outside. Through a blur of tears and sweat and spinning wheels, he caught sight of Poros' face turned back towards him, and the open cave of his mouth.

'Lean out further. Bring your chariot out.'

There *was* space. Poros was creating it, even as he pushed his own horses round the turn. Ajax was leaning too, but the other way, levering the last pairs of horses into the space Poros left for them. The Blues' driver shouted again, 'Math, lean out, damn you!'

Math didn't trust Poros, but Akakios had said they would all die together if any one of them crashed and he didn't think Poros wanted to lie pegged on the sand with his skin stripped any more than Math did.

And so he tried the impossible, and let go of the rail and hooked his right ankle on something that felt firm and, stretching his arms up, reached further out.

The rail was hooked under his ribs now, seated in the curve of his waist. His hair streamed back. A slipstream cooled his armpits. His eyes spewed tears and his face was scrubbed clean and raw with the flying dust.

But the juddering stopped and then the corner was over and all he had to do was bring himself in again smoothly, to be in balance for the long drive down the straight.

The chariot wobbled. In the fight to hold the team in line, Math felt Ajax shift his own weight and realized that the rock-steady thing he had hooked his ankle round was Ajax's shin and that, by easing it sideways, the driver was helping him back in to the chariot again.

And he was there, safe, standing on knees that threatened to buckle but did not, heaving great gulps of gritty air and grinning stupidly in relief.

'Three more corners,' Ajax shouted past Math to the

drivers and seconds on either side, over the boiling chaos of cheers from the trackside. 'Let's see if we can do them safely, shall we?'

They did. Nobody, on the track or off it, had the stamina for more excitement. They took the corners with plenty of space between and they paced themselves to perfection, so that the lead horses were not only in line but were matched stride for stride as they crossed the finish.

Gradually, the teams slowed and stopped. Steam came off them in ripe clouds. Ajax was laughing, Poros too. Lentus was threatening his boy with every bad death he could think of, but quietly, so that nobody beyond the three chariots could hear. They existed in a bubble of their own; the almost-hysteria of the watching crowd couldn't reach them yet, nor the fact that Nero was climbing down into a litter, ready to be brought to the front of the throng.

Math leaned back on the rail and looked up at the dirty sky. His palms had crescent nail marks gouged across the width of each, his face felt as if Akakios had already stripped it of skin and his ribs were bruised where the rails had bitten into them. He was as happy as he could ever remember.

He took a deep breath. 'It's not about losing the fear, is it? It's about feeling it and still being able to think.' He spat grit from his mouth that had been there since the beginning. 'And calling to the gods, obviously. I did hear you do that.'

Math felt the heat of Ajax's gaze and turned his face up. 'Am I too much like my father?'

Ajax looked away. 'You're very like him. But not too much. You reminded me of . . . someone else.'

'You?'

'No. My mother's brother. He would have had your courage, I think, when he was young. It was a great thing you did today.' Ajax looked away, smoothing the reins straight. 'Nero's coming.'

Math made himself stand up tall. He wanted to straighten his tunic, but he wasn't wearing one. He wasn't, in fact, wearing nearly enough, but then none of them was. He straightened his loincloth instead, and ran his hand through his hair.

Ajax jumped down from the chariot and turned to offer him his hand. 'I want to meet your mother's brother,' said Math, as he climbed down.

'One day you will.' Ajax's lips barely moved as he spoke. 'If we survive this afternoon. I'll lay you two denarii that Nero's going to invite us to join him in the baths.'

CHAPTER THIRTY-ONE

'The kithara is played by Rhemaxos,' Nero said languidly. 'Do you like it?'

They were in the private imperial baths, exactly as Ajax had predicted, and, despite his best efforts to cleave close to the rest of the Green team, Math was alone with Nero, standing up to his chest in scalding water that sought out every scrape and cut and lapped at them viciously.

He wanted to lie down, to savour again the moments of flying, to find if they might, at last, portend the beginnings of his success as a driver. Instead, he shifted his weight to lean back against the pink marble of the pool's edge and let one filthy foot rise up. Scrubbing at it with the heel of his hand, he said, 'The music is beyond words, lord. All of Alexandria is. Compared to Coriallum, this is a city for the gods.'

He spoke Latin with the inflections of court. A winter in the compound had taught him that. He had learned a measure of diplomacy, too, although he had no idea if it was enough to keep him safe.

Each time he looked at Nero, he saw in his mind's eye an image of the baker, who had died by imperial order, and heard in his mind's ear Pantera's warning that if he ever gave way to Nero's blandishments the emperor would tire of the chase and have Math slaughtered afterwards, or do it himself in the throes of lust.

He had met men like that before and survived them, but in Coriallum, if he had made eyes at a client and then changed his mind, he could simply have vanished into the alleyways and both would have forgotten it within a day.

Here, now, there was no possibility of quiet anonymity. By Akakios' decree, Math was a hostage to Hannah's 'good behaviour', his life inextricably linked to hers. He wondered if Nero knew that too, and decided he probably did.

He scraped the mud from his toenails with his fingers, dropped his foot back into the water and lifted the other one. Under Nero's limpid gaze, even something so grubbily basic as cleaning his feet was, it seemed, to be transformed into an erotic invitation. If Math had any doubts on that score, the echoes were above and all around, in mosaics and murals of lechery.

Here on the side wall, the nymph Echo lay naked before Narcissus, her fingers resting lightly on her groin. A little further away, wing-heeled Mercury disported himself with human maids and youths, beguiling them with his brilliance. High up in the domed ceiling, satyrs joined with water spirits, gods with goddesses and mortal women, all modelled on the same tight-breasted girl. The men all had hair that curled about their heads, as Nero's did.

To bring it all from the walls to reality, white linen cloths lay at the pool's edge, ready for whomsoever should leave first. Beyond, bedrooms furnished with silk lay with their doors open and beautiful slaves waited tactfully in the background. The lyre's notes drifted down from the high gallery, at times light as wild blossom in spring, at others stirring as a martial anthem.

A crash of military chords sent a hero to his death. In the lull afterwards, Nero rolled over on to his stomach sending waves teasing across the pool towards Math. Beneath the water, his skin was broiled to the same pink hue as the marble that walled the pool.

'Alexandria is indeed made for the gods,' he said pensively. 'It's unsurpassed in our empire, except only for Rome. You will see that soon for yourself.'

'To see Rome, lord, we must win the race against the Blues and the Whites,' Math said. 'As you saw today, we are well matched.'

'No.' Nero blew on the water, making complex patterns of ripples. 'What we saw today was that you are all capable of appearing well matched, that the White boy is prone to indulgences of exhilaration, while you and the Blues' second held your nerve. Above all, we saw that Ajax and Poros are drivers of exceptional talent. We did not see all three teams well matched.'

Math felt his bladder tighten. He remembered something Pantera had said about being honest with this man. Truthfully, he said, 'The Greens and the Blues are well matched, Lord. If it's true that the baker was selling information, he couldn't have sold news of which would win, because none of us knows.'

'Which is exactly what he sold. That, and news of a damaged tendon that was healed before he ever got word of it.'

'So, why—'

'He died for the principle that our compound remains sealed, not for the value of what he knew.'

Abruptly, Nero kicked out towards the deepest end of the pool. There, goat-footed Pan in bronze played his reed pipes to a trio of nymphs. They were polished often, but still the heated water spread green rust on the tips of their elbows and in the creases of their knees.

Easing himself round Pan's raised right hoof, Nero came to sit on a ledge that let him submerge up to his neck. He crooked a finger, calling Math to him. Math checked again on the positions of the others in case he had the chance

301

to call on them. At the pool's shallower end, the artful pages still held Ajax, Poros and Lentus in a group. The other boys were playing dice with a pair of guards. Caught between them, Akakios looked no more bitter than any man who was forced to disport himself naked with boys he has ordered flogged and men who would see him dead in a heartbeat if they but had the power.

'Does Akakios frighten you?' Nero asked, as Math splashed round to join him.

'He does, lord. Only a fool would not fear him. Except my lord, of course, who need fear no man.'

'Indeed. Such is his bane and his bounty and the reason he is so useful to us. But you should not be afraid of him. Remember that, whatever he threatens; you have our protection. But we asked how you thought you might best get to Rome?'

Nero turned to lie on his back, letting his hands drift across the oily water, keeping his linen cover decently over his groin as if either one of them might be surprised at the wonder they found there. There was a question in his eyes.

Creasing his brow, Math said, 'Ajax is the better of the two drivers. Poros has been here longer and has the fitter team. To beat him, we must use our horses to their best advantage. I think we might take some spars from the race-chariot to make it lighter and that way give Brass and Bronze a better chance.'

Nero shook his head. 'That won't do it. Not unless you take so much wood from the chariot that it falls apart.' At his signal, a slave brought him wine in a goblet that might have been carved from a single piece of amber. He drank, and spilled a little in the pool as a libation to the gods. It stained the water, thin as blood. Nero slid through it to Math's side and gripped his arm.

'Listen to me,' he said. 'Poros runs fours stallions in his team while Ajax runs only Brass and Bronze, with two geldings behind. We believe that if he were to run Brass and Bronze in front, with Sweat and Thunder behind, he would win, and you would come to Rome. We wish you to come to Rome, but it must be done fairly.'

It was framed as a suggestion, but emperors never made suggestions; they gave orders which were followed. So Math frowned as if the concept of running all four of the Green team's colts together were a new one, not something he chewed over once every half-dozen days with Ajax until the arguments on both sides were worn thin and his ears dulled with all the reasons why it wouldn't work.

One reason, actually: Bronze hated Thunder with a vast and deadly passion and was hated equally in his turn. However much both stallions might give to their racing, if ever they were harnessed to the same rig there would be carnage.

The northern tribes of the snow wastes, it was said, bred horses for fighting. They set stallions one against the other in a pen and then ate the loser, letting only the final victor of a season's battles mate with their mares. The men mated with the mares first, apparently.

Math wasn't sure he believed that, but if ever Bronze was stolen away in the night, he was sure he would only have to search the nearest northmen's camp to find him serving their mares, having killed every other stallion in single combat.

None of which was worth saying aloud. There was, in fact, no way out. For the fifth or sixth time, he strove to catch Ajax's eye. Miraculously, he succeeded, but it came to nothing. Ajax blinked twice, to show he had seen, and then tilted his head a little to his left, to where Akakios had clearly positioned himself between him and Nero.

'The horses would need to be schooled for such a thing, but it's not impossible.' Math chewed his lip as a thought came to him. 'We have three days until the trial against Poros is due to run. Perhaps if it could be put back for a further two days, that would give us time to try out your idea and make it work?'

Across the pool, something had changed. Akakios had taken a step to the left and Ajax was coming at last, drifting slowly through the chest-high water, his colour pinked by the heat from torso to gleaming scalp. Nero saw him and let go of Math's arm.

Relief made Math reckless. He splayed his hands and slid them through the water, making of them chariots and horses that raced side by side. 'Could you do such a thing? Could you set the trial back by another two days so we can try out the four colts together a few times before we have to race?'

'We are emperor. We can do anything.' The water surged as Nero levered himself up on to the tiled pool side. Slaves ran forward, bringing towels for his torso, his shoulder, his hair. Behind them, the pool emptied as other men, too, brought their bathing to a close.

Math lifted himself out and sat naked at the pool's edge. Nero handed him his own towel, reeking of rose-oil, wine and hot sweat.

'But we cannot do as you ask,' Nero said sadly. 'The senate makes demands on us that we cannot ignore. We leave for Rome on the fifth day from now and would take you with us. You may therefore have one day extra, so four in total. It is not beyond you and Ajax to work your magic with the horses by then, surely?'

Chapter Thirty-Two

'It's madness! It can't be done. Bronze will kill Thunder or be killed in his turn. Math, you know this. Hannah, he *does* know; don't look at me like that. It'll be carnage. We'll lose the horses and the rig before we ever get near the race. I'll be dead and Nero will hang the rest of you for making him look like an idiot. Pantera will be left alone to do . . . whatever it is he has to do.'

They were in the stables, in shade and relative privacy, soaked in the smells of hay and horse dung, with only the faint flavour of rose-oil from the baths.

Ajax was running both hands over and over across his still-pink crown, pacing the length of the stalls. Hannah was the only breath of calm and Math let her soothe the shivering, shuddering ague that had been on him since he had left the baths and walked back to the compound with Ajax, Poros and the retinue of huge Ubian guards who had taken them there in the first place.

Hannah sat on an empty harness box. Outside, the compound buzzed with busy contentment, like a bee skep on a warm day. 'Could it not be done just once, to win the trial?' she asked, reasonably.

'Absolutely not. If we do it once and win, we'd have to do it again in Rome.'

'So then—'

'So we won't get any second chances with Bronze. Once he understands what's coming, he'll be ready. If we win here, all we're doing is postponing the carnage till Rome.'

'It can't be undone now,' Hannah said. 'You have to at least appear to try. If you spend the next four days trying, and then fail, will it be enough to ward off Nero's vengeance, do you think?'

'We can't. We have to win now.' Ajax stepped away from Hannah and Math. He was brown as an Egyptian, the scars on his back thinned down to pale threads. His eyes were bright as copper, his brows thinly black. If he had hair enough to cover his absent ear, of the same colour and shine, he would have been the very image of Apollo. Math felt him catch Hannah's eye in a question, and the subtle shift of her answer.

She said, 'This isn't just about the race, is it?'

'Not any more.' Ajax smoothed his palm across his scalp. 'Math's going to Rome and there's nothing we can do about it. Nero will have him, one way or the other. If we're to stay together, we have to win.'

'You could do that with two colts.'

'I believe I could. Nero, however, believes otherwise and Nero is our emperor. So if we're going to avoid a bloodbath' – Ajax lifted a headstall from the rack on the wall and threw it to Math – 'we'll have to spend the next three days running all four colts round that bloody track until they're on their knees, too spent to fight.'

Math caught the headstall that was thrown him. It was the last thing his father had made, pliable and beautiful and very light. 'We're using the racing harness?' he asked, wide-eyed. 'And the racing rigs?' In his dreams. In his best and wildest dreams . . .

'The racing harness and the racing rigs,' Ajax agreed. He didn't look as if it would be the fulfilment of every boy's wish. 'You'll drive Brass and Bronze, they're the better

306

schooled. I'll drive Sweat and Thunder in the spare racing chariot. By the time we're finished, they'll be so bored of each other's company, they won't bother to fight. Get everything ready today. Make sure you can wind the reins in your sleep. We'll start tomorrow morning at dawn.'

'Go Bronze! Go Brass! Go! Go! *Go!*'

Math was flying. Out of control, without Ajax to help him, he was flying. The light racing chariot bounced under his feet, light as a leaping deer. On any other day, he would have fallen and, in falling, killed himself. But today, at last, his body seemed to have its own knowing.

The parade race with Ajax had given him that, so that here, now, he could stand with his hands spread wide and his head back and he was not falling but flying, leaning into the turn, letting Bronze, hugely powerful, made of muscle, bone and teeth, made of rage and blood and hate, letting all of that go into pulling the light racing rig tight round the bend and up into the straight.

Where he met Ajax, coming the other way, racing right-handed, with the sun, which was quite astonishingly difficult and went against all his horses' training, but they needed to do it, so that they might pass each other twice on each circuit, letting Bronze and Thunder pass each other, left hand to left hand, so they could meet and match, but not fight. For only when immersed in a race did the blood-mist of winning rise higher in each of the colts than the blood-mist of killing his rival. And Ajax's alchemy seemed to be working. For three circuits now they had met and met again, and while both colts flattened their ears to their heads as they passed there was no war yet; nobody had died.

Nero's watching men could report that they were genuinely trying and Poros could stand at the edge and fume and do nothing. Math didn't have time to see if he was.

He barely had control. Actually, he had no control. If the horses hadn't known the track as well as they knew their own stables, they would have crashed into the walls at the end of the first short straight.

But they did know it, and without the need to manoeuvre round other rigs Math had nothing to do but stand still and ride the wind. On the next long straight, he leaned forward and risked one single cast of his long thin whip to crack in the air above Bronze and Brass, to ask of them yet more speed.

As a ship surges forward from a newly unfurled sail in a greater breath of wind, so did his horses give him a burst of power to take him faster down the straight so that he was more than flying and the tears streaming past his temples were for joy as much as speed and he knew at last, in the seat of his soul, what it was to fly loose from his body, freed from all the weights and sorrows of the earth.

He understood in his soul why it was that Ajax came so alive out here on the sands and why his father had so loved battle.

Lifting his head, Math screamed out his father's name and heard it lost in the thunder of his own movement. Flying over the red hot sands, he knew, with an indescribable elation, that nobody could ever take from him the memory of freedom.

Standing at the side rails, away from Poros and the emperor's men, Hannah heard Caradoc's name in the high hawk's cry and wept for the joy of it, and the pain of a boy finding freedom who was too young to have lost it.

She bent her head to rest her forehead on her loosely clenched fists and so neither heard the footsteps nor saw the shadow at her side until a voice said, 'It was Xenophon, I believe, who said a horse's hooves should sound as cymbals on the sand. He was an exceptional horseman, but I'm not sure he heard cymbals as I hear them. I'd have said those four colts sound more like mallets driving pegs into wood.'

'Akakios.' Hannah kept her eyes on the track. Akakios came to lean on the rail by her side.

'I've been speaking to men in Alexandria,' he said conversationally. 'Scholars of ancient wisdom, apothecaries, astrologers, priests. I have been honest with them about who I am, and what I want. They, in turn, have been honest with me. Five different men and one woman have independently told me the same thing so that even I begin to believe it.'

Hannah squeezed her hands together to keep them still. Math was on the far straight. His team passed Ajax at the middle marker, as they needed to. The horses noticed each other less each time.

Akakios waited until the two chariots were clear, then, 'Can you guess what they told me?'

'That if you enter the maze of the Oracle beneath the Temple of Serapis,' Hannah said flatly, 'you will never emerge alive.'

'Exactly so. I did not kill Ptolemy Asul, but he was a man much valued by the Sibyls and they already know the part I played in his demise. Even if I were to reach the Styx – which I gather is unlikely – I would not cross it alive.' He turned round, leaning back against the top rail with his arms folded. 'Why did you not tell me this?'

'I was about to. If you remember, we were interrupted.'

'There has been time since then.'

'In which you have been closeted with the emperor to the exclusion of anyone else, or abroad in Alexandria where I am now forbidden to go. You know, that's what matters. We will cancel our arrangement. Nobody will be hurt.'

Hannah turned away, as if to leave. Akakios caught her wrist. His fingers left livid prints on the burns he had made six days before.

'I need to know what the Oracle knows,' he said. His

eyes held exactly the quality of humanity they had in Ptolemy Asul's house, which was none. 'I will find that out, and you will help me to do so.'

'Then we will both die.' She let the scorn show in her voice. 'I thought you might value your own life more highly than that.'

'I do. And because I do, I value your life highly also. You should be grateful.' He released her arm. The marks of his fingers stood out white against the healing burns. 'My sources tell me that I can send a surrogate, a man who is not as . . . tainted as I am. Is this true?'

'It may be . . . if you can find someone prepared to take the risk. Crossing the Styx is not without its dangers, even for a man pure of heart.'

'You'd be surprised who will take risks on my behalf.' Akakios' smile made the gorge rise in her throat. 'Saulos, in this instance, has professed himself glad to do so.'

'Saulos?' Hannah stared at him in frank astonishment. 'Why?'

'Because I told him you would die if he did not.' Akakios tipped his head. 'In case you hadn't noticed, he holds you in high esteem. He is, in fact, besotted. He'll take whatever risks are asked of him to keep you safe. Is love not a wonderful thing?' He turned again, to gaze out at the track where the horses were moving smoothly. There was still an obvious disparity between Ajax's skill and Math's, but it was growing less with each circuit.

Akakios turned back to face Hannah. 'And whereas you might not return Saulos' love,' he said, 'I know that I can rely upon you to do whatever you can in your turn to keep Ajax and Math safe. Have you petitioned the Oracle yet, to ask if you might conduct in a supplicant?'

Hannah shook her head.

'My sources say that you must, and soon. When is appropriate?'

She found her voice. 'The dawn of any day.'

'Then tomorrow at dawn, you will ask for and receive permission to escort Saulos into Hades. At the time appointed, you will be his guide in all ways and will ensure that he remains alive and returns with the answer that I require. You will do this willingly and well or those whom you love will die as Ptolemy Asul died. You know I can do this, and I will.'

Ajax found her later, being sick into a bowl in her own quarters. He was alight with the success of his venture, with Math's skill, with hope for the race, so that she didn't want to tell him what had happened and he had to draw it out of her word by word.

When she was done, he sat on the edge of her bed staring straight at the wall. His face had taken on the smooth blankness she saw before a race, when his mind was turned inward. He said, 'I could kill him, here, today, now. He wouldn't threaten you then.'

'He'll have thought of that. If he dies, there will be an order left for you and Math to die. It's the way men like him work.'

'What will you do, then?'

Hannah set the bowl down and wiped her mouth with the heel of her hand. Making herself meet Ajax's eyes was harder than giving her word to Akakios had been. Ajax could read her in ways Akakios never could; he knew the cost of what she was doing. She was glad Math wasn't there.

'I'll do exactly what he asks,' she said. 'I'll take Saulos into the tunnels beneath the Serapeum that lead to Hades, there to cross the Styx and meet with the Oracle. What happens after that is between him, the Ferryman and the Sibyl. If he dies, it won't be of my doing.'

311

CHAPTER THIRTY-THREE

Dawn came slowly to the man lying in the rubble of the half-built building that backed on to the Temple of Serapis in Alexandria.

Pantera had settled there in the dark, feeling his way, lit by grey stars. By feel, he had come to a place he had noted during the day, and to the oiled cloth he had hidden between the scattered stones. Then, feigning the appearance of a clerk sent to examine the site, he had made a space for himself, clearing it free of broken bricks and other debris so that he could lie unseen through an entire day if necessary.

Before dawn, he had eased himself in, and drawn the pale cloth over his head, for shade and camouflage together. He had laid his knife where he could reach it then rested his chin on his fists and prepared to wait.

And wait.

Dawn was a pale thing, scented with eucalyptus and juniper, brought to life by mosquitoes flying in droves from Lake Mareotis and then cicadas that hid with the scorpions in the walls. After the insects, songbirds came in great profusion, to blast the temple and its surround, to shake it awake, and all the priests who attended the god.

White-clad novices emerged and began to sweep the

temple steps. Satisfied, the birds went away to sing other, less violent songs, except for one full-throated warbler that stayed behind to warn the priests and whoever else might listen of the man lying still under the canvas.

Unless, of course, the warning was meant for the man, to tell him he was not alone. It had been true once, in Britain, when Pantera had lain in wait for a small band of Roman auxiliaries and the clucking of a blackbird had warned him of the scout who might have run over him if he had not listened to the bird and moved in time.

He lay still, therefore, listening, scenting the breeze coming in off the lake, and so was not surprised when a single pebble bounced in front of his face and a light, acerbic voice said, 'Leopard, must you lie in your lair in the full glare of the sun or will you come with me into privacy and shade?'

'How may I come without being seen by the three men Akakios has set on watch?' Pantera asked.

'Slide backwards two lengths of your body and turn to your right eighty degrees. There you will find a stack of oak planking set at an angle against the wall. Behind it is an entrance such as a boy might crawl down. If your body will fit, you can go in there and nobody will ever see you.'

'And if I don't fit?'

'Try it,' said Hypatia of Alexandria from the thin air near the temple. 'There's no point in taking risks if what you desire can be achieved easily without.'

It wasn't easy. He had never been happy in confined spaces, particularly not those fashioned by men, but he inserted himself feet first into the small round portal and slid-wriggled through into the room below. A woman's hands caught his ankles and he let them guide him down on to a ledge and thence to the floor.

He stood in darkness made more complete by its contrast to the morning's fierce sun. When he stretched his

313

hands out his fingertips found smooth, flat limestone at each quarter. The roof was a bare hand's breadth over his head. The walls were within reach on three sides. He could feel warmer air from the fourth, but also a hint of a fresh current that cut across to cool his right side, and brought with it the peppery tang of incense.

Hypatia left him and returned from an outer chamber bearing an oil lamp of soapstone with a good wick that didn't smoke too much. The light pushed outwards, showing the small, perfect room into which she had brought him, the bench cut into the far wall, and the paintings.

The paintings: images of life, and greater than life. Behind him, instantly engaging, stood Cerberus, three-headed hound-guardian of Hades, made lifelike in a way men never were.

Each head was of a different kind of hound, one a great, broad-jawed mastiff, the next wise Anubis, the last a running dog from Britain. They had teeth to rend and their throats were red with blood. But the birds flying across the other walls unsettled him more.

'Three herons,' he said, tracing the outline of the first with his finger. 'They're souls, travelling to the underworld – am I right? And when they come down out of the sky, Charon, the Ferryman, takes them in his craft across the Styx to the landing stage guarded by the triple-headed hound. And this . . .'

He took the lamp from her hand and brought it close. The paint was old, and worn, but as clear as anything he had seen in Ptolemy Asul's house. Around and above, ghosted images of birds and sexless men, of cats, ibis, oxen and hounds, ran all towards the third and final panel of the frieze.

There, the three herons came to rest, standing in a high domed room, with their wings spread as covers over the lying figure of a sleeping youth. He or she – it was impossible to tell which – had dark hair bound at the brow with a fillet of silver, and was covered from neck to foot by a thin white shroud, except where the arms were folded over the breast, hiding what might lie beneath.

'This is the soul, brought home at death,' Pantera said hoarsely, and wondered why it moved him so.

'You're right.' He thought Hypatia sounded surprised, possibly impressed. 'What you see there are the Ka and Ba – the first two herons – seeing the soul safely home, that it might not be lost in the world. We who are alive fear the manner of our death, when what we should fear is an unwitting death, in which our soul does not know itself free and cannot navigate its way forward. In which case—'

'In which case it roams the place of its death, seeking to return into life.' Pantera shivered and watched the shadows float about the room. 'In Britain, the dreamers can speak with such lost souls and send them home. Here, I know of no one who could do that.'

'Such people exist,' Hypatia said drily, 'but we'd be sewn into sacks and thrown into the Nile for heresy if we revealed ourselves openly.'

She stood close enough to touch. Her scent was the same as it had been when they had first met: a breath of wild roses, with ever more subtle tones of other flowers beneath. She wore it sparely, so that she smelled also of brick dust and eucalyptus and water from a cold, deep well.

Pantera turned his back to the herons. 'The sisters have been here a long time, then.' He made it half a question.

Hypatia took back the lamp. 'We were here before Alexander ever set foot on the isthmus,' she said. 'We will be here long after Rome is dust.'

'So the tale of the wheat flour poured on the sand to draw the streets of a city is a myth?'

'No, the wheat flour is true; Alexander wanted to see how to lay out a city. What's false is that he did it on an empty land. We were here, and had been so since before the pyramids were built. And it's also not true that Ptolemy Soter alone decided to build the Serapeum.' She waved her hands upwards. Pantera had a sense of a great weight pressing down on this room. 'He was helped in the making of his new god.'

Pantera tried not to imagine the entire Temple of Serapis falling in on his head, heavier than the sky, and far more likely to collapse. He swept his arms overly wide, encompassing the room and its old, old murals. 'The sisters designed the Serapeum to hide this?'

'And all that it leads to.' Unexpectedly, Hypatia smiled. 'You *are* clever. And I am a poor host. Wait.' She took the lamp and left him in darkness with her voice echoing in his ears.

She returned with two pewter mugs. The sides made satin mirrors, curving her reflection around her hand. She was still the most beautiful woman he had ever seen. And still the most unreadable.

Formally, she handed him a mug, saying, 'I swear by the god we both believe in that this is untainted, and so safe for us to drink.'

'Thank you. They say the oracles drug their petitioners to make them suggestible. I'm glad to hear it's not true.' He sipped self-consciously, tasting stone and the deepest earth. 'Do we both believe in the same god? I didn't know the Sibyls were given to Mithras.'

'We're not. But if you don't know by now that the god's name and shape is a shield, a bright pattern to catch the eyes and deflect them from the greater truth behind, then you shouldn't be here.'

Pantera was considering the truth of that when a single stone fell – or was dropped – in the outer chamber. It bounced once, destroying any semblance of privacy.

Pantera had his knife half out when Hypatia caught his arm. 'No. This isn't for you.' She set her beaker steadily on the floor. Three different shadows passed across her face.

316

'Although it may be the other reason you came. Will you wait here a moment?'

She did not take the lamp this time. Her eyes, it seemed, could see into the blackness at the room's margins. She became a moth's wing, leaving, a soft shade that stepped up to the wall and through it and was gone.

Left to himself, Pantera set the lamp in a niche in the wall and stood with his back to it, blocking the light. He closed his eyes for a count of ten heartbeats and when he opened them the black had shades of grey within it, and he could see that the room in which he stood had not one but two other doorways besides the small, cramped tunnel that had given him entrance.

Two strands of air passed him, one from each doorway. He followed the cooler, fresher of the two, tasting juniper and sunlight on the incoming air. It gave way to a tunnel, which bent round to his left. He saw grey, hazed daylight and walked towards it.

'You came,' Hypatia said, as he neared the turn.

Pantera stopped still, as he had once in childhood, when his only fear had been of a falling sky, and the love he had sought was his father's.

'I came,' agreed a woman he knew, in a voice he had never heard. 'Akakios made me. He holds Math's and Ajax's lives against my good behaviour.'

'You came only for that?' asked the cooler voice. 'For love of the Briton?'

Pantera closed his eyes and wished himself elsewhere, but in the long silence that followed, he did not walk away.

'What must I do?' Hannah asked at last.

'Bring Saulos, as Akakios demands. Make sure he's properly prepared. Take him to the Styx. The Ferryman will be there to conduct you over if he answers the questions correctly.'

'He'll answer if anyone can. Akakios chose well.'

'In that case, the Oracle will be in the Temple of Truth as she has always been. If he approaches her properly, he will be given what he seeks.'

'Pantera needs to know it also,' Hannah said, from further away. 'Could you . . . has he asked . . . ?'

'Yes. The prophecy can only be spoken once, but I will bring your leopard to the temple and he can hear what Saulos hears.'

He heard a pause, and a woman's footsteps, pacing. Hannah said, 'But then Akakios will kill him.'

'There are ways and ways to bring a man to the Oracle. You will know Pantera while Saulos will not, and so will not be able to betray him to Akakios. In so far as any man can be, Pantera will be safe in this. And Ajax.'

'Thank you.' Hannah's slow breaths filled the tunnel in which Pantera stood. She said, 'Will I see you again?'

'I'll be in the temple.'

'You know I didn't mean it like that.'

'I do, but also you know there are some things we are not allowed to see.' It seemed to Pantera, listening, that Hypatia hovered on the brink of tears. With a strength of will that hurt to hear, she said, 'My dear, you were followed when you came here. You will have to go back to Akakios and tell a story of such power that he'll be too afraid to send in his men to wrest the information he wants by force. Can you do that?'

My dear.

We were lovers.

It was enough. Rising, Pantera walked back through the tunnel to a darkness where he could be alone.

The lamp had gone out in the room of the three herons. By touch, he sought and found the bench cut in the far wall and sat down. His hands roamed over it, coming to know the smooth edges of its surface and the patterns cut there of gods he barely knew. They gave him calm, whether he honoured them or not, so that when Hypatia came back he could rise and offer her the salute of one warrior to another that he had learned in Britain.

'Is that what I think it is?' Her face carried the strain he had heard in her voice.

He inclined his head. 'An honouring of your courage.'

'Not courage. Did you think it was courage that caused Ptolemy Asul to remain in his house, knowing what was to come?'

'Could he have left?'

'Of course, but they would have tracked him wherever he went. He didn't want to spend a life in hiding, but rather preferred to die where his friends might find him. Also, he wished to give you . . . what he gave.'

The candlestick shaped as a golden dancer remained beneath the elephant in Ptolemy Asul's house. He believed she must know that. He said, 'I will honour her.'

'You will reclaim her and pass her one day to your daughter.'

His only daughter was dead. Pantera looked down at his hands, which, by the god's grace, did not shake.

Hypatia gave a small, husked laugh. 'Thank you for not asking more. I have had enough, today, of helping people with their futures.'

Suddenly ungainly, as if the strings that held her up had been severed, she sat on the floor with her arms balanced on the points of her knees and her head bent between them.

From there, muffled, she said, 'At dawn on the day of the new moon, Hannah will bring Saulos into the Temple of Truth and I will bring you. You must be in your place amidst the rubble before he gets here. Can you do that?'

'I can be here through the night if it will help.'

'I think it might, although we can't enter before dawn. You must not eat for two nights and the day between them. You must take no wine from henceforth, only water. You must come clean in bowels and bladder. You will need the customary gifts for the Ferryman and the Oracle. Take care how you come by them. If Akakios comes to hear that you are searching the markets of Alexandria for frankincense and myrrh, it will bring danger to all of you, not least Hannah.'

She stopped, her gaze searching his face. He saw her reach a decision. 'If you want one piece of advice from me, it is this: from this moment on, cultivate with every fibre of your being the ability to hear the voice of your god. And make sure that it is the voice of truth that speaks to you, not the lure of power. Men make their own gods, and not all of them lead to the heart. Remember that, when the time comes.'

'I have met the truth hanging on a cross. I know it.' Pantera stood. 'I will do my utmost to bring it alone into your domain.'

CHAPTER THIRTY-FOUR

Bronze was ready to race. Fat veins pulsed on his skin in the rising heat of the morning. His ears were funnels, scooping up the sounds of birds on the dormitory roof, of mice in the feed stores, of distant gulls at the harbour, of clouds traversing the sky and the soft song of the sun's motion: he heard everything, and knew the meaning of each part.

Never had the colt been so well. Never had Math loved him so much. He led him out of the stalls into the cool evening. The other three horses were already harnessed, all three in the same traces, ready for the one horse, inside at the front, who led the team.

After two days of agonizing indecision, that lead space had been kept for Bronze. He was the best: Math knew it and Ajax had come to accept it. He alone had the power of character, the strength of bone and sinew, the towering mind to lead the other colts and bend them to his will, which was Ajax's will, so that they might win.

And yet it had to be tested. Ajax would have left it to the day of the race and taken the risk, but Nero had let it be known that he wished a report to be given him of the team's progress under its new driving regime and so, with exultation from Math and deep misgivings from Ajax, they were here, on the eve of the race, ready to try out Nero's idea.

Hannah had taught Math how to breathe to keep himself calm, but now, in the heat of the moment, he didn't need it. Stepping out into the full sun, he walked on air, beside a colt who danced in the light of the gods. The rope was a thread of silk between them, charged with lightning. As one, they turned the corner and walked on to the training track. As one, they saw the four geldings harnessed to the spare racing rig and smelled the presence of the other colts and knew it was time to race properly.

Bronze did not scream, or rear or strike. The smell of his sweat did not turn rank with the need to kill. He danced forward in the wide arc Ajax had marked out in the sand that brought him out past the four geldings held steady by Nexos, the loriner's wall-eyed son, and only after that did he see his enemy harnessed in behind his brother and still he did not fully understand.

He screamed briefly, but more in confusion than true rage, and Thunder answered, but did not fight free of the harness. Math let out a long-held breath and uncramped his hands.

Bronze's place was next to Brass, in front of Sweat, as far from Thunder as it was possible to get and still be in the same team. The big colt backed in like a green and innocent yearling with only a roll of his eyes to show he was uncertain of the new situation. With Math's prayers streaming into his ears, he accepted the harness without a fight, did not try to bite or kick, opened his mouth for the bit as a child accepts the breast.

Math buckled tight the racing rein that had been his father's handiwork and was still better than anything Saulos could make.

The marks of the Osismi were tooled on every thong and thread. Curl-necked birds and lean hounds ran along, giving their flight and fleet passage to the horses. He saw each one with the sharpness of new making and first seeing. He felt them as if he had never touched anything before, as if the pads of his fingers were sucking in the luxury of lightly oiled leather for the first and only time, leaving his skin tingling to the roots of his hair.

The buckles lay flat. The traces were straight, with no twists. Finished, Math wiped his oily fingers on his tunic that he might not blemish the colt's perfect hide as he gave Bronze his last caress.

A wafting breeze carried the sharp smell of pine resin over the oil and horse-sweat. Ajax was there, naked to the waist, oiled as the horses were oiled. The aged alabaster jar of pine resin had been a gift from a merchant in Coriallum, presented with much bowing on the docks before they boarded the ships.

Ajax held it out. 'Would you . . . ?'

To put the resin on the driver's hands was the last anointing, the culmination of the weeks, months, years of training that led to any race. Always before, Ajax had done it himself. Now, Math accepted the jar in his cupped hands. The sides were warm, and the resin inside was soft, like honey. Taking the leather pad from inside the lid, he swept it round and round on Ajax's palms as he had seen the other do so often.

When he was done, Math turned the pot over and took the smaller lid from the base and the cotton pad that was in it and swept the powdered chalk between the driver's fingers. Like that, with his palms able to hold the reins against all the slick horse-sweat and his fingers chalked to wick away any sweat of his own, Ajax was ready.

Handing back the jar, Math made a stirrup of his hands and Ajax used it to vault neatly up on to the chariot.

The colts knew the ritual as well as anyone. Scenting the resin and the chalk, they grew taller, brighter, sharper.

Math looked up. Ajax was speaking to him. 'Will they do it?'

'Run?' Math asked.

'Fight.'

'I don't think so.'

'Let's see then,' Ajax said.

Math stepped back, taking the looped rope with him. Bronze watched him go, showing the whites of his eyes, but still the volcano of his rage did not erupt. Math breathed again, deep in, slowly out, needing to do it now.

'Well, that wasn't too bad, was it? Can we move now, do you think, you four-legged lumbering oxen?'

Speaking obscenities gently, Ajax lifted the reins and clucked his tongue. Walking in step as they had been trained to do, the team stepped out on to the empty track. Nobody fought. Over his shoulder, tersely, Ajax said, 'Math, get mounted.'

Math took moments to chalk his own hands – he didn't need resin for the geldings – and let Nexos give him a leg up into the spare racing rig. The geldings were kind horses, and tried their hardest; he had never been afraid when he drove them.

He set them out on the track. Ajax was waiting for him, holding his team to a slow walk. Watching him was like watching the first moments of a fire in bundled straw, when the flames lick and spit but have not yet roared to life.

'Walk your team alongside mine,' Ajax said. 'See if we can hold them slow and calm for the first half,' and they did, passing side by side towards the imperial box, as they must if the emperor was there.

Feeling the changed mood, the colts allowed the geldings alongside, watching them, but not racing. Math let his mind stretch beyond them, tentatively, and found the Green team gathered silently along the track's edge.

A handful of Blues stood further out, pushed back to the margins because this wasn't a race and it wasn't their team and they were not supposed to be showing an interest.

Poros remained where he had always been, at the western bend, standing on a bench halfway up to the back wall with his arms folded and his face a mask of boredom.

They passed the podium above the eastern bend and saluted their absent emperor. On the back straight, Ajax leaned over a little, testing and altering the lie of the thongs that held him. He practised once with the small knife, to make sure he could cut himself out. The horses flicked their ears, but held to a walk.

Looking down at their rumps, Ajax said, 'I met Pantera this morning. He says they're going tomorrow into the Temple of Truth that lies beneath the Temple of Serapis. Hannah will take Saulos. Hypatia, who was Ptolemy Asul's cousin, will take Pantera secretly by another route. I thought you should know.'

Bronze tossed his head. The whites of his eyes showed. His walk lifted almost to a trot. Math breathed as Hannah had taught him, in and out, slowly, freeing the cold knot in his abdomen. The big colt settled.

Math said, 'You'll go, won't you? You'll follow Hannah?'

In profile, he saw the flash of Ajax's teeth. 'Lean forward and talk to the horses. People are watching, and some of them may know how to read a word by its shape.'

The kind geldings listened to him, fluting their ears back and forth. To their chestnut tails, Math said, 'But will you?'

'I'd have to be back in time for the race, of course, but she'll be going in at dawn.'

'Does Pantera think you'll be back in time?'

'I didn't ask him.'

'So why . . . ?'

They were heading west along the straight. Ajax pushed his team up to a cautious trot. With the horses blocking him from Poros' view, he said, 'Hannah thinks she doesn't need protection. But Akakios is not to be trusted. He'll kill

325

her simply to prove he can. If you stay on the inside for this bend, and let me move half a length in front of you, we could race three circuits from when we pass the line. Try to let me win. Poros will think it's a set-up otherwise.'

'Let you win? Ha! With those four to handle, you'll be lucky to make one circuit. Are you ready? Go! Go! *Go!*'

They raced, slowly. Math handled the four geldings as well as he had ever done in his life. Ajax won easily. The colts did not fight.

Math slept in the drivers' room in the Green dormitory that night. As second driver, it was his right. He woke before dawn, and lay listening to the slide of linen on skin and then of iron on leather as a knife was taken from its sheath and slid back again. The smell of newly honed metal caught at his throat. Beyond the small knife that cut him free from the traces if he fell, he had never seen Ajax go armed. He didn't know he carried a knife.

'Ajax?'

'I'll be back before the race.' A shadow leaned over Math's bed. Cool, dry lips pressed on his temple. From the dark, Ajax said, 'Get the colts harnessed and ready. You know everything we need by now. I'll be back to race them. We all will. I promise you that.'

CHAPTER THIRTY-FIVE

The rising sun carved a thin red band across an ochre sky as Hannah watched Saulos feel his way down the road leading to the Temple of Serapis.

She waited for him at a small, anonymous doorway along the temple side. Behind her, a long, sloping corridor led down into the room in which she had met Hypatia which led in turn to an underground maze of tunnels and rooms in which an untutored man – or a forgetful woman – could become fatally lost. In her youth, she had seen the cluttered grey bones of those who had done so, left where they lay.

Death by thirst was not the worst way of passing, but still not one to invite without cause. And so, because she was bound by the same rules as Saulos – more so because she knew the penalties – she hadn't slept, or eaten, and had drunk only water in the time since she was last here. In addition, she had spent the previous night laying her mind open to the gaze of the stars, making of herself the empty vessel, cleared of all loves and hates, thoughts, cares and terrors.

Saulos saw her and veered off course.

'This is it?' He was expecting something larger, greater, more imposing; everyone did. In its very understatement, the entrance to the Oracle's temple was intimidating. 'I thought the lamps would be lit.'

'I'll light them when you come inside and we can let fall the hide that covers the door.'

Already, Hannah's voice was changing. She heard it clear as a flute, and cold as a frosted morning. She had no idea what Saulos heard, but his eyes showed white at the rims and he avoided her gaze. He was afraid of her.

'What must I do?' he asked.

'Have you fasted?' It was the necessary question. Everything now was prescribed.

He ran his tongue across his teeth. 'For a night and a day and a night I have taken no food and drunk only water. I have passed dung and urine and have no need to pass either again. I am dressed only in linen, with neither wool nor silk nor leather, nor anything of animalkind about me. My hair is combed with water and my cheeks are freshly shaved. I am as pure as any man can be who was not given to God at birth and has not spent his life on his knees in prayer.'

'Purity is an aspect of the heart, not only of the body,' Hannah said, but she stepped back and Saulos followed her in under the low lintel. She let fall the hide across the doorway, blocking out the strands of grey starlight and the peach fuzz of dawn.

In perfect darkness, she moved about, finding by feel flint and tinder and iron and the small, stubbed wick of the first lamp. Long before, she had done this. To do it now was to move backwards in time, to become younger, to re-find innocence and the joy that came with it.

Both youth and innocence departed as the first light brought her Saulos' green-white face. His eyes followed her from lamp to lit lamp around the room, flinching from the walls and the things he read there.

He licked his lips for the second time. 'The walls show

death. I see treachery and slaughter, the punishment of innocence, the dominance of kings. Is there no chance of hope? Of life?'

'We are the hope, you and I.' The final lamp was lit. Hannah turned, watching her shadow spiral the room. 'The way to life is across the river into death.'

'Ferried there by Charon, who will ask me three questions.' Even here, Saulos couldn't resist a display of his learning.

'Ferried there only if you can answer each of the three questions correctly.'

'And if I don't?'

Hannah stared at him flatly. 'If you speak less than the truth, if you fail to answer any question correctly, you will not leave this place alive. As to the manner or duration of your death, I couldn't say; a man can live a long time alone in darkness, I believe. But you needn't face that. If you wish to walk away now, you may do so. Is that your wish?'

She had to ask; it was part of the entering and required truth as its answer, but she had never done so with so much of herself hanging on the answer. 'Well?'

He closed his eyes, shutting her out. 'Truthfully – is it the wish of my heart to leave this place? Of course. What sane man would not wish himself back in his bed, asleep, with dawn yet to come? Is it the wish of my courage? No. I was sent here by Akakios' command, but having arrived I will not walk away at the first hurdle; we both know the cost of that.'

'Are you sure?'

'Yes.' His eyes sprang open. 'That's my truth and I stand by it. If it's not enough, then you can seal the door and leave me here now.'

'It's enough.'

'May I ask you a question now, before we go in?'

'I can't see why not.'

'Have you conducted others into here? Or am I the first?'

That made her laugh, warming the air between them. 'Would you like to be the first?'

'Of course.' Saulos pulled a wry face. 'But I think I'd feel safer if there had been others before me.'

'There were three,' Hannah said. 'Two men and a woman. I can't tell you their names or which of them lived and which died – but more lived than died. Let that cheer you as we pass down into Hades.'

On that, she lifted a single lamp from its niche and stepped past him to the opening that led deeper into the heart of the maze.

'Have you fasted?'

Pantera lay under his oiled cloth cover in the building site behind the Temple of Serapis, beneath which lay the greater, more secret, Temple of Truth.

From the sound of her voice, Hypatia was less than ten feet away. He turned his head to where he thought she might be. 'As you instructed,' he said, 'I have eaten nothing, and drunk only water. I have also passed dung and urine and found the first ridiculously easy and the second ridiculously hard. I thought I had faced all evils a man could suffer, and so was without fear, which of course was hubris on my part. Do men usually find themselves rendered weak with terror when they come here?'

'The wise ones understand their own terror,' Hypatia said. 'The others enter and never leave.' He heard her move a little. 'Were you going to lie there all day? Saulos has already gone in.'

'I know. And three of Akakios' men watched him do so. But they're not watching here. You chose your entrance well.'

'Then you are free to join me in it.'

A block of granite the size of a ram and ten times its

weight had been Pantera's company through the night. Giving it a final, friendly pat, he eased out from under his oil cloth and crawled towards the leaning planks that hid the entrance he had used before.

Framed in the shadows of the oak planking, Hypatia was the same sculpted perfection as when he had first seen her in a hidden house in Alexandria. As then, she was dressed in white linen, but had added a broad belt woven through with gold threads. Like his, her feet were bare. Her hair was swept back from her face and fell in a silk sheen to her shoulders. She smelled faintly, as ever, of un-named wild flowers.

The entrance to the underground room lay at her feet, as uninviting as it had been before – more now that Pantera knew the uncomfortable wriggle that led from it, and the room beyond, with its images of herons that had disturbed his sleep these past nights. He found his mouth aswill with nervous saliva and swallowed.

'If this is Hades, the beginning will be the least of it, I imagine?' His voice was not as shaken as he had feared it might be.

Hypatia raised one brow. 'I imagine you may be right. If you—'

An owl called nearby. In daylight. Hypatia spat an oath in a language Pantera didn't know. A small, wicked blade sprang into her hand; he hadn't known she was armed.

He caught her wrist. 'Wait.'

She twisted free, her face frozen with fury. 'We must not be followed. This matters more than your life or mine.'

'This man won't follow if we don't want him.'

He dropped her arm and, putting his cupped hands to his lips, blew a soft, answering cry. The reply came immediately. Relieved, Pantera said, 'If you don't want him to come in here, I'll go out and tell him so.'

'If you can find him.' Hypatia had her eye to a crack in

331

the wood. Her voice was thoughtful now. 'How many men could have tracked you here, do you think?'

'Until a moment ago, I would have said none.'

'Exactly. So there's a reason your young Briton has found us. Let him come.'

Ajax made a brief silhouette in the triangle of oak and then was on one knee before Hypatia.

'Lady . . .' He spoke in Egyptian, language of the Sibyls, which Pantera only barely understood. 'I have fasted and drunk only water this past day. I am cleansed in body and of clear intent. If it is your will, I would enter this place.'

Astonished, Pantera said, 'How do you know—'

'He was trained on the island of Mona.' Hypatia had laid her hand on Ajax's crown. 'The dreamers there know more of the oracles than anyone else on earth.'

'Lady, I spent my youth badly and did not learn as much as I could have done. There may be ways in which I am in error. If so, I will leave this place and undertake not to return.'

'You have come to protect Hannah?'

'I have, lady. And to offer whatever other service I may.'

There was a weight to his voice that Pantera did not understand. Hypatia, though, clearly did. She was silent a long moment and Pantera saw her lips move twice, as if in conversation with someone or something unseen.

'Do you have the questions and their answers?' she asked, eventually. A sense of wonder lit her voice.

Ajax said, 'I do.'

'And you could navigate the two paths that lead to the river, the one straight as a staff, the other coiled like a snake and branched as often as an oak?'

'I believe so.'

'Then, by all means, you should go and take the role allotted. Tell Alexandros you come with my blessing.'

*   *   *

Step by slow step, caught in a shivering bubble of lamplight, Hannah and Saulos moved on and in and down through the labyrinth of ancient, man-made tunnels with their smooth stone walls and barely perceptible incline that took them ever deeper beneath the Serapeum.

Following a memory laid down in her childhood, they turned and wove, taking a right here, or a left there, with the lamp always pushing back the dark, but never so much that they could see more than two steps ahead.

Warm air swept Hannah's ankles, so that at times she felt as if she were walking through tepid Nile water. She had been there before and knew it was not so, but Saulos looked down as often as he looked forward, and soon began to lift his feet higher, not trusting the evidence of his eyes and the patchy lamplight.

Not only their feet were affected. From their knees up, tendrils of warm air, even heat, snaked up from the tunnel's depths to wrap their chests, their arms, their necks, to caress their faces and kiss their cheeks. The air was damp, with the smell of old breath.

'Like walking into the mouth of a god,' Hannah observed, as they turned yet another corner and faced a wall of damp air.

Archly, Saulos said, 'My god does not open his mouth thus, but rather— *Hannah!*'

He clutched at her arm. The wall of air had become, briefly, a gale, and had blown out the lamp. With Saulos clinging as a dead weight on one arm, Hannah reached out her free hand and sought the smooth wall, searching forward amidst the fine cracks and old scars until her questing fingers found the first in a series of small cupped depressions up at shoulder height that told her where she was.

She followed them forward, counting, dragging Saulos with her, step by unwilling step.

'Have you no fear?' His voice quavered, full of tears.

'If I have fear in this place,' Hannah said, 'you are dead. Pray that I don't.'

They walked on in silence. The air became intolerably humid. A wind soughed past, like the premonition of a desert storm, hissing, whispering, deafening.

Eight hundred blind paces, two left turns and a right-angled, right-sided bend later, Hannah's fingers dropped into the deepest yet of the dimples on the wall. She stopped. Saulos slammed into her shoulder and backed off, cursing.

She said, 'Don't move. The river Styx runs at your feet, flowing at right angles to this path. If you step forward, you'll drown. If, instead, you reach to your left, you'll find a lamp. You must light it. Everything from here on must be done by you.'

Saulos found the lamp and struck the iron truly. The lamp took his spark and fed on it, sending a tall flame up the wick in a way that augured well. Hannah saw him smile, and say something to himself, or his listening god.

Then he turned, and saw the steaming water of the river, and the caped, hooded figure who stood by its edge and the ferryboat beside him, and the smile fell from his face.

'Welcome to the Styx, Saulos of Idumaea,' said the Ferryman pleasantly. 'For due payment, I will take you across.'

Which was exactly as it should have been.

Except that the shadowed figure spoke in the voice that lined the halls of her sleep and carved its own path through her heart, and no part of Hannah's training had prepared her for that.

CHAPTER THIRTY-SIX

'Where's your driver?'
It was an hour after dawn. Poros leaned at his ease against the barn's doorpost. His beard shone with oil and the garlic on his breath swept four stalls down to where Math was washing Sweat ready for the race trial.

'He's gone to pray,' Math said. 'He'll be back in time for the race.'

'He prays in Alexandria now, does he?' Poros sauntered down the aisle as if he owned it. The stench of garlic filled the entire box. 'Strange thing for an Athenian,' he said, leaning in over the stall door. 'I didn't know they worshipped Serapis in Greece?'

Math kept his head down, below Sweat's neck. It gave him a view of the barn while keeping him clear of his enemy; there was nobody around who could help him.

'Ajax has travelled a lot. On the boat, he prayed to Manannan of the waves. In the city, I think he calls to the spirit of Alexander himself.'

Poros pursed his lips and raised his brows. Leaning over the door, he lifted a green ribbon from the rack and began idly to braid one into the colt's tail. 'So we will find him at Alexander's tomb, if we go to look?'

Math hefted his bucket of water, threw the entire

contents down Sweat's neck and stood back. 'Why would you choose to disturb his prayers? I'm second driver. If you have a question for the team, I can answer it.'

Poros' laugh sent doves clattering from the rafters. With his head thrown back and his beard jutting forward, he was Zeus in all his thunderous glory.

'Boy, you're ten years old! You did well enough in the display the other day, but there are still things that are beyond you.' He finished his braid and slapped Sweat on the rump. By a miracle, the colt did not kick him. He pushed himself away from the door. 'Find your driver. Bring him to Akakios below the emperor's podium one hour before the race.' At the doorway he paused, caught half in the shadows, half in colour. With an unusual gravity, he said, 'Don't try to run this race. You're not ready yet. Remember what happened to Icarus when he flew too near the sun.'

Math finished braiding Sweat's mane and went round to his tail. The ribbon Poros had set was perfect. Math ripped it out with shaking hands and set about replacing it. At the fifth attempt, he had one that was almost as good. He had no idea who Icarus was, but he had no wish at all to try to fly towards the sun.

The midday meal passed without sign of Ajax and the grooms took themselves off to lie down for an hour out of the day's worst heat.

Math couldn't sleep and didn't try, but took advantage of the rare privacy to sit on one of the benches in the tack room, close his eyes and pray to his father, to the more distant memory of his mother and most urgently to Ajax, that he might hold true to his promise.

Get the colts harnessed and ready. You know every-thing we need by now. I'll be back to race them.

But he wasn't back, and the race was coming ever closer and Math had a new nightmare now; that if Ajax wasn't there when the colts were led on to the track, Nero would name Math as the substitute driver.

In complete darkness, Pantera followed Hypatia through the tunnel that led to the Temple of the Oracle, which lay beneath the Temple of Serapis.

As far as he could tell, they had walked downward for the entire labyrinthine journey, but Hypatia had declined to light the lamp and they had walked in darkness the whole time, with the walls smooth as a tomb on either side and the weight of Serapis' temple overhead, waiting at every step to crash down on the heads of those beneath.

Light-headed with hunger, disoriented by the dark, Pantera found himself seeing the shade of his mother, who had taught him to fear that the sky might fall on his head. She walked beside him, through the wall of solid rock, and promised the earth was not as fallible as the sky, and would not fall.

Later, she was joined by Aerthen, who walked on his other side, carrying his daughter, Gunovar, so that, when he finally lost count of his steps and the litany of turns he thought they had made, he came to rely on their joint presence to keep his courage bright.

'Stop.' Hypatia's voice carried the ring of authority. He stopped before he ran into her. The tunnel was cool. His back ran wet with sweat.

A peppery incense tickled the air and, from round a corner in front of them, a faint torchlight banished the ghosts on either side. Pantera closed his eyes, trying to bring them back.

Hypatia called out, 'Alexandros?'

Footsteps shuffled in the dark tunnel ahead. A man's stilted voice said, 'Whom do you bring?'

'The Leopard,' Hypatia answered.

'Not the Bear?'

'The Bear came before us, by the direct path.'

'Then I have met him and did not know it.' A slight, stooped figure detached itself from the shadows by the wall. 'The Bear is the one who came to take the Ferryman's cloak? Who knew the questions and their answers?'

'I believe so. You are spared the task you hate.'

Alexandros was older than Seneca. He was possibly older than any man Pantera had seen, although the dim light made it hard to tell. He carried an oak staff as high as his head and bore no weight on his right leg. He stood back, as if to let Hypatia past.

'Wait.' Pantera caught her arm. 'Is that true? Has Ajax taken the Ferryman's place at the crossing of the river Styx?'

'In this place and this time,' Hypatia said, 'Ajax *is* the Ferryman. There are prophecies that speak of this. It happens only at the turning of the earth.'

'What makes you think *Ajax* will let Saulos cross the river? He loathes him.'

'Today, he is the Ferryman,' Hypatia said again. 'He is bound by laws greater than love or hate to put the questions that will bring the supplicant to deepest knowledge of himself. If Saulos can find the answers, Ajax will do what he must. As will we. Will you follow Alexandros into the temple? It's not far along the tunnel from here. I'll join you as soon as I may.'

CHAPTER THIRTY-SEVEN

'Reject me. But know that I cannot be forsaken.
To lose me is to lose life's greatest gift.
Embrace me, and know that you are blessed.
For is it better to yearn for me unheeded
Or to run from me, and yet be overtaken?
What am I?'

The Ferryman's voice lacked any trace of humanity, but echoed from the river to the tunnel's high, curved roof and back. He stood upright, his pole reaching up into the dark. Behind him, the water of the Styx rushed past in near silence. His ferry was long and slender and lilted back and forth in the current. His eyes were black lights beneath his hood.

To Saulos, he said again, 'What am I?'

'That's not . . .' Hannah let her hand fall. The black eyes turned to her, frightening in their soullessness.

The hollow voice said, 'I have asked the first question. The supplicant need not answer, but if he does, his response must be correct.'

Saulos' head swivelled from the cowled figure to Hannah and back. His body was frozen in place. She couldn't tell if he had recognized Ajax, or – more likely –

if he was simply overwhelmed by the presence of a figure from his childhood nightmares. Had he fainted at her feet, he would not have been the first.

He said, 'This is it? That's all of the question?' He had thought it would require knowledge, something to be drawn from the pool of his learning; the men always did.

'This is all of it,' Hannah agreed. 'And I cannot help you.'

His pallid eyes searched her face, as might a blind man's fingers, seeking clues to something heretofore unknown. His mobile hands were speechless. 'May I hear it again?'

'No.' She shook her head. 'Each riddle can be spoken only once by the Ferryman, although you may speak it aloud to yourself if you wish.'

'If I choose not to answer, I must leave?'

'You must. You will go safely, returning as we came.'

'But if I answer incorrectly . . . ?'

Kindly, she said, 'You've got this far. The water is deep and the currents strong. The Ferryman is permitted to strike you once with his pole. Your death will be swift.'

Saulos gave a short, harsh laugh. 'Whereas yours at Akakios' hand most certainly won't be. I would recommend you to join me in the water should I fail.' He surprised her by sitting suddenly on the tunnel's floor with his back pressed tight to the wall. He pushed his head back, flattening his hair. 'But since I don't wish either of us to die, fast or slow, I will think on this riddle.'

The silence that followed was greater than the water's rush. When at last he spoke, Saulos directed his answer to the river, rather than the Ferryman.

'I could not forsake you, for in doing so I would lose life's greatest gift. I will embrace you when you come, for to yearn for you when you are denied is every man's greatest fear. I cannot run from you, however I might wish to when life's colour enchants me, for I will always be overtaken.' He waited a moment longer, watching the water's surface and the lamp's wild reflection. Then, raising his head, he said clearly, 'You are death.'

The Ferryman inclined his head. 'I am death,' he agreed. 'The first is yours.'

Pantera stood alone at the threshold to the Temple of Truth, home of the Alexandrian Sibyl, trying to gauge how big the place was, and failing; a haze of wood smoke and incense smothered the floor and rose in clouds that obscured the walls and ceiling so completely, he couldn't see where the one left off and the other began.

At his best guess, Pantera thought that it was a perfect replica of the Temple of Serapis that grew from the ground above it. The array of fluted columns supporting the roof was the same, and the rows of brackets holding the lit torches on the wall. But here, no statue of the god stood tall to impress the populace. In its place was a circular stone altar ringed by glowing braziers that stood to one side of the vast open space.

In its stark simplicity, it was far more terrifying than any god could have been and Pantera found himself drawn unwillingly towards it. He had only ever once felt as he did now, when he had been similarly drawn into a circle of standing stones on a moor near the hill fort of the Dumnonii. By the gods' grace, he had left that place alive, although Aerthen had scolded him endlessly after for going near it uninvited, always with tears in her eyes.

He wanted her to scold him now, there in the circle of tight, cold air that took no warmth from the braziers. In her absence, he made himself study the altar, so that at least he could know what he faced. This close, it was clear that the stone was far denser than the local sandstone, and a deep grey, almost black. That, too, was like the standing stones of Britain and Gaul.

The top surface was a map of the moon, showing the

hare that lives on its surface, but with marks at the edges to show the directions. The north wind and a stag at one edge were balanced by a salmon opposite. Pantera stood in what he thought was the east, marked by a rising sun that gave birth to a phoenix. To the west a hare leapt over a crescent moon. Between each of these ran smooth channels, black as old blood.

Across the room, near the door by which he had come in, a foot scuffed on a stone, deliberately. Pantera spun round – and found himself in the presence of the Oracle.

A tall, slender wraith, she emerged from what looked very like a blank wall, nearly hidden by the smoke, and came towards him, gliding effortlessly across the uncertain floor.

He thought he recognized her scent, and something in the carriage of her head, but there was no way to be sure; she was completely concealed in white linen that fell in thin drapes from her crown to her ankles and he could see no living part of her but her feet and narrow ankles. Most disturbingly, although he couldn't see her eyes, he had no doubt at all that she could see his.

'Did you bring the incense of life and death?'

Pantera fumbled in his belt pouch. The quarter-grain of frankincense nesting there had cost him all of his remaining money. He had stolen the myrrh, incense of death, at the risk of losing his right hand if he had been caught; in Alexandria, myrrh was valued more highly than a horse or a house.

He brought the two nuggets of resin out as if they were newborn fledglings, too frail to be held by more than cupped hands.

The Oracle – it was Hypatia, he was almost certain now – pointed over his left shoulder. 'Give them to Alexandros.'

Pantera spun round and found himself facing the stooped figure, leaning on his staff. In a day of escalating terrors the fact that a lame man who walked with a stick could get within arm's reach and Pantera not know it was as frightening as all the rest put together.

Weakly, he gave his two nuggets into the old man's care. Alexandros limped past, circling the altar until he came to stand at the Oracle's left hand. Two braziers stood in front of him, one each to left and right.

'Watch now,' said the Oracle, as Alexandros raised both his hands high and, with the dexterity of decades' practice, crushed the resins in either fist and let loose the tiny seeds in two perfect, even streams on to the red hot braziers below.

Left and right, life and death, hope and trust; two skeins of white smoke leapt to the roof, sweet and sharp and beautiful.

Pantera breathed in and the ropes became veils that stretched wide, from wall to wall of the temple. On the second breath, they became windows to other worlds, to places past and gone and never seen, to the lost haunts of his youth. He felt his heart sing. He strained his eyes, looking for the ghosts that must arise in a place like this.

'Don't.' The Oracle's voice pierced the smoke, clear as cut ice. 'Watch. Don't think. If you become lost, we won't be able to find you.'

It was hard to watch and not become lost. Pantera found himself staring down at the braziers, believing they might hold him in place, but the veils drew him in whatever he did; his home was there, and his mother – not as a ghost, but as she had been when he was young – and the friends of his boyhood. Under summer dawns and winter moons, his father had taught him to shoot his first arrows, and later to stalk lizards in the desert, and then men. He was joyful in ways he had forgotten and his grown self wept for the loss of who he had been.

The veils moved, and time with them, and he watched a living man brought from a tomb and felt the first thread of the Oracle's meaning. Later, bitter-hearted, he left his home and walked across a desert to find a man who had once seemed a friend.

Friendship became apprenticeship became a profession. And in that profession a moment passed, a small thing, one meeting among many, held in a hostel on the border between Galilee and Syria, at the start of the road to Damascus. One idea was discussed. One theory floated. One solution proposed to the many crises that plagued that war-torn place. So small a thing, on which a world might turn. He clutched tightly to the image, to remember it later.

'Pantera?'

Hypatia's voice brought him back. The veils ripped apart, and all their joy with them. He found it hard to stand upright. Alexandros was at his side with his oak staff, holding him steady.

Somewhere in the distance, a dog barked, once, and then twice more.

Hypatia – it was she, not the ageless voice – asked, with true compassion, 'Can you stand?'

'Yes.'

'Then do so, swiftly. Saulos is coming.'

Like a child caught in an act of theft, he looked round in alarm. 'Where should I hide?'

Hypatia smiled at him then; he felt the full force of it through her cowl. 'In the Chamber of Truth,' she said, 'there is no hiding. You will be here, aiding him in his request. Alexandros has all the cover you need.'

Alexandros stood steady as a rock at his side. Over his arm lay a cloak of coarse black cloth, with a hood that fell forward as a cowl.

CHAPTER THIRTY-EIGHT

The cowl was both a blindfold and a disguise.
Pantera made himself breathe, and counted the scents of incense and old spittle and unwashed hair and found them strangely comforting, like the harsh wool scratching his face.

And then, just as the smokes of frankincense and myrrh had become a vellum on which his past had been painted, so the cowl's dense screen became a window to eyes other than the ones he was born with, so that he could see the true dimensions of the Oracle's temple, and know how much greater it was than the one that housed the false god above; he could see the Oracle herself, and know how much greater she was than any one woman, even Hypatia; he could see Alexandros, and know that his lame leg was the gift that had led him to this place, and that his soul was light as a feather, held in balance on Osiris' scales.

And with his new vision, he knew too the names and essences of the two men and a woman who were walking up the long corridor from the rushing river below.

Hannah came first, forging through the knee-high smoke with the hound's baying draped all around her like a cloak.

In daylight, Pantera would have known her by the straightness of her back, by the curve of her neck, by the sweep of her black silk hair. Here, cloaked into blindness, he saw instead her courage and the texture of the peace that sustained her, even as sparks of red terror shot through when she saw him standing black-robed and silent behind the altar; she hadn't expected him to be part of the Oracle.

Pantera hadn't considered himself as a part of it before that moment either, but now, with neither arrogance, nor pride, nor fear, he knew it to be true; he was there because he was needed, because he was wanted, because time and the gods had ordained that it be so. And, because he had seen the past in the veils of smoke, he knew how to see at least part of the future written on the black screen of the cowl.

It was with that far-sight, therefore, that he saw Saulos emerge from the tunnel.

At Hannah's murmured order, he walked between the pillars and came to kneel before the altar. There was nothing humble in his supplication. He was faint from hunger and still weak from his own terror, but in his own estimation he was a man who had successfully battled the Ferryman to win his passage across the Styx and he entered the chamber of the Oracle alight with his own power, as if he had just earned the keys to all its wealth of worldly knowledge.

Arrogance blazed from him, as peace had from Hannah. Pantera strove to see what lay beneath, but had no time, for a third soul was walking up the long tunnel that led from the Styx. Forewarned, Pantera lifted his head in time to see a third black-cowled figure enter the chamber, and knew that this was beyond all precedent; that even more than his own presence, that of the Ferryman changed the delicate balances of past, present and future.

To Pantera's left, Hypatia hissed out a long, slow breath,

346

like the exhalation of a mountain as the sun's light leaves at dusk.

'You come as a supplicant. Have you the incense of life and of death?' Her voice was the raw essence of power, greater than any man might carry, however great his arrogance. It filled the temple to the furthest reaches of the roof.

Wordless, Saulos held up the two resins in his cupped palms.

'Give to your left the Sense of Life and to your right the Sense of Death.'

Without any volition on his part, Pantera found himself taking a step forward. Saulos' eyes flew wide. For the first time he looked uncertain. Moved by forces beyond his own control, Pantera stretched out his hands to accept the frankincense as it was offered.

His hands . . . that were not his hands.

If he had had any command of his own body, he would have fallen in fright, then. The hands cupped together in the red light of the brazier were old and mottled and the fingers were longer than his had ever been.

He stared at them even as he accepted Saulos' offering, held the rich nugget high above the flames, crumbled it between finger and thumb, and, with a dexterity that amazed him, sent the fragments flowing down to the burning heart of the fire. To the Oracle's left, Alexandros matched him grain for grain, spill for spill.

Two columns of white smoke streamed evenly to the ceiling. Saulos breathed in the new scent, coughing. His eyes streamed and his nose began to run. He stared open-mouthed at the visions that were sent him. Whatever they were, Pantera could not see them.

Presently, the Oracle's ageless voice said, 'You may ask one question. It will be answered with the truth.'

'*Only one?*'

By a clear act of will, Saulos managed not to give voice

347

to the panic that flooded his mind. Instead, he gathered himself and bent his considerable intellect towards finding a single question that would give him the answers he needed. Oracles were famed for their ambiguity; on the precise framing of a question, whole kingdoms prospered or died.

Pantera saw the shape of the words before they were spoken aloud, so that the hearing was an echo of something already asked and answered.

'At what time of what day of what year must Rome burn to fulfil *this* prophecy as it was written?'

Saulos drew from his tunic the copied prophecy with all its gaps and ambiguities and promises and held it out to the Oracle.

Pantera could have recited it by rote, but in this place the power of the writing was made manifest, drawn as images across the veil of white smoke, and, this time, he could see where it led.

He saw Jerusalem drenched in blood, Rome scarred and burned, rising again from the ruins of a fire, saw men and women burned within it, and again, and again, in cycles of death and violence spreading down the centuries for a hundred generations and more.

The Oracle disdained to take the paper. 'We issued this prophecy. We know where it leads. Are you sure that you do?'

'Lady, I know only what is required of me.' Dark passions curdled Saulos' soul; arrogance, contempt, vengeance and a pure, unadulterated hatred, all of them hidden in daily life, all of them on view here, in the Temple of Truth. Ignoring them, he said, 'If the Oracle issued these words, it must have been with a reason.'

'We saw the beginnings of a great evil and sought to deflect it,' the Oracle agreed. 'If a god is drenched in blood, his kingdom will likewise be bloody, but a prophecy is only one path among many and, as men and women can bring it into being, so also can men and women prevent it. Such men and women as are here in this chamber today may not have it in their power to keep this evil from the world, but, knowing what may come, they can at least create a seed of hope to stand against the darkness. You have seen the bloodshed on which the new kingdom is built. Are you certain you wish me to answer your question?'

Saulos clasped his hands together, cracking the knuckles. His arrogance blazed. 'Lady, for the sake of one man and one woman who stand before you, I must say that I am.'

'Hear this then.' The Oracle raised her arms. Her leaf-light voice drifted out across the smoke, carrying to Saulos, to Pantera, to Hannah and, last, to Ajax, dressed as the Ferryman, who stood by the entrance to the tunnel that led to the Styx.

'One comes who brings wrath and destruction, who brings death in the name of life, hate in the name of love, pain in the name of compassion. His time is not endless, but will seem so. And thus will it come about in the Year of the Phoenix, on the night when the Great Hound shall gaze down from beyond the knife-edge of the world, that in his sight shall the Great Whore be wreathed in fire and those who would save her will stoke the flames.'

'The Great Hound?' Saulos closed his eyes in concentration. 'Sirius, Hound of the Sky, known in Egypt as Sopdet? You have not given me a day or a date, nor even a year.'

'You know already that this is the Phoenix Year,' the Oracle said, not unkindly. 'Sopdet rises this year over Rome on the eighteenth night of the month once known as Quintilis, but now named after Gaius Julius Caesar, who believed himself a god. You have until then to prepare – nearly four months. At least two of those months will, of necessity, be spent in a sea journey, but it will be no different for anyone else who strives to reach Rome in time.'

349

'My lady, I offer my deepest thanks.' Saulos' bow was the lowest and most extravagant Pantera had ever seen. His relief rolled over them all.

'You should leave,' Hypatia said. The exhaustion in her voice was her own. 'And you,' she raised her head and looked directly at Ajax, 'have a race to run.'

Chapter Thirty-Nine

Nero sat on a golden dais high up on the newly built stands at one end of the oval race track, under a banner of cloth of gold above it.

Immediately beneath, in a display of unmatched arrogance, Bronze was throwing himself back and forth in a frenzy, with Math on the end of the lead rope, fighting to bring the big colt past Thunder and into his place in the Green team, last to be harnessed, last before the race began, last because Math had to lead Bronze himself – last because Ajax wasn't there.

Which meant he was truly going to have to drive the four colts in the race trial. Which meant, at best, he would lose, and at worst he would kill himself and his horses. If he lived long enough even to start.

At the moment, that seemed unlikely. Bronze screamed again. A front hoof split the air by Math's head. He threw himself sideways. The leather reins sliced his palm.

'Let go. I've got him. Let go of the reins. *Let go*. Well done. See? Nothing's impossible with a tight hand on the reins.'

Math's fingers relaxed their death-grip on the rope. His knees did not support him. Only the now-still head of his horse kept him upright.

He opened his eyes. Poros was there, holding Bronze; the only man besides Ajax who could hope to catch and hold the colt when he was lost in his rage and the need to fight.

Math stared at him in confusion. 'Why . . . ?'

'Don't ask stupid questions. Have you the racing bit in?'

'Of course!' That he could even ask such a thing gave Math the strength to stand straight.

'Then get that flapping idiot away from the other horses, get the harness tied and get up on the rig before he breaks loose. I can't hold him for ever.'

Nexos had heard himself being referred to as a flapping idiot. Actually, everyone within twenty yards had heard it. The boy flushed an ugly scarlet but let go of Thunder, smartly. At Poros' signal, two of the Blue grooms ran forward. The lead horse was buckled into the harness faster than it had ever been done.

Math found he could tie leather and plait the reins and started to do just that.

'No,' Poros said, as he reached for the reins. 'Mount first. I'll pass you the reins once you're up. After that, you're on your own. We have one circuit to warm up, then slow as we come to the start line, and wait for the emperor to drop his white rag. For your horses' sake if not your own, don't cross the line early. You don't want to have to set it all up again.'

'I won't.' Math accepted a leg up into the fragile cage of the chariot. Planting his feet in the corner stays, he looked back down at Poros. 'Why are you helping?' he asked again.

The man frowned up at him. His hair flopped down over his eyes. His beard covered most of the lower half of his face like a fungus. Between them, ruddy cheeks lifted in a raw, angry humour.

'Because I want this race over and won. Your entire

team's only here because Nero wants to bed you, not for your horses or the skill of your driver. Now you're going to lose and I'll have been seen to win honestly and fairly. I can wear the Red banners in Rome and nobody, not even the emperor, will be able to stop me. Now fix your reins and get ready before your bloody horse goes wild again.'

As he had predicted, Bronze went wild. Thunder went wilder, straining forward to reach his enemy so that, had it not been for Poros' slur, Math would have been thrown from the bucking chariot before it ever reached the track.

Your entire team's only here because Nero wants to bed you, not for your horses or the skill of your driver.

If that had been false, Math would not have been so angry, but the truth spoken so baldly made him livid, and rage gave him a balance he otherwise lacked, so that he stayed upright, and kept his hold on the reins, and burst past the watching slaves in the first two strides.

Which was good except that he wasn't on the track, but had cut across it and was heading straight for the central wooden spina around which they raced.

Throwing his full weight on the reins, Math hauled the team right, spinning it round Thunder as the outside rear anchor, then let them have two strides straight on the newly raked sand before he began the longer swing left, to follow the track's counter-sun direction.

So far did his fury last, but no further. A battle raged in the traces and he was powerless to control it. *Watch their ears*, Ajax had said once. *Their ears show which way they'll go. If you can change that, you have control. Use your body and your voice.*

Chaos had come to his chariot and their ears were everywhere; Bronze's mane was plastered back against his head, so that he looked more like a snake than he had ever done. He was thrashing, trying to turn in the shafts, bucking, striking backwards, missing Sweat who was right behind him only because Ajax had thought to reset the traces so that they were too far apart for such kicks to reach their target.

Even so, Sweat was doing his best to retaliate, straining forward to bite at Bronze's bucking rump, but it was Thunder who was causing most havoc; he struck and struck across the diagonal, in his desperation to draw first blood.

As a result, they were not racing at all, not even moving forward properly. All their energy was going upwards and outwards, more up and more out with each stride until they were moving no faster than a trot, but explosively, so that the chariot's fragile wicker basket was shaken at every stride.

To underline Math's incompetence for anyone who hadn't noticed yet, Poros brought his Blue team on the long, lazy route round the outside at an easy canter, performing his warm-up by the book. It was as insulting as anything he had ever done; nobody passed to the outside even in a warm-up unless their horses were five times better than their opponent's.

Over the screaming madness of his team, Math heard muted catcalls from the Blues and a collective sigh from the Greens. He was too afraid now to be angry, but fear was a goad of sorts and in the madness of his terror he conceived an idea.

With a swift prayer to the watching spirit of his father, he fixed one sweating hand on the reins, leaned forward, and with the other flicked his whip out over the lead pair.

Never hit them. *Never*. It was the one unbreakable rule.

Math broke it. With an accuracy born of desperation, he flicked the whip's end directly at Bronze, drawing blood from his heaving quarters. The great colt screamed and bucked so high that the soles of his hooves showed cleanly to Math up in the chariot. The whole team nearly stopped.

Math did it again. Over cries of horror from the Green team, and of derision from the Blues, he did it a third time.

And didn't die. In his new rage, Bronze slewed the chariot round so tightly that it tilted and nearly fell. Brass tumbled to his knees and was dragged along the sand. Sweat screamed at the pressure put on his hocks and his inside cannon. Thunder had to battle to hold his feet and had no strength left for fighting Bronze.

But they did it, all of them, and when the rig straightened out Math was on his feet and sent the whip singing forward one more time, not at Bronze now, but between the two lead horses, snapping them forward as they had been trained, so that their ears all faced the same way and the chariot surged ahead. It was ragged, and barely controlled, but they were racing at last – just nowhere near the track.

When he had time to take his mind from the horses, Math discovered that he was careering down the middle of the track, along the side of the Spina, heading in a straight line directly towards the solid oak palisade of the compound's perimeter.

To hit that at any speed meant certain death; at racing speed . . . there wasn't time to think how bad it would be. Math slewed the team into a turn so hard he thought his horses' legs might shatter under the strain. They didn't, but at the apex of the turn, when all his skill went into keeping the chariot upright, a stray lance of afternoon sunlight struck the emperor's golden dais and rebounded, dazzlingly bright. A cacophony of light hit all four horses, and spooked them into a bolt that made racing speed seem like a sedate canter.

Coming out of the bend, Math lost all hope of control. Eyes streaming, he headed at a flat gallop up the length of the oval towards the stands that held Nero, which were as matchwood to racing colts. Immediately beyond them was the oakwood palisade, solid as a stone wall.

Math tilted his body and tilted and tilted, trying desperately to bring the trajectory of the team's panic on to a line that would not hit Nero. He managed that much but little else and at a certain point, when he thought no one else was in danger, he stopped trying and sought instead the freedom of flying that had so exhilarated him the day before.

As he had then, Math called for his father, and felt his presence, and tasted the glory of a death bravely faced. Mourning only for his horses, he relaxed all grip on the reins and gave himself to the last, long gallop up the full length of the track.

As he passed the halfway point on the Spina, he realized that Hannah must be watching, and that she would grieve, not only for him, but for Ajax, who must be dead, or he would have come to take over the race by now. He was consoled by the thought that she would be left with Pantera, which would save her having to choose between the two men. Because she would have had to choose; he saw that with sudden clarity and could not think how he might ever have thought otherwise. It was not that Ajax and Pantera were lovers, but that both men loved Hannah, and she them. Just as Math did.

He carried the thought with him towards death, to give him courage; that Hannah would have the spy and Math would have Ajax, and all that he was. He thought death would be a good place, with Ajax there to greet him.

It was Ajax's ghost, then, that came running out across the sands, clad only in a loincloth, scalp shining pink under the late afternoon sun, shouting in a language Math didn't know, which must be the language of the dead, except that it sounded a lot like the songs that Math's father used to sing, and the words were those Math had heard spoken softly in the nights before his mother had died, words of war and battle and glory and loss that reached into his chest and plucked at the strings of his heart.

He began to weep hot tears of fierce, painful joy, that filled his eyes and blurred his vision so that he thought he saw Ajax running alongside the chariot with his arm reaching up, and thought he heard him shouting out, 'Give me your hand!'

Death was more exciting than he had dared imagine. Math reached out his hand as the ghost of Ajax grasped his wrist and, shouting 'Hold tight!', used it as an anchor by which to haul himself into the fragile wicker basket that was made for one man, not two.

'Give me the whip! Lean your body to the left. Left. Left! *Left!* Good. Now stand very still. I need to take the reins from your waist.'

Math's vision was still blurred, but there was no mistaking Ajax's voice, nor Ajax's nimble fingers unwinding the reins and retying them round his own body, nor Ajax's whistle to the horses, that caused all of their ears to come straight, nor Ajax's command for more speed that did things to the chariot Math had never even dreamed about.

Somewhere, a great many throats were cheering themselves hoarse. Math thought he heard Hannah's voice within the cacophony. Certainly he heard Nero's. It came to him in a dawn of wonder that neither he nor Ajax was dead, and that they were, in fact, racing. Two of them, racing in a one-man chariot. He dashed the tears from his eyes and looked around for Poros, and saw him four lengths ahead.

Ajax had the horses under control, if racing this fast was ever under control. He was standing spread-legged across the width of the wicker, with his feet braced on either side. Math was caught in the back corner. He looked up, just as Ajax glanced down and grinned at him. 'You're going to have to act as second man. Just don't lean as far on the corners as you did before. This rig isn't built for that.'

'What are we doing?' Math asked.

'Racing. To win.'

But Math was watching Poros. The Blues' driver was the only other person who mattered just now and he, too, had truly begun to race. He was one man, and they were two. Even with better horses, they couldn't hope to make up four lengths.

A corner was coming. Seeing it, Math's mind became startlingly clear. He let go of the chariot's sides and shifted his weight to the inside. To Ajax, over the speed of their racing, he shouted, 'You can't win with two of us on board!' and launched himself out across the sand.

He had six months of training; six months that were, really, a daily practice in throwing himself from a moving chariot without dying, although none of it had been anywhere close to the speed and angle and sheer insane danger of this.

For a moment, Math truly flew and, flying, curled himself into a ball as he had been taught, bringing his chin to his chest and bending his arms round so that his elbows made a circle rather than a corner, squeezing his knees up to his chest—

His world, briefly, was full of sound and light and the screams of the onlookers. The circling track and the palisade turned upside down. A voice he didn't recognize said, 'Math, curl tighter, *now*!'

He did his best. Soon after that, he hit the ground sickeningly hard, and knew nothing.

'Math?'

The voice came from behind him. Nexos. It sounded like Nexos.

'Math . . . wake up.' A warm, friendly hand shook his

358

shoulder twice, and then withdrew. In grief, Nexos said, 'I can't get him to wake.'

'He's as awake as he's going to be. Let me see.' It was Hannah. Math felt her hand on his brow, on his neck, on his wrist. He tried to grasp her fingers but his own hand had no strength. She lifted it and held it. 'Math? Can you hear me?'

He could, but only just. Mostly what he could hear was the sound of a crowd going wild in a kind of delirious ecstasy, and somewhere over it a big colt, screaming his victory.

He said, 'Is the race over?'

'It is. You missed the best bit.' Hannah was trying to sound cheerful, but in truth she was worried. Math frowned.

'Ajax lost?'

'No. Not at all. Not even close. He overtook Poros on the second to last lap and came in three lengths ahead. Nero was right; our four colts were more than a match for Poros' when they were all raced together. It was the best race there's ever been in Alexandria, everyone says so. Nero is a very happy man. I think you might be made an honorary member of his family.'

Math's mind was too fuddled to make sense of everything all at once. He worked through it, step by step by step, and—

'We're going to Rome? The Green team's going to race for Nero in Rome?' There were all kinds of reasons why that was a very bad idea, but just now his chest ached with a burning, bursting pride.

'We are.' Hannah leaned down and kissed his cheek. 'For better or worse, we are all going to Rome.'

III

ROME AND ANTIUM
17–19 JULY, AD 64

CHAPTER FORTY

Rome's cattle market opened at dawn two days after the ides of July to a bellowing of cattle, calves and bulls that easily drowned out the Tiber's sullen mumble from the foot of the hill.

Dressed in the plain cloth of a rural farmer, Pantera sat on an upturned barrel beside a pen full of newly weaned heifers, whittling at a stick that might one day become a bull-goad. Around him, weather-beaten men steeped in the aroma of cow manure came to lean on the pen gates and shake their heads at the dismal quality of the stock displayed therein.

For the most part, they ignored him. When they tried to bargain, he grinned foolishly and spoke in fast, accented Gaulish, pointing to a red-haired man nearby who took their money and sold them his lean heifers. One or two of those who thought they had driven a good bargain threw a coin at the whittling fool as they left. Pantera scooped up the copper pieces and grinned his thanks and never took his eyes from the entrance to an alleyway a hundred paces away that he had been watching since daybreak.

Farmers and stockmen passed back and forth across the alley's mouth, but not until the sun began to give colour to the cattle did anyone enter it. Then, Pantera laid down his bull-goad with a silver coin beneath, hobbled ungainly down the row of pens, ducked under a guard rope at the market's edge and followed the solitary figure into the alley.

Akakios walked a hundred paces ahead of him, tall and bitter as the day was new. He wore a cloak against the morning's chill and carried a short stabbing sword at his belt, angled tight to his leg, where it could be drawn with most speed.

Old stables and byres lined both sides of the narrow street, abandoned when the new stock buildings were put up in Caligula's reign and long since fallen into disrepair. Pantera waited in a disused doorway and watched Akakios pause before each broken, unhinged door, examining it for scratch marks.

The last building, a long, low barn set at the alley's foot, stood out amongst the rest. Mould grew on its walls and paint peeled from its door as much as from any of the others, but the roof was whole, and the gaps in its walls had recently been boarded over.

It was here that Akakios found the marks he wanted. As he lifted the wooden bar to let himself in, Pantera walked back out of the alley and turned right through the ghetto, towards a line of empty donkey stables, recently mucked out.

The door to the second hung ajar. Inside, Hannah and Shimon sat opposite each other on the straw, neat and clean in the patched linen of household slaves.

'We were beginning to think you'd taken a liking to cattle dealing.' Hannah passed Pantera a beaker of clean water and received a hunk of dried spiced beef in return. She split it three ways and they shared it comfortably.

Shimon leaned his staff near the door and sat cross-legged with his back to the far wall. 'Poros is less than a mile away,' he said. 'Where's Akakios?'

'Heading for the cattle barn at the foot of the alley,'

Pantera answered. 'Someone's repaired the roof since I was there yesterday.'

'Ha!' Shimon clapped his hands. 'The letter could be real, then. I had prayed so. You will have arranged a way for us to enter unseen?'

'There's a door at the back hanging open just enough to admit a man,' Pantera said. 'I put a pile of old roof beams in front when I checked it last night. If you're careful, you can crawl in unseen and lie behind them.'

Shimon looked up sharply. 'Am I going alone?'

'No.' Pantera finished the last of his breakfast, wiping his mouth with the back of his hand. 'We need credible witnesses, or Nero will hang us for treason.' He turned to Hannah. 'The Emperor mustn't know you're a part of this. Could you go back to the goose-keeper's cottage? If it goes well, I'll meet you there after I've visited the imperial palace in Antium.'

The two officers of the Watch who leaned against the railings near the calf pens had not patrolled the market at any point in the morning. As far as Pantera could tell, they had been there for the sheer pleasure of a summer's morning steeped in the stink of cattle; country men made to live too long in the city and glad of a respite.

Even so, they had kept their eyes open and their wits sharp: half a dozen times, they had noticed pickpockets working the crowd and had alerted their men subtly, so that the thieves could be arrested without fuss at the market's edge.

The smaller, darker of the two was the sharper. He had olive skin and black hair curled ram-tight about his head. If it wasn't for the fact that the men of the Watch were always recruited from families of Latin descent, Pantera would have said he was Syrian.

His colleague was taller by a head and broader by the worth of an ox. He had the build of a gladiator, with the fair skin and sun-shy complexion of a northern Latin. Neither of them wore any badges of rank and, early on, Pantera laid a private bet with himself that the smaller one outranked his taller, broader, more Latin colleague. Through the morning, he had seen no reason to change that view.

The pen nearest them held a cow in milk with a pair of twin calves at her side. Pantera hobbled up with a pail of fresh water and tipped it messily into the trough, then dumped the bucket to the ground and leaned both elbows on the rail.

'When I was in Britain,' he observed affably, 'the stock-breeders of the tribes believed that the heifer calf of twins was always infertile.' And then, into the silence that followed, 'If you give me your names and ranks, we can proceed more swiftly.'

'And you are . . . ?' It was the small, dark one who asked. He had the tattoo of the Twentieth legion on his right wrist and was the right age to have served in Britain.

'If you open the pouch at my right side,' Pantera said, 'you'll find the emperor's ring wrapped in a white silk square. I wear his seal on a thong about my neck. If you wish to examine that, I suggest we leave the market. I have no wish to destroy an identity that's taken me four days to create.'

'We asked who you were.'

The taller guard spoke this time; his colleague was already occupied. With the smooth dexterity of a street boy, he lifted the ring from Pantera's pouch, examined and returned it. Anyone watching would have seen him lean forward on the rails and look into the pen, nothing more.

'He's telling the truth,' he said. 'He's the emperor's man, however little he looks like it.' And then, to Pantera, 'We don't need to see the seal; the man who bears Nero's ring already outranks anyone else in Rome.'

He turned round, hooking his elbows over the rail and

his thumbs in his belt. 'I'm Appius Mergus, centurion of the first century, the first cohort of the Vigiles, tasked with care of the city at night and with protection against fire. I served three years with the Twentieth in Britain. This is Marcus Tullius Libo, my aquarius. He was with the Ninth when they lost to the Eceni. The market's almost over. Unless the Lusitanian who's just bought your cow discovers that the heifer calf is sterile and demands his money back with interest, we can leave now. What do you need us to do?'

Pantera said, 'Bear witness to an execution. The emperor will question you afterwards.'

'Who's to die?' Libo asked.

Looking thoughtful, Mergus said, 'We don't need to know that. We're there as witnesses, not members of a conspiracy. The emperor will need to be clear about that.' He tilted his head to Pantera. 'And you, too, need to be clear. We'll watch, but not help. Are we going far?'

Pantera lay with Shimon and the two watchmen behind a clutter of old roof beams, peering through the gaps between, breathing air thick with dust and the loamy smell of old cow dung. The barn loomed low over them. Largest of the line, it had wooden walls that reached the height of a man, and then slatted boards above that let in long, linear strands of morning sun to slice the dust into lozenges.

A forgotten consignment of old cow hides was stacked in bales, four deep at the end nearer the other door. Akakios had pulled two of them down and sat at his ease on the bench they made, an ankle hooked over one thigh and his fingers looped over the knee.

Behind his right shoulder, the door ground open on old, hard hinges. A bluff, broad-shouldered man stood framed in the light, his face made square by a beard.

'Poros,' Shimon whispered. 'God is good.'

Pantera eased himself half a hand's breadth sideways, so that he could see both men through a narrow slot between the roof beams.

Akakios hadn't moved from his makeshift couch. 'We'll need to replace the door,' he said. 'The hinges won't last the use of ninety men.'

'Ninety?' Poros took care as he pushed the door shut. He spoke from the depths of his barrel chest behind his black beard, and his voice easily reached the back wall where Pantera lay waiting. 'Are you sure we have so many?'

'At least.' Akakios smirked. 'Our friend has a wide reach. The first sixty reached the docks at Ostia with the morning tide. They'll be here by this evening, the rest tomorrow morning.' He rose and stepped out into the centre of the open space. An angled shaft of sunlight sprayed dust motes across his high, bald brow. 'The Oracle was precise: the fire must begin as Sirius, the dog star, gazes on to Rome. I have consulted a dozen different astrologers from as many schools and all are agreed that the star first rises tomorrow night. Between now and then, we must house, feed and water upwards of ninety men, together with whatever they will need to stoke a blaze.'

Poros had begun to pace the length of the building, checking the walls as he went. From the far end, he shouted back, 'If we clear this place out, we can fit in a hundred beds, with room for a kitchen. There are no latrines, but we can dig a pit in the yard. The risk of infection will be low in the beginning, and by two days from now this place will have burned to the ground.'

'Not if you're sensible. Unless you choose to martyr yourselves in the conflagration, you'll need somewhere safe to retire when the work is done. This is by far the best option.'

'This tinder box?' Poros' laugh echoed the length of the barn. Here, he showed no deference to Akakios, but seemed to outrank him, at least in his own mind. 'You

would have us roast along with the rest of Rome's unbelievers?'

'Not at all.' Akakios paused less than ten paces from
the beams behind which Pantera and the others lay. He
stood in the cleft between two shafts of sunlight, so that
his voice came from darkness. 'There's a water tank uphill
of here. If it is left unattended, you can—'

'It won't be left unattended. The Watch are the best-
drilled force in the empire. They—'

'I own the Watch.'

'All six cohorts?' Disbelief rendered Poros shrill.

'No, only the commanding officer. Which is enough.'
Akakios' disembodied voice rolled fat with satisfaction. 'If
you would own an army, you need only buy the man who
gives the orders. The prefect of the Watch is as loyal to me
as you are. His men will abandon the water tanks for long
enough for yours to act. If you close off the water supply
from the aqueduct and then breach the tank, ten thousand
cubic feet of water will flow down through this building.
If you have left the hides stacked up at the top end there'
– Akakios swept his arm across the short end of the barn,
furthest from where Poros now stood – 'they may soak in
the water and thus form a barrier that will keep the fire
from consuming your quarters. If not, you'll have a clear
route through the back door and into the Tiber. Unless
your god can create fire out of water, you should be safe
enough.'

Akakios was on the move again, coming closer to the
haphazard muddle of planks and beams near the back
door.

With each coming pace, Pantera could see more clearly
the open pores stretched along the beak of his nose, could
hear his feet scuff the dried earth. But more, with each
coming pace, too, he could feel Mergus coil tighter, a
spring compressed past the point of destruction.

The prefect of the Watch is as loyal to me as you are.

In all the days of planning on the ship from Alexandria, Pantera had not considered that Akakios might have suborned the city's firefighters. Faced with proof of that fact, it occurred to him that if Mergus had been bought along with his commander, then he, Pantera, and Shimon were as good as dead. He held his breath, waiting to discover whether his ability to judge a decent man had abandoned him.

Two heartbeats later, still alive, he concluded to his satisfaction that it had not; Mergus' rage was all for Akakios and the prefect.

Akakios had paused eight paces away. Pantera turned his head and caught Shimon's eye. Together, they began to edge back away from the beams. They were bracing themselves to rise when Mergus caught hold of Pantera's arm.

Pantera craned his neck round, shaking his head. Mergus nodded back, his eyes blazing. Curtly, Pantera pointed at Mergus, and made the horned-owl sign that had been used to signify reconnaissance by the Cornovii in Britain.

Mergus' eyes widened in shock. Pantera made the universal sign for cutting a throat, then pointed to himself and Akakios in sequence.

Mergus jabbed his own thumb towards Poros, his brows raised in question, then caught sight of Shimon, who was already drawing his sicarius from his sleeve. Pantera made the sign for watching a second time, with emphasis, and Mergus, lips pursed and nostrils flared white, sank back to the dry earth.

Pantera let his knife weigh in his hand. His father had first bought him a dagger small enough to practise with when he was five years old and still too small to draw a bow. He had thrown it from ten paces at a target as wide as he was tall, and had missed. By the time he was six, ready for a bigger knife, he could hit a linen square the size of his own palm from thirty yards.

By the time he left Judaea, he could throw from a bad

angle on a dull night at a running man shouting orders and hit his larynx, silencing him in the breath between words. More than archery, more than spying, this skill was his father's greatest gift. And the advice that went with it: *Don't think. Let your body make the throw. If you think, you'll miss.*

Don't think. Akakios was walking again; six paces away and closing. From the far end of the barn, Poros said something scathing in reply to the earlier jibe at his god. Pantera couldn't make out the words over the rush of blood in his ears.

Five paces. Pantera lifted three fingers of his free hand and felt Shimon's nod.

Three. His mouth tasted of desert sand. His eyes pricked hotly, as if he might weep.

Two. His pulse pounded in his neck, his legs, his hands . . . and

One!

He exploded from lying to standing in one fluid movement. Akakios spun in shock that became rage that became the first fractions of attack.

He should have died then, but Pantera's knife remained in his hand. He was five years old and his father's voice spoke with terrible calm in his ear.

You're too close. If you're close enough to touch a man, then don't throw your knife away. Stab him!

He did more than that. Akakios was incandescent with rage and hate. His sword whistled from its sheath, slicing forward and up; his mouth flew wide, shouting insults, probably, but Pantera was too lost in battle rage to hear them.

He heard nothing and saw little for, in those first moments of movement, Akakios' cloak had whipped back, revealing a mail shirt shining beneath, and Pantera was no longer five years old, practising his first throw in his father's ox barn, but a warrior of the Dumnonii, facing the

371

men of the Fourteenth legion, with his wife and child dead in the blood-soaked dirt at his feet.

Howling their names as his battle cry, he vaulted the small wall of roof beams and hurled himself at the hated enemy. His body was his shield, ready to block the sword strike, with no care if he died doing it, only that it would buy him time to bury his knife in Akakios' throat.

Akakios came as hard at Pantera and they slammed together, solid as bulls in the rut, driving the wind from each other's lungs so that breathing became impossible.

Through the red haze of suffocated pain, Pantera grappled for Akakios' head, gouging his thumb towards the eye socket. He shrieked as his legs were kicked from under him, but his hand clutched tight and, falling, he found a grip on Akakios' meagre hair.

It was enough to hold him upright, enough even to pull him higher and higher in a thrusting leap, so that when his left hand slammed his knife vertically down into the one place that was always free of armour, it had his full weight behind it.

Akakios died with Pantera's blade embedded in the unarmoured gap between his neck and his collar bone. Little blood spilled from the wound, but the blade's tip sliced through the great vessels feeding his heart and his life's blood pumped into his chest so fast that he didn't know himself dead.

One hand scrabbled at Pantera's face, and fell away. His knees buckled. The hate faded last from his eyes as he sank into Mergus' waiting embrace.

Pantera knelt on the earth, fighting to breathe. His world was a black tunnel with silver lightning bolts seared across. His own blood made a storm in his ears.

Shimon's voice pierced it, loudly. 'Would that we could all die so swiftly, with so little care.'

Shimon shouldn't have been so close.

372

Pantera dragged his head up. 'Poros?' The word came out hoarsely, on a precious, hoarded breath.

He saw Shimon shake his head. 'Poros ran for the door as soon as he saw you rise up with a knife in your hand. I had a choice: to block Akakios' sword hand, or to run after Poros. You and I have an oath, so I chose the former. Would you prefer I had not?'

Pantera shook his head and, closing his eyes again, gave himself over to breathing.

A while later, hearing a movement behind him, he opened them. Mergus who had been kneeling by Akakios' body, was standing.

'I am a witness,' he said, wiping blood from the heel of his hand. 'And Libo. We will come with you to Antium, and make our report to the emperor, but I'm damned if I'll be the one to tell him he needs to find a replacement for Akakios. I'm not sure there's another man like him in the entire empire.'

CHAPTER FORTY-ONE

The Greek physician called always in the late afternoon. He had yellow eyes, a stringy beard, and stiff, unfriendly hands, exactly the opposite of Hannah's. They moved around Math's body with a mechanical thoroughness, testing, pulling, twisting, jabbing and, finally, winding the bandage round Math's aching chest with ruthless efficiency.

'Well done.' He stepped back from the bed and began to pack his equipment. 'If you keep doing the exercises with Constantin, you'll be fit to race before the end of the month. You may not appreciate my techniques, but the Egyptian witch treated you every day for a two-month voyage and you were as sick the day you came off the boat as you were when you got on to it.'

As a point of principle, Math didn't speak to the physician except in the monosyllables required to explain his bowel movements and bladder function.

Just now, he chose not to point out that he was still sick when he came off the boat because it was neither safe nor sensible for him to be well in Nero's company; and that Hannah could have cured him far faster than any goat-eyed Greek had not she and Math worked out a strategy of feigned illness designed to keep him safe from the emperor

374

at least until Pantera and Ajax were free to take him back to Hibernia.

There was a time, when his father was alive, when the threat of being taken to Hibernia would have been enough to cause Math to run away from home. These days, fed by Hannah's promises, he dreamed nightly of green hills and grey loughs and a wild, free land populated by wild, free warriors.

But Hannah was gone, banished to Rome at the goat-eyed Greek's insistence, and Nero had taken a dislike to Ajax after the race in Alexandria, so it wasn't safe for him to leave the horse barns, and even Saulos had gone, sent away by Akakios in a moment of spite.

All of which left Math sore and afraid and alone in the unfamiliar world of Nero's palace, attended only by Constantin, the young Nubian body slave who had been sent to massage his torn muscles and, later, help him to perform the hourly exercises that were part of his pre-scribed treatment.

Constantin was four years older than Math and two heads taller, with black skin that shone like satin, and huge, laughing eyes. His hands were friendly and his constant presence an unexpected joy that made the days and nights more bearable.

He had a spy's knack of becoming invisible and had become Math's eyes and ears, stretching out beyond the tiny second-floor infirmary room with its quiet murals and the screened balcony that looked out over the garden to the garish, noisy, profligate seaside palace that was Nero's favoured residence.

Math was watching the physician pack away his copper bowls, but he kept half an eye on Constantin, so that he saw the moment when he cast a meaningful glance side-ways at the screens that hid the balcony.

The garden lay below, a place of fascinating activity over which the infirmary provided a perfect viewing point, but only if you pressed your eyes to the holes in the screens, which wasn't something to be done in the physician's presence. Constantin caught Math's eye and flicked his own gaze from the physician to the door.

Math said, 'I'm tired. My ribs ache and I want to sleep. Constantin will help me do my exercises later, when the sun's less hot.'

That was more conversation than he'd offered in the entire month of their stay. The physician straightened, slowly. A smile transformed his face. 'Then naturally I will leave you to rest and expect to see you tomorrow, restored to full health, ready to race for your emperor. Make sure you complete the exercises before tomorrow's dawn. Good day to you both.' He gathered up his equipment and departed, striding to the chimes of his copper bowls.

Constantin drifted ghost-like to fill the physician's place. 'Two men came fast on tired horses a short while ago,' he murmured. 'They are here now. Nero has entered the garden. The two others are with him, stinking of horse-sweat.' Constantin wrinkled his nose. 'One is armed, like a guard. The other is lame on his left leg and his right shoulder—'

'Pantera!' Math was a good deal fitter than the Greek doctor realized. He vaulted out of bed and across the room and thrust his face against the screen in the one spot where each eye could line up with a slot and he could view the whole garden.

The place was washed in buttery afternoon light that roasted the pink marble to the colour of oranges. In the garden's centre a wide oval pool lay sheathed in water lilies and flowering grasses. Dressed in full toga with amber beads ranged in cascading layers about his neck and wrists, Nero leaned out over it, holding titbits between his fingers for the delicate, kissing carp.

Behind him, with his back to the balcony, Pantera stood

awkwardly to attention beside a small, wiry, dark-haired man wearing the scale mail and iron-banded greaves of a watchman. The plumes in his helmet were yellow and white, chopped small, so that they stood up like a boar's tail, adding nothing to his height. Math couldn't see his face, but he stood at ease with his arms clasped loosely behind him and looked far more relaxed than either Pantera or Nero.

Hearing what went on in the garden was even harder than seeing it; birds sang in giant cages just below the balcony and the nearby sea roared its muted counterpoint. Today, to make life more difficult still, a solitary gull mewed in the harbour just down the hill so that Math had to screw his eyes half shut and send all his thoughts down the line of his hearing to sort out the words from the background chaos.

'. . . letter does not constitute proof of any kind. Akakios may well have written it specifically in order to draw the scum to the surface of their cesspit and destroy them. You acted beyond your remit. We *will* have restitution.'

Nero stood, wiping his fingers on a towel. His movements were stiffly truncated, not at all the painted languor of the theatre. He spun round and thrust his fist at Pantera. 'Read the letter aloud. We would hear it again before we sentence you.'

'As my lord commands.' Pantera gave a brief bow and drew a scroll from under his arm. Looking down from the balcony, Math could only see the back of his head, but he didn't need to see his face to know that it would be a model of humility, nor his eyes to know how angry he was: two angry men in one place and one of them the emperor. His palms began to sweat on Pantera's behalf even as the steady voice floated up to the balcony.

'*The moment of our joined endeavour grows near. The men will gather in Rome on the day before the blaze must*

377

be lit. They will need somewhere to sleep, to eat, to drink – and to be hidden. Find a suitable location close to the river. We shall meet there on tomorrow's dawn after the second trumpet to make ready.'

Pantera raised his head. 'Akakios signed this letter with his own hand. A gold coin bearing my lord's countenance accompanied it. The coin was used to rent a sizeable cattle barn by the river in which the conspirators held their tryst this morning.'

'That is not proof,' Nero said mulishly.

'It's not,' agreed Pantera. He rolled the scroll and tucked it under his arm. 'But it's the best we were ever likely to get. If it makes any difference, I, too, was sure someone else was the source of the infamy. But we followed Akakios and saw him meet Poros, driver of the Blues, and there was no doubt—'

'We will *not* believe Poros a traitor.' Nero hurled his towel across the floor. None of the slaves made a move to pick it up. Pantera continued in the same even voice with which he had started.

'My lord, both men spoke of starting the fire, and of the preparations they would make to ensure it destroyed Rome, but I think perhaps my lord would best hear that at first hand from someone unimpeachable, that he may know the truth when he hears it.'

'Is there such a man in all Rome?' Nero asked, bitterly.

Pantera turned to his left and drew the watchman forward. 'My lord, allow me to present Appius Mergus, centurion of the first century, the first cohort of the Watch. In all of Rome, there is no man more loyal to my lord. Together with his aquarius, he accompanied me as witness. He took no part in the violence that followed, but can report to you accurately what he heard.'

'Then he should do so.' Nero's voice was high again, and querulous.

'My lord.' The man named Appius Mergus sank to one

knee, unbuckled his sword and laid it at Nero's feet. 'I swear by the genius of my emperor that I have served Rome loyally for twenty-two years, first in the legions and then in the Guard. In the name of Jupiter Best and Greatest, I further swear that I hold office in the emperor's name and would not besmirch it, and that I hold as sacred my role as witness.'

Mergus' voice held no trace of fear, which meant, in Math's opinion, that either he was immune to fear or he didn't know the way Nero adored brave men on some days and, on others, was so afraid of their courage that he had them slaughtered out of hand.

'Get up.' Nero snapped his fingers. 'We will hear you give your testimony directly and we will establish the veracity of it as you speak. A man's eyes speak the truth, whatever lies his voice might spill.'

'As my lord commands.' Mergus stood fluidly, leaving his sword belt on the ground. 'My aquarius and I were on watch at the cattle market this morning when this man' – he gestured towards Pantera – 'made himself known to us as an agent of our emperor, to whom we owed the duty of rank. He ordered that we act as witnesses to an execution. He led us a short distance away to an abandoned cattle barn, wherein a man waited, and was presently joined by another. Akakios was the first. We did not, at that point, know the name of the other. As my lord knows, it was Akakios who died.'

'That much is true,' Nero said grimly. 'We are in possession of his severed head. Continue.'

'We lay within earshot and overheard these two men discuss their intention to light a fire that would consume the whole of the city. They argued over whether the barn was safe to act as a refuge for their men after the fire was lit. Poros said not, that it would burn with the rest. Akakios claimed it could be made safe if a cistern were to be breached further uphill, so that the water might flood

down and inundate the bales of cow hides in the warehouse, thus protecting him.'

'No!' Nero slapped Mergus hard across the cheek. The
noise cracked like thunder across the garden, frightening
the birds. Behind the screen, Math felt Constantin flinch.
He held himself still, as he thought his father would have
done.

'The traitors cannot breach a water tower!' Nero
screamed. 'The loyal men of our Watch protect the city's
water with their lives. No rabble, however large, could
destroy them.'

'They can if the officers order their men elsewhere,'
Mergus said grimly, and for the first time Math heard
passion tremble his voice. 'Akakios said he owned the
prefect of the Watch.'

Nero let his hand fall slowly. 'The prefect is dead, I presume?'

Pantera said, 'Not yet, lord. We don't know who else
Akakios may have suborned. To arrest one is to alert them
all. And we can't be sure of any man's loyalty now. Save
this one, whom I have brought.'

'You are so sure of him?' Nero jabbed a vicious finger at
Mergus. 'Kneel!'

Mergus knelt.

'Look into the eyes of your emperor and tell us that you
are loyal to our body and soul, that you have not sold
yourself to Akakios or his cause.'

Math gripped tight to the gaps in the screen. If ever Nero
had looked like a man about to kill, it was now.

'My lord, with a glad heart I do so swear. I have never –
and will never – assault the person of my emperor. I have
never taken gold, or promise, or threat from Akakios, or
any of his men. My life is given to your protection, and
Rome's. I would die before I saw my city burn.'

'As you should.' Nero turned his back on Mergus and
Pantera and leaned over his pond. The perfect surface

showed the moment when he began to weep. Ghost-grey carp kissed his tears as they fell.

A long time later, when a slave had brought him a rinsed towel for his face, Nero turned back to the waiting men. 'He speaks the truth.' And then, at Pantera's nod, 'You were right to kill Akakios. All that remains is to execute the prefect, appoint a replacement, and Rome is safe.'

'My lord knows that is not so.'

'Why not?'

'Because there is a third man, the "friend" Akakios spoke of, to whom the ninety give their loyalty and to whom Poros of the Blues will have returned with news of Akakios' death. This is the man who hates Rome and Jerusalem enough to see them both destroyed to bring about his Kingdom of Heaven. He must be found and stopped.'

'Then you will find him.'

'My lord, I will try.'

'You have our seal. Use it in our name. Rome must not burn.' Nero snatched up Mergus' belt and drew the short sword in a flicker of fast light, laying the tip on Pantera's shoulder. 'Use the loyal men of the first cohort to help you fight such flames as may arise. Do this, and you will have your heart's greatest desire. Fail and . . . it would be best for us all that you not fail.'

Without warning, Nero raised his eyes, so that Math, straining to hear, found his gaze locked by his emperor's. It lasted no more than a heartbeat and there was no lust to be read in it, no pity, no real malice, but its very emptiness left Math clutching at the screen, his bowels made uncertain and his palms wet with sweat.

He clung there still as Nero left the garden, so that when Pantera, too, looked up and met his eyes, with a glance that held pity and a promise together . . . that was when Math found his legs would no longer hold him and the tears

381

he had held back since the crash in Alexandria could not be stopped by himself, or Constantin, or even the Greek physician summoned back to tend him in the stultifying silken prison of the infirmary.

CHAPTER FORTY-TWO

The trumpeter of the Watch marked the first hour after midnight with a burst of brief notes. Hearing it, Seneca moved his numbed buttocks against the hard earth floor, seeking some feeling. The small noise he made soaked into the mud-brick around him and the night fell silent again.

'When he comes,' he said to the dark, 'don't ask his name. Just let him in.'

Nearby, a woman laughed. 'You've said that every hour for the past three,' she said. 'I know what to do if he comes. What if he does not?'

'He asked for this meeting. He'll come.' Seneca's voice fell flat in the small room. The woman huffed another laugh but some time later, when they heard footsteps in the narrow alley outside, she was standing before the knock came at the door.

Thinly, Seneca said, 'If it's not for me . . .'

'Then you will be privy to my business.' The woman's voice was musical in the dark. 'You'll not see anything you haven't before.' She pushed a way through the beaded curtain that made the single room into two and walked unerringly to the door.

It cracked ajar and a murmured conversation broke the hush. The woman padded back, her naked feet scuffing the earth. Seneca felt her fresh amusement before she spoke. 'They are two. Both for you. I have no names, but the taller will come in and the small, dark one will wait outside the door as a guard. Already, this night brings great wonders; my door has never been guarded before.'

To honour her guest, she struck iron to flint and lit the saved stub of a candle. The newborn light was kind to her face, easing away the decades, making her the woman Seneca had first met when both were young. She stepped back and their guest parted the curtain and ducked into the room.

'Pantera.' Seneca stood uncertainly. 'You brought company.'

Pantera stank of horse-sweat and harness oil and dust. He jerked his head backwards. 'I brought Mergus, centurion of the Watch. He'll keep us safe. May I come in?'

'Of course.'

The candle showed the single small bed, big enough for one man and half a woman. Pantera sat on the edge and then, with a glance for the woman's approval, lay back with his hands looped behind his head. When no one spoke, he closed his eyes and there was a moment when he looked as if he slept. His face was not quiet in repose.

'We have wine,' Seneca said. 'Would you like some?'

'Watered. Please.'

'You intend to stay awake after this?'

'We have the rest of tonight and all of tomorrow to find the man I seek. The dog star rises two hours after dusk tomorrow. I intend to stay awake as long as necessary to keep Rome from burning.'

Seneca had brought the wine from his own cellar. It was heresy to water it, but Pantera's tone did not allow for dissent. At Seneca's signal, the woman furnished two beakers and a jug of well water and took herself to the far side of the curtain so they could pretend privacy. She left the candle stub on an upturned barrel.

'She's a friend,' Seneca said, speaking to Pantera's raised brows. 'We can talk safely here. I have some food. Here . . .' From beneath the bed, he brought a tray of goat's cheese dipped in crushed hazel nuts with slices of lemon, a ham and a small clay pot of olives. He laid it on the barrel by the candle and wished he had brought more so that it might not seem as if he had doubted there would be two eating, not one. 'Have you news?'

'No, but I need something from you, something I didn't want to put in writing.'

Seneca blinked, that he might not seem to stare. Not once in all the time of their relationship had Pantera asked him for anything: not an olive, not a coin, not a knife, not a posting. Uncertainly, he said, 'What have I that you would value?'

'A name.' Pantera sat up and reached for a hunk of ham. 'Nero's given me a century of the Watch as my personal guard and the rest of their cohort are under my orders. I have five hundred men who will search the whole of Rome to find the man who wants to burn their city – but I don't know who they should be looking for.'

'And you think I do?'

'I'm sure of it. The Oracle told me so.' The candle flickered up to Pantera's face from below, sharpening the angles of his cheeks and the hollows about his eyes. His eyes rested on Seneca's face with alarming acuity. 'Think back to the early years of Claudius' reign . . . I was in Syria, you had just been to Judaea. We met in a drovers' hostel on the road to Damascus. You told me of an agent of yours, one of Herod's kin—'

'Half of Judaea is Herod's kin and half of them were agents of mine at one time or another.'

'This one was in trouble: he couldn't do what you'd set him to do. You and I talked through the night over a

385

jug of wine; we shared wild, impossible ideas, thoughts and theories, hypothetical situations. In the morning, you went back the way you'd come. You didn't say if you were going to see him and I never asked. I'm asking now. I think you went back and told him the way he might bring the Hebrews to Rome using their belief against them instead of force.'

'It was such a long time ago . . .' Seneca sat against the wall again, resting his elbows on his knees and his face in his hands. His gaze passed through Pantera, seeing the past paint itself across the candle-warmed walls; a man's forgotten face, the tapestry of his history, his needs and wants, the things that had brought him to Rome and set him against his own people.

Slowly, as if the whole were a mosaic blown apart and he must find the pieces in order, Seneca said, 'He was young; twenty-three, maybe twenty-four. He'd been interrogating the Galilean's Sicari rebels, striving to suppress their insurrection against Rome. He was losing his battle: there were too many rebels, too willing to die. We gave him a different means to his end, you and I.'

'We did.' At a rustle on the bed, Seneca opened his eyes to find that Pantera had pushed himself to sitting. Candlelight brightened him from breastbone to hairline, wild-faced with sleeplessness and hope. 'We told him to invent a religion that would turn the Hebrews towards Rome. And now he wants to burn the city, to give his blood-soaked god rule over all the earth.' He caught Seneca's wrists. 'I need his name . . . I need everything about him. I need to know how he thinks and what he'll do, what he eats and drinks, how he dresses, what kind of shoes he wears . . . everything.'

Seneca pressed his palms to his eyes, shutting out Pantera's fervour. He said, 'It's too long ago. All those things will have changed.'

'But you must have known his name.'

386

'I knew him as Herodias, but that was an alias and he'll have used a hundred others since then.'

'Tell me what he looks like.'

Helpless, Seneca let his hands drop. 'He's a spy, just as you are. He looks how he chooses to look. If he wanted to make an impression, you'd pick him out of a crowd of thousands. If he didn't want to be noticed, you could share a bath with him and hardly see he was there.'

Pantera stabbed a piece of cheese and chewed on it. 'How did he think?'

'Sloppily. He wanted to be a Pharisee but the rabbis wouldn't have him: his logic was too shaky. He's insecure, but arrogant. More than most men, he's driven by the need to be loved by others. By now, if you're right, he's surrounded himself with sycophants who believe every word and who'll die on his behalf.'

'Not if we can stop him first.' Pantera looked as if his mind was already out in the streets, directing the searches. He pressed his fingers to his temples. 'No man is invisible to those closest to him. Does he have family? Whom does he love? Women? Men? Boys? What did he do to earn money? What skills did he have? Something? Anything?'

Seneca stared at his own hands, the better to sift the rush of images that assailed him now; of covert meetings in marketplaces, of ciphered letters, of reports sent by others of this one man among many, a single thread in the vast web of his network that must be drawn tight and examined for what set it apart from the rest.

'He doesn't love anyone,' he said, slowly. 'He's too much in love with himself for that. As for family, he was a cousin to Herod, of the royal house of Judaea, but the Herodians are Idumaean first; they have their roots in the desert. He learned the skills of the desert early and can pass himself off as a middle-ranking tent-maker, but I don't know if he—'

'No!' Pantera slammed both hands against the wall, as

he threw himself upright. 'An *Idumaean*! Invisible except when he wants to be seen . . . Why didn't I see it?' He swept back the curtain in a clatter of beads. The startled woman ducked out of the way. 'I have to go. You should leave too. Both of you. It isn't safe to stay.'

'Wait!' Seneca sprang through the curtain after him. 'You mean you don't think you can stop the fire?'

'I don't know.' Pantera was already at the door, framed in the candle's pale light. 'I have to try. There's a chance . . . If I can find this man and keep Rome from burning, Nero might let me take Math from Antium.'

There was too much uncertainty in that. 'Is he working alone?' Seneca asked.

'He has ninety men with him, maybe more by now.'

'So even if you stop him, you'll never—'

'Stop the fire completely. I know. We can minimize it, save lives, save property. If possible, we can save the best part of Rome. It may be enough.'

'It may not.'

'I know.' Pantera dragged his hands through his hair, leaving it in wild disarray. 'If I were to ask you . . . If I begged another favour? Something that might put you at personal risk? Would you consider . . .'

To be asked twice in one night, when he had never been asked before. To be trusted enough. 'Sebastos . . .' Seneca took a single step forward. His heart hurt. He had to clear his throat to speak. 'Whatever it is. You have only to ask.'

CHAPTER FORTY-THREE

Dawn broke quietly over the goose-keeper's cottage, as it had done for nearly six centuries.

Here, generations of keepers had bred the geese for Juno's sacred temple since before Rome was a republic. It would have vanished along with those around it in the centuries that followed but for the fact that Juno's geese had warned the besieged Romans of a Gaulish attack, for which service their keeper's cottage had been preserved unchanged while Rome grew around it.

Since the beginning, the keeper had always been a woman. For the past twenty-seven generations that woman had been a Sibyl, and now, in the month of July in the tenth year of the reign of the Emperor Nero, that Sibyl was Hannah.

It was a peaceful place and she had thought she could rest here. Instead, she found the living ghosts of her present followed her from the cottage to the meadow, to the goose house on its alder-shrouded island in the pond, back to the cottage, giving her no respite.

Math was there always: Math flying from the chariot, Math on the scarred sand, dead and then not-dead, Math sick on the ship from Alexandria to Antium and hating it, Math's face as she left him in the care of the Greek physician.

In the gaps between Math, she was met by Ajax in the places she would not have thought to look: his shaved head reflected in the smooth perfection of a recovered goose egg, the sharpness of his glance in the first prickle of sunlight on the water, his fast, boyish smile in the fire she lit in the evenings to read by. She read a lot, in the days of waiting.

In between reading, Shimon came to visit, an intruder from the world of the living who, daily, brought her no news at all of Math and Ajax, but endless detail of Pantera . . .

'Pantera is in Rome, I have met him. Pantera is stalking Akakios as a hunter stalks a boar in deep forest. Pantera has followed Akakios to three meetings, each with a different man. Pantera has intercepted a letter from Akakios to Poros. He copied it and sent on the copy, keeping the original to show to Nero; you couldn't tell them apart.'

'Then how do you know the original was authentic?' Hannah had asked.

Shimon had shrugged amiably. 'If Poros and Akakios both come to the meeting place tomorrow, then it was authentic. Pantera will be at the cattle market in the morning. We'll know then.'

'I want to come,' Hannah had said, and she had gone and had met Pantera and he had sent her back to the goosehouse, and she had waited until late in the afternoon before Shimon had come to the gate.

'Is he alive?' She had sat half a day on her terror that he might not be.

'He's alive. Akakios is dead. Pantera has gone to deliver the news to Nero. If the emperor doesn't hang him for his presumption in killing Akakios, he will come here tomorrow.'

Tomorrow fast became today and now it was Pantera

who filled the uncertain moments as Hannah slid from sleeping to waking and back again, Pantera's river-brown eyes that became the tunnel she could not walk down, Pantera's calloused hands that held hers as she washed her face in the basin on rising, Pantera's voice that greeted the geese with her, each by name.

Pantera still stood in her mind's eye an hour after dawn when she heard someone rap an uneven tattoo on the oak gate at the far end of the wall.

Bees followed her down the path and under the honey-suckle arch. White geese stretched their necks to watch her pass. Goslings in yellow fluff piped and chirruped and were sleepily admonished.

She had wanted Pantera, but it was Shimon's shock of old-snow hair that greeted her, and his staff that was raised ready to knock again. Hannah stepped back and welcomed him in. 'Have you seen Pantera?'

'Here,' said the voice of her mind and she heard the latch fall on the gate and spun back to it, smiling.

And then not.

He didn't fill the space around the gate as he had done in her imaginings and his eyes drew her nowhere except to his face, which was lined with exhaustion and the weight of bad news.

He said, 'I saw Seneca last night. He gave me a name.' And then, 'Could we go in?'

He shook his head at the questions in Hannah's eyes and would say no more. Heartsick, she shooed the geese from under their feet and led the way down the path and under the low lintel into the single room that was her home.

Stone walls a yard thick and a flagged floor kept the cottage cool in the day and warm at night. A window at one end gave out on to the meadow, the pond, the somnolent geese. Inside, a bed, a table and a bench occupied most of the small space. A vase of blue meadow flowers stood on the table, filling the room with a delicate scent; it seemed a lifetime since she had picked them on rising. A fireplace, a well and a basin for washing made the rest of the ornament.

Hannah filled a ewer from the well, poured into three beakers and set them on the table.

'What name did Seneca tell you?' she asked.

Shimon leaned against the door. His quiet voice spoke before Pantera's. 'It's the Apostate, am I not right? The man who would burn Rome. Is he an agent of Seneca's?'

'He was once. Not any more.' The bed lay under the window. Pantera sat on it with his elbows on the window ledge, looking out at the garden. All Hannah could see of him was his back.

'It's someone we know.' She felt her heart strike a hammer-blow on her sternum, hard enough to knock her cold. 'Ajax?'

'No.' Pantera turned at the sound of her voice. 'Ajax is a bear-warrior of the Eceni. He might not grieve Rome's loss, but he isn't trying to burn it.'

A bear warrior? She had to let that pass. 'Then who?' she asked.

'Someone more dangerous, because he's less obvious. He's a cousin of Herod the Tetrarch, an Idumaean by birth. He served his apprenticeship mending tents and progressed to cutting harness, until he was recruited by Seneca and became an agent of Rome. He's a small man of no consequence, who could walk into a room and not be seen, but his arrogance gets the better of him, so that he craves crowds who adore him. Until these last days, he has been with the—'

'Green team in Alexandria and then Antium,' Hannah finished for him, hoarsely. 'And is presently in Rome, having been dismissed by Akakios, who claimed to be acting in Nero's name.' She held her mug with whitened fingers. 'Saulos is the Apostate. *Saulos.* I took him in to the Oracle to learn the date when Rome must burn.'

392

'And before that, I led him to Ptolemy Asul's house,' Pantera said. 'I suggest we not compete in our guilt.'

'Saulos tortured Ptolemy Asul?' Hannah said. 'Not Akakios?'

'Of course he did.' In agitation, Shimon paced the length of the small room. 'The Apostate used crucifixion and hot irons exactly like that in Judaea. I saw the bodies so often, and yet in Alexandria I believed what I was led to believe without question. That shame is mine.'

'Then we are all at fault.' Hannah raised her eyes to Pantera's grey-tired face. 'Where is he now?'

'I don't know. The first cohort of the Watch has been searching the city since the second hour after midnight. They are searching still.'

'They won't find him,' said Shimon. 'If Seneca trained him, a cohort of men is not enough. The entire Roman army could comb Rome and not find him by tonight. Do you even know where to look?'

Pantera shook his head. 'Only that he needs an alternative to the barn that Akakios had found: big enough and safe enough to hold ninety men. He'll want it downhill from a water tower if he can, and within reach of the river, which narrows it down a little, but not enough. We're searching the ghettos, but we're not getting any help: the Watch isn't popular there and the men can't say there's going to be a fire or there'll be riots. He'll need a source of food and water for at least ninety men, which means—'

Hannah said, 'He'll also need a source of spikenard or something else very close to it and he'll need to find a physician who's competent to treat chronic ulcers. There are very few of those and I know which markets they work from.' And then, as they stared at her, 'Did you not know about his wound?'

'What wound?' they asked together, staring.

They continued to stare as she told them, and when, somewhere partway through her description of the ulcer and

393

how it must be treated, and by whom, their minds caught up with hers, they spoke over themselves to stop her.

They were too slow and too late.

Hannah said, 'I've stayed here tending geese while you two have been hunting Akakios across the city. This I can do. You can't. Saulos trusts me, as a physician and as the Sibyl who guided his path to the Oracle. If anyone can get near to him, it's me.' She was already moving round the cottage, packing a satchel with things she might need. 'I dressed the wound before we both left Antium, but if he hasn't seen someone else before now, it'll stink. He won't risk going to his death with a suppurating wound; he'll be looking for an apothecary and a physician. If he sees me, he'll think I've been sent by his god to help him.'

Pantera rose from his chair. 'If we follow you at a safe distance, we can—'

'No!' Hannah hammered her palm on the table. 'If he sees either of you, he'll kill you, or me, and disappear. We don't have time for that. Let me do this. The markets are open and the apothecaries all know me. I'll find out where he's staying and where his men are, and I'll get news back to you here. Don't speak.' She laid a hand on Shimon's arm. 'I have the right to do this, for Ptolemy Asul. And for my father.'

'I know.' Shimon's eyes carried all kinds of concern, but he didn't speak any of it aloud. 'I was going to wish you well. And to say you are truly your father's daughter.'

No one had ever said that before. Her eyes began to sting. Before she could weep, Hannah reached for her cloak, which hung on a hook on the back of the door.

'Hannah . . .' Pantera stood and opened the door, so that she must pass him to leave. Exhaustion scored lines across his forehead. 'This is the man who crucified Ptolemy Asul. I think it's likely he set the fire at the inn in Gaul that killed Caradoc. He is without mercy. Please don't underestimate him.'

CHAPTER FORTY-FOUR

The grubby girl thief appeared out of the early morning mist, holding her hands out, palm up. Her clothes barely covered her nakedness. If she had washed in her life, it was not this year. Her eyes were bright as a jackdaw's and her instincts as sharp.

Hannah said, 'Where?'

The girl jerked her head roughly northwards, uphill, into the chaos of the Palatine market where the dawn mist rising from the river draped itself wetly over the stalls, saturating them all in the Tiber's morning bouquet of drowned rats and duck shit and mud. Already, the aisles were too crowded to see more than a few paces in any direction.

'You're sure it's him?' Hannah asked.

The girl rolled her eyes; they were blue, like the Gauls', though her hair was black. She never spoke. Hannah had no idea if she could.

Hannah said, 'Show me,' and the girl vanished, fast as a rat, and then came back to find her because Hannah couldn't push a way through the crowd quickly enough.

They moved swiftly enough once they were together. Hannah worked doubly: first to keep an eye on the flash

395

of greasy black hair ahead of her and second to get her bearings so she could find her way back.

In fast succession, they passed a baker lifting trays of flat bread from the oven, a stall selling olives at one end and olive oil at the other, another selling fish sauce in vast amphorae, another offering mushrooms, picked this morning and driven by fast cart into the city. Men and women stepped aside as Hannah passed, thinking her on the way to a woman in childbirth, or some other like emergency. She wore the green cloth of her calling wound round her upper arm and carried her bag and they pressed bread into her hand as she passed them by, or olives or cheese, for luck and for the novelty of seeing a healer in the slum market.

The girl thief stopped. She had more sense than to point, but she drew a line in the dust with her foot and Hannah looked along it, between a wine merchant and a pair of Gaulish brothers selling black olives and garlic to where a man leaned against a stall, haggling over a barrel of cheese.

His head was out of sight, but a buzz of flies attended his back and, over the warm, ripe bouquet of grape and garlic, olives and veined blue cheese, Hannah caught the sweet-sick horror of rotting flesh.

'Thank you.' Hannah dropped the promised piece of silver into the waiting palm. The girl did not leave. Hannah said, 'I need to speak to him alone.'

The girl looked at her a moment, then, in perfectly acceptable Latin, said, 'If you need help, raise your arm.'

'He's dangerous,' Hannah said. 'You shouldn't be close to him.'

The girl shrugged, her eyes lit with scorn. 'He's only one man,' she said. When Hannah looked again, she was gone.

Hannah walked past the cheese stall and on to the potter who sold small clay jars for salve, and the beeswax to seal them. The vendor recognized her and even as she reached him had produced the box with medical jars for her to examine. She lifted one up, testing its weight.

'Hannah!' A man called her name. Hannah set the pot aside and asked the price for a dozen wax seals, folded in dried oak leaves. 'Hannah, it's me! Wait! Don't go!'

She paid for the pot and the seals and turned away, sliding them into a pocket of the bag hung from her shoulder. Saulos caught up and tugged at her sleeve, holding her back. 'My dear! I never thought I'd see you in Rome! What are you doing here?'

She turned in evident surprise. He was dressed as a merchant, with a skein of wool at his belt to show his interest in all things woven. His hair was oiled and newly washed. Flies hung about him but dared not settle on the wound; a smear of camphor kept them at a distance.

Hannah backed away. 'Math has another physician. I am no longer welcome at Antium.'

'No more than I was.' Saulos grimaced. 'You left Math with Nero?'

She looked stricken and it was not only an act. 'I had no choice. I was told a Greek physician would care for him, but I've heard nothing since. Nero's men won't speak to me and Math himself can't write to send a message.'

Saulos' eyes were fixed on her face. 'And Ajax? He would send you word, surely? In his solicitude . . .'

Hannah looked away. 'Ajax is . . . That is, I no longer seek succour from Ajax. He and I . . .' It took her a moment to find the right words. 'We see the world differently. He seeks Roman citizenship. It's all he desires.'

'Citizenship?' Saulos barked a laugh. 'I thought he despised Rome and all it stands for?'

'He resents what he cannot join. And he has not the learning of the Sibyls, to see how Rome's decadence is a rot that endangers all we have built, all the beauty and the knowledge, and . . .' Hannah's gaze snapped back to

Saulos. A sharp wind swept between them. She shivered, sending away ill-said words, and drew her cloak around her. 'I should go,' she said. 'Perhaps another time . . .'

Saulos clutched at her arm. 'Don't leave. Please. Not yet.'

She had a list of things to buy. She let her eyes fall to it and then looked up the aisle, to see where she must go. 'Really, I didn't mean to hold you. You must be busy.'

'No! That is, I have things I must . . . Hannah! Please!' He caught the front of her cloak and backed away, drawing her with him, coaxing as if she were a frightened child. 'Come with me. We should talk somewhere . . . safer. I won't keep you long, I swear it.'

Hannah let herself be taken to the edge of the market, where a Lusitanian wine merchant sold poor Falernian in jugs, but also by the beaker. Saulos bought one, and brought it to share with her on the shaded benches set nearby for the clientele.

'We can talk safely here,' he said. 'This man is mine.'

Hannah let her eyes widen a fraction. 'What need have you of a man such as this?'

'He has boys throughout the markets who tell me when the Watch search parties are near.' They were on a slope and Saulos on the uphill side of it. His eyes were level with hers, flat and calm and sure. He spoke briskly, with no trace of a stammer and with a certainty that the Saulos of Gaul and Alexandria had lacked.

He read confusion on her face and smiled. 'I have something to tell you,' he said. 'After it, you may wish to leave, and may do so freely; it may be best and safest if you do. But I would ask that, whatever you think, whatever you do, you not betray me. For our friendship, would you do this?'

'For our friendship.' Hannah agreed.

He leaned back, kneading his brow with his knuckles. The wind curved around them, bringing her the smell of his wound.

He said, 'You are familiar with the Sibyls' prophecy regarding the requirements for bringing about the Kingdom of Heaven?'

'The one for which we risked our lives in Hades?' Hannah said drily. 'It would be hard to forget.'

'Then you should know that Akakios was my man, not I his.'

Hannah frowned. 'I don't understand.'

'I found the prophecy and I gave the orders. Akakios was never going to enter Hades; it was to our advantage that he could not approach the Oracle and must send me in his place. It was I who needed to find the date, and I did so.'

'You lied to the Oracle?'

He shook his head. 'Every word I spoke was true. I would be dead, else, you know that. But I was not asked for my motives in entering, and did not give them.'

The air grew thick between them. Hannah looked down first. For a while, she studied her fingers. 'I risked my life to lead you to the Styx. I did it in good faith.'

'And I went in good faith! Hannah, you must believe that. Rome must burn. It *must*. You said yourself that its decadence is destroying all that is beautiful and worthy. And the Oracle alone had the date. The dog star rises over Rome tonight. I can do all that is needed to bring about the Kingdom of Heaven.'

'You can burn Rome?'

'And then destroy Jerusalem. Yes.'

'The Kingdom of Heaven.' Hannah studied Saulos' face as if seeing it for the first time. 'Do you believe in a world where the god of Abraham rules alone, where his laws reign inviolate?'

'My men do. They are sworn to the new covenant and the Kingdom that will arise from it. They will die to make that happen.'

Abruptly, Hannah stood. Saulos remained on the bench.

She felt his gaze pierce between her shoulder blades as she walked downhill through the market to the old Syrian apothecary.

Returning, she held her purchases in her cupped hands, a gift not yet given. 'I dressed your wound in Antium,' she said. 'I think it has not been dressed since.'

Saulos blushed deeply.

Hannah said, 'It may be you have a physician . . . ?'

'I have Poros.' Saulos spread his hands.

'So my presence may not add anything to your cause.' Hannah turned away.

'No!' Saulos' fingers gripped white on her forearm. 'You would add everything. Everything. But I question my right to ask you to take the risk of staying.'

'You're not asking,' Hannah said, 'I am. You only have to say yes.'

They completed their errands together. At the end, close to noon with the high sun a blazing pyre roasting the city to tinder dryness, Hannah had everything she needed for the dressing and Saulos had food, wine and bread for two hundred men.

'Two hundred?' Hannah asked as they walked down from the market through the maze of tiny alleyways that marked the ghettos of the Palatine.

'And more arriving through the day.' Saulos caught her elbow, turning her to the side. 'Turn left there, under the cow-hide flap. And then right immediately after. You'll have to duck down, the ceiling is low. This pen was made for sheep and goats, not Alexandrian healer-women.'

Inside, cool air met them like a welcome lover, so that Hannah only noticed the stench as an afterthought. Under Saulos' direction, she passed through a narrow channel that stank of goat manure and out into a second alley. A little way down, two men in legionary dress stepped out of the shadows to stop them. Saulos gave the passwords, and introduced Hannah to each in turn. 'You're well protected,' she said, as he led her on down the hill.

'We need to be.' Saulos' face clouded over. 'Yesterday, we were betrayed. Akakios had rented a cattle barn half a mile downriver from here. He was slain there and Poros was lucky to escape with his life. You'll meet Poros at the warehouse. He's as loyal a man as I have ever met, but we may have traitors within our ranks. For safety, we must assume so.'

Hannah looked about. The alleyway was so narrow they could barely walk down it together. 'This isn't an easy place to assault.'

'It's almost impossible,' Saulos said, with grim satisfaction. 'Nothing short of the entire Praetorian and Urban Guards could assault us here. And even then there are ways out of this place that even I haven't found yet. I think five men, left living, could burn Rome if they were properly prepared, and we are nothing if not that. Excuse me—'

He leaned past her and pushed open a door. Noise spilled out, loud as a rushing tide. A wall of heat gave them momentary pause.

'This is the warehouse,' Saulos shouted, over the din. 'I apologize for the disarray. Until yesterday, it housed bales of wool. Poros is there.' He pointed through the throng. A big bluff man looked up at the sound of his voice. He frowned a moment, then a wide smile split his beard across and he began to push his way through the mass of men.

Saulos said, 'He's my quartermaster. He'll introduce you to the men. I have some arrangements to make and then I must pay a visit to the water tower beside the Claudian temple further up the hill. You are welcome to join me. With Akakios gone, securing the city's water supply is my responsibility. Before that—'

'Before anything, we will dress your wound.'

'Of course.' He flashed a grin. 'As my physician directs, so shall it be. There's a dais over by the rear door that

I'll use to speak to the assembly tonight. It has a curtain round it now for privacy. We can use it, perhaps, so as not to alarm the men?'

The dais was bare boards laid on bricks, but it was tolerable and there was light enough from a row of vents set high in the roof. Saulos' wound had not liquefied as much as she had feared and the dressing went on cleanly. The old one was taken out and dropped in the river to keep its foulness from spreading.

When she was done, Saulos stood, stretching his arms as he had done each time in Alexandria. He was turning away when Hannah grimaced in evident distress.

'Hannah!' He spun back. 'Are you all right?'

'The heat . . .' Hannah forced a tight smile and waved her hand in the way all women use to dismiss the things they can't discuss in men's company.

'My dear.' Saulos grasped her wrist and her elbow. 'You must leave Rome. I should have said so earlier, but selfishness held me back. Go now. I've got gold enough to buy you a good horse and an escort.'

'No.'

'But, Hannah—'

'No!' All around, men arrested their activities to stare. She dropped her voice. 'I'm not leaving now,' she said. 'You can't make me.'

'The fire—'

'Must start tonight. I know the risks better than you do. I'm a Sibyl. Never forget that.'

'How could I? Your courage shames me.' Saulos took her elbow and guided her away from the gaggle of watching men. 'If you won't leave, then at least rest here, behind the curtains. This isn't a palace, or even the compound at Alexandria, but—'

'Please . . .' Hannah shook her head. 'Allow me what little pride I have. In any case, walking helps ease the pain.' She nodded back towards the door. 'Perhaps I might walk up the Aventine and see the city from above? If I'm going to be useful tonight, I could identify the routes of the aqueducts nearest to here.'

'You would do that?' Saulos took her hand and bent to kiss it. When he rose, his smile was radiant. 'I have to visit the water engineer,' he said. 'I will escort you that far.'

Hannah lifted her satchel. 'I'll make sure I'm back before you talk to the men.'

'It'll be more than talk.' Saulos' eyes shone. 'Tonight, I will tell them God's truth one last time. They will eat of his flesh and drink of his blood, and go to the fire as living memories of their saviour.'

CHAPTER FORTY-FIVE

Two men followed Hannah through the hot, dry morning as she left the warehouse and walked up the hill towards the high, white wall of the goose-keeper's garden halfway up the Aventine.

A lumpen, gap-toothed merchant lounged against a wall opposite Juno's gardens, peering at her from under the hat's brim. Hannah knew him and he knew that she knew him. His presence made no sense, except in the context of a warning Pantera had offered in Gaul.

If you know of one person following you, then there's at least one more, probably two. The first is a decoy. If you're arrogant, you'll believe yourself clever to have seen him and not look for the others.

He had been talking to Math in the strange light of a fire-washed Gaulish meadow, with a dead man lying at peace beneath an oak tree. It had been the first of the promised tutorials, a small nugget, given out of mercy to a boy who was drowning in mourning.

At the time, Hannah had barely listened. Now, she tensed her abdomen and slumped against the wall in apparent pain, cursing just loudly enough to be heard.

The lumpen spy opposite spat into the dust and looked away, but not before he had locked eyes with a sour-looking boy inexpertly fingering bolts of coloured linens in the doorway of the cloth merchant a few doors down.

Two then, at least.

Hannah levered herself from the wall and, looking round, appeared to notice the weathered oak gate for the first time. Hesitantly, she smoothed down her tunic, ran her fingers through her hair and pushed the gate inward.

'Hello?' The shout was designed to be heard from the street outside, not inside. 'Do you have any water?'

The geese came to greet her, nuzzling her hand. She had no crusts to give them, but picked grass and let them tease it from her fingers.

The cottage stood at the very back of the garden, down the length of the wall. Thick-walled and ancient, it lay slumbering in the sun with its windows half shuttered against the sun and its only doorway curtained by a hanging hide. No windows from neighbouring buildings overlooked the garden either; it was not considered either wise or lucky to look down on the gods' geese.

Hannah was halfway there when she heard a woman's voice, raised in anger. '*No!*'

She began to run, and then stopped as a man spoke, calming, his voice so soft that it was lost in the stream's song.

The woman's answer came sharply again. 'How can you say that, you who gave up love for the sake of a man who escaped early into death?'

And so Hannah knew who it was, and that Hypatia must be truly shaken to use such knowledge as a weapon.

She moved neither forward nor back, but stood frozen, listening, as from the cottage Shimon said mildly, 'I wouldn't call crucifixion an escape, but you're right, I gave up love for the Galilean and would do so again. And I will die to preserve what is left of him if I must.'

'Hannah is all that's left of him,' Hypatia said.

'I know.'

A chill raised the hairs on Hannah's arms. After a long while, Shimon went on, 'You will die for her too, if you have to, when the time comes. Why else are we here?'

'What if I fail?' Hypatia sounded close to despair. 'My courage isn't like yours, able to give my life for a dream that may never be real.'

'Then do as much as you can. It's all that is asked of us. If I get you water, will you drink?'

There was a murmuring of quiet conversation. Water splashed into fine clay and a cup was set down.

Hannah backed along the path to the bleached oak gate through which she had entered. There she rattled the handle once, and then again louder until the geese hissed alarm and, at last, someone in the cottage pushed open the door.

Shimon came to greet her as she walked along the path. Before he could speak, she said, 'I'm here with menstrual pains, seeking help from the goose-keeper. Saulos doesn't trust me fully yet. Two of his men followed me up the hill. They're outside now, so I don't have much time. Is Pantera here?'

Shimon shook his head. Gently, he said, 'He's with Mergus, organizing a fire drill. But you should know Hypatia is here. You don't have to come in if you don't want to.'

His compassion, as much as anything, moved her to tears. 'I'll come,' Hannah said. 'The world is bigger than my grief.'

The cottage was mercifully cool after the noonday heat. Hannah stood in the single sparse room, looking out at the pond. Older goslings sported in the noisy water, racing each other to the island behind the weeping alder.

She said, 'I have to leave before the men outside start to ask what I'm doing here.'

Hypatia came forward from the shadows by the fire-

406

place. 'You can tell them that the keeper of Juno's geese gave you something for your condition,' she said. 'And you could take this, which would make it true.' She held a mug of foaming sherbet balanced on her hands. Shreds of marigold petals clung to the crease across her palm that marked her heart, her spirit, her life. It was as deep and long as Hannah remembered it.

Hannah is all that's left of Judas the Galilean. You will die to preserve her . . .

You will too.

Hypatia misread her hesitation. 'I wouldn't drug you.'

'I know.' Hannah took the mug and set it on the table. 'I've just spent a morning soliciting the company of the man who killed Ptolemy Asul. I feel filthy and murderous together. Would you . . . ?' She opened her arms. Hypatia stepped forward to meet her.

There was no passion in their embrace, but a world of kindness, and strength. Hypatia showed no sign of her earlier grief, and presently Hannah rested her forehead on her cool shoulder and let go the weight of the morning's deceptions.

Shimon stood at the window watching the goslings with his back turned to them. Hannah studied him over Hypatia's shoulder. Her mother had spoken often of this man who had been her father's lieutenant; how he was the most savage in a fight, and the most loyal to her father's cause. In Gaul he had seemed a threat, sent to drag Hannah into a life and a conflict she didn't want to be part of. Over the past six months, he had become a friend without her noticing.

'Thank you.' Hannah pressed a kiss to Hypatia's neck and stepped back. Hypatia offered her the sherbet again and she accepted. Her mouth ached at the memory of flavours. She said, 'When will Pantera come back?'

'I don't know,' Shimon said. 'He left after you did. He's still got Mergus' century of the Watch at his command.

407

He'll bring them when we have the location of Saulos and his ninety.'

'Two hundred,' Hannah said.

'Two—?' Shimon's mouth snapped shut. 'Where?'

'In the old wool warehouse that backs on to the river below the Palatine market. It's the central one of the line and Saulos has filled the ones on either side with traps. His men know at least sixteen ways out but anyone trying to get in would lose ten men for every one that got through. A frontal attack is almost impossible; the only entrance is down a narrow alley that won't take more than two men side by side and his door-guards are all ex-legionaries, so he—'

'He has legionaries in his group?' Hypatia gave a sour laugh. 'Are they believers?'

'They believe in the power of his gold,' Hannah said. 'What else they may believe will become clear tonight when he preaches. He's planning a Dionysian rite, with bread as flesh and wine as blood.'

'Cannibalism.' Shimon spat on the floor.

'But powerful. When he's finished, his men will believe themselves god-filled and immune to danger. It will be . . . interesting to watch.' As she spoke, Hannah backed towards the door until her hand lay on the latch. 'The warehouse could be destroyed by fire,' she said, thinking aloud. 'If it was done properly, with men ringing it, you might be able to trap Saulos and his two hundred, but the alleys are so narrow there the fire would surely spread.'

'It would be unfortunate if Rome were burned by those trying to save it,' said Hypatia.

Hannah nodded. Her fingers worked the latch, easing it up. The geese crooned from the meadow outside. 'There's an alternative that might work,' she said. 'But it needs someone on the inside. I'll go back now and do the best I can. If I haven't come out to you by sunset, then burn the warehouse and do what you can with the water towers to

408

stop the fire spreading. Make a firebreak first. Pantera will know what to do. Tell him this is for Math: the living matter more than the dead.'

Hannah stepped smartly back, pushed the door shut and dropped the oak stave across that barred it from the outside. It wasn't impossible to escape; Shimon was already climbing out of the window as she reached the gate in the wall, but it stopped either him or Hypatia from asking what she was going to do, or trying to stop her when she gave the answer.

CHAPTER FORTY-SIX

'Math?'

It was the middle of the afternoon and Math was asleep, as his physician directed. He had been ordered not to wake until dusk.

He eased his eyes open a fraction and closed them against the sun's brilliance. It definitely wasn't dusk, but Constantin tapped his collar bone in their private signal that meant it was safe to rise. 'Math, you must wake up.' He fumbled, lost in a sea of white silk.

If his health had been predicated on the luxury around him, Math would have been immortal by now. The bed was crafted from cedar and ebony, the headboard carved to show hunting scenes in the Egyptian fashion, with flat-faced archers and gem-collared leopards coursing lean, long-necked deer.

Beyond its foot, the afternoon sun shone in from Nero's garden to glance brilliantly off a polished bronze war shield placed artfully on a pedestal for just that purpose. Nero liked his rooms to be brightly lit at all times of day and night; he hated darkness.

Math, by contrast, had found that since the accident in Alexandria he couldn't bear bright light. Always, when he woke in the afternoons, he kept his eyes half shut against the shield's glare. It helped ease the tenderness in his head, although it did nothing to stop his ribs hurting, particularly now, when Constantin was being unaccountably clumsy.

Always before the boy's touch had been deftly sensuous, but not today. Math caught his breath and hissed it out slowly as he came to sitting.

Having got him upright, Constantin stepped back, which was more unusual still. Belatedly remembering what Pantera had taught him, Math listened to his surroundings before he opened his eyes any further.

Clearly, he was still in his sleeping chamber in Caesar's palace: the gilded, marbled, perfumed bower set at the sea's edge thirty miles from Rome. Listening to the hush of an ebbing tide, the peep of wading birds and the gulls screaming over the fishing boats returning to the harbour, Math decided it was mid-afternoon, another departure from the normal, but there was more, if he could only find out what it was.

On the physician's orders, Constantin had bathed him in rosewater that morning and the faint scent covered the harsher, cleaner scent of the sea. But Math could also smell a tinge of oiled iron, garlic and leather. And behind the sea's song, he heard the faint chink of mail and the creak of boots.

'Math?'

Math jerked more upright. Ajax was there, in the palace, from which Nero's hatred had banished him, and wearing chain mail – except that couldn't happen. Nero wouldn't allow it.

'Math. Will you open your eyes now? Please.'

Ajax was being patient, which was a lot more frightening than when he was angry, in the way that falling off a horse was never quite as bad as the fear that came before it.

Math turned his head away from the shield's glare and opened his eyes a fraction more.

411

And then wide.

Ajax was in the middle of the room, naked, flanked on either side by two of the giant Germanic guards. Their knives jutted loosely under his chin, drawing paired straggles of blood, but it was his eyes that caught Math; in their pale amber light burned a rage that caught his breath.

'Ajax?' Math said softly.

'You need to dress. The emperor wishes to see you. Crystal will help.'

'Cryst—'

Math's head jerked round. And so he found that Constantin was not Constantin, but a younger, clumsier boy, who lacked Constantin's long hair and ready smile. Who was, in fact, quite clearly terrified.

But he had tapped Math's collar bone in a way only two people in the world had known.

'Where's Constantin?' Math asked.

The boy who was Constantin's replacement shook his head. He could have been his younger brother, but Constantin's eyes had been a source of constant joy and this boy's held only grief.

A single tear damped one black cheek. Wiping it away, Crystal thrust forward a bundle of clothing; a chiton in the Greek style, with keyed patterns at hem and neck, a copper belt inlaid with garnets and sapphires, subtle by Nero's standards.

The metal shimmered and chimed as the shaking boy held it out. Constantin was dead, or dying; better dead. Ajax was held prisoner. And the belt buckle was a gift from Nero.

Math had been in the palace long enough to know that showing terror was a strategic catastrophe. Besides, if Ajax could keep calm with two knives at his throat, then Math could do at least as well.

He forced a smile. 'Why are you called Crystal?' he asked.

412

Either Crystal didn't know palace intrigue well enough to smile back, or he was too scared. 'The lord named me for his favourite horse,' he said.

Nero's favourite horse was an ageing grey mare. Math decided not to point this out. 'It's a good name,' he offered. 'He must favour you.'

'He does,' said Ajax crisply. 'It's why he's sent him to wake you.'

Math's smile fell away. Crystal held out the chiton as if it burned his hands. 'You will dress? Please?'

'Of course. I'll—'

'Don't lift your arms too high,' Ajax said helpfully, and then, as if they were alone and free to gossip, 'Poros has gone into Rome to oversee arrangements for the race at the month's end. He sends you his regards and best wishes for your recovery. You should let Crystal fix the belt. Your shoulder isn't up to it yet although the physician says your mind is well now, which is good. We all rejoice.'

Math tried not to gape. Ajax had always been good at slipping in the vital information among a clutter of useless gossip. On this occasion, what mattered was that Poros had gone, because Poros' bluff good manners had been a restraint on Nero. Math shuddered, suddenly cold.

Crystal was lifting his arms, sliding the chiton over his head. Math was not Ajax, to go naked into battle. He took a shallow breath and pushed his hands ahead of himself and dived in through the tunic's mouth, wriggling out the other side with as little hurt to his ribs as he could manage.

As he emerged, Crystal's shaking hands held out the belt. 'My lord . . .'

Math had never been 'my lord' to Constantin. He was about to correct the boy when he caught sight of Ajax, who had bowed his head. Ajax never, ever bowed, except . . .

'Put on the belt,' said Nero's voice from behind him.

413

Crystal stepped back, forcing his hand into his mouth. Math's hair sprang stiff on his scalp.

'Lord . . .'

Nero stood in the open space between the sun-shield and the door, eyeing him as a butcher eyes a fattened goose. 'Our physician informs us that you are fit to engage in discourse. We have been watching you these past two days and we deduce you are well enough now to walk and to talk with us, even if you are perhaps not entirely well enough yet to race a chariot.'

'To race? My lord, I—'

'To race.' Nero nodded to the two Ubian guards who held Ajax. They grabbed his arms and rammed them high up behind his back. Ajax gave one explosive grunt and was silent.

Math sprang forward. Astonishingly, Crystal grabbed for him, but it was the look on Ajax's face that brought him up short.

'Ajax?'

Ajax shook his head. It was impossible to think of him as merely a driver now. That guise had been stripped away on the sands of the race track in Alexandria.

He was a warrior, and Nero knew it, who hated men of courage.

The strings of Ajax's shoulders showed as white glistening ropes under the tension from his hard-held arms. Sweat gathered in fat drops on his flanks. None of it showed on his face. 'Do as your emperor asks,' he said. 'Your life and mine depend upon it.'

'Your driver speaks the truth. Listen to what he says.'

Nero floated across the floor as if it were the stage of his private theatre. Long ago, someone had told him he looked good walking thus and had been believed.

An antique vase stood on another pedestal, behind the bronze sun-shield. It was half Math's height and as wide across as the girdle of his hips. The image painted in blue around its brick-red circumference was from the time of Athens' ascendancy and showed a thin, bearded man grasping a boy's chin in one hand, and his genitals in the other. Nero had never spoken of it directly to Math, but he had let it be known that he valued it highly, and that it was reckoned to be worth at least as much on the open market as Ajax's entire chariot team.

Now, the emperor lifted it on the palm of one hand. On the plinth it had been sturdy. Held aloft, it became fragile as the thinnest egg shell.

'Your driver's life is in my hand,' Nero said. 'It hangs on your good behaviour as much as does your own. If I so choose . . .' He tilted his hand. The Greek vase shattered on the marble floor.

In spite of himself, Math flinched. Crystal cried aloud and leapt back. Neither the Ubian guards nor Ajax so much as blinked.

Nero gave a tight smile. 'Will you behave for me, Math?'

415

CHAPTER FORTY-SEVEN

Grey smoke smeared the sky in a broad ribbon from the peaked roof of Augustus' forum in the east to the temple of the vestals on the Sacred Way that lay to the south of where Pantera stood.

Beside him, Mergus lifted a deer-bone whistle to his lips and shrilled a long, high blast. A chain of men in boiled leather armour lifted their tarred rope buckets so smoothly, so completely in unison, that it was as if a giant beast had rolled on its side, exposing a black band along one flank.

A shouted order followed, and another and another and another so close together that if Mergus had not told Pantera the sequence beforehand, he would have missed it.

Lift empty. Drop. Lift full. Pass.

Libo, Mergus' broad-shouldered aquarius, was one of the eight men surrounding the open-topped water tank. They were all equally huge. On the drop, each man filled his bucket. On the lift and the pass, their muscles stretched and grew as they raised them, full now, and sent them back down their lines. Not a single drop of water fell to blacken the dusted pavings around the cistern.

The chain of full buckets rippled and grew in a way that was opposite in every respect to the gaggle of old men and

416

boys in Gaul who had done their best to keep an inn from burning.

Here, the fire was a pile of old straw mattresses. Only lice died and most of those were drowned before they could burn, so fast and so complete was the deluge poured upon them. A larger fire, a hundred paces away, was put out as fast by a team working a horse-drawn fire engine with an eight-man pump that was worked in relays by three teams, so that there was time for each to recover before they had to step up again.

Pantera watched, mesmerized by the near-mechanical precision of the work. To his surprise, he found that he was still moved to see that men could be so trained, could entertain such pride in their work; that they could reach for perfection, and find it, and hold it, and not let the beauty of their own success bring them down. He thought of his father's endless drilling with the bow, and his heart ached as it had when he was a child in Judaea and wanted nothing more than to join the legions.

Mergus' whistle sounded three short blasts and one long. Before the last note died, the men stood down. An obstinate drizzle of smoke marred the high point of the sky but beneath it was unblemished blue, sharp as crystal, clear as a mountain stream.

A final blast blew, on a different note. As one, the line of men turned and bowed to their tribune, temporarily made prefect of the Watch, who stood on an ox-cart a little away from the action.

From his place a hundred paces away, Mergus murmured, 'That was as good as it gets. Calpurnius will hate it on principle, he always does.'

Pantera squinted into the sun. Gnaeus Calpurnius, tribune of the first cohort of the Watch, was an awkward, angular figure, with a high patrician brow and an unfortunate nervous tic that left him sneering even when he smiled. 'He doesn't look particularly—'

417

'This is insane!' A voice like a bullhorn cut over the hush of stacking buckets. 'Do you think Rome's made of water? Did you enquire of the engineers if they had sufficient to spare? What will you do if there's a real fire? Throw feathers at it?' A grey-haired bull of a man ran past Pantera and Mergus to the ox-cart and hurled his ire at Calpurnius.

Pantera watched with open curiosity. 'Don't they decimate men for insubordination in the Guard?' he asked.

'Not the officers,' Mergus said, 'only the men. And it's not been done yet. That's Quinctillius Varus, tribune of the second cohort. And beyond him, looking just as upset, is Annaeus of the sixth. I think we can safely say that neither of them wants his cohort to hold a drill.'

'Which is either immensely sensible, given the obvious paucity of water, or it's insane given the obvious likelihood of a fire. I think I should confess my role in this, don't you?'

Pantera strode forward past the line of watching men. At the ox-cart, he vaulted up to take the space alongside Calpurnius, gaining height over the two complaining tribunes.

'Allow me to introduce myself,' he said, untying the pouch at his belt. 'Sebastos Abdes Pantera, currently acting under order from his imperial majesty.'

The belt had been a parting gift from Nero. The new pouch thereon bore the imperial mark of the lyre and the chariot. Sight of that alone cut both men silent, but the seal he drew out of it caused them to salute, and then to bow.

Pantera took his time retying the pouch. The silence grew painful.

'I rode in from Antium this morning. The prefect' – he nodded to Calpurnius – 'will vouch for my bona fides. The emperor is rightly concerned with the risk of fire amongst

418

his subjects. I assured him that with his trust and bearing his goodwill' – he tapped the pouch with his forefinger – 'I could arrange a fire drill. Vigilance is everything, as I'm sure you know.'

That was the motto of the Watch and if they didn't hate him already, the two tribunes did so then. But he carried the imperial seal and they had each sworn fealty to it and its holder. They bowed their way back towards their waiting cohorts.

Gnaeus Calpurnius, who was far from a stupid man, waited until they were out of earshot. 'Did that tell you what you needed to know?' he asked mildly.

'A little.' Pantera blew out his cheeks. 'Of the six cohorts, the second and sixth are led by men who are either exceptionally thoughtful and have full care of Rome—'

'Or they wish to see it burn. And either way,' Calpurnius said, 'traitors or not, you'll die for what you just did if they find you alone.'

Pantera ran his fingers through his hair, teasing out the particles of soot. 'Then I will endeavour to ensure that they don't.'

CHAPTER FORTY-EIGHT

If Hannah had not spent years learning to navigate the Sibylline labyrinths, she would never have found her way back through the warren of narrow alleys and broken buildings that protected the entrance to Saulos' headquarters.

For a while, even with the map laid out in her mind, she thought she had got lost, and that she might have to abandon her plan in its infancy. She stopped then, on the corner of an alley, and stared up at the high, blue sky, letting the colour clear her mind so that she could be certain she was not, after all, acting rashly, or purely for vengeance.

Vengeance was there; a vision of Ptolemy Asul stained her mind whenever she saw Saulos now, and it cried for vengeance. So, too, did the more distant, hazier image of the father she had never known, who had given his life for his men, and had his death traduced for political gain.

But it wasn't only for them. Staring up into the limitless blue, Hannah knew that she was here because she had spent nearly a year with Pantera and Ajax, because their cause had become her cause, and she was as bound now to its success as they were.

A collared dove flew over, from north to south, heading

towards the river. She followed its path down the alley. At the foot, she found the ox-hide door with the mark of the tent-maker on its upper right hand corner and knew she was not, in fact, lost. She passed through it into the low-roofed goat-pen and then out again into the knife edge of sunlight that lit the final alley leading down to the warehouse.

At first glance, the only sign of life was a group of grubby urchins playing with a tan and white, floppy-eared hound whelp that ran back and forth across the narrow passageway. One of the girls looked up and grinned, showing blue eyes beneath matted black hair. Hannah flipped her a silver coin as she pushed between them and felt the shadow of their presence behind her; children were everywhere, invisible as slaves. The smell of the river reached her over the low warehouse roofs, and somewhere, not far away, men shouted as they loaded or unloaded a boat.

The guards were there, but well hidden. These were not the men who had seen her in Saulos' company in the morning. Like their predecessors, these were legionaries, but younger, fitter, better armed, with shields and short javelins in addition to their gladii. Their passwords had changed and she had no idea what the new ones were, but they had orders to let her past. She had each tell her the word, in case she had need of it later.

The last of them stood a dozen paces from the warehouse, not quite beyond reach of the stench of wet wool. A red ram's head marked the wool-merchant's door. More recently, some wag had scratched a wine jug on it and more recently still, another had drawn an image of Nero with his lyre. Strictly speaking, that was an offence against the person and god-head of the emperor, but here, where no emperor ever came, even incognito, there was little danger that the owner of the warehouse would be arrested, even if he could ever be tracked down.

421

The urchins' young hound gave song and dashed past in noisy pursuit of a rat, or a mouse, or a cockroach, or simply a thrown pebble; it was impossible to tell. In the ensuing commotion, Hannah repeated her final code word clearly, stepped past the guard and rapped out on the red ram's head the rhythm that gave her entrance into Saulos' headquarters.

Pantera reached the goose-keeper's in the late afternoon. Shimon met him at the door with a beaker of well water and the news he didn't want to hear.

'Hannah came when you were away. She went back to Saulos.'

Pantera felt his heart clench. 'You let her go?'

'We had no way to stop her,' Hypatia said. She came out of the shadows at the back of the cottage, where the herbs were kept. The light touch of her scent lit the air before Pantera saw her. 'She said the warehouse is close to impregnable, that Saulos has two hundred men and can send them out through the maze of the ghetto so fast you'd need two legions to stop him and even then only if you surrounded the whole of the dockside. You're to burn the warehouse if she hasn't come out by dusk.'

'With Hannah inside?' Pantera stared from Shimon to Hypatia and back again.

'That was the implication.' Hypatia's black gaze raked across his face. 'She said to tell you she was doing it for Math.'

'Of course she did.' When, momentarily, Pantera closed his eyes, he saw Hannah standing in a burning inn, with Math tumbling down a ladder, begging for help for his father. He opened them again; Hypatia's pitiless gaze was preferable. 'Did she say what she was going to do before we set fire to everything around her?' he asked.

'No. But it isn't hard to guess. She is the Galilean's

daughter. Who else can undermine Saulos' credibility in front of his people?'

'If she denounces him as a liar, he'll kill her.'

Hypatia nodded. 'Unless you can stop him. I thought you had a century of men?'

'They won't be enough. We won't get so much as a handful in without alerting them well in advance.' Pantera dragged his hand through his hair. 'When did she leave?'

'An hour ago.' Shimon had gathered his olivewood staff from the room's furthest corner. 'But I followed her down the hill, behind Saulos' two spies. There were children playing at the entrance to the alley. One of the girls had followed Hannah and heard the passwords. She sold them to me. I can get you and me past the sentries, at least as far as the door. After that—'

'After that, we're two men against two hundred, but if we can get Hannah out, the narrow alleys will work in our favour. I'll see if I can set Mergus' men outside.' Pantera turned to Hypatia. 'Will she do this? Will she name Saulos a liar in front of his own sworn men?

Hypatia nodded. Her black eyes were wide and full of helpless rage. 'She'll do whatever it takes to stop Saulos, even if it means she's going to die trying.'

Hannah stepped into the warehouse as a gladiator steps on to the sands: outwardly calm and inwardly taut as a bow string. As the door swung shut on its new hinges, she was assaulted by the heat, sweat and thunderous noise of two hundred hungry men devouring their evening meal. The smells of cooked garlic, fish sauce, stewed beans and honey rose over the rank, sodden wool.

Poros was near the doors with half a dozen members of his Blue team. They waved to her with enthusiasm, who had barely exchanged two words with her when she was on the opposing team in Alexandria. She waved back, and exchanged welcomes with other men she had met in the morning.

The warehouse was transformed. When she had last seen it, the place had been darkly damp, and disorganized. Now, it was like a temple at Passover; full to capacity, but buzzing with order. Racks of wall candles pushed back the dark, scenting the sweaty air with beeswax, while the horizontal slats high up in the wooden walls let in the evening sun.

Dust motes sparked in the angled beams and men were sliced across their lengths by the light, seeming to dance in jerking steps as they moved among the military camp beds laid out in ordered rows across the floor, carrying bowls of stew to stand in huddles or sit on their blankets and eat.

Saulos himself was hammering the last nails into the dais that had been their treatment room. The curtain was gone now, and a lectern had been set up at the front, ready for an oration. Saulos reached for a new nail as she approached.

'Hannah!' He swung round to embrace her. 'How are you?' He held her at arm's length, searching her face.

'Better. I went into a cottage on the Aventine for water and the woman there gave me herbs for the pains.' She told half the truth, and no lies, exactly as he had done in Hades. She found she could still hold his gaze cleanly, which was a relief.

'Then you feel less . . .' His hands filled in the words he couldn't find.

'Much less, thank you.'

'Good. Come and see what we've got.' He took her arm and ushered her across the floor to the far corner.

The crowds parted again to let him through. They were in his fiefdom now, among his chosen comrades, the foot soldiers ready to give their lives in the coming fight.

He knew them all by name. Here and there, he stopped

424

to ask after a man's wife, or his children, to enquire whether he had brought his son with him, or his brother, his nephew, uncle or distant cousin, whether some chore had been carried out, whether the auspices were good.

In all cases, the answer was *yes*; brothers, fathers, uncles, cousins and sons were here, or were on their way, and they had done everything he had asked of them. They waited now only to finish eating and to be given their final orders. As far as Hannah could tell, they would have been content without the meal; if Saulos hadn't ordered them to eat, they would willingly have left on empty bellies.

They reached a wall, and so the end of the men. In the quiet, Saulos drew Hannah closer. 'Did you see the line of the aqueduct when you were up the hill?'

'I saw it and the Aqua Marcia, where it comes to an end on the Capitoline. If you want to prevent water from reaching the centre of Rome, you'll have to destroy them both.'

'Excellent!' He beamed at her. 'I'll order Poros to take his men up there at the start. In the meantime, perhaps if you could help carry the candlesticks to the dais?'

The candlesticks were silver, taken from some temple. Each was taller than Saulos, taller even than Hannah, made from solid silver, with many-branching arms that held aloft more candles than she could count.

They carried them to the dais and set them up on either side of the lectern. The candles weren't lit yet, and the warehouse was already as hot as the noonday. Hannah said, 'If you're going to light those, I should open the back door for a while. The men need clean air to breathe or the sour humours will stifle their courage before the evening's work.'

'Of course.' Saulos waved a hand towards the door even as more men clamoured around him with questions. Poros ploughed a way through the crowd carrying wine jugs on a tray across both arms. Two broad-shouldered youths of the Blue team followed bearing another piled high with loaves of flat bread. Wine and bread. Hannah thought of Shimon, spitting, and wondered what he would do if he were here.

The area by the back door was quiet, away from the crush of men. Cobwebs draped the wall and door in one vast, dusty curtain, thick as silk. Fighting her way through, Hannah found the hinges were of old leather, gone hard with disuse, and that the iron catch was rusted shut, but not locked.

It gave way after some effort and she braced her shoulder against the jamb to force it open, letting in a rush of light and humid air from the river.

A shallow courtyard lay beyond, full of debris, surrounded by an oak palisade with gates that hung awry on torn hinges. Nobody was guarding this entrance. Hannah pushed through the broken gates and stepped out of the courtyard to the jetty beyond and found, as she had thought, that there was a direct route along the riverside, joining up all the warehouses and leading out eventually to one of Rome's main arteries.

'Hannah?'

She spun back towards the warehouse. Saulos stood in the doorway. His tunic was a clean one, belted with bleached linen cord, and his hair had been combed, but it was not the clothes that made her stare; they were the least of the changes in him. In all ways, from the set of his shoulders to the planes on his face, Saulos was as different from the stuttering fool she had met in Gaul as Pantera was from Nero. Here was a man who could kill Ptolemy Asul and revel in it.

He is without mercy, Pantera said in the ear of her mind. *Please don't underestimate him.*

She thought of her father, and of Math, and looked

up to the clear sky. The river ran close, and a path to freedom.

'Hannah?' Saulos came forward and took her hand. 'Will you come and help me give out the bread and wine? As we do so, I would ask you to think of the saviour whose death will free us all.'

CHAPTER FORTY-NINE

In fulfilment of his promise to Pantera, Seneca reached Antium with the last of the sunlight on the night Sirius rose over Rome. Tethering his horse away from the road, he crawled in through a forest of thorn bushes until he lay in the dark behind the guardhouse with his head pressed to the earth, watching for an opportunity to act.

Ahead, Nero's palace complex stretched out for a hundred paces on either side, a vast sprawl of torchlit marble, lying just beneath the horizon. To Seneca's left, at the southernmost end of the houses and slave rooms, was the open-ended horse barn that housed the emperor's chariot teams and in which, if he had understood Pantera correctly, Ajax was being held captive.

Guards marched back and forth at both ends. The pair nearest the palace were not soldiers, but the two eldest sons of a particular senator, whose father had paid for the privilege of their being allowed to pace back and forth in the dark. They were bored, and easily distracted. Three pebbles tossed towards the far end of the latrines sent them running down with their swords drawn, each trying not to outpace the other.

Ignoring the stiffness in his hips and a knifing pain in his left knee, Seneca slipped inside the stable block, and slid along the starlit aisle between the stalls. He dodged the snapping teeth of the brassy colt halfway down, and around the time the senator's sons returned, grumbling, to their posts he reached the last stall on the left, where the oak doors had been reinforced with iron bars set from floor to ceiling. The bolt was padlocked securely in place.

He knew that lock. He knew where its key was kept. He could no more get to it than he could reach for the moon.

He heard a movement inside the stall. A finger scraped on the wall, drawing his attention to a knothole in the wood. He put his mouth to it.

'It's Seneca,' he whispered, 'sent by Pantera to free you so we can both free Math. I can't get to the key. I'll need to find some other way to pick the lock.'

'Tiberius.'

Pantera stood in the alley leading to Saulos' warehouse and spoke the code word in a hoarse whisper. A legionary guard eyed him with suspicion. 'Throw back your hood.'

He did so, tilting his head in the way men do to appease their superiors. At his side, Shimon did the same, although his evident arthritis and stooped back meant the guard did not have a clear look at his face.

On the street behind, three children played noisily with a young hound. Pantera told them to leave. They ignored him. He turned and made shooing motions with his hands. They laughed and the girl stuck her tongue out.

The guard was old enough to have children and grand-children of his own. Shaking his head, he waved the two men on.

'Caligula.'

The second guard was half the age of the first. He, too, watched the children. The girl lifted her tunic and exposed herself. She was too young to be a whore and, in any case, the man had orders not to leave his post. He sent Pantera and Shimon on down the alley.

'Claudius.'

The third guard was near the door, listening to a voice echoing from inside the warehouse. He waved them past and on, and in.

A moth fluttered in through the high vents, sailing on the last of the sun.

Hannah watched it briefly, but her attention was on Saulos, who had poured the wine for the front row of men and was back on the dais, preparing to preach. He was vibrating with a passion that filled the warehouse, so that it was impossible to look anywhere other than at this man standing between the tall, brilliant candle-sticks.

For a while, the evening's quiet was punctuated by the soft percussion of clay on beaten earth as the last of the newly filled beakers was set down on the floor. Then silence enveloped the crowd. Two hundred and thirteen men sat rapt. Their waiting was a palpable thing. If Hannah had not opened the back door, the pressure would have been unbearable.

'Thank you.' Saulos' voice sailed high overhead. 'You have come here so that, tonight, we can fulfil the new covenant that began with the death of a man thirty years ago. We will speak of that presently, but first I want to remind you of everything we have overcome to reach this place.'

Hannah expected tales of Saulos' battles with the Sicarioi. What she heard was a litany of names and acts of personal courage that meant nothing to her, but every-thing to the men who were named.

He had been trained well, asking questions to which his men knew the answers at least in part, but giving them always more than they had before so that amongst the growing nods and murmurs of agreement was always surprise, and indignation, and, soon, a tide of righteous anger that rose to meet Saulos' own passion as they cheered each rhetorical flourish.

He was not the best Hannah had heard – the priests of Isis and Serapis did the same thing better – but it was more than enough to rouse the warehouse and Hannah felt herself carried high on a wave of urgent, impatient need.

The moth slid down the sun. Unnoticed, it danced in the candlelight behind Saulos' head. Two hundred and thirteen men stood spellbound, and did not see it.

'. . . and so, as we go out to make manifest the prophecy of ancient times, as we strive to bring closer the Kingdom of Heaven, I say that the least of you will ascend to the highest place, that each tongue of flame that you light is a blessing, a kiss from our god even as *this* is his kiss to us now . . .'

Breaking off, Saulos cast his arm out, staff-straight, over the crowd and the moth's giant shadow fell forward, kissing the back of his outstretched hand, his arm, and his brow.

Hannah didn't know if he had seen the moth before he moved, or had guessed it was there, or somehow had control of it or was simply monumentally lucky; anything seemed possible. What was clear was that every one of the men in the room believed they had just witnessed a sign of divine favour.

They began to kneel. First was Poros, who stood directly in front of the dais, and then another, younger man, and another; and then row upon row, in a susurration of rumpled linen, they were all on their knees, bending forward to touch their brows to the ground.

Saulos prayed over them, in a voice that rose to the rafters and beyond. His fervour lit his face. His voice was a risen flute, played for his god, played *by* his god, bewitching his men.

He raised his arms to the heavens. His voice sang back and forth across the crowd, naming men and their families, speaking to them personally. Somewhere in the centre, a youth barely in his first beard fainted.

Hannah alone remained standing, at her place in the doorway, between the candlelight and the greying dusk of the courtyard. A small flame of outrage blossomed and grew as Saulos spoke of her father, taking his name in vain. She fanned it until her anger at least matched her fear.

Out of nowhere, she remembered Math's face in the dark of a Gaulish night as he spoke of *his* father, and the sooty taste of his forehead as she kissed it, flavoured with smoke and boyish sweat.

'Math.' She spoke the name aloud, a final gathering point for her courage.

Nobody heard her. Outside, a cicada chirruped. Inside, the moth bumped against the back wall, lightly. Saulos widened his spread arms, gathering the crowd into his embrace. '. . . in drinking the wine which is his blood and eating the bread which is his flesh, we thereby remember the anointed one, our saviour, who gave himself for our sins, who died on the cross and was resurrected on the third day—'

'No, he didn't.'

Her words fell as a hammer's blow across the crowd. Saulos froze in mid-sentence, his arm beckoning to the sky.

Hannah stepped half a pace sideways, so that the remaining light from the courtyard might cast her shadow across him.

'He didn't,' she said succinctly, 'and he didn't and he wasn't.'

CHAPTER FIFTY

The warehouse door shut behind Pantera, letting him into the dark. Saulos' voice filled his ears, echoing. Hannah was at the back, standing in shadow by the door. Ten rows of kneeling men separated him from her.

Saulos was speaking to his god. Shimon tugged his sleeve. Harshly, he whispered, '*Kneel!*'

Pantera knelt. More slowly, making the most of a supposed arthritis, Shimon did the same. The men around them were bowing. Pantera followed their lead and, with Shimon, pressed his head to the beaten earth, noses full of dust and old wool and stale urine.

Like that, kneeling in candlelit darkness, trying not to sneeze, Pantera heard Saulos invoke a dead man's name, and heard Hannah's voice cut past him like a sliver of glass.

'No, he didn't.'

The man to Pantera's right jerked as if hit, and lifted his head.

'He didn't, and he didn't and he wasn't.'

The words fell each apart, shocking and hard as hail from a summer's sky.

Nobody moved, not even Saulos.

Pantera reached for Shimon, who turned towards him, haggard in the poor light. His hands flashed a brief and unmistakable message. It wasn't a good plan, but it was all they had. Pantera counted to three and pushed himself upright.

Saulos turned to Hannah with dream-like slowness, his eyes full of hurt. Speechless, he waited for her to speak again, while his men shuffled restlessly in their kneeling lines.

Hannah didn't step up on to the dais; the grey-gold evening light from the back door was still her ally. She didn't shout, either; the Sibyls had taught her how to be heard in a crowd. Lightly, distinctly, she cast her voice beyond Saulos to the front wall, where the door-keeper still knelt and the last few men had just drifted in.

'The Galilean, whom you have claimed as your saviour, did not die for your sins; he would never have chosen to do such a thing, nor was it ever asked of him. Who would knowingly serve a god who requires the death in agony of one man for the supposed sins of many?'

Whispers flew in the dim light. She went on, a little louder.

'He didn't die on the day of his execution at all; he was taken down at the procurator's orders after only six hours. You've all seen crucifixions. No man dies that quickly unless he is already dying or his legs have been broken. Neither of these was the case. He lived. He was taken to a nearby tomb. Later that night, his friends removed him under cover of darkness.'

'That isn't—' Saulos began.

She glared him to silence. 'Your "saviour" was *not* resurrected on the third day as Saulos teaches, because he wasn't dead. He lived for another forty days, cared for by Mariamne, his wife, in the caves at Masada until his blood turned sour and he couldn't be saved. He died peacefully

434

then, surrounded by those who loved him and had fought for him. He died for what he believed in, which was that Rome and all things Roman should be driven from Judaea for ever. He died for his men, not for a god who revels in torture. He—'

'Hannah.' Saulos' eyes burned into her, lacking all soul. His voice was smooth as honey. 'This is completely untrue. The Lord God has spoken to me. I have been our saviour's apostle for nearly twenty years, preaching his word. I have known—'

'You know nothing. What colour was your messiah's hair?'

'I—'

'What colour were his eyes?'

'How could—'

'Where was he born? Who were his parents? What were the names of his brothers and sisters? When was he married? What were the names of his children? Answer me any one of these!'

'Why?' Frustration cracked Saulos' voice. 'Why do they matter?'

'Because you don't know the answers! Not one. You know *nothing* about this man you claim to revere. Not a single thing about his life except his death, which you have twisted for your own ends!'

Hannah had to raise her voice now; two hundred and thirteen men were all speaking at once. 'If you don't know how he lived, how can you possibly know why he died? You never met him. You never spoke to him. And you are *not* his apostle. You despise and are despised by the men who fought at his side; Shimon the zealot, Yacov his brother, his grandsons, his nephews, all those who shared his life. He was dead before you had ever heard of him. You've built a temple on your own fantasy, and gulled these men into believing you. Tonight, they will give their lives for your lies.'

'Hannah, he was dead before you were born. You have no better way of knowing how he lived than—'

'*He was my father.*'

Silence fell, hard as an axe. Saulos' mouth snapped shut.

'I was born five months after his death,' Hannah said. 'His eyes were the same colour as my eyes. His hair was my hair. I know this because my mother told me. My mother, who was his wife. She bore him two sons before me, either of whom would have killed you on sight for what you have done to our father's name.'

'Is it true?' a voice shouted from the crowd, muffled by cloth, but distinct. 'Is it true that our lord did not die for us?'

'Of course it's not true.' Saulos shouted louder, as if volume made the truth. 'This woman wasn't born when he died for our sins. His resurrection—'

'He did *not* die for your sins!' Hannah's voice cut across his. 'He was *not* resurrected. He was carried living from his tomb and died in Masada.'

She had no intention of getting into a shouting match, but the Sibyls had taught her the power of simple repetition. She watched the words course through the crowd, snagging more men with their meaning each time.

Saulos saw it as well. The effort it took to rein in his anger was both remarkable and clear.

'Hannah.' He was the soul of reason. 'In this assembly, you have no credibility. It's my word against yours. Unless you have some proof, can bring forward someone who shares your view—' He spread his hands, in invitation. As if on his signal, Poros and the Blue team began to shout a single word.

'Lies! Lies! Lies!'

Just as when they had knelt, the men took their cue from these at the front. Others took up the chant and others, until it thundered to the roof.

'*Lies! Lies! Lies!*'

Saulos raised a brow. Under the growing chaos, so that only Hannah could hear, he said, 'You've lost. Retract it all and I'll let you live.'

Hannah shook her head. 'A shouting rabble doesn't make truth into lies or lies into truth. You *know* I'm right.'

'But without support, you have no way of—'

'She is not lying! I will testify to the truth!' A single voice, pitched high above the mob, cut over it.

It was the man who had called out before. He was scything through the crowd towards her, shoving his comrades to left and right, clearing a path to the front, where, in a move as ostentatiously dramatic as anything Saulos had done all evening, he sprang on to the podium and threw back the hood of his cloak, revealing a shock of old-snow hair and the beaked shelf of a nose.

The chant faltered. The man raised his arms as Saulos had done. 'I am Shimon of Galilee, zealot and follower of the man you call your saviour. You know me, and know I am given only to the truth.'

He didn't control his pitch as Saulos and Hannah had done, but there was a powerful honesty in his words. 'Many of you have met me on my travels. The rest of you have heard of me. You know that I served the Galilean, and fought with him against the tyranny of Rome. So you know I speak the truth when I testify that Hannah of Alexandria is his daughter and that he did not die on the day he was crucified.'

His voice felled them with its power. Each man looked to his neighbour for courage, for direction. Shimon spoke into a new silence, raw with indecision. 'Know now that Saulos, whom you follow, is the Apostate. He was excommunicated from the Assembly for his lies. He has spent years spreading lies against the man I served and I swear to you now in the name of the god of Abraham that what he says is untrue. If you know me at all, you know

I would suffer any death before I would defame an oath made in the name of our god.'

His hot old eyes roamed the crowd. His arm struck out, pointing to the fourth row. 'Mattathias, you know me. Have I ever lied?'

Mattathias had no choice. He shook his head mutely, his eyes flaring with alarm. Others around him were picked out with the same forensic accuracy.

'Abraham? Philotus? David? Antonius? Manasseh? You all know who I am and that I speak the truth?' Man after man nodded as his name was called out.

Hannah saw a movement in the front row. She reached up to the dais. 'Shimon! Watch Poros—'

'Don't listen to this man! He lies! You know he lies!' Saulos screamed, drowning out her warning. The crowd buzzed like a kicked hive at his words. 'He has no proof! God himself has spoken his truth to me. Can you doubt his word over a mere man of flesh and blood? Nobody here can give credence to these lies, to this—'

'I can. I was twelve years old when two men and a woman carried a living man from a tomb in the garden above Jerusalem. My father was a guard there. I lay hidden in the gardens and saw it. I swear now that Shimon of Galilee, zealot in the service of Yaweh, speaks the truth.'

Pantera!

Hannah heard a choking noise from the dais and spun round in time to see Saulos' face pass from grey terror to scarlet fury, even as he raised the arm with the knife.

'Pantera! He's got a—'

And then Poros was there with a knife in each hand and vengeance wrought across his face. 'Murderers! Traitors! These are the men who tried to kill me!'

Saulos leapt off the dais. Hannah jumped back—

And was slammed against the wall as Pantera and Shimon each hurled himself between her and the danger.

Crushed in the hot sweat of their dual embrace, Hannah

couldn't speak or hear or think. But she saw the blistering half-moment when Pantera's eyes met Shimon's and something utterly private passed between them, beyond words, or fear, or bravado. A thing that only men who lived on the edge of death might know.

Each of them looked across at Saulos, at Poros, at the candlesticks and back again. Each nodded to the other. And then turned in, shoulder to shoulder, with her behind them and Saulos, Poros and a mob bent on murder in front.

CHAPTER FIFTY-ONE

Fire blossomed in the warehouse, the colour of mari-golds. In the moment's held breath before violence broke out, Pantera had toppled the nearest candlestick, sending fire across the floor. Shimon had hurled a broken bale of old, tired wool after it. A curtain of flame kept the mob back for a heartbeat, two, three . . .

'Poros!' Hannah saw him through the sudden bright-ness, blades like living flames in either hand. She remem-bered the courtyard, and the debris near the door.

She backed out. A rusted iron bar as thick as her wrist rested against the wall. In more prosperous times, it had been needed to bar the door. She grabbed it with both hands and prised it free of the mess around it.

Inside, Pantera had thrown at least one of his knives. A man lay dead across the band of fire, damping it down; one of the Blue team. Poros was at his side, screaming obscenities, trying to push through the gap in the flames.

Shimon stood in front of him swinging his oak staff in a complex arc, with such a look of wild glee on his face that Poros recoiled a step and then another. Shimon followed him up, shouting past him in Aramaic, naming men and listing Saulos' crimes.

In those first moments, Hannah couldn't see if he was

having any impact; in the crowd, men were flinging water on the spreading fire, raising clouds of white smoke that snaked sideways and up, filling the warehouse from floor to rafters, obscuring the shouting, fighting mob.

Because now they were fighting amongst themselves; there was a battle going on in the body of the warehouse that kept more men from assaulting the small group at the front. They were three against Poros and the Blue team with Saulos somewhere in the smoke, invisible and dangerous. Pantera was nearby, but Hannah couldn't see him, only heard him to her left, shouting in the mayhem.

Poros had found a sword and was swinging it, matching Shimon's staff in a delicate, lethal dance. With her iron bar held near its end, Hannah slid in through the door and sideways with her back to the wall. The fire scorched her face. Smoke choked her. She fought against panic, against memories of Gaul. Poros loomed ahead, made bigger by the warping shadows. The iron bar spun in her sweat-wet hands as, ducking under Shimon's cudgel, she put the full force of her back, her shoulders, her legs, into a swing aimed at his head.

She missed.

Poros saw her and ducked under the swing. Hannah was thrown off balance, spun further round and crashed into the dais. The iron bar flew from her hands, skittering across the oak boards. The second candlestick toppled over, spraying beeswax and fire into the dark space to her right.

'*Hannah! Move!*'

She rolled sideways, out, down, away from the fire and the dais, into a flickering dark. A knife hissed past and stuck in the wall, shuddering. Shimon stepped over her, protectively, cudgel blurred in the bad light. Smoke crowned him. He was dancing with Poros, who was better armed. Pantera was there, fighting to Shimon's left, protecting his shoulder as warriors did in battle. He had fought in Britain, where men died for the honour of saving each other. It was his voice that had shouted her name through the mayhem.

The knife sagged from the dry wood in the wall above her. Hannah grabbed the hilt and wrenched it out and this time she didn't stand up where she could be seen, but kept to her belly beneath the wavering ceiling of smoke and crept forward along the edge of the dais until she could see Poros' blunt, bearded silhouette.

Shimon was opposite him. Seeing her, he dropped his guard a fraction. Poros lunged forward, his blade a slice of vengeance, cutting straight for Shimon's heart.

There was no time to think, to regret, to imagine the ending of a man's life. Hannah thought of Math, made to race when he wasn't ready. With his broken face in her mind's eye, she thrust herself upwards, aiming for the broad back, midway down, just off centre to the left.

Her stolen knife grated on a rib, glancing out and up in another miss. Already Poros was turning away from it, wrenching round. His face loomed over hers, his teeth a slash of white in his beard. But the knife still had purchase.

Math loomed between them, bright blood clotting in his hair.

'*No!*' Hannah brought her other hand up and rammed her balled fist on top of the first and felt the blade slide forward with sickening ease into the sheath of flesh and lung and heart.

The end flipped like a landed fish, once, twice, with the steady beat of his heart, and then, even as he roared a name she did not know, the rhythm stuttered and sprang, wildly erratic.

Hannah still had hold of the handle, wet now with his blood. She dragged the tip sideways, to make the hole in his heart bigger, to let the blood out faster, to bring death with greater mercy; her only gift.

The twitching stopped and, moments later, Poros fell like a tree, stunning the ground at her feet. Over the smoke and sweat and fear, she smelled the sharp iron-sweetness of blood, and then urine. She had never killed before except in mercy: Ptolemy Asul, and, once, a child born with its legs fused together. Nobody had ever known. The parents had burned myrrh at the statue of Serapis in thanks that their child was born dead. And now—

'Hannah!' A hand caught her wrist. 'Back! Now!' It was Pantera, a shape in the smoke. His face was shining with heat and sweat. 'The fire's gone wild. The roof's coming down. It's the inn at Gaul all over again. Shimon's already in the courtyard. Will you come out? Come out with us now? Please?'

The courtyard was empty of men. To the right of the door stood a barrel, half full of spring rain. Hannah grabbed it, rolling it on its edge. 'The door . . . block . . . the door.' She was coughing now that they were in the clear air, as if her lungs preferred the smoke.

Pantera grabbed the barrel's rim. Together they swung it across the door, holding it shut. Men hammered on it from the inside. The damaged hinge was breaking.

'Come on,' Shimon called from the courtyard gate. 'That won't hold them for long.'

'Where's Saulos?' she asked, running.

Pantera was at her side, barely lame. They passed out of the courtyard together. 'Escaped through the front door. A dozen with him.'

Hannah said, 'He'll go for the water towers. He's the only one who knows how to turn the taps off. We have to—'

'I set Mergus there. Twenty men are guarding each of the five closest towers. It's the fire that matters. Where will they start the blaze?'

443

'Everywhere. They have wool and pitch set at a dozen places nearby. Five men would be enough.'

'Then a dozen will be a disaster.'

'Maybe Mergus' men will stop them?'

'If they're not betrayed by others of the Watch.' Pantera ran on her left. To her right, the Tiber ran slick and slow under the evening sun. 'Mergus was at the tower by the Claudian temple. We should reach him as soon as we can.'

'It's another quarter-mile up the hill,' Hannah said. 'Can you run that far?' This last to Shimon, who was bent double with his hands on his knees, choking in the aftermath of the smoke.

'Anywhere you can lead, I can run.' His eyes streamed with smoke-born tears, but behind that they were ablaze with a fire of their own. 'Just let us stop Saulos and I will ream out my lungs and spit blood for the rest of my life.'

The first rush of water met them at a crossroads below Claudius' temple; a shining snake, slithering down the street, gathering dust and children and thirsty dogs.

Three men of the Watch came fast after it; an officer and two others skidding down on wet pavings. Pantera waved them to a stop. All three bled from new-made wounds. The officer was small, dark, wiry.

'Mergus!' Pantera gripped his arms. 'The second or the sixth?'

'The second. A century came at us. We were outnumbered four to one. We chose not to die protecting a cistern.'

'Good. Is Libo alive?'

'He should be. I left him in charge of the water engines at the forum.'

Hannah asked, 'Did you see Saulos?'

'How would I know him?'

'You wouldn't,' Pantera said shortly. 'That's his strength.

444

And you won't—' He stopped suddenly, looking west. 'Damn,' he said softly. 'It's begun.'

Hannah turned to look. A thread of black smoke angled straight as a drawn line from the foot of the hippodrome.

'The wind's heading inland from the river. It'll spread faster than Ajax's mad colts.' Pantera bent to catch water from the flood about his ankles and dashed it over his hair and the shoulders of his tunic. 'This may be Saulos' fire, but if a portion of the Watch is supporting it, the Urban Guard may follow. Mergus – you know what to do?'

'We do. We'll meet in the forum still?'

Pantera eyed him, shaking his head. 'I have to find Saulos. When that's done, I'll come to the forum. But first . . .' He spun in a circle. 'We need Nero. The emperor's presence still counts for more than gold or promises. For that, we need someone with a horse who can ride thirty miles in the dark and be believed when he gets to Antium.'

'Faustinos,' Mergus said. 'The water engineer. He's Iberian. They're born on horseback. He lives here somewhere. I don't know exactly.'

'I do.' Hannah grabbed Pantera's arm. He shot her a look of surprised appreciation. 'He's two streets from here,' she said. 'Saulos went there after I dressed his wound this morning.' She was already running. 'Come *on*.'

CHAPTER FIFTY-TWO

Soot fell in great, fat flakes, like soft snow. Already – *already* – the stench of burning flesh pierced the smoke and the screaming panic of men, women, children, mules, pigs, dogs, rats sliced the air.

It was Gaul again, only greater.

Hannah wiped the grime from her face and considered how it would feel to strangle Faustinos, the Iberian water engineer, with her bare hands.

He had been unbearably slow to rouse from his dinner couch. In that first bubble of time, in the agony of explanation, while Pantera selected and saddled a horse from his stable, while Mergus and Shimon together impressed on him the truth of the catastrophe, while Faustinos finally saw the water flooding past his open door and grasped the fact that his trust had been betrayed and that only the emperor could save his beloved aqueducts, while he was physically lifted into the saddle by Pantera and made to repeat his mission and finally, tardily, departed . . . in that time, the lazy thread of smoke stitching the evening sky had been joined by a dozen others and others and each had broadened to a feather, to a flag, to a tidal wave of flame, sent roaring east towards the heart of the city by the rising wind.

An early tide of refugees flooded with them. The children came first; the street urchins who were always fastest, not sure if it was serious, running backwards, shouting jests and wagers, throwing trophies to each other and to the adults, slaves and beasts who came after them.

They ran over the uneven pavings in front of Faustinos' meagre house, past the officer and two men of the Watch, past Hannah, Shimon and Pantera.

The fire hadn't reached here yet; the breached settling tank was keeping the flames and heat at bay. But the smoke came where the fire could not. Hannah swept her arm across her face, pressing the coarse wool of her tunic to her nose and mouth, and even so she could barely breathe. For a moment, she was in Gaul again, standing beneath a ladder, waiting for a man and his son to come down to her.

Pantera's hand was on her shoulder, as it had been then. He turned her away from the fire. 'Were you thinking of Math or Caradoc?' he asked. 'Or both?' He was bright again, filling her mind, for all that the soot lay in the lines about his eyes, in savage paint.

'Both.' Hannah dropped her tunic from her face. 'We've done all we can here. We need to find Math and Ajax and get out. There are boats running on every tide from Antium. We could be halfway to Gaul by this time tomorrow.'

'You should go. There are horses here. Shimon will take you.'

'Not you?'

He shook his head. 'I can't leave while Saulos lives. I made him what he is. No one else can stop him now.'

Hannah shook her head. 'If you're staying, I'm staying,' she said.

Pantera's smile fell away. Briefly, she thought he might argue, but he looked past her to Shimon. The two men's eyes met as they had done in the warehouse, their silent dialogue too complex for the time it took, too profound for the quiet on their faces.

Pantera broke away first. 'Shimon will help you get to the coast,' he said. 'I will see to Saulos. Seneca's gone to Antium. If humanly possible, he'll free Ajax and Math and buy passage for them on a ship. He'll get you to Britain if I can't join you.'

'You weren't listening. I said—'

'I was listening. Hannah, the city is *burning*! There's nowhere safe.'

'Yes there is. The goose-keeper's cottage has survived every fire for the past four centuries. Is Hypatia still there?'

'She was when we left.'

'Then I'll go there. Shimon can go to the coast to meet Ajax and Math.'

'They have Seneca, they have no need of me.' Shimon's old-snow hair was full of soot, turning him young again. When he shook his head, black flakes flew around them. 'Where you go, I go. I owe it to your father. No—' He held up a hand, forestalling Pantera. 'We have as much right to stay as you do. We'll wait at the goose-keeper's house until dawn. Send us word when you can. If we hear nothing, we will assume you dead. In which case, I give you my word that I will protect Hannah with my life.'

Pantera's face was unreadable. The sky behind him was the perfect, crystalline blue of night-fall; the smoke had not reached there yet. His cheeks were burnished orange from the fire. His hair, lit from above, glowed gold as a Gaul's.

Hannah saw him nod to himself; then, amid the smoke and the mayhem, he lifted her hand. She felt the grit on his palm, and the hard rhythm of his pulse and the slip of saddle oil from Faustinos' harness.

He took Shimon's hand too, joining them in a triangle. 'I'll hunt Saulos and when I find him I'll kill him.

Tomorrow morning we'll leave here, whether the fire is out or not. Nero can find himself another spy.' Pantera kissed the back of Hannah's hand and let it fall. Shimon's, he gripped a moment longer. 'Take care of each other.'

Chapter Fifty-Three

Tiers of beeswax candles blazed on both sides of Nero's bed, sweetening the night air. Two polished silver mirrors on either wall took the dancing lights and multiplied them back and forth until Math's eyes hurt.

He was trying not to frown, which was harder than he might have expected, but gave him something to concentrate on that wasn't the part-naked Nero, lying breadthways across the wine-red silk with his head by Math's knee and his feet dangling over the far edge of the bed.

After a day's intimate attendance, the slaves had finally been banished. Left alone, Nero was smiling up at the Bacchus painted on the ceiling, fingering his favourite lyre. He played better than he sang.

A flagon of Falernian lay empty by the bed and Math had drunk none of it. Nero had not been fully sober since early afternoon and now he was cheerfully and comprehensively drunk.

If you ever let the emperor become familiar, if you ever come to see him intimately, in all the contortions and stupidity of a man consumed by his desires, then you will have to die.

Pantera had said that in Gaul, and Math had believed it.

Now, he hoped the spy was wrong and had some basis for his optimism. If rumour was even half correct, the Empress Poppaea had seen Nero in the 'contortions of desires' long before they were married, and she wasn't dead yet, and some of the slave-boys might also have survived a night in this room, on this silk-ridden bed, caught between the silvered mirrors and the honey-scented candles. Math thought hard about who might have been here before him, in order not to think of Constantin. Or Ajax.

Behind the darkness of his closed lids, Math saw Ajax, stripped of his skin, and Constantin, battered to death, and a baker, lying out in the sun with—

He stopped. He was a street whore. He knew exactly how important it was to seem whole, clean, healthy, humble and, above all, cheerful, in the company of a client; the more powerful the client, the more important it was to be serene.

With an effort, he set Ajax behind a bulwark in his mind and worked on keeping it solid and impregnable. Ajax had said that both their lives depended on his behaviour, and while intimacy with the emperor might yet mean certain death, Math wanted to believe that if he did all that was required of him, Ajax might be allowed to live afterwards.

The emperor stopped playing and rolled on his side. He raised his gaze to meet Math's. 'What would you like?'

'Lord?'

'We wish to play music for you. What would cheer your heart?'

A month living in the palace had taught Math more of courtly ways than the whole six months in Alexandria. Smoothly, he said, 'My knowledge of music is too narrow to make a considered choice, lord. Perhaps something that Rhemaxos played in Alexandria? That was a good time.'

'A good choice.' Nero smiled, remembering. 'He played the Air of Perseus while we were in the baths, as we remember. It's difficult, and more suited to the kithara, but we shall assay it now.'

The emperor's fingers were thick and stubby, set about with a profusion of rings in silver, jet, copper, gold and coral. Softened by the candlelight, they became a blur of glistening colour, dancing across the strings. Wine had lubricated them just enough to enable him, in fact, to play quite well.

Perseus slew the Gorgon in a crash of candle-shaking chords. In the quiet afterwards, Nero said, 'You will disrobe.'

'Yes, lord.'

Nero was still playing when Math finished; even allowing for his hurt shoulder, it hadn't taken long. Not knowing what else to do, he slid under the wine-red silk. There was a trick to this that he had learned a long time ago, which was to concentrate only on the room, so that whoever else was in it might seem distant and small.

Perversely, the brightness of the light here made it easier. And even after nearly a month in the palace, he had never experienced silk of quite this quality before.

Pinching a thick loop, he let it slip through his fingers. Abruptly, he thought of Hannah's hair and so of Hannah and so, unforgivably, of Ajax. Tears pricked the corners of his eyes. He dared not wipe them away; the mirrors showed everything and Nero's eyes rested on him, twice reflected.

The music sank to its thoughtful end.

'Do you wish to be a father?' Nero asked, in the silence that followed.

'Lord? I'm too young to marry.'

'But when you're older, would you want that? Would you wish to sire a child?'

They were stepping round a question nobody had ever asked Math before. In panic, he reached for an answer that might suffice. 'Alexander, the great god-king of

452

Macedon, fathered a child on Roxanne although he loved Hephaistion. It was his duty, so he did it.'

The emperor thumbed his lyre. Three notes sprayed across the gulf between them. His foot, by chance, came to rest on Math's calf.

'Who amongst the Gauls,' he asked, 'relayed to you the tales of Alexander?'

'My father did, lord.' Math's hands were sweating. Black marks smeared the silk where he had gripped it. Somewhere distant, he heard, or felt, the beginnings of a vibration that was the earth, shaking. He wanted to believe it was the earth, and not Ajax held somewhere under torture, shaking the foundations of the palace in his torment.

Thinking of his father, who was safely dead, he said, 'He told me Gaulish tales too, but he said we were becoming Roman and so I should know the heart of Rome. Every Roman of worth strives to model himself on Alexander.'

'He said that?'

'He did, lord.' Inspired, Math remembered something Pantera had told him on the night of the fire. 'He was proud of me. It's good for a man to have a child to come after, to bear his name. I am proud to be my father's son. Who else has the same pride, and carries the same love as a father for his son, and the son for his father?'

Math surprised himself. Evidently, he surprised Nero, too. After a moment's pause the emperor set his lyre against the wall, then rolled over on the bed until his head came level with Math's hip.

His breath was warm and smelled of wine. His drink-fuddled eyes were damp.

'Your father was a wise man. We could wish . . .' With a flick of his tongue, Nero licked away a tear that had dribbled to the corner of his mouth. 'To have a father's pride, and to feel it in return, that would be something remarkable. I would have liked to have met your father.'

Another line crossed. When Nero ceased to be 'we' and 'us' and became 'I' and 'me', there was no turning back.

Math unglued his tongue from the roof of his mouth as Nero reached out and gripped his ankle. It was not an accidental move; Ajax had done the same in the mornings, to wake Math up. Nero lifted his gaze. His eyes were more focused now, and they asked a question.

Answering it, Math said, 'My father is dead, but his place is taken by Ajax now, who is as a brother to me.'

'A brother?'

'Or perhaps a second father.'

Most emphatically not a lover, not a rival, not worthy of imperial envy or jealousy. Math made all of these things clear in his voice.

Satisfied, Nero's gaze came away from Math's face and drifted downwards. His hand followed more slowly where his eyes led.

Math made himself breathe. The bed shook in a steady rhythm. He did not think he was shivering, but he was no longer sure. With his eyes on the brilliant, much-reflected candles, he prayed to the spirit of his dead father for fortitude and courage and the ability to forget come morning.

Distantly, as through a fog, he heard Nero, suddenly peevish, say, 'Can you hear a galloping horse?'

CHAPTER FIFTY-FOUR

Seneca stood in the dark and felt through his feet the stamp of the guards marching back and forth at both ends of the barn. The two senator's sons were not remotely in step, but they were making enough noise to cover the slight sounds he made in trying to find a means to pick the lock that kept Ajax imprisoned.

A fingertip search of the empty stall in which he stood offered nothing. Across the aisle was the tack area in which, searching by starlight, he found the racing chariot, the training chariot and two complete sets of harness. With a little more effort, he found six beautifully crafted, leaf-light racing bits hanging together from a hook on a slender hoop of wire, high up on the wall.

In the traditional way, the hoop on which they hung was made from a single strand of wire bent into an eye at one end and a hook at the other; when the hook snagged the eye, it made a circle. And when straightened it could, with any luck at all, make a lock pick.

Seneca was a man for whom luck was made, not given. With slow care, he slid the hook from the eye and the six racing bits from their wire. One by one, he laid them on soft hay where the rattle of sweet-iron would not alert the guards. With them gone, he turned his attention to the wire.

An age later, he stood in the aisle outside Ajax's prison holding his new lock pick in one hand. He ran his dry tongue around his drier teeth, found a knot hole in the wood and put his mouth to it. 'It's me. I think I can open the lock.'

There was a moment's surprised pause, then Ajax whispered, 'I'll piss in the bucket. The sound will give you cover.'

Seneca's instincts were not those of a thief as were Math's, or even Pantera's, but the lock was flashily big, made to withstand crowbars and axes, not to hold off a wire. Shortly after Ajax began noisily to spray his urine into the bucket Nero's guards had provided, the padlock sprang open.

If he had expected thanks, Seneca was disappointed. Lean as the wind, Ajax slid past him, patting his shoulder lightly as he crossed the aisle to the tack room.

The man was feral, and preternaturally silent, and Seneca, who had trained the best assassins in the Roman empire, watched him as a circus-owner watches an exotic beast. He had met chariot-drivers aplenty. None of them had inspired in him the hope and fear that this man did.

He was halfway to an idea when Ajax returned, carrying a set of reins from the harness on the wall. The thin, pliable leather smelled lightly of oil.

'What are you going to do?' Seneca whispered.

'Kill the guards.' Ajax's amber eyes flashed in the starlight. 'We can't get Math out with them there. You were planning to get Math?'

'Of course. Pantera sent me to—'

Ajax's iron grip caught his wrist. It took a long, long moment before Seneca heard what Ajax had heard.

When he did, he said, 'That's a horse, coming fast.'

Ajax frowned. 'Nero doesn't like interruptions at night,' he said. 'Everybody knows that.'

'Then Rome is burning. Nobody would come that fast for anything else.' Seneca tugged his still-held wrist. 'We must leave. We can come back for Math later.'

'What will he do?' Ajax asked.

'Nero? That depends on whom he's with and whom he's trying to impress.'

'Nero is with Math.'

'Ah.' Seneca blew out his cheeks. He wished he didn't feel so old. 'If they are already . . . occupied, nobody will dare to disturb him. If he is not yet engaged, and is halfway to sober, he will want to prove himself the great warrior, saviour of his people.'

'Will he go back to Rome? Or organize relief from here?'

'He hasn't the power to do it from here. He'll have to go to Rome.'

'Can he ride well enough to get there in a hurry in the dark?'

'No. He'll take the chariot. Tonight, perhaps even the racing chariot.'

Ajax laughed, a soft huff of derision that barely moved the night air. 'Who'll he take as driver?'

'You. Except you're in prison and he's not likely to decide to let you out. So—'

'*Math.*' Ajax smacked his balled fist into his palm with a force that was no less frustrated for being silent. 'He'll have Math drive him with all four colts, it'll be his greatest love-gift.' He turned on his heel. 'I need to be back in the prison. They'll notice if I'm gone and rip the place apart looking for us. Lock me in again and then hide somewhere safe if you value your life. Quickly. The guards have noticed that someone's coming.'

*   *   *

'You will drive for us. You wished to race for your emperor, and you will do so, not against other drivers, who might slow their horses and lose for fear of our displeasure, but against fire, which is driven by the gods.'

Nero, fully dressed, and sober, stood in the aisle of the horse barn. Two dozen pitch-pine torches flared and spat, chasing the shadows. Grooms sprinted to do his bidding. The race chariot stood at the end of the barn, ready to drive. The two senator's sons held Sweat and Thunder. Nexos, thick with sleep and fear, had been woken to harness Brass and Bronze and was doing so, badly.

Math stood to one side, kept out of the way by men who treated him with undisguised contempt.

'You should take the practice rig,' a clear voice said from the far end of the barn. 'The racing one will disintegrate on the roads long before you get to Rome.'

That was true, but nobody had dared say so aloud. They didn't say so now, but kept their heads down and worked on with the horses.

Nero turned slowly.

'Who speaks?' His voice was uncommonly low.

'I do, lord. Ajax of Athens.'

They had locked Ajax in a stable with no food and no water. Nero had told Math so. He had three days' life, at most, before he died of thirst. For a man under sentence of lingering death, he sounded inhumanly composed.

Nero stalked down the aisle to the last box. Two of the vast Germanic guards followed, each bearing a torch in one hand and his naked sword in the other. Nero lifted a chain from about his neck and used the key thereon to unlock the padlock that held Ajax's stable-prison closed.

'Come out.'

'I am at your service—'

'Down!'

Before he could move, the larger of the two guards

458

slammed the hilt of his sword against the driver's head. Ajax dropped to his knees like a poleaxed ox. Math kept his eyes on the horses and dug his nails into his palms against the stinging in his eyes.

'You are alive at my whim. For this insolence, you will die.'

'We all die, lord. But if the emperor dies before he reaches Rome, the empire will lose its father. A racing chariot is not built to survive thirty miles on metalled roads. It will break before the halfway mark.'

'*Math!*'

'Lord.' Math sprinted down the length of the barn.

'Will the racing chariot break apart on the roads?'

'Yes, lord.'

'You didn't tell me.'

'Forgive me, lord.' Math knelt as far from Ajax as he could. It mattered now to divert everyone's attention to the chariots. 'I was thinking only of speed. It would be safest for my lord if he used the practice vehicle.'

'But slower?'

'It matters not how fast you travel, lord, if you die before you reach the gates of Rome.'

'Of course. Such wisdom from a child.' Nero looked at the taller of the two guards. If he nodded, Math didn't see it, but the effect was immediate.

Faster than Math had seen any trackside team, the racing chariot was wheeled away and the practice rig made ready. Bronze and Brass backed into the traces ahead of Sweat and Thunder as if it were any normal day. There was no warfare, no screaming, only a bloodless, terrifying efficiency.

Somewhere along the way, Ajax was returned to his cell. The guards beat him first, efficiently and nastily and silently. Nobody paid them any attention.

Nero demanded the drivers' resin and was given it. He smeared some on his own hands and, with no ceremony whatsoever, handed the pot to Math. The torches lit them both. Nero was sweating, exactly as he had been in the bedroom. His pupils were just as dilated.

'We ride, then,' he said casually. 'Rome awaits us. You, Math of the Osismi, will race for me against the fire, and you will win.'

For Seneca, picking the lock on the stable door the second time was faster than the first, if no less quiet. Two of the guards were at their station at the head of the barn, marching back and forth as they had been. The senator's sons had gone from the other end, taking horses to follow the emperor's racing chariot. Their absence made little difference to the danger.

The lock sprang open in his hand. He slid into the stall, easing the door shut behind him. Ajax was lying in the straw, breathing harshly. With Seneca's help, he eased himself to sitting. The shadows were kind to him, hiding his face.

'Are you fit to ride?' Seneca whispered. He impressed himself with his own calmness. He was filthy, his tunic was torn, grain husks scoured his skin and his hair, he was sure, was in utter disarray. His consolation was that, even in the half-dark of the stall, Ajax looked far worse; clotted blood made dark streaks around the point on his left temple where the guard had clubbed him and a spreading bruise flared scarlet across his ribs where he had been kicked.

'I'm fit enough,' he said, and stood up.

'In that case, you'll need this.' Seneca handed Ajax the loop of harness the driver had previously chosen as his means of assassination.

'What's that for?'

'To kill the guards, as you planned before.'

Ajax took a long breath of barely held impatience. 'We can't. The whole palace is awake. If we kill them now,

460

someone will notice and follow us. If we leave them, they won't notice I've gone before morning.'

'But they'll hear us as soon as we bring the first horse out of its stall.'

'Exactly. So we'll have to walk.'

'To Rome? Are you insane? You're barely fit to—' Seneca lunged forward as Ajax's legs gave way, and caught him before he hit the ground. The noise of that alone would have brought the guards at a run.

'Are you all right?'

'No. Yes . . . Give me a moment.'

They wrestled together, ineffectively, until Ajax found his feet again. Standing, he swayed back until his shoulders met the wall. A band of light filtering through the bars that made the stall a prison flared across his face, illuminating, at last, the clear signs of pain.

Seneca made to touch the bruise and took his hand away.

'Your ribs,' he asked. 'Are they broken?'

'No.' Ajax pulled a face. 'We were discussing how to leave in a way that wouldn't alert the guards. We can't take a horse, so we'll do it on foot. If we walk nine paces then run nine, then walk nine then run again, we can do it.'

'That's impossible,' Seneca said.

Improbably, Ajax grinned. 'You'll only think it is for the first ten miles. The last ten are the easiest. The ten in the middle you will hate. But you will want to tell the world of your prowess when you finish. Are you coming? Soonest started is soonest finished and—'

Seneca laid his hand on Ajax's shoulder. 'I have a better idea. My horse is less than a mile away. Near enough to reach and far enough away not to be heard by the guards. I suggest we share it, one on foot, one riding, changing every mile. If you want to run for your mile, you're more than welcome. I'll walk for mine.'

*　　*　　*

Later, as they passed the eighth milestone, with Ajax jogging and Seneca riding, the philosopher, looking down, observed thoughtfully, 'Your hair is growing back and neither of us has a razor with which to shave it. What are you going to do when the world finds you are as gold-fair as a Gaulish warrior, and not possessed of the night-black locks that herald a true son of Greece?'

He got no answer; he had not expected one. A dozen miles later, when he had thought some more, he said, 'What is Math going to do when he finds you share his colouring?'

Ajax said nothing this time, either, but that was as much of an answer as his previous silence had been. Reaching the twenty-second waymark on the route to Rome, Seneca found himself smiling.

CHAPTER FIFTY-FIVE

I'll hunt Saulos and when I find him I'll kill him.
Pantera had meant what he said, and still did. But how do you find one man in a city of thousands? How do you find him when that city is on fire, with the wind driving the blaze ever inland, ever higher, ever hotter?

He turned a slow circle with his eyes half shut, blurring his vision, working to remember each time he had seen Saulos, from the mewling, stammering idiot who had been introduced by Nero in Gaul to the wild-haired, wilder-eyed orator on the podium in the warehouse and all the minor meetings in between. He weighed what little Seneca had told him, and all that he knew of the training the old spymaster had given to the men who worked for him.

And last, because all he knew was too little to be of use, he stopped thinking and let his instinct roam free; the sense, far beyond the other five, tingled at the back of his neck and pulled him northwards, to the Forum Romanum that was the heart of the city.

He opened his eyes. A half-dressed merchant ran past, smoke plaiting his hair. Pantera caught his elbow and wrenched him aside from the herd. 'Go to the forum,' he shouted. 'To the forum! The fire won't reach there.'

The man struggled free. He wore no shoes nor tunic,

only his bath robe, badly wrapped. Deaf to good advice, he cast one frantic look behind and hurled himself back into the flood tide of fleeing humanity.

Pantera took a step back and was surprised to find that Mergus had not yet left.

'I've sent the men to find the prefect,' Mergus said, lifting one shoulder, as if that had been the plan all along. His face was deeply lined, far more than his age allowed. When he smiled, as he did now, it creased his features, obliquely. 'I thought you might want help hunting your mad arsonist.'

It was tempting. And impossible. 'Mergus, no.' Pantera gripped the smaller man's arm. 'Calpurnius will need you to organize the defence against the fire. And if he dies, you'll need to do everything you can to keep yourself and your men safe from the tribune of the second. He's Saulos' man, without a doubt. He'll kill you if he gets the chance. Go now. I'll meet you in the forum when I'm done.'

Mergus eyed him flatly. 'This is too personal to accept help?'

That was too close to the truth. Pantera said, 'One man alone can become part of the crowd. Two together can't, particularly when one of them is a centurion of the Watch. I can do this better on my own.'

'I'll wager Saulos is waiting for you to do just that.' Mergus gave the salute the legions had used in Britain. 'Good luck. Against that one, you'll need it.'

The first cohort of the Watch had control of the Forum Romanum, centre of Rome's law, of its commerce, of its worship.

All down the side of the Via Sacra, past the full and ancient length of the Temple of the Vestals, men replicated the human bucket-chain they had practised at Pantera's command. In the dark now, with the panicked crowds already growing thick, the rope and tar buckets passed effortlessly from hand to swinging hand on a single note from the whistle. The bath-house sizzle of hot steam was competing with the stench of smoke and burning flesh. In places, the water chains were winning. In other places, clearly not.

Pantera spotted one of Mergus' men ahead in the crowd and, putting his hands to his mouth, shouted, 'The Basilica Julia needs a pump machine!'

The man spun, pointing. 'Behind you!'

Pantera leapt out of the way just in time.

'Make way! Make way!'

The crowd ripped apart to let through a team of blinkered, smoke-shy horses dragging a water cart. It cannoned past Pantera and slid to a halt by the Basilica Julia, where flames twenty feet high were lashing at the stone.

Vast, half naked, with his helmet jammed on his head as an afterthought, Libo rode at the head of the engine. He saw Pantera and waved a greeting even as he directed his men towards a water tank set at ground level.

Another stream of commands saw a siphon from the back of his cart lowered into the tank and four uniformed watchmen set themselves to pumping the handles. Two further men held the nozzle. Water drizzled from the mouth like the poor end of a piss.

Astonishingly – insanely – a crowd gathered to watch, growing larger with every stroke of the pump. Having tried to push through them and failed, Pantera turned back, shouting, 'Hose the crowd!'

Libo had jumped down and was working with the men at the water tank, too far away to hear. The two watchmen holding the hose stared at him and did nothing. A lifetime's training had taught them to take orders from their aquarius, not from a lame man with a crooked right shoulder wearing a torn and filthy tunic who lacked even the most basic symbols of rank.

Pantera drew a fresh breath. 'Hose the crowd, damn

you! Make them wet. Save them from the fire. It'll take two strokes of the pump. Then you can go back to keeping Caesar's basilica and all the forums safe. *Do it!* Nero will know of it if you let the people burn for want of a little water.'

The emperor's name worked magic. The two men turned the hose on to the crowd just as the full power of the pump engine began to bite. A fountain's spit of water arced up, over and down, wetly. Children screamed, but only briefly. Their parents had heard Pantera and understood what he was doing for them. Someone somewhere roused a cheer.

The crowd loosened and Pantera broke his way through. Reaching the far side, he called out, 'Move on! Get to the Field of Mars! Safety beckons at the Field of Mars!'

When he began to run, men and women from the crowd ran with him. Behind them, the watchmen at the pump machine turned their hoses on the basilica.

Pantera pushed on. He was soaked to the skin and glad to be so; too soon his tunic felt warm again and he smelled of steam more than smoke.

At the head of the Via Sacra, he stopped a moment and turned a circle, seeking Saulos, or signs of Saulos or thoughts of Saulos; anything that might bring them together.

A wash of flame lit the sky behind him, casting shadows forward, and there, to the east, he caught a clear sight of the gilded statue of Augustus, perched atop his own forum, which housed the Temple of Mars Ultor where all Rome's wars were begun.

To lose the seat of Mars was to lose Rome's soul. Even after the light died away and smoke shrouded the city anew, Pantera's instinct drew him there: the eleventh sense that thought now as Saulos thought, and hated as he hated; that sought, above all else, to rip the beating heart from Rome's corpse.

He had told Mergus that a single man could progress

faster and more secretly than two and it was true, but here he was without family, which set him apart from the rest. He ran on, skirting the bucket chains and the men who commanded them. Rounding a corner, he saw the Temple of Minerva directly in front of him and, sitting on the bottom step below the colonnades, a copper-haired boy of around ten years old, holding tight to a big tan-coloured hound bitch at his one side and a girl of no more than three years at his other.

'Are you lost?' Pantera crouched down, offering his hand to the hound to sniff. It whined and licked a graze on his wrist, where the skin had been scraped off in the warehouse fight. He addressed his question only to the boy. The girl had stuffed the back of her hand in her mouth and was staring at him with pebble-wide eyes.

'Father told me to find a safe place.' The boy had the crystal-pure voice of a singer. 'He said he'd find us after the fire.'

'You've done well, then, to find this place. Minerva always protects the young. But I think the Forum of Augustus might be safer. The Temple of Mars Ultor is there.'

'Thank you, but we are content to remain here.'

The boy turned his head away, signalling to anyone of good breeding that the conversation was closed. Lit by the coming fire, the side of his face shone wetly from the corner of his eye to his chin. His cheeks were thickly freckled and his hair shimmered in a particular shade of reddish blond that Pantera had most recently seen beneath an aquarius' helmet.

'Is your father Marcus Tullius Libo, aquarius to the first century, first cohort of the Watch, serving under Centurion Mergus?' he asked.

The boy's eyes flew wide.

'I just left him.' Pantera waved a hand back into the chaos. 'He's working hard to save the Basilica Julia. I'm

467

sure he'll succeed and then come to find you, but even so you'd be better waiting at the Forum Augusta. Minerva is good to children, but Mars Ultor and Venus support the soldiers and the sons of soldiers. I could escort you both, if you wish?'

'How do you know my father?' The boy gazed up at Pantera, wanting to believe.

'We met in Britain during the final battles there. Tonight, he was fighting the fire as bravely as any of the legions fought the Boudica's warriors.'

That was true, loosely, and every child knew of the bloody war in Britain. To mention it was to lay claim to valour beyond the shabbiness of the night.

The boy stood, smartly. To his sister, he said, 'We should go to the Forum of Augustus and wait for Father there.'

'Perhaps you would allow me to carry her?' Pantera put his hand on his own sternum, where his brand had been burned away. 'I swear in Mithras' name that I won't let her come to harm.'

The bull-god's name carried more magic even than the Boudica's. At last, the boy remembered his manners. 'Her name is Sulla,' he said. 'I am Sextus.'

'I am Sebastos Abdes Pantera, in service to the emperor.' Pantera crouched down. 'Sulla, if I lift you on to my shoulders, could you look ahead and tell me when we're coming to Augustus' forum? Look for the very tall marble colonnades with the gilded statue of the god Augustus on top of the triangular bit above the columns. He's pointing east to the rising sun, showing the dawn, which will be the fire's end.'

Thus, in perfect disguise, with a girl-child balanced on his better shoulder and a boy with a hound at his side, anonymous and unremarked as any father saving his family, he made his way through the chaos towards the long flight of steps that led up to the marbled majesty of Augustus' monument to himself.

There, he set Sulla down on the lowermost step. She gazed up at him with a wobbly smile. Once, in the naïveté of his youth, Pantera would have thought her docile and been grateful for it. Then he became a father and discovered the depths within the very young. Now, he knew that the girl was in shock, but that a thaw was on its way and promised to be spectacular when it arrived. He laid a hand on Sextus' shoulder.

'Here would be a good place to wait,' he said. 'Your father will see you easily when the fires have died down, and in the meantime there are many officers of the Watch around. When you see an officer who isn't too busy, go to him and give your names and make sure the prefect learns that you're here.'

'Where are you going?'

'Inside the forum. The Temple of Mars is in there. I would speak to the god, and perhaps find a man I have been looking for.'

The crowd thinned suddenly near the top of the steps and, without warning, Pantera stepped from relative shadow into a wall of light cast by a dozen pitch-pine torches. In Augustus' time, they had been set along the front of the forum to illuminate the gilded statue of the god-emperor that it might draw the eyes of all Rome to his memory throughout the hours of darkness.

In recent years, they had been left unlit except at the Saturnalia, but tonight an officer of the Watch had ordered them lit early on, that the crowds might find their way to the relative safety of the forum. Now, the fire outshone any torches, and nobody in the city looked up except Pantera, who gave one brief salute, for memory's sake, before he passed beneath the statue's feet into Augustus' forum.

He stood still, letting his eyes adjust to the dark and his ears to the tomb-like quiet. Here, the air was dry and light, peppered with incense and expensive tallow, almost free of the stench of roasted flesh that rolled over the men, women and children outside.

It was too dark to see all the way down the broad hallway but Pantera had visited the Temple of Mars in daylight a decade before. A building within a building, gilded and martial at once, it had left him with a greater respect for the gods of war and peace.

His instinct had led him there, and a pair of torches set either side of the doorway drew him on. There was no sign of Saulos, nothing to hear, nothing to see, but Pantera felt as if his skin had been flayed from his body, leaving every nerve screaming. If a mouse had moved within a thirty-foot radius, he would have known it.

Softly, he padded down one side of a long hallway, squeezing between the colonnades and the life-sized bronze statues of Rome's hallowed past. Here were Cincinnatus, Virgil, Cicero, Pompey, Caesar, Marc Antony. And in the very centre of the hallway, twice as large as life, a second bronze Augustus drove his four-horse chariot single-handed into eternity.

Pantera was squeezing past Claudius Centho, an early dictator of Rome, when he caught the scent of blood beneath the incense.

Fresh blood; in a place with no sign of life.

He turned towards it, easing the knife from the sheath on his left arm. In the stillness, fainter than his own heart-beat, he heard a drop splash on to marble.

The sound came from the centre of the hall, where Augustus' giant chariot raced into eternity, drawn by the horses of the sun.

There was no cover at all between the colonnades at the sides of the hall and its centre. Pantera dropped to a crouch and made his way across as silently as he might. On the way, he heard three more drops, each one slower than the last. The iron-sweet smell of spilled blood became stronger with each yard crossed.

The chariot's sculptor had modelled his horses for drama, not speed; all four stood on their hind legs, thrashing. Pantera ducked under the rearmost pair and lay in the clutter of their racing feet looking back down the hall to the stuttering torches that lit the Temple of Mars. They were smoky and unstable, but they sent light enough to burnish the bronze, and to cast in silhouette the clotted strings of blood that hung down from the back of the chariot. Here, the smell was loud and brash as a slaughterhouse.

Barely breathing, Pantera rose up and pressed his ear to the chariot's shell, moving backwards until he felt a heartbeat that was faster than his own, and heard a quiet, careful breath, slower than his own erratic respiration, punctuated once by a sniff, as of a man whose nose perpetually runs.

Drawing his second knife, he crept to the chariot's open back.

Gnaeus Calpurnius, lately made prefect of the Watch, lay curled like a sleeping child with his cut throat a dark gash against the burnished bronze. Behind him, nestled in the bowed front of the chariot, shielded by Augustus' knees, was a living man. Two eyes shone in the torchlight. White teeth glimmered in a grimace, or a smile.

'Saulos,' Pantera said aloud, and threw both of his knives.

Chapter Fifty-Six

Math was living his dream, and it was a nightmare.
A roaring dragon devoured Rome. Wings of flame scorched the sky. Its tail destroyed houses, men and horses alike, smashing them to bloody bone. And Math was racing towards it.

He was racing as badly as he had done in Alexandria, probably worse. All four colts were bolting, entirely out of control, just as they had done in the final trial, with the difference that the road was clear in front of him, Poros was not trying to squeeze him on the corners – and there was not the slightest chance that Ajax could come to help him.

His ribs ached; they hadn't stopped aching since he had woken in the palace with Crystal tapping his shoulder. His feet were bruised from bracing against the constant buck and dive of the chariot, and his tongue was sliced on both sides by his clattering teeth. Cut raw by the reins, his hands had long ago lost all feeling, and his ears hurt from the hammering hooves on the solid road, the slashing wind and, above both of these, the screaming encouragement of Nero, his emperor, who clung to the wicker at his side, goading him on like a madman.

They had a train of mounted men behind them, striving

472

to keep up, of whom Faustinos, the water engineer, was the only one within reach. He had been given the big grey gelding, favoured son of Crystal, that Math thought the best of Nero's riding horses. Driven by his need to get back to the city and repair his beloved cisterns, he hurled his mount at insane speeds after the chariot, shouting at Math to go faster.

The two Germanic guards and the detachment of dress cavalry detailed to guard Nero were hopelessly outdistanced. Inferior horsemen on inferior horses, they trailed a quarter of a mile behind with no chance of catching up, while Nero, who held their lives in his hand, rode with one hand on the wicker rail and one high in the air, brandishing a flaring torch, declaiming his love for the night, for himself and for Math.

Oblivious of danger, god-like in his euphoria, Nero had bellowed his promises to the city he was coming to save for the past thirty miles and continued unabated even as they reached the outer streets of Rome and felt the fire's first breath scorch their faces and the stench of burning people began to send the horses wild.

Math was exhausted. Simply to stand in a chariot for thirty miles tested the limits of his endurance, but once in the city the challenge of keeping the smoke-maddened horses in line, keeping them from running anyone down, keeping them on the main streets, turning corners as Nero directed, required feats of concentration he had never considered possible.

But he survived each threat and surprisingly soon they were careering down a broad, open street, with the marbled villas on either side glowing red as if cast from molten metal. The sight of them caused Nero to let go of the rail and lunge at Math, brandishing what looked at first sight like a cudgel.

The chariot slewed off balance. Fighting for control, Math heard Nero shout, 'Can you sound a horn?'

The thing blocking Math's view of the road wasn't a cudgel, but a bull's horn of quite fantastic length, chased with silver at tip and rim, carved with intricate sigils across its belly.

'Can you—' Nero shouted again.

'*Watch out!*' Math threw his whole weight on the reins. Bronze screamed. Math thought Thunder's foreleg buckled, but the colt took the weight of the turn and the chariot wrenched round, missing the family they had nearly run down. The man snatched his three children from the road. The woman sprang inelegantly into the gutter.

Nero fell sideways, hard. The chariot rocked and rolled as he clawed at Math and pulled himself upright. By a miracle, he had not dropped the horn.

'You will announce my entry.'

The side of Nero's face was bruised. Tears sparked in his eyes, and the first flickers of rage.

Math already had the reins tied to his waist. He worked his right hand free from the plaited leather rein and held it out.

Nero pressed the horn on to his palm. It was smooth as polished marble, but warm, with the silver worn by years of use.

'Can you sound it?'

'I've blown one like it.' Twice, in fact, most recently when his mother died. Then, his father had given him a horn far smaller than this one, with only a single band of silver at the mouthpiece, and had bade him play it. It was to help his mother find the gods, apparently. Math had not believed it, but had played for his father's sake.

He knew how because he had learned on the night his mother had last been well, when the tall, silver-haired man in the stained cloak had come from Britain and had given Math's father news of a death, or perhaps of many deaths.

Later, when he had gone, Math's father had blown the

474

horn. Math had got up and gone to him and so it was that, before dawn, he had learned how to sound the lament and had done so, finding solace in the way it wrapped them together.

Now, for the third time in his life, as he rounded a bend with fire on two sides and people scattering before his horses like hogs before hounds, he lifted the long, elegant horn and pressed the silver to his lips and blew the only notes he knew: his father's lament for the war-slain dead.

Bright, rippling horn music sang to the smoky stars. Falling back, it became by turns the sound of his father, weeping, and then a man's voice, singing.

By a small, but necessary, miracle, the four colts slowed and became controllable.

Math took the horn from his lips but the music did not stop. At its behest, the crowd thinned, and moved aside, as corn moves before the wind, so that Math's chariot passed through without bringing hurt to anybody.

A single man stood at the roadside, sounding his own horn. He was Ajax's height but Pantera's leaner build. He had Pantera's hair, grown long, but Ajax's mouth and the same slant to his nose. He had straight shoulders, which was entirely unlike either of them, and eyes that were black as the night sky seen in a millpond.

Math felt his gaze and turned his head and his eyes locked with a man who was neither Ajax nor Pantera, but an amalgam of both.

He wanted to call out, but his voice failed him. He had only the horn. He blew it again in a long, fine note and, as the sound fell away, the other music stopped.

CHAPTER FIFTY-SEVEN

Head down, legs pumping, Pantera sprinted up the marble hallway towards the door.

Saulos came after, fast, hard, unhurt. Pantera's knives had flown true, striking the place where his body should have been, but they bounced off a shield that had been covered by Calpurnius' cloak so that in the dark it had looked like a torso.

Instinct made Pantera jink sideways. A knife clattered on the floor where he had been. He grabbed and missed and it skittered forward out of reach; he had no weapons left and Saulos had them all.

He ran on. The door was still thirty paces away; too far. He cannoned sideways again, curling an arm round Virgil, pushing the bronze off its plinth to crash forward on the marble. Behind him, Saulos laughed and leapt over the debris. A second knife cut the air between them.

'You should have stayed in Britain.' Saulos' voice clattered among the colonnades, not far behind. 'You were safe there.'

'Safe? I was crucified.'

Saulos barked a laugh. 'Then at least you know what's coming. I'm not going to kill you. The tribune of the second can do that, as one of his first acts as prefect. I shall merely provide proof that you killed Calpurnius before I leave Rome.'

'Where are you going?'

'Jerusalem. You read the prophecy. That, too, must fall. Stop hiding, damn you!'

Saulos had discovered the curse of the statues: that every one cast the life-sized shadow of a man. Pantera stood behind Anthony, and then Pompey, and then Crassus. The closer he came to the door, the brighter became the light, the stronger the shadows.

'What about Hannah? Will you abandon your love so easily?' Pantera sent the words back to bounce on the statues far behind. 'Saulos? You've gone quiet. I thought you loved Hannah. Was I wrong?'

Talking covered the soft sounds of his movement as he undid his belt and wound one end round his hand. The pouch came free. Nero's ring was inside, nestled in the hank of wool that once more kept his coins silent.

From the hallway, Saulos' voice came brittle and cold. 'Hannah is no longer your concern. We shall find her before the night's out.'

'We?' Given more time, Pantera could have played Saulos as the emperor played his lute: badly, but well enough to hear the tune. He had no time. He hefted his pouch in one hand, testing the weight, letting Saulos' own voice cover the sound of his movements.

'The tribune of the second owns the Watch now.' Saulos was pleased with himself; his voice rang off bronze and marble. 'His men are already combing the city. They're outside with orders to arrest you on sight. If you go out on to the steps, you're a dead man. Surrender to me and we can come to an accommodation.'

Pantera laughed aloud. 'An accommodation like the one you offered Ptolemy Asul? Do I look like a man who seeks death by hot irons? Seneca said you had no sense of logic. Is that why the Pharisees refused to let you train with them? Because you let your guts rule your head?'

'They didn't—' Saulos spun and threw exactly at the place where Pantera's pouch had bumped softly against the base of Julius Caesar's statue. Even before his knife hit Caesar's bronze chest, Saulos launched himself after it, slicing his sword in a long oval that made the air sing.

Pantera rose behind him, his belt taut between his two hands, and looped it over Saulos' neck.

'*No!*' Saulos jabbed one elbow back with savage force. Pantera jerked away, his hands breaking free from the belt. He used his elbow and then his knee and felt both make satisfying contact.

Writhing, Saulos gouged for his eyes with one hand and with the other stabbed a knife up at his chest.

Pantera threw himself sideways, biting hard on the nearest sight of skin: a thumb. He tasted blood. Saulos screeched. Another man's shout echoed it, and the sound of running feet in the hall.

Pantera kicked and wrenched away, rolling across the marble. Saulos' blade hacked at his face, grazing his scalp. A trickle of blood joined the others on his cheek as he rolled free and ran for the wide gape of firelight that was the hall's door.

Two men ran at him with the fire at their backs: officers, wearing the double carnelian flash of the treacherous second cohort. They converged on him from either side, shouting orders to stop, to surrender, to lie down if he valued his life. Pantera ducked between them, so that, turning, they crashed into each other in a clamour of dented armour.

He reached the doorway and the flood of light, with the dazzling Augustus above. Behind, the officers and Saulos were running together in the last yards of the hallway.

'Murder!' Pantera hurtled down the stairs zig-zagging like a hare, leaping over sleeping children and their white-faced, silent parents. He heard Saulos call his name and put his hands to his mouth to shout again, 'Murderers! Treason! The prefect is—'

Saulos' arm slammed across his mouth, silencing him. His hand reached for Pantera's hair, dragging his head back, exposing his throat to the light, to his slashing blade.

Pantera fought back by instinct, as he had in his childhood in the stews of Jerusalem, in his youth in the ghettos of Alexandria, in his adulthood in the hell of a torture room in Britain. There wasn't a single dirty move he hadn't practised then or that he didn't use now, gouging, biting, kicking, striking. By sheer weight of sustained attack, he got his fingers on Saulos' knife hand, and twisted it in and round and down, aiming for the sweet spot to the left of his breastbone where—

'Stop!' Someone kicked his leg. It wasn't Saulos. Pantera pressed on. The same booted foot kicked him in the kidneys, harder.

He screamed. Pain crashed over him. Vomiting, he dropped the knife.

A hand drew his head back. The air sang to the sound of a blade.

'No! He must live! He knows where Hannah is.' The singing ceased. The pain did not.

Pantera opened one eye; the other was glued shut with his own blood. Saulos was kneeling on the steps less than a yard away, gasping as if he had run the length of Rome. His face was bleeding from a cut along his cheek. His eyes burned with a flat hate. The sword that had come so close to killing Pantera was held by the ox-broad tribune of the second cohort.

Pantera moved his gaze to meet the tribune's. He scrabbled for the cord at his neck, but couldn't reach it. 'I hold . . . emperor's seal. You owe . . . fealty.'

The tribune laughed. Saulos pushed himself up and

came to stand over Pantera, wiping blood from his nose with the back of his hand. 'He owes fealty to a higher power than a golden seal.' More loudly, for the benefit of the listening crowd, he said, 'You killed Calpurnius, the prefect. I will testify.'

The crowd knew Calpurnius. Their voices sighed in the night.

'Will you testify before the emperor?' asked the tribune.

'If I must.'

'You must. He's here now. No other man is permitted to blow the war horn in the city of Rome.'

Pantera closed his eyes. He heard the horn sound once, and then again. And he heard the sound of hoofbeats, individual as a signature, and knew that Math had brought Nero to Rome.

CHAPTER FIFTY-EIGHT

'There, in front of the steps. Beneath the statue of Augustus. Stop there!'

The horses were beyond exhaustion. Black with sweat and ash, their flanks heaving like fire bellows, their paces raggedly uncoordinated, they barely pulled the chariot forward.

Math spoke to them over the fire's roar, begging them to give him another step and another, but slowly, carefully, because the ground was slick with water and the press of people so great.

Like that, slowly, with care, he brought them broadside on to the wide stairway leading up to the blazing statue. Thunder tripped as he came to a halt. Math thought his tendons had burst.

'The horses . . . May I . . . ?'

'Do what you must. We will not forget what you have done for us this night.' Nero's face was radiant, even as he surveyed the wreckage of his city. He stood tall in the chariot, cradling the war horn to his chest like a victory spear. His voice carried out over the crowd with the benevolence and certainty of a father.

On the steps the people were standing, then kneeling. Someone set up a cheer, lost at first in the roar of the fire, but stronger as others took it up and others until the sound outdid the fire.

The six-man guard that had followed the chariot all the way from Antium chose that moment to arrive. Wrenching their horses side-on to the crowd, they dismounted in a flurry of hooves and threw themselves forward, forming a human chain between the emperor and his people.

Math knelt at Thunder's feet, running his hands down his legs. The rank smell of horse-sweat outdid the fire. The colt's hooves were red hot and his legs shuddered, finely, like leaves in an autumn storm, but the tendons were not bowed and Math could find no points of pain in either forelimb.

Some men passed him, dragging another. He ignored them and walked round to Sweat, who was in better shape and might race again, and then last to Brass and Bronze, who had done the best part of the work for the last two miles. The colts drew huge, shuddering gasps, each one slower than the last, each one a greater effort. Their heads drooped to touch the ground. Their ears hung flat.

'I'll get you water,' Math said. 'Just wait. Please wait. Don't die now.' There was water everywhere, and he had seen the bucket chains. Frantically, he looked round, searching for someone who might care about Nero's horses at a time when fire ate Rome on three sides, and Nero was dispensing judgement on a traitor.

Three officers of the Watch were stacking buckets not far away. Math waved to catch their attention and turned to forge a way through the crowd where it was thinnest, in front of the chariot—

And so nearly stepped on Pantera, who knelt at sword-point on the cobbles in front of him.

Math jumped back in panic, biting off a cry. Nobody looked at him; everyone was watching the emperor.

'Our city burns.' Nero was weeping – *weeping!* – shaking

with rage or grief or both. 'We engaged you to stop this fire.'

'Majesty.' Pantera bowed forward, pressing his brow to the pavings. Every visible part of him was bruised. His voice was a broken whisper. With an effort, he spoke more loudly. 'You engaged me also to protect the new prefect of the Watch, and he is slain. His body is in Augustus' chariot inside the forum. Someone should recover him and give him due honour.'

'Is that true?' Two officers stood behind Pantera. Nero's gaze raked them both. When neither of them answered immediately, the Germanic guards broke through the crowd, ran up the steps into the forum and came back again.

Pantera closed his eyes. Math thought he saw his lips move in prayer.

'Calpurnius is there, lord. His throat is cut.'

'Who did this? You—' Nero used the war-horn as a pointer, stabbing it at Pantera. 'Answer me. Who did this?'

Pantera raised his head. 'Saulos the Idumaean, lord. When Seneca trained him, he was known as Herodias. In Judaea they know him as the Apostate. I tried to kill him. As you can see, in this, too, I failed, although only within the last moments.'

'Where is he now?'

'He was with us on the steps beneath the father Augustus. He vowed to testify before your majesty as to the cause of Calpurnius' death. Anyone within earshot will attest to that.' Men in the crowd agreed, vocally, and then stopped, blanching, at Nero's bellow.

'*Where is he?*'

The horses flinched. The officer who had arrested Pantera stared at the ground and would not answer.

Levelly, Pantera said, 'I believe he chose to leave before your majesty arrived here.'

'You did not hold him prisoner?'

Nero spoke over his head and the tribune, directly addressed, could not avoid giving an answer. 'Lord, this man bore a knife in the sacred hallway. He refused to submit to us and fought when we tried to detain him. We thought he alone was guilty. There was no need to arrest—'

'Take them.'

The tribune's sword was already turning as the Germanic guards stepped forward. They didn't see his face from the angle Math did, and so were not fast enough to stop him from falling on to his knees, and from there on to his own blade.

It pierced him just below the breastbone and came out at the top of his back, by his shoulder blades. His breath frothed red at his mouth and nose and his blood flowed black on the pavings.

Nero licked his lips, watching the man die. It took longer than Math had expected. By the time the man's eyes turned up, he had thought of Ajax and Constantin, and his father. He was not sick, and thought that each of them would be proud of him in their own way.

Nero nodded as the German guards took the body away. 'He failed us. He deserves this. Take the centurion. Find out if he was bought by Akakios or was acting in good faith. You will remain kneeling.' His eyes raked Pantera's bruised and bloody face. 'What have you done?'

Pantera blinked once. He was clearly in considerable pain, so that Math thought he might faint there, in front of the emperor, and knew without doubt that if he did the German guards would be ordered to kill him where he lay.

Surprisingly, his voice rang clear, as if the pain belonged to someone else. 'I have prevented the utter destruction of Rome, lord. No man could have done more.'

'Explain.'

'The first cohort was loyal to you: we were sure of that.

Calpurnius and I divided the centuries among the water towers and across the city, to protect the vital sites. In this we succeeded. Four districts out of fourteen are aflame. No more.'

'Calpurnius is dead.' Nero's eyes were flat, like a fish.

'And Saulos still lives. In that I have failed you. But I thought it more important to save the city of Rome than to hunt down one man within it.'

'We do not consider *this* to be saved!' Outraged, Nero flung out his left arm, letting his toga slide from his shoulder so it took on the shape and style of a stola. Like that, he turned a full circle, showing his palm to the audience.

On the stage, the move was known as 'the woman's revolve'. Good actors played it slowly, while their musicians sounded a particular note of the horn, the better to underline the woman's anguish after the loss of her husband or son.

In this setting, surprisingly, Nero did not look effeminate, but rather gave voice to an otherwise unspeakable pain. The crowd sighed with him in a long, ululating note that mirrored his grief with theirs. The fire stood behind them as a backdrop. The moment was perfect.

'Lord, may I speak?' A centurion of the Watch pushed untimely through the crowd, shattering the spell.

Nero jerked round, his face aflame. Math recognized Mergus, the small, dark centurion who had been at Antium, and uttered a prayer for his life; few men interrupted Nero's play-acting and lived to see another dawn.

Out of instinct, the Germanic guards stepped back a wary pace, leaving Mergus to stand beside the kneeling Pantera at the foot of the chariot. The flashing uniform of one contrasted greatly with the torn and filthy tunic of the other.

Caught in the open, focus of a thousand eyes, Mergus saluted with military precision. 'I would speak for the sake of the city,' he said.

485

Nero's right brow danced high. 'Yes?'

'Our prefect is dead. The tribune of the second, his successor, has just died at his own hand – rightly so, for he was a traitor. But the fire grows apace and we need an officer to lead us. May I ask that one be appointed with all celerity?'

'Who?'

'My lord, that is not for me to say.' As he spoke, Mergus took a single pace to his left and Math's jaw dropped.

Perhaps later than the men and women on the steps, certainly later than Nero, he saw what Mergus had done. For the man was, if not an actor, then at least an aficionado of the stage, and, exactly as Nero had made of his chariot a pulpit, so he had made one of the space at the foot of the chariot. Now Pantera was at its centre and anyone who had ever seen a play would have recognized the kneeling man as the hero of a tragedy.

Pantera was staring at the ground. Math, who sat now at his horses' feet, saw his eyes flare wide in surprise as he, too, understood what had happened. The crowd held its breath.

Nero ran his tongue round his teeth. A life, perhaps two lives, hung on his whim. Quietly, he said, 'What would you advise that we do?'

'Me, lord?'

'You. The Leopard. My oath-sworn spy. The man who failed to keep Calpurnius alive.'

Pantera looked up slowly. 'Evacuate the city to the Field of Mars. Throw open the gates to your gardens on the crest of the Capitoline nearby. Order the Watch to make the saving of life their first priority and the saving of property a distant second. Thereafter, promote the tribune of the sixth cohort to the prefecture and have his men follow their standing orders in case of a fire out of control; use the water to saturate buildings ahead of the fire and where that cannot be done, order thirty feet ahead of the flames brought down to make a firebreak. Beyond these things, there's nothing any of us can do.'

'We can pray.'

There was a hidden meaning to that and everyone heard it. Pantera bowed his head. Linear bruises on the side of his neck showed where someone had tried to strangle him. Nero's gaze rested on him, waiting.

At length, struggling for words, Pantera said, 'Your excellency holds in his hand that which is most dear. What more could a man ask but that it is held gently and with due care? I pray for that to the god who holds most power.'

The crowd thought he was begging for his life. As they might have done in the circus, men here and there began to hold their fists at an angle with thumb out, to show that he should live. Some kept their thumbs hidden, for death, but they were few; they had heard him argue a good case against Saulos, and a better one for saving Rome.

Math knew that they were not discussing Pantera. The skin beneath his armpits prickled nastily and hot blood flushed his cheeks.

Nero said, 'We always hold such a thing gently.'

Math shivered with a cold nausea.

Pantera murmured, 'I know, lord. And yet it would show great compassion if—' A building fell then, and the crash of falling masonry drowned out all other sounds, but Math saw Pantera's lips frame a question that looked more like a statement. There was a brief flurry of haggling that no one else could possibly hear. To Math's eyes, it seemed that Nero capitulated, and was not happy with it. None the less, as the noise of falling masonry abated, he ordered Pantera to stand.

'My lord has orders?'

'You offered us a strategy,' Nero said. 'We accept in its

fullest with one exception. We will not yet promote the tribune of the sixth to be prefect.'

'Who then, lord?'

'You. The strategy is yours. Its success or failure rests on your head. You promised us a city saved to the best of your ability. Make it so.'

CHAPTER FIFTY-NINE

'With Math's help, we shall protect the children.'

Thus, standing at the porticoed entrance to the Forum Augustus, with flames lighting his face and great black crow-feathers of soot falling softly about his shoulders, did Nero Claudius Caesar Augustus Germanicus, emperor of Rome and all her provinces, announce his part in the night's drama.

Math had no choice but to play the part allotted to him. He, too, was caught in the fire's flare, as much the focus of the crowd as Nero whose hand rested on his shoulder. Children were already flocking towards them. Their eyes had fed on Math's face, as if, having magically appeared, he and Nero could now magically extinguish the fire, or at the very least lead them all to safety.

Pantera stood nearby, gathering information and issuing a steady stream of orders to the men newly under his command. Someone had given him a helmet and cloak marked with the signs of the Watch. He held both in the crook of his left arm and even so, dressed as he was in a torn tunic, with his right shoulder crooked, not taking all his weight on his left leg, he commanded more respect than any of the officers who stood around him awaiting their orders.

At Nero's new pronouncement, Pantera abandoned his conversation with a short, wiry guard and bowed to his emperor.

'Your excellency shows his greatness,' he said. 'A nation's children are its future. If I might offer a suggestion, it might be prudent to—'

'Lead them up the Capitoline hill to the imperial gardens that stand adjacent to the Field of Mars.' Nero gave an acid smile. 'We are aware of that; you have said so already. We shall take our own guardsmen and as great a detachment of the Urban Guard as you can spare. We shall organize a route to the gardens. There, we shall provide food and water for all who take shelter. History shall record that this emperor did everything possible for his people in their extremity.'

'My lord has the wisdom of all great Caesars,' Pantera said. 'If he wished to mount, I believe the grey gelding ridden by the water engineer is the most fit of the riding horses and, given its pale colour, will be most readily seen by my lord's people as he leads them to safety. Math, perhaps, could hold the beast?'

At a nod, Math left his own beleaguered colts and walked back to take the reins from one of the guards. Faustinos the water engineer had already gone, taking two aquarii and their detachments to see if the broken cisterns could be repaired.

The horse was exhausted. In Antium, it had been given everything it could need and more. Here, there wasn't even water, certainly no feed.

Math let it lick the salt sweat from his hand, feeling the tightness of its lips across his palm. He scratched it behind the ears, in the sweaty place where the bridle lay, and it rested its forehead on his shoulder so that each shuddering breath reached down to his feet.

Pantera's shadow fell across the horse's neck. Math said, 'He's not fit to be ridden. You can't let—'

'He's the best we have. Nero rides well enough and you'll be at his side to see he goes no faster than a walk. There's a water trough in the garden and stables at the side of the Field of Mars. Collect your colts next time you come down. The guards that came with Nero will take care of you.'

All of that was said loudly, for the benefit of anyone listening. Under the fire's crackling, Pantera breathed, 'Where's Ajax?'

'In Antium.'

'But held prisoner against your good behaviour?'

'Did Nero tell you that? When the building fell?'

'No. But Ajax is his best lever to use against you. It's what I would do if I were Nero. Did Seneca reach you? He came to Antium earlier in the evening.'

'I didn't see him.'

'Then he and Ajax are beyond our help.' He gripped Math's arm at the elbow, as he had once gripped Ajax's in a pool in Gaul, with an inn blazing nearby and a dead man beneath an oak tree in the meadow. 'Get through tonight alive,' Pantera said. 'Nothing else matters.'

'We are ready to mount.' Nero approached with three of his guards and a wake of small children behind him.

'Lord, your horse awaits.'

Pantera released Math's arm and made a stirrup of his looped hands. Nero swung himself lightly up and settled in the saddle, waving the gathered children to follow them.

Nero did ride better than Math had expected; he was fully sober, and sharply aware of the children stumbling in his train. Twice, he instructed Math to bring one to him who had fallen faint from too much smoke. Both were lifted up to ride in front of their emperor as they paced at a slow walk up the hill, away from the flames.

Six men of the Watch ran ahead, keeping the route clear. At the hill's top, they threw open the bronze gates to the imperial gardens, where, among the flowering trees and

491

frantic trills of the caged birds, was a water trough for the horses and the children.

Nero passed down the silent, owl-eyed child he had been holding. His toga was stained with saliva, tears and blood. It made him more regal than he had ever been, a credit to the Caesars who had gone before.

He gave sensible orders to the nearest watchmen, and then said to Math, 'See that each child has enough water. Food will be brought. You need not go down the hill. The Watch will bring your horses up. You will remain here and care for the weakest of the children. We believe you have the skills for that.'

'Lord.' Math bowed as he had seen Pantera do. 'I will do my best.'

It was the last sane conversation he had that night. The rest was conducted in hoarse shouts where three words threaded together was a long sentence and more often than not his orders from Nero came as a nod, or a meeting of eyes or, once, a single shout of his name, in time to catch a falling girl-child who had breathed too much smoke and had toppled off the emperor's horse.

Math carried her at a run to the imperial gardens, spat water from his own mouth between her blue lips until she choked, and breathed and came alive again, stark-eyed and screaming.

He spat life into a great many children over the course of the next few hours. Very soon, his existence had narrowed to a dash from the gates to reach the nearest of the incomers, seeking out those who could no longer walk, carrying them back to the place kept clear beside the horse trough under the olives where the scent of foreign flowers was lost beneath the stench of smoke and blood and death except once in a while when, breathing in, he found a sweetness that made him want to weep.

He became skilled at scooping water into his own mouth, savouring the sudden splash of cold in the hot night, then spitting it quickly in a sprayed rush into the waiting mouth in the hope that the cold and wet might restore life that the fire's heat had taken.

Not all of them came back to cough on his shoulder. Three were lost that he knew of; two boys and a girl. Their deaths pierced his heart. Each one dragged him down until the next half-living child was brought, and he must leave the dead to their own fortunes and run and run and lift and run and drink and spit . . . and wait to see the first flutter of the eyelids, and the choke, and then turn them over and bounce his balled fist between their shoulder blades, to push the water out again and let them live.

With Nero and the Watch, Math worked through the night. Somehow, somewhere, a nameless watchman kept count of the hours, sounding each one with a trumpet. The brazen notes cut the night into manageable parts, so that Math began to look forward to them, counting down to each one as he had once counted down the clamouring water clock in Alexandria.

He saw Pantera barely at all; the newly appointed prefect of the Watch spent the night traversing the city across and across, marshalling his men to ever greater feats of endurance and courage. Word amongst those sent back to Nero's gardens said that he had personally led the centuries of the first cohort to the inferno's edge to hack new firebreaks.

The men were full of his praise and it seemed for a while that Pantera had made of himself a god, able to be in more than one place at a time, Once, at the sixth hour of the night, when all was darkest, he brought up half a dozen children, carrying one of them himself. He was lamer than Math had ever seen him.

Of the one he carried, he said hoarsely, 'This is Libo's daughter. Her name's Sulla. I don't know how— She should have been safe. Care for her well.'

Libo was the big, bluff guard who had gone to get the

493

colts and bring them to safety halfway through the night. He was weeping now, but less wildly than he had been earlier when his son and daughter were lost.

The child was barely dressed and not breathing. Mute, Math showed where she should be laid on the woollen cloak beside the horse trough and spat water into her as he had done with all the others. After, when she had choked and begun to breathe, he sat down, taking her head on his lap, and began dribbling water in the corners of her lips.

Pantera crouched down beside him. 'You're doing well,' he said. 'I'm proud of you.'

Around them, guards were listening. Pantera pulled Math into an embrace. Into his ear, he said, 'Hannah and Shimon are at the goose-keeper's cottage on the Aventine. It's clear of the fire so far. If you need help, go there.'

'What about you?'

From behind, Libo clapped him brusquely on the shoulder. 'Never worry, boy. Pantera will save us all from the fire and come back to you safe and well.'

Libo believed it, because he needed to believe that his daughter might live. But Math was close enough now to see Pantera's face, to read the deadness about his eyes and the line etched between his brows that had grown deeper with each hour of the night. Not even in Gaul, when the two of them had sat through the nights together without sleep, had he seen such exhaustion as he saw now.

'Is it bad?' he asked, when he found his voice.

Pantera pulled a wry smile. 'It's not good. A dozen of Saulos' men escaped the warehouse. They're stoking the fires. And there's at least a century of the Watch who are actively working for him. They're harder to find, but at least we know now who their centurion is.'

He leaned forward and kissed Math's head. 'I'm keeping Mergus with me; he's the small, wiry guard with hair like a horse's mane and a scar across the bridge of his nose.

494

He's sharper than Libo, but has no children. If anything happens to me, Libo will get you to the goose-keeper's cottage on the Aventine. If it's burned, he'll give his life to get you away from Rome. You can trust him.' Pantera squeezed Math's arm. 'I found his children – twice.'

Chapter Sixty

The fire that ate Rome had first become visible as Seneca and Ajax passed the tenth milestone. Then, it was only a whisper of colour, pale as a boy's hair in the morning, streaked along the horizon, barely outshining the stars.

The closer they had come, the greater it had grown in size and colour until, at five miles' distance, jagged flames had played clearly along the spine of the horizon.

At the three-mile mark, Seneca could smell smoke peppering the air.

Ajax tapped his arm. 'You should leave your mare here,' he said. 'There's a farm with neat fields. She'll be well cared for. Tether her near the water trough so she can drink before they find her.' He had, Seneca observed, a Gaulish care for animals.

Seneca had dismounted before it occurred to him that he could have refused, indeed that the protocols of rank and station demanded that he do so to restore his waning authority.

He had tied the tether lines at the mare's ankles before he had spelled out for himself the reasons why he couldn't refuse at all, the most acceptable of which was that he had several questions currently nagging at his curiosity and wished to remain in Ajax's company long enough to find their answers; to ignore an order now, clearly, was to be left behind.

He patted the mare's wither and left her to graze. Peering into the night, he picked out the outlines of the farmhouse and three sheds clustered in a hollow that Ajax had already seen. Closer, a kennelled dog whined, but did not bark. As they left, a cockerel coughed its way to an early crow, deceived by the fire's false dawn.

Half a mile later, they met the first refugees: whole families sitting on the turf at the roadside, watching fire paint the horizon in brightening shades of amber as if it were a display put on for their benefit.

These ones were the furthest out, those most able to walk, and to carry their children. The closer they came to Rome, the thicker became the crowd, the less mobile and the less decorous.

At the two-mile mark, progress was almost impossible; grown men tugged at their tunic hems, begging them not to walk on into the hell that was Rome.

'If we turn off here,' Seneca said, 'we can find a route through the fields. There will be fewer people to see us, or slow our progress.'

Ajax glanced at him sharply. 'Do you know a path, or do we simply cut across country?'

'I think that if we turn right at the stone in the shape of a boar, there should be a farm path down through the groves of nut trees. At the gap at the foot of the hill, we turn left at the twisted olive that turns against the wind. From there the track should take us up to the Via Tiburtina. If it's still there. I heard of it more than thirty years ago from a man who used to spy for Julius Caesar. I've never walked it myself.'

'What better time than now?' Ajax favoured him with a brief, dry smile; the first of the thirty miles. 'Can you run nine and walk nine again, do you think?'

He showed no signs of tiring, or of pain: Seneca had passed beyond surprise at that twenty miles ago. 'If I have to,' he said, and set off, to prove it.

Beyond the nut trees, the track was old and barely used. Thick with weeds and olives, it wound through irrigated farmland, and ended abruptly at a wooden stile, beyond which was an alley serving the slave quarters between two large villas at the side of the Via Tiburtina.

'We should walk now,' Ajax said. 'And not speak unless we have to.'

Subdued, Seneca took second place going over the stile and walked as he was told. He was too tired to think clearly, but he missed the conversation of earlier.

For the duration of the thirty miles, whether he was running or walking or riding, the two of them had talked. Their dialogue had been fragmented, but always interesting, shifting from the experience of Alexander in the far distant lands where he had met the ascetic priests of outlandish gods to the warriors of Britain to the politics of Rome. Here, in the city, that easy rapport had ended without warning. Here, Ajax was hunting.

Silent as a shadow, he never stayed long on the path, but regularly stepped off sideways into silent buildings, or loped ahead to check the way was clear, leaving Seneca feeling unusually ineffectual. Once, he thought he saw blood on Ajax's hands, but wasn't sure. An hour before, he could have enquired as to its origin. Now, he walked on, accepting an object lesson in stealth.

'Did I hear someone sound the watch hours?' he asked presently.

'The tenth hour just sounded,' Ajax said, his voice slotting beneath the sounds of the city. 'Dawn comes in two hours. Night is our friend; we shouldn't waste it.'

They were moving as fast as any sane man could do, given the dark and the debris and the need for secrecy. Even as the brazen notes of the watch trumpet melted into the fire, empty villas gave way to merchants' booths and those in turn became by degrees the slums of the suburra.

'Look.' Seneca pointed, and then, feeling foolish, let his arm fall; only a blind man could have failed to see the barricade of flame ahead, and even the blind would have felt the wall of heat. There, the fire was a true inferno, sucking in air to make its own wind, roaring fit to match the gods.

Between them and it, like a demon's playground, lay a hundred feet of broken buildings, demolished by the Guard to create a firebreak.

'We can't cross that,' Ajax said.

'Follow me,' Seneca said, seeing a way to be useful again. 'I can find us a path past the breaks.'

The next half hour was a hell to haunt dreams for a lifetime as Seneca turned back and then left, navigating a twisting death-walk through the smoke-hazed huddle of huts and shops and three- or four-storey tenements, all empty as if visited by plague, with the pall of death chokingly thick; the fire had not reached here yet.

Then, at one alley's end, they came to the places it had reached, where the stench of raw smoke made Seneca sneeze, and all around was the greater horror of burned and burning buildings, decked about with burned and burning bodies, some of them still living.

Out of mercy, Ajax killed those he could reach, climbing two storeys up once on to charred and smouldering beams to reach a woman who stretched out a charred arm to them as they passed. She couldn't speak. Seneca was glad. The stench of burned hair and flesh made him retch.

After that, they kept moving uphill towards the parts the fire had not yet reached. There, in a back alley, they came upon the Watch cutting firebreaks and Ajax hid as Seneca played the part of a grieving father soliciting news of the fire and the welfare of those caught in the city centre.

'Nero's thrown open the imperial gardens and is

offering safety and food while "his boy" – I trust that's Math – is marshalling the orphaned children in there. The adults with children are going up to the Field of Mars. Calpurnius is dead. Tonight, the emperor's spy is prefect of the Watch.'

'And by that, we sincerely hope they mean Pantera.' They stood at a street corner. Ajax surveyed the surroundings. 'If memory serves, the Field of Mars is due north of here. Am I right?'

He had already set off. Seneca followed him at a trot; they were in a hurry again, evidently. Catching up, he said, 'May I ask how you come to know the geography of Rome?'

'I was here in Claudius' time. With my father.'

'I see,' said Seneca, who did not see at all for at least the next two blocks and then suddenly saw too much.

'My dear boy . . .' They were nearly at the gardens. Ajax had become a hunter again, merging with the shadows. Striving for a matching skill, Seneca slid into an alcove behind him and, reaching out, caught the crook of Ajax's elbow, holding him still. Stray firelight reached them. Thus lit, the halo of gold hair was clearly visible on Ajax's unshaved head. 'Are you quite mad?' Seneca whispered. 'If Nero discovers who you are . . .'

'Then being skinned alive will seem like a blessing. I know. So if you can manage not to shout it from the rooftops, I would be grateful.'

He edged forward, drawing Seneca with him, ducking them both down behind a broken water trough. 'Nero's ahead, I can hear him, so we need to keep hidden, although I think the more pressing need is to keep hidden from Saulos, who would appear to be watching Pantera, who in turn is talking, I think, to Math. You see?' Ajax smiled. 'The gods are good if we give them our all.'

500

CHAPTER SIXTY-ONE

Pantera stopped near the top of the hill in a place where the light of the fire did not meet the light from Nero's gardens and the road passed through a dozen paces of darkness and peace in which he could assess his condition.

Eight times already in the night, he had paused in this place. Each time, he had come to the same conclusion: that he was still alive, and so capable of going on, but had no idea how much longer that might continue. His body answered him after a fashion; nothing was broken that had not been broken before, but the places that had been broken a long time ago in Britain were white hot and screaming. His left ankle felt as if the tendon had split again while his right shoulder burned as if Saulos had branded it in the fight. He knew neither of these to be true, but he knew also the finite limits to his own stamina.

He was not there yet, and he had two good reasons to keep moving. For them, he levered himself away from the wall against which he was leaning, and set his mind on things other than pain. Specifically, because he was nearest and most vulnerable, he went looking for Math.

He found him by the horse trough where he had been all night, still tending burned children who had lost their hair to the fire and breathed in too much smoke. He turned before Pantera reached him, and offered a wan smile.

'Libo's daughter—'

'Is in the care of her brother. I know. The worst is over here, although not in the Aventine. I have to go there.'

'Now? You're not . . . Can't someone else go?'

'Not this time; it has to be me. Dawn's two hours away. I'm fitter than you think.' That was a lie, and they both knew it.

Math's face crumpled. 'Please . . .' He beckoned and, when Pantera came close, pulled him into a tight embrace. Into his ear, he whispered, 'Saulos is—'

'Somewhere nearby. I know. I've seen him once, just not close enough to kill him, and when I got there, he'd gone.' Pantera kissed the top of Math's head. 'That's why I have to go. He'll follow me. He's trying to find Hannah.'

'Is she—'

'She's with Shimon. He'll keep her safe, but we think the century of the Watch that's loyal to Saulos knows where she is.' Two men of the second century, the second cohort had been found, injured by falling debris. Each of them had told the same tale before he died.

Math grabbed Pantera's arm. 'Then they'll—'

'Try to find her. I know. I'm going there now, and I'm going to draw Saulos away. You can help me.' Pantera eased himself out of Math's clinging grip and stood holding him at arm's length. In a whisper pitched to carry, he said, 'I'm going to find Hannah. After that, we're going to get you all out of Rome.'

'You can't. You're . . .' Math ran out of words. A single tear rolled down his cheek, leaving a shining snail's track in the mask of soot and filth.

With his own throat tight, Pantera took his hand. 'I'll come back, I promise. Stay safe.'

*   *   *

502

At the garden's edge, Pantera signalled Mergus, and they worked their way down the hill, seeking a route to the Aventine that went behind the worst of the fire, in the lanes soaked by the water engines of the Watch.

They had both been in Britain; they knew what it was to fight in hostile territory, where every tree and bush hid a spear waiting for blood. Tonight, they treated Rome as if it were an enemy encampment, taking care at each junction, finding cover in the shadows, the demolished buildings, the smoke.

Partway down a broken alleyway, Mergus touched Pantera's sleeve. 'We're being followed by more than just Saulos.'

'I know. There are two others behind him.'

A beam blocked their path, a smouldering mess of charred, wet wood. Mergus ducked under it neatly and, for a moment, was lost in the dark. Four paces on, behind a stack of burned-out barrels, he joined Pantera again. 'I still see only one: old and lame in his hips.'

They edged over a fallen pigsty, replete with dead, part-roasted piglets, picked their way through the rubble of a house. On the flat ground beyond, Pantera said, 'That's Seneca. The other one's a bear warrior of the Eceni.'

'Here?' Mergus cast a disbelieving glance over his shoulder. At the next flat piece of ground, he turned round and walked backwards.

'Don't.' Pantera caught his arm, turning him forward again. 'You won't see him unless he wants you to and if he does you may take it as a compliment; they show themselves to adversaries they consider worthy before they kill them. The unworthy simply die.'

'Does Saulos know they're there?'

'He'll know about Seneca. My sincere hope is that he doesn't know about Ajax.'

A broken cistern blocked their path. The water had long since become steam. Pantera climbed over it stiffly. On the far side, two men lay side by side. Mergus knelt to be sure they were dead. Catching up, he said, 'We should kill Saulos now.'

'We could try. And in the meantime, the men of the second cohort will take Hannah. Given the choice between the satisfaction of killing Saulos and saving Hannah, I choose the latter. Can you run up the hill if you have to?'

'I can.' Mergus huffed a derisory laugh. 'Can you?'

They were in the corner of the cattle market. Nothing was left of it. Stepping over the bodies of an old woman and a dog, Pantera flexed his left ankle. The pain transcended anything he could remember. He thought it probably wasn't as bad as it had been in Britain, only that his body, out of mercy, had forgotten.

He said, 'If I can't, don't wait for me. There are two women and a man in the goose-keeper's house. Escort them to safety in the emperor's name.'

'I can't do that if they're already taken,' Mergus said. 'Centurion Appollonius is the son of a consul. I don't have the authority to arrest him, or even obstruct him in the prosecution of his duties.'

'You do now. Here—'

Pantera pulled open the pouch at his belt, retrieved earlier from Augustus' forum. Nero's gold and sapphire ring danced in a fading bloom of firelight.

Mergus gazed at it, unimpressed. 'Tonight,' he said drily, 'it may be that the emperor's authority is not what it was. And I wouldn't trust him to take my word over Appollonius' if it comes to an argument.'

Pantera was coming to like Mergus a great deal. 'Take it anyway.' He placed the ring in the other man's hand, closing his fingers over it. 'It may keep you from being crucified in the morning.'

'Maybe.' Mergus hid the gold beneath his leather jerkin. 'And if it can't, then— *Mithras!* Is the entire Aventine on fire?'

They had just turned a corner. Aghast, Mergus looked up the hill. 'They've set a new blaze,' he said, in horror. 'The wind's blowing in our faces; it would never have driven the fire up here. The bastards are ahead of us, setting fire to the streets behind them as they go.'

Smoke swirled around them, sucked this way and that by the fire. They could see nothing but burned and burning buildings, and, ahead, a wall of savage flame. And then from high up at the fire's leading edge, they heard the voices of men raised in anger – and a woman scream.

Pantera put his hand on Mergus' shoulder and pushed him up the hill. 'That's Hannah! *Go!*'

CHAPTER SIXTY-TWO

On the Aventine hill, the gander, his geese and their sacred goslings slept safely in a stone goose-house that stood on a tiny island in the centre of the pond at the meadow's far end, accessed by a wooden causeway. The goose-keeper's cottage seemed similarly secure, encircled by water and far away from any of the neighbouring buildings from which burning debris might fall.

'This place has withstood seventeen fires since it was first built,' Hypatia had said when Shimon and Hannah had first knocked on the oak gate at the night's beginning. 'An eighteenth won't touch it. Come in. You'll be safe from the fire here.'

They had, indeed, been safe from the fire. Hannah had even managed to sleep, fitfully, until an hour or two before dawn, when the sound of falling masonry had woken her and, with Shimon and Hypatia, she had gone outside in the pre-dawn dark to watch the fire's progress.

It came fast, and against the wind, but even when the saddler's stall just down the hill burst into wild, greasy flame, it was clear that Hypatia had been right; it was never going to reach across Juno's wide meadow to touch the geese or their keeper's cottage.

Wide awake now, Hannah stood huddled with Hypatia

and Shimon in the doorway watching flames scour the night sky, gauging the fire's progress towards them by its colour and heat. Soon after the saddler's, the silversmith's took light. The workshop at the back was full of precious metals that burned in a rainbow cacophony of colours: acid greens lanced through deeper shades of blue and violet; red spheres rose to hover like bloody ghosts in the heat; a sheet of white washed through once, and was gone.

The fire moved on and the colours faded until only the spectrum of reds and paler golds remained, like a hearth fire, but so vast that it roused its own wind, growing ever fiercer until a fire-made gale seethed through the rafters loud enough to overwhelm the crash of tumbling masonry and falling beams in the street outside.

Which was how three people used to subterfuge, trained to hear the sounds beneath the murmur of the world, did not hear the guards who came to find them until six armoured men began to break down the oak gate with their fire axes.

Hypatia reacted first. 'That's not Pantera. Go!' She shoved Hannah ungently in the small of the back. 'We can hide in the goose-house on the island.'

Hannah ran across the meadow towards the bridge. Hypatia kept by her side all the way, urging her on, catching her elbow when she fell, hauling her up, pushing her ever faster, as if they were young again, running from some shrill Sibyl bent on revenge.

With her nose and throat full of gritty soot and her hair grey with smoke, Hannah stumbled across the bridge and under the weeping alders towards the mossy stone goose-house.

The stone hut was cloaked in darkness, hidden from the firelight by a fringe of hanging branches. Hypatia could see in the dark, it seemed. She reached forward and twisted and a door opened, dark on dark. The mellow smell of sleeping geese feathered out, thinning the smoke and soot.

'Inside.' Hypatia's mouth was next to Hannah's ear. 'There's a space to your right by the perches. Try not to tread on a gosling. They scream like wounded deer.'

Hannah squeezed in on her hands and knees, feeling ahead of herself for anything living. She touched hot goose faeces and an old, cold egg, and the scrawny leg of an adult goose that snibbed at her ribs, and then there was only the stone wall, old with cobwebs and dust.

She felt for the corner and turned round slowly, cramped by the stone on two sides and a wooden perch on the other. The door to the goose-hut swung shut, cutting off the fire and the smoke and the sounds of axes crashing on wood, and men committing violence.

Hannah's eyes began slowly to find fragments of light and to build from them images of geese and wood, stone and flesh. Hypatia was very close. Her breath smelled pleasantly of wood smoke, as if the charnel house stench outside hadn't touched her. Her elbows rested on Hannah's knees. Nobody else was in the small space beyond her; there wasn't room. Which meant . . .

'Where's Shimon?' Hannah whispered.

'Fulfilling his oath to your father.'

'*Hypatia!* Where is he?'

Hypatia kept her eye pressed to a gap in the door, from which she could watch the garden. She said, 'He's doing what the gander would do if the geese were attacked; he's sacrificing his life that we might— *No!* – Your death won't stop his, or make it any swifter, or— Hannah, will you be still and *listen*?' She grasped both of Hannah's wrists, and physically prevented her from leaving the goose-house.

Cramped, scared, still whispering, Hannah was furious. 'Why must he die for me? We despise Saulos for pretending that my father gave his life in sacrifice for people he

508

could never know, why is this different? Hasn't there been enough blood?'

'He believes you are worth saving.'

'But I don't—'

'Hush.' Hannah felt Hypatia fumble to reach and lift her hand. Her cool, dry lips pressed briefly to the heel of her thumb. Her mother used to kiss her like that, a way to restrain, to hold, to keep Hannah quiet and safe at times when hot blood and youth might have caused her to speak or act out of turn. In all their time together, Hypatia had never kissed her thus. 'This is his choice. Let him make it.'

Outside in the meadow, men shouted, one of them in pain. Hypatia dropped Hannah's hand and pressed her eye to the gap in the door. Presently, easing back, she whispered, 'He's lied to them, told them we've gone. It may be enough to stop them searching any further. Sit very still.'

They sat crushed together in the dark with the fidgeting geese, holding cramped hand to cramped hand, barely breathing, with their hearts loud enough for each to hear the other and their tears dried with terror.

It wasn't enough.

Whatever Shimon had said, he was not believed. Orders were shouted and on that command six men searched Juno's garden, a place they defiled by their mere presence.

Hannah, who couldn't see, heard their voices sweep ever closer. She found Hypatia's sleeve in the dark and gripped it.

'What do we do if they find us?'

'You sit still and let the geese keep you safe.'

'What will you do?' Suddenly, horrifyingly, Hannah knew the answer. 'No. No. No, you mustn't—'

'My love . . .' Hypatia turned to face her. The kiss she gave then was a lover's kiss, full of memories and hope and promises for the future. 'I have to go now. They're hunting for a man and a woman and they must find them. I asked

509

for this time with you and it was given. For that we should be grateful.'

There was a scuff of nails on wood, not unlike the scratch of a mouse, and a brief, billowed draught as the door opened and shut.

'*Hypatia!*'

Her first instinct was to hammer, screaming, on the door until someone – anyone at all – came to open it and let her out. But the geese had shifted in the dark and got in her way, so that she couldn't reach the door in time to stop the bar settling down to keep it shut.

Stuck, she had no choice but to crawl forward on her hands and knees, reaching blindly ahead until she felt the change in texture that was stone giving way to wood.

'Hypatia?'

Childlike, Hannah whimpered aloud to the dark. Fast, hot tears washed her face clean and made her head pound with the same unstable rhythm as her heart so that her pulse surfed in her ears, washing out the muttering geese, and the fire, and the distant shouts of the guards rising over a woman's single scream.

CHAPTER SIXTY-THREE

'That's Hannah! *Go!*'

Seneca heard Pantera's voice clearly over the demolition of the fire and, as if it spoke to him, launched himself forward.

'Don't be a fool!' Ajax jerked him to a halt, his fingers iron-hard on Seneca's forearm. They were hiding under a broken cistern at the foot of the hill. The river mumbled sullenly behind, outdone by the majesty of the fire ahead. 'Saulos is between us and Pantera. What we heard, he has heard. He loves Hannah. What will he do?'

Seneca blew out a breath. 'If he truly loves her, then I think he won't kill her or let her be killed, but he will certainly kill Pantera if he has the chance. His only regret will be that it can't be done slowly, over days.'

'And he will want to gloat before he kills. He hasn't the strength of mind not to.' Quiet as a ghost, Ajax had risen to his feet. Near naked, with the firelight sharp on the first new growth of his hair, with his scars like living silver across all parts of his torso, he looked barely human. Seneca was terrified of him. He had denied this half the night. Now, he allowed himself the honesty.

He drew a sharp breath. 'You're right; Saulos won't

throw his knives from a distance. We can follow him and Pantera as they both ascend the hill.'

'Then we shall do so.' Ajax smiled, grimly. 'This time, you don't have to run, but you do have to follow exactly where I go, and make no sound.'

If the whole of the night had been a preparation for this, it was inadequate, but still Seneca succeeded in the tasks that were set him, and exulted in them. He was burned across his forearms and face, his scalp was singed, he trod on glowing embers so that his sandals burned through to his feet. His nose was clogged with noxious many-coloured smoke and his eyes streamed red raw. He wormed under dangerously unstable walls, stepped past pools of liquid pitch and clambered over dead men and hounds, and was as happy as he could ever remember being.

Always, Ajax was ahead, finding the best path. And always Saulos was ahead of him, and Pantera ahead again and his wiry companion ahead of both, all three of them visible now that Seneca had the art of seeing them.

And because he had the art of seeing, he saw the detachment of the Watch emerge from the gate in the whitewashed hall. And he saw their two prisoners.

Ajax was a half-seen glimmer of pale skin lying prone beneath a fallen roof beam. Gathering his courage, Seneca crawled forward to join him.

'That's—'

'Shimon and Hypatia, I know. But not Hannah.' Ajax watched a moment, then said, 'The centurion's stoking up the fire at the next-door shop.'

'He can't burn the goose-keeper's house – Juno keeps it immune to fire.'

'Does she? If I were a Roman, I'd worship her ahead of Mars. The centurion's doing his best to make it burn, though. Either he thinks nobody's left inside . . .'

'Or he's trying to make sure that whoever's in there doesn't come out. Pantera thinks that. Look.'

Pantera had caught up with the wiry, dark-haired officer who was his companion. Both were watching the centurion as he stoked the new fire. They were animated in their conversation, pointing, gesticulating, shaking their heads.

The centurion leapt back smartly. A smouldering beam fell, as if at his command, and blocked the gate in the whitewashed wall. He stayed a heartbeat longer, to be sure the fire had caught, and then left at a run, following the route his men had taken.

In his hiding place, Pantera made a point, with emphasis. The small, wiry man saluted and followed the centurion at a discreet distance. Pantera waited, fidgeting, until they were out of sight, then ran to the gate.

Seneca said, 'We have to unblock the gate. He's going to try to—'

'He's going to try to climb the wall and he won't succeed.'

'You could go in his stead. You're fitter than he is.' Even in the half-dark, with the fire making the shadows jump, it was obvious that Pantera was at the limit of his resources.

Ajax was looking somewhere else. 'Where do you think Saulos has gone?'

'He's over there.' Seneca pointed to his left.

'Not any more.'

Blinking his eyes clear of the smoke, Seneca looked up the hill to the place where Saulos had been tucked discreetly behind a broken wall, and found it empty.

In his ear, Ajax whispered, 'There.'

Up ahead fresh fires blazed, men shouted and smoke billowed thickly. Through it, Seneca saw Pantera trying to find a way past the smoking beam to the blocked door in the whitewashed wall.

And there, too, less than ten yards further on, Saulos was crouched in a doorway, a knife in either hand.

Chapter Sixty-Four

The only route in to find Hannah was over the wall. To that end, Seneca gave him a leg up. Feeling for handholds, he discovered that the top was not covered in spikes, as he had feared it might be.

On the far side, he dangled for a moment, hanging by his hands. He had no idea how far he was from the ground. On a prayer, he let go. The fall was just far enough to jar his ankles, but not so far as to break them. He landed hard on the paved path below, rolled a little and pushed himself up to standing.

The gardens were not as fire-bright as the street outside; the same walls of the neighbouring houses that kept the meadow safe also shaded it from the flames. Neither were the moon and stars any use for light; the entire sky was blurred to bloody mess by the smoke.

He stood still, breathing the cleaner air. Had he been asked earlier in the day – by Seneca, say, or Math – he would have said he knew exactly, to the nearest heartbeat, the limits of his own exhaustion; that he had plumbed his own depths so often that he knew when it was impossible to push himself further.

The night had proved him clearly wrong; several times he had thought he must stop and rest, and had found the necessary reserves to continue. In the cold light of sanity, he permitted himself the honest appraisal that climbing the wall had been a push too far.

He thought he had enough left to walk to the cottage, and perhaps lie down. Except that he had to find Hannah first. If she was alive. If the Watch hadn't slaughtered her out of hand.

He thought he should know if she were dead. He wasn't certain of it.

He walked slowly towards the cottage, feeling the warm grass underfoot, then cool paving stones and more grass and—

He spun towards the dark, drew the knife that he had carried through the night, jerked his arm back to throw . . .

And let it down again.

I am too tired for this.

He blinked the sweat from his eyes and still he couldn't tell if the shape coming at him across the meadow was a ghost from his past, or the first of the night's dead come to find him.

The ghost stopped in the centre of the meadow.

'Ajax? Ajax of Athens?'

Hannah's voice. Her living voice. He sank to his knees on the hot, cindered grass.

'Ajax?' She flowed across the grass, jerkily.

Something more painful than loss blocked his throat. He tried to speak her name and it came out as a wordless croak of the kind he had heard too often through the night from inside burning buildings.

Rising, he met her coming down to him. They stumbled together to kneel on the grass.

Pantera said, 'Not Ajax. I'm sorry.'

Light fingers strayed over his face, his eyes, his hair, feeling things he could not see. Her face was almost dizzily happy. He didn't understand why.

515

She said, 'Don't be sorry. Please, please don't be sorry. At least one prayer this night is answered. But you're weeping. Who's died? Is it Math?'

'No. Math's well.' He caught his breath and coughed and said, 'You. I thought you were dead. Not true. Obviously.' And then she was kissing his neck over and over, saying his name. Her hands wrapped his body, her fingers dug in tight. Suddenly, entirely unexpectedly, probably hopelessly, he wanted other things, too, and wasn't sure how to ask.

He found her chin and brow by feel, framing her with his hands. As his eyes cleared of tears and smoke, he found her face by sight, and he was able to kiss her cleanly, on the cheek, in greeting, in offering, asking the question he dared not speak aloud.

'I'm covered in ash,' he said, and he was laughing now, but only a little, and then he had to stop because she had found him at last, lip to lip, nose to nose, brow to brow, and her answer left him no air to breathe, or mind to think, or heart to grieve.

He felt her fingers lock in his hair, drawing his head back. 'I think that's just as well. If you weren't, you'd be able to tell that I'd just spent part of the night hidden in the goose-house.'

He leaned back a little, so he could see her properly, and make sense of the smears on her arms.

'The Watch took Shimon and Hypatia,' she said.

'I know. Mergus has gone after them. He has Nero's ring. If they can be saved, he'll do it.' And then, closing his eyes, 'Saulos was outside.'

'Is he dead?'

'He might be by now. Ajax has gone after him. Either one of us could have come over the wall to you. I was here first, so he chose to let me.'

This time he could not read her face, only that whatever warred within her was complex.

'I'm sorry. If you'd have preferred—'

Her fingers stopped his mouth. 'Tell me Saulos won't kill him?'

'He won't kill him. He might escape, but he hasn't got what it takes to kill Ajax.'

'Or you?'

He looked down at his hands that she might not read the shame in his eyes. 'Tonight, he might be able to kill me. He came close once already. I think that's why Ajax chose the way he did.'

She let her gaze fall. 'What now?'

Dawn was coming. Even had the distant trumpeter not marked the passing hours, Pantera had sat through the sunrise often enough to know the earliest signs of day: the growing contours in the grass where it was no longer a black velvet carpet, ripples on the pond that allowed a first tinge of silver, a shape under the trees on the island that must be the goose-house, the first colour to Hannah's eyes.

He tugged his hand through his hair. 'We can't leave here yet. The gate's blocked and the centurion set fire to the house next door. What was it, a bakery?'

'A carpenter's.'

He nodded. 'It's burning hard. We're stuck here until the worst of it dies down.'

Hannah lifted his fingers, and kissed them. 'Hypatia always said this was the safest place in Rome.'

'And Hypatia, as we both know, is always right. And . . .' he kissed her hand in his turn, and let his gaze meet hers, still testing what he thought he saw there, 'you're here, and alive, and I would like us to have time to celebrate that. Might we go into the cottage?'

They lay crushed together on the narrow bed beneath the window. The shutters hung open to the dawn. The gander was out on the water, but not yet the geese. The fire still cast its glow in the west, to rival the eastern sun.

Pantera lay on one side, propped on one elbow, with his back to the cold wall and Hannah's breasts soft on his chest. His lower lip was swollen. He tasted blood where she had bitten it, or he had. He had thought himself too drained for anything but sleep, and had been powerfully wrong. Neither of them had slept yet.

The world was a new place, and he had not yet found his way in it. He had forgotten what it was to lay himself bare to another's view, to be given freedom to discover the contours of another's body. He had forgotten the soul-blinding beauty of a woman, freely given, and what that could do to him.

He explored every part of her even as she studied his scars, the misshaped shoulder, the flat white mess that had once been a brand of Mithras. He wanted to believe she wasn't looking with a physician's eye, or at least not only with that.

He felt the touch of her look and matched it with his free hand, tracing lines in their pooled sweat on her torso, about her navel, across and across the lines of her pelvic bones to her hips, and up to her breasts and then, when she was still looking, he leaned down and traced his lips along the line his fingers had marked, teasing and teasing until she gave the same throaty cry she had earlier in the dark and rolled over, finding him blindly with hands and tongue and teeth and then with all of her, pressing him flat on the goosefeather mattress, rising over him to greet the dawn again in her own way, with their hands entwined, palm to palm, fingers interlaced . . .

'What is it?' He felt the change in her hands first, and then the rest of her. 'What's the matter?'

'Nothing. Not you.' They were still locked together. She slumped against him, pressing her forehead to his chest.

518

'You don't want a child?' He studied her, searching, trying to see inside. 'There are ways to be sure. We don't have to—'

'Hush.' She kissed him to silence. 'It's not about a child, and anyway it's too late for that. She's made. What we do now is for us.' Absently, she smoothed his hair over his brow. He watched her weigh a difficult choice and wished his heart did not crash so hard in his chest.

Biting her lower lip, she said, 'Did you think of Aerthen when we . . . earlier?'

'I tried not to,' he said, truthfully, and then, because he couldn't slow the speed of his mind, even when it worked against him, he said, 'and you thought of Hypatia. But I would be with Aerthen if she weren't dead, and Hypatia's still alive, so' – he pushed himself up on his elbow again – 'you should go to her.'

Hannah was looking away from him, out of the un-shuttered window. 'I can't. I don't know where she is, and in any case we can't leave. You said so.'

'I also said that Mergus has orders to do whatever it takes to keep them safe. When he finds them, he'll take them to the forum.'

'What if he doesn't find them?'

'Tonight, I am prefect of the Watch. As soon as we can leave here, I'll find them.'

In his mind, Pantera was already out in the charred streets, setting the Watch – his Watch – to find a Sibyl with black hair and the scent of lilies. He didn't think she would be dead; she was too clever for that.

We were lovers . . . Earlier, at the height of her passion, Hannah had spoken a word and he had not heard it. Only now did he know it as a name. He closed his eyes and then opened them again, staring up at the ceiling.

'Don't. Please.'

Hannah caught his hair, painfully, and brought his head round to hers. A dozen heartbeats ago, he would have loved her for that, and met her with his own power. Now, his gaze skidded over her face.

She pulled him back a second time. 'Please . . . I need to be truthful, that's all. What's this' – her sweeping arm took in the bed, and shut out the world – 'without truth? Neither of us comes to this unscarred, or completely whole. We are who we are. Don't let it destroy us. Please.'

'But you love her.'

'And you love Aerthen.'

'Who is dead. Hypatia is not.'

'But here, now, she may as well be. Will you allow me to have a past, and believe me that it is past? Please?' She said it more quietly this time, and reached across the finger's-width gap that had become a chasm between them. 'Some things are always going to be of her. And from tonight, some things will always be of you.'

He was in uncharted water, with nothing to show him the way. His attention was caught by the curve of her collar bones, by the shine of her sweat and his, caught in a stray shard of firelight, by the pool of dark just above it, curtained by the raw smoke-silk of her hair. Unthinking, he asked, 'Has there ever been another man?'

'Never.' She squinted at him. 'You?'

'A man?' Astonishingly, he found himself laughing. 'I'll make you a promise,' he said. 'I'll leave your past alone if you'll leave mine. How does that sound?'

'It sounds good.' She glanced down at him. 'Did you know when Aerthen died?'

'I killed her.'

She shut her eyes. 'I'm sorry.'

'Don't be. Are you telling me you'll know if Hypatia dies?'

'I hope so. It's not happened yet, but she thought it would be soon and was trying not to be afraid.' Her smile was infinitely sad. 'Can we lie together again? Please?'

He lowered her down to lie on him, sternum to sternum.

For a long time, they pressed together, motionless, skin on skin, so that he could feel her heartbeat against his own ribs.

He thought she had fallen asleep until abruptly she roused and, shaking herself like a dog out of water, propped up on her elbows and bent to kiss him.

He said, 'Hannah, we don't have to—'

'I want to. Be still. Let me do this.' Her kisses drifted down to his chest, to the scar of Mithras, and below it.

For a long time, he did lie still until it became unbearable not to move, and even then he waited until she made it clear beyond doubt what she wanted of him.

Then he was not still at all, and when they linked fingers again they were both aware of what they did, but lost in the wildness, with their pasts kept apart from the present, and when she arced up high over him, taut as a drawn bow, the name she spoke was clearly his, and he did not think of Aerthen.

CHAPTER SIXTY-FIVE

'Hannah? Can you wake? Someone's coming.' Pantera touched her shoulder. His face hovered over hers, bright with care, wet from washing in the ewer by the bed. He was sharply awake, scrubbed clean of the night's fatigue. In the pale morning light, his age had receded ten years. Here, now, he was the man who had filled the quiet of her mind, in the nights of waiting before the fire.

One hand still lay on her shoulder, the thumb describing circles on her collar bone. His other held the knife Hannah had found strapped to his forearm in the early part of their time together. Only later, near dawn, had he allowed her to remove it, and then would not let her lay it far from the bed.

A sound came from the gate outside, of wood being broken. 'The fire's gone down enough to let them near the gate,' Pantera said. 'Someone's taking an axe to the beam that's blocking it.'

Hannah sat up, too quickly. 'We can hide in the goose-house.' The thought appalled her.

Pantera laughed, reading her face. 'Not unless you want to.' He leaned over to kiss her. The laughter was swiftly gone. He said, 'I think it's Ajax. Anyone else would come over the wall. It means we can start looking for Shimon and Hypatia.'

'And Math,' Hannah said.

'And Math,' he agreed.

She took his hand and let him raise her to her feet. He helped her to wash, found her a fresh tunic and laid it out, the one clean garment in the room. Blue irises worked in silk thread at hem and sleeves said it was Hypatia's.

Hannah tied the belt of roped silk. From the window, she could see flames stitch the horizon to the south and west. Elsewhere, plumes of smoke bellied on the wind, but the raging fire-storm of the night was gone. Outside, the sounds of breaking wood were growing more urgent.

Pantera stood at the door, looking out. 'When Ajax went to hunt Saulos, we didn't know if you were still alive in here.'

'So it would be a kindness to go to him now.' The idea made her stomach lurch.

Pantera turned. His eyes sought her face. 'Have you regrets?' he asked.

'None.' She thought it was true.

He said, 'It would be better to go out, I think, than to be found sitting side by side on the bed's edge like errant children.' Reaching out, he drew her into an embrace. His kiss mimicked Hypatia's last kiss in the goose-house; full of hope and love and the bittersweet grief of parting.

Seneca saw her first: the dark-haired woman to whom he had lost both Ajax and Pantera.

Had he not been expecting her, he would barely have recognized the quiet physician of Coriallum. Here was a woman wrought fine and new, emerging from the wreckage of the fire as Athena from the waves.

Ajax hadn't seen her yet. He was wielding the axe with a fury against the beam that blocked the gate. They had found only one axe, and even after the night they had both experienced, he still had more strength to wield it. The difference between them was less than it had been, though.

Seneca had set himself the task of cataloguing Ajax's waning energy with scientific precision. As Aristotle had examined the bodies of dead and living animals for their secrets, so Seneca was bringing the same objectivity to his study of his night's companion.

Thus it was that he had moved a little to one side as the beam began to fall from the gate, and so saw Hannah before Ajax did, and saw her see him, and saw the sudden ache written across her face, sharp and sore as a knife's cut. He saw it wiped clear as fast as it appeared so that when Ajax paused to sluice the sweat from his eyes and chanced to look through the gap, she was smiling for him in greeting.

'Ajax.'

'Hannah.'

They were formal as distant cousins. Then Hannah moved and Seneca saw what Ajax had already seen: that Pantera stood beside Hannah, and that he, too, was rendered clean and clear by the dawn, and was just as uneasy in Ajax's presence.

'Saulos is still alive.' Ajax addressed Pantera, sparing them both. 'He led us back to Math. We had a choice to leave and follow Saulos, or to stay and keep watch over the children. We chose the latter.'

'Thank you. He'd have killed Math if he could. Where is he now? Is he safe?'

'Math? Nero has him. Seneca thinks you could negotiate now for his release. He says that after the night's work, you'll have best success.'

'And you? Where will you go?'

Ajax looked at Hannah and then back at Pantera. Seneca, who thought the night had taught him how to read the smallest nuanced changes of Ajax's moods, read nothing at all.

He said, 'A merchant ship rides at anchor at Ostia, on the mouth of the Tiber, ready to sail for Hibernia, via Gaul. It has been there since the last month's end, waiting for word. My uncle is on it. He will wait until the next new moon and then leave.'

'How on earth did he know to come here?' Seneca asked.

Ajax's eyes never left Hannah's face. 'My sister had a dream. Amongst my people, she is accorded the greatest of her generation. She said that my brother and I would sail on it together, back to our family.'

Pantera blinked in surprise. 'And did your sister see more than you two on this ship?'

'Others were with us. It's hard to say exactly who. Dreams are rarely explicit; the interpretation is everything.'

'Like prophecies,' Pantera said.

'Exactly like them.' Ajax's pale hawk's eyes were unusually bright.

Seneca thought his head might break under the tension. Tentatively, he said, 'If I might make a suggestion? The best tide from Ostia is the second hour after noon. The distance from here to there is eleven miles. There is therefore a limited time in which to reach the ship. I believe Pantera alone has the best chance of wresting Math from Nero's grasp. Ajax can't risk being seen and moreover he has to get some sleep – don't argue, you're only standing now out of pride – before he travels that far. He could perhaps stay here a while with Hannah while I find horses that might take them to the port. Pantera, you can join them there with Math if it is possible. If not, send a message with the necessary information so that the ship might sail.'

'I can't leave without Math,' Ajax said simply.

'And we can't leave without Hypatia and Shimon,' Hannah said. 'Will you be able to wrest them from Nero too?'

'If he has them,' Pantera said, 'I will certainly try.'

There was a heartbeat of silence, in which Pantera dared meet Hannah's gaze. Whatever passed between them was private. What was not remotely private was the fact of its passing.

Colouring slightly, Pantera raised his hand to Ajax in the kind of salute Seneca had seen from the older warriors of Britain, brought as captives to Rome. 'I leave her in your care. We'll meet you at Ostia with Math and whoever else we can bring.'

CHAPTER SIXTY-SIX

Math thought the dark-haired woman was Hannah when Libo and his men carried her bodily under the archway into Nero's private garden. Her face was bright with new bruises, half hidden by hair so full of ash that it looked white, with only streaks of black.

Then she raised her head, and the eyes that met his were not Hannah's, nor was the hard, angry smile. He could breathe again.

He was breaking his fast with the emperor in the hedged area away from the rest of the morning's havoc. There were no singing birds here, but wild roses twined over the arch and all around flowers opened to the growing dawn.

Math had not washed on waking, but nor had Nero; he smelled of smoke and grit and a night's work. He kept his hand on Math's knee as they ate, and only removed it when Libo ushered in the woman who was not Hannah. The big watchman treated her with respect bordering on fear; Math didn't think it was he who had beaten her before she was brought here.

After her, other men brought Shimon, who had been beaten far more badly. And then they dragged in someone else, small, wiry, dark-haired, his face purpled by bruises.

Math shot to his feet. 'That's Mergus! Pantera took him up on to the Aventine to rescue . . .'

He tailed to silence. The woman who wasn't Hannah put a finger to her lips. Math was trying to work out who she could be when a centurion of the Watch marched under the rose arch and stamped to a salute in front of the dining table.

Nero ignored him, pointedly. His gaze was on Mergus and it was not kind. Opening his hand, he showed a fat, sweat-marked ring on his palm. Gold greeted the morning, and a blue cabochon sapphire with stars at its heart. Apollo played his lyre at the sides.

To Mergus, in the stilted voice he had always used to address Akakios, he said, 'You have used this, our token, against our officer. We might say you have abused our token.'

'Lord, such was not my intention.' Wisely, Mergus dropped to both knees. 'Pantera, our new prefect, gave me the ring and with it your authority. Such was my understanding. His best concern was that the woman and man who had given their services to Juno should be restored to safety and dignity. I was ordered to do whatever that took, up to and including the arrest of Centurion Appollonius.' Mergus gave the faintest of nods in the direction of the man who had just marched in.

'He outranks you,' Nero said.

'And yet he was lighting fires on the Aventine hill, lord. I have witnesses who will attest to that. He was following his tribune's orders even after that man had died by his own hand. In doing so, he forfeited his position.'

Nero's flat eyes swivelled round. 'Is this true?'

'Lord.' The centurion named Appollonius did not kneel, but bowed stiffly. 'I had information that a Hebrew had ordered the fires to be lit. I was further informed that this Hebrew and his Egyptian whore had evicted the true keeper of Juno's geese and appropriated her dwelling. I went there and found this man, Shimon of Galilee, known also as Shimon the zealot, long an enemy of Rome. I found also this Hypatia, his whore. She cursed my men in the name of Isis when they arrested her. I am satisfied she is Egyptian.'

Hypatia. That was the name. A friend of Hannah's. And the centurion was afraid to look at her directly. And he hadn't denied lighting the fires. Math noticed that. He hoped Nero had too.

The woman had certainly noticed. Under the light of the pitch-pine torches, her caustic gaze would have shrivelled the centurion had he dared to catch her eye.

Math, who did dare, studied the bruises on her wrists and one vivid weal on the side of her face. She saw him looking and shrugged one shoulder, wryly. Math nodded back the same dry appraisal of the lunacy of adults; a secret between them.

Everyone else was watching Nero, whose word could kill them speedily or slowly, or not at all.

He crooked a finger at the guards. 'Bring the woman. We would question her.'

'Lord.' Appollonius extended a warning hand. 'She is dangerous.'

'Then we look to you to keep us safe.' Nero's smile was thin as a snake's. 'She does not appear to us dangerous.' Three men of the Watch brought her forward. 'Who are you?'

She stood straight and tall and beautiful. 'I am a Sibyl, lord. Keeper of the flame of Isis.'

A Sibyl! The word hissed around the garden with no one giving it voice. Math thought his own eyes might start from his head from shock.

'A Sibyl?' Nero spoke what everyone else dared not. 'One of those who wrote the prophecy?'

'Lord, I ordered that the prophecy be copied, nothing more. The words were spoken a hundred generations ago and circulated widely at that time. We released them again now in such a way that those who cared most for Rome might have an opportunity to prevent the conflagration and all that it prefaced. Our intent was honourable.' Her voice was the perfect chime of a cymbal at dawn, but Math caught the fine edge of a tremor in her hands and her shoulders.

'You could have come directly to us with the information.'

'No, lord. Akakios prevented it. We had to use subtlety to find who else was a traitor.' Her eyes strayed to Appollonius. He flushed a deep, unfetching crimson.

'Nevertheless . . .' Nero tapped his lips. 'The conflagration was not prevented. We hold you responsible for this fire and will exert our justice. You will be taken from here and—'

'*No!*' Shimon stepped forward – and collapsed on to the hard earth as three watchmen clubbed him to the ground.

Math turned away.

'Leave him!' Nero snapped his fingers. 'Let the Hebrew rise.'

With noticeably less enthusiasm, the men who had knocked Shimon down levered him up. His nose bled messily down his chin. Fresh bruises purpled both arms. He stood erect, held by his own pride, and made no effort to clean himself.

Math sat with his teeth clamped on his lower lip. Nero had no legal training, but believed himself to be the ultimate arbiter of Rome's justice, and a competent counsel. He believed himself to be a god, too, on exactly the same basis: he was emperor and his word was law.

He stood now, with one hand on his hip, after the manner of the courts. 'You are Shimon of Galilee, also known as Shimon the zealot?'

'I am.'

Math winced, and stared straight ahead. Everyone else

530

was gazing at Shimon in varying degrees of disbelief, waiting for him to say what he had not. Clearly, he hadn't misspoken. Even in Coriallum, it was known that the Hebrews were particularly difficult in this regard.

Nero alone seemed untouched. Amiably, he said, 'Did you know of the Sibylline prophecy before this night?'

'I did.'

Again, the aching, painful gap.

'He is your *lord*! You will name him as such.' The centurion, Appollonius, cracked the back of his hand across Shimon's face, sending strings of bloody mucus across Nero's toga.

Math was beginning to hate that man. Nero, he thought, was not impressed either. Nor, it seemed, was someone else, newly come to the garden. A crisp, cold voice rang out through the silence.

'Lord, why is this man still at liberty to assault your loyal subjects when he has spent the night burning your city?'

Three watchmen drew their blades and spun, then stood down. Their prefect stood at his ease under the rose arch with the glare of the rising sun behind casting him in living gold.

'*Pantera!*'

Math ran past all the others. It might have been forbidden, it probably *was* forbidden, but some joys cannot be contained, some relief is impossible to hide.

He threw himself into the man's arms and Pantera, a newly shining Pantera, lifted him high and hugged him and set him down lightly at his side. He did not send him back to Nero.

'Lord, Appollonius has impeached himself by his actions of the night. He and his troop lit fires, not only on the Aventine, but in the suburra and around the forum. I have men aplenty who will testify in your name that this is true. I will personally testify that Shimon of Galilee was

531

working to help prevent the fire, not to light it. And he saved my life in the fight with Akakios.'

A miracle had happened in the night, clearly, because Pantera was restored to himself again and sharply awake, which gave him an advantage over everyone else in the garden. He spoke with an authority that brooked no denial.

Nero looked a moment at the ring that lay on his palm, flecked now by Shimon's blood. He crooked a finger. 'You will approach us.'

At the dining couch, Pantera sank down on both knees with an elegance that stole Math's breath.

Clasping Pantera's head in both hands, Nero gripped a great fistful of hair on either side of his face, twisting it until Math saw the skin blanch where it took root. Pantera's lips made a thin, hard line.

'You are our prefect, the saviour of Rome.' True grief roughened the emperor's voice. 'We have lost four precincts, but could have lost ten more – and would have done without you.'

'My lord is kind.' Pantera raised a brow; it was all he could move. He said, 'Last night I had the honour to serve my emperor and did so with all my heart. This morning, as was agreed, I resign my post.'

'Then we shall give it to Centurion Appollonius.'

A child's threat. Pantera smiled. 'My lord is too astute to do such a thing. He can smell treachery when it comes near him.'

Nero nodded. Appollonius jerked and was still. With so small a gesture, he had lost and everyone knew it. Nobody knew yet who might win.

'Who then?' Nero asked. 'Who is fit to take your place?' His hands were still knotted in Pantera's hair.

Pantera pursed his lips. 'Mergus is well placed. He excelled himself during the night and ill deserves the treatment he has had since dawn. To grant him the prefecture would undo the hurt he has suffered. But he is perhaps better a free agent, not weighed down with the duties of rank. And he is a centurion. It would be better to elevate a tribune. Annaeus of the sixth proved his loyalty many times over in the past hours and, as I said last night, he is a capable man. Either would suit.'

'Which?' The emperor's hands tightened again. His knuckles grew white.

As much as a man can do who is held to kneeling by hands tearing at the roots of his hair, Pantera gave it thought. To those watching, it seemed that, without turning his head, he cast his eyes over the two men he had named. Exhausted and filthy, each came to parade attention.

'I would choose Gaius Annaeus, tribune of the sixth cohort, as my successor to the post of prefect of the Urban Guard,' he said.

With his words, it was so. Nero's assent was a formality, haphazardly given.

'Lord, the Centurion Apollonius . . . ?' Libo sought out three of the Watch with his eyes. With swift and subtle movements, they blocked the rose arch. Had Appollonius intended to leave, he had lost his opportunity.

Answering a glance from Nero, Pantera murmured, 'As my lord knows, he was the son of a consul. He should be given the opportunity to fall on his sword as did his tribune. Mercy and compassion strengthen the giver as much as the receiver.'

Nero had already lost interest. His gaze had returned to Shimon and rested there, hotly.

Pantera still knelt at the emperor's feet, his head still held in the rigid grip. Carefully, not looking at Shimon, he said, 'My lord, parting is a grief, but it cannot be delayed for ever.'

'Do not leave us!' Early sunlight shimmered on trembling tears.

'Lord, I have done all I can. As you said, the fire is less than it might have been. It may smoulder a while before the water tanks can be repaired and supplies restored, but no further precincts will be lost. A great many lives have been saved and my lord can rebuild a new Rome, with greater care for fire, and be known for a thousand years as the one who did so.'

'But Akakios did not plot alone! He had succour and support amongst the Hebrews. In Gaul, you told us so, and again in our garden at Antium.' Nero was scarlet with anguish. Foam gathered at the corners of his mouth. His hands, holding Pantera's hair, were shaking.

'I may have misspoken.'

'You did not! This man, Shimon, is guilty.' Made rash by grief, Nero flung out his arm, pointing at Shimon. 'Guards! Take this man. We name him the source of the fire.'

'Lord—' With no apparent difficulty, Pantera was standing. Mergus had not moved and the only other watchman left, unwilling to act alone, flushed scarlet, but held his ground. Ignoring them both, giving all his attention to the man-child in front of him, Pantera said, 'Shimon did not light the fire, excellency. I will swear that on anything you wish.'

'On my name, claiming me as your god?'

'If you desire it.'

'But he will not swear so!' Nero's lips trembled. 'He would not name me lord.'

Pantera stood with his hand pressed to his own sternum, near where Math knew there to be a burn mark the size of his palm. He kept his eyes on the emperor, and so held at least a thread of his attention.

'Whatever Shimon's other failings' – his voice made them minor – 'he did not light last night's fire; indeed, he has aided the fight against it. Saulos is the arsonist, who was an agent of Seneca's, loyal to Rome. He engineered

534

every part of the blaze and our efforts to stop it, from first beginnings in Gaul. He and his followers are known to your officers. Libo will hunt down those who survived the fire and deliver them to my lord for his justice.'

'They will burn, every one of them, as they made my people burn!'

'And they will deserve it, lord.'

'But Saulos will not be among them. Annaeus, our new prefect, cannot deliver to us a man schooled by Seneca; he has not the skill. Only you can find him, and bring him to us, fit for retribution.'

'Lord, there are others equally capable who—'

'No there are not!' Nero swung round, suddenly searching. Math tried to will himself invisible, and failed.

By a snap of the emperor's fingers, Math was summoned forward. He came on stilted legs that moved without any volition on his part. At Pantera's side, he began to kneel, but Nero's arm curved round his waist, drawing him in, and, openly, Nero's hand stroked his hip.

For the barest fraction of a moment, Math saw desperation writ raw on Pantera's face, gone before he truly understood it. A smile took its place, made for the moment. Pantera said, 'My lord gave his word . . .'

'We gave our word that you could take the boy to his brother, who had heard of the father's death and come to look for him. Where is that man now?'

Pantera scratched the side of his nose, thinking. An old memory from Coriallum echoed in Math's ear. Seneca saying, *He is an actor. He can smell deceit from a hundred paces. Never risk it.*

Math repeated the words over and over in his mind, trying to send them to Pantera, that he might remember.

Pantera frowned. 'I believe he is at the port of Ostia, or will be so by early afternoon. Of course, if he spent the night in Rome, the fire may have delayed him.'

He spoke the truth. It shone from him and Nero believed

it. It made no difference to what came next.

Looking back, long after it was over, Math thought there was nothing else Pantera could have done or said that would have made any difference, and that Pantera had known it from the moment Nero called Math to his side. Possibly, he had known it before he ever stepped into the garden.

'Then we see an obvious answer to Rome's dilemma.' Nero's smile was joyful. 'We gave our word and we will keep it. We grant you permission to take Math, for whom we have a great affection, to Ostia, after which we require that you return and undertake to hunt down for us the man Saulos, who so inflamed our mercy. Unless you wish to break the night's covenant and depart from us now? In which case our agreement is void and the boy remains in our company. We will bless him with all possible care.'

Math swayed. His knees turned to water.

Nero's grip kept him upright. Nero's softest, most dangerous voice said, 'See how greatly he desires to stay?'

Pantera stood very still. His face had lost all colour, except for the two flaring patches of red at the hairline just above his ears where Nero had held him. 'My lord will accept my sworn word that I will return after Math's ship has sailed?'

'We shall.'

'The boat, of course, must reach its destination unhampered and without delay.'

A man does not make bargains with his emperor. Nero's lips tightened. Stooping, he kissed Math on the cheek. 'If it does not, it shall be through no agency of ours.'

'My lord?'

A woman's voice rang out across the garden. 'It may be that the former prefect, Pantera, is required to travel with the boy to keep him safe and deliver him to the womb of his family. If that were the case, I would undertake to hunt

536

Saulos the Herodian for you in his stead. The Sibyls have resources no man can match.'

Math drew a tortured breath. A man may perhaps bargain with this emperor, but a woman would do well to remember that Nero had ordered his own mother slain; that he routinely took lovers of both sexes without care for his wife's shame – his second wife. The first, too, had died by his word.

Nero's head turned to Hypatia with dangerous slowness. 'You wrote the prophecy that destroyed our city. Your life is forfeit. We shall have retribution. The people require it.'

Pantera stepped between them. 'Lord, she did not speak the prophecy. What does my lord gain by her death? Is harmony served by insulting the Sibyls?'

'Ha!' Clinging to Math, Nero spun round in a circle, jabbing a finger at Pantera's chest, and then at Shimon's. 'But this Hebrew insults us and you say it is nothing! Doubtless, you would have us free him too?'

'I seek only justice, lord, done and seen to be done, for the greater glory of our emperor and of Rome.'

'Then we shall release him' – Nero clapped his hands to the sky – 'when he names us his lord.'

Shimon's smile was full of pity for the tortured youth in front of him. Math wished he hadn't seen it. 'It is my very great regret,' he said, 'that I cannot do that. There is no lord but the god of Israel whose name alone is for ever held in awe. You are Caesar, a man, ruler of men, lord only of the material world. You hold temporary ownership of our lands, nothing more. I cannot name you lord.'

In the garden, nobody moved except Nero, who turned with a dreamlike slowness back to face Shimon. His face was blotched white and red; his breathing had the jerkiness of a man who has just slaked his lust.

When he spoke, it was in a whisper, yet easily heard. 'Then you will die,' he said. 'You will burn on the Field of Mars this night to light the darkness of those who survived this fire, wrought by your countryman. All those who aided him will die at your side.'

Releasing Math, Nero subsided on to his dining couch and selected an olive. To those standing in attendance, to Pantera, to Math, to Hypatia, and to Mergus, who gently held Shimon, he said, 'Leave us. Take the boy to the docks and return before dusk. We would contemplate alone the ills brought upon our city and how we may best repair them.'

CHAPTER SIXTY-SEVEN

Ostia lay white and blue at the mouth of the Tiber; a mirage of shimmering marble caught between blue sky and bluer sea. An uneven line of ships' masts needled the southerly horizon. The horses caught the breath of sea air before Hannah did, and quickened their pace, so that the harbour came into view more suddenly than she expected.

'There.' Ajax rose up in the saddle and pointed. 'Towards the back. The banner of the Sun Horse rides at the mast head.'

That had a history; his voice resonated with a lifetime's stories just of that banner. Hannah wanted to ask what they were, but they were moving too swiftly now, and there was no time, and in any case they had not yet spoken, except the barest words needed to find their way here.

For eleven miles, she had wanted to ask a lot of things, to talk, to explain about the night, to find out if she would be welcome on the ship, whether Pantera might come too. If she wanted him to come. If he wanted to come with her. If the world were not so hopelessly divided and she caught on the blade's edge, unable to tilt either way.

She needed to speak and could not until Ajax spoke to her, and he had not done so yet, except once, at the cottage to ask her if she needed a hand to mount, and then to speak directions in single words that she didn't need. She wanted to ask how he knew the way to Ostia, too, and couldn't.

The ship he had pointed to was not the greatest of those swaying at anchor in the bowl-shaped harbour, but far from the least. Lean and racy, it looked good enough to outsail most of those there, to cut through the waves rather than having to roll over their crests as had the ship that had borne them all to Alexandria so long ago.

A man sat on a fisherman's stool nearby. She wouldn't have noticed him, but that he stood and shaded his eyes, looking towards them, and then waved.

She said, 'Who is it that waits?'

'My mother's brother.'

'He looks like a Roman.' From a distance, Hannah thought he was not unlike a somewhat older Pantera, but taller, with longer, blacker hair that shone like a raven's wing in the sun.

'He served with the legions for many years,' Ajax said.

His tone was too even. 'You don't like him?' Hannah asked.

'I don't know.' For the first time that morning, he sounded human. 'It wasn't only my sister's dreams that sent me here; Valerius' dreams of many nights mirrored hers and it was by his leave that I came. By his order, you might say. Very little happens amongst our people now without his blessing.'

'I find it hard to imagine you taking orders from any man.'

Once, Hannah could have said that and they could have laughed at it together, seeing a truth that applied to both of them. Now, it sounded like an embarrassing attempt to curry favour.

Ajax ignored it. 'When I left Britain, I would have said that, while I respected him, I would not have grieved at news of his death. Today, I find that I'm glad to see him.' He smiled, not at her. 'Some good has come of this, then.'

'Ajax, stop.' Hannah put her hand on his arm. He braced against her, but did slow his horse. The man, Valerius, let his hand fall and sat down again.

Hannah said, 'I won't say I regret last night because that would be untrue. But it wasn't . . .'

Throughout the eleven-mile ride, Hannah had rehearsed this. Under his bright hawk's gaze, she lost her tongue. Gathering herself was an act of will.

On a taken breath, she said, 'It wasn't an ending. Unless you want it to be. I can ride away now and we can never see each other again. But if you want that, it might be best if I didn't come to meet your mother's brother.'

'And then Pantera can meet you at the place you have arranged. After he has delivered Math.' Ajax's face was blank as polished stone. The morning sun marked out the bruises of the night, the burns on his cheek, the welts where he had been struck, but not a whisper of anger or of grief. Either would have been better than this.

'I haven't arranged anything with Pantera,' she said. 'He may be detained in Rome, or he may join us on the ship. I don't have any more idea than you do.'

'But do you want him to be on the ship? Does he? We're travelling beyond Gaul. The voyage won't take nearly as long as it took to get to Rome from Alexandria although it may seem like it for a while. In my experience, ships can become . . . crowded after the first days.'

'We managed before.' She sounded like a child and could do nothing about it.

'But Pantera wasn't with us on either voyage. In fact, we have never been all three together for long. You have had my company or his. Only in the Temple of the Oracle under the Serapeum at Alexandria did you truly have us both.'

'I don't think that counts.'

541

'I don't think so either.' No softening showed in the marble stillness of his face, but his voice became unbearably gentle. 'You had to choose, Hannah. Neither of us could do it for you. And you have. We all must live with that.'

'Is there no going back?' In full daylight, her world had become dark.

He shook his head. 'I don't think so. Among my people . . . it would be different. In the roundhouse, men and women join for love or lust, a child is made, and perhaps by the time the child is born the man has gone and the child is reared by a man she names father who was not her sire. But we are not in the roundhouse now and you have not lived like that. Pantera, I think, would not share you. And if I am honest, I would find it hard. Some stay with their first love for life. I think I would be one such.'

He lifted his hand from the reins. His horse took a step forward. 'You should go,' he said. 'I will ride down to meet my mother's brother and let him know that at least one part of the dreaming came to pass. We will each remember that we parted with courage. It is best that way.'

Hannah's breath was searing her chest. She heard horses on the road behind, and prayed as hard as she had ever done, to the god in whom Hypatia believed, that it was who she thought it was.

To Ajax, she said, 'Which part of the dream will be lost?'

'The part which said that I would return to the care of my family bringing with me the other half of my heart, and that I would be father to the child conceived in Rome.'

She counted four horses. Ajax must have heard them, too – he could hear a fly alight on a leaf a mile away. She made her own mare stand still.

'That wasn't your sister's dream,' she said. 'You told me she dreamed only of Math.'

'Graine is eight years old. And she has reasons of her own for not dreaming the making of a child. In that detail, her dreams were different from Valerius', but in all other respects they were identical. And you have what you wanted. We are no longer alone.' Ajax closed his eyes. She thought she heard him speak a prayer, or an oath, but not with her ears, only with her mind.

Presently, without opening his eyes, he said, 'Seneca's leading: he leans to the left and unbalances his horse. Pantera, just behind, is exhausted close to the point of incapacity, but not quite there yet. Math, as ever, rides as if his passion gave the horse wings. He's sad now. He has left his chariot horses behind in Rome under Nero's care.'

'And the fourth rider?' Hannah asked. 'Is it Shimon?'

'Not Shimon. Someone lighter than him, with more facility on a horse. If I had to guess, I'd say it was the guard who was with Pantera through last night.' Ajax spun his horse slowly on its haunches and looked at her properly at last. 'Shall we find out?'

Math saw Hannah first; since the last milestone, he had been searching the horizon for the sight of black hair and her smile beneath it. Coming round the final bend, he saw her cast sharp against the deep blue sea behind, with the sun spinning her hair to gold and sparking off a fragment of metal at her belt. She was too far away to see her face, but he knew from the set of her shoulders that she was unhappy.

Pantera saw them too. He murmured '*Mithras*' in a way Math had not heard before. His horse broke stride with the word then quickened straight after; he was always a man to face his own terrors.

Mergus, who had travelled all the way at Pantera's side, kept pace as if he were already bound to Pantera's shadow. Math let his own horse have its head, cantering on the firm road. Seneca swore by a haphazard assortment of other gods, and followed.

The old man hated riding; anyone could see that, but

nothing short of death would have stopped him coming to the docks to see Math depart. At least, that was what he had said when he brought them their horses; not the four chariot colts, they must be left in Rome, but good riding horses, given by a tribune Pantera knew.

Seneca had been uncommonly helpful. Math thought now that he had engineered everything so he could see Pantera meet Ajax in Hannah's presence.

Even this far away, with fifty yards still between them, the air was thick with things unspoken, sharp with care and fiercely fragmented passions, so that riding the last few strides to the dock in the hotly humid noon felt like breaking through ice on the horse trough at midwinter.

Nobody had spoken. Nobody, Math thought, was going to speak. Having least to lose, he opened his mouth, ready to take that burden himself, when the shadows at the dockside shifted, and a man stepped forward, and said, simply, 'Hello, Math.'

Math gaped, and swallowed and gaped again and stared as if his eyes might break. The man was Ajax's height, or even taller, but had Pantera's colouring: a skin that favoured the sun. He had Pantera's hair, grown long, but Ajax's mouth and the same slant to his nose. He had straight shoulders, which was entirely unlike either of them, and eyes that were black as the night sky seen in a millpond.

'You were in my dreams,' Math said. His voice was strained, needing water. Everyone was looking at him. 'You blew the horn for me at the roadside in Rome when we raced against the fire. And before that, in Alexandria, you called to me to roll tighter when I fell from the chariot. I thought you were Ajax. Or Pantera.'

'I was trying to help. I apologize if it was improper.' The man's eyes said more than his words. Here, Math thought, was someone who had known grief and pain and unbearable loss and yet still felt himself beloved of his god.

Math was staring again. He tried to look away and couldn't.

The man made a small, apologetic movement. 'I'm sorry. With so many months to prepare, I had thought I might do this better than this. You've lost a father and I bring you news of your family, and even that I haven't delivered yet.' The man gave the formal salute of the Britons. 'I am—'

'You're Valerius!' Pantera pushed his horse past Math's. Disbelief transformed his face. 'Julius Valerius, decurion of the first troop, the First Thracian cavalry, stationed at Camulodunum. You're a Lion of Mithras! You brought me to the god. You gave me the brand, and then later burned over it, so that the warriors of Britain might not know me as a servant of Rome, but would believe me one of their own. What in the god's name are you doing here?'

Valerius blinked. Math had not known him more than a dozen heartbeats, but already it was interesting to see him taken aback; it wasn't something he could imagine happening often.

'Sebastos Abdes Pantera. I had thought you dead four years since. I'm glad to see it not so.' When nobody spoke, Valerius rubbed the side of his nose. 'As to your question, I profoundly hope I'm here for the same reason you are, namely to return Math to his family. He has lost a father, but gained a brother and two sisters. The first of these, he knows. The others are waiting for him on Mona, where the legions have not yet returned.'

'They'll return soon enough,' Pantera said. 'When Nero is no longer emperor . . .'

'Of course. And we'll go to Hibernia, where Rome will never come. It is all ready. We wait only for Math. And those others who will come with us?' His black gaze glanced off Seneca and Mergus, but lingered on Pantera, Hannah and, last, and longest, Ajax.

Math was lost in a maze of words and meanings. Something Nero had said in the garden buzzed between his ears. He had thought it was another lie and given it no thought.

We gave our word that you could take the boy to his brother, who had heard of the father's death and come to look for him.

Math pushed his horse a pace closer. 'Are you my brother?' he asked of the tall man who had been a decurion of the cavalry.

Valerius frowned. He stood close enough for Math to see the lines about his eyes, and the thin web of old battle scars on his neck and hands.

'It would be my very great honour to be Caradoc's son,' he said. 'But no. The burden and joy of that fall to Cunomar.'

Math stared at him, uncomprehending.

'He doesn't understand,' Ajax said, from somewhere behind. 'He knew our father as Caradoc. But he knows his brother as Ajax.'

Math's world melted, slow as ice in the noonday sun, each word a drop that made only lately gathered sense. Numbly, he turned on his horse, all the way round with his back to the mane and his feet pointing towards the tail, to face back to where Ajax was. It was a good horse. It stood and let him do it.

'You're not Ajax?' he asked. He sounded like a small child.

'I'm who you know me to be.' Ajax brought his own horse close. He touched the back of Math's wrist. His amber eyes were uncommonly warm. 'As Ajax I came to Gaul to look for you, ready to follow wherever you went. But before I was Ajax I was Cunomar, son of Caradoc and Breaca, who was known as the Boudica, and who led the armies of Britain until her death three years ago. You are the son of Caradoc and Cwmfen, a warrior of the Ordovices. And you are my brother.'

In the hot day, Math shivered. 'My father was a warrior,' he repeated. He had always known that. Here, now, it mattered to say it aloud.

'The greatest,' Ajax said.

'But you're a bear-warrior. You're the greatest.'

'I'm a small shadow compared to our father or either of our mothers.' Ajax was smiling at last, which was a relief greater than anything else. 'Come to me, little brother, who carries the world on his shoulders. Come to me.' He pushed his horse alongside and, leaning over, swept Math off his own mount.

'Little brother,' he said again, with his lips on Math's hair. 'I saw you born, and saw our father fight for you, but I never held you or called you what you were. I should have done it sooner than this.'

He pressed a kiss to Math's crown, and then wrapped him close in a tight embrace. Slowly, it came to Math that he was weeping. *Ajax* was *weeping*. Seagulls watched them, keening. Lazy waves slapped against the dock. Ropes creaked with the swaying ships. Math clung to his brother in a blind, swooning joy, and was held.

There was a way the joy could be made greater. Squirming free, Math eased back so that he could see Ajax's face, in all its complex not-quite-hidden passion. 'Will Hannah come with us to . . . the place where we're going?' The island's name was still too foreign to speak. 'Will Pantera?'

He was half prepared for what might come, but even so the change in Ajax was still a shock; like a door slammed shut in his face, just as he was stepping through.

He found himself set back on his horse. With his face set, Ajax said, 'I don't think that will be possible. Some things must—'

A shadow slid between them. 'You don't know what's possible or impossible,' Pantera said. 'Not yet. Ajax, we need to speak in private. Will you come with me, please?'

*　　*　　*

547

The sound of Math speaking his name jerked Pantera from the shocked stillness that had bound him.

Under the gaze of Valerius, who had first brought him to Mithras – Pantera needed several days to become used to the idea of that – he found the strength to reach Ajax.

Taking the man he had once called his brother by the shoulder, he signalled Mergus, who stepped back to let them pass and did not try to follow.

They didn't go far; only round the back of the harbour-master's house, to the southern, sunny side of the dock, where women were still cleaning the last of the morning's catch, under a cloud of mewling gulls. Here, they could speak without being heard.

'Ajax . . .' Pantera still had no idea what to say.

'No.' Ajax put a hand on his shoulder, keeping him at a distance, keeping him quiet. 'You are still my brother. There is no need for conflict. When the boat leaves, Hannah will stay with you here in Ostia. Math will come with us to Mona, to join his sisters and to learn his birthright. You will, of course, raise Hannah's child well and if it chances that she comes to us in adult life, Math will be ready for her. Already he is dreaming with Valerius. These things do not happen often, or lightly.'

'Did Hannah say that she wanted to be parted from you and Math?' He could say her name. For that, Pantera gave private thanks to his god.

'Hannah is . . . ambivalent.' Ajax said. 'I am grateful, naturally, for her kindness in that. But she made her choice last night in the goose-keeper's—'

'Stop.' If they spoke of that, Pantera knew he would lose what courage he had. 'If she had made any kind of choice, she would have told you so clearly. She has more courage than either of us.'

A muscle twitched on Ajax's cheek. 'She does.'

'So we can agree about something.' Pantera sat down on the dusty stone harbour, leaning his back against the

548

harbourmaster's house. Ajax stood outlined by the crystal sky, and the sea. He burned with life; it was not hard to see why a woman might love him.

Pantera said, 'It's not only Hannah who has to make a choice. I made mine this morning in Nero's garden. Math's freedom comes at the expense of my own. To Nero, I have given my word to hunt Saulos. To Shimon, I have promised to do whatever I can to keep Jerusalem intact. Hypatia and Mergus have pledged to help me.'

Ajax shook his head. 'Shimon and Hypatia would release you from your pledges, and from what I've seen of Mergus, he will follow where you lead and count himself lucky. As to Nero – you don't have to keep your word to that . . . filth.'

'I do. He's emperor and his word is law. Your father escaped him, but Math has a family to meet and he can't do so if he's constantly running from Nero's agents. So I must go, and Hannah can't come with me. Even if she wanted to, I wouldn't take her; the risk is too great. I give her to your care. Whether you choose to love her or to abandon her out of false pride is entirely your own affair.'

Ajax watched the gulls a while. 'Her child,' he said. 'In Valerius' dream I was the father, but—'

'When I was with the Dumnonii, a child's father was the man who reared her, who taught her, who protected her, who cared for her as she grew. Who sired her mattered not. If that has changed . . .' Pantera shrugged.

'It hasn't.' Ajax crouched down on his heels. Their eyes were level. His gaze searched the crannies of Pantera's soul. 'You love her as I do,' he said. 'Why are you doing this?'

Under the merciful touch of his god, Pantera gave the best and only gift in his possession. 'When she reached the height of her passion,' he said, 'she spoke a name. It wasn't mine.'

'Truly?' Ajax's eyes did not let go.

'I swear it in the name of my god, and by the oath I gave

your father. Nothing is more sacred to me.' By that same god, by that same memory of Caradoc, Pantera hid deep in his own memory the name he had heard and prayed that Ajax not ask it.

He didn't.

They were silent a long time. Neither of them broke the thread of their joined gaze. At the end, Ajax held out his hand. They hooked their fingers together and, like that, using each other as a lever, they stood.

'If you need help in killing Saulos,' Ajax said, 'you know the ways to ask.'

'I know some of them, I think. But I'll try not to impose.'

'Helping a brother is never an imposition. And when you have killed him, there will always be a place for you amongst the bear-warriors of Britain, wherever we are. Hannah's daughter will be there. She will grow knowing who sired her; that Sebastos Pantera was first among his peers in the skills of life, and war.'

Pantera found his throat dry, and speech difficult. 'If you were to name her Gunovar,' he said, 'it would be a great kindness. One day, perhaps I will tell her why.'

CHAPTER SIXTY-EIGHT

'Hannah?'

She heard Pantera call her name, and could read nothing in it. But then she watched them come round the side of the harbourmaster's house together as brothers, and knew there was only one way that could have come about. She was already weeping when Pantera reached her and drew her aside.

'Why?' she asked.

The others turned their backs, giving them privacy. Pantera's hands stroked her hair as they had done in the night, and under the veiled gaze of dawn. His eyes fed on her face.

'Nero had Math,' he said. 'The only thing I had to bargain with was myself. I have pledged to hunt Saulos. Hypatia and Mergus have sworn to come with me.'

'Shimon?'

'Shimon will die this evening. He is Nero's scapegoat; a man on whom all blame can rest.'

'Oh, Shimon . . .' She pressed her head to his chest where the even beat of his heart reached her. 'I don't want to lose you.' The words were jagged in her throat.

He kissed the crown of her head. 'I'll be with Hypatia. We can talk of you together. Ajax couldn't have done that.'

He leaned back, and tilted her head up. 'I promised I'd bring her to greet you. She's here, she'll come if you want her, but she said it would be easier on both of you not to meet again. You said your goodbyes in the goose-hut.'

Hannah said nothing; speech was impossible. Pantera read the answer in her eyes. 'I'll tell her,' he said.

He stepped back. She caught his wrists, thinking he was leaving. 'Will your daughter never know you?' she asked. 'What do I tell her?'

'Tell her the truth. That you loved two men, one of whom sired her, one of whom fathered her. Ajax has said he will tell her the same.' He eased his hands free, kindly. 'Ajax said I could come and find you when Saulos is dead. I'll send word first. If you don't want me, if it will make your lives too difficult, tell me so and I will find somewhere else to go.'

'I won't do that.' She was frantic now, feeling the end. 'I couldn't.'

'Don't sell your future to the present. Only raise our daughter well, knowing love, and not war. You and Ajax can do this. It's what matters most.'

He bent his head and kissed her and straightened and walked away to speak to Math. Hannah did not move until he was gone.

Without knowing, Pantera had saved the hardest to last.

Math came to him slowly, as one who expects a beating. As he crossed the white stone, Pantera had time to think how long he had known it would come to this. Entering Nero's garden, certainly, it had been clear there was no other way out. Leaving the goose-keeper's cottage, he was fairly sure he had already known it. And then perhaps before he got there, in the night when he made his bargain with Nero and was prefect for the duration of darkness, with a promise that a boy would be freed with the dawn. Or before that, even, before he'd returned to Rome, when he saw the race in the compound at Alexandria, and Nero's grief. Or in Coriallum, giving his oath to a dying man in a fire. Or stepping on to the dock, to see a gold-headed, filthy dock thief pretending to fish with the stink of horses in his hair. Or—

'Must you go?' Math's voice was breaking. For the first time, Pantera heard it slide down and crack and come back again. 'Nero won't find us if you don't do as he said.'

'I'm afraid he will. And there's no honour in giving an oath and then breaking it. Even to such as he. Valerius and Ajax will teach you that.'

'I want to learn it from you.' Math's face was pinched and white under the violent afternoon sun. Blued echoes of sleeplessness and anguish laid their prints beneath his eyes. The joy with which he had held Ajax was burned away in a loss for which he felt responsible.

Pantera felt himself too tall, but did not want to crouch. He sat on a stone bollard set into the dockside and so brought his face level with Math's. 'You've learned almost as much as I can teach you,' he said. 'But I promise you now that if it's possible to come back after we've killed Saulos, I will do it. And an oath to you given from the heart is worth ten to other people.'

Math bit his lip. 'Will you really kill Saulos?'

'I swear to you I will do everything I possibly can to kill Saulos.'

'And not let him kill you?'

'Not if I can help it, no. Math—' He caught his hand awkwardly. He was not Math's brother, and had never known how to hold him. 'You can blame yourself for this, and become bitter and sour. Or you can accept the gift of freedom and know that bitterness will not sweeten any-thing for anyone. Will you try not to be bitter, if I try not to get myself killed?'

Math's grey eyes were swollen and red. A single tear spilled from one corner. 'I'll try.'

553

'Which is the best anyone can do. If I can free the chariot colts, I'll do it. If I get them, I'll send them to Britain; that way you'll know I'm still alive and hunting Saulos. You should go now. I think they're waiting.' He put his arm round Math and hugged him. It felt right. 'Don't forget this.'

Math walked alone down the dockside and up the wooden plank that led to the ship.

The *Sun Horse* was manned by eight Gauls; big blond men who spoke little and moved about the boat with soft feet and deft hands and took their places willingly at the rowing benches to take the ship from harbour; on this boat, there were no slaves. Her master knew Ajax by his other name, and greeted Math as if he were royalty.

'Son of Caradoc,' he said, 'we have waited for you these ten long years. Welcome.'

Math found a place at the stern, where he could still watch the shore. A yard away, on the dockside, separated from them by an arm's length of sea that could have been stepped over with ease, Pantera had remounted.

With Seneca on one side and Mergus on the other, he waited to see the ship leave and it seemed to Math that the spy's grief hung around him like raven's wings, as Hannah's did. She had gone to the front of the boat, and would not look back. So much hurt, and so much joy. Math thought he might tear apart, pulled by each of them.

Pantera caught his eye and waved. Math waved back, and on that signal the ship's master blew a whistle. Seven men moved into place with military speed. Last, the Gaul remaining on shore cast off the rope and jumped aboard and they pushed off from the harbour.

The oars dipped and pulled. The boat lurched forward and again, and then settled into the surge and ebb of smooth rowing.

The tall man of Math's dreams came to stand at his

side. 'There's a woman standing in the shade of the harbourmaster's house,' Valerius said. He didn't point, but directed his eyes a little south. 'Hannah knows she's there, but not, I think, your brother. He sees what he needs, and it seems he does not need to see that. Who would she be?'

Math looked where he was shown. 'It's Hypatia,' he said. 'She's going to Jerusalem with Pantera to help kill Saulos.'

'Thank you. I had hoped it would be so. I'll leave you now. Segoventos says we'll have good weather for the full voyage. He was trained by his father, who was the best ship's master I've ever met. Even so, I shall spend the days puking over the side. You would be doing me a kindness if you did not offer me food.'

EPILOGUE

The ship sailed due west, down the line of the setting sun. Late in the evening, Math moved to the bow to catch the last of the failing light. Between one breath and the next, he saw the sun set fire to the world. What had been tints of flame on the bow-wave spread out and out across the wide sea until the whole blue-grey glittering ocean became a bed of living flame too bright to bear.

He closed his eyes. The fire grew stronger behind the dark of his lids, rising from sea to sky. A hand reached through it. He extended his own hand in response and felt it grasped by a dry, firm grip.

'Welcome. I had hoped it would be you.'

The voice was Shimon's, the peaceful voice of a man come home to himself.

Math opened his eyes. Hot fire continued to rise to the sky, blotting out the sunset. It filled the whole of the world, from horizon to horizon, with living flame; the ship was gone.

Shimon was the fire's centre, standing upright, bound to a stake. Beyond and behind, men and women watched in their straggling hundreds, huddled in groups together. Their mouths were open, shouting. No sound came, not even the roaring flames.

'Math?' Shimon spoke in the silence in his head. 'Could you assist me?'

Math had no idea what to do, and then did. He reached a hand out to untie the bindings that held his friend. The fire did not touch him.

'Thank you.'

Stepping free, Shimon rinsed his hands and face in the flames as he might at the morning's water trough. He looked past Math. His face, cast in shimmering gold by the fire, became radiant with a new joy.

'Lord.' He made to kneel. A man came forward from Math's left, and caught him, saying, 'Don't kneel, my friend. All kneeling is done. You have done all that could have been asked of you, and more. Be safe now, and well.'

They embraced, two men of same height and same build, only that Shimon was the elder by three decades.

A woman came, wreathed in flame and sun. Her hair was black smoked silk. Her eyes were almonds. She said, 'Shimon,' and it was a summoning and a welcome and a thanks. The fire consumed them, all three.

'Math.' Valerius' voice reached for him. 'You need to come back now.'

Hannah's face grew from the fire. Ajax was a bear, hunting the sunset. Pantera had blood dribbling down over one eye.

Math closed his own eyes and opened them again. The faces vanished, replaced by the darkling waves. The sun was old and almost set. It laid beaten copper on the ocean.

Valerius sat beside him looking vaguely ill. 'What did you dream?' he asked.

'Shimon's dead,' Math said. 'He wants us to know that he's safe and beyond pain. And Hannah's mother sends her love to all of us.' He turned, to look into the black eyes. 'Pantera will come and find us, won't he? Later, when he's killed Saulos?'

'The god holds that man close,' Valerius said. 'When he's killed Saulos, if he can travel to join us, he will.'

He left soon after that. Math stayed at the bow until the sun's last bruise left the waves and the moon rose to salt them silver, colour of new hope, and new life.

Then he sent his mind forward to the land ahead, to the sisters he had never met, that she might know he was coming, and might dream a safe journey home.

THE END

AUTHOR'S NOTE

The Emperor's Spy has had a long gestation period. The first seeds were set while I was writing the first novel in the four-part Boudica cycle, when I was looking forward to a time beyond Boudica, and wanting to revisit some of the surviving characters beyond the events of AD 61.

I knew very little of the great fire of Rome apart from the useful fact that it was three years after the end of the Boudican revolt, which seemed a good time frame for a sequel. Later, while researching the life of the Emperor Nero for the second Boudica novel, I found more – for instance that there's no way Nero fiddled while Rome burned, in part because fiddles hadn't been invented in AD 64, but mainly because, contrary to popular opinion, he was doing his level best to help his people. Nero was a chariot racer as well as an actor/singer and I spent most of *Boudica: Dreaming the Bull* with an image in the back of my mind showing a boy racing his chariot against a background of flames.

True to that image, at the end of *Boudica: Dreaming the Bull* I left Caradoc and his newborn son, Math, in Gaul with plans to come back later. In the four years that followed, I gathered snippets of useful information. In particular, I watched a television documentary in which it was pointed out that the fire was lit on the first night in AD 64 in which Sirius, the dog star, rose over Rome – and that there were in circulation at the time 'apocalyptic manuscripts' which predicted that the Kingdom of Heaven would arise only if Rome were to burn under the eye of the dog star.

Even for a hardened cynic, that was too much of a coincidence to be accidental. The programme went on to suggest that 'one of the many sects of Christianity' had lit the fire on the grounds that they were the only ones with a vested interest in bringing about the Kingdom of Heaven, which in turn seemed entirely reasonable.

Thus, when it came time to begin *The Emperor's Spy*, there were two primary routes of research. The first was to create the characters who could successfully carry through what was by then looking like a spy thriller. The second was to come to grips with the history of very early Christianity – that period between the death of the man we know today as Jesus Christ and the development of the 'many sects' who battled it out for control of the new religion in the second and third centuries.

The first of these was by far the easier. Quite early on, I discovered references to the gravestone of an archer named Julius Abdes Pantera. He died in Germany, but he had served in Judaea and there are mentions in early Christian texts that Christ was in fact the son of Pantera. I chose not to carry that through (it was a complication too far), but 'the Leopard' was such a perfect name for a spy that I couldn't let it go completely. Sebastos Abdes Pantera arrived early, bright and shiny and whole – a writer's dream.

Others grew around him: I have followed Ajax from childhood and wish to follow him through his adulthood into old age, if he survives that long. Valerius is an old friend and I considered bringing him back, but decided that he had grown through the great learning of his life and deserved some peace, so we see him only at the end.

And so I began to investigate the 'many sects' of Christianity, to find which one might have started the fire. I had an idea that Peter, Paul and Mary might each have founded their own traditions by then, each teaching something different, and that this might have been a source of conflict.

I was wrong. In fact, I was completely wrong, and so was the TV documentary. There were, it turns out, dozens of early sects, each claiming a monopoly on the truth – but none of them got off the ground until the early second century. At the time we're talking about – the mid-60s of the first century AD, thirty years after the crucifixion – there were no sects at all, just two competing groups of people.

The first, much larger group was composed of the Sicari zealots who had lived, worked and fought with the man known then as Judas the Galilean, and continued his work after his death. They were supported by the many, many thousands of followers who had joined what the contemporary historian Josephus calls 'the Fourth Philosophy'.

The second, smaller group was led by the man we know as St Paul, self-proclaimed 'apostle to the Gentiles' who had been sprinting around the eastern Mediterranean doing his utmost to undermine the Galilean's followers, preaching a new covenant based on the abjuration of the old Hebrew laws and the creation of a new faith. Reading between the lines of Acts, Paul's attested letters and the book of James, it seems clear to me that he hated them and they hated him to the point where they tried to kill him and only swift action by the local Roman legions in Jerusalem got him out alive.

I therefore decided to look more closely at the two men central to the Christian myth: St Paul – referred to here as Saulos – and Judas the Galilean, known to later generations by the Greek name Jesus, an adaptation of the name Yeshu or Yeshua (Joshua) which means 'saviour' in Hebrew.

I should say that nowhere is there any concrete proof of either man's existence, never mind their lives and deaths, in the way there is, say, for Nero, whose life – and death – were recorded in a number of different classical sources, some of which were written by men who were alive at the time. We can also still visit the monuments that were built in Nero's name, complete with the inscriptions. And if we need to know what Nero looked like, we have a series of coins that were struck during his reign showing his progress towards maturity. On a grander scale, we know which legions marched where on his orders, which governments were overthrown as a result, and what politics ebbed and flowed around him.

He was a giant figure, is gigantically recorded, and that's as good as historical proof ever gets, short of an inscribed tomb with bones that could be DNA-tested. Thus, in so far as we believe anything in history to be an objective fact, we can say that Nero was indeed emperor of Rome. How he ruled is open to interpretation and is the stuff of heated academic argument, but nobody doubts his existence.

We cannot however say the same about Judas/Jesus or any of the men, women and children associated with him – which may be one reason why the arguments as to the truth are a lot more heated and not restricted to the academic field.

Taking Paul first, we have seven authenticated epistles – which is to say those letters that scholars conclude were all written by the same man who may have called himself Saulos/Paul and may have been instrumental in spreading the Christian myth around the eastern Mediterranean.*

*See 'Sources' for a list of the relevant letters.

Few men of the early church are viewed with such varied passions. At one end of the scale, St Paul is the founding father of the Christian church, the 'Apostle to the Gentiles' who brought the faith to Rome, at huge personal risk.

At the other end, he's a delusional 'seer of visions' who took upon himself the role of 'educating' the Greek-speaking Hebrews of the Mediterranean and in the process demolished all the hope, compassion, equality and mercy that the man we know as Jesus Christ taught, thus setting the tone for future generations of hate, misogyny and homophobia.

There is a third view, developed in more depth by Robert Eisenman and Hyam Maccoby, which seems most plausible to me and is the one I have developed in *The Emperor's Spy*. It holds, in essence, that Paul/Saulos was a Roman agent tasked with suppressing the growing anti-Roman insurgency fomented by the Sicari rebels of the movement Josephus calls 'the Fourth Philosophy'.

A failed Pharisee who lacked the necessary grasp of logic to be taken on as a rabbi, the embittered Paul joined what was, in effect, the military police run by the Sadducees under the auspices of the High Priest. In this role, he spent several years pursuing and torturing members of the Fourth Philosophy in an effort to subdue the insurrection. But he failed – they were stronger than anything the Romans could do to them and every man, woman or child tortured only recruited more to their cause.

If he wasn't a Roman agent to begin with (in my fiction, I have said that he was), then it was around now that he was recruited and given the more complex task of turning the Hebrews' famed religiosity against them, making it a weapon that would bind them more closely to Rome, removing the necessity for revolt.

To do so, he created a new religion, basing it on the death of the Galilean, a man he had never met; a man whose *followers* he barely met until he was summoned to Jerusalem in the early 60s and asked to explain himself.

Failing, he would certainly have been executed had not a Roman detachment taken him into protective custody and escorted him to safety in Caesarea. He languished in prison for two years and then vanished from history well before the date of the fire.

Nevertheless, it seems to me that of the two groups around at the time of the fire, the one which was fixated on the imminent arrival of the 'Kingdom of Heaven', the one which had most to gain – and least to lose – by burning Rome, was Paul's.

He had the motive and the means and I don't think Nero was as mad as everyone says, or at least not in this: if he crucified anyone afterwards, it was because they were intimately involved in the fire. He won't have known them as Christians because I don't think they'd begun to take on that name yet, but even if they had, they were Paul's creation, not related to the real thing.

If you're interested in more detail, I'd recommend reading Robert Eisenman's book *James, the Brother of Christ* for a far more intricate look at the enmity between Paul and James, and Hyam Maccoby's *The Mythmaker* for a more detailed look at Paul the man.

Judas the Galilean is less easy to pin down. The historian Josephus is our only source for him, in the way that the Christian gospels are the only source for Jesus.

Daniel Unterbrink, in his book *Judas the Galilean: the Flesh and Blood Jesus*, argues that Judas was the basis for the Christian story, while I think that the man who led the Sicari zealots in their audacious raid on the armoury at Sepphoris in AD 6 was not the same man who, say, preached the Sermon on the Mount or gave rise to the aphorisms in the gospel of Thomas. That, I believe, was Judas' pacifist vegetarian brother, the Nazirite James, but

I share Unterbrink's view that Judas was the basis for the part of the story that relates to the crucifixion.

Josephus tells us nothing of Judas' death but he does tell us that his grandson, Menahem, raided an armoury to arm his men and that he rode into Jerusalem on a donkey proclaiming himself the messiah, from which we might infer that nobody thought there was only one messiah or that he had been and gone – and that he was probably following a family tradition.

For me, the clinching argument that Judas' death was taken and usurped by men who had never met him is that they twisted his name. He was Judas, leader of the Sicarioi. By stroking a T across the last letter and inverting the first two, we have Judas Iscariot – a surname not known in Hebrew histories to that point. If you wanted to hide the origins of your sect, if you wanted to make it as pro-Roman as you could, while removing all stain of an anti-Roman past, what better way than to hide the name of the man who had founded it, than in the name of his own worst enemy?

I don't think Paul did this – he was using the moniker 'Christ Jesus' which means 'saviour saviour' in Greek, and then the Greek version of the Hebrew Yeshua. Another example is 'Thomas Didymus', which means 'twin twin' in the same two languages – clearly there was a habit at the time of saying the same thing twice. That said, I think that, like 'Boudica' which means 'victory' and was a name acquired after the fact, this was a name given by Paul to highlight the role of the man whose death he had usurped. It became current only after the fall of Jerusalem and the utter destruction of the Fourth Philosophy.

By then, if we follow Joseph Atwill's theories in *Caesar's Messiah*, Paul was gone from the scene, but Titus Vespasian and Josephus together saw the value in continuing what he had begun and it was they who put together the mix of fact and fiction that became the gospels. In creating a religion that could be acceptable under Roman rule, it was in their interests to paint it as pro-Roman and anti-Semitic as they could, while distancing it as far as possible from the insurrection that had been at its heart. They changed a lot of names, but turning the name of the hero Judas of the Sicarioi into a traitor was the greatest act of spin, and the most successful.

Judas had at least three sons and a number of grandsons, the last of whom was crucified at around ninety years of age. His daughters are not recorded, but then Josephus doesn't ever tell us much about women unless it's to point out how flaky they were, so I have allowed myself to assume that he had at least one daughter. Hannah was always going to take a central role in my novel – although I didn't know until I was writing her story which of the possible men in her life would climb the wall into the goose-keeper's garden and become the father of her child.

Of the other characters taken from history, Shimon is Simon, also known as Simon Peter, Cephas and, latterly, St Peter. It seems to me that, next to Judas the Galilean, Shimon's memory has been most traduced by those who came after him. In *The Emperor's Spy*, St Peter is restored to his original character as Shimon the zealot, referred to by Josephus as Sadduc/Zadok, the Galilean's lieutenant and a senior figure in the Sicari zealots, a man who devoted his life to expelling Rome from his country and restoring a theocracy based on Hebrew texts.

As with all good books, the era has drawn me deeper than I had ever imagined, which means there are at least three more books in plan that will see Pantera, the Leopard, pursue Paul into Jerusalem and out again and then across the empire in his quest for fulfilment and peace.

SOURCES

My sources are too numerous to list individually, but the primary texts are as follows:

- Tacitus, who provides most of the detail of the fire. In fact, as with the burning of Colchester and London in the Boudican revolt, without his account we would barely know it happened. I have based my timeline of the conflagration itself on his account.
- The writings of Josephus, both 'Antiquities' and 'War', particularly those parts of 'Antiquities' that deal with the rise of what he terms the 'Fourth Philosophy' of Judaism, also known as the 'Assembly of the Poor' or 'the Way'.
- Acts, particularly the so-called 'we' document beginning at Chapter 16 which is narrated in the first person plural and which contains details of St Paul's actions until the early 60s, concluding with his excommunication from the Assembly headed by James, and his flight from Jerusalem.
- The epistles of Paul which are generally considered to be authentic, these being: 1 Thessalonians, Galatians, Philippians, Philemon, 1 and 2 Corinthians, 1 Romans 15/16. I am assuming that the insertion into 1

Corinthians 14 v 34–36 regarding the role and actions of women is a later addition. Apparently this is absent from the earliest manuscripts of this text, is added as a marginal note later, and is inserted into a number of other places before settling in its current position. The text reads perfectly acceptably without it, in fact, it makes a great deal more sense. It also clears Paul of the charge of misogyny, which otherwise doesn't stick.

Other early sources have provided insight into the times, particularly Suetonius and Philo.

The works of Joseph Atwill (*Caesar's Messiah*), Bart D. Ehrman (various, particularly *Lost Christianities*), Robert Eisenman (*James, the Brother of Christ* and *The New Testament Code*), Hyam Maccoby (*The Mythmaker*) and Daniel T. Unterbrink (*Judas the Galilean: the Flesh and Blood Jesus*) were key to my reconstruction of events at the time.

I don't agree in their entirety with any of them, but an amalgamation of the concepts outlined by Eisenman, Unterbrink and Atwill in particular have enabled me to envisage a time frame and event cycle that makes sense of what is otherwise a historical morass. Elaine Pagels and Karen L. King were also immensely instructive and Paul Cresswell very kindly sent me the chapter concerning St Paul from his then unpublished work *Jesus the Terrorist* (now in press and due for publication in early 2010).

I am persuaded by Bart Ehrman that the earliest existing versions of Luke contain no reference to the Eucharist. (http://rosetta.reltech.org/TC/extras/ehrman-pres.html)

Given that Luke post-dates Paul's letters, it may be that Paul was not its progenitor and that the instructions on its practice given in 1 Corinthians 17 are a later addition, but Paul still seems to me the most likely progenitor – only a committed anti-Semite would both annihilate the

Hebrews' covenant to their God *and* incorporate into his newly minted religion a rite that, while normal among the Greeks in their worship of Dionysus, was an abomination to the Hebrews.

For the rest, I am indebted to Justin Pollard and Howard Reid for their magnificent text on Alexandria, and particularly for the revelation that the Romans had all the technology to create a hydraulic engine, or even a steam locomotive, but that slave power was cheaper than wood and so they never took it forward.

The Oracle under the Serapeum at Alexandria is a fiction, but it is based on the one recently excavated at Baia near Naples, which replicates almost exactly the details of Virgil's trip to Hades. The Serapeum itself was a dominant feature of Alexandria, but was destroyed by a Christian bishop some centuries later.

Quadrigas were of course driven four abreast rather than four in-hand, but the latter fitted the story better, so I have re-arranged the driving style.

A Note From The Author

In the early part of 2010, I was asked to write a short story for a 'What if . . .' compilation: what if various turning points in history had turned the other way. Mine, of course, was 'What if the Boudica's armies had won?' I spend half of my life talking to people at literary festivals or in reading groups about the *Boudica: Dreaming* books, and about Pantera's 'Rome' series, and we often end up discussing how life might have been had the Romans not kept their foothold in Britain, so I jumped at the chance of writing about it.

The short story went on to be published by the BBC *History* Magazine as their first item of fiction, but we include it here as something for those of you who knew Ajax when he was Cunomar, and Valerius when he was Bán, and who watched the Boudica's daughter, Graine, from her birth, through the trauma of her rape, to her part in the final battle. It is here, too, for those of you who have only known Ajax as he is here, who have come to know only a fraction of Valerius, and Graine barely at all. For you, this is my vision of how Pantera might have been had he remained in Britain, part of a victorious army, and chosen to remain – but as a Briton, not a Roman.

I wrote this in a short gap between sections of *Rome*:

The Coming of the King, and completed the editing after the first draft was done. For me, it's a breath of freedom, to return to Britain, to return to people I know better than most of those I come across in real life, and to return to a world where the gods and the dreaming hold true. It is, in fact, sheer, glorious self-indulgence. I offer it for your entertainment.

Manda Scott, Shropshire, mid-summer 2010

The Last Roman In Britain

The girl was not a ghost; she only looked like one. Wreathed in mist, she stepped out of the storm, and crouched at his side. 'Are you Hywell of the white scar?'

'I am.' Her eyes were grey and seemed too grave to be the eyes of a child. Unsettled, Hywell said, 'How did you know my name?'

'They said you were controlling the fighting. Who else could it be?' She pointed down the slope into the bowl of flat land where the remaining men of the Second Legion fought to their late, swift deaths. They died for nothing, not even to defend their standard: they had not brought the Eagle with them on either of the last two sallies from the fort.

'I am to tell you that the Boudica's army is within reach. If you need more warriors, they will come.' She had a light, grave voice, that put him in mind of winter breezes, and starlight at dusk.

'Thank you.' He looked at her more closely. She was small and slight and would have been blonde if the rain had not plastered her hair darkly to her head. Her face was oval, with high cheeks, her eyes the grey of a sky after rain. He imagined her adult, and knew then, who she was.

He wiped rain from his eyes. 'Do you think we'll need your mother's warriors?'

'Maybe.' Her cloak was of oiled wool. The water ran off it in fat drops. She settled it around her shoulders and stared down onto the battlefield, assessing it much as he had done.

The Roman legionaries were clustered in a ring with their shields locked tight and their gladii stabbing out between. The pride of the Dumnonii, Hywell's tribe, stood about them in a wider circle, unshielded for the most part, without helmets, without any of the stolen mail they had worn earlier in the day when there had still been a chance they might lose the battle. Now they were naked in the fray, men and women equally, that their children might tell of this in their dotage; how their mothers and fathers slew the last century of the last legion armed only with the blades of their ancestors, and claimed the land back for their own.

They fought under a storm-sky, on bloody earth, and behind them, in the west, the fortress of the Second Legion was a black void haloed with scarlet; the fires that had been lit in the early morning were feeding on whole oak limbs now, and the summer storm had not the power to extinguish them.

Such a simple thing to end a siege; if he had known all it would take was a good, hot fire, Hywell would have lit it far sooner. But then he was inclined to think that if he had lit it sooner, the men inside would have had the wit to reach buckets down into the southern sea below the cliffs that held their backs, and empty them onto the flames, leaving the wood to smoke in useless ruin.

It had taken this long; four months of warriors camped around the fort, just out of missile range, so that the defending legion had to rely on their well water, and their reducing rations to eat and drink. It had taken the steady flow of message birds flying into the high lofts on the fort's roof, telling of the defeat of the Ninth legion, the fall of Camulodunum and then Lugdunum, of Suetonius Paulinus' failure to take the stronghold of Mona, sacred to the gods, of his decision to turn back and confront the Boudica's warriors; of his long, slow drawn-out defeat as those warriors had harried and hunted his legions so that they could not march from one night camp to the next without losing men.

Later, reading the smokes of camp fires and hearing the skull drums and the victory horns of night encampments in the forests beyond their fort, they had learned of his final defeat.

When they killed and ate their cavalry horses, when the flow of deserters grew from a trickle to a river, and each one ready to tell him of the humiliation, the desperation, the waning discipline, of the few who held out for Nero to send reinforcements, of the greater mass who knew they had been abandoned – then Hwyell had known they were ripe for the picking.

And when the Boudica's brother had sent down the Eagles of the Ninth, the Fourteenth and the Twentieth legions for him to set about the fort as proof that they were alone on this foreign soil, the last legion in Britain, then he had known the time was perfect.

He had ordered that the biggest of logs not be used for the fire, but dragged out onto the flat plain at the dark of the moon. The remnants of the Second legion had sallied out through the main gates at dawn, when the ground was still dry and they could hold their ranks in good order. Under the morning light, the great, hewn trunks lay in a haphazard pattern across the battlefield, giving cover to the waiting warriors.

Under Hywell's watching gaze, the first three centuries had marched forward in good order, aiming for the oaks. The leading ranks only discovered the ditches that had been dug ahead of the logs by falling into them, losing men to the stakes and loose boulders set beneath the latticework of willow and turf.

The centurions were seasoned men, used to acting in adversity. They pulled their troops back and sent them forward again in narrow columns, testing the ground, in the course of which, they discovered that there was method in the chaotic patterns of the logs. Thus they advanced in a long, winding snake – not line abreast, which was their strength.

Hywell's warriors had waited and waited, and only when he had set the bull horn to his lips and sounded the note had the first hundred risen from behind the felled trees.

The battle had not been fast or clean; the legionaries of the Second legion had fought with the ferocity of men with nothing to lose, slashing out like cornered stags, calling on Jupiter, Mars and Mithras to help them to die with honour, and to kill as many as they might while doing it, but they were against warriors who had nursed their hatred for twenty years, who cared not if their lives were the cost of victory.

The men and women of the Dumnonii fought for the future of their children and the land under their feet. They fought for their gods and their ancestors and their language. They fought for their roundhouses and the chance once again to bear weapons in the open. They fought with their hounds at their sides and their children at their backs and they were winning with such ease now because they had worked through the night to drag forward the trees on Hywell's orders, for he had the best understanding of Rome and its legions.

Which was why he was lying here on the warm, wet earth with the stench of blood and entrails rolling over him in steaming waves. And why the Boudica's daughter had come to find him.

She turned to him now. Her grey eyes rested on his face.

'Your warriors need no help,' she said, 'The Romans will all be dead by dusk.'

A shadow crossed his soul, stirred from a darkness he had not explored in all his time with the Dumnonii.

Her eyes saw all of him. 'You're Gunovar's father?' she asked. 'Aerthen is her mother?'

'Yes,' he said, 'And yes.' Aerthen, love of his life, was on the battlefield. The hardest part of his morning had been their parting. He carried her scent in his nostrils, flavoured with sweet apple smoke from the first fire. Gunovar was safe, away from the carnage. His daughter was three years younger in her body and a thousand years younger in her soul than this child who had come to find him.

He said, 'You are Graine, the dreamer.' He did not say, *You are Graine, the Boudica's youngest daughter who was raped by an entire century of men and nearly died. You are Graine, who held her mother as she died on the battlefield, leading the charge that broke the shield wall when the last three centuries of the Twentieth finally turned at bay.* It did not help to speak such things aloud, but she read them anyway, in his face.

'I am both of those,' she said, nodding. 'My brother and my uncle are here now, waiting at the forest's far edge. They wish to speak with you.'

He made himself smile for this small, terrifying child. 'They wish to ask how best to find the lost Eagle of the Second?'

She smiled back, teasing, and raised a brow. 'Mostly.'

The storm ended as Hywell stepped out of the forest and into the Eceni camp. The clouds cleared on the back of a freshening wind. The stench of battle swept eastwards, leaving rain-cleaned air and the mellow autumn scents of forest, horse and hound.

It was not the whole of the Boudica's army; most of them had gone now, to bring in a late harvest. But a few

577

hundred had gathered, bringing with them wagons of corn and hunting hounds, and had dug their own fire pits and latrines as if they were a Roman unit on scouting duty. The Boudica's brother, Valerius, had fought for twenty years for the legions before he came back to his people: his hand showed in everything.

Hywell counted the numbers of horses, of standards, planted in the earth, of men and women mending harness or hammering swords and it crossed his mind that if ever they wanted to assault Rome itself, this was the time to do it.

Two men waited among the tethered horses on the camp's margins. The younger was blond and naked to the waist, with the marks of the bear-warriors on his back and arms. His right ear was missing and his hair had been shaved back on both sides to show it.

Hywell did not kneel, but only because such things were not done here.

He said, 'Son of the Boudica, the Dumnonii are honoured by your presence.' It was safest to say these things; the bear-warriors of the Eceni were known from one land's end to the other and their leaders were chosen by prowess, not by age or standing or lineage. Legend said they could not be killed, and their presence on a battlefield assured victory. Their trackers were said to take the guise of a bear and to move through a forest so silently that the grazing deer would not move out of their way. The Boudica's son was said to have crushed the Ninth legion single handed, and while that could not possibly be true every single report said that he went bear-mad in battle and was not entirely sane the rest of the time. It was wise, therefore, to honour him.

The youth smiled, and was clearly Graine's brother. 'We have come too late, it seems, to be of much assistance.' Cunomar. His name was Cunomar; Hound of the sea.

'You kept the Fourteenth and the Twentieth Legions

578

from our backs while we held the siege,' Hywell said. 'That was all that we needed. We . . . owed a great deal to the Second. It's good to have been able to pay.'

'We need to look ahead, though.' Cunomar wore a knife at each hip. He drew one now and, knelt, smoothed the back of it across the mud to make a smooth plate and drew a circle with the tip thereon. Beside it, separated by a hand's breadth of mud, he drew another, smaller circle. 'This is us,' he said, 'Britain. And this—' His knife stabbed the larger circle, 'is Gaul and the Germanies, with Rome behind them. We've defeated the legions now. But we have to keep them away. How can we do that when they have already crossed the water twice?'

Cunomar drew a few lines on the mud that became troopships under full sail. When he looked up, his eyes were amber, not at all like his sister's, but frank and open.

Hywell said, 'Is it true that the bear warriors of the Eceni must fight a she-bear in her den before they are allowed to bear the scars in battle?'

'No.' Cunomar shook his head. 'But it is useful to have the Romans think so. Is it true that Hywell of the white scar can kill with the stealth of a hunting cat so that the enemy souls walk the earth, not knowing they have died? Is it true he knows more about Rome than the Romans, and that he can set traps that even the wiliest of centurions may not escape from?'

'No,' Hywell said, 'but it is useful to have the warriors think so.'

'So!' Cunomar rose, grinning, and took a step back. 'They said you were clever. It's good to know that much at least was right. So, with your cleverness and your knowledge of Rome, what would you do to stop the Emperor from attacking us afresh next year, or the year after?'

'I would change the Emperor for someone who understood the foolishness of such an act,' Hywell suggested, and waited for them to laugh at him.

Nobody did.

'How very strange,' Cunomar said, softly. 'That's exactly what Valerius said.'

The Boudica's son looked to his left, where stood the man whom Hywell had been avoiding since he stepped out of the forest. This man was taller, leaner, older, and altogether less open than his companion. A black and white colt stood behind him, resting one hind leg. He leaned on its haunch with his arms folded across his chest. His eyes were black, and if the girl-child's grey gaze had troubled Hywell's soul with its touch, under this man's look, his soul burned bright as the fires around the fortress.

Valerius, the Boudica's brother, had served half his life in the Roman Auxilliary. Once, he had been a Lion in the service of Mithras. In Camulodunum one summer when Britain had seemed at peace, this man had acted in rites for the god, bringing novices to an underground temple where they knelt in darkness for the brand, and through the pain, came to know the light.

It had been dark in the temple. There had been forty novices, and the Lion had been masked. It was one rite in dozens, maybe hundreds, he had conducted over ten years. It was possible, therefore, that he might not recognise one of his initiates if that man was wearing different dress and speaking a different language than the one he spoke now. Hywell, who had not always been Hywell, prayed that it was so.

'How did the Boudica's brother imagine he might achieve the change of an Emperor?' he asked.

'I had hoped to ask you.' Valerius said, 'Will you walk with us? I believe the fortress of the Second is safe now, for such as we three to enter.'

The fortress of the Second lay with its back to the sea. Cliffs held its southern and western borders with the bowl of the battlefield stretched to north and east.

It was quiet now, all fighting done. Children moved across the bloodied turf, stripping the dead. Warriors made fires at the edges and honed their weapons out of habit, more than need. If a new legion came at Nero's behest, it would have to land somewhere safe, and this coast was not that.

Valerius said, 'We've set watchfires all along the coast. If a galley tries to land, we'll know before the first horses hit the water.'

'Was I thinking aloud?' Hywell asked.

'No. But you were looking at your wife and your concern was clear.'

Hywell waved. Aerthen waved back and, after her, Gunovar, three years old now, light of his days and his nights. He wanted to be with them. He made signals that he would join them presently and hoped that it was true.

The two fires either side of the entrance gate to the Fortress had been quenched, which made it possible to enter. Inside, dead men leaked blood and urine and gut-spill onto the earth. Each wound told a story, each starved body a lifetime's tales. The stench of ordure and old sweat told of the months under siege.

'There's no wood,' Valerius said, turning to look. 'They've burned everything they could take without actually dismantling the fortifications. I wonder what they cooked?'

'Their horses,' Hywell said. 'Some of them defected. They told us.'

'Did you kill them?'

'Of course. They knew we would, but it was a faster, more honourable death than if they'd stayed in here and died of hunger.'

The fortress was twenty years old and had been built, layer on layer, like an onion. The outer wall was hollow, containing rooms on three floors. Within it were barracks, stables, feed rooms, harness rooms, workshops, the central headquarters, with parade grounds on three sides, and a locked room on the fourth for legionary pay.

Its doors were barred and locked. In silence, Valerius and Hywell lifted the bars and stood back to let Cunomar kick in the doors. Inside, eight chests gaped open, wide as a dead man's breath. Every other piece of wood in the room had been torn up to use as firewood.

Hywell said, 'Where's the gold? They haven't left this place in three months so they haven't spent it.'

'Buried?' Cunomar offered. 'With the Eagle?'

'Or in the officer's rooms,' said Valerius. 'We must at least look.'

It took longer to break open the doors to the head-quarters, and they had to use a broken sword as a lever. Inside was empty and dry. The echoes of men's prayers hugged the corners, causing the shadows to move. The standards of the centuries were there, and the genius of Nero, stacked in a corner.

'No Eagle,' Cunomar said.

Valerius caught Hywell's arm. 'Where would you put it, if you had to hide the thing you valued most?'

'It wouldn't be in here,' Hywell said.

Valerius turned on his heel. 'If I were under siege here, in this fort – and I might have been if things had been different – I would put the Eagle in the Mithraeum if I wanted to hide it. But if I were alive, and wanted to keep it at all costs from the enemy. I would—'

'The battlements!' Hywell was already running. 'I'd take it up to the battlements and, if someone came, I'd throw myself into the sea.'

At the foot of the stairwell, a cluster of dead warriors waited for someone to take them away. Further up, beyond the open door, a tighter knot of legionaries lay in their armour, still warm. Cunomar reached them first. He was rising as Hywell came up, wiping his knife on a dead man's cloak. One of the fallen had a newly opened throat.

'Stop!'

Valerius called out in Latin while Hywell and Cunomar were still on the steps. In Latin. 'Don't leap. There is no need. We will send you to Nero with your Eagle.'

'Will we?' Cunomar asked, as they stepped up the last few wooden steps onto the high battlements of the fortress, where they looked over the sea. Hywell looked down. He had never felt safe at great height. The waves dashing to their deaths on the rocks below looked tiny, no bigger than a child's finger, when in life they were the height of a bull. He stepped back from the edge and looked elsewhere.

Valerius was standing just in from the stair head. Opposite him, the Prefect of the Second legion, stood with one knee on the battlements. 'One step closer and I'll go,' he said.

'You can go if you wish,' said Cunomar, in perfect Latin, 'But we just offered you your life, your Eagle and a safe conduct to the Gaulish coast. Might you not wish to ask my uncle his reasons for offering that?'

He leaned his back against the grey stone that looked down over the sea and folded his arms. In the language of the Eceni, he said to Valerius, 'What do you plan?'

Possibly it was the language that pushed the Prefect, or simply that the Prefect could not face returning to Rome as the last of his legion. Whichever, he spoke his last word to his god and, in that same breath, abandoned the battlement and threw himself on his upended sword.

'No!' Three men said it, in three languages. Cunomar reached the Prefect first and slid his own knife up, into the man's heart. Death came faster like that than the ragged, imperfect sword wound that had opened the liver, but not his chest.

They were quiet after. Valerius sat a while, holding the dead man's hand with his eyes closed, his lips moving in a prayer to Mithras that Hywell knew without hearing the words.

Cunomar bit his lip and looked down at the crashing sea below; the Eagle was already gone beyond reach and the coast was too treacherous for swimmers to try for it.

Hywell moved away, softly, to the small stone hut set back from the battlements where the message birds were kept. He was not one of those who could see a spirit leave this life and move to the next, but he knew when it was happening, and the closeness of this, the intensity, brought him to a decision.

'The Prefect was not only here to throw the Eagle out of our reach, he was trying to send a message-dove to Rome,' he said, presently.

With the other two watching, he reached for the pouch at the dead man's belt and lifted from it the small quill and the block of ink and the tiny cylinders that were the tools of his trade. 'There are three birds left in the loft,' he said. 'Two are pied black and white, from the Emperor's dove-cote. One is the colour of red sandstone. That one goes to the spymaster, Seneca.'

'Seneca?' Valerius' gaze met Cunomar's over Hywell's shoulder. 'I thought you might know how he could be reached.'

Cunomar smiled, and shrugged, as one who had just lost a substantial wager. His amber gaze studied Hywell with a fresh intensity. 'So if we wished to send a message to Rome, who should we send it to, and what should it say?'

To the Emperor Nero from the Boudica: greetings. Your legions are defeated. Britannia is no longer a province of Rome. We hold the Eagles of the Second, Ninth, Fourteenth and Twentieth legions. Do not attempt their rescue unless you wish to lose more.

Hywell released the pied dove. It rose fast, startled by

584

the unfamiliar touch and turned south across the water. Its wings clapped a staccato tattoo and it was gone, fast as an arrow.

Valerius held out the fine-pared quill to Hywell. 'I have written to Nero. Would you care to write to your spymaster?'

Hywell looked at his feet, at the sea, at the two men, armed, waiting. He thought of Aerthen, and Graine and how much he wanted to live. He thought of running, and unthought it; the bear-warriors of the Eceni were the best runners in the land and Cunomar led them: he was best of the best. He said, 'How did you know?'

'I branded you for Mithras. Did you think I would forget?'

'I had prayed that you would.'

'I might have done, but then I burned the brand away less than six months after it was done, so that you could join the tribes, as if you were one of them. It was dark then, and you were looking away. Did you know it was me?'

Hywell closed his eyes. 'No.'

'Pain does that, sometimes,' Valerius said. 'It robs a man of knowledge he might need. And it was dark.'

'Am I to die?'

'You might if one of you doesn't tell me exactly what has just happened,' Cunomar said, from his other side. 'Who is this man?'

'I knew him as the Leopard,' Valerius said. 'He was one of Seneca's foremost agents, sent to spy on the southwestern tribes. He lived with us in Camulodunum for six months, learning the languages of Britain. In that time, he came to follow Mithras, but we had to burn the brand away when he left us.' He turned to Hywell. In Latin, he said, 'What did you tell the Dumnonii when they found you?'

In the language of Britain, Hywell answered, 'That I had been held down by four Roman cavalrymen and a

585

fifth had poured fire on my chest. It is always best to tell the truth.'

Cunomar blinked. 'You're Roman?'

Hywell shrugged. It was easier now that the truth was out to look him in the eye. 'My father was an archer in Judea, my mother was a Gaulish slave. I don't have Roman citizenship, but I spied for years for Rome. So yes, in terms of your question, I was Roman.'

'And now you are a Dumnoni warrior,' Valerius said, helpfully, against Cunomar's amber glare.

'I am. I have a Dumnoni wife and a daughter who knows me as her Dumnoni father. When the revolt began, I could have walked into the fortress and told the Legate of the Second everything I knew. I did not. When Paulinus marched his men south and your scouts were following him, sending word to us, I could have told them what was happening and the legionaries of the Second could have marched out to meet him: he might not have lost his last two centuries then. I did not. I am Hywell of the white scar. The Leopard is gone.'

'But will you write to Seneca now? Will you tell him what he needs to know to help him become Emperor?'

He could have wept, for relief, for joy greater than any the god had brought him. In this company, it would have been acceptable. He bit his lip and shook his head, and found words that said enough. 'I will try.'

To the spymaster Seneca, from the Leopard, greetings. Britain is lost. Your wealth is not. The Eceni have no use for gold, except to give it to the gods. Of the twenty-six million sestertii you lost here, eight tenths might be returned to you – if you provide the means. If, in addition, you undertake that Rome shall never again send her legions against us, trade might resume to the benefit of both Britain and Rome.

'Is that it?' Cunomar was reading the first unencoded

draft. Hywell wrapped the second in a cylinder of ivory and bound it to the leg of a bird the muted red of soft sandstone. 'You haven't said he should make himself Emperor.'

'If I did and someone else read it, Seneca would die. But only the Emperor can give an undertaking not to send the legions anywhere. Seneca knows that and he knows that I know it. And with twenty million sesterces in his hand, with Nero facing the loss of four legions, he can take the throne. If I were a betting man, I'd say Nero will be dead by his own hand before the winter.'

'You said that Seneca should not send his legions against "us". Will he know now, that you are . . . not who you were?'

'That is the first thing he will know, and the most dangerous. He thought of himself as my father. It will not be an easy loss.'

The rock-red message-dove winked one ice-blue eye. Hywell held it a moment more, counting the heartbeats against his fingers, before he raised both his hands and opened them, letting it go.

'What now?' he said to Valerius. 'We won't have an answer this side of the full moon. Maybe not next.'

'Now we must gather the warriors and march again. Cogidubnos holds the lands of the Belgae east of here, where the legions first landed. He was reared in Rome. He thinks of himself as Roman. There was a time when Britain was big enough for those who loved Rome and those who hated her and those who simply didn't care, but that time is over; his people need a new ruler. To a similar end, Ardacos has gone north with half a thousand warriors, to rid us of Cartimandua who was Rome's whore in the north. We shall do the same in the south.'

'I'll come with you,' Hywell said, 'If I may?'

'You would be welcome. But should someone not stay here and wait for a dove to return with Seneca's answer?'

'Seneca is Rome's spymaster. If it matters to him, he'll get us word. We don't have to stay here waiting.'

From the Emperor Seneca to his son, the Leopard, Greetings. A ship named The Sun Horse has lately sailed from Gaul to Mona bearing the father of the bear. If that same ship were to return with an investment, we would have an accord. There is much that could be traded to our advantage, and Rome does not need to extend her northern boundaries if those boundaries are not themselves under threat.

'The father of the bear?' Hywell stood alone with Valerius on the southern shore, at a place where an island of white cliffs lay within site of the headland. The last warmth of summer lifted up off the sea. Cormorants fished from the rocks below. Gulls mewed overhead. The late autumn air smelled of frost, and life, and hope.

Valerius said, 'Cunomar's father. His name is Caradoc. Cartimandua betrayed him to Rome. He escaped death, but he was injured and chose not to return to the warriors less than whole. He has been sheltering in Gaul ever since. A man named Luain mac Calma took ship to bring him home as soon as we knew the land was secure.' He took Hywell's note and read it again. *'If those boundaries are not themselves under threat.* Will Seneca keep the peace if we keep it?'

'As long as he can levy taxes on trade, he will keep the peace. It's not in his interests to wage expensive wars.'

'What if Gaul and the Belgae see Britain free and seek the same for themselves?'

'Seneca needs to be well rooted in his power before he can give up land. If Gaul would have her freedom, she would do well to wait – ah, I think the bear himself has found his prey.'

There, in the red-blood sunset, stood Cunomar, with his spear held aloft. At its top, lolled a human head, with fresh wounds to the crown. 'Cogidubnos is dead.' Hywell said it to hear it spoken, rather than because there was doubt. 'After Cartimandua's death, he called himself the last Roman in Britain.'

'But he didn't know us.' Valerius looked south, across the water, to the white island. 'What was your name, before you were the Leopard?'

'My given name was Sebastos Abdes Pantera. But that man died in the forests of the west. Now, I am Hywell of the white scar, father to Gunovar of the Dumnonii, who will grow to be a warrior one day, in a roundhouse kept safe by her mother's people. So that leaves you,' Hywell faced him. 'You were Bán, brother to the Boudica long before you were Valerius.'

'But it was as Valerius that I lived and saw the Boudica die and it is as Valerius that I shall remain. There needs to be one Roman left alive in Britain, to speak with the spy-master who will be Emperor, and whoever comes after him. As long as the legions stay away from these shores, I am happy to be that man.'

Valerius turned, shading his eyes against the low Western sun. 'Shall we go now, to join the warriors? They will want to celebrate the news that our island is ours once again.

ROME

THE
COMING OF THE KING

M.C. Scott

AD 65, SEBASTOS PANTERA, known to his many enemies as the Leopard, is the spy the Emperor Nero uses only for the most challenging and important of missions. Hunting alone, not knowing who he can trust, he must find the most dangerous man in Rome's empire and bring him to justice.

But his prey is cunning, subtle and ruthless. Saulos has pledged to bring about the destruction of an entire Roman province and has even now set the means to do so in motion.

It will take the strategies of a master hunter to combat the brilliance of Saulos' plan, and so Pantera must set forth into the wild lands of Judaea to set an equally deadly trap for his arch-enemy and nemesis . . .

'Religious and political tensions, passion and intrigue, superb action sequences and real and imagined characters are seamlessly woven together to create a fascinating and exciting story on a truly epic scale'
Guardian

'A dramatic new version of the past . . . grippingly sustained'
Independent

'Why's that?'

'People react strangely to being asked to become a spy. It calls into question your prior relationship: Did he become my friend just to recruit me? It also implies moral duplicity. You, as the recruiter, have a singular purpose, which requires asking someone to lie and deceive on your behalf. It's an odd relationship.'

'Got any advice?'

'It's like going out on a date. It's all in the timing. You move in too early and the girl will accuse you of being too fresh. You come on too late and you might have bored her, shown her your uncertainty. It's a delicate process and, like dating, you only get better at it by doing it . . . a lot.'

'You've just filled me with confidence, Mark. I haven't been out on a date for more than a year.'

'Some people say it's like riding a bicycle,' said Flowers. 'But there's a big difference between an eighteen-year-old taking up cycling and a middle-aged man going back to it. I wish you'd change your whisky, Javier. This stuff is like drinking peat bog.'

'Maybe you'd like some Coca Cola to go with it?' said Falcón.

Flowers chuckled.

'Do your people know whether your Moroccan friend is "safe"?' he asked.

'Did I say that I was recruiting a friend, and that he was Moroccan?' asked Falcón.

Another chuckle from Flowers, followed by a big snort of whisky.

'You didn't say, but given our present circumstances it was a safe bet.'

'They seem to have researched him pretty well,' said Falcón, giving up quickly on the game.

'That's not how you find out if someone is "safe",' said Flowers. 'Research is like trying to learn how to succeed in business by reading a self-help book.'

'I know he's safe.'

'Well, you're a homicide cop, so you should know when someone is lying to you,' said Flowers. 'What sort of conversations have you had about terrorism, Iraq, the Palestinian question, that have led you to believe that your friend is "safe"?'

'None in which the outcome of the conversation has been crucial, if that's what you mean.'

'I can find thousands of Muslims in the tea houses of North Africa who would condemn the actions of these extremist groups and their indiscriminate violence, but I would struggle to find one who would give me information that might lead to the capture and possible death of a jihadi,' said Flowers. 'It's one of the strange contradictions of this kind of spying: it takes a profound moral certitude to behave immorally. So, how do you know he's "safe"?'

'I'm not sure what I can tell you that would help you believe, without sounding foolish,' said Falcón.

'Try me.'

'We recognized something in each other from the first moment we met.'

'What does that mean?'

'We've had comparable experiences, which have given us a level of automatic understanding.'

'Still not sure,' said Flowers, closing an eye over his raised glass.

'What happens when two people fall in love?'

'Take it easy, Javier.'

'How do two people sort out all that necessarily complicated communication that lets them know that they will be going to bed together that night?'

'You know the problem with that? Lovers cheat on each other all the time.'

'What you're saying, Mark, is that we can never know, we can only be as certain as possible.'

'The love analogy is right,' said Flowers. 'You've just got to be sure that he doesn't love someone more than you.'

'Thanks.'

'Who are we talking about, by the way?'

'You took your time.'

'Had I known you were going to be so coy, I'd have taken you out to dinner.'

'This isn't *my* business, it's CNI business.'

'Do you think you'll be able to get out of Casablanca airport without my guys spotting you?' asked Flowers.

'I'm surprised you haven't had me followed before.'

Silence. Flowers smiled.

'You knew all along,' said Falcón, throwing up his hands. 'Why do you play these games with me?'

'To remind you that, in my world, you're an amateur,' said Flowers. 'What are you hoping to get out of Yacoub Diouri?'

'I don't know. I'm not even sure whether I'm going to accept the task and, if I do, whether my superiors will allow me to do it.'

'What about the investigation here?'

'There's a lot still to be done, but at least we know

what went on inside and outside the mosque in the days leading up to the explosion.'

'Was that why you wanted me to research I4IT?'

'They're in the background . . . quite a long way in the background,' said Falcón, who filled him in on Horizonte and Informáticalidad.

'I4IT are not, in fact, based in Indianapolis,' said Flowers. 'The company headquarters is in Columbus, Ohio, due to its proximity to Westerville, Ohio, which was where the US temperance movement started, and from where National Prohibition took off back in the 1920s.'

'You're making this sound significant.'

'The corporation is owned and actively run by two born-again Christians, who discovered their faith through the excesses of their youth,' said Flowers. 'Cortland Fallenbach was a computer programmer who used to work for Microsoft until they "let him go" due to problems with alcohol and other substances. Morgan Havilland was a salesman for IBM, until his sex addiction got out of control and he had to be removed before the company ended up in court on the end of a sexual harassment suit.'

'Did these guys meet in therapy?'

'In Indianapolis,' said Flowers. 'And having both worked for the most powerful IT corporations in the world, they decided to set up a group to invest in hi-tech companies. Fallenbach was a software king and Havilland understood hardware. At first they just invested and took profit from their inside knowledge of the industry. Later they started buying companies outright, merging their strengths, and either selling them or setting them up in groups of their own. But there was, and is, one important stipulation if you want to be a part of I4IT . . .'

'You have to believe in God?' asked Falcón.

'You have to believe in the *right* god,' said Flowers. 'You have to be a Christian. That doesn't mean they don't buy companies owned by Hindus, Muslims, Buddhists or Shintoists – if that's what they're called – it just means that they don't become a part of I4IT. They either strip out what they want and, if they're still valuable, they sell them on; if they're not, they let them rot into the ground.'

'Ruthless Christians,' said Falcón.

'Crusaders might be a good word,' said Flowers. 'Very successful crusaders. I4IT has world-wide assets in excess of $12 billion. They showed a profit in the first quarter of this year of $375 million.'

'What about politics?'

'Fallenbach and Havilland are members of the Christian Right and therefore deeply Republican. Their ethos, though, is based on religion. As long as you prac-tise the same religion they believe you can understand each other. If one is a Muslim and the other a Christian there will always be fundamental differences which will prevent perfect communication. Athcists are off the page, which means communists are unacceptable. Agnostics can still be "saved" . . .'

'Is this the level of discussion in board meetings before a take-over?'

'Sure. They take company culture very seriously and religion is the foundation of that culture,' said Flowers. 'Where they can get away with it, they don't employ women in the workplace, other-wise they keep to the bare legal minimum. They don't employ homosexuals. God hates fags . . . remember, Javier?'

'I don't remember that line from the Bible.'

'Their success and profitability is a manifestation of their righteousness.'

'How active are they outside their own corporation?'

'As far as we know, it's limited to *not* doing business with people whose principles they don't agree with. So they produce a lot of ultrasound equipment, for instance, and they won't sell to clinics known to perform abortions,' said Flowers. 'As far as any *active* anti-religious movement goes, we haven't heard of anything.'

'Do you think Informáticalidad using this apartment for brainstorming sessions is weird?'

'If you ask me what's weird, it's companies and governments spending billions of dollars and euros a year on management consultancies, who come in and give them the kind of common sense that my grandmother could have told them for free,' said Flowers. 'Informáticalidad sound like a company who haven't bought into the bullshit industry and have come up with a cheaper, and probably more productive, solution which leaves them with an asset at the end of it all. If you can place any of those Informáticalidad brainstormers in the mosque, now that's a different story . . .'

'Not so far,' said Falcón. 'Another thing: have you got any information on an organization called VOMIT?'

'VOMIT . . . yes, I've seen their website. We thought it stood for Victims of Muslim and Islamic Terror until one of our operators saw the Spanish. They can only be accused of not presenting the full picture, but that's just a matter of imbalance. It's not criminal. There's no incitement to take revenge, no bomb-making advice, weapons training or active recruitment to "a cause".'

'If it's just a few geeks with some phones and a computer, that's one thing,' said Falcón. 'If it's a multi-billion-dollar corporation with world-wide resources, wouldn't that be different?'

'First of all, I don't see that connection. Second, there'd have to be more of a perceived threat to get us to do any digging on VOMIT,' said Flowers. 'And anyway, Javier, why are you sniffing around the wacky fringes of this attack instead of getting stuck into the guts of it? I mean, VOMIT, I4IT . . .'

'The guts of the problem are under a few thousand tons of rubble at the moment,' said Falcón. 'Informáticalidad was an unignorable part of the scenario outside the mosque. VOMIT were introduced into the frame by the CNI. We have some suspicious occurrences in the mosque, which have not been adequately explained.'

'Like what?'

Falcón told him about the council inspectors, the blown fuse box and the electricians.

'I know what you're thinking,' said Flowers.

'No, you don't, because I haven't decided on a scenario yet myself. I'm keeping an open mind,' said Falcón. 'We know that two terror suspects – Djamel Hammad and Smail Saoudi – made deliveries to the mosque, which could be innocent or could have been bomb-making material. A deposit of hexogen – or cyclonite, as you call it – was found in the back of their van . . .'

'Fucking hell, Javier,' said Flowers, sitting up. 'And you don't call that damning evidence?'

'It looks bad,' said Falcón, 'but we're not talking about looks here. We've got to get beyond appearances.'

'Is there any more of this whisky? I'm getting the taste for this liquid-charcoal stuff.'

Falcón topped him up and gave himself another jolt of manzanilla. He sat back, feeling as he always did in his conversations with Flowers – stupid and flayed.

'You know, Mark, you still haven't told me anything I couldn't have found out for myself inside half an hour on the internet, whereas I've told you . . . everything. I know you like to keep your account with me in the black, but I'd appreciate some real help,' said Falcón. 'Why don't you tell me something about the MILA, or Imam Abdelkrim Benaboura?'

'There's a good reason why you don't get as much information from me as I do from you,' said Flowers, who let those names flash past him without a flicker. 'I'm running a station that covers southern Spain and its relations with Morocco, Algeria and Tunisia. I have no idea what is going on in Madrid, northern Spain or southern France. I only see a small corner of the whole picture. London, Paris, Rome and Berlin make their contributions, but I don't see any of it. Like you, I'm just a contributor.'

'You're making yourself sound very passive.'

'I'm getting information from all sorts of different sources, but I have to be very careful how I use it,' said Flowers. 'Spying is a game, but I never forget that it's being played with real people, who can get killed.

So *you* only get information that doesn't endanger you or any of my other sources. If I'm in any doubt, you won't be given it. Be glad that I'm not a risk-taking station head.'

'Thanks for that, Mark. Now why don't you tell me about Los Mártires Islámicos para la Liberación de Andalucía?'

'I first heard about them at the end of last year as El Movimiento rather than Los Mártires. My source in Algiers told me that they were a disaffected faction of the Algerian GIA, the Armed Islamic Group, who had crossed the border into Morocco and teamed up with a local group, whose goal at the time was the liberation of the Spanish enclaves in Morocco: Ceuta and Melilla. The Algerians brought with them a network, with operatives already installed in Madrid, Granada, Málaga and Valencia.'

'But not Seville?'

'I'm coming to that,' said Flowers. 'My source told me that what the Moroccans could supply was finance. They were cash rich from their connections in the hashish trade in the Rif mountains. What they didn't have was a network and a strategy. Both Ceuta and Melilla are small enclaves, well protected and well supplied by the Spanish mainland. The Algerians saw the money and told them to think big. Liberate Andalucía, cut off the Spanish supply line to Ceuta and Melilla, and this Western corner of the Islamic kingdom is whole once again.'

'You'd need an army and a navy to take Andalucía.'

'And there's the British in Gibraltar, who might have an opinion on the matter, too,' said Flowers. 'But that is not the point. The liberation of Andalucía is an inspiring *ideal* that fills the hearts of Islamic fanatics with a warm Allah-infused glow. It is the *dream* that will draw followers to the cause. My source also read the Algerians' intentions wrong. They didn't want access to the hashish trade because of finance, they wanted to tap into their smuggling routes to get people and material across to Spain.'

'Has that been happening?'

'Nobody's been caught,' said Flowers. 'Smuggling routes generally exist because they're allowed to. There's a constant stream of hashish from Morocco and cocaine from South America coming into the long, unpatrollable Iberian coastline, and there's plenty of money to keep the authorities happy and quiet.'

This talk made Falcón's sweat run cold. The money, organization and corruption were all in place to make a devastating campaign on Andalucía seem likely rather than crazy.

'What about Seville and the MILA?' asked Falcón.

'Some Afghans arrived in Morocco in January.'

'Where in Morocco? How do your sources get such information? Why aren't we getting it?'

'There's no base. There's no town hall with posters outside advertising "MILA Meeting Tonight". I have one source, at the wrong level, who is able to give me bits and pieces. You don't just walk into these groups off the street. You have to be vouched for. It's all to do with family and tribal ties. I believe my source's information, but I'm wary of sharing it because he's peripheral to the group's leading council.'

'Which means it could be invention?'

'You see, Javier, being given information doesn't necessarily make the picture any clearer.'

'Tell me about the Afghan connection.'

'Some Afghans arrived, offering the group a Seville connection. They said he was capable of giving recce and logistical support, but did not have the capacity to carry out an attack.'

'Name?'

'He couldn't give me one.'

'One of the worshippers in the mosque here told me that there had been a visit from a group of Afghans and that the Imam had spoken to them in Pashto.'

'I'd be careful about putting those two pieces of information together without more corroboration,' said Flowers.

'What's the news on Abdelkrim Benaboura?' asked Falcón. 'He doesn't seem to be high risk and yet there's a clearance problem with his history. What does that mean?'

'That they don't know who he is from a certain date, which is normally around the end of 2001 and the beginning of 2002 when the US went into Afghanistan and the Taliban regime broke up and dispersed. You have to remember, until 9/11 the US and European intelligence network in the Islamic world was negligible. We sorted out who was who on our own turf in the years that followed, but there were, and still are, very large gaps – as you'd expect from an introverted religion that stretches from Indonesia to Morocco and Northern Europe to South Africa. Factor in the difficulties of identification, given the clothes these people wear, the headgear and facial hair, and histories are not so easily matched to people.'

'You still haven't told me anything about Abdelkrim Benaboura.'

'Why do the CNI think it's so important for you to recruit Yacoub now, right at the moment when you're supposed to be heading the biggest murder enquiry of your career?'

'The CNI think they might have discovered something even bigger.'

'Like what?'

'They weren't prepared to say.'

'What have they got that's made them think that?'

'You don't miss much, Mark, do you?' said Falcón, but Flowers didn't answer. He was deep in distracted thought until he looked at his watch, knocked back his whisky and said he had to go. Falcón walked him to the door.

'Have you tried to recruit Yacoub Diouri yourself?' asked Falcón.

'Something worth remembering,' said Flowers, 'he doesn't like Americans. Now, who was that beautiful woman who left just as I arrived?'

'My ex-wife.'

'I've got two ex-wives,' said Flowers. 'It's funny how ex-wives are always more beautiful than wives. Think about that, Javier.'

'That's all you do, Mark, leave me with more to think about than when you arrived.'

'I'll give you something else to roll around your brain,' said Flowers. 'The CNI planted the story about the MILA in the press. How about that?'

'Why would they do that?'

'Welcome to my wonderful world, Javier,' said Flowers, walking off into the night.

He stopped at the end of the short avenue of orange trees and turned back to Javier, who was silhouetted in the doorway.

'One last piece of advice,' said Flowers. 'Don't try to understand the whole picture . . . there's nobody in the world who does.'

19

Manuela lay in bed alone, trying to ignore the faint click of Angel's fingers on the keys of his laptop in another room. She blinked in the dark, holding back the full contemplation of something very horrible: the sale of her villa in El Puerto de Santa María, an hour's drive south from Seville on the coast. The villa had been left to her by her father, and every room was packed with adolescent nostalgia. The fact that Francisco Falcón didn't much like the place and loathed all the neighbours, the so-called Seville high society, had been erased from Manuela's memory. She imagined her father's spirit writhing in agony at the proposed sale. It was, however, the only way that she could see of repairing her financial situation. The banks had already called her before close of business, asking where the funds were that she'd told them to expect. It was the only solution that had come to her, in the death and debt hour of four o'clock in the morning. The estate agent had told her the obvious: the Seville property market would be stalled until further notice. She had four possible buyers for her villa, who were constantly reminding her of their readiness to purchase. But could she let it go?

Angel had been calling her all day, trying to restrain the excitement in his voice. His conversation was full of the ramifications of Rivero's retirement and the great new hope of Fuerza Andalucía, Jesús Alarcón, who he'd been steering around all day, after interviewing him for the profile in the *ABC*. Angel's media manipulation had been brilliant. He'd kept Jesús off camera when he visited the hospital and got him to talk privately to the victims and their families. His greatest coup had been to get him through to Fernando Alanis in the intensive care unit. Jesús and Fernando had talked. No cameras. No reporters. And they'd hit it off. It couldn't have been better. Later, when the Mayor and a camera crew got through to intensive care, Fernando had mentioned Jesús Alarcón, on camera, as the only politician who hadn't sought to make any media capital out of the victims' misery. It was pure luck, but a total masterstroke for Angel's campaign. The Mayor had just managed to squeeze back the nervous smile that wanted to creep across his face.

Consuelo couldn't stop herself. Why should she? She couldn't sleep. What better way to remember carefree sleep than to watch the experts; the calm faces of the innocents, eyelids trembling, softly breathing, deep and dreamless in their beds. Ricardo was first, the fourteen-year-old, who'd reached the gawky age, where his face was stretching in odd directions, trying to find its adult mould. This wasn't such a peaceful age, with too many hormones shooting around the body and sexual yearning fighting with football in his mind. Matías was twelve and seemed to be growing up quicker than his elder brother; easier to walk in somebody else's footsteps than to tread out one's own, as Ricardo had done with no father to guide him.

Consuelo knew where this was heading, though. Ricardo and Matías took care of themselves. It was Darío, her youngest at eight years old, who drew her in. She loved his face, his blond hair, his amber-coloured eyes, his perfect little mouth. It was in his room that she sat down in the middle of the floor, half a metre from his bed, looking into his untroubled features and easing herself into the uneasy state she craved. It started in her mouth, with the lips that had kissed his baby head. She drank it down her throat and felt the twinge in her breasts. It settled in her stomach, high up around the diaphragm, an ache that transmitted its pain from her viscera to the tingling surface of her skin. She scoffed at Alicia Aguado's questioning. What was wrong with such a love as this?

Fernando Alanis sat in the intensive care unit of the Hospital de la Macarena. He watched his daughter's vital signs on the monitors. Grey numbers and green lines that told him good things, that she was capable of lighting up a machine, if not her father. His mind crashed and fell about like a hopeless drunk in a bin-filled narrow alleyway. One moment it was gasping at the catastrophic destruction of the apartment building, the next it was buckling at the sight of four covered bodies outside the pre-school. He still couldn't quite believe what he had lost. Was this a mechanism of the mind that suspended things too unbearable to comprehend, almost to the point of a barely remembered nightmare? He'd been told by people who'd survived bad falls from scaffolding that the rush of the ground coming to meet you was not so terrifying. The horror was in the eventual awakening. And with that he would lurch sickeningly forward to the bruised and battered face of his daughter, her oval mouth slack against the clear plastic concertina of tube. Everything inside him felt too big. His organs were jostled by the colossal inflation of hate and despair which had no direction, other than to make themselves as uncomfortable as possible. He went back to a time when his family and the building had been intact, but the thought of the third child he'd been proposing made him break down inside. He couldn't bear to take himself back to a state that would never exist again, he couldn't bear the notion of never seeing Gloria and Pedro again, he couldn't stomach the finality of that word 'never'.

He concentrated on his daughter's beating heart. The jumping line. Be-dum, be-dum, be-dum. The thready skip of the green fuse against the terminal blackness of the monitor made him rear back in his seat. It was all too fragile. Anything could happen in this life and did . . . and had. Perhaps the answer was to retreat into emptiness. Feel nothing. But that held its terror, too. The monstrous negativity of the black hole in space, sucking in all light. He breathed in. The air expanded his chest. He breathed out. His stomach wall relaxed. This, for the time being, was the only way to proceed.

Inés lay where she had fallen. She hadn't moved since he'd left. Her body was a miasma of pain from the pummelling it had sustained from his hard, white knuckles. Nausea humped in her stomach. He'd punched her through her flailing hands; one of her fingers had been bent back. In an escalation of his fury he'd torn off his belt and lashed her, with the buckle digging into her buttocks and thighs. With each stroke he'd told her through clenched teeth: 'Never . . . speak . . . to my girlfriend . . . like that . . . ever again. Do you hear me? Never . . . again.' She'd rolled to the corner of the room to get away from him. He'd stood over her, breathing heavily, not so different from when he was sexually aroused. Their eyes met. He pointed his finger at her as if he might shoot her. She didn't pick up what he said. She'd taken in the purity of his hatred from his blank, basilisk eyes, the colourless lips and his red, swollen neck.

No sooner had he left the apartment than she started to rebuild her illusion. His anger was understandable. The whore had told him some nonsense and set him against her. That was the way these things worked. He was just fucking the whore, but she wanted more now. She wanted to be in the wife's shoes, on the wife's side of the bed, but she was just the whore so she had to play her little games. Inés hated the whore. A line came into her head from an old conversation with Javier: 'Most people are killed by people they know, because it is only they who are capable of arousing the passionate emotions that can lead to uncontrollable violence.' Inés knew Esteban. My God, did she know Esteban Calderón. She'd seen him gilded with the laurel wreath, and cringing like the village cur. That was why she could arouse such emotions in him. Only she. That old cliché holds true. Love and hate have the same source. He would love her again once that black bitch stopped meddling with his mind.

She raised herself on to all fours. The pain made her gasp. Blood dripped from her mouth. She must have bitten her tongue. She crawled up the bed to stand on her feet. She unzipped her dress and let it fall. Unhooking her bra was a torture, bending to slip off her panties nearly made her faint. She stood in front of the mirror. A massive bruise spread across her torso where he'd hit her that morning. Her chest ached through to her spine. A criss-cross of weals covered her buttocks and upper thighs, broken by punctured skin where the buckle had dug in. She put a finger to one of these marks and pressed. The pain was exquisite. Esteban, in that passionate moment, really had given her his fullest attention.

Javier lay in the dark, with images from the late news still present in his mind: the demolished building under the surgical glare of the floodlights; the smashed plate-glass windows of a number of shops with Moroccan wares for sale; the fire brigade spraying a flaming apartment which had been fire-bombed by kids on the rampage; a cut, bruised and swollen-faced Moroccan boy, who'd been set upon by neo-Nazi thugs with clubs and chains; a butcher's selling halal meat with a car rammed through the metal blinds of the store front. Falcón shunted all the images out of his mind until all that was left was the ultimate remnant of terror – deep uncertainty.

He cast his mind back to before the bombing, looking for a clue amongst all those extraordinary emotions that might help him make sense of what was happening. His mind played tricks. Uncertainty had that effect. Human beings always believe that an event has been

prefigured in some way. It's the necessary part of redis-
covering the pattern. Mankind cannot bear too much
chaos.

He had the illusion of the impenetrable darkness
receding from him, like the endlessly expanding
universe. This was the new certainty, the one that sent
all the old narratives, with which we structured our
lives, down into the black hole of human understanding. We have to be even stronger now that science
has told us that time is unreliable, and even light
behaves differently if you turn your back. It was a
terrible irony that, just as science was pushing back the
limits of our comprehension, religion, the greatest and
oldest of human narratives, was fighting back. Was it
because of resentment at being found on the discard
pile of modern European life that religion was making
a stand? Falcón closed his eyes and concentrated on
relaxing each part of his body until, finally, he drifted
away from the unanswerable questions and into a deep
sleep. He was a man who had made up his mind and
had a car arriving early to take him to the airport.

The car, a black Mercedes with tinted windows, turned
up at 6 a.m. with Pablo sitting in the back in a dark
suit with an open-neck shirt.

'How did your talk with Yacoub go last night?' asked
Pablo, as the car pulled away.

'Given that a bomb went off in Seville yesterday, he
knows I'm not coming over on a social visit.'

'What did he say?'

'He was pleased that we were going to see each
other, but he knows there's an ulterior motive.'

'He's going to be a natural at this business.'

'I'm not sure he'll take that as a compliment.'

'Because of your investigation this is time-critical, so we've arranged a private jet to take us down there. The flight to Casablanca will be less than an hour and a half as long as we get good air-traffic clearance. You've got diplomatic status so we'll get through any formalities quickly, and you'll be on the road to Rabat within two hours of take-off,' said Pablo. 'I presume you're meeting Yacoub in his home?'

'I'm a friend, not a business associate,' said Falcón. 'Although that might change after this meeting.'

'I'm sure Mark Flowers gave you some good tips.'

'How long have you known about Mark . . . and me?' asked Falcón, smiling.

'Since you first outwitted him back in July 2002 and he made you one of his sources,' said Pablo. 'We're not worried about Mark. He's a friend. After 9/11 the Americans said they were going to put someone in Andalucía and we asked for Mark. Juan has known him since they were in Tunis together, keeping an eye on Gaddafi. Did Mark give you any ideas on how to approach Yacoub Diouri?'

'I'm pretty sure he tried to recruit him and was rebuffed,' said Falcón. 'He said that Yacoub didn't like Americans.'

'That should make your task easier, if he's used to being approached.'

'I don't think Yacoub Diouri is someone you "approach". He's the sort of guy who would see you coming a long way off if you did. We'll just talk, as we always do, about everything. It will come out in the way it does. I'm not going to use any strategies on him. Like a lot of Arabs, he has a powerful belief in honour, which he learnt from the man who became his father. He is someone to whom you show respect, and not just as a gesture,' said Falcón. 'Perhaps you should tell me the sort of thing you want him to do, how you want him to operate, what contacts you're expecting him to make. Are you hoping to get information about the MILA from him?'

'MILA? Has Mark been talking to you about the MILA?'

'You're all the same, you intelligence people,' said Falcón. 'You can't take a question, you have to answer it with another. Do you exchange *any* information?'

'The MILA has nothing to do with what we want from Yacoub.'

'The TVE news said they were responsible for the bomb,' said Falcón. 'A text was posted from Seville to the Madrid office of the *ABC*, about Andalucía being brought back into the Muslim fold.'

'The MILA are only interested in money,' said Pablo. 'They've dressed their intentions up in jihadist rhetoric, but the reason they want to liberate Ceuta and Melilla is that they want the enclaves for themselves.'

'Tell me what we're trying to achieve,' said Falcón.

'For the purposes of this mission, what is crucial is not *who* destroyed that apartment building in Seville and *why*, but rather *what* the explosion has revealed to us,' said Pablo. 'Forget the MILA, they're not important. This is not about your investigation into yesterday's bomb. This is not about the past, but the future.'

'OK. Tell me,' said Falcón, thinking that Flowers may have been right about the CNI planting the MILA story.

'Last year the British held their parliamentary

elections. They didn't need the example of the Madrid bombings to know that these elections were going to be the target of a number of attempts by terrorists to change the way a population thinks.'

'And nothing happened,' said Falcón. 'Tony Blair, the "little Satan", got in with a reduced majority.'

'Exactly, and nobody knew that there were three separate cells with active plans, who were prevented from carrying out their attacks by MI5,' said Pablo. 'All those cells were sleepers, dormant until they received their instructions in January 2005. Every member of the cell was either a second- or third-generation immigrant, originally from Pakistan, Afghanistan or Morocco, but now British. They spoke perfect English with regional accents. They all had clean police records. They all had jobs and came from decent backgrounds. In other words, they were impossible to find in a country with millions of people of the same ethnicity. But they *were* found and their attacks *were* prevented because MI5 had a codebook to help them.

'When they were searching some suspects' properties after a series of arrests made in 2003 and early 2004 they came across identical editions of a text called the *Book of Proof* by a ninth-century Arab writer called al-Jahiz. Both editions had notes – all in English, because the accused didn't have a word of Arabic between them. Some of the notes in each copy were remarkably similar. MI5 photocopied the books, replaced the originals, released the accused and set their code-breakers to work.'

'And when did they share that information with the CNI?'

'October 2004.'

'So what happened with the London bombings of 7th and 21st July 2005?'

'The British think they stopped using the *Book of Proof* after the May 2005 elections.'

'And now you think you've discovered a new codebook,' said Falcón. 'What about the new copy of the Koran found on the front seat of the Peugeot Partner?'

'We think they were going to prepare another codebook to give to someone.'

'The Imam Abdelkrim Benaboura?'

'We haven't finished searching his apartment,' said Pablo, shrugging.

'That's taken some time.'

'The Imam lived in a two-bedroomed flat in El Cerezo and almost every room is full, floor to ceiling, of books.'

'I don't feel any closer to knowing why you want to recruit Yacoub Diouri.'

'The jihadis are in need of another big coup. Something on the scale of 9/11.'

'But not as "small scale" as a few hundred people killed on trains in Madrid and the underground in London,' said Falcón, not quite able to stomach this level of objectivity.

'I'm not diminishing those atrocities, I'm just saying that they were on a different scale. You'll learn about intelligence work as you do it, Javier; you're not in the trenches, seeing your friends getting killed. It has an effect on your vision,' said Pablo. 'Madrid was time-targeted, with a specific goal. It wasn't a big, bold statement. It was just saying: This is what we can do. There's no comparison to the operation that brought down the Twin Towers. No flight or hijack training. They just had to board trains and leave rucksacks. The most difficult aspect of the operation was to buy and deliver the explosives, and in that we now know they had considerable help from local petty criminals.'

'So what is the big coup?' asked Falcón, uneasy at this breezy talk of death and destruction. 'The World Cup in Germany?'

'No. For the same reason that the Olympics in Greece was untouched. It's just too difficult. The terrorists are competing with specialists who have been planning security at these events for years. Even the buildings are constructed with security in mind. The chances of discovery are increased enormously. Why waste resources?'

Silence, as the Mercedes tyres ripped over the tarmac towards the airport, which was smudged out by the early-morning haze.

'You don't know what it is, do you?' said Falcón. 'You just know it's coming, or maybe you "feel" it's coming.'

'We have no idea,' said Pablo, nodding. 'But we don't just "sense" their desperation, we know it, too. The design of the Twin Towers attack was to generate a fervour in Muslims all over the world, to get them to rise up against the decadent West, which they feel has humiliated them so much over the years, and to turn on their own dictatorial leaders and corrupt governments. It hasn't happened. The disgust level is rising in the Muslim world at what the fanatics are prepared to do – the kidnapping and beheading of people like the aid worker Margaret Hassan, the daily slaughter of Iraqis who just want to have a normal life – these things are not going down well. But the demographics of the Muslim world lean heavily on the side of youth, and a disenfranchised youth likes nothing better than a demonstration of rebel power. And that is what these radicals are in need of now: another symbol of their power, even if it's the last bang before they die out with a whimper.'

'So what has this bomb in Seville indicated to you?'

'The fact that hexogen was found is a cause for concern and, judging by the level of destruction, it was not a small quantity. Just the use of this material, which the jihadis have never used before, makes us think that the design was *not* to frighten the population of Seville, but something bigger,' said Pablo. 'The British have also revealed that local sources have heard talk about something "big" about to happen, but their intelligence network has picked up no changes in any of their communities. We have to remember that, since the July 7th London Underground bombings, those communities are more aware, too. This makes MI5 and MI6 think that it will be an attack launched from the outside, and Spain has proven to be a popular country for terrorists to gather and plan their campaigns.'

'So how are you expecting Yacoub Diouri to help you?' asked Falcón. 'He doesn't do much business in England. He goes to London for shopping and the two fashion weeks. He has friends, but they're all in the fashion industry. I'm assuming, by the way, that you want Yacoub to act for you because he's *not* involved in international terrorism, but that he might have contacts with people whose involvement in these activities he is unaware of.'

'We're not going to ask him to do anything unusual or out of character. He attends the right mosque and he already knows the people we want him to make contact with. He just has to take it a step further.'

'I didn't know he attended a radical mosque.'

'A mosque with radical elements, where it is possible, with a name like Diouri, to become "involved". As you know, Yacoub's "father", Abdullah, was active in the independence movement, Istiqlal, in the fifties; he was one of the prime movers against European decadence in Tangier. His name carries huge weight with the traditional Islamists. The radicals would love to have a Diouri on their side.'

'So you know who these radical elements are?'

'I go to church. I'm a moderate Catholic,' said Pablo. 'I don't have much time to get involved in church-related business or socialize with other members of the congregation. But even I know all the people who hold strong views, because they can't keep them in and they can't disguise their history.'

'But you can have powerful convictions and have enthusiasm for radical ideas without being a terrorist.'

'Exactly, which is why the only way to find out is to be involved and get to the next level,' said Pablo. 'What we're trying to find is a chain of command. Where do the orders come from to activate the dormant cells? Where do the ideas for terrorist attacks originate? Is there a planning division? Are there independent recce and logistical teams who move around, giving expert help to activated cells? Our picture of these terrorist networks is so incomplete that we're not even sure whether a network exists or not.'

'Where are the British in all this?' asked Falcón. 'They're expecting another major assault from the outside. They must know about Yacoub from his trips to London. Why haven't they tried to recruit him them-selves?'

'They have. It didn't work,' said Pablo. 'The British are very sensitive to anything that happens in southern Spain and North Africa because they're in the middle, with their naval base in Gibraltar. They are aware of the potential for attacks, like the explosive dinghy launched at the USS *Cole* in Yemen in October 2000. They have sources in the ex-pat criminal communities operating between the Costa del Sol and that stretch of Moroccan coast between Melilla and Ceuta. The nature of the drug-smuggling business is that it is cash heavy and requires access to efficient money-laundering operations. Other criminal communities are inevitably involved. Information comes from all angles. When we told the British that hexogen had been used in the Seville bomb yesterday, it resonated with something they already knew, or rather something they'd heard.'

'Did they tell you what that was?'

'It needs to be corroborated,' said Pablo. 'The most important thing, at this stage, is to find out whether Yacoub is prepared to act for us. If he's already turned down the Americans and the British, it could be that he's not interested in that sort of life, because, believe me, it is very demanding. So let's see if he's a player and take it from there.'

The car had arrived at a private entrance to the airport, beyond the terminal buildings. The driver talked to the policeman at the gate and showed a pass. Pablo dropped the window and the policeman looked in with his clipboard. He nodded. The gate opened. The car drove into an X-ray bay and out again. They drove beyond the air cargo area until they arrived at a hangar where six small planes were parked. The car pulled up alongside a Lear jet. Pablo picked up a large plastic bag of that morning's newspapers from the floor of the Mercedes. They boarded the jet and took their seats. Pablo flicked through the newspapers, which were full of the bombings.

'How about that for a headline?' he said, and handed Falcón a British tabloid.

THE SECOND COMING? COUNT THE NUMBER
OF THE BEAST: 666
6 JUNE 2006

20

The plane touched down just after 8 a.m. Spanish time, two hours ahead of Moroccan time. They were met by a Mercedes, which contained a member of the Spanish embassy from Rabat, who took their passports. They were driven to a quiet end of the terminal building and after a few minutes they were through to the other side. The Mercedes drove to where the rental cars were parked. The man from the Spanish embassy handed over a set of keys and Falcón transferred to a Peugeot 206.

'We can't have an embassy vehicle turning up at his residence,' said Pablo.

The diplomat handed over some dirhams for the tolls. Falcón left the airport and joined the motorway from Casablanca to Rabat. The sun was well up and the heat haze was draining the colour from the dull, flat landscape. Falcón sat back with the window open and the moist sea air baffling over the glass. He overtook vastly overloaded trucks farting out black smoke, with boys sitting on top of sheet-wrapped bales, their legs hooked around the securing ropes. In the fields a man in a burnous sat on a bony white donkey, which he tapped and poked with a stick. Occasionally a BMW flashed past, leaving a flicker of Arabic lettering on the retina. The smell was of the sea, woodsmoke, manured earth and pollution.

The outskirts of Rabat loomed. He took the ring road and came into the city from the east. He remembered the turning after the Société Marocaine de Banques. The tarmac gave out immediately and he eased up the troughed and pitted track to the main gate of Yacoub Diouri's walled property. The gate-man recognized him. He swung up the driveway, lined with Washingtonian palms, and stopped outside the front door. Two servants came out in blue livery with red piping, each wearing a fez. The hire car was driven away. Falcón was taken inside to the living room, which overlooked the pool where Yacoub swam his morning lengths. He sat down on one of the cream leather sofas, in front of a low wooden table inlaid with mother-of-pearl. The servant left. Birds fluttered in the garden. A boy dragged a hose out and began spraying the hibiscus.

Yacoub Diouri arrived, wearing a blue jellabah and white barbouches. A servant set down a brass tray with a pot of mint tea and two small glasses on the table and left. Yacoub's hair, which he'd allowed to grow long, was wet and he now had a close-cropped beard. They embraced with an enthusiastic Arabic greeting and held on to each other by the shoulders looking into each other's eyes and smiling; Falcón saw warmth and wariness in Yacoub's. He had no idea what was readable in his own.

'Would you prefer coffee, Javier?' asked Yacoub, releasing him.

'Tea is fine,' said Falcón, sitting on the other side of the table.

Falcón's question was humped up in his mind. He felt an unaccustomed nervousness between them. He knew for certain now that Spanish directness was not going to work; a more spiralling, philosophical dynamic was called for.

'The world has gone crazy once again,' said Diouri wearily, pouring the mint tea from a great height.

'Not that it was ever sane,' said Falcón. 'We've got no patience for the dullness of sanity.'

'But, strangely, there's an unending appetite for the dullness of decadence,' said Diouri, handing him a glass of tea.

'Only because clever people in the fashion industry have persuaded us that the next handbag decision is crucial,' said Falcón.

'*Touché*,' said Diouri, smiling and taking a seat on the sofa opposite. 'You're sharp this morning, Javier.'

'There's nothing like a bit of fear for honing the mind,' said Falcón, smiling.

'You don't look frightened,' said Diouri.

'But I am. Being in Seville is different to watching it on television.'

'At least fear provokes creativity,' said Diouri, veering away from Falcón's intended line, 'whereas terror either crushes it or makes us run around like headless chickens. Do you think the fear people experienced under the regime of Saddam Hussein made them creative?'

'What about the fear that comes with freedom? All those choices and responsibilities?'

'Or the fear from lack of security,' said Diouri, sipping

278

his tea, enjoying himself now that he knew Falcón was not going to be too European. 'Did we ever have that conversation about Iraq?'

'We've talked a lot about Iraq,' said Falcón. 'Moroccans love to talk to me about Iraq, while everybody north of Tangier hates to talk about it.'

'But *we*, you and I, have never had the *original* conversation about Iraq,' said Diouri. 'That question: Why did the Americans invade?'

Falcón sat back on the sofa with his tea. This was how it always was with Yacoub when he was in Morocco. It was how it was with Falcón's Moroccan family in Tangier; with all Moroccans, in fact. Tea and endless discussion. Falcón never talked like this in Europe. Any attempt would be greeted with derision. But this time it was going to provide the way in. They had to circle each other before the proposal could finally be made.

'Almost every Moroccan I've ever spoken to thinks that it was about oil.'

'You learn quickly,' said Diouri, acknowledging that Falcón had acquiesced to the Moroccan way. 'There must be more Moroccan in you than you think.'

'My Moroccan side is slowly filling up,' said Falcón, sipping the tea.

Diouri laughed, motioned to Javier for his glass, and poured two more measures of high-altitude tea.

'If the Americans wanted to get their hands on Iraqi oil, why spend $180 billion on an invasion when they could raise sanctions at the stroke of a pen?' said Diouri. 'No. That's the facile thinking of what the British like to call "the Arab street". The teahouse huffers and puffers think that people only do things for immediate gain, they forget the urgency of it all. The invention of the Weapons of Mass Destruction pretext. Haranguing the UN for more resolutions. Rushing the troops to the borders. The hastiness of the planned invasion, which made no provision for the aftermath. What was all that about? Where was Iraqi oil going to go? Down the plug hole?'

'Wasn't it more about the *control* of oil in general?' said Falcón. 'We know a bit more about the emerging economies of China and India now.'

'But the Chinese weren't making a move,' said Diouri. 'Their economy won't be larger than America's until 2050. No, that doesn't make sense either, but at least you didn't say that word that I have to listen to now when I go to dinners in Rabat and Casablanca and find myself sitting next to American diplomats and businessmen. They tell me that they went into Iraq to give them democracy.'

'Well, they did have elections. There is an Iraqi assembly and a constitution, as a result of ordinary Iraqi people taking considerable risks to vote.'

'The terrorists made a political mistake there,' said Diouri. 'They forgot to offer the people a choice that didn't include violence. Instead they said: "Vote and we will kill you." But they had already been killing them anyway, when they were walking down the street to get some bread with their children.'

'That's why you have to swallow the word democracy at your dinners,' said Falcón. 'It was a victory for the "Occupation".'

'When I hear them use that word, I ask them – very quietly, I should add – "When are you going to invade

Morocco and get rid of our despotic king, and his corrupt government, and install democracy, freedom and equality in Morocco?"'

'I bet you didn't.'

'You see. You're right. I didn't. Why not?'

'Because of the state security system of informers left over from the King Hassan II days?' said Falcón. 'What *did* you say to them?'

'I did what most Arabs do, and said those things behind their backs.'

'Nobody likes to be called a hypocrite, especially the leaders of the modern world.'

'What I said to their faces were the words of Palmerston, a nineteenth-century British prime minister,' said Diouri. 'In talking about the British Empire he said: "We have no eternal allies and no perpetual enemies. What we have are eternal and perpetual *interests*."'

'How did the Americans react to that?'

'They thought it was Henry Kissinger who'd said it,' said Diouri.

'Didn't Julius Caesar say it before all of them?'

'We Arabs are often derided as impossible to deal with, probably because we have a powerful concept of honour. We cannot compromise when honour is at stake,' said Diouri. 'Westerners only have *interests*, and it's a lot easier to trade in those.'

'Maybe you need to develop some *interests* of your own.'

'Of course, some Arab countries have the most vital interest in the global economy – oil and gas,' said Diouri. 'Miraculously this does *not* translate into power for the Arab world. It's not only outsiders who find us impossible to deal with – we can't seem to deal with each other.'

'Which means you're always operating from a position of weakness.'

'Correct, Javier,' said Diouri. 'We behave no differently to anyone else in the world. We hold conflicting ideas in our heads, agreeing with all of them. We say one thing, think another and do something else. And in playing these games, which everybody else plays, we always forget the main point: to protect our interests. So a world power can condescend to us about "democracy" when their own foreign policy has been responsible for the murder of the democratically elected Patrice Lumumba and the installation of the dictator Mobutu in Zaire, and the assassination of the democratically elected Salvador Allende to make way for the brutality of Augusto Pinochet in Chile, because they have no honour and only interests. They always operate from a position of strength. Now, do you see where we are?'

'Not exactly.'

'That is another one of our problems. We are very emotional people. Look at the reaction to those cartoons which appeared in the Danish newspaper earlier this year. We get upset and angry and it takes us down interesting paths, but further and further away from the point,' said Diouri. 'But I must behave and get back to why the Americans invaded Iraq.'

'The half of my Moroccan family that doesn't think it was about oil,' said Falcón, 'thinks that it was done to protect the Israelis.'

'Ah, yes, another notion that seethes in the minds of the tea drinkers,' said Diouri. 'The Jews are running everything. Most of my work force thinks that 9/11 was a Mossad operation to turn world opinion against the Arabs, and that George Bush knew about it all along and let it happen. Even some of my senior executives believe that the Israelis demanded the invasion of Iraq, that Mossad supplied the false intelligence about weapons of mass destruction, and that Ariel Sharon was the commander-in-chief of the US forces on the ground. Where the Jews are concerned, we are the world's greatest conspiracy theorists.

'The problem is that it is their rage at the Israeli occupation of Palestine that blinds them to everything else. That fundamental injustice, that slap in the face for the Arab's sense of honour, brings up such powerful emotions in the Arab breast that they cannot think, they cannot see. They focus on the Jews and forget about their own corrupt leadership, their lack of lobbying power in Washington, the pusillanimity of almost all dictatorial, authoritarian Arab regimes . . . Ach! I'm boring myself now.

'You see, Javier, we are incapable of change. The Arab mind is like his house and the medina where he lives. Everything looks inward. There are no views or vistas . . . no visions of the future. We sit in these places and look for solutions in tradition, history and religion, while the world beyond our walls and shores grinds relentlessly forward, crushing our beliefs with their interests. People will look back on the twentieth century and gasp. How was it, they will say, that a race that held the world's most powerful resource, oil, the resource that made the whole system run, allowed most of its people to live in abject poverty, while its political, cultural and economic influence was negligible?

'You know the last people in the world who should be sent to talk to the Arabs are the Americans. We are polar opposites. In becoming an American, part of the pact is to walk away from your past, your history, and totally embrace the future, progress, and the American Way. Whereas, to an Arab, what happened in the seventh century or 1917 is still as vivid today as it was when it first occurred. They want us to embrace a new future, but we cannot forsake our history.'

'Why is it that, when you talk about the Arabs, sometimes you say "we" and sometimes "they"?'

'As you know, I have one foot in Europe and the other in North Africa, and my mind runs down the middle,' said Diouri. 'I perceive the injustice of the Palestinian situation, but I can't emotionally engage with their solutions: the intifada and suicide bombings. It's just a terrifying extension of throwing stones at tanks – an expression of weakness. An inability to draw together the necessary forces to bring about change.'

'Since Arafat has gone, things have been able to move forward.'

'Stagger forward . . . lurch from side to side,' said Yacoub. 'Sharon's stroke signified the end of the old guard. The vote for Hamas was a vote against the corruption of Fatah. We'll see if the rest of the world wants them to succeed.'

'But despite all these misgivings, *you* still have no desire to live in Spain.'

'That's my peculiar problem. I've been brought up

in a religious household and I've benefited from the daily discipline of religious observance. I love Ramadan. I always make sure I am here for Ramadan because for one month of the year the workings of the world drift into the background and the spiritual and religious life becomes more important. We are all joined together by it in communal fasting and feasting. It gives spiritual strength to the individual and the community. In Christian Europe you have Lent, but it has become something personal, almost selfish. You think: I'll give up chocolate or I won't drink beer for a month. It doesn't bind society like Ramadan does.'

'Is that the only reason you don't live in Spain?'

'You are one of the few Europeans I can talk to about these things, without having you laugh in my face,' said Diouri. 'But that is what I have learnt from my two fathers, the one who forsook me, and the one who taught me the right way to be. That is the difficulty for me in both Europe and America. You know, there's been a big change here recently. It was always the dream to get to America. Young Moroccans thought their culture was cool, their society much freer than racist-bound Old Europe, the attitude of Immigration and the universities more open. Now the kids have changed their minds. They were attracted to Europe, but now, after the riots in France last year and the disrespect shown in Denmark, their dreams are of coming home. For myself, when I'm alone in hotel rooms in the West and I try to relax by watching television, I gradually feel my whole being dissipating and I have to get down and pray.'

'And what's that about?'

'It's about the decadence of a society consumed by materialism,' said Diouri.

'To which you yourself make a considerable contribution, and from which you derive great benefit,' said Falcón.

'All I can say is, if I lived anywhere other than Morocco, I would be drained of will within a few weeks.'

'But then you rage against the lack of progress and the inability to change in the Arab world.'

'I rage against poverty, the lack of work for a young and growing population, the humiliation of a people by –'

'But if you give a young guy work, he'll make money and go out and buy a mobile phone, an iPod and a car,' said Falcón.

'He will, once he has made sure that his family is taken care of,' said Diouri. 'And that is fine, as long as the materialism doesn't become his new God. A lot of Americans are profoundly religious whilst being driven by materialism. They believe it goes hand in hand. They are wealthy because they are the chosen people.'

'Well, that's confused everything,' said Falcón.

'Only the extremist polarizes through simplification,' said Diouri, laughing. 'Extremists understand one thing about human nature: nobody wants to know about the complexity of the situation. The invasion of Iraq was about oil. No, it wasn't. It was all about democracy. The two extremes are a long way from the truth, but there's enough in both statements to make people believe. It *is* all about oil, but not Iraqi oil. And it is about democracy, but not the strange beast that will have to be cloned in order to hold Iraq together.'

'I think we've come full circle,' said Falcón. 'We must be close by now.'

'Oil, democracy and the Jews. There's truth in all of them. It was part of the brilliance of the plan,' said Diouri, 'to create such a colossal diversionary arena that the world would look nowhere else.'

'The problem with most conspiracy theories is that they always award phenomenal intelligence and foresight to people who've rarely exhibited those qualities,' said Falcón.

'This action didn't require huge intelligence or foresight, because it simplified all complexities down to a single perpetual interest. There's also a terrifying logic to it, which conspiracy theories always lack,' said Diouri. 'I told you that it was all about oil, democracy and protection, but none of it was to do with Iraq.

'For the Americans to maintain their world domination they need oil in a continuous supply at a competitive price. Democracy is a very fine thing, as long as the right person wins, and that means the person who will look after American interests most ably. Democracy in the Arab world is dangerous, because politics is always bound up with religion. It is only promoted in Iraq because the installation of another, more pliable, despot than Saddam Hussein would not be acceptable to the outside world.'

'At least it introduces the *concept* of democracy.'

'There have been attempts at democracy in the Arab world before now. It breaks down when it becomes clear that the winners in the elections would be the

Islamic candidates. Democracy puts power in the hands of the most numerous, and for them Islam will always come first. That doesn't offer much security to American interests, which is why the democratically elected Iraqi assembly and their constitution have had to be . . . wrestled into position.'

'Do you think that's the case?'

'It doesn't matter whether it is or not. It's the common perception in the Arab world.'

'So who are the Americans seeking to protect with all this activity in the region, if it isn't the Israelis?'

'The Israelis can take care of themselves as long as they have American support – which they are guaranteed, because they're so powerfully represented in Washington. No, the Americans have to protect the weak and the flabby, the decadent and the corrupt, who are the guardians of their greatest and most sacred interest: oil. I believe – and I'm not a mad, lone conspiracy theorist – that they invaded Iraq to offer protection to the Saudi royal family.'

'It's not as if Saddam Hussein had shown himself to be the most accommodating neighbour.'

'Exactly. So a perfect pretext was invented on the basis of past performance,' said Diouri. 'Anybody could see that after the first Gulf War in 1991 Saddam was a spent force, which was why Bush senior left him there, rather than create the unknown quantity of a power vacuum. Fortunately, Saddam still strutted about on his little stage with all the arrogance of a great Arab icon. He was cruel and genocidal: gassing the Kurds and massacring Shias. It was easy to create the image of an evil genius who was destabilizing the Middle East. I mean, they even managed to frame him for 9/11.'

288

'But he *was* cruel, violent and despotic,' said Falcón.

'So when are the coalition forces going to turn their attention to, say, Robert Mugabe in Zimbabwe?' said Diouri. 'But that's how the Americans play the game. They confuse the picture with elements of truth.'

'If Saddam was a spent force, why did the Saudis believe they needed protecting?'

'They were scared of the militancy that they themselves had created,' said Diouri. 'To maintain credibility as the guardians of the sacred sites of Islam, they bankrolled the medressas, the religious schools, which in turn became hotbeds of extremism. Like all decadent regimes, they are paranoid. They sensed the antipathy of the Arab world and its extremist factions. They couldn't invite the Americans in as they had done in 1991, but they could ask them to install themselves next door. The double reward for the Americans was that they not only secured their perpetual interest, the oil, but also drew the forces of terror away from the homeland by offering a target in the heart of Islam. Bush has repaid his corporate debts to the oil companies, the American population feels safer, and it can all be dressed up as the forces of Good crushing those of Evil.'

Silence, while Diouri lit his first cigarette of the morning and sipped some more tea. Falcón sucked on the sweet, viscous liquid in his own glass, his question crammed tight in his chest.

'Tea, cigarettes, food . . . they're all negotiating tools,' said Diouri, mysteriously.

Falcón studied Yacoub over the rim of his tea glass. Spies were necessarily complicated people, even those with a clear motive. The worrying and yet crucial aspect of their personality was their need, and therefore ability, to deceive. But why spy? Why did he himself provide information for Mark Flowers? It was because he had begun to find the illusion of life tiresome. The supposed reality of tussling politicians, beaming businessmen and fatuous pundits was exhausting to watch on TV when its veneer had been worn so thin. He spied, not because he wanted to exchange one facile illusion for a slightly more knowing one, but because he needed to remind himself that acceptance was passive, and he'd already discovered the dangers of denial and inaction in his own mind. But what he was asking his friend Yacoub to do was real spying, not just giving Mark Flowers some detail to fill in his little pictures. He was asking Yacoub to pass on information that could result in the capture, and perhaps death, of people that he might know.

'You're thinking, Javier,' said Diouri. 'Normally, at this stage, Europeans are writhing in their seats with ennui at having to talk about Iraq, the Palestinian question and all the rest of the insoluble horror. They have no appetite for polemic any more. In my world of fashion, all they want to talk about is Coldplay's new album or costume design in the latest Baz Luhrman movie. Even business people would rather talk about football, golf and tennis than world politics. It seems that we Arabs have created an interest that nobody wants. We've cornered the market in the most boring conversations in the world.'

'It's riveting to the Arabs because you haven't got what you want. The comfortable never want to talk about stuff that will make them feel uncomfortable.'

'I'm comfortable,' said Diouri.

'Are you?' said Falcón. 'You're wealthy, but do you have what you want? Do you know what you want?'

'I associate comfort with boredom,' said Diouri. 'It might be to do with my past, but I cannot bear contentment. I want change. I want a state of perpetual revolution. It's the only way I can be sure that I'm still alive.'

'Most Moroccans I've spoken to would like to be comfortable with a job, a house, a family and a stable society to live in.'

'If they want all that, they'll have to be prepared for change.'

'None of them wanted terrorism,' said Falcón, 'and none of them wanted a Taliban-type regime.'

'How many did you get to condemn acts of terrorism?'

'None of them approved . . .'

'I mean outright condemnation,' said Diouri firmly.

'Only the ones who had persuaded themselves that the terrorist acts had been committed by the Israelis.'

'You see, it's a complicated state, the Arab mind,' said Diouri, tapping his temple.

'At least they didn't find terrorism honourable.'

'You know when terrorism *is* honourable?' said Diouri, pointing at Falcón with the chalk stick of his French cigarette. 'Terrorism was considered honourable when the Jews fought the British for the right to establish their Zionist state. It was considered dishonourable when the Palestinians employed extreme tactics against the Jews in order to reclaim the land and property that had been stolen from them. Terrorists are acceptable once they've become strong enough to be perceived as freedom fighters. When they are weak and disenfranchised, they are just common bloody murderers.'

'But that's not what we're talking about here,' said Falcón, fighting back his frustration at how the conversation had spiralled off again.

'It will always be part of it,' said Diouri. 'That hard pip of injustice scores at the insides of every Arab. They know that what these mad fanatics are doing is wrong, but humiliation has a strange effect on the human mind. Humiliation breeds extremism. Look at Germany before the Second World War. The power of humiliation is that it is deeply personal. We all remember it from the first time it happened to us as a child. What extremists like bin Laden and Zarqawi realize is that humiliation becomes truly dangerous when it is collective, has risen to the surface and there's a clear purpose in venting it. That is what the terrorists want. That is the ultimate aim of all their attacks. They are saying: "Look, if we all do this together, we can be powerful."'

'And then what?' said Falcón. 'You'll be taken back to the glory days of the Middle Ages.'

'Forward to the past,' said Diouri, crushing out his cigarette in the silver shell of the ashtray. 'I'm not sure that's a price worth paying to have our humiliation assuaged.'

'Have you heard of an organization called VOMIT?' asked Falcón.

'That's the anti-Muslim website that people here get so enraged about,' said Diouri. 'I haven't seen it myself.'

'Apparently the site enumerates the victims of Muslim attacks on civilians, not just in the Western world but also Muslim-on-Muslim attacks such as the suicide bombings of Iraqi police recruits, women murdered in "honour" killings, and the gang-raping of women to inflict shame . . .'

'What's your angle, Javier?' asked Diouri, through narrowed eyes. 'Are you saying this organization has a point?'

'As far as I know, they are making no point other than keeping count.'

'What about the name of the website?'

'Well, "vomit" expresses disgust . . .'

'You know, Muslim life is regarded rather cheaply in the West. Think how valuable each of the 3,000 lives was in the Twin Towers, how much was invested in the 191 commuters in Madrid or the 50-odd people who died in the London bombings. And then look at the value of the 100,000 Iraqi civilians who lost their lives in the pre-invasion assault. Nothing. I'm not sure they even registered,' said Diouri. 'Was there a website that enumerated the victims of Serb slaughter in Bosnia? What about Hindu attacks on Muslims in India?'

'I don't know.'

'That's why VOMIT is anti-Muslim. It has singled out the acts of a fanatic few and made it the responsibility of an entire religion,' said Diouri. 'If you told me they were responsible for blowing up the mosque in Seville yesterday, it wouldn't surprise me.'

'They've established a presence,' said Falcón. 'Our intelligence agency, the CNI, are aware of them.'

'Who else are the CNI aware of?' said Diouri, uneasy.

'It's a very complicated situation,' said Falcón. 'And we're looking for intelligent, knowledgeable and well-connected people who are willing to help us.'

Falcón sipped his tea, grateful for the prop. He'd

finally got it out into the open. He almost couldn't believe he'd said it. Nor could Yacoub Diouri, who was sitting on the other side of the ornately decorated table, blinking.

'Have I understood you correctly, Javier,' said Diouri, his face suddenly solid as a plastic mask and his voice stripped of any warmth. 'You have presumed to come into my house to ask me to spy for your government?'

'You knew from the moment I called you last night that I wasn't coming here on a purely social visit,' said Falcón, holding firm.

'Spies are the most despised of all combatants,' said Diouri. 'Not the dogs of war, but the rats.'

'I would never have thought of asking you if for one moment I took you to be a man who was satisfied with what we are being asked to believe in this world,' said Falcón. 'That *was* the point of your discourse on Iraq, wasn't it? Not just to show me the Arab point of view, but also your appreciation of a greater truth.'

'But what has led you to believe that you could ask me such a question?'

'I ask it because, like me, you are pro-Muslim and pro-Arab and anti-terrorism. You also want there to be change and to make progress rather than a great regression. You are a man of integrity and honour . . .'

'I wouldn't normally associate those virtues with the amorality of spying,' said Diouri.

'Except that, knowing you, your purpose would not be financial reward or vanity, but rather a belief in bringing about change without pointless violence.'

'You and I are very similar people,' said Diouri, 'except that our roles have been reversed. We have both been wronged by monstrous fathers. You have suddenly discovered that you are half Moroccan, while I should have been brought up Spanish, but have *become* Moroccan. Perhaps we are the embodiment of two entwined cultures.'

'With messy histories,' said Falcón, nodding.

21

The radio promised the Sevillanos a day of towering heat, in excess of 40°C, with a light Saharan breeze to sting the eyeballs, dry the sweat and render the site of the destroyed building a serious health hazard. Consuelo was still groggy from the pill she'd taken at three in the morning, when she'd realized that watching Darío's fluttering eyelids was not going to help her sleep. As always, she had a busy day ahead, which would now be enclosed by the parentheses of sessions with Alicia Aguado. She did not think about them. She was removed from what was happening. She was more aware of the bone structure of her face and the snug mask of her skin, behind which she hoped to keep operating.

The mood of the radio presenter was sombre. His words of reflection did not penetrate, nor did his announcement of a minute's silence for the victims of the bombing, which had been called for midday. Her eyelids closed and opened as if she was expecting a new scene with every blink, rather than the same scene, minutely changed.

The sleeping pill dulled the adrenaline leak into her system. Had she been any sharper, the terrifying sense of coming apart that she'd experienced yesterday would have been too powerful a memory, and she would have glided past Aguado's consulting room and driven straight to work. As it was, she parked the car and let her legs carry her up the stairs. Her hand engaged with Alicia Aguado's white palm as her hips fitted between the arms of the lovers' chair. She bared her wrist. Words came to her from some way off and she didn't catch them.

'I'm sorry,' she said. 'I'm still a little tired. Can you repeat that?'

'Last night, did you think about what I told you to?'

'I'm not sure that I remember what I told . . . what you told me to think about.'

'Something that made you happy.'

'Oh, yes, I did that.'

'Have you been taking drugs, Consuelo? You're very slow this morning.'

'I took a sleeping pill at three this morning.'

'Why couldn't you sleep?'

'I was too happy.'

Aguado went to the kitchen and made a powerful café solo and gave it to Consuelo, who knocked it back.

'You have to be sharp for our meetings, or there's no point,' said Aguado. 'You have to be in touch with yourself.'

Aguado stood in front of Consuelo, tilted her face up, as if she were positioning a small child for a kiss, and pressed her thumbs into her forehead. Consuelo's vision brightened. Aguado sat back down.

'Why couldn't you sleep?'

'I was thinking too much.'

'About all those things that made you "too happy"?'

'Happiness is not my normal condition. I needed a respite.'

'What is your normal condition?'

'I don't know. I cover it too well.'

'Are you listening to yourself?'

'I can't help it. I have no resistance.'

'So you didn't do what I told you to do last night.'

'I told you. Happiness is not my normal condition. I'm not drawn to it.'

'What *did* you do?'

'I watched my children sleeping.'

'What does that tell you about the condition that you *are* drawn to?'

'It's uncomfortable.'

'Do you drive yourself hard in your work?'

'Of course, it's the only way to be successful.'

'Why is success important to you?'

'It's an easier measure . . .'

'Than what?'

Panic rose in Consuelo's constricting throat.

'It's easier to measure one's success in business than it is to measure, or rather to see . . . perceive . . . You know what I'm trying to say.'

'I want you to say it.'

Consuelo shifted in her half of the seat, took a deep breath.

'I balance my failures as a person by showing the world my brilliance in business.'

'So, what is your success to you?'

'It's my cover. People will admire me for that, whereas if they knew who I really was, what I had done, they would despise me.'

'Do your three children sleep in separate bedrooms?'

'Now they do, yes. The two older boys need their own space.'

'When you watch them sleeping, who do you spend most time with?'

'The youngest, Darío.'

'Why?'

'He is still very close to me.'

'Is there an age gap?'

'He's four years younger than Matías.'

'Do you love him more than the other two?'

'I know I shouldn't, but I do.'

'Does he look more like you or your late husband?'

'Like me.'

'Have you always looked at your children sleeping?'

'Yes,' she said, thinking about it. 'But it's only become . . . obsessive in the last five years, since my husband was murdered.'

'Did you look at them any differently, compared to now?'

'Before, I would look at them and think: these are my beautiful creations. Only after Raúl's death did I begin to sit amongst them – I put them all in the same room for a while – and, yes, it was then that the pain started. But it's not a bad pain.'

'What does that mean?'

'I don't know. Not all pain is bad. In the same way that not all sadness is terrible and not all happiness that great.'

'Talk me through that,' said Aguado. 'When is sadness not so terrible?'

'Melancholy can be a desirable state. I've had affairs with men which have satisfied me while they lasted and when they finished I was sad, but with the knowledge that it was for the best.'

'When can happiness not be so great?'

'I don't know,' said Consuelo, twirling her free hand. 'Maybe when a woman comes out of a courtroom saying that she's "happy" her son's killer was sentenced to life imprisonment. I wouldn't call that . . .'

'I'd like you to personalize that for me.'

'My sister thinks I'm happy. She sees me as a healthy, wealthy and successful woman with three children. When I told her about our sessions she was stunned. She said: "If you're nuts, what hope is there for the rest of us?"'

'But when do you see *your* happiness as not being so great?'

'That's what I mean,' said Consuelo. 'I should be happy now, but I'm not. I have everything anybody could wish for.'

'What about love?'

'My children give me all the love I need.'

'Do they?' asked Aguado. 'Don't you think that children *take* a lot of loving? You are their guiding light in the nurturing process, you teach them and give them confidence to face the world. They reward you with unconditional love because they are conditioned to do that, but they don't know what love is. Don't you think that children are essentially selfish?'

'You don't have children, Alicia.'

'We're not here to talk about me. And not every point of view that comes from me is my own,' said Aguado. 'Do you think life can be complete without adult love?'

'A lot of women have come to the conclusion that

300

it can be,' said Consuelo. 'Ask all those battered wives we have in Spain. They'll tell you that love can be the death of you.'

'You don't look like the battered type.'

'Not physically.'

'Have you suffered mental torment from a man?'

A tremor shuddered through Consuelo and Aguado's fingers jumped off her wrist. Consuelo thought that she'd kept the content of this session at a remove. What she'd been saying was in her head, of course, but it was confined there, fenced in. But now somehow it had broken out. It was as if the mad cows had realized the flimsiness of the barriers and crashed through to stampede around her body. She felt the wild terror of yesterday. The sense of coming apart – or was it the fear of something that had been contained getting loose?

'Keep calm, Consuelo,' said Aguado.

'I don't know where this fear comes from. I'm not even sure whether it's associated with what I've been saying, or if it's from some other source that's suddenly leaked into the mainstream.'

'Try to put it into words. That's all you can do.'

'I've become suspicious of myself. I'm beginning to think that a large chunk of my existence has been kept satisfied, or perhaps tied down, by some illusion that I've devised to keep myself going.'

'Most people prefer the illusory state. It's less complicated to live a life feeding off TV and magazines,' said Aguado. 'But it's not for you, Consuelo.'

'How do *you* know? Maybe it's too late to start breaking things down and rebuilding them.'

'I'm afraid it's too late for you to *stop*,' said Aguado. 'That's why you've ended up here. You're like someone

301

who's walked down an alleyway and seen a naked foot sticking out of a rubbish bin. You want to forget about it. You don't want to get involved. But unfortunately you've seen the foot too clearly and you'll get no peace until the matter is resolved.'

'The reason I came here was because of the man in the Plaza del Pumarejo – my bizarre . . . attraction to him and its danger to me. Now we've talked about other things, unrelated to that, and I have the feeling that I've got nowhere to go. Nowhere in my head is safe. Only my work takes my mind elsewhere, and that's only temporary. Even my children have become potentially dangerous.'

'None of it is unrelated,' said Aguado. 'I'm teasing out the threads from the tangled knot. Eventually we'll find the source and, once you've seen it and understood it, you'll be able to move on to a happier life. This terror has its rewards.'

Inés woke up in a convulsion of fear. She blinked, taking in the room a piece at a time. Esteban wasn't there. His pillow was undented. She creaked up on an elbow and threw off the sheet. The pain made her whimper. She panted like a runner, summoning energy for the next lap, the next level of pain.

There didn't seem to be a pain-free position. She had to think her way around her body, trying to find new pathways to limbs and organs that didn't hurt. She got up on to all fours and gasped, hanging her head, staring down the tunnel of her falling hair. Tears blurred her vision. There was a circle of diluted red on her pillow. She got a foot down on to the floor and slid off the bed. She shuffled to the mirror and pushed her hair back. She could not believe it was her head on top of that body.

The contusions were gross. An abstract of purple, blue, black and yellow had spread out over her entire chest area and now joined the bruise on her torso, which reached down as far as her pubic hair. It was true, she did bruise easily. It wasn't as bad as it looked. The pain was more from stiffness than actual damage. A warm shower would help.

In the bathroom she caught sight of her back and buttocks. The welts looked angrier and uglier. She would have to disinfect the punctures left by the buckle. How easily this new regime came to her. She ran the water, held her hand – still puffy from where her finger had been bent back – underneath the flow. She stepped in and held on to the mixer tap, gasping at the pain of the water falling on her. She wouldn't be able to wear a bra this morning.

Tears came. She sank to the floor of the shower. The water seethed through her hair. What had happened to her? She couldn't even think of herself in the first person singular any more, she was so distant from the woman she used to be. She slapped the shower off and crawled out like a beaten dog.

She found reserves she didn't know she had. She took painkillers. She was going to work. It was impossible to stay in the hell of this apartment. She dried herself off, got dressed and made up. Nothing showed. She went out and caught a cab.

The driver talked about the bomb. He was angry. He hit his steering wheel. He called them bastards, without knowing who 'they' were. He said that the time had come to stop fucking about and teach these people a lesson. Inés didn't engage. She sat in the back, gnawing at the inside of her cheek, thinking how much she needed somebody to talk to. She went through all her friends. They were hopeless. Not one could she describe as intimate. Her colleagues? All good people, but not right for this. Family? She couldn't bear to reveal her failure. And it came to her out of the blue, a thought she'd never allowed herself before: her mother was a stupid person and her father a pompous ass who thought he was an intellectual.

The office was empty. She was relieved. Her schedule told her she had two meetings and then nothing. She'd made sure there was nothing because she had to prepare for a court appearance the next day. She headed for the door and one of her male colleagues blundered in with an armful of files. The pain of their collision detonated in her head. Fainting seemed like the only option to wipe clean the pain circuit. She dropped and held on to her foot as a distraction. Her colleague was all over her, saying he was sorry. She left without a word.

Meetings passed. Only at the end of the second one did the judge ask her if she was all right. She went to the lavatory and tried to ignore the trickle of blood she saw slowly dissipating in the water. Her period? She hadn't had one. It wasn't due. She didn't care. She took more painkillers.

She went across the avenue to the Murillo Gardens. She knew what she was after: she wanted to see the whore again. She wasn't sure why. One part of her wanted to show the whore what he'd done to her, the other part . . . What did the other part want?

The whore wasn't there. It was hot. The street signs

told her it was 39°C at 11.45. She walked through the Barrio Santa Cruz, amongst the ambling tourists. How was she going to find the whore? The painkillers were good. Her mind floated free of her body. Reality eased off a few notches. It hadn't occurred to her that painkillers killed all manner of pain.

Her lips tingled and did not feel like her own. Street sounds came to her muffled, her vision was soft focus. She was being drawn along by a great multitude of people who were crowding into the Avenida de la Constitución and heading for the Plaza Nueva. They carried banners, which she couldn't read because they were turned away from her. In the square there were hundreds of placards held up in the air, which said simply: *PAZ*. Peace. Yes, she would like some of that.

The clock struck midday and the crowd fell totally silent. She walked amongst them, wondering what had happened, looking into their faces for signs. They returned her gaze, stone-faced. The traffic noise had stopped, too. There was only the sound of birds. It was quite beautiful, she thought, that people should be gathering together to ask for peace. She wandered out of the square just as people returned to a state of animation and the murmur of humanity rose up behind her. She went down Calle Zaragoza thinking she would go to El Cairo for something to eat. They liked her in El Cairo. She thought they liked her in El Cairo. But everybody liked everybody else in bars in Seville.

It was then that she saw the whore. Not the whore herself, but a photograph. She stepped back into the street, confused. Could whores do that now? Advertise themselves in shop windows? They pipe porn into your living room after midnight now, but do they let whores tout for business like this? She was surprised to find it was an art gallery.

A car gave her a light toot. She stepped back up to the window. She read the card next to the photograph: *Marisa*. Just that – Marisa. How old was she? The card didn't say. That's what everybody wants to know these days. How old are you? They want to see your beauty. They need to know your age. And if you're talented, that's a bonus, but the first two are crucial for the marketing.

Beyond the window display was a young woman at a desk. Inés went in. She heard her heels on the marble floor. She'd forgotten to look at the whore's work, but she was committed now.

'I love that Marisa,' she heard herself say. 'I just love her.'

The young woman was pleased. Inés was well dressed and seemed harebrained enough to pay the ridiculous prices. They veered off together to admire Marisa's work – two woodcarvings. Inés encouraged the woman to talk, and in a matter of minutes had found out where Marisa had her workshop.

Inés had no idea what she should do with this information. She went to El Cairo and ordered a stuffed piquillo pepper and a glass of water. She toyed with the bright red pepper, which looked obscene, like a pointed, inquisitive tongue looking for a moist aperture. She hacked it up and forked it into her cotton-wool mouth.

She went home, turned on the air conditioning and lay on the bed. She slept and woke up in the chill of the apartment, having dreamt and been left with an overwhelming sense of loneliness. She had never been as lonely as in that dream. It occurred to her that she would only be as lonely as that in death.

The painkillers had worn off and she was stiff with cold. She realized that she was talking to herself and was fascinated to know what she'd been saying.

It was 4.30 in the afternoon. She should go to the office and work on the case, but there didn't seem much point now. For some reason tomorrow had begun to seem unlikely.

She heard herself say: 'Don't be ridiculous.' She went to the kitchen and drank water and swallowed more painkillers. She came out of the apartment and into the street, which was thick with heat after the thin, chilled air inside. She caught a cab and heard her voice ask the cab driver to take her to Calle Bustos Tavera. Why had she asked to be taken there? There was nothing to be gained . . .

There was something jutting out of the gathered neck of her handbag, which she held on her lap. She didn't recognize what it was. She pulled open the bag and saw a steel button set flush in a black handle and a straight steel blade next to her hairbrush. She looked up at the driver, their eyes connected via the rear-view mirror.

'Have you seen that?' said the driver.

'What?' said Inés, in shock at the sight of the knife.

But he was pointing out of the window.

'People hanging hams outside their front doors,' he said. 'If they can't afford them, they're hanging pictures of hams. A ham manufacturer in Andalucía is distributing them. This guy on the radio was saying it's a passive form of protest. It goes back to the fifteenth century when the Moors were driven out of Andalucía and the Catholic Kings promoted the cooking and eating of pork to signify the end of Islamic domination. They're calling today *El Día de los Jamones*. What do you think of that?'

'I think . . . I don't know what I think,' said Inés, fingering the knife handle.

The driver switched the radio to another station. Flamenco music filled the cab.

'I can't listen to too much talk about the bomb,' he said. 'It makes me wonder who I've got in the back of my cab.'

22

Yesterday's emotionally charged workload, followed by the three evening meetings, an uneven night's sleep, the flight and the tension caused by the uncertainty of his mission had left Falcón completely drained. He'd briefly told Pablo that Yacoub had agreed to act for them, but not without conditions, then he'd hit his seat in the Lear jet and passed out instantly.

They landed at Seville airport just before 2.30 p.m. and split up agreeing to meet later that night. Back at home, Falcón showered and changed. His housekeeper had left him a fish stew, which he ate with a glass of cold red wine. He called Ramírez, who told him there was to be another big meeting at 4.30 p.m. and gave him a very thin update, of which the best news was that Lourdes, the girl they'd pulled out of the wreckage yesterday, had regained consciousness for a few minutes just after midday. She was going to be all right. There was no news on the electricians or the council inspectors, except that Elvira had arranged a press release and there'd been announcements on TV and radio. Nothing extraordinary had come out of the interviews with the Informáticalidad sales reps. The one remarkable element in Ramírez's report was his praise for Juez Calderón, who had been handling a very aggressive media.

'You know I don't like him,' said Ramírez, 'but he's been doing a very good job. Since our big news yesterday the investigation has been completely stalled, but Calderón is making us look competent.'

'Realistically, what's the earliest we can expect to get to the epicentre of the bomb?' asked Falcón.

'Not before 9 a.m. tomorrow,' said Ramírez. 'Once they get down to the rubble directly over the mosque they're going to be working by hand, under bomb squad and forensic supervision. That's going to take time and the conditions are going to be horrible. In fact, they already are. The stink down there gets into you like a virus.'

'It's been confirmed with 99 per cent certainty that one of the dead in the mosque is a CGI source,' said Comisario Elvira, opening the 4.30 p.m. meeting. 'We won't have complete confirmation until the DNA samples are matched to those taken from his apartment.'

'And what was he doing in there?' asked Calderón.

'Inspector Jefe Barros has the report,' said Elvira.

'His name is Miguel Botín, he's Spanish, thirty-two years old and a resident of Seville,' said Barros.

'Esperanza – the woman who gave Comisario Elvira the list of men believed to be in the mosque – she had a partner who was in the destroyed building,' said Falcón. 'Was that Miguel Botín?'

'Yes,' said Barros. 'He converted to Islam eleven years

ago. His family came from Madrid and his brother lost a foot in the March 11th bombings. Miguel Botín was recruited by one of my agents in November 2004 and became active just over fourteen months ago, in April 2005.'

The only noise in the pre-school classroom was from the mobile air-conditioning units. Even the steady grinding of the machinery outside had receded as Barros began his report.

'For the first eight months Botín had very little to tell us. The members of the congregation, most of whom were of non-Spanish origin, were all good Muslims and none of them were in the slightest bit radical. They were all sympathetic to the story of his brother and they were all outraged by the London bombings, which occurred not long after Botín became active.

'It was in January this year that Botín first started to detect a change. There was an increase in outside visitors to the mosque. This had no noticeable effect on the congregation, but by March it seemed to be having a discernible effect on Imam Abdelkrim Benaboura. He was preoccupied and appeared under pressure. On 27th April my agent made a request to plant a microphone in the Imam's office. I had a discussion with the Juez Decano de Sevilla, who was issued with my agent's report. The evidence was deemed to be largely circumstantial and a bugging order was refused due to a lack of hard evidence.

'On my agent's request, Botín stepped up his activities and started following Imam Abdelkrim Benaboura outside the mosque. Between 2nd May and the date of this report, which was Wednesday, 31st May, Botín saw the Imam meet with three pairs of men, on ten separate occasions at ten different locations around Seville. He has no idea what was said at any of these meetings, but he did manage to take some photographs, only two of which show clearly visible people. On the basis of this report, with the photographic evidence, another bugging request was made last Thursday, 1st June. We did not receive a reply prior to the explosion yesterday morning.'

'How many men are visible in these two shots?' asked Falcón.

'Four,' said Barros, 'and since the CGI in Madrid have sent down a set of shots from the apartment they raided yesterday, we've been able to identify two of them as Djamal Hammad and Smail Saoudi. We have no idea yet who the other two men are, but the shots are currently in the hands of the CNI, MI6 and Interpol. Obviously I would like to have made this information available sooner, but . . .'

'What about these ten different locations?' said Calderón, cutting in on the self-pity. 'Is there anything exceptional about them? Are they near public buildings, addresses of prominent people? Do they appear to be part of a plan of attack?'

'There's a significant building within a hundred metres of each meeting place, but that's the nature of a big city,' said Barros. 'One of the meetings was in the Irish pub near the cathedral. Who knows if that was the perfect cover for three Muslims who didn't drink alcohol, or whether their meeting outside the only remaining structure of the twelfth-century Almohad mosque was significant.'

'When was the first request to bug the Imam's office turned down by the Juez Decano?' asked Falcón.

'On the same day it was applied for: 27th April.'

'And why wasn't the second bugging request author-ized and acted on?'

'The Juez Decano was away in Madrid at the time. He didn't see the application until Monday afternoon – 5th June.'

'What was Miguel Botín's description of the Imam's state of mind during this month when he observed him more closely?' asked Falcón.

'Increasingly preoccupied. Not as engaged with his congregation as he had been the previous year. Botín became aware of him taking medication, but wasn't able to find out what it was.'

'We found Tenormin on his bedside table, which is a prescription for hypertension,' said Gregorio from the CNI. 'We also found an extensively stocked medicine cabinet. His doctor says that he has been treated for hypertension for the past eight years. He'd recently been complaining of heart rhythm problems and was on medication for a stomach ulcer.'

'When will we get access to the Imam's apartment and your findings?' asked Falcón.

'Don't worry, Inspector Jefe,' said Juan, 'we've been working with a forensics team since the moment we opened the apartment door.'

'We'd still like to get in there,' said Falcón.

'We're nearly finished,' said Gregorio.

'Does the CNI have an opinion about Botín's find-ings and the Imam's doctor?' asked Calderón.

'And has someone gained access to his mysterious history?' asked Falcón.

'We're still awaiting clearance on his history,' said Gregorio.

'The Imam was under a lot of pressure,' said Falcón, before Calderón could mount another attack on Juan. 'Hammad and Saoudi were known operators in the logistics of attacks. They met with the Imam. Were they asking the Imam to act in some way? Perhaps they were calling in a favour, or a promise made some time ago in his inaccessible history. Under those circumstances, what do you think would put a man like the Imam under severe stress?'

'That they were asking him to do something that would have very grave consequences,' said Calderón.

'But if he believed in "the cause" surely he would be happy?' said Falcón. 'It should be an honour for a radical fanatic to be asked to participate in a mission.'

'You think the pressure came from being a reluctant accomplice?' said Gregorio.

'Or the nature of what he was being asked to do,' said Falcón. 'There's a different pressure in storing an unknown product for a week or two, say, and being asked to actively participate in an attack.'

'We need more information on the Imam's activities,' said Elvira.

'It hasn't been confirmed yet, but we think it likely that Hammad and Saoudi were in the mosque when the building was destroyed,' said Falcón. 'Confirmation will come with DNA testing. The other two men photographed by Miguel Botín have to be identified and found if we want to know how the Imam was implicated.'

'That is in hand,' said Gregorio.

'I'd like to talk to the agent who ran Miguel Botín,' said Falcón.

Inspector Jefe Barros nodded. Comisario Elvira asked

314

for a résumé of the situation with the electricians and the council inspectors. Ramírez gave the same very thin update he'd just given to Falcón.

'We know the CGI antiterrorist squad did not have the mosque under surveillance,' said Falcón. 'We have two men posing as council inspectors, who were clearly intent on gaining access to the mosque. The electricians were responding to a blown fuse box. We have to look at the possibility of a link between the fake council inspectors and the electricians. I cannot believe that a legitimate electrician would not have come forward by now. The obvious advantage of being an electrician is that you can bring large quantities of equipment into a place, and witnesses have confirmed that this was the case.'

'You think that *they* planted the bomb?' asked Barros.

'It has to be considered,' said Falcón. 'We can't ignore it just because it doesn't fit with the discoveries we've made so far. It also does not exclude the possibility that there was already a cache of explosives in the mosque. We must talk to your agent. What state of mind is he in?'

'Not good. He's a young guy, only a little older than Miguel Botín. We've been recruiting in that age group because they can connect more easily with each other. His relationship with Botín was close. The two of them had a religious connection.'

'Were they both converts?'

'No, my agent was a Catholic. But they both took their religion seriously. They respected and liked each other.'

'We'd like to speak to him *now*,' said Falcón.

Barros left the room to call him.

'The forensics need to make contact with the wives

and families of the men who were in the mosque,' said Elvira. 'They have to start extracting DNA as soon as possible. The woman who represents them, Esperanza, says she will only talk to you.'

Elvira gave him the mobile number. The meeting ended. The men dispersed. Elvira hung on to Falcón.

'They're sending me some more people down from Madrid,' he said. 'No reflection on you or your squad, but we both know the demands that are being made. You need more foot soldiers and these are all experienced inspector jefes and inspectors.'

'Anything that's going to relieve pressure, I'm happy with,' said Falcón. 'As long as they don't complicate things.'

'They're under my jurisdiction. You don't have to deal with them. They'll be assigned where they're needed most.'

'Have the Guardia Civil been able to get more information on the route of Hammad and Saoudi from Madrid to Seville?'

'It's taking time.'

Barros pulled Falcón aside as he left the room.

'My agent's not back from lunch yet,' he said. 'They'll call me as soon as he gets in.'

'It's just gone 4.30 p.m.,' said Falcón, giving him his mobile number. 'He's running a bit late, isn't he?'

Barros shook his head, shrugged. Things were not going well for him.

'What's your agent's name?'

'Ricardo Gamero,' said Barros.

Falcón called Esperanza and they arranged to meet in some nearby gardens. He asked to bring a female police officer with him.

Cristina Ferrera was waiting for him outside the preschool. He briefed her on the way. Esperanza recognized Falcón as he got out of the car. Introductions were made. They piled back in. Esperanza sat next to Falcón, Ferrera was behind, staring at Esperanza as if she recognized her.

'How are the women holding up?' asked Falcón. 'I imagine the circumstances are very difficult for them.'

'They oscillate between despair and fear,' she said. 'They're devastated by the loss of their loved ones and then they see the news – the assaults and damage to property. They feel a little more secure since your Comisario came on television and announced that violence against Muslims and vandalizing of their property would be dealt with severely.'

'You're their representative,' said Ferrera.

'They trust me. I'm not one of them, but they trust me.'

'You're not one of them?'

'I'm not a Muslim,' said Esperanza. 'My partner is a convert to Islam. I know them through him.'

'Your partner is Miguel Botín,' said Falcón.

'Yes,' she said. 'He wants me to convert to Islam so that we can get married. I'm a practising Catholic and I have some difficulties, as a European, with the treatment of women in Islam. Miguel introduced me to all the women in the mosque to help me understand, to help me get rid of some of my prejudices. But it's a big leap from Catholicism to Islam.'

'How did you meet Miguel?' asked Ferrera.

'Through an old school friend of mine,' said Esperanza. 'I ran into the two of them just over a year ago, and after that Miguel and I started seeing each other.'

317

'What's your friend's name?' asked Falcón.

'Ricardo Gamero,' she said. 'He does something in the police force – I don't know what. He says it's administrative.'

Seville was a village, thought Falcón. He told Esperanza what they needed from the women and said that Ferrera would accompany her to collect and mark up the DNA samples.

'We'll need a sample from Miguel Botín as well,' said Falcón. 'I'm sorry.'

Esperanza nodded, staring into space. She had a clear, unadorned face. Her only jewellery was a gold cross at her neck and two gold studs in her ear lobes, which were visible as her slightly crinkly black hair was scraped back. She had very straight eyebrows and it was these that first gave away her own emotional turmoil, and then the moisture flooding her dark brown eyes. She shook hands and got out of the car. Falcón quickly told Ferrera how Ricardo Gamero fitted in and asked her to find out if Esperanza knew what her partner had been doing.

'Don't worry, Inspector Jefe,' said the ex-nun. 'Esperanza and I recognize each other. We've been on the same path.'

The two women moved off. Falcón sat in the air-conditioned cool of the car and breathed the stress back down into its hole. He made himself believe that he had time on his side. The terrorist angle of the attack was not, at the moment, in his hands, nor was the Imam's history, but progress had been made. He had to concentrate his powers on finding a link to the fake council inspectors and the electricians. There had to be another witness, someone more reliable than Majid

318

Merizak, who'd seen the inspectors and the electricians. Falcón called Ferrera and asked her to find out from the women if there was anybody else who might have been in the mosque on the mornings of Friday 2nd June and Monday 5th June.

He went back to his notebook, too much occurring to him for his brain to have any chance of remembering detail. The first bugging request the CGI made to the Juez Decano was submitted and refused on April 27th. When did Informáticalidad buy the apartment? Three months ago. No date. He called the estate agency. The sale went through on the 22nd of February. What was he expecting? What was he looking for? He wanted to apply pressure on Informáticalidad. He was still suspicious of them, despite the performance by the sales reps in the police interviews. But he didn't want to apply pressure directly. It had to come from another source, other than the homicide squad. He wanted to see if they would react.

Maybe if he could find someone who'd been recently fired, or had "moved on"', from Informáticalidad they would still know people at the company, perhaps even some of the guys who'd used the apartment on Calle Los Romeros. He found the lists given to him by Diego Torres, the Human Resources Director. Names, addresses, home telephone numbers and the dates they left the company. How was he going to find these people at this time of day? He started with the employees who'd left the company most recently, reasoning that they might still be out of work until after the summer. He hit answer machine after answer machine, number no longer in use, and then, finally, a ringing tone that went on for some time. A female voice answered sleepily. Falcón asked for David Curado. She shouted and threw down the phone, which took a soft landing. Curado picked it up. He sounded just about alive. Falcón explained his predicament.

'Sure,' said Curado, waking up instantly. 'I'll talk to anybody about those wankers.'

Curado lived in a modern apartment block in Tabladilla. Falcón knew it. He'd been there years ago to observe a hostage situation across the street. Curado came to the door stripped to the waist, wearing a pair of white short trousers as seen on the tennis player Rafael Nadal. Like Nadal, he looked as if he went to the gym. Beads of sweat stood out on his forehead.

The apartment was hot. The girl who'd answered the phone was lying splayed across the bed in a pair of knickers and a tiny vest. Curado offered a drink. Falcón took some water. The girl groaned and rolled over. Her arms slapped against the mattress.

'She gets annoyed,' said Curado. 'When I'm not earning I don't turn on the air conditioning during the day.'

'Dav-i-i-id,' said the girl in a long whine.

'Now that you're here,' he said, rolling his eyes.

He got up and flipped the switch on the fuse box. A light mist appeared at the vents. The girl let out an orgasmic cry.

'How long did you work for Informáticalidad?' asked Falcón.

'Just over a year. Fifteen months, something like that.'

'How did you get the job?'

'I was head-hunted, but I did the research to make *sure* that I was head-hunted.'

'What was the research?'

'I went to church,' said Curado. 'The sales guys at Informáticalidad were the best paid in the business, and it wasn't all commission-based money. They paid a good basic salary of close to €1,400 a month and you could triple that if you worked hard. At the time I was working like a slave for €1,300 a month, all commission. So I started asking around and it was weird; nobody knew anything about how this company recruited. I called all the agencies, looked through the press and trade magazines, the internet. I even called Informáticalidad themselves and they wouldn't tell me how they recruited. I tried to get friendly with the Informáticalidad sales crew, but they brushed me off. I started looking at who they sold to, and it didn't matter what prices I offered, I could never make a sale. Once a company started buying from Informáticalidad, they bought exclusively. That's why they can offer the high basic salary. They don't have to compete. So, I began looking at the individuals in the companies they sold to and tried to get friendly with them. Nothing.

'I couldn't get anywhere until a buyer from one of these companies got fired. It was she who told me how it worked: you've got to go to church, and you mustn't be a woman. So I qualified on one score, but I hadn't been to church for fifteen years. There were three churches they used: Iglesia de la Magdalena, de Santa María La Blanca and San Marcos. I bought myself a black suit and went to church. Within a couple of months I'd been approached.'

'So you got the job, the money, the nice apartment,' said Falcón. 'What went wrong?'

'Almost immediately they started to cut in on my free time. We were sent on courses – sales training and product information. Normal stuff. Except that it was almost every weekend and there was a lot of repetitive company ethos shit *and* religion, and it wasn't always easy to differentiate between the two. They also did this other thing. They'd partner you off with a senior guy who'd been with the company for two or three years, and he would be your mentor. If you were unlucky and got one of the "serious" ones, they'd fill your head with even more shit. I saw people recruited at the same time as me who just disappeared.'

'Disappeared?'

'Lost their personality. They became an Informáticalidad man, with a glassy look in their eye and their brain tuned to one frequency. It gave me the creeps. That,' said Curado, leaning forward conspiratorially, 'and the total lack of women in the whole sales force. I mean, not one . . .'

'How did you get along with your mentor?'

'Marco? He was a good guy. I still talk to him occasionally, even though it's *forbidden* for Informáticalidad men to talk to ex-employees.'

'Why did you leave?'

'Apart from the lack of women and all the brainwashing shit,' said Curado, 'they wouldn't let me into where the big money was being made. Like I said, they sold to companies without having to compete, so you got the good basic salary. But if you wanted to make the big commissions, *that* was all in converting new prospects to the Informáticalidad way. Once they'd been

322

converted, you got commission on everything that was sold to that company – *ever*.'

'And how did that work?'

'I never found out. I never got beyond the lowest tier of salesmen. I did not have the right mentality,' he said, tapping his forehead. 'In the end they forced me out through boredom. I was nothing more than a form-filler and a post boy. Taking orders, passing them on to "supply". It was the way they got rid of you at Informáticalidad.'

Falcón took a call from Inspector Jefe Barros.

'I'm on my way to an apartment on Calle Butrón,' said Barros. 'You'd better come along as well.'

'I'm in the middle of an interview,' said Falcón, annoyed.

'Ricardo Gamero *was* late coming back from lunch, so I sent another of my agents round to his apartment. There was no answer. The woman in the apartment below let him in. She said she'd seen Gamero going up, but hadn't seen him leave. The agent called back and I told him to get in there any way he could, which was when the woman started screaming. There's a central patio in the block. She'd opened the window to shout up the well. He was hanging out of his bedroom window.'

23

Marisa left her apartment. It was hot, easily over forty degrees, and the perfect time for her to work in her studio. Her tight mulatto skin yearned to sweat freely. Out in the street she walked in the sun and breathed in the desert air. The streets were empty. She stumbled on the cobbles of Calle Bustos Tavera until her eyes got used to the sudden shade. She turned up the alleyway to the courtyard. The light at the end was blinding. The sun had sucked out even the edges of the buildings beyond the arch. She shivered a little at the sensation she always had walking down this tunnel.

At the end, where the huge cobbles turned pewtery on the threshold, she stopped. The courtyard should have been empty at this hour. Instinct told her that someone was there. She saw Inés, halfway down the steps leading to the entrance of her studio.

Rage shuddered through her and bunched up behind her flat chest. This fatuous middle-class bitch now wanted to infect the sanctity of her work place with the received opinions of her bourgeois upbringing, with the soulless rant of her consumer needs, with

324

her self-righteous smugness of 'being thin'. Marisa stepped back into the full darkness of the tunnel.

In turning back to go up the stairs to the studio, Inés revealed the lowest welts on the backs of her thighs. These people deserve each other, thought Marisa. They wander through life with total belief in their brilliant control of the reality around them, without ever seeing the iridescence of the illusory bubble in which they float. They might as well be dead.

Marisa suppressed the temptation to run up the steps, beat the wretched woman senseless, throw her down the stairs, break her skull open and discover the smallness within. My God, she hated these people, grown from tradition, sporting their fancy names – Inés Conde de fucking Tejada – surname *and* title rolled into one.

Inés reached the top of the steps, put her handbag down, tugged open the neck and drew out a black-handled knife. Now this was interesting. Had the bitch come to kill her? Maybe the skinny-legged cow had some *cojones* after all. Inés scored something on the front door of the studio, stepped back and jutted her chin at her work. She put the knife back in the bag and walked down the steps. Marisa backed away, snarling, and retreated to her apartment for an hour. By the time she returned the courtyard was empty, the heat more intense. She ran up the stairs to see Inés's message. Scored into the door was the predictable word: *PUTA*. Whore.

It was time this was over, she thought. She couldn't have the bitch turning up at her place of work.

The news of Gamero's suicide had so disconcerted Falcón he'd left Curado with barely another word. Now, as he drove across town, ideas occurred to him and he called Curado on his mobile.

'Have you heard of someone called Ricardo Gamero?'

'Should I?' he asked. 'Was he at Informáticalidad?'

Maybe that had been too lurid an idea.

'I want you to do something for me, David,' said Falcón. 'I want you to call your old friend at Informáticalidad – Marco . . .?'

'Marco Barreda.'

'I want you to tell Marco Barreda that you had a visit from the Inspector Jefe del Grupo de Homicidios, Javier Falcón. The same cop who's investigating the Seville bombing. I want you to tell him what we discussed in a "thought you'd like to know" sort of way. Nothing sensational, just matter of fact. And tell him what my last question to you was.'

'About Ricardo Gamero?'

'Exactly.'

The Médico Forense was already up the ladder, carrying out his preliminary examination of Ricardo Gamero's body, as Falcón arrived on the crime scene. There was no doubt that he was dead. The CGI agent who'd found him, Paco Molero, had checked for a pulse. Even if Gamero had survived jumping off his window ledge with a rope tied around his neck, he would not have lived for long. On the floor were twelve empty trays of paracetamol. Even if they'd got him to hospital and pumped his stomach, he would probably have remained in a coma and died of liver failure within forty-eight hours. This was not attention seeking. This was an experienced policeman making sure. His apartment had been locked and chained. His bedroom door was also locked, with a chair tilted under the handle.

Falcón shook Inspector Jefe Barros's hand.

'I'm sorry, Ramón. I'm very sorry,' said Falcón, who'd never lost anybody from his squad, but knew that it would be terrible.

Two paramedics manoeuvred the body on to the ladder and pulled it up through the bedroom window. They laid him out on his living-room floor while the forensics went through the bedroom. Falcón asked the instructing judge for permission to search the body.

Gamero was wearing suit trousers and a shirt. He had a wallet in one pocket, loose change in another. As Falcón turned the body to check the back pockets, the head lolled with sickening flexibility. There was a ticket to the Archaeological Museum in the right-hand back pocket. Falcón showed it to Inspector Jefe Barros, who couldn't get rid of the dismay in his face. The ticket had today's date on it.

'He's a citizen of Seville,' said Falcón. 'He doesn't need to buy a ticket to get into this museum.'

'Maybe he didn't want to show his ID,' said Barros. 'Stay anonymous.'

'Was that where he met his informers?'

'They're taught not to follow a routine.'

'I'd like to talk to the agent who found him – Paco Molero?'

'Of course,' said Barros, nodding. 'They were good friends.'

Paco was sitting at the kitchen table with his face in his hands. Falcón touched him on the shoulder, introduced himself. Paco's eyes were red.

'Were you worried about Ricardo?'

'There's been no time for that,' said Paco. 'Obviously

327

he was upset, because he believed he'd lost one of his best sources in the mosque.'

'Did you know his source?'

'I've seen him, but I didn't know him,' said Molero. 'Ricardo asked me to come with him a few times, to check his back – just a routine precaution to make sure he wasn't being watched or followed.'

'Did he leave the office at all today, apart from going to lunch?'

'No. He went out at one thirty. He was due back two hours later. When he hadn't showed by four thirty, and his mobile was turned off, Inspector Jefe Barros sent me over here to find out what had happened.'

'What time did you find him?'

'I was here by ten to five, so maybe just gone five o'clock.'

'Tell me what happened yesterday . . . after the bombing.'

'We were all at work when it happened. We called our sources to arrange meetings. Ricardo couldn't get through to Botín. Then we were told not to leave the office, so we drafted up-to-date reports from what our sources had told us the last time we'd seen them. Lunch was brought in. We weren't released to go home until after 10 p.m.'

'Were you aware of any pressure on Ricardo, apart from the usual work stress?'

'Apart from the *unusual* work stress, you mean?'

'Why unusual?'

'We were being investigated, Inspector Jefe,' said Molero. 'We wouldn't be much of an antiterrorist outfit if we didn't know when our own department was being investigated.'

'How long have you known about this?'

'We reckon it probably started around the end of January.'

'What happened?'

'Nothing . . . just a change in attitude, or atmosphere . . .'

'Did you suspect each other?'

'No, we had total trust in each other and a belief in what we were doing,' said Molero. 'And I would say that, out of the four of us handling Islamic terrorist threats, Ricardo was the most committed.'

'Because he was religious?'

'You've had time to do some homework,' said Molero.

'I just met his source's partner, who happened to be an old school friend of Ricardo's.'

'Esperanza,' said Molero, nodding. 'They were at school and university together. She was going to become a nun before she met Ricardo.'

'Did they ever get together?'

'No. Ricardo was never interested in her.'

'Did he have a girlfriend?'

'Not that I know of.'

'Esperanza told me that the relationship Ricardo had with his source was based on a mutual respect for each other's religion.'

'Religion had something to do with it,' said Molero. 'But they were both against fanaticism, too. Ricardo had a special understanding of fanatics.'

'Why?'

'Because he'd been one himself,' said Molero and Falcón nodded him on. 'He believed that it came from a profound desire to be good, which interacted with a deep concern and constant worry about evil. That was where the hatred came from.'

'Hatred?'

'The fanatic, in his deep desire for goodness, is in constant fear of evil. He begins to see evil all around him. In what we think of as harmless decadence, the fanatic sees the insidious encroachment of evil. He begins to worry about everybody who is not pursuing good with the same zeal as himself. After a while he tires of the pathetic weakness of others and his perception shifts. He no longer sees them as misguided fools, but rather as ministers of the devil, which is when he starts to hate them. From that moment he becomes a dangerous person, because then he is someone receptive to extreme ideas.

'Ricardo had long conversations with Botín, who described a fundamental difference between Catholicism and Islam, which was The Book. The Koran is a direct transcription of the Word of God by the Prophet Mohammed. The word Koran means "recitation". It is not like our Bible, a series of narratives laid down by remarkable men. It is the actual Word of God as taken down by the prophet. Ricardo used to ask us to imagine what that would be like to a fanatic. The Book was not the inspired writing of gifted human beings, but the *Word of God*. In his desperation for goodness, and his fear of evil, the fanatic penetrates deeper and deeper into the Word. He seeks "better", more exactingly good interpretations of the Word. He works his way out, by degrees, to the extremes. That was Ricardo's strength. He'd been a fanatic himself, so he could give us an insight into the minds that we were up against.'

'But he wasn't a fanatic any more?' said Falcón.

330

'He said he'd once reached the point where he'd begun to look down on his fellow human beings and not just found them lacking but thought them subhuman in some way. It was a form of intense religious arrogance. He realized that once you've reached the point where you don't regard all humans as equals, then killing them becomes less of a problem.'

'And had he reached that point?'

'He'd been pulled back from it by a priest.'

'Do you know who this priest was?'

'He died of cancer last September.'

'That must have been a blow.'

'I suppose it must have been. He didn't talk to me about it. I think that was too personal for office consumption,' said Molero. 'He worked harder. He became a man with a mission.'

'And what was that mission?'

'To stop a terrorist attack *before* it happened, rather than helping to catch the perpetrators *after* a lot of people have been killed,' said Molero. 'In fact, last July was a bad time for Ricardo. The London bombings affected him very badly and then at the end of the month his priest was diagnosed with cancer. Six weeks later he was dead.'

'Why did the London bombings affect him like that?'

'He was disturbed by the bombers' profile: young, middle-class British citizens, some with small children, and all with family ties. They weren't loners. That was when he became focused on the nature of fanaticism. He developed his theories, bouncing ideas off one friend, the dying priest, and the other, the convert to Islam.'

'So, he would have taken this explosion as a personal failure.'

'That, and the fact that it also took the life of Miguel Botín, with whom he'd developed a very close relationship.'

'He'd just applied a second time for a bugging order.'

'We thought the refusal of the first was strange. Since the London bombings, we've been told to look for the slightest change of . . . inflexion in a community. And there was plenty going on in that mosque to justify a bug being placed there – according to Ricardo's source, anyway.'

'Do you think it had something to do with the department being under investigation?'

'Ricardo did. We didn't see the logic of it. We just thought he was angry at being turned down. You know how it is: your brain plays tricks and you see conspiracies wherever you look.'

'He had a ticket in his back pocket for the Archaeological Museum, which he must have visited in his lunch break today,' said Falcón. 'Any thoughts about that?'

'Apart from the fact that he didn't have to *buy* a ticket, no.'

'Would that be significant?' asked Falcón. 'Was he the sort of person who would leave something like that as a sign?'

'I think you're reading too much into it.'

'He met somebody in his lunch break and then killed himself,' said Falcón. 'His mind wasn't made up before the meeting; why would you bother to go if you were planning to kill yourself? So something happened *during* this meeting to tip him over the edge, to make him believe, perhaps with his mind in an emotional turmoil, that he was in some way responsible.'

'I can't think who that person could be, or what they could possibly have said to him,' said Molero.

'What church did his friend the priest belong to?'

'It's close. That's why he took this apartment,' said Molero. 'San Marcos.'

'Did he still attend that church, even after the priest's death?'

'I don't know,' said Molero. 'We didn't see much of each other outside the office. I only know about San Marcos because I offered to go with him to his priest's funeral Mass.'

To understand why Gamero had committed suicide they needed to talk to the person he'd met in the Archaeological Museum. Falcón asked Barros to find out from the rest of the antiterrorism squad if they'd seen Gamero with anybody they didn't recognize. He also wanted all names and telephone numbers from Gamero's office line, and in the meantime they'd check his mobile and the fixed line in his apartment. Barros gave him the mobile numbers of the other two officers in the anti-terrorism squad and left with Paco Molero. The instructing judge signed off the *levantamiento del cadáver* and Gamero's body was removed. Falcón and the two forensics, Felipe and Jorge, began a detailed search of the apartment.

'We know he committed suicide,' said Felipe. 'All the doors were locked from the inside and the prints on the water glass next to the paracetamol trays match the body's. So what are we looking for?'

'Anything that might give us a lead to the person he met in his lunch break,' said Falcón. 'A business card, a scribbled number or an address, a note of a meeting . . .'

Falcón sat at the table in the kitchen with Gamero's wallet and the museum ticket. The tendons of his hands rippled under the cloudy membrane of the latex gloves. He felt sure that there were connections to be made out there, which he was just missing. Every lead they were pursuing failed to unfold into the greater narrative of what was going on. There were movements, like seismic aftershocks, that brought about casualties such as Ricardo Gamero, a man dedicated to his work and admired by his colleagues, who'd seen . . . what? His responsibility, or was it just the recognition of his failure?

He teased out the contents of Gamero's wallet: money, credit cards, ID, receipts, restaurant cards, ATM extracts – the usual. Falcón called Serrano and asked him to get the name and number of the priest of the San Marcos church. He went back to the wallet, turning over the cards and receipts, thinking that Gamero was a man who was used to a high level of secrecy in his life. Vital phone numbers would not be written down or stored in his mobile but either memorized or encoded in some way. He wouldn't have, or couldn't have, made contact with the person he saw in the museum on the day of the bomb. His department was being watched and they were all being kept in the office. He could have called at night after they were released from work. He would probably have used a public phone. The only chance was that he might not have remembered an infrequently used mobile number. He turned over the last ATM extract in the wallet. Nothing. He thumped the table.

'Have you got anything out there?' asked Falcón.

'Nothing,' said Jorge. 'The guy's in the CGI, he's not

going to leave anything hanging around unless he wants us to find it.'

A call came through from Cristina Ferrera. She gave him the name and number of another Spanish convert, who would normally have been in the mosque at that time in the morning but had gone to Granada on the Monday evening. He was now back in Seville. His name was José Duran.

A few minutes later Serrano called with the name and number of the priest of the San Marcos church. Falcón told him to stop what he was doing and come to Calle Butrón, pick up Gamero's ID and take it to the Archaeological Museum, where he should ask the ticket sellers and security guards if they remembered seeing Gamero and anybody he might have met.

The priest couldn't see him until after evening Mass at about 9 p.m. It was already 6.30. Falcón couldn't believe the time; the day almost gone and no significant breakthrough. He called José Duran, who was in the city centre. They agreed to meet in the Café Alicantina Vilar, a big, crowded pastelería in the centre.

Serrano still hadn't showed up. Falcón left the ID with Felipe and decided it was quicker to walk to the pastelería than get stuck in evening traffic. As he walked he put a call through to Ramírez and gave him a quick report on Ricardo Gamero, and told him he'd stolen Serrano for a few hours.

'We're not getting anywhere with these fucking electricians,' said Ramírez. 'All this manpower to find something that doesn't exist.'

'They do exist, José Luis,' said Falcón. 'They just don't exist in the form we expect them to.'

'The whole world knows we're looking for them and

they haven't come forward. To me that means they're sinister.'

'Not everybody is a perfect citizen. They might be frightened. They probably don't want to get involved. They couldn't care less. They might be implicated,' said Falcón. 'So *we* have to find *them*, because they are the link from the mosque to the outside world. We have to find out how they fit into this scenario. There were three of them, for God's sake. Somebody, somewhere, knows something.'

'We need a breakthrough,' said Ramírez. 'Everybody's making breakthroughs except us.'

'You found the biggest breakthrough of all, José Luis – the Peugeot Partner and its contents. We have to keep up the pressure and then things will start to give way,' said Falcón. 'And what are all these other break-throughs?'

'Elvira's called a meeting for 8 a.m. tomorrow. He can't talk until then, but it's international. The web's spreading wider by the hour.'

'That's the way these things go now,' said Falcón. 'Remember London? They were rounding up suspects in Pakistan inside a week. But I tell you, José Luis, there's something homegrown about this, too. The intelligence services are equipped to deal with all that world-wide web of international terrorism. What we do is find out what happened on our patch. Have you read the file on the unidentified body found at the dump on Monday morning?'

'Fuck, no.'

'Pérez wrote a report on it and there's an autopsy in there, too. Read it tonight. We'll talk about it tomorrow.'

The waiter brought him a coffee and some sort of sticky pastry envelope with pus-coloured goo inside. He needed sugar. He had to wait half an hour for José Duran, in which time he took calls from Pablo of the CNI, Mark Flowers from the US Consulate, Manuela, Comisario Elvira and Cristina Ferrera. He turned his mobile off. Too many of them wanted to see him tonight and he had no more time to give.

José Duran was pale and emaciated, with hair plastered close to his head, round glasses and a fluffy beard. Deodorant was a stranger to his body and it was still 40°C outside. Falcón ordered him a camomile tea. Duran listened to Falcón's introduction and twizzled his beard into a point on his chin. He breathed on his glasses and wiped them clean with his shirt tail. He sipped his tea and gave Falcón his own introduction. He'd been to the mosque every day of last week. He'd seen Hammad and Saoudi talking to the Imam in his office on Tuesday, 30th May. He hadn't heard their conversation. He'd seen the council inspectors on Friday, 2nd June.

'They must have been from Health and Safety, because they looked at everything: water, drains, electricity. They even looked at the quality of the doors . . . something to do with fire,' said Duran. 'They told the Imam he was going to have to get a new fuse box, but he didn't have to do anything until they issued their report and then he had fifteen days to put it right.'

'And the fuse box blew on Saturday night?' said Falcón.

'That's what the Imam told us on Sunday morning.'

'Do you know when he called the electricians?'

'On the Sunday morning after prayers.'

337

'How do you know that?'

'I was in his office.'

'How did he find their number?'

'Miguel Botín gave it to him.'

'Miguel Botín *gave* the Imam the number of the electricians?'

'No. He reminded the Imam of the card he'd given him earlier. The Imam started to search the papers on his desk, and Miguel gave him another card and told him that there was a mobile number he could call any time.'

'And that was when the Imam called the electricians?'

'Isn't this sort of detail just a bit ludicrous in the light of . . .?'

'You've no idea how crucial this detail is, José. Just tell me.'

'The Imam called them on his mobile. They said they'd come round on Monday morning and take a look and tell him how much it was going to cost. I mean, that's what I assume from the questions the Imam was asking.'

'And you were there on Monday morning?'

'The guy turned up at eight thirty, took a look at the fuse box –'

'The guy was Spanish?'

'Yes.'

'Description?'

'There was nothing to describe,' said Duran, searching amongst the empty tables and chairs. 'He was an average guy, about 1.75 metres tall. Not heavy, but not thin either. Dark hair with a side parting. No facial hair. There was nothing particular about him. I'm sorry.'

'You don't have to try to tell me everything now, but think about it. Call me if anything occurs to you,' said Falcón, giving him his card. 'Did the guy say hello to Miguel Botín?'

Duran blinked. He had to think about that.

'I'm not sure that Miguel was there at that point.'

'And later, when he turned up with the other guys?'

'That's right, he needed help. The Imam wanted a socket in the storeroom and he had to cut a channel from the nearest junction box which was in the Imam's office,' said Duran. 'Miguel was with him in the office. I presume they said hello.'

'What about the other guys, the labourers – were they Spanish, too?'

'No. They spoke Spanish, but they weren't Spaniards. They were from those Eastern bloc countries. You know, Romania or Moldavia, one of those places.'

'Descriptions?'

'Don't ask me that,' said Duran, running his hands down his face in frustration.

'Think about them, José,' said Falcón. 'Call me. It's important. And have you got the Imam's mobile phone number?'

24

Seville – Wednesday, 7th June 2006, 20.30 hrs

Falcón called Inspector Jefe Barros to see if anybody had searched Miguel Botín's apartment. Nobody from the CGI had been there. He called Ramírez, gave him Botín's address, told him to get round there and look for the electrician's card. He called Baena, gave him the Imam's mobile number and told him to get the phone records. He called Esperanza, Miguel's partner, she'd never heard of any friends of his who were electricians. By the time he'd made these calls he was at the doors of the Iglesia de San Marcos. It wasn't quite 9 p.m. He flicked through his messages to see if Serrano had called. He had. At the museum they'd remembered Ricardo Gamero at the ticket desk. Two security guards had seen him speeding through rooms taking no notice of the exhibits. A third security guard had seen Gamero talking to a man in his sixties for some twenty minutes. The guard was now at the Jefatura with a police artist working up a sketch of the older man.

Father Román was in his early forties. He was out of the robes of office and in an ordinary dark suit with the jacket folded over his arm. He was standing in the nave of the brick interior of the church, talking to two women dressed in black. On seeing Falcón he excused himself from the conversation, went over to shake hands, and led him up to his office.

'You look exhausted, Inspector Jefe,' he said, sitting at his desk.

'The first days after something like this are always the longest,' said Falcón.

'My congregations have doubled since Tuesday morning,' said Father Román. 'A surprising number of young people. They're confused. They don't know when this will end or *how* it can possibly end.'

'Not just young people,' said Falcón. 'But I'm sorry, Father, I must press on.'

'Of course you must,' said Father Román.

'You may know that one of your congregation committed suicide today – Ricardo Gamero. Did you know him?'

Father Román blinked at the swift devastation of this news. It left him dumb with shock.

'I'm sorry I wasn't able to break it to you more gently,' said Falcón. 'He took his life this afternoon. Obviously you knew him. I understand he was a very . . .'

'I met him when my predecessor was taken ill,' said Father Román. 'They were very close. My predecessor had helped him resolve a number of issues to do with his faith.'

'How well did *you* know Ricardo?'

'He didn't appear to be seeking the same sort of relationship with me as he'd had with my predecessor.'

'Did you know what these issues to do with his faith were?'

'That was between them. Ricardo hasn't spoken to me about them.'

'When was the last time you saw Ricardo?'

'He was here on Sunday for Mass, as always.'

'And you haven't seen him since?'

Silence from Father Román, who looked as if he was coping with a distressing nausea.

'Sorry,' he said, snapping out of it. 'I'm just trying to think of the last time we spoke . . . and if there was any indication that he was still troubled to the same extent as he had been in my predecessor's time.'

'You didn't happen to see him today, did you, Father?'

'No, no, not today,' he said, distracted.

'Have you heard of a company called Informáticalidad?' asked Falcón.

'Should I have done?' asked Father Román, frowning.

'They actively recruit personnel from amongst your congregation,' said Falcón. 'Is that without your knowledge?'

'Forgive me, Inspector Jefe, but I find it rather confusing the way this conversation has developed. I'm feeling the pressure of your suspicion, but I'm not sure about what?'

'It's better just to answer the questions rather than trying to understand what they're about. This has become a very complicated situation,' said Falcón. 'Have you ever met a man called Diego Torres?'

'It's not such an unusual name.'

'He happens to be the Human Resources Director at Informáticalidad.'

'I don't always know the profession of the members of my congregation.'

342

'But you have someone of that name who attends this church?'

'Yes,' said Father Román, squeezing it out like a splinter.

Falcón went through the list of board members of Informáticalidad. Four out of the ten were members of Father Román's congregation.

'Would you mind telling me what exactly is going on here?' said Falcón.

'Nothing is "going on here",' said Father Román. 'If, as you say, this company is using my church as an informal recruiting agency, what can I do? It is the nature of people that they will meet at a church and that there will be a social exchange. Quite possibly invitations are made and it's conceivable that jobs might be offered. Just because the Church seems to have less influence in society, doesn't mean that some churches don't perform in the way that they used to.'

Falcón nodded. He'd overreached himself in his excitement at finally realizing a connection, only to find it a little too loose.

'Did you know Ricardo Gamero's profession?'

'I knew from my predecessor that he was a member of the police force, but I have no idea what he does, or rather, did. Was he a member of your squad?'

'He was an agent with the CGI; specifically, the antiterrorism group,' said Falcón. 'Islamic terrorism.'

'I doubt that was something he talked to many people about,' said Father Román.

'Did you happen to notice if he mixed with any of the people I mentioned who worked for Informáticalidad?'

'I'm sure he would have done. When people leave church they go to the two cafés around the corner. They socialize.'

'Did you notice regular meetings?'

Father Román shook his head.

Falcón sat back. He needed more ammunition for this conversation. He was tired, too. The flight to Casablanca and back seemed to have been from a month ago. The fullness of every minute, with not only his own findings but the ramifications of concurrent investigations under the colossal concentration of manpower rolling out all over Spain, Europe and the world, made hours feel like days.

'Were you aware that Informáticalidad not only used your church but two others inside the old city for the same purpose?' said Falcón.

'Look, Inspector Jefe, it's quite possible that this company has an unspoken employment policy of only taking on practising Catholics. I don't know. These days, I believe, you're not allowed to ask a recruitment agency to discriminate on your behalf. What would *you* do?'

'They *do* have an unspoken employment policy,' said Falcón. 'They don't take on any women. I suppose that's not dissimilar to the Catholic Church.'

On the walk back to his car, Falcón called Ramírez, who was still searching Miguel Botín's apartment.

'We're not getting anywhere here,' said Ramírez. 'I don't know what it is about this place, but we're sure somebody's been around here before us. It's a bit tidy. We've turned the place upside down and we're going through his library now.'

'I have a witness who saw him give a card to the Imam.'

'Maybe they're still with him in his bag under the rubble.'

'What state was the bombsite in when you last saw it?'

'The heavy work is over. The crane has gone. They're working by hand now, with just a couple of tippers standing by. They've put scaffolding up and sheeted off the remaining rubble. About six teams of forensics are ready to go in. They reckon they'll get into the mosque itself by mid-morning tomorrow.'

'When you've finished at Botín's apartment, let everybody go home and get some sleep,' said Falcón. 'It's going to be another big day tomorrow. Have you seen Juez Calderón?'

'Only on television,' said Ramírez. 'He's been giving a press conference with Comisario Lobo and Comisario Elvira.'

'Anything we should know?'

'There's a job waiting for Juez Calderón as a chat-show host if he gets bored of being a judge.'

'So he's not telling them anything, but it looks as if he is.'

'Exactly,' said Ramírez. 'And given that we've come up with fuck-all today, he's making us sound like heroes.'

The drive back home was eerily quiet. At nearly 10 p.m. the streets should have been alive and the bars full of people. A lot of places were closed. There was so little traffic Falcón went through the centre of town. Only a few young people had gathered in the Plaza del Museo under the trees. The mood was sombre and the narrow streets tense with anxiety.

An investigation of his fridge revealed some cooked prawns and a fresh swordfish steak. He ate the prawns with mayonnaise while drinking a beer direct from the bottle. He fried up the fish, squeezed some lemon over it, poured himself a glass of white rioja and ate, his mind picking over the detail of the day. He went over the dialogue with Father Román. Had the priest been trying to avoid the sin of lying by omission, evasion and ducking the question? It felt like it. He poured himself another glass of white wine, pushed back his plate and folded his arms and had just started to contemplate the big event of the day – the suicide of Ricardo Gamero, when his first visitor arrived.

Pablo had come on business. He refused a beer and they went into the study.

'You mentioned Yacoub had some conditions before you fell asleep on the plane this morning,' said Pablo.

'The first condition is that he will only talk or deal with me,' said Falcón. 'He won't meet any other agents, or take phone calls from anyone but me.'

'That's quite normal except, of course, you'll be in different countries. I'll talk you through the communication procedure later, but it won't exactly be direct contact,' said Pablo. 'It puts *you* under a lot of pressure.'

'He also says he's not making a lifelong commitment,' said Falcón.

'That's understandable,' said Pablo. 'But you know, spying can have an addictive effect on certain personalities.'

'Like Juan,' said Falcón. 'He looks like a man with a few secrets. As if he's running two families that don't know about each other.'

'He does. He has his wife and two kids and the CNI,

and they don't know *anything* about each other. Keep going with the conditions.'

'Yacoub will not give us any information that could jeopardize the life of any of his family members,' said Falcón.

'That was to be expected,' said Pablo. 'But does he suspect any of his family members?'

'He says not. But they're all devout Muslims and they lead very different lives to him,' said Falcón. 'It could be that he finds out that they are closely involved or at some remove, but he will not be an instrument in their downfall if they are. These people have totally accepted him as one of their own and he won't give them up.'

'Anything else?' asked Pablo.

'My problem: Yacoub doesn't have any training for this work.'

'Most spies don't. They just happen to be in a position where information comes their way.'

'You make it sound easy.'

'It's only dangerous if you're careless.'

Falcón had to raise his concentration levels to take in Pablo's briefing about the method of communication with Yacoub. He got him to boil it down to the basics, which were: they would communicate via email, using a secure website run by the CNI. Both Falcón and Diouri would have to load their computers with different encryption software. The emails would go to the CNI website to be decrypted and passed on. The CNI would obviously see all emails and make their recommendations for action. All Falcón had to do this evening was to call Yacoub and tell him to go to the shop in Rabat and pick up a couple of books. These books would give Yacoub all the information he needed. Falcón made the call and kept it short, saying he was tired.

'We've got to get him working as soon as possible,' said Pablo. 'This whole thing is moving fast.'

'What whole thing?'

'The game, the plan, the operation,' said Pablo. 'We're not sure which. All we know is that, since the bomb went off yesterday, the level of encrypted emails on the web has gone up fivefold.'

'And how many of those encrypted emails can you read?'

'Not many.'

'So you haven't cracked the code from the Koran found in the Peugeot Partner?'

'Not yet. We've got the world's best mathematicians working on it, though.'

'What do the CNI make of Ricardo Gamero's suicide?' asked Falcón.

'Inevitably we're thinking that he was the mole,' said Pablo. 'But that's just a theory. We're trying to work up the logic around it.'

'If he was the mole, from what I know about him, I'd find it hard to believe he was passing information to an Islamic terrorist movement.'

'Right, but what about Miguel Botín? What do you know about him?'

'That his brother was maimed in the Madrid train bombings, giving him good reason to be operating *against* Islamic terrorism,' said Falcón. 'That his girl-friend was a school friend of Gamero who remains a devout Catholic, having so far been reluctant to convert to Islam. And it was Botín who followed the Imam and

348

took shots of Hammad and Saoudi and these other two mystery men, which he handed over to the CGI. He was also prompting Gamero to get the Imam's office bugged. That's about it.'

'He doesn't sound like a promising candidate as a terrorist, does he?'

'Have you searched Botín's apartment?' asked Falcón.

Pablo cradled his knee, nodded.

'What did you find there?'

'I can't say.'

'But you found something that makes you think Botín was acting for the terrorists while working for Gamero?'

'This is what it's like, Javier,' said Pablo, shrugging. 'The Hall of Mirrors. We constantly have to revise what we're actually seeing.'

'You found another heavily annotated copy of the Koran, didn't you?' said Falcón, sitting back, dazed. 'What the hell does that mean?'

'It means you cannot say a word about this conversation to anybody,' said Pablo. 'It means we have to get our counterintelligence up and running as soon as possible.'

'But it also means that the terrorists, whoever *they* are, were letting Miguel Botín serve up information to the CGI that compromised the Imam, Hammad and Saoudi, along with whatever operation was being planned in the mosque.'

'We're still conducting our enquiries,' said Pablo.

'They were sacrificing them?' asked Falcón, nauseated by his inability to think his way around this new development.

'First of all, we live in an age of suicide bombing – there's sacrifice for you,' said Pablo. 'And secondly, intelligence services all over the world have always had to sacrifice agents for the greater good of the mission. It's nothing new.'

'So this electrician, whose card Miguel Botín handed over to the Imam, was the agent of their destruction? The electrician was sent by Botín's Islamic terrorist masters to bomb the building? That's just fantastic.'

'We don't know that,' said Pablo. 'But as you know, not all suicide bombers realize that they *are* suicide bombers. Some have just been told to deliver a car, or leave a rucksack on a train. Botín had just been told to give an electrician's card to the Imam. What we need to find out is *who* told him to do that.'

'Are we wasting our time here?' asked Falcón. 'Is this whole investigation just a show, for whichever terrorist group decided to abort their mission and blow up any possible leads back to their network?'

'We're still very interested to find out what's in the mosque,' said Pablo. 'And we're very keen to get Yacoub up and running.'

'And how do you know that Yacoub is approaching the right group, even?' asked Falcón, exhausted and close to rage from frustration.

'We have confidence in that because it has come from a reliable detainee and has also been verified by British agents on the ground in Rabat,' said Pablo.

'What group are we talking about?'

'The GICM, Groupe Islamique de Combattants Marocains, otherwise known as the Moroccan Islamic Combatant Group. They had links to the bombings in Casablanca, Madrid and London,' said Pablo. 'What we're doing here is not something that was thought up yesterday as an idea worth trying, Javier. This represents months of intelligence work.'

Pablo left soon after. Falcón was almost depressed by their exchange. All the man-hours put in by his squad were beginning to look like a waste of energy, and yet there were unnerving gaps in what Pablo had told him. It was as if each group involved in the investigation put most trust in the information that they themselves uncovered. So the CNI believed in the annotated Koran as the codebook, because of the example of the *Book of Proof* uncovered by British intelligence, and that coloured everything they looked at. The fact that the witness in the mosque, José Duran, had described the electrician and his labourers as a Spaniard and two Eastern bloc natives, who did not sound anything like Islamic terrorist operatives, held little water for Pablo. But then again, it had been local Spanish petty criminals who'd supplied the Madrid bombers with explosives, and what does it take to leave a bomb? A little care and a psychotic mind.

After the press conference on TVE with Comisarios Lobo and Elvira, Juez Calderón had taken a taxi round to Canal Sur, where he was miked up and eased on to the set of a roundtable discussion about Islamic terrorism. He was the man of the hour and within moments the female chair of the programme had drawn him into the discussion. He controlled the rest of the programme with a combination of incisive and informed comment, humour, and a savage wit he reserved for so-called security specialists and terrorism pundits.

Afterwards he was taken out to dinner by some

executives from Canal Sur's current affairs department and the female chair of the programme. They fed and flattered him for an hour and a half until he found himself alone with the female chair, who let it be known that this could continue in more comfortable surroundings. For once Calderón demurred. He was tired. There was another long day ahead of him and – the main reason – he was sure that Marisa was a better lay.

Calderón sat in the middle seat in the back of the Canal Sur limousine. He felt like a hero. His mind was racing with endorphins after his TV performances. He had a sense of the world at his feet. Seville, as it flashed past in the night, began to feel small to him. He imagined what it must be like to be as high on success as this in a city like New York, where they really knew how to make a man feel important.

The limousine dropped him off outside the San Marcos church at 12.45 a.m. and, for once, rather than take his usual little deviation around the back, he strode past the bars on the other side, hoping that friends of Inés would be drinking there who would stop him and congratulate him. He really had been exceptionally brilliant. The bars, however, were already closed. Calderón, in his heightened state, had failed to notice how quiet the city was.

As he went up in the lift he knew that the only way he was going to sleep was after a strenuous, crazy fuck with Marisa, out on the balcony, in the hall, going down in the lift, out in the street. He felt so on top of the world he wanted everybody to see him performing.

Marisa had watched the TV programmes in a state of insensate boredom. She could tell that the press conference revolved around Esteban, as all the questions from journalists were for him. She could also see that he was controlling the roundtable discussion, and even that the female chair was dying to get into his trousers, but the drivel that was being talked had reduced her to a vegetative state. Why do Westerners have to get so exercised about things and talk them to death, as if it's going to be any help? Then it struck her. That was what irked her about Westerners. They always took things at face value, because that was what could be controlled, and what could be measured. They just served up their lies all round and then congratulated each other on 'their command of the situation'. That was why white people bored her. They had no interest beyond the surface. 'What are you doing, sitting there all day, Marisa?' had been the most frequently asked question she'd faced in America. And yet in Africa they'd never asked her that question – or any question, for that matter. Questioning existence didn't help you live it.

She looked down on Calderón's arrival from her balcony. She saw his jaunty steps, his little preparations. When he said his usual: 'It's me,' into her entry phone, she replied: 'My hero.'

He burst into her apartment like a showman, arms raised, waiting for the applause. He drew her to him and kissed her, pushing his tongue between the barrier of her teeth, which she did not like. Their kissing had only ever been lip deep.

It wasn't difficult to tell that he was still on the crest of the media wave. She let him drive her out on to the balcony, where they had sex. He looked up at the stars, holding on to her hips, imagining even greater glory. She participated by hanging on to the railings and making a suitable amount of noise.

As soon as he was finished, he was rendered mentally and physically drained, like someone coming off a coke high. She managed to steer him to the bed and get his shoes off before he fell into a deep sleep at 1.15 a.m. She stood over him, smoking a cigarette, wondering if she'd be able to wake him in a couple of hours' time.

She washed herself in the bidet, closing her right eye to the smoke rising from the cigarette. She lay on the sofa and let time do what it was good at. At 3 a.m. she started trying to rouse him, but he was completely inert. She held a lighter to his foot. He writhed and kicked out. It took time to get him to come round. He had no idea where he was. She explained that he had to go home, he had an early start, he had to get changed.

At 3.25 she called a taxi. She put his shoes on, got him standing, put his arms into his jacket and called the lift up to her floor. She stood outside with him, his head dropping and jerking off his chest and her shoulder. The taxi arrived just after 3.30. She put him in the back and instructed the driver to take him to Calle San Vicente. She said he was exhausted, that he was the leading judge in the Seville bombing, and that gave the driver a sense of mission. He waved away her €10 note. For this man it was going to be free. The cab pulled away. Calderón had his head thrown back on the rear shelf. In the yellowish street lighting he looked as he would when dead. The whites of his eyes were just visible below the lids.

At that time of the morning, with Seville as silent as a ghost city, there was no traffic and the cab arrived at Calle San Vicente in just under ten minutes. After much cajoling, the cab driver had to reach in and physically haul Calderón out into the street. He walked him to the front door of the building and asked him for his keys. The driver got the door open and realized he was going to have to go all the way. They crammed themselves into the hall.

'Is there a light?' asked the driver.

Calderón slapped at the wall. Light burst into the hall and the ticking sound of a timer started up. The driver supported him up the stairs.

'This one here,' said Calderón, as they reached the first floor.

The driver opened the apartment door, which was double locked, and returned the keys to Calderón.

'Are you all right now?' he asked, looking into the judge's bleary eyes.

'Yeah, I'm fine now. I'll be OK, thanks,' he said.

'You're doing a great job,' said the driver. 'I saw you on the telly before I started my shift.'

Calderón clapped him on the shoulder. The driver went down the stairs and the light in the hall went out with a loud snap. The cab started up and pulled away. Calderón rolled over the doorjamb into the apartment. The light was on in the kitchen. He shut the door, leaned back on it. Even in his exhausted state, with his eyelids as heavy as lead, his teeth clenched with irritation.

25

Calderón came to with a start that thumped his head into the wall. His face was pressed against the wooden floor. The smell of polish was strong in his nose. His eyelids snapped open. He was instantly wide awake, as if danger was present and near. He was still dressed as he had been all day. He couldn't understand why he was lying in the corridor of his apartment. Had he been so exhausted that he'd slept where he fell? He checked his watch: just gone four o'clock. He'd only been out for ten minutes or so. He was mystified. He remembered coming into the apartment and the light being on in the kitchen. It was still on, but he was beyond it now, further into the flat, which appeared to be completely dark and cold from the air conditioning. He struggled to his feet, checked himself. He wasn't hurt, hadn't even banged his head. He must have slid down the wall.

'Inés?' he said out loud, puzzled by the kitchen light.

Calderón stretched his shoulders back. He was stiff. He stepped into the rhomboid of light on the corridor floor. He saw the blood first, a huge, burgeoning crimson

356

pool on the white marble. The colour of it under the bright white light was truly alarming. He stepped back as if expecting an intruder still to be there. He lowered himself and saw her through the chair and table. He knew immediately that she was dead. Her eyes were wide open, with not a scintilla of light in them.

The blood had spread to the right side of the table and underneath it. It was viscous and seemed to be sucking at the chair and table legs. It was so horribly bright that it throbbed in his vision, as if there was still life in it. Calderón crawled on all fours round to the left of the table to where Inés's feet lay, slack and pointed outwards in front of the sink. Her nightie was rucked up. His eyes travelled from her white legs, over her white cotton panties, beyond the waistband – and that was where the bruising started. He hadn't seen it before. He'd had no idea his fists had accomplished such horrifically visible damage. And it was then that he thought he might have seen this before after all, because his whole body was suddenly consumed with a remembered panic that seemed to constrict his throat and cut off the blood supply to his brain. He reared back on his knees and held his head.

He crawled back out of the kitchen and got to his feet in the corridor. He went swiftly out of the apartment, which required him to unlock the door. He hit the stair light, looked around and went back in. The light was still on in the kitchen. Inés was still lying there. The blood was now one floor tile's width from the wooden floor of the corridor. He pressed the balls of his palms into his eye sockets and ripped them away, but it made no difference to the horror of what lay before him. He dropped to all fours again.

'You fucking bitch, you stupid fucking bitch,' he said. 'Look what the fuck you've gone and done now.'

The noisily bright blood resounded in the hard kitchen. It was also moving, consuming the white marble, reaching towards him. He went back around the table. The ghastly purple of the contusions seemed to have deepened in colour in the interim, or his constant toing and froing in and out of the light was playing tricks. Between her splayed thighs he now saw the welts from his belt lashing. He sank to his knees again, pressed his fists into his eyes and started sobbing. This was it. This was the end. He was finished, finished, finished. Even the most incompetent state judge couldn't fail to make a watertight case against him. A wife-beater who'd gone a step too far. A wife-beater who'd just come back from fucking his mistress, had another confrontation and this time . . . Oh, yes, it might have been an accident. Was it an accident? It probably was. But this time he'd overdone it and she'd smashed her stupid head open. He pounded the table.

It cleared as suddenly as it had arrived. Calderón sank back on his heels and realized that the terrible panic had gone. His mind was back on track. At least, he felt it was back on track. What he hadn't realized was the nature of the damage done by the panic, the way it had opened up electronic pathways to the flaws in his character. As far as Calderón was concerned, his mind was back to the steel-trap clarity of the leading judge in Seville, and it came to him that, with no chest freezer, the only solution was to get her out of the apartment, and he had to do it now. There was just over an hour before dawn.

Weight was not the problem. Inés was currently 48

kilos. Her height at 1.72m was more of a difficulty. He stormed around the table and into the spare room, where the luggage was kept. He pulled out the biggest suitcase he could find, a huge grey Samsonite with four wheels. He grabbed two white towels from the cupboard.

One of the towels he laid across the kitchen doorway to stop the blood from seeping into the corridor. The other he wrapped around Inés's head. It nearly made him sick. The back of her head was a flat mush and the blood soaked gratefully into the towel, consuming the whiteness with its incarnadine stain. He found a bin liner and pulled it over her head, securing it with cooking string. He washed his hands. He put the case on the table, picked Inés up and laid her in it. She was far too big. Even foetally she didn't fit. He couldn't cram her feet in and, even if he could, her shoulders were too broad for the case to shut. He looked down on her with his considerable intellect surging forward, but fatally, in the wrong direction.

'I'll have to cut her up,' he said to himself. 'Take her feet off and break her collar bones.'

No. That was not going to work. He'd seen films and read novels where they cut up bodies and it never seemed to work, even in fiction where everything can be made to bloody work. He was squeamish, too. Couldn't even watch *Extreme Makeover* on TV without writhing on the sofa. Think again. He walked around the apartment looking at everyday objects in a completely new light. He stopped in the living room and stared at the carpet, as if willing it not to be the cliché of all clichés.

'You can't wrap her up in the carpet. It'll come

straight back to you. Same with the luggage. Think again.'

The river was only three hundred metres from Calle San Vicente. All he had to do was get her in the car, drive fifty metres, turn right on Calle Alfonso XII, go straight up to the traffic lights, cross Calle Nuevo Torneo and there was a road he remembered as quite dark, which ran down to the river and veered left behind the huge bus station of Plaza de Armas. From there it was a matter of metres to the water's edge, but it was a stretch used by early-morning runners, so he would have to act quickly and decisively.

The decorators. The memory of his irritation at them leaving their sheet up the stairs a few days ago juddered into his brain. He ran out of the apartment again, slashed on the stairwell light and stopped himself. He put the apartment door on the latch. That would be too much to bear: locked out of his apartment with his dead wife on the kitchen floor. He leapt down the stairs three at a time and there it all was, under the stairs. There were even full cans of paint to weigh down the body. He pulled out a length of paint-spattered hessian sheeting. He sprinted back up the stairs and laid it out on the clean half of the kitchen floor. He lifted her out of the suitcase, where she'd been lying like a prop in an illusionist's trick, and laid her on the sheet. He folded the edges over. He gasped at the momentary peak of horror at what he was doing. Inés's beautiful face reduced to a scarecrow's stuffed bin liner.

The blood had reached the towel across the doorway and he had to leap over it. He crashed with the deranged heaviness of a toppled wardrobe into the corridor, cracking his head and shoulder a glancing blow on the wall. He shrugged off the pain. He went into his study, tore open the drawers, found the roll of packing tape. He kissed it. On the way back he steadied himself and hopped more carefully over the blood-soaked towel.

He wrapped the tape around her ankles, knees, waist, chest, neck and head. He pocketed the cooking string and tape. He didn't bother to admire his mummified wife, but ran out of the apartment, grabbing his keys and the garage remote as he left. He took the door off the latch. Slapped the fucking light on again – tick, tick, tick, tick, tick – and rumbled down the stairs. He sprinted down Calle San Vicente to the garage, which was just around the corner. He hit the button of the remote as he rounded the bend and the garage door opened, but so slowly he was jumping up and down in towering frustration, swearing and punching at the air. He rolled underneath the quarter-open door and hurtled down the ramp, pressing another button on the remote for the light. He found his car. He hadn't driven the damn thing for weeks. Who needs a car in Seville? Thank *fuck* I've got a car.

No mistakes. He reversed out calmly, as if suddenly on beta-blockers. He eased up the ramp. The garage door was only just fully open. The car hopped out on to the street, which was deadly quiet. The red digits on the dashboard told him it was 4.37. He pulled up outside the apartment, clicked the button to open the boot. He sprinted upstairs, in the dark this time, fell and cracked his shin such a blow on the top stair that the pain ricocheted up his skeleton to the inside of his skull. He didn't even stop. He unlocked the door, slowed down at the kitchen and stepped over the bloody towel.

Inés. No, not Inés any more. He picked her up. She

was absurdly heavy for someone who was less than fifty kilos and had lost at least three kilos of blood. He got her into the corridor, but she was too heavy to cradle-carry her. He hoisted her over his shoulder and closed the apartment door. He stepped carefully down the stairs in the dark again. That fucking tick, tick, tick of the light just too unbearably stressful at this stage. He stuck his head out into the street.

Empty.

Two steps. In the boot. Shut the boot. Close the apartment building door. Wait. Slow down. Think. The tins of paint to weigh down the body. Open the boot. Back under the stairs. Pick up the two cans of paint. As heavy as Inés. Heave them into the boot. Close the boot. In the car. Rear-view mirror. No headlights. Calm. Nice and slow. You're nearly there. This *is* going to work.

Calderón's car was alone at the traffic lights by the Plaza de Armas, which were showing red. The lights from the dash glowed in his face. He checked the rear-view again, saw his eyes. They were pitiful. The lights changed to green. He eased across the six empty lanes and took the ramp down to the river. It was first light. It wasn't quite as dark as he would have liked down by the river. He would have preferred something subterranean, as black as antimatter, as utterly lightless as a collapsed star.

There was still plenty to do. He had to get the body out, attach the cans of paint, and push it into the river. He had a good, long look around until he couldn't believe that everything wasn't moving. He shook the paranoia out of his mind, opened the boot. He lifted the body out and laid it down on the pavement close to the car for cover. He heaved out the cans of paint with superhuman strength. Sweat cascaded. His shirt was stuck to him. His mind closed off. This was the home stretch. Get it done.

He didn't see the man at the back of the bus station, was not aware of him making his fatal call to the police. He worked with savage haste while the man muttered what he was seeing into his mobile phone, along with Calderón's registration number.

With no traffic it took less than a minute for a patrol car to arrive. It had been cruising down by the river less than a kilometre away when the two officers were notified by the communications centre in the Jefatura. The car rolled down the ramp towards the river with its headlights and engine switched off. Only Calderón's car was visible. He was kneeling behind it, taping the second can of paint to Inés's neck. His sweat was dripping on to the hessian sheet. He was finished. All he had to do now was hump close to 100 kilos about a metre across the pavement and then up over a low wall and into the water. He summoned his last reserves of strength. With the two paint cans attached, the body had become incredibly unwieldy. He jammed his hands underneath, not caring about the skin he tore from his fingers and knuckles. He drove forward with his thighs and, with his chest and pelvis close to the floor, he looked like an enormous lizard with some unmanageable prey. Inés's body shifted and thumped into the low wall. He was panting and sobbing. Tears streamed down his face. The pain from his stubbed fingers and torn nails didn't register, but when the headlights of the patrol car finally came on and he found himself encased in light, like an exhibit in the reptile house, he stiffened as if he'd just been shot.

The policemen got out of the patrol car with their weapons drawn. Calderón had yanked his arms out from under the body, rolled over, and was now lying on his back. His stomach convulsed with each racking sob. A lot of the emotion he was coughing up was relief. It was all over. He'd been caught. All that hideous desperation had flowed out of him and now he could relax into infamy and shame.

While one patrolman stood over the sobbing Calderón, the other ran a torch over the taped-up hessian sheet. He put on some latex gloves and squeezed Inés's shoulder just to confirm what he already knew, that this was a body. He went back to the patrol car and radioed the Jefatura.

'This is Alpha-2-0, we're down by the river now, just off the Torneo at the back of the bus station in Plaza de Armas. I can confirm that we have a male in his early forties attempting to dispose of an unidentified body. You'd better get the Inspector Jefe de Homicidios down here.'

'Give me the car registration number.'

'SE 4738 HT.'

'Fuck me.'

'What?'

'That's the same number given to me by the guy who reported the incident. I don't fucking believe this.'

'Who's the owner of the vehicle?'

'Don't you recognize him?'

The patrolman called out to his colleague, who passed a torch over Calderón's face. He was barely recognizable as human, let alone a specific person. His face bore the contortions of a particularly agonized flamenco singer. The patrolman shrugged.

'No idea,' the patrolman said, into the radio.

'How about Juez Esteban Calderón?' said the operator.

'Fuck!' said the patrolman and dropped the mouthpiece.

He shone his own torch in the man's face, grabbed him by the chin to hold him still. Calderón's agony slackened off with surprise. The patrolman let a sly grin spread across his face before he went back to the car.

Falcón had to claw his way out of sleep like an abandoned potholer, desperately trying to reach a star of light in a firmament of blackness. He came to with a jerk and grunt of disgust, as if he'd been spewed up by his own bed. The bedside light hurt him. The green digits on his clock told him it was 5.03. He grappled with the phone and sank back into his pillow with it clasped to his ear.

The voice was of the duty officer in the communications centre of the Jefatura. He was babbling. He was speaking so fast and with such a heavy Andaluz accent that Falcón only picked up the first syllable of every other word. He stopped him, got him to start again from the top.

'We have a situation down by the bus station at the Plaza de Armas. Behind the bus station, down by the river near the Puente de Chapina, a man has been apprehended attempting to dispose of a body. We have a positive identification of the owner of the vehicle used to bring the body to that point, and we have a positive ID of the man who was attempting to dispose of the body. And the man's name, Inspector Jefe, is . . . Esteban Calderón.'

Falcón's leg spasmed as if some high voltage had shot up it. In one movement he was out of bed and pacing the floor.

'Esteban Calderón, the judge? Are you positive?'

'We are now. The patrolman at the scene has checked the ID and read the number back to me. That and the car's registration confirm the man as Esteban Calderón.'

'Have you spoken to anyone about this?'

'Not yet, Inspector Jefe.'

'Have you called the Juez de Guardia?'

'No, you're the first person. I should have –'

'How was the incident reported?'

'An anonymous phone call from a guy who said he was walking his dog down by the river.'

'What time?'

'It was timed at 4.52 a.m.'

'Is that when people walk their dogs?'

'Old people who can't sleep do, especially in this heat.'

'How did he report it?'

'He called in on his mobile, told me what he was seeing, gave me the registration number and hung up.'

'Name and address?'

'Didn't have time to ask him.'

'Don't talk to anyone about this,' said Falcón. 'Call the patrolmen and tell them there is to be radio silence on this matter until I've spoken to Comisario Elvira.'

The bedroom seemed to fill up with the catastrophe of scandal. Falcón went out on to the gallery overlooking the patio. The morning was warm. He felt sick. He called Elvira, gave him some seconds to wake up and then told him the news in the most measured tone he could muster. Falcón broke the ensuing silence himself, by telling Elvira how many people, at this point, knew what had taken place.

'We have to get him, the body and the car off the street as soon as possible, whatever happens,' said Elvira. 'And we need a judge and a Médico Forense to do that.'

'Juez Romero is reliable and neither a friend, nor enemy, of Esteban Calderón.'

'This mustn't look like a cover-up,' said Elvira, almost to himself.

'This isn't something that can be covered up,' said Falcón.

'We have to do things absolutely by the book. The investigation might have to be taken off your hands, given Esteban Calderón's status.'

'I think it better for me to initiate the proceedings,' said Falcón.

'Let's go for normal procedure, but nobody, absolutely nobody, is to talk about this. We must have no leaks until we can get a press statement together. I'll speak to Comisario Lobo. Tell the communications officer to make the usual calls but not, under any circumstances, to inform the press. If it gets out before we're ready there'll be hell to pay.'

'The only person we can't control is the anonymous caller who reported the incident,' said Falcón.

'Well, *he* shouldn't know who it was he was reporting, should he?' said Elvira.

This was too big a scandal to contain. Elvira was asking too much. This was going to come sweating out of the Jefatura walls. Falcón called the communications centre, gave the instructions and asked the officer to call Felipe and Jorge to the crime scene. He showered, standing under the drilling water, trying to think of any plausible, innocent explanation for Calderón being discovered down by the river with a dead body.

It was 5.30 and the dawn was well advanced by the time he walked across the Plaza de Armas to the incident. The traffic on the Torneo was still very light. A patrol car had parked at the top of the ramp and some cones had been put out to stop any traffic from turning down the road. The duty judge was already at the scene, as was a police photographer, who was taking some shots. Jorge and Felipe arrived and were allowed down the ramp.

There was no sign of Calderón. Two patrolmen were making sure no early-morning joggers came past the scene along the riverbank. The duty judge told Falcón that Calderón was sitting in the back of the patrol car with one of the policemen who'd first come across the incident.

'We're just waiting for a Médico Forense to arrive and inspect the body.'

A set of tyres squeaked at the top of the ramp and a car rolled down and parked up. The Médico Forense got out with his bag. He was already dressed in a white hooded boiler suit and had a mask hanging from his neck. He shook hands, put on gloves, and they proceeded to the body. An ambulance arrived with no siren or flashing lights.

The Médico Forense used a scalpel to cut the tape wrapped around the body. He worked from the feet up to the head. He laid open the hessian sheet. The head wrapped in the black bin liner looked sinister, as if the body had been the subject of some sexual deviancy. Falcón started to feel dizzy. The Médico Forense murmured into his dictaphone about the heavy bruising on the torso. He put his scalpel through the cooking string at the neck of the body and eased away the bin liner. A darkening at the edges of his vision made Falcón clutch at the duty judge's sleeve.

'Are you all right, Inspector Jefe?' he asked.

Under the bin liner the head was wrapped in a towel. The front was white, with blood smears over it. The Médico Forense lifted up one corner of the towel and folded it back. The outline of the face was visible, as under a shroud. He pulled away the other corner of the towel and Falcón dropped unconscious to the floor, with the features of his ex-wife imprinted on his retina.

Falcón came to on the ground. The duty judge had managed to catch him and break his fall. The paramedics from the ambulance were over him. He heard the duty judge above their heads.

'He's in shock. This is his ex-wife. He shouldn't really be here.'

The paramedics helped him up. The Médico Forense continued to murmur into his dictaphone. He checked the thermometer, made a calculation and muttered the time of death.

Tears welled up as Falcón looked down once more on Inés's inert body. This was a scene from her life that he'd never imagined – her death. Over the years he'd done a lot of thinking and talking about Inés. He'd relived their life together ten times over, until he'd nearly driven Alicia Aguado insane. He'd only been able to get rid of her permanent occupation of his mind by finally seeing her for what she was, and realizing how badly she'd behaved and treated him. But this was not how it should have ended. No amount of selfishness deserved this.

The paramedics moved him away from the body and got him sitting on the low wall by the river, away from where the Médico Forense was working. Falcón breathed deeply. The duty judge came over.

'You can't handle this case,' he said.

'I'll call Comisario Elvira,' said Falcón, nodding. 'He'll appoint somebody from the outside. My entire squad is an interested party.'

Elvira was speechless until he finally managed to come up with his condolences. The catastrophe was so much worse than he'd imagined and, as he spoke, first to Falcón and then the duty judge, the hideousness of the morning press conference began to spread like a malignancy through his innards.

The duty judge finished the call and handed the mobile back to Falcón. They shook hands. Falcón took one last look at the body. Her face was perfect and undamaged. He shook his head in disbelief and had an image from years ago, when he'd come across Inés in the street. She'd been laughing; laughing so hard that she was doubled up with her hair flung forward, staggering backwards on her high heels.

He turned away and left the scene. He walked past the patrol car where Calderón was being held. The door was open. The radio squawked. Calderón's wrists were cuffed, his torn and bleeding hands lay in his lap. He stared straight ahead and his vision did not deviate even when Falcón leaned in.

'Esteban,' said Falcón.

Calderón turned to him, and said the sentence that Falcón had heard more times from the mouths of murderers than any other.

'I didn't do it.'

26

The classroom in the pre-school had been reglazed and new blinds put up. The air conditioners were already working full blast, which was the only way to keep the sulphurous stink of the corrupted bodies still in the destroyed apartment building at a bearable level. It was already past eight o'clock and still Comisario Elvira had not arrived. Everybody was tired, but there was a buzz of expectation in the room.

'Something's happened,' said Ramírez, 'and I've got the feeling it's something big. What do you think, Javier?'

Falcón couldn't speak.

'Where's Juez Calderón?' said Ramírez. 'That's what makes me think it's big. He's the man for the press conference.'

Falcón nodded, appalled to silence by what he'd seen down by the river. The door opened and Elvira came in and made his way to the blackboard at the far end of the room, followed by three men. Already present at the meeting were Pablo and Gregorio from the CNI, Inspector Jefe Ramón Barros and one of his senior officers from the antiterrorist squad of the CGI, and Falcón and Ramírez from the homicide squad. Elvira turned. His face was grim.

'There's no easy way to put this,' he said, 'so I'm just going to give you the facts. At around six o'clock this morning Juez Esteban Calderón was placed under arrest on suspicion of murdering his wife. Two patrolmen found him earlier this morning, attempting to dispose of his wife's body in the Guadalquivir. Given these circumstances, he will no longer be acting as the Juez de Instrucción in our investigation. It will also be impossible for our own homicide squad to conduct the murder enquiry, which will be carried out by these three officers from Madrid, led by Inspector Jefe Luis Zorrita. Thank you.'

The three homicide officers from Madrid nodded and filed out of the room, stopping briefly to introduce themselves and shake hands with Falcón and Ramírez. The door closed. Elvira resumed the meeting. Ramírez stared at Falcón in a state of shock.

'We have decided to appoint a Juez de Instrucción from outside Seville,' said Elvira, 'and Juez Sergio del Rey is on his way down from Madrid now. On his arrival an announcement will be made to the press at a conference to be held in the Andalucian Parliament building and until that time I would ask you to keep this information to yourselves.

'Following the suicide yesterday of Ricardo Gamero of the CGI, there have been some major developments and the CNI will now explain these to us.'

Something had been sucked out of Elvira's face overnight. The staggering import of his announcements had left him haggard. He sat back in the teacher's chair, inanimate, with his chin resting on his fist, as if his head needed that sort of support to keep it in place. Pablo made his way to the front.

'Just prior to the suicide of the CGI agent, Ricardo Gamero, we had received information from British intelligence that they had successfully identified the other two men photographed by Gamero's source, Miguel Botín. These two men are of Afghan nationality, living in Rome. They were known to MI5 because they were arrested in London two weeks after the failed 21st July bombings and held for questioning under the Terrorism Act. They were released without being charged. The British were not able to establish what these men were doing in London at the time, other than that they were visiting family. The known addresses of these two men in Rome were raided by the Italian police last night and found to be empty. Their current whereabouts is unknown. What concerns us about these suspects is that they are believed to have connections to the high command of al-Qaeda in Afghanistan, and are believed by the British to have forged links with the GICM in Morocco. In the last year they are known to have visited the UK, Belgium, France, Italy, Spain and Morocco. All these countries are believed to have GICM sleeper cells. There is considerable intelligence work still to be done to ascertain Miguel Botín's role, Imam Abdelkrim Benaboura's relationship to these two men, and their involvement with what has happened here in Seville.

'After Ricardo Gamero's suicide we conducted a search of Miguel Botín's apartment and discovered a heavily annotated copy of the Koran which matches the edition found in the Peugeot Partner driven by

Hammad and Saoudi. Large chunks of the notes are exact transcripts and we believe that this is a codebook. It is now thought that as each sleeper cell is activated they are issued with a new codebook, which they use until their mission is complete.

'The significance of finding this copy of the Koran in Miguel Botín's apartment is that it *could* mean that Ricardo Gamero's source was a double: working with the CGI and operating for a terrorist cell. This throws considerable confusion into the current investigation, because it would mean that the only intelligence Botín was communicating to Gamero was what his commanders *wanted* us to know. This would mean that Hammad and Saoudi, the two Afghans, and the Imam were all expendable.

'There is one final confusing detail about Botín's actions in this scenario. As you know, a great deal of manpower has been spent trying to find the fake council inspectors and the electricians. Inspector Jefe Falcón has found a witness who was in the mosque on the Sunday morning, after the fuse box blew on the Saturday night. This witness saw Botín give the electrician's card to the Imam, and he watched as the Imam called the number and made the appointment. Inspector Jefe Barros has informed us that this was not something sanctioned by him or anyone in his department. The CGI was still waiting for authorization to bug the mosque.

'We now have to examine the possibility that the council inspectors and the electricians were members of, or in the pay of, a terrorist cell. It could be – and we might only have a chance of verifying this when the forensics have reached the mosque – that the council inspectors laid a device to blow the fuse box and that the electricians were brought in to set a bomb that would wipe out the Imam, Hammad and Saoudi, and Botín himself.'

'There seems to be a break in the logic chain of that scenario,' said Barros. 'It might just be believable that Botín was the unwitting agent of their destruction, but I don't see any terrorist commander allowing that quantity of hexogen, brought into this country at what one imagines was considerable risk and expense, to be destroyed.'

'The electricians and council inspectors would constitute a type of terrorist cell we've never come across before, too,' said Falcón. 'The witness said they were a Spaniard and two Eastern Europeans.'

'And how does Ricardo Gamero's suicide fit into this scenario?' asked Barros.

'A profound sense of failure at his inability to prevent this atrocity,' said Pablo. 'We understand that he took his work very seriously.'

Silence, while everybody wrestled with the CNI's possible scenario. Falcón snapped out of his shocked state and burned with his theory that too much weight was being attached to the copy of the Koran as a codebook. But it was impossible to understand how two identical copies could have ended up in the Peugeot Partner and Botín's apartment.

'Why do you think this cell self-destructed?' asked Barros.

'We can only think that it was a spectacular diversionary tactic, to occupy our domestic investigating teams and all European intelligence services while they plan and carry out an attack elsewhere,' said Pablo. 'If

Botín was a double agent, his terrorist masters would have known that the mosque was under suspicion. They fed that suspicion further by bringing in the hexogen and Hammad and Saoudi, two known logistics men. They then blew it up. They don't mind. They're all going to paradise, whether as successful bombers or magnificent decoys.'

'What about the Afghans?' asked Barros. 'They've been identified, but not exactly sacrificed.'

'Perhaps Botín intended the shot of the two Afghans to be interpreted by us as an indication of an attack planned for Italy. Botín supplied those photographs when he was a trusted CGI source.'

'So, another diversionary tactic?'

'The Italians, Danish and Belgians are all on red alert, as they were after the London bombings.'

'So this letter sent to the *ABC* with the Abdullah Azzam text and all the media references to MILA – was that all part of this grand diversion?' asked Barros, nearly enjoying himself at being able to finally needle the CNI, who had so humiliated him and his department.

'What we're working on now is the real target,' said Pablo. 'The Abdullah Azzam text and the idea of MILA are powerful tools of terror. They inspire fear in a population. We see this as part of the escalation of this particular brand of terrorism. We are fighting the equivalent of a mutating virus. No sooner do we find one cure than it adapts to it with renewed lethal strength. There is no model. Only after we have sustained attacks do we become aware of a modus operandi. The intelligence gathered from the hundreds of people interviewed after the Madrid and London bombings is no help to us now. We are not talking about an integrated organization with a defined structure, but more of a satellite organization with a fluid structure and total flexibility.'

'Are you sure you're not reading too much into the diversionary tactic?' said Elvira. 'After the Madrid bombings –'

'We're pretty sure that ETA provided the diversion which led to the devastating success of the Madrid bombings. We don't think it was a coincidence that, 120 kilometres southeast of Madrid, the Guardia Civil stopped a van driven by two ETA incompetents, and loaded with 536 kilos of titadine for delivery to Madrid; and on the same day, 500 kilometres away in Avilés, three Moroccan terrorists were taking delivery of the 100 kilos of Goma 2 Eco used on the Madrid trains,' said Pablo. 'British security forces and intelligence were focused on an attack on the G8 Summit in Edinburgh when suicide bombers blew themselves up on the London Underground.'

'All right, so there is a history of diversion,' said Elvira.

'And a diversion that is prepared to sacrifice 536 kilos of titadine,' said Pablo, looking pointedly at Barros.

'The reality,' said Elvira, 'is that we have no idea who we are dealing with most of the time. We call them al-Qaeda because it helps us to sleep at night, but we seem to have come up against a very pure form of terrorism whose "goal" is to attack our way of life and "decadent values" at whatever cost. There even seems to be competition between these disparate groups to think up and carry out the most devastating attack possible.'

'This is what we're concerned about here,' said Pablo, enthused by Elvira seeing his point of view. 'Are we experiencing a series of diversionary jabs prior to the main attack – something on the scale of the World Trade Center in New York?'

'What *we* need to know,' said Ramírez, tiring of all the conjecture, 'is where our investigation here, in Seville, should be heading.'

'There is no Juez de Instrucción until Sergio del Rey arrives from Madrid,' said Elvira. 'The Madrid CGI have been pulling in all contacts of Hammad and Saoudi for interviews, but so far they appear to have been operating alone. The Guardia Civil have successfully plotted the route taken by the Peugeot Partner from Madrid to the safe house near Valmojado, where it is believed they were keeping the hexogen. They are having difficulties plotting the route taken by the vehicle from Valmojado down to Seville. There are concerns that it diverted on its route.'

'Where was the last sighting of the Peugeot Partner?' asked Falcón.

'Heading south on the NIV/E5. It stopped at a service station near Valdepeñas. The concern is that ninety kilometres later the road forks. The NIV continues to Cordoba and Seville, while the N323/E902 goes to Jaen and Granada. They are looking at both routes, but it's not easy to track a particular white van amongst the thousands on the roads. Their only chance is if the vehicle stopped and the two men got out so that someone could identify them, as happened at the service station near Valdepeñas.'

'Which means there's a distinct possibility that there's more hexogen elsewhere,' said Pablo. 'Our job at the moment is to find out what connections Botín made, and we'll be speaking to his partner, Esperanza, this morning.'

'That's great,' said Ramírez. 'But what are *we* supposed to do? Keep searching for the non-existent electricians and council inspectors? We're looking like incompetents at the moment. Juez Calderón was doing a good job of protecting us from too much media attention. Now he's in a police cell. A CGI antiterrorist agent has committed suicide and *his* source *could* be a double agent. We're at crisis point here. Our squad can't just carry on as we were.'

'Until we receive forensic information from inside the mosque, there's not a lot else we can do,' said Falcón. 'We can go back to the congregation of the mosque and interview them about Miguel Botín, see what that throws up. But I believe we *should* keep hammering away at the electricians and council inspectors – who *do* exist. They *have* been seen. And if I understand the CNI correctly, the council inspectors created a pretext so that the electricians could plant a bomb. They are the perpetrators of this atrocity. We *have* to find them and the people who sent them. *That*, as the Grupo de Homicidios, is our goal.'

'But possibly one that you can only achieve through quality intelligence,' said Elvira. 'Are they part of an Islamic terrorist cell or not? Perhaps the answer lies somewhere in the history of Miguel Botín, who gave their card to the Imam.'

'And what *about* the Imam?' said Ramírez, not wanting to be thwarted. 'Where is he in all this? Has the CNI search of his apartment been completed? Can we have their findings? Has access to his history finally been granted to someone who's allowed to tell us?'

'We can't access it because we do not hold it,' said Pablo.

'Who does hold it?'

'The Americans.'

'Did you find a heavily annotated copy of that edition of the Koran in the Imam's apartment?' asked Falcón.

'No.'

'So you don't think he was in the loop?' said Ramírez.

'We don't know enough to be able to answer that question.'

The meeting broke up soon after that exchange. The CNI and CGI men left the pre-school together. Elvira asked Falcón to attend the press conference in the Andalucian Parliament building when the new judge arrived, to show a united front. Ramírez was waiting outside the classroom.

'I'm sorry for your loss, Javier,' he said, holding him by the shoulder and shaking his hand. 'I know you and Inés had grown apart, but . . . it's a terrible thing. I hope you didn't go to the crime scene.'

'I did,' said Falcón. 'I don't know what I was thinking. They told me over the phone that he'd been identified as Juez Calderón and that he'd been trying to dispose of a body. I don't know why . . . I just didn't think it would be Inés.'

'Did he do it?'

'I went to talk to him in the patrol car. All he said was: "I didn't do it."'

Ramírez shook his head. Denial was a very common psychological state for husbands when they murdered their wives.

381

'There's going to be a feeding frenzy,' said Ramírez. 'A lot of people have been waiting for this moment.'

'You know, José Luis, the worst thing . . .' said Falcón, struggling, 'was that she was very badly bruised over her torso, down her left side . . . and it was old bruising.'

'He'd been *beating* her?'

'Her face was completely clear.'

'You'd better take the riot squad with you into that press conference,' said Ramírez. 'They're going to go mad if they hear about that.'

'Inés came round to my house the other night,' said Falcón. 'She was behaving very strangely. I thought for a moment she wanted to get back with me, but now I think she was trying to tell me what was happening to her.'

'Did she seem in pain at all?' asked Ramírez, preferring to stick to the facts.

'She was swearing like I'd never heard her swear before and, yes, she did hold on to her side at one point,' said Falcón. 'She was furious with him for all his . . .'

'Yes, we know,' said Ramírez, who hadn't banked on this level of intimacy.

Falcón's eyes filled, his mind taking its grief in gulps. Ramírez squeezed his shoulder with his huge mahogany hand.

'We'd better start thinking about today,' said Falcón. 'Did you manage to read that file about the unidentified body found at the dump on Monday?'

'Not yet.'

'We don't get that many dead bodies in Seville,' said Falcón. 'And in my career I have never come across such a disfigured corpse, and poisoned with cyanide, too. And all this happens days before a bomb goes off in the city.'

'There doesn't *have* to be a connection,' said Ramírez, wary of letting himself in for more fruitless work.

'But before we get a ton of forensic information from the mosque, I'd like to see if there is one,' said Falcón. 'At least I'd like to identify the victim. It might open up another pathway into this situation.'

'Any pointers before I start reading?'

'The Médico Forense thought he was mid forties, long-haired, desk bound but tanned and didn't wear shoes very much. He had traces of hashish in his blood. There was also tattoo ink in the lymph nodes, which is the reason his hands were severed: they had tattoos on them, small ones, but presumably distinctive.'

'Sounds like a university type to me,' said Ramírez, who was suspicious of anybody with too much education. 'Post-graduate?'

'Or maybe a professor trying to recapture his youth?'

'Spanish?'

'Olive-skinned,' said Falcón. 'He'd had a hernia op. The Médico Forense removed the mesh. See if you can get a match for it, find the company that supplied it and to which hospital. Of course, he might have had it done abroad . . .'

'Do you want me to do this on my own?'

'Take Ferrera with you. She's done some work on this already,' said Falcón. 'Pérez, Serrano and Baena can tour the construction sites of Seville, especially any with immigrant labour. Tell them they *have* to find the electricians.'

'Didn't I hear someone say that you were having a

model made of this guy's head – the one from the dump?'

'The sculptor's a friend of the Médico Forense,' said Falcón. 'I'll follow that up.'

'You missed your session last night,' said Alicia Aguado.

'Something cropped up,' said Consuelo. 'Something very upsetting.'

'That's why we're here.'

'You told me to make sure I had a family member to look after me when I came home after my session on Tuesday evening,' said Consuelo. 'I asked my sister. She was there, but couldn't stay for long. We talked about the session. She could see that I was calm and so she left. Then yesterday afternoon she called me to check that I was still OK, and we chatted and she remembered something she'd meant to ask me about the night before. My new pool man.'

'Pool man?'

'He looks after the pool. He checks the pH levels, hoovers the bottom, skims the surface, cleans the . . .' said Consuelo, getting carried away on the detail.

'OK, Consuelo, I'm not going into the pool-cleaning business,' said Aguado.

'The point is, I don't *have* a new pool man,' said Consuelo. 'The same guy has been coming round every Thursday afternoon since I bought the house. I inherited him from the previous owners.'

'And what?'

Consuelo tried to swallow, but couldn't.

'My sister described him, and it was the same disgusting *chulo* from the Plaza del Pumarejo.'

'Very upsetting,' said Aguado. 'It unnerved you, I'm

384

sure. So you called the police and stayed with your children. I can understand that.'

Silence. Consuelo was slumped to one side of the chair, as if she'd lost some stuffing.

'All right,' said Aguado. 'Tell me what you did, or did not do.'

'I didn't call the police.'

'Why not?'

'I was too embarrassed,' she said. 'I'd have to explain everything.'

'You could have just told them that an undesirable person was snooping around your home.'

'You probably don't know very much about the police,' said Consuelo. 'I was a murder suspect for a couple of weeks five years ago. What they put you through is not so different to what you're doing to me here. You start talking and they smell things. They know when people are hiding the shit in their lives. They see it every day. They'd ask a question like: "Do you think it possible that you know this person?" and what would happen? Especially in my fragile mental state.'

'I know you might find this difficult to believe, but to me this is a positive development,' said Aguado.

'It makes *me* feel like a failure,' said Consuelo. 'I don't know whether this person could be a danger to my children, and just because of my own shame I'm prepared to put them at risk.'

'But at least now I know that he's real,' said Aguado.

Silence from Consuelo, who hadn't considered this alarming possibility.

'Our minds have ways of correcting imbalances,' said Aguado. 'So, for instance, a powerful chief executive who controls thousands of people's lives may redress the balance by dreaming of being at school and the teacher telling him what to do. This is a very benign form of balancing things out. More aggressive forms exist. It's not unusual to find successful businessmen who visit a dominatrix in order to be tied up, rendered powerless and punished. A New York psychologist told me he had clients who went to nurseries where they could wear nappies and sit in oversized playpens. The danger comes with the uncertainty between the fantastic, the real and the illusory. The mind becomes confused and cannot differentiate, and then a breakdown can ensue, with possible lasting damage.'

'What you mean is, I've had the fantasy and I may take the next step and seek out the reality.'

'But at least you weren't describing an illusion to me,' said Aguado. 'Before your sister confirmed his existence, I wasn't sure how advanced you were. I told you not to allow yourself to be distracted on your way here because, if he was real, then the reality you were seeking was very dangerous for you . . . personally. This man has no idea of the nature of your problems. He has sensed some vulnerability and is probably just a predator.'

'He knows my name and that my husband is dead,' said Consuelo. 'Those two details came out when he accosted me on Monday night.'

'Then you really should talk to the police about it,' said Aguado. 'If they think you're strange, refer them to me.'

'Then they'll know I'm a lunatic and take no notice,' said Consuelo. 'There's been a bomb in

Seville, and a rich bitch is worried about a *chulo* in her garden.'

'Try talking to them,' said Aguado. 'This man might assault or rape you.'

Silence.

'What are you doing now, Consuelo?'

'I'm looking at you.'

'And you're thinking . . .?'

'That I trust you more than I've trusted anyone in my life.'

'Anyone? Even your parents?'

'I loved my parents, but they knew nothing about me,' said Consuelo.

'So who have you trusted in your life?'

'I trusted an art dealer in Madrid for a bit, until he moved down here,' said Consuelo.

'Who else?' asked Aguado. 'What about Raúl?'

'No, he didn't love me,' said Consuelo, 'and he lived in a closed-off world, trapped by his own misery. He didn't talk to me about his problems and I didn't reveal my own.'

'Was there anything between you and the art dealer?'

'No, our attraction was nothing remotely sexual or romantic.'

'What was it then?'

'We recognized that we were complicated people, with secrets we couldn't talk about. But he did once tell me that he'd killed a man.'

'That's not an easy thing to do,' said Aguado, sensing that they might be closer to the heart of the tangled knot than Consuelo suspected.

'We were drinking brandy in a bar on the Gran Via. I was depressed. I'd just told him everything about my abortions. He traded this secret of his, but he said it was an accident when, in fact, it was much more shameful than that.'

'More shameful than appearing in a pornographic movie to pay for an abortion?'

'Of course it was. He'd killed somebody for –'

Consuelo stopped as if she'd been knifed in the throat. The next word wouldn't come out. She could only cough up a croak as if there was a blade across her windpipe. A powerful shudder of emotion rippled through her. Aguado released her wrist, grabbed her by the arm to steady her. A strange sound came from Consuelo as she slid to the floor. It was something like an orgasmic cry, and, in fact, it was a release, but not one of pleasure. It was a cry of acute pain.

Aguado had not expected to reach this point so quickly in the treatment, but then the mind was an unpredictable organ. It threw things up all the time, vomited horrors into the consciousness and, this was the strange thing, sometimes the conscious mind could hurdle these terrible revelations, side-step them, leap across the sudden chasm. Other times it was scythed to the ground. Consuelo had just experienced the equivalent of being hit by a half-ton bull from behind. She ended up in the foetal position on the Afghan rug, squeaking, as if something enormous was trying to get out.

27

The pressroom in the Andalucian Parliament building was filled to capacity, and there were more people outside in the corridors. The double doors had been left open. It was inconceivable to Falcón that something hadn't leaked. The heaving level of interest in a routine press conference could not be so vast.

The gravity of the revelations had brought Comisario Lobo to the conference and his glowering presence was a comfort. Lobo commanded respect. He induced fear. Nobody took his huge frame and coarse cumin complexion lightly. He was the most senior policeman in Seville and yet he seemed to be a man just managing to keep the lid on an extremely violent temperament.

On the raised platform were six chairs set behind two tables, on which had been placed six microphones. The six stars of the press conference – Comisarios Lobo and Elvira, Juez del Rey, the Magistrado Juez Decano de Sevilla Spinola, Inspectores Jefe Barros and Falcón – were standing in the wings, occupying themselves with the folded lengths of card on which their names were printed. Del Rey had arrived only five minutes earlier,

389

having taken a cab straight from the Estación Santa Justa. He looked remarkably calm for a man who'd been woken up at 6.15 in the morning and told to catch the next AVE train to Seville and take control of the largest criminal investigation Andalucía had ever seen.

At exactly 9.30 Lobo led them out, like a cadre of gladiators being presented to the public. There was a clatter of shutters and flickering of flashes from the photojournalists. Lobo sat in the middle, held up a large finger and surveyed his audience, who instantly battened down to total silence.

'The prime objective of this press conference is to introduce the new team who will be conducting the investigation into the Seville bombing, now referred to as 6th June.'

He presented each member of the team, explaining their role. There was a human tremor at the introduction of Sergio del Rey as the new judge directing the investigation, which meant that Falcón's role was lost in the aftershock.

'Where's Juez Calderón?' shouted a voice from the back of the room.

Lobo's huge finger was raised once again, this time with a slightly admonishing edge to it. Silence fell.

'The Magistrado Juez Decano de Sevilla will now explain the reason behind the change in our Juez de Instrucción.'

Spinola stood up and gave a similar, terse and factual description of the events of the early morning down by the Guadalquivir river as Elvira had done an hour earlier. When he'd finished there was a missed beat and then a roar, as of a crowd in an enclosed basketball arena who'd just witnessed a heinous foul. Their hands came out waving pens, notebooks, and dictaphones. When their shouting failed to penetrate they started screaming, like maddened traders in the bear pit of a crashing *bourse*. It was impossible to hear any questions. Lobo stood. The Colossus of the Jefatura made no impact. The scandal was just too vast, and the herd too demented, to care about his immense authority. The journalists rushed the platform. Falcón was grateful for the barrier of the table. Lobo was decisive. The six men left the stage just managing not to break into a run for the door at the back. Barros was the last man out and he had to wrest his arm from the clutches of a woman's blood-red nails. The door was shut and locked by security. The journalists hammered from the other side. The double doors seemed to swell, as if they might be about to burst open.

'There's no talking to them,' said Lobo. 'And, anyway, there's nothing to be said beyond that statement. We'll hold another press conference later and ask them to present their questions beforehand.'

They left the building and all except Lobo, Elvira and Spinola were driven back to the pre-school. Juez del Rey still hadn't completed his reading of the case file, which was already huge. He said he'd need until midday to complete it and then he would like a meeting with the investigating team.

Falcón called Dr Pintado, the Médico Forense who'd handled the unidentified corpse from the dump, and asked for Miguel Covo's number, saying he had to see anything that the sculptor had been able to accomplish as soon as possible. Pintado said that Covo would call if he had anything to show.

A call came through on his personal mobile. It was Angel. He should have turned the damn thing off.

'I was there,' said Angel. 'I've never seen anything like that in my life.'

'I thought we were going to have to fire tear gas at you lot,' said Falcón, trying to keep it light.

'This is a disaster for your investigation.'

'Juez del Rey is a very capable man.'

'You're talking to me, Javier – Angel Zarrías: public relations expert. What you've got on your hands is . . .'

'We know, but what can we do? We can't turn the clock back and bring Inés back to life.'

'I'm sorry,' he said, her name reminding him to be solicitous. 'I'm really sorry, Javier. I just got carried away with the madness in there. It must have been hard for you. Not even your experience could have prepared you for that.'

The saliva thickened in Falcón's mouth as the bitterness of his grief hit him again in another unexpected wave. He was surprised. He'd thought he'd rid himself of all emotional entanglements with Inés and yet here were these odd residues. He'd loved her, or at least he thought he'd loved her, and he was amazed at how that seemed to have stood the test of her cruelty and selfishness.

'What can I do for you, Angel?' he said, businesslike.

'Look, Javier, I'm not a fool. I know you can't talk about anything even if you did know what had happened,' he said. 'I just want you to know that the *ABC* is on your side. I've spoken to the editor. If Comisario Elvira needs help we're prepared to give our full support.'

'I'll tell him, Angel,' said Falcón. 'I've got to go now, I've got another call.'

Falcón closed down that mobile and opened the other. It was the sculptor, Miguel Covo. He had something to show him. He gave Falcón directions to his workshop. Falcón said he could be there in ten minutes. He called Elvira on the way and mentioned the conversation with Angel Zarrías.

'Nothing comes for free in this world,' said Elvira, 'but we *are* going to need all the help we can get. I've just read the autopsy report and . . . I'm sorry, Javier, I shouldn't have mentioned that.'

'I saw her,' said Falcón, his stomach lurching.

But he didn't want to hear it. He'd read autopsies before of battered wives and girlfriends and been stunned at the body's capacity to absorb punishment and still keep going. He tuned himself out from Elvira's voice. He really didn't want to know what Inés had suffered.

'. . . a civilized man, a respected and brilliant legal mind, a cultured person. We used to bump into each other at the opera. There's no telling, Javier. It's a terrifying thought that even these certainties cannot be trusted.'

'Perhaps I shouldn't have told you about Angel Zarrías's offer.'

'I don't follow you.'

'That's Angel Zarrías's talent. He has a genius for the manipulation of image.'

'The suspicion is going to be that we knew about Calderón's behaviour and condoned it with our silence because of his exceptional ability,' said Elvira, who seemed more panicked by the power of the media now that he'd lost Calderón, his brilliant front man. 'Things are going to come out once Inspector Jefe Zorrita starts

digging. And then there'll be all the women he was . . .
you know . . .'

'Fucking?'

'That wasn't the word I was after, but, yes, I understand it wasn't just one or two,' said Elvira. 'Less scrupu-
lous newspapers than the *ABC* might get hold of them
and there'll be more stories stretching back over the
years . . . We'll all look complete idiots, or worse, for
not having spotted the flaws in his character beforehand.'

'None of us *did* know about it,' said Falcón. 'So we
shouldn't feel guilty about presenting our case. And it's
the way of the world that these things have to be
conducted through the media. But at least some good
will come out of it.'

'How's that?'

'It will change people's perceptions. They'll now
know that anyone can be an abuser of women. It's not
the preserve of uneducated brutes with no self-control,
but possibly civilized, cultured, intelligent men who
can be moved to tears by *Tosca*.'

They hung up. Covo's workshop was near the Plaza
de Pelicano, an ugly, modern square of 1970s apartment blocks, whose central sitting area had become a
place where dog owners brought their pets to shit.
Falcón parked outside Covo's studio in an adjacent
compound of small workshops and took a digital camera
out of the glove compartment.

'I used to keep it all in the house,' said Covo, as he
led Falcón through a steel-caged door into a room that
was completely bare of any decoration and had only
a table and two chairs. 'But my wife started to complain
when I worked my way into other rooms.'

Covo made some strong coffee and broke the filter off a Ducado and lit it. His head was shaved to a fine white bristle all over. He wore half-moon glasses with gold rims, so that he looked like an accountant from the neck up. He was slim with a nut-brown body, and his arms and legs were all sinew and wiry muscle. This was all visible because he wore a black string vest, a pair of running shorts and sandals.

'The only problem with this place is that it gets very hot in the summer,' he said.

They drank coffee. Covo didn't volunteer any more information. He studied Falcón's face, eyes flicking up and down, side to side. He nodded, smoked, drank his coffee. Falcón did not feel uneasy. He was glad to have a respite from the madness of the world outside in the company of this strange individual.

'We're all unique,' said Covo, after some minutes, 'and yet remarkably the same.'

'There are types,' said Falcón. 'I've noticed that.'

'The only problem is that we live in a part of Europe where there has been a lot of genetic exchange. So that, for instance, you will find the Berber genetic marker e3b both in North Africa and on the Iberian peninsula,' said Covo. 'Much as we'd like to, we're not going to be able to tell you where exactly your corpse comes from, other than that he is either Spanish or North African.'

'That's already something,' said Falcón. 'How did you find the genetic marker?'

'Dr Pintado has been calling in some favours from the labs,' said Covo. 'Your corpse has good teeth. You already know that he's had corrective work to make them straight; expensive and unusual for someone of his generation. The work was not done in Spain.'

'You've been very thorough.'

'I presumed that this man's death has something to do with the bomb, so I have been working hard and fast,' said Covo. 'The important thing is to work out how this affects the shape of the face and the overall effect of good teeth is impressive. Hair is also important, head and facial.'

'You think he was bearded?'

'The job they did with the acid was not as thorough as it could have been. I'm certain he was bearded, but that presents other problems. How did he keep it? All I can say is that it wasn't long and shaggy. The teeth perhaps indicate a man who cared about his appearance.'

'And he kept his hair long.'

'Yes, and he had high cheekbones,' said Covo. 'A prominent nose – part of the septum was still intact. I think we're talking about a rather striking individual, which was why they probably went to such lengths to destroy his features.'

'I'm surprised they didn't smash up his teeth.'

'They would have had to extract each one to make sure. It was probably too time-consuming,' said Covo. 'Let me show you what I've done.'

Covo stubbed out his Ducado after a last long drag and they went into the studio. Lights came on in certain areas. In the centre of the room was a block of stone from which a number of faces were emerging. They all gave the impression of struggle, as if they were inside the rock and nosing out into the world, desperate to be free from the stultifying substance. Around the walls, in the gloom, were the spectators. Hundreds of heads, some in clay, others frighteningly real in wax.

'I don't let many people in here,' said Covo. 'They get spooked.'

'By the silence, I imagine,' said Falcón. 'One would expect so many faces to be expressing themselves.'

'It reminds people too much of death,' said Covo. 'My talent is not artistic. I am a craftsman. I can recreate a face, but I cannot give it life. They are inanimate, without the motivation of soul. I embalm people in wax and clay.'

'The faces coming out of the rock seem animated to me,' said Falcón.

'I think I've started to feel the restraint of my own mortality,' said Covo. 'Let me show you our friend.'

To the right of the block of stone was a table with what looked like four heads under a sheet.

'I made up four copies of his faceless head,' said Covo. 'Then I made a series of sketches of how I thought he looked. Finally, I started to build.'

He lifted the sheet off the first head. It had no nose, mouth or ears.

'Here I'm trying to get the feeling for how much skin and fat would cover the bones,' said Covo. 'I've looked at the whole body and estimated the extent of his covering.'

He lifted the sheet off the next two heads.

'Here I've been working with the features, trying to fit the nose, mouth, ears and eyes together on the face,' said Covo. 'The third one, as you've probably noticed, is more decisive. Once I've reached this stage I do more sketches, working with hair and colour. This fourth figure I made last night. I painted him and attached the hair just this morning. It's my best guess.'

The sheet slipped off to reveal a head with brown

397

eyes, long lashes, aquiline nose, sharp cheekbones, but with the cheeks themselves slightly sunken. The beard was clipped close to the skin, the hair long, dark and flowing and the teeth white and perfect.

'I'm only worried that I may have got carried away,' said Covo, 'and made him too dashing.'

Falcón took photographs, while Covo made a selection from the sketches of other possible looks. By 11 a.m. Falcón was heading back across the river to the Jefatura. He had the sketches scanned and the image of the victim transferred to the computer. He called Pintado and asked him to email the dental X-rays. He put together a page with the corpse's approximate age, height and weight, the information about the hernia op, tattoos and skull fracture. He called Pablo, who gave him the email address of the right man in the CNI in Madrid who would distribute it to all other intelligence agencies, the FBI and Interpol.

Ramírez called just as he was leaving.

'I've spoken to the vascular surgeon at the hospital,' he said. 'He's identified the hernia mesh taken from the body as one known by the trade name SURUMESH, made by Suru International Ltd of Mumbai in India.'

'Does he use them?'

'For inguinal hernias he uses a German make called TiMESH.'

'You're learning stuff, José Luis.'

'I'm completely fascinated,' said Ramírez, drily. 'He tells me Suru International would probably supply hospitals through medical supplies wholesalers.'

'I'll speak to Pablo. The CNI can get a list from Suru International.'

'Then they've got to contact the hospitals supplied

by those wholesalers. It's quite possible that a hospital takes meshes made by a number of different manufacturers. Then there are the specialist hernia clinics. This is going to take time.'

'We're moving on a lot of fronts,' said Falcón. 'I have a face to work with now. We have dental X-rays. I'm thinking more about America. He had orthodontic work done –'

'Most inguinal hernias occur over the age of forty,' said Ramírez. 'Dr Pintado estimates the guy's hernia op as three years old. So we're only looking at, say, the last four, maximum five years of hernia operations. Maybe two and a half million ops worldwide.'

'Keep thinking positively, José Luis.'

'I'll see you next year.'

Falcón told him about the meeting with Juez del Rey at midday and hung up. He sent another email about Suru International to his contact in the CNI. He got up to leave again. His personal mobile vibrated, no name came up on the screen. He took the call anyway.

'*Diga*,' he said.

'It's me, Consuelo.'

He sat down slowly, thinking, my God. His stomach leapt, his blood came alive. His heart beat loudly in his head.

'It's been a long time,' he said.

'I saw the news about Inés,' she said. 'I wanted to tell you how sorry I am and to let you know that I'm thinking of you. I know you must be very busy . . . so I won't keep you.'

'Thank you, Consuelo,' he said, willing something else to come to mind. 'It's good to hear your voice again. When I saw you in the street . . .'

'I'm sorry for that, too,' she said. 'It couldn't be helped.'

He didn't know what that meant. He needed something to keep her on the phone. Nothing seemed relevant. His mind was too full of the corpse, hernia meshes and two and a half million ops world-wide.

'I should let you go,' she said. 'You must be under a lot of pressure.'

'It was good of you to call.'

'It was the least I could do,' she said.

'I'd like to hear from you again, you know.'

'I'm thinking of you, Javier,' she said, and it was all over.

He sat back, looking at the phone as if her voice was still inside it. She'd kept his number for four years. She was thinking of him. Do these things have meaning? Was that just social convention? It didn't feel like it. He saved her number.

The car park at the back of the Jefatura was brutally hot, the car windscreens blinded by the sun in the clear sky. Falcón sat in the car with the air conditioning blasting into his face. Those few sentences, the sound of her voice, had opened up a whole chapter of memory which he'd closed off for years. He shook his head and pulled out of the Jefatura car park. He headed for El Cerezo the back way, via the Expo ground, crossing the river at the Puente del Alamillo. He arrived at the bombsite at the same time as Ramírez.

'Any news about the electricians?' asked Falcón.

'Pérez called. They've been through seventeen building sites. Nothing.'

'What's Ferrera doing?'

'She's chasing down witnesses who might have seen

400

our friend with the hernia being dumped in the bin on Calle Boteros.'

They went into the pre-school. Juez del Rey was alone, waiting for them in the classroom. They sat down on the edges of the school desks. Del Rey folded his arms and stared into the floor. He gave them a perfect recap of the major findings of the investigation so far. He didn't use notes. He got all the names of the Moroccan witnesses correct. He had the whole timetable of what had happened in and around the mosque, in his head. He'd decided to make an impression on the two detectives and it worked. Falcón felt Ramírez relax. Calderón's replacement was no fool.

'The two most significant recent developments in the investigation concern me the most,' said del Rey. 'Ricardo Gamero's suicide and the belief that his source was working as a double agent.'

'We had a sighting of Gamero by a security guard in the Archaeological Museum in the Parque María Luisa,' said Falcón. 'We've got a police artist working on some sketches of the older man he was seen talking to.'

'I'll call Serrano,' said Ramírez, 'see how that's going.'

'I'm not convinced that a sense of failure at preventing this bomb attack from taking place was enough to drive a man like Gamero to suicide,' said del Rey. 'There's something more. Failure is too general. Feeling personally responsible is what drives people to kill themselves.'

'The police artist didn't have much luck with the security guard last night,' said Ramírez, coming back from his call. 'He's been with him again this morning. They should have something by lunchtime.'

401

'I'm not convinced by Miguel Botín as a double, either,' said del Rey. 'His brother was maimed by an Islamic terrorist bomb, for God's sake. Can you see someone like that being turned?'

'He was a convert,' said Falcón. 'He took his religion very seriously. It's difficult to know what sort of impression a charismatic radical preacher could make on someone like that. We have the example of Mohammed Sidique Khan, one of the London bombers, who was transformed from a special needs teacher into a radical militant.'

'We don't know what the relationship between Miguel Botín and his injured brother was like, either,' said Ramírez.

'I'm also uncomfortable about the electricians and the fake council inspectors. I don't buy the CNI line that they were a terrorist cell. The CNI seem to me to be trying to cram square information into a round hole.'

There was a knock at the door. A policeman put his head round.

'The forensics have been working their way through the rubble above the storeroom in the mosque,' he said. 'They've found a fireproof, shock-proof metal box. It's been taken to the forensic tent and they thought you might like to be there when they open it.'

28

Outside the pre-school everybody was wearing masks
against the stench and Falcón, Ramírez and del Rey
walked with their hands clasped over their mouths
and noses. There was an anteroom to the main body
of the forensics' tent, where they all dressed in white
hooded boiler suits and put on masks. The interior of
the tent was air conditioned down to 22°C. Five
forensic teams were currently working at the site. All
of them had stopped for the opening of the box.
Something within the human psyche making it impossible, even for forensics, to resist the mystery of a
closed, secure container.

A dictaphone was tested and set in the middle of
the table. The leader of the forensic team nodded to
the judge and detectives as they gathered around. His
hands, in latex gloves, were spread on either side of a
red metal box. Next to him was a shallow cardboard
evidence box, dated and with the address of the Imam's
apartment on the lid. Inside were three small plastic
bags containing keys. A white-suited figure nudged into
Falcón. It was Gregorio.

'This could be interesting if those keys open that box,' he said. 'Two sets came from the desk and one from the kitchen of the Imam's apartment.'

'Are we ready?' asked the forensics team leader. 'Here we are on Thursday, 8th June 2006 at 12.24 hours. We have a sealed metal box, which has sustained some blast damage to the lid, although the lock still appears to be sound. We are going to attempt to open this box, using keys taken from the Imam's apartment during a search of those premises on Wednesday, 7th June 2006.'

He rejected the first sachet of keys but selected the next one and poured the two keys into his hand. He fitted one of the identical keys into the lock, turned it, and the lid sprang open.

'The box has been successfully opened by a key found in the kitchen drawer of the Imam's apartment.'

He opened the lid and lifted out three coloured plastic folders, thick with folded paper. This emptied the box, which was removed to another table. He opened up the first green folder.

'Here we have one sheet of writing in Arabic script, which has been paper-clipped to what appears to be a set of architect's drawings.'

He opened out the drawings, which proved to be a detailed plan of a secondary school in San Bernardo. The other two folders followed the same pattern. The second set of drawings featured the plan of a primary school in Triana, and the third, the biology faculty on Avenida de la Reina Mercedes.

Silence, while the men and women of the forensic teams contemplated their find. Falcón could feel the minds in the room working their way towards more and more uneasy conclusions. Each Islamic terrorist atrocity had released new viral strains of horror into the body of the West. No sooner had the West become reconciled to men as bombs, than they had to accept women as bombs, and even children as bombs. It seemed sickeningly obvious now that car bombs would transmute to boats as bombs, and then planes as bombs. Finally the atrocities would no longer remain at a distance in the Middle East, Far East or America, but come to Madrid and London. Then there was the unimaginable. The stuff that would make a horror novelist tremble at night: executions beamed around the world of men and women being beheaded with kitchen knives. And finally Beslan: children held hostage, given no food or water, explosives hung over their heads. How is an ordinary mind supposed to work under these conditions of easy contagion?

'Were they going to blow these places up?' asked a voice.

'Take hostages,' said a woman. 'Look, they're after kids from five years old up to twenty-five years old.'

'Bastards.'

'Is there nothing these people won't do? Are there no fucking boundaries?'

'I think,' said Juez del Rey, quick to put a lid on the mounting hysteria, 'that we should wait until we have translations of the Arabic script in our hands before we jump to conclusions.'

It was not the voice of reason that people wanted to hear. Not just yet, anyway. They'd been waiting a long time to get their hands on solid evidence and now they'd found something spectacular they wanted to vent some of their anger. Del Rey sensed this. He moved things along once more.

'As a precaution, these three buildings should be searched. If there was a plan to seize them it's possible that weaponry has been stored there.'

Everybody nodded, glad to see that even the man from Madrid suffered the same paranoia, the same corrupted brain circuit as themselves.

'Let's get these drawings and the Arabic texts through the forensic process as soon as possible. We need those translations fast,' he said.

'There's something else,' said the forensics team leader. 'The bomb disposal people have come across something interesting on the explosives front.'

An army officer in white overalls with a green armband pushed his way through to the table.

'So far we've only had full access to the area above the storeroom, because there's no evidence of bodies or human tissue. We still believe that the main destructive explosion was caused by a large quantity of hexogen being detonated, but we have also found trace evidence of Goma 2 Eco, which is the mining explosive that was used in the Madrid bombings.'

'Did one set off the other?'

'It's certainly possible, but we have no way of proving it.'

'Is there any reason why two types of explosive would be used?'

'Goma 2 Eco is industrial quality, whereas hexogen is military. If you have a large quantity of hexogen, which has greater brisance than Goma 2 Eco, I don't see why you'd use a lower grade explosive, unless your intention was to cause other distracting explosions, or to hold people in a state of fear.'

'You estimated the hexogen stored in the building to be in the region of 100 kilos,' said del Rey.

'Conservative estimate.'

'What sort of damage would 100 kilos do to these schools and the university faculty on these drawings?'

'A real expert, who understood the architecture of the buildings, could probably raze them to the ground,' said the army officer. 'But it would be a demolition job. They would have to drill into the reinforced skeleton of the building and wire the charges together for a simultaneous explosion.'

'And what about people?'

'If everyone was herded into one or two rooms of each building, with 30 kilos of hexogen there would be no, or only very few, survivors.'

'Is it possible for you to tell how much Goma 2 Eco exploded in the storeroom of the mosque?'

'Personally, I would say 25 kilos or less, but I wouldn't be able to stand up in court and say that, because the hexogen trace is too dominant.'

'Is hexogen manufactured in Spain?'

'No. The UK, Italy, Germany, USA and Russia,' he said. 'They probably make it in China, too, but they're not telling us if they are.'

'Why go to the trouble of importing it?'

'Its availability,' said the army officer. 'Wherever there's conflict in the world, there's ordnance, and hexogen can easily be extracted from it. You end up with low-volume high explosive which is untraceable, easy to transport, hide and disguise. Domestic gunpowder magazines are more tightly controlled since 11th March, although there have been thefts – for instance in Portugal last year. I would also say that the chances of hexogen being spotted in an open European transport system are slim. Whereas mounting a robbery of a gunpowder magazine in this country would get you lower grade explosive, and draw the immediate attention of the authorities.'

'What about the home-made variety, used in the London bombings?' asked del Rey. 'Wouldn't it be easier to mix up easily available ingredients than go to the trouble and risk of bringing in hexogen, or stealing Goma 2 Eco?'

'You're right, triaceton triperoxide can be made quite easily, but I wouldn't like to be around someone dealing with it, unless he had a chemistry post-graduate degree and we were operating in temperature-controlled laboratory conditions. It's volatile,' he said. 'Also it depends on what sort of atrocity you want to commit. TATP is fine if you're intent on killing people, but if you want a spectac-ular explosion, with serious destruction and loss of life, then hexogen is much more capable of doing that. Hexogen is also stable and not temperature sensi-tive, something that's important at this time of year in a place like Seville, where daytime temperatures can vary by as much as twenty degrees.'

The work rate was increasing. Material was coming in at a constant rate from the bombsite. Bits of credit card, scraps of ID, driving licences, strips of clothing, shoes. The more macabre findings, such as body parts, were taken to the tented morgue next door. While del Rey watched the forensic work, Falcón briefed Elvira, who'd just arrived from a meeting in the town hall with the Mayor, Comisario Lobo and Magistrado Juez

Decano Spinola. Elvira ordered searches of the three buildings immediately. Evacuation would be carried out by the local police and searches conducted by the bomb squad in case of booby traps. Elvira was concerned that other terrorist cells might have become active, preparing to take over the buildings. The CGI had to be alerted. Gregorio of the CNI was already in touch with Pablo, who was asking for the translations to be sent to him by secure email as soon as they were ready.

Falcón, Ramírez and del Rey stripped off their boiler suits in the forensic tent's anteroom and went back to the pre-school to resume their meeting.

'What do you make of *that* development, Inspector Jefe?' asked del Rey.

'We were asked to keep an open mind in this investigation, especially by the senior CNI man,' said Falcón. 'And yet, since we found the Peugeot Partner and its contents, almost all subsequent findings have directed us towards the belief that an Islamic terrorist campaign was being planned in this mosque.'

'*Almost* all subsequent findings?'

'We cannot satisfactorily explain the fake council inspectors and the electricians, and yet we are very suspicious of their involvement,' said Falcón. 'They seem to be an intrinsic part of the actual explosion. Now that we've spoken to the bomb squad officer it seems clear that a smaller device was planted, which set off the stored hexogen. We have a link between Miguel Botín and the electricians. He was seen handing over the card to the Imam. But who was he working for?'

'You don't buy the CNI line either?'

'I would if there was any proof for it, but there's none.'

'What about those keys from the Imam's apartment opening the box?' said Ramírez. 'Where does that place the Imam now?'

'As part of the plot,' said del Rey.

'Except that the keys were found in a kitchen drawer,' said Falcón. 'I find that strange when all the other keys were kept in his desk. And the two keys were identical. Would you keep them together?'

'If we are to believe that Botín was a double agent and that he was serving up the Imam to the CGI on behalf of another terrorist commander, as the CNI seem to think, then what are we to make of the drawings in the metal box?' asked del Rey.

'The Imam's keys opened the box, therefore whatever is in that box is an expendable operation,' said Falcón. 'The CNI would be forced to admit it was another part of the diversion.'

'And what do you think, Inspector Jefe?'

'I don't have enough information to think anything,' said Falcón.

'You said you were keeping an open mind, Inspector Jefe. What does that mean exactly? That you've been conducting other enquiries?'

Falcón told him about Informáticalidad, giving the background on Horizonte and I4IT. He gave their reasons for buying the property and how the sales reps used it. He also told him about Informáticalidad's recruiting procedure.

'Well, all that sounds strange, but I can't see anything in particular that's pointing to their involvement in this scenario.'

'I've never heard anything like it,' said Ramírez.

'So far, the only illegal thing I can find is that they used black money to buy the apartment,' said Falcón. 'I've been trying to find something that links them to what was going on in the mosque.'

'And you haven't found it.'

'The only connection is that one of the churches used in recruiting employees for Informáticalidad was the same one used by the CGI antiterrorist agent Ricardo Gamero – San Marcos.'

'But you have no proof that Gamero met anyone from Informáticalidad?'

'None. I spoke to the priest from San Marcos and I would describe some of his responses as extremely guarded, but that's all.'

'Are you hoping that the police artist's drawing of the man Gamero met in the museum is going to provide that link to Informáticalidad?'

'That's a tricky process: to extract a likeness from a museum security guard's view of a person he wasn't particularly interested in,' said Falcón. 'They're looking for troublemakers, not two adults having a conversation.'

'Which is why, after five hours, we still have nothing,' said Ramírez.

'We're also pushing forward with an enquiry we started the day before the bomb,' said Falcón, and described the circumstances of the mutilated corpse.

'And because of the timing, you think that there might be a link to the bombing?' asked del Rey.

'Not just that; after this particularly brutal treatment to hide the victim's identity, the body had been sewn into a shroud. That struck me as respectful and religiously motivated. The corpse also had what is known as a Berber genetic marker, which means that he was either from the Iberian peninsula or North African.'

'You said he was poisoned.'

'He ingested it,' said Falcón, 'which could imply that he didn't know he was being "executed". Then they removed his identity but treated him with respect.'

'And how will this help us to identify the fake council inspectors and the electricians?'

'I won't know that until I identify the murdered man,' said Falcón. 'I'm hoping that can be done now that an image of the victim's face and a full set of dental X-rays have been sent out to intelligence services world-wide, including Interpol and the FBI.'

Del Rey nodded, scribbled notes.

'We're not getting anywhere looking for these electricians through conventional channels,' said Ramírez.

'While the bomb squad officer was talking, it occurred to me that an explosives expert would have to know about electronics and therefore probably electrics in general,' said Falcón. 'Goma 2 Eco is a mining explosive, so perhaps we should sit our witnesses down in front of photo IDs for all licensed explosive handlers in Spain.'

'Have your witnesses been able to describe the electricians?'

'The most reliable one is a Spanish convert called José Duran, but he couldn't describe them very well. There didn't seem to be anything particular about them.'

'Witnesses plural, you said.'

'There's an old Moroccan guy, but he didn't even spot that the two labourers weren't Spanish.'

'Maybe we should send an artist along to see José Duran while he looks at the licensed explosive handlers,' said Ramírez. 'I'll get on to it.'

Falcón gave him his mobile to extract Duran's number. Ramírez left the room.

'I'm concerned that the CNI are either not seeing things straight, or they're not telling us everything we should know,' said del Rey. 'I don't know why they haven't let you into the Imam's apartment yet.'

'They're not concerned about what happened here any more,' said Falcón. 'This explosion was either a mistake or a decoy, and either way there's no point in expending energy to find out very little when there's possibly another, more devastating attack being planned elsewhere.'

'But you don't agree with the CNI's point of view?'

'I think there are two forces at play here,' said Falcón. 'One force is an Islamic terrorist group, who appeared to be planning an attack using hexogen, brought here in the Peugeot Partner and stored in the mosque . . .'

'An attack on those schools and the biology faculty?'

'Let's see what forensic information we get, if any, from the drawings and the texts,' said Falcón. 'And also the content of the translations.'

'And the other force?'

'I don't know.'

'But how does this force manifest itself?'

'By a breakdown of logic in the scenario,' said Falcón. 'We can't fit the council inspectors and the electricians into our scenario, nor can we explain the Goma 2 Eco.'

'But who do you think this force is?'

'What are these Islamic terrorist groups fighting for,

413

or who do you think they're fighting against?' asked Falcón.

'It's difficult to say. There doesn't seem to be any coherent agenda or strategy. They just seem to be meting out a series of punishments. London and Madrid were supposedly because of Iraq. Nairobi, the USS *Cole* and the Twin Towers because they believe that America is an evil empire. Bali because of Australian action in East Timor against the Islamic nation of Indonesia. Casablanca was supposedly against Spanish and Jewish targets. Karachi . . . I don't know; it was the Sheraton, wasn't it?'

'And that's our problem here,' said Falcón. 'We have no idea who their enemy is. Perhaps this other force is just a group of people who've had enough and decided they don't want to be passively terrorized any more. They want to fight back. They want to preserve their way of life – whether it's considered decadent or not. They could be the people behind the VOMIT website. They could be an unknown local Andalucian group who've heard about the MILA and perceived it as a threat to them and their families. Maybe it's a religious group who want to maintain the sanctity of the Catholic faith in Spain and drive Islam back into North Africa. Or perhaps we are even more decadent than we know and this is pure power play. Somebody has seen the political or economic potential in terrifying the population. When those planes hit the Twin Towers everything changed. People see things differently now – both good and bad people. Once a new chapter in the human history of horror has been opened, all sorts of people start applying their creative powers to the writing of its next paragraphs.'

29

'Did you manage to talk to your ex-mentor, Marco Barreda, at Informáticalidad?' asked Falcón.

'I did better than that,' said David Curado. 'I went to see him.'

'How did that go?'

'Well, I called him and started to tell him what you and I talked about, and he stopped me, said it was a pity we hadn't seen each other since I'd left the company and why didn't we meet for a beer and a tapa?'

'Has that happened before?'

'No way, we've only ever talked on the phone,' said Curado. 'I was surprised; you're not even supposed to talk to ex-employees, let alone meet them for a beer.'

'Was it just the two of you?'

'Yes, and it was odd,' said Curado. 'He'd been all enthusiastic on the phone, but when we met it was almost as if he'd changed his mind about the whole thing. He seemed distracted, but I could tell it was an act.'

'How?'

415

'I told him about our conversation and he barely took any notice,' said Curado. 'But then I asked the question about Ricardo Gamero and he was stunned. I asked him who this Ricardo Gamero was, and he said he was a member of his church who'd committed suicide that afternoon. As you know, I used to go to San Marcos myself and I'd never come across Ricardo Gamero, so I asked him if he'd killed himself because the cops were after him and Marco said that the guy *was* a cop.'

'How do you think he'd taken the news of Ricardo Gamero's suicide?'

'He was sick about it, I could tell. Very upset, he was.'

'Were they friends?'

'I assume so, but he didn't say.'

Falcón knew he had to speak to Marco Barreda directly. Curado gave him his number. They hung up. Falcón sat back in his car, tapping the steering wheel with his mobile. Had Gamero's suicide made Marco Barreda vulnerable? And if that was a weakness and Falcón could get some leverage, would it reveal enough, would it, in fact, reveal anything?

He had no idea what he was getting into. He had spoken to Juez del Rey about these two forces – Islamic terrorism and another, as yet unknown – both of whom had demonstrated a ruthlessness in their operations, but he knew nothing about their structures, nor their aims, other than a preparedness to kill. Had the one movement learnt from the other: declare no coherent agenda, operate a loose command structure, create self-contained, unconnected cells who, having been remotely activated, carry out their destructive mission?

Talking this through to himself produced a moment of clarity. *That* was one cultural difference between Islam and the West: whenever an Islamic attack occurred, the West always looked for the 'mastermind'. There had to be an evil genius at the core, because that was the order that the Western mind demanded: a hierarchy, a plan with an achievable goal. What was the chain?

He worked back from the electrician who'd planted the bomb. He'd been brought in by a call from the Imam, who in turn had been given the electrician's card by Miguel Botín. The card was the connection between the mission and the hierarchy who'd ordered it. Neither the electricians, nor the council inspectors for that matter, had been in the building at the time of the explosion, and both sets of people were as much a part of the plan as the card. This would not be how an Islamic terrorist cell would operate. That would mean, logically, that the only other person who could have activated Miguel Botín was Ricardo Gamero. Why had Gamero committed suicide? Because, in activating Miguel Botín with the electrician's card, Gamero did not realize that he was making him the agent of destruction of the building and all the people inside.

That would be reason enough to take your own life.

On the day of the bombing, the CGI antiterrorist squad couldn't move because of the possibility of a mole in their ranks. Only on day two could Ricardo Gamero have got out and demanded to see someone senior – the older man in the Archaeological Museum – from whom he demanded an explanation. That explanation had not been good enough to prevent his suicide. Falcón called Ramírez.

'Has that police artist come up with a sketch of the man Gamero met in the museum yet?'

'We've just scanned it and sent it to the CNI and CGI.'

'Send a copy to the computer in the pre-school,' said Falcón.

'The witness José Duran is due here any moment. We'll show him the shots of the licensed explosive handlers, but I'm not holding out much hope,' said Ramírez. 'The bomb could have been made up by somebody else and left in the mosque, or he could have been an assistant to an explosives expert and learnt everything necessary.'

'Keep at it, José Luis,' said Falcón. 'If you want a really impossible task, try looking for the fake council inspectors.'

'I'll add that to the list of two and a half million hernia ops I've still got to go through,' said Ramírez.

'Another thought,' said Falcón. 'Contact all the Hermandades associated with the three churches: San Marcos, Santa María La Blanca and La Magdalena.'

'How's that going to help?'

'Whatever's happening here has some religious motivation. Informáticalidad recruits from church congregations. Ricardo Gamero was a devout Catholic attending San Marcos. The Abdullah Azzam text was sent to the *ABC*, the main Catholic newspaper, and it included a direct threat to the Catholic faith in Andalucía.'

'And what do you think the Brotherhoods in these churches could have to do with it?'

'Maybe nothing. You'd be too exposed as a known Brotherhood but, you never know, they may have heard of a secret one, or seen strange things going on in the churches that might give us some leverage with the priests. We have to try everything.'

'This could get ugly,' said Ramírez.

'Even uglier than it is already?'

'The media are all over us again. I've just heard that Comisario Lobo and the Magistrado Juez Decano de Sevilla are going to give another press conference to explain the situation following Juez Calderón's dismissal,' said Ramírez. 'I heard the one at the Parliament building earlier today was a disaster. And now the television and the radio are full of arseholes telling us that since Calderón's arrest on suspicion of murder and wife abuse, our investigation has completely lost credibility.'

'How has all this got out?'

'The journalists have been all over the Palacio de Justicia, talking to Inés's friends and colleagues. Now they're not just talking about the evident physical violence, but also a prolonged campaign of mental torture and public humiliation.'

'This is just what Elvira was frightened of.'

'A lot of people have been waiting a long time to get Esteban Calderón down on the ground and, now they've got him there, they're going to kick him to death, even if it means our investigation is effectively destroyed.'

'And what do Lobo and Spinola hope to achieve in this press conference?' asked Falcón. 'They can't talk about a murder investigation that's in progress.'

'Damage control,' said Ramírez. 'And they're going to talk up del Rey. He's due to come on afterwards, with Comisario Elvira, to give a recap of the case so far.'

'No wonder he was so word perfect with us,' said Falcón. 'Maybe it wouldn't be such a good idea for him to talk about what we're working on now.'

'You're right about that,' said Ramírez. 'You'd better call him.'

Del Rey had switched his mobile off. Maybe he was already in the studio. Falcón called Elvira and asked him to give a rather cryptic message to del Rey. There was no time to explain the detail. Falcón picked up the sketch from the computer operator in the pre-school. At least it looked like a drawing of a real person. A man in his sixties, possibly early seventies, in a suit and tie, some hair on top with a side parting, no beard or moustache. The artist had included the man's height and weight as given by the security guard, he was on the small side at 1.65m and 75 kilos. But did it look like the man they wanted to find?

Back in the car he took a look at the lists given to him by Diego Torres, the Human Resources Director at Informáticalidad. Marco Barreda was not one of the employees who'd spent time in the apartment on Calle Los Romeros. Maybe he was too senior for that. He called the mobile number David Curado had given him and introduced himself with his full title.

'I think we should talk face to face,' said Falcón.

'I'm busy.'

'It'll take fifteen minutes of your time.'

'I'm still busy.'

'I'm investigating an act of terrorism, multiple murder and a suicide,' said Falcón. 'You have to make time for me.'

'I'm not sure how I can help. I'm neither a terrorist, nor a murderer, and I don't know anybody who is.'

'But you did know the suicide, Ricardo Gamero,' said Falcón. 'Where are you now?'

'I'm in the office. I'm just on my way out.'

'Name a place.'

Deep breath from Barreda. He knew he couldn't brush him off forever. He named a bar in Triana.

Falcón called Ramírez again.

'Have you got the printout of all calls made on Ricardo Gamero's mobiles?'

Ramírez crashed around the office for a minute and came back. Falcón gave him Barreda's number.

'Interesting,' said Ramírez. 'That was the last call he made on his personal mobile.'

'While I think about it,' said Falcón, 'we need the list of calls the Imam made on his mobile. Especially the one he made in front of José Duran on Sunday morning, because that is the electricians' mobile number.'

The bar was half full of people. Everybody was looking at the television, ignoring their drinks. The news had just finished and now it was Lobo and Spinola. But Ramírez had been wrong, it wasn't a press conference; they were being interviewed. Falcón walked through the bar, looking for a lone young man. Nobody nodded to him. He sat down at a table for two.

The interviewer, a woman, was attacking Spinola. She could not believe that he hadn't known about the campaign of terror conducted by Calderón against his wife. The Magistrado Juez Decano de Sevilla, an old-school pachyderm with saurian eyes and an easy, but quite alarming, smile, was not uncomfortable with his moment in the hot seat.

Falcón tuned out of the pointless argument. Spinola was not going to be drawn. The female interviewer had lost herself in the emotional aspect of the case. She should have been hitting Spinola on Calderón's ability to perform and his integrity as a judge in the investigation. Instead she was looking for some riveting personal revelation and she had gone to precisely the wrong man for it.

A young guy in a suit caught Falcón's eye. They introduced themselves and sat down. Falcón ordered a couple of coffees and some water.

'You people are having a hard time,' said Barreda, tilting his head at the TV.

'We're used to it,' said Falcón.

'So how many times has it happened that a Juez de Instrucción has been found trying to dispose of his wife's dead body during a major international terrorism investigation?'

'About as many times as a valued member of an antiterrorist squad has committed suicide during a major international terrorism investigation,' said Falcón. 'How long have you known Ricardo Gamero?'

'A couple of years,' said Barreda, subdued by Falcón's swift response.

'Was he a friend?'

'Yes.'

'So you didn't just see him at Mass on Sundays?'

'We met occasionally during the week. We both like classical music. We used to go to concerts together. Informáticalidad had season tickets.'

'When did you last see him?'

'On Sunday.'

'I understand that Informáticalidad use San Marcos and other churches to recruit employees. Did anybody else from the company know Ricardo Gamero?'

'Of course. We'd go for coffee after Mass and I'd introduce him around. That's normal, isn't it? Just because he's a cop doesn't mean he can't talk to people.'

'So you knew he was in the antiterrorist squad of the CGI.'

Barreda stiffened slightly as he realized he'd been caught out.

'I've known him two years. It came out eventually.'

'Do you remember when?'

'After about six months. I was trying to recruit him to Informáticalidad, making him better and better offers, until finally he told me. He said it was like a vocation and he wasn't going to change his career.'

'A vocation?'

'That was the word he used,' said Barreda. 'He was very serious about his work.'

'*And* his religion,' said Falcón. 'Did he feel the two were bound up together?'

Barreda stared at Falcón, trying to see inside.

'You were a friend he met at church, after all,' said Falcón. 'I would have thought you were bound to talk about the Islamic threat. And then once it came out . . . the nature of his work, I mean. It would seem a natural progression to at least discuss the connection.'

Barreda sat back with an intake of breath and looked around the room, as if for inspiration.

'Did you ever meet Paco Molero?' asked Falcón.

Two blinks. He had.

'Well, Paco,' continued Falcón, 'said that Ricardo, by

his own admission, had been a fanatic, that he'd only just managed to transform himself from being an extremist to being merely devout. And that he'd managed to achieve this through a fruitful relationship with a priest, who died recently of cancer. Where would you describe yourself as being on that integral scale between say, lapsed and fanatical?'

'I've always been very devout,' said Barreda. 'There's been a priest in every generation of my family.'

'Including your own?'

'Except mine.'

'Is that something you feel . . . disappointed by?'

'Yes, it is.'

'Was that one of the attractions of the culture at Informáticalidad?' said Falcón. 'It sounds a bit like a seminary, but with a capitalist aim.'

'They've always been very good to me there.'

'Do you think there's a danger that people with like minds and with the same intensity of faith might become, in the absence of a balancing outside influence, drawn towards an extreme position?'

'I've heard of that happening in cults,' said Barreda.

'How would you describe a cult?'

'An organization with a charismatic leader, that uses questionable psychological techniques to control its followers.'

Falcón left that hanging, sipped his coffee and took the top off his water. He glanced up at the television to see that Lobo and Spinola had now been replaced by Elvira and del Rey.

'The apartment which Informáticalidad bought on Calle Los Romeros near the mosque – did you ever go there?'

'Before it was bought they asked me to look at it to see if it was suitable.'

'Suitable for what?' asked Falcón. 'Diego Torres told me . . .'

'You're right. There wasn't much to look at. It was entirely suitable.'

'How upset were you by Ricardo's death?' asked Falcón. 'That's a terrible thing for a devout Catholic to do: to kill himself. No last rites. No final absolution. Do you know *why* people commit suicide?'

A frown had started up on Marco's forehead. A trembling frown. He was staring into his coffee, biting the inside of his cheek, trying to control emotion.

'Some people kill themselves because they feel responsible for a catastrophe. Other people suddenly lose the impetus for carrying on. We all have something that glues us into place – a lover, friends, family, work, home, but there are other extraordinary people who are glued into place by much bigger ideals. Ricardo was one of those people: a remarkable man with great religious faith *and* a vocation. Is that what he suddenly lost when that bomb exploded on 6th June?'

Barreda sipped his coffee, licked the bitter foam from his lips and replaced the cup with a rattle in its saucer.

'I was very upset by his death,' said Barreda, just to stop the barrage of words from Falcón. 'I have no idea why he committed suicide.'

'But you recognize what it means for a man of his faith to do that?'

Barreda nodded.

'You know who Ricardo's other great friend was?' asked Falcón. 'Miguel Botín. Did you know him?'

425

No reaction from Barreda. He knew him. Falcón piled on the pressure.

'Miguel was Ricardo's source in the mosque. A Spanish convert to Islam. They were very close. They had great respect for each other's faith. I have a feeling that it was as much Miguel Botín as Ricardo's old priest, that pulled him back from the brink of fanaticism to something more reasonable. What do you think?'

Barreda had his elbows up on the table, his fingertips pressed into his forehead and his thumbs pushing into his cheekbones, hard enough for the skin to turn white.

Falcón had Barreda right there on the brink, but he couldn't get him to move that last centimetre. His mind seemed locked in a state of great uncertainty and doubt. Falcón still had his ace up his sleeve, but what about the drawing? If he showed it to him and the man was unrecognizable he would lose his present advantage, but if it was a close likeness it could blow the whole thing open. He decided to play the ace.

'The last time you saw Ricardo was on Sunday,' said Falcón. 'But it wasn't the last time you spoke to him, was it? Do you know who was the last person on earth that Ricardo spoke to before he hanged himself out of his bedroom window? The last number on the list of mobile calls he made?'

Silence, apart from the television burble at the far end of the café.

'What did he say to you, Marco?' asked Falcón. 'Were you able to give him absolution for his sins?'

The whole bar suddenly erupted. All the men were on their feet, hurling insults at the television. A couple of empty plastic bottles were thrown, which glanced off the TV, whose screen was full of del Rey's face.

'What did he say?' Falcón asked the man nearest to him, who was shouting: '*Cabrón! Cabrón!*' in time with the rest of the men in the bar.

'He's trying to tell us that it might not have been Islamic terrorists after all,' said the man, his tremendous belly quivering with rage. 'He's trying to tell us that it could have been our own people who've done this. Our own people, who want to blow up an apartment block and schools, and kill innocent men, women and children? Go back to Madrid, you fucking wanker.'

Falcón turned back to Marco Barreda, who looked stunned by the reaction around him.

'Fuck off back to Madrid, *cabrón*'!

The bar owner stepped in and changed the channel before someone put a glass bottle through the screen. The men settled back into their chairs. The fat guy nudged Falcón.

'The other judge, he beat his wife, but at least he knew what he was talking about.'

The television showed another current affairs programme. The interviewer introduced her two guests. The first was Fernando Alanis, whose introduction was lost in applause from the bar. They knew him. He was the one who'd lost his wife and son, and whose daughter had miraculously survived and was now fighting for her life in hospital. Falcón realized that this was the man they were all going to believe. It didn't matter what he said, his tragedy had conferred on him a legitimacy that Juez del Rey's vast experience and command of the facts totally lacked. In the other chair was Jesús Alarcón, the new leader of Fuerza Andalucía. The bar was silent, listening intently. These were the people who were going to tell them the truth.

Barreda excused himself to go to the toilet. Falcón sat back from the table in a state of shock. He'd lost all the leverage he'd just created. Why hadn't Elvira given del Rey the message that he shouldn't mention the other angle of the investigation? Now that the mistake had been made, it was clear that, even as an enquiry, let alone a possible truth, it was totally unacceptable to the local populace.

The topic of the TV discussion was immigration. The interviewer's first question was irrelevant, as Fernando had come to the cameras well primed. There wasn't a sound in the bar as he started to talk.

'I'm not a politician. I'm sorry to say this in front of Sr Alarcón, who is a man I've grown to respect over the days since the explosion, but I don't like politicians and I don't believe a word they say, and I know I'm not alone. I am here today to tell you how it is. I'm not an opinion-maker. I am a labourer who works on a building site, and I used to have a family,' said Fernando, who had to stop momentarily as his Adam's apple jumped in his throat. 'I lived in the apartment block in El Cerezo which was blown up on Tuesday. I know from the media people I've met over the last few days that they would like to believe, and they would like the world to believe, that we live in a harmonious and tolerant modern society here in Spain. In talking to these people I realized why this is the case. They are all intelligent people, far more intelligent than a mere labourer, but the truth of the matter is that they do not live the life that I do. They are well off, they live in nice houses, in good areas, they take regular holidays, their children go to good schools. And it is from this point of view that they look at their country.

They want it to continue in the way that it appears to them.

'I live . . . I mean, I lived in a horrible apartment in a nasty block, surrounded by lots of other ugly blocks. Not many of us have cars. Not many of us take holidays. Not many of us have enough money to last the month. And *we* are the people living with the Moroccans and the other North Africans. I am a tolerant person. I have to be. I work on building sites where there is a lot of cheap immigrant labour. I have a respect for people's rights to believe in whichever god they want to, and to attend whichever church or mosque they want to. But since 11th March 2004 I have become suspicious. Since that day, when 191 people died in those trains, I have wondered where the next attack is coming from. I am not a racist and I know that the terrorists are very few out of a large population, but the problem is that . . . I don't know who *they* are. They live with me, they live in my society, they enjoy its prosperity, until one day they decided to put a bomb under my apartment block and kill my wife and son. And there are many of us who have lived in suspicion and fear since 11th March until last Tuesday, 6th June. And now it is we who are angry.'

Barreda came back from the toilet. He had to go. Falcón followed him out into the heat and fierce light of the street. All his advantage and initiative had gone. They stood under the awning of the bar and shook hands. Barreda was back to normal. He'd recomposed himself in the toilet and perhaps been strengthened by listening to Fernando Alanis's speech on his way back.

'You didn't tell me what Ricardo said to you in that final phone call,' said Falcón.

429

'I'm embarrassed to have to talk about it after . . . what we've said about him.'

'Embarrassed?'

'I didn't realize how he felt about me,' said Barreda. 'But then . . . I'm not gay.'

30

'So why weren't all these other lines of enquiry written up in a report?' asked Comisario Elvira, looking from del Rey back to Falcón.

'As you know, I've been helping the CNI with one of their missions,' said Falcón. 'I've had to maintain the enquiry into this murder which happened prior to the bombing, and I've since acquired a suicide to investigate. However, all these enquiries, I believe, are linked and should be moved forward together. At no point have I deviated from my initial intention, which was to find out what happened in the destroyed building. You have to agree that there has been a breakdown of logic in the scenario, and it's my job to create different lines of enquiry to find the necessary logic to resolve it. I didn't hear what happened on television, but it has now been explained to me that it was the interviewer who interrupted Juez del Rey and said: "So you believe it was one of our own people that committed this atrocity?" It was *that* question which caused this public relations problem.'

'Problem? Public relations catastrophe,' said Elvira. 'Another one, on top of this morning's debacle.'

'Did you talk to Angel Zarrías of the *ABC*?' asked Falcón.

'We're a bit shy of the media right now,' said Elvira. 'Comisario Lobo and I are having a strategy meeting after this to see how we can repair the damage.'

'Juez del Rey has done a great job bringing himself up to speed on a very complicated and sensitive investigation,' said Falcón. 'We can't allow the thrust of our enquiry to be dictated by the media, who have seen an opportunity to manipulate a nervous population by playing games with us on television.'

'What we're playing with here is the truth,' said Elvira. 'The presentable truth and the acceptable truth. And it's all a question –'

'What about the *actual* truth?' said Falcón.

'And it's all a question,' said Elvira, nodding at his little slip, 'of timing. Which truth is released when.'

'Have the translations of the Arabic script attached to the drawings been completed?' asked Falcón.

'So you didn't see the news *before* we went on,' said Elvira. 'And nor did we, which was why the wretched interviewer seized on what Juez del Rey was saying. Only afterwards did we find out that the evacuations of the two schools and biology faculty had been filmed, *and* a translation of one of the Arabic texts was aired with it.

'Each text gave full instructions on how to close off each building, where to hold the hostages and where to place the explosives in order to ensure maximum loss of life, should special forces storm the building,' said del Rey. 'There was a final instruction in each text,

432

which was that one hostage – starting with the youngest child in the case of the schools – was to be released every hour and, as they made their way to freedom, they were to be shot, in full view of the media. This process was to continue until the Spanish government recognized Andalucía as an Islamic state under Sharia law.'

'Well, that explains why there was nearly a riot in the bar I was in,' said Falcón. 'How did the media get hold of the text?'

'It was delivered by motorbike to Canal Sur's reception in a brown padded envelope, addressed to the producer of current affairs,' said del Rey.

'An enquiry is underway,' said Elvira. 'What were you doing in this bar?'

'I was interviewing the last man to speak to Ricardo Gamero before he killed himself,' said Falcón. 'He's a sales manager at Informáticalidad.'

'This isn't the old guy who was seen talking to Gamero in the Archaeological Museum?' said del Rey.

'No. This was the last call Gamero made on his personal mobile,' said Falcón. 'I presume that all members of the CGI's antiterrorist squad would be vetted, Comisario, including their sexuality?'

'Of course,' said Elvira. 'Anybody with access to classified information is vetted to make sure they're not vulnerable.'

'So it would be known if Gamero was homosexual?'

'Absolutely . . . unless he was, you know, not practising . . . so to speak.'

'The guy I was talking to, Marco Barreda, was at cracking point when the bar went crazy. He knows something. I think he feels that whatever it is that *he* or *they* have got involved in, it has spiralled out of control. He's sick about Gamero's death, for a start. That was not part of the script.'

'And what script is that?' asked Elvira, who was desperate for one.

'I don't know,' said Falcón. 'But it's something that explains what happened in that mosque on Tuesday. If we had the manpower, I'd have the whole of Informáticalidad down at the Jefatura and interview them until they broke down.'

'So what did Marco Barreda say were Gamero's last words?' asked Elvira.

'That Gamero was in love with him,' said Falcón. 'He'd been reluctant to say anything because he was embarrassed about it. I thought it was significant that he'd been to the toilet. I'm sure he called someone and was given advice about what to say. He was at cracking point and then suddenly he seemed to be back on the rails.'

'So what have we got on Informáticalidad?'

'Nothing, apart from the fact that the apartment was bought with black money.'

'And what do you think this apartment was used for?'

'Surveillance of the mosque.'

'With what purpose?'

'With the purpose of attacking it, or enabling others to attack it.'

'For any particular reason?'

'Other than that they are an organization recruited from the Catholic Church and therefore representative of the religious Right and opposed to the influence of Islam in Spain, I'm not entirely sure. There might be a political or financial angle that I don't, as yet, know about.'

'You haven't got enough,' said Elvira. 'You've interviewed all the sales reps and you've tried to capitalize on Marco Barreda's vulnerability without success. All you have is an unsubstantiated theory to go on. How could you apply any more pressure? If you brought them down here, they'd come with lawyers attached. Then there'd be the media to contend with. You're going to need something much more solid than your instinct to break open Informáticalidad.'

'I'm also concerned that that was *all* they did,' said Falcón, nodding. 'Provide surveillance information and nothing more. In which case we could interview them for days and get no further than that. I need another link. I want the old guy seen talking to Gamero in the museum.'

'Did you show the drawing to Marco Barreda?' asked del Rey.

'No. I was concerned that it might not be a close enough likeness and I wanted to apply pressure to his vulnerable point, which was Ricardo Gamero.'

'What's your next move?'

'I'm going to take a look at all the board directors of Informáticalidad and the other companies in their group, including the holding company, Horizonte, and see if I can find a likeness to the sketch,' said Falcón. 'What are the CNI and CGI doing?'

'They're concerned with the future now,' said Elvira. 'Juan has gone back to Madrid. The others are using the names from this investigation to try to get leads to other cells or networks.'

'So we're on our own with this investigation here?'

'They'll only come back to us if we find, from the DNA sampling, that the Imam, or Hammad and Saoudi, weren't in the mosque at the time of the explosion,' said Elvira. 'As far as they're concerned, there's nothing more for them to extract from this situation and they're more worried about future attacks.'

Back in his office, Falcón ran an internet search for Informáticalidad and Horizonte and extracted photographs of the directors of all the individual companies, their groups and the holding company. As he scrolled through the search engine's results for Horizonte he came across a web page dedicated to the celebration of their fortieth anniversary in 2001. As he'd hoped, the page showed a banquet with more than twenty-five shots of the great and the good at their tables.

The memory is a strange organ. It seems to be random and yet it can be jogged into patterns by other senses. Falcón knew if he hadn't just seen him on television he would never have picked him out from all the other faces at the Horizonte candlelit, floral dinner. He stopped, scrolled back. It was unmistakably Jesús Alarcón, with his beautiful wife sitting three places to his right. He looked at the caption, which said nothing, other than this was a table belonging to Horizonte's bankers – Banco Omni. Well, that figured. Alarcón had been a banker in Madrid before he came to Seville. He printed out the page with all its photographs and left the Jefatura, Serrano having given him the name of the security guard at the Archaeological Museum.

The security guard was called to the ticket desk and Falcón showed him the photographs, which he flipped through quickly, shaking his head. He ran his finger over the fortieth anniversary banquet shots. Nothing jumped out at him.

It was too hot even for a quick snack under the purple flowers of the jacarandas in the park, and Falcón drove back into town with too much on his mind. Pablo from the CNI called and they agreed to meet in a bar on Calle Leon XII near the destroyed apartment building.

Falcón was there first. It was a downtrodden place. The staff hadn't bothered to clear away the ankle-deep fag butts, sugar sachets and paper napkins after the coffee-break rush. He ordered a gazpacho, which was a little fizzy, and a piece of tuna, which had less flavour than the plate it was served on, and the chips were soggy with oil. Things were going well. Pablo arrived and ordered a coffee.

'First thing,' he said, sitting down. 'Yacoub has made contact and we've given him his instructions on your behalf. He knows what to do now.'

'And what is that?'

'Yacoub belongs to two mosques. The first is in Rabat: the Grand Mosque Ahl-Fès, which is attended by the powerful and wealthy. It's not known for any radical Islamic stance. But he also belongs to a mosque in Salé, near his work, which is a different kind of place altogether, and Yacoub knows it. All he has to do is step over to the other side and start getting involved. He knows the people . . .'

'How does he know the people?'

'Javier,' said Pablo, with an admonishing look, 'don't ask. You don't have to know.'

'How dangerous is this going to be for him?' asked Falcón. 'I mean, radical Islam isn't known for its forgiving nature, and I imagine they're especially unforgiving when it comes to betrayal.'

'As long as he maintains his role there's no danger. He communicates with us at a distance. There's no face to face, which is where things normally come unstuck. If he needs to see anybody then he can organize a business trip to Madrid.'

'What happens if they take him over and start feeding us emails of disinformation?'

'There's a phrase he has to use in his correspondence with us. If that phrase isn't employed then we know it isn't him writing and we react accordingly.'

'How quickly will they come to trust him?' said Falcón. 'You've always been of the opinion that this bomb was a mistake, or a diversion. Maybe you're expecting an information return too quickly if you think that he can help you with attacks which have already been planned.'

'They'll recognize his value immediately . . .'

'Has he been approached by the GICM before?' asked Falcón, these things only just occurring to him.

'He's in a unique position because of his business,' said Pablo, pointedly ignoring Falcón's question. 'He can travel freely and is widely known, respected and trusted by his business partners. He will arouse no suspicion from the Moroccan authorities looking for radicals, or European authorities looking for terrorists or their planners. He's the perfect person for a terrorist organization to make use of.'

'But they'll test him first, surely?' said Falcón. 'I don't know how it works, but they might give him some valuable information and see what he does with it. See, for instance, if it appears elsewhere. Just like the CNI did with the CGI here in Seville, come to think of it.'

'That's *our* job, Javier. We know what we can use from him and what we can't. If we have information that could only possibly have come from him, then we know to be careful,' said Pablo. 'If he tells us that there's a GICM cell operating from an address in Barcelona, we don't just storm the building.'

'What's the other thing?'

'We want you to communicate with Yacoub tonight. There's nothing to be said, but we want him to know you're here and in touch with him.'

'Is that it?'

'Not quite. The CIA have come back to us with the identity of your mystery man with no hands or face.'

'That was quick.'

'They've developed quite a system over there for tracing people of Arabic origin, even when they've become American citizens,' said Pablo. 'Your model man did a good job with the face, and his identity was corroborated by the hernia op, tattoos and dental X-rays.'

'What were the tattoos?'

'On the webbing between thumb and forefinger he had four dots configured in a square on his right hand, and five dots on his left hand.'

'Any reason?'

'It helped him count,' said Pablo.

'Up to nine?'

'Apparently women never failed to comment on them.'

'*That* is on his *file*?' said Falcón, amazed.

'You'll see why when I tell you he was a professor in Arabic Studies at Columbia University until March last year, when he was fired after being found in bed with one of his students,' said Pablo. 'And you know how they found out? He was shopped by one of his other students who he was bedding at the same time.

'You don't do that sort of thing at an American university and get caught. The police were brought in. The girls' parents threatened to sue the university and then him personally. It was the end of his career – and it cost him, too. He managed to settle out of court on advice from his lawyers, who knew he would lose and that they wouldn't get paid. He had to sell his mid-town apartment, which had been left to him by his parents. The only job he could get after the case blew over was teaching maths privately in Columbus, Ohio. He lasted three months of a Mid West winter and then flew to Madrid in April last year.

'After that, our information gets a little sparse. We've a record of him taking a trip to Morocco for three weeks at the end of April. He took the ferry from Algeciras to Tangier on 24th April and he came back on 12th May. That's it.'

'Does he have a name?'

'His real name is Tateb Hassani,' said Pablo. 'When he became an American citizen in 1984 – which was also the year both his parents died, one in a car crash and the other of cancer – he changed his name to Jack Hansen. It's not so unusual for immigrants to anglicize their names. He was born in Fès in 1961 and his parents left Morocco in 1972. His father was a businessman who went back and forth frequently. Tateb only went back to Morocco twice in thirty years. He didn't like it. His parents forced him to maintain an Arabic educa-tion and his mother spoke to him only in French. He wrote and spoke Arabic fluently. He graduated in mathematics, but couldn't get a place as a post-graduate, so he switched to Arabic Studies and wrote a thesis on Arab mathematicians. He came out of Princeton with a doctorate in 1986. He spent time in the universities of Madison, Minnesota and San Francisco before ending up in New York. He had a good life: a university salary, with the rent from his parents' apartment coming in. Then, when he landed the professorship at Columbia, he took over the apartment and had the perfect existence, until he started sleeping with his students.'

'What about his religion?'

'He's down as a Muslim, but, as you might have gathered from his history, he'd let that lapse.'

'Was he known for any opinions about radical Islam?'

'You can read the file sent over by the CIA,' said Pablo, taking it out of his briefcase, laying it on the table. It looked to be about ten pages long.

'Are there any samples of his handwriting in here?' asked Falcón.

'Not that I've seen.'

'Can the CIA send some across to us?' asked Falcón, flicking through the pages. 'In both Arabic script and English.'

'I'll get them on to it.'

'Any other languages, apart from French, English and Arabic?'

'He spoke and wrote Spanish, too,' said Pablo. 'He used to give a maths course every summer over here at Granada University.'

'Comisario Elvira told me that you're not much interested in our investigation any more and that Juan has gone back to Madrid,' said Falcón. 'Does that mean you've cracked the code in the annotated versions of the Koran?'

'Juan's been called back to Madrid because there have been reports of other cells, not connected with Hammad and Saoudi, which are now on the move,' said Pablo. 'We're still interested in your investigation, but not in the way you are. And, no, we haven't cracked the code.'

'How's the diversion theory going?'

'Madrid have hit dead ends with the Hammad and Saoudi connections,' said Pablo. 'Arrests have been made, but it's the usual thing. They only knew what *they* were doing. They received encrypted emails and did what they were told to do. So far we've only picked up a few "associates" of Hammad and Saoudi, which hardly constitutes unravelling the whole network – if there was one to unravel. We're hoping Yacoub can help us there.'

'What about the MILA?'

'A story invented by the media based on some truth – that this group does, in fact, exist – but they weren't involved in any way,' said Pablo. 'It was a neat follow-on from the Abdullah Azzam text sent to the *ABC*. Something to capture the public's imagination, but, in the end, bogus. If you ask me, it's irresponsible journalism.'

'And VOMIT?' asked Falcón. 'Did you break them down, too?'

'That's not a priority for us,' said Pablo, riding over Falcón's irony. 'We're more concerned about future attacks on European countries which emanate from Spain rather than an enumeration of the past.'

'So nothing has changed?' said Falcón. 'You still

believe that Miguel Botín was a double, and he was instructed to give the electrician's card to the Imam by someone in his radical Islamic network?'

'I know you don't have any faith in it,' said Pablo, 'but we have more information than you do.'

'And you're not going to give it to me?'

'Ask your old friend, Mark Flowers,' said Pablo. 'I've got to go now.'

'You know, it was a set of keys from the Imam's kitchen drawer that opened the fireproof box recovered from the storeroom of the mosque,' said Falcón. 'Gregorio was with me when they opened it and he was very interested by that, although, as usual, he didn't say why the CNI was so fascinated.'

'This is just the way we have to be, Javier,' said Pablo. 'It's nothing personal, it's just the nature of our work and the work of others in our business.'

'Make sure you call me when the handwriting comes through from the CIA,' said Falcón.

'What do you want us to do with it?'

'You've got a handwriting expert back in Madrid, haven't you?'

'Sure.'

Falcón bowed his head and started flicking through Tateb Hassani's file. He knew it was childish, but he wanted to show that two could play at the withholding information game.

'Gregorio and I will come by your house tonight.'

He nodded, waited for Pablo to leave. He closed the file, sat back and let his mind wander. The television was on and the four o'clock news showed the evacuations of the schools and the biology faculty while the bomb squad went in with their dogs. Gradually, a palimpsest of the Arabic script found with the architect's drawings appeared over the action images with a voice-over of their translations. Cut to a journalist outside the school, trying to make something out of the fact that nothing, as yet, had been found on the premises.

The chair recently vacated by Pablo slid into Falcón's vision. He went back to the photographs of Horizonte's fortieth anniversary and the shot of Banco Omni's table. That's what he'd noticed: an empty chair next to Jesús Alarcón's wife, Mónica. A closer look showed that the chair had just been vacated by a man in a dark suit who was walking away. Against the dark background, only a cuff of shirt, a hand and his collar with some grey hair above it was visible.

The pre-school was empty, apart from a policewoman at the door and another on the computer in one of the classrooms. The stink from the bombsite did not make it a popular location to hang out. Falcón logged on to the internet and entered: *Horizonte: fortieth anniversary*. He clicked on the first article, which was from the business pages of the *ABC*. The byline jumped out at him because it was A. Zarrías. He read through the article just looking for a mention of Banco Omni. It was there, but no names. The photograph was of the Horizonte board at the dinner. He went for another article, which had been published in a business magazine. Again the byline was for A. Zarrías. Falcón clicked on five other articles, of which three had been placed by Angel. He must have been doing the PR for Horizonte's fortieth anniversary. Interesting. He entered Banco Omni and Horizonte into the search engine.

There were thousands of hits. He scrolled down

through the pages of hits until he got to articles written in 2001. He clicked on the articles, not reading them but checking who placed them. Angel Zarrías had written 80 per cent of them. So, when Angel had quit politics he'd gone into journalism, but he'd also picked up a lucrative sideline in PR with Banco Omni, who presumably put him in touch with Horizonte. He entered 'Banco Omni board of directors' into the search engine. He went back through the years, pulling up articles on to the screen. There were names, but never any photographs. In fact, the only photograph he could find of any employees of Banco Omni was from the table shot taken at Horizonte's fortieth anniversary banquet.

31

'It's taken me hours to get to speak to this person,' said Ferrera, 'but I think it's been worth it. I've got a . . . reliable witness to the dumping of the body which was later found on the rubbish dump outside Seville.'

'We now have a name for that body. He's called Tateb Hassani,' said Falcón. 'You didn't sound very sure of that word "reliable".'

'He drinks, which is never a good thing for a court to hear, and I'm not sure we could ever get him to court anyway.'

'Tell me what the guy saw and we'll worry about his credentials if it gets us anywhere.'

'He lives in an apartment at the end of a cul-de-sac just off Calle Boteros. His daughter owns the third and fourth floors of this building. She lives on the third and her father lives above. Both apartments have the perfect view of those bins on the corner of Calle Boteros.'

'I'm sure that's why the daughter bought them,' said Falcón. 'And what's this guy doing awake at three in the morning, looking out of his window?'

'He's an insomniac, or rather he can't sleep at night, only during the day,' she said. 'He sleeps from eight until four. The daughter wouldn't let me disturb him until she'd given him lunch. She knows that if she breaks his routine it'll be hell for her for a week.'

'He goes straight into lunch?' said Falcón. 'She doesn't give him breakfast?'

'He likes to drink wine, so she gives him something substantial to eat with it.'

'So, what's his problem exactly?'

'Quite unusual for a Sevillano: he's agoraphobic. He can't go outside and he can't bear more than two people in a room.'

'I see the problem with the court appearance now,' said Falcón. 'Anyway, he was awake at three in the morning, but not so drunk that he couldn't see what was going on by the bins.'

'He was drunk, but he says it doesn't affect his vision,' said Ferrera. 'Just after three o'clock on Sunday morning, he saw a large, dark estate car pull into the cul-de-sac and reverse back towards the bins. The driver and passenger got out of the front, both male, and a third man got out of the back. The driver stood in the middle of Calle Boteros, and looked up and down. The other men opened the boot. They checked the bins, which were empty at that time of night, tipped one of them on its side and leaned it against the rear of the car. They reached into the back and dragged something into the bin. They manoeuvred the bin, which now appeared heavy, back up to the pavement and returned to the rear of the car. They removed two black bin liners, which the witness described as bulky but light, and swung them into the bin on top of whatever they'd just put in there. They closed the bin. The driver slammed the boot shut. They got back into the car, reversed into Calle Boteros and headed off in the direction of the Alfalfa.'

'Could he give you anything on the three men?'

'He thought, from the way they moved, that the two guys who did the work were young – by that he meant around thirty. The driver was older, thicker around the waist. They were all dressed in dark clothes, but seemed to be wearing what looked like white gloves. I assume he means latex gloves. The driver and one of the younger men had dark hair and the third was either bald or had had his head shaved.'

'Not bad for an old drunk in an attic,' said Falcón.

'There's some street lighting on that corner,' said Ferrera. 'But, still . . . not bad for someone who his daughter says will drink until he falls over.'

'Just don't include that in his witness statement,' said Falcón. 'What about these two "bulky but light" bin liners they threw on top of the body?'

'He thought they probably contained something like gardening detritus – hedge clippings, that sort of thing.'

'Why?'

'He's seen that sort of stuff thrown in there before, but at the end of the afternoon, not at three in the morning.'

'Have you found any large houses in that area which might have that quantity of gardening detritus?' asked Falcón. 'It's mostly apartments around the Alfalfa.'

'They could have picked up a couple of bin liners of stuff from anywhere,' said Ferrera.

'If they'd done that, those bin liners would have

448

come out first, whereas, according to your friend, they dealt with "something heavy" first.'

'I'll see what I can find.'

'Come to think of it, Felipe and Jorge said they had a bin liner of clippings that they'd picked up near the body on the rubbish dump,' said Falcón. 'I'll see if they've had time to have a look at it, yet.'

Ramírez called as Falcón was on his way out to the forensics' tent.

'The Imam's mobile phone records,' said Ramírez. 'The CNI have got them and they won't release them to me. Or rather, Pablo said he would look into it, but now he doesn't take or return my calls.'

'I'll see what I can do,' said Falcón.

The forensic tent was filled with more than twenty masked and boiler-suited individuals who were impossible to differentiate. Falcón called Felipe and told him to come outside. Felipe remembered the gardening detritus, which he'd also had a chance to look at.

'It was all from the same type of hedge,' he said. 'The kind they use in ornamental gardens. Box hedge. Small, shiny, dark green leaves.'

'How fresh was it?'

'It had been cut that weekend. Friday afternoon or Saturday.'

'Any idea how much hedge we'd be looking at?'

'Remember, that might have been just part of the clippings,' said Felipe. 'And I live in an apartment. Hedges are not my speciality.'

Calderón was lying on the fold-down bed in his police cell. His head was resting on his hands, while his eyes stared at four squares of white sunlight high on the wall above the door. When he closed his eyes the four squares burned red on the inside of his eyelids. If he looked into the darkness of the cell they smouldered greenly. He was calm enough for this. He had been calm since the moment he'd been caught trying to get rid of Inés. Get rid of Inés? How had that phrase broken its way into his lexicon?

They'd brought him down to the Jefatura in the early-morning summer light. He was shirtless because the forensics had bagged that horrifically blood-stained garment. The cops had the air conditioning on even at that hour and his nipples were hard and he was shivering. As they crossed the river, two rowing eights, out for early training, slipped under the bridge and he had the sensation of an enormous weight coming off his shoulders. The relaxing of the muscles in his neck and between his scapulae was almost erotic. It was a powerful post-fear drug that his body chemistry had concocted, and it had the awkward result of arousing him.

He had gone through the process of incarceration dumbly, like an animal for slaughter, moving from transport, to pen, to holding cell with no idea of the implications. A DNA swab had been taken from the inside of his cheek, he'd been photographed and given an orange short-sleeve shirt. The relief of finally being left alone, with no possessions, his belt removed, and just a pack of cigarettes, was immense. His tiredness drew him to the bed. He kicked off his loafers and sank back on the hard bunk and fell into a dreamless sleep, until he was woken at three in the afternoon for lunch. He'd eaten and applied his ferocious intellect to what he was going to say in his interview with the detective before falling into this dazed state of looking at the squares of light on the wall. It was unexpectedly pleasant to be released from the oppression of time. At five o'clock the guard came to tell him that Inspector Jefe Luis Zorrita was ready to interview him.

'You are, of course, allowed to have your lawyer present,' said Zorrita, coming into the interview room.

'I *am* a lawyer,' said Calderón, still with all his pre-crime arrogance. 'Let's get on with it.'

Zorrita made the introductions to the tape and asked Calderón to confirm that he'd been given the opportunity to have a lawyer present, and had declined.

'I didn't want to talk to you until I'd had the full autopsy report from the Médico Forense,' said Zorrita. 'Now I've got that and had the opportunity to conduct my preliminary enquiries . . .'

'What sort of preliminary enquiries?' asked Calderón, just to show that he wasn't going to be passive.

'I've more or less established what you and your wife had been doing over the last twenty-four hours before her murder.'

'More or less?'

'There are still some details to fill in on what your wife was doing yesterday afternoon. That's all,' said Zorrita. 'So what I'd like you to do, Sr Calderón, is to tell me, in your own words, what happened last night.'

'From what time?'

'Well, let's start from the moment you left the Canal Sur studios and arrived at your lover's apartment,' said Zorrita. 'The time before that is well accounted for.'

'My lover?'

'That was the word Marisa Moreno used to describe your relationship,' said Zorrita, looking through his

451

notes. 'She was firm about not wanting to be called your mistress.'

That admission from Marisa made him feel quite sentimental. How ridiculous it was that a police enquiry had drawn that from her. Having not thought about her very much since being arrested, he suddenly missed her.

'Is that a fair description?' asked Zorrita. 'From your point of view?'

'Yes, I would say that we were lovers. We'd known each other for nine months or so.'

'It would explain why she was doing her best to protect you.'

'Protect me?'

'She was trying to make out that you'd left her apartment later than you had, which would have made it more difficult for you to have murdered your wife . . .'

'I did *not* kill my wife,' said Calderón, summoning the full severity of his professional voice.

'. . . but she "forgot" that she'd called a taxi for you and that we can access all the phone records, as well as the cab company logs, and talk to the driver himself, of course. So her attempts to help you were, I'm afraid, quite futile.'

The interview was not following the pattern that Calderón had outlined to himself in his lawyer's mind while lying on his bunk. He'd witnessed only a few police interrogations in his time as a judge and so had little idea of the way in which they moved. It was for this reason that, barely a minute into his interview with Zorrita, he was in a quandary. Warmed by the thought that Marisa had called him her lover, but chilled by the idea that she believed he needed her help, which had ugly implications. The effect of these two extremes of temperature alive in his body was to undermine his equilibrium. His thoughts would not line up in their usual orderly fashion, but seemed to mill around, like shoals of children careering around the school playground.

'So, Sr Calderón, please tell me when you arrived at your lover's apartment.'

'It must have been about 12.45.'

'And what did you do?'

'We went out on to the balcony and made love.'

'Made love?' said Zorrita, deadpan. 'You didn't indulge in anal sex, by any chance?'

'Certainly not.'

'You seem very firm about that,' said Zorrita. 'And I only ask you such a personal question because the autopsy revealed that your wife seemed to be accustomed to being penetrated in this fashion.'

Panic rose in Calderón's chest. He had lost control of the interview in a matter of a few exchanges. His arrogance had cost him dear. His assumption that he could trounce Zorrita in any mind or word game had proved to be wide of the mark. This was a man who was used to the wiliness of criminals, and had come to the interview with a clear strategy, which made Calderón's analytical brain seem worthless.

'We made love,' said Calderón, unable to add anything more without making it sound like some biological transaction.

'Would you say that these two relationships generally worked in this fashion?' asked Zorrita. 'You treated your lover with respect and admiration, while abusing your wife as if she was some cheap whore.'

453

Outrage was the first emotion that leapt into Calderón's throat, but he was learning. He saw Zorrita's two interrogating weapons: emotional stabs, followed by logical bludgeon.

'I did not treat my wife like a cheap whore.'

'You're right, of course, because not even a cheap whore allows herself to be beaten up *and* sodomized for no money at all.'

Silence. Calderón gripped the edge of the table so hard his nails whitened with the pressure. Zorrita was unconcerned.

'At least you don't have the temerity to deny that you treated your wife in such shameful fashion,' said Zorrita. 'I presume your lover didn't know these two sides to your personality?'

'Who the fuck do you think you are, to presume to know anything about my relationship with my wife, or my lover?' said Calderón through lips gone bloodless with rage. 'Some fucking Inspector Jefe, come down from Madrid . . .'

'Now I can see why your wife would be terrified of you, Sr Calderón,' said Zorrita. 'Underneath that brilliant legal mind, you're a very angry man.'

'I am not fucking angry,' said Calderón, pounding the table hard enough to jog a hank of his hair loose. '*You* are *goading* me, Inspector Jefe.'

'If I'm goading you, I'm not doing it by shouting at you or insulting you. I'm only doing it by asking you questions based on proven fact. The autopsy has revealed that you sodomized your wife and that you beat her up so badly that some of her vital organs were damaged. There's also a history of humiliation, which even extended to pursuing an affair with another woman on the same day that you announced your engagement to your wife.'

'Who've you been talking to?' asked Calderón, still unable to control his fury.

'As you know, I've only had today to work on this case, but I've managed to talk to your lover, which was a very interesting conversation, and a number of your colleagues and your wife's colleagues. I've also spoken to some of the secretaries in the Edificio de los Juzgados and the Palacio de Justicia, and the security guards, of course, who see everything. Of the twenty-odd interviews I've conducted so far, not one person has been prepared to defend your behaviour. The least emotional description of your activities was "an incorrigible womanizer".'

'What was so interesting about your conversation with Marisa?' asked Calderón, unable to resist the bait of that remark.

'She was telling me about a conversation you had about marriage. Do you remember that?' asked Zorrita.

Calderón blinked against the rush of memory; too much had happened in too short a time.

'The reason you married Inés . . . Maddy Krugman? How Inés represented stability after that . . . catastrophic affair?'

'What are you trying to do here, Inspector Jefe?'

'Jog your memory, Sr Calderón. You were there, I wasn't. I've only spoken to Marisa. You talked about "the bourgeois institution of marriage" and how she, Marisa, wasn't interested in it. You agreed with her, didn't you?'

'What do you mean?' asked Calderón.

'You weren't happy in your marriage, but you didn't want to get divorced. Why was that?' asked Zorrita.

Calderón couldn't believe it. He was in the elephant pit again. He pulled himself together this time.

'I believe that once you've made a commitment before God, in church, you should adhere to it,' he said.

'But that wasn't what you said to your lover, was it?'

'What did I say to her?'

'You said: "It's not so easy." What did you mean by that, Sr Calderón? It's not as if we're living in fear of excommunication any more. Breaking your vows wasn't your concern. So what were you worried about?'

Even Calderón's giant brain couldn't compute the numerous possible answers to this question in less than half a minute. Zorrita sat back and watched the judge agonize over everything except the truth of the matter.

'It's not that difficult a question,' said Zorrita, after a full minute's silence. 'Everybody knows what the repercussions of divorce are. If you want to extricate yourself from a legal commitment, you're going to lose out. What were you afraid of losing, Sr Calderón?'

Put like that, it didn't seem so bad. Yes, it *was* a common fear for men facing divorce. And he was no different.

'The usual things,' he said, finally. 'I was worried about my financial situation and my apartment. It was never a serious possibility. Inés was the only woman I'd ever . . .'

'Were you concerned, as well, that it might affect your social status, and perhaps your job?' asked Zorrita. 'I understand your wife had been very supportive of you after the Maddy Krugman debacle. Your colleagues said she helped you to get your career back on track.'

His colleagues had said that?

'There was never any serious threat to my career,' said Calderón. 'There was no question that I would be appointed as the Juez de Instrucción for something as important as the Seville bombing, for instance.'

'Your lover offered you a solution to the problem, though, didn't she?' said Zorrita.

'What problem?' said Calderón, confused. 'I just said there was no problem with my career, and Marisa –'

'The awkward problem of the divorce.'

Silence. Calderón's memory baffled around his head, like a moth seeking the light.

'"The bourgeois solution to the bourgeois problem",' said Zorrita.

'Oh, you mean that I could kill her,' said Calderón, snorting with derisive laughter. 'That was just a silly joke.'

'Yes, on *her* part,' said Zorrita. 'But how did it affect your mind? That's the question.'

'It was ridiculous. An absurdity. We *both* laughed at it.'

'That's what Marisa said, but how did it affect *your* mind?'

Silence.

'It never, for one moment, entered my mind to kill my wife,' said Calderón. 'And I *didn't* kill her.'

'When did you first beat your wife, Sr Calderón?'

This interview was like a steeplechase, with the fences getting higher as he progressed around the course. Zorrita watched the internal struggle that he'd seen so many times before: the unacceptable truth, followed by the necessary delusion, and the attempt to construct a lie from those two unreliable sources.

'Had you beaten her before the beginning of this week?' asked Zorrita.

'No,' he said firmly, but instantly realized that it implied some admission of guilt.

'That's cleared something up,' said Zorrita, making a note. 'It was difficult for the Médico Forense to establish the occurrence of the first beating you gave her because, well, as I understand it, old bruising isn't as easy to measure as say . . . body temperature. Dating old bruising is a difficult business . . . as is organ rupture and internal bleeding.'

'Look,' said Calderón, inwardly gasping at these shocking revelations, 'I know what you're trying to do.'

'I'd really like to establish a specific time when you first beat Inés. Was it Sunday night or Monday morning?'

'They weren't beatings, they were accidents,' said Calderón, aghast that he'd used the plural now. 'And, whatever the case, it does not mean that I murdered my wife . . . I didn't.'

'But did the first beating occur on Sunday or Monday?' asked Zorrita. 'Or was it Tuesday? Of course, you used the plural. So it was probably Sunday, Monday, Tuesday and then, finally and tragically, Wednesday, and we'll never be able to attribute what bruise to which day. What time did you get back on Tuesday morning, having spent the night with Marisa?'

'It was around 6.30 a.m.'

'Well, that squares with what Marisa said. And was Inés asleep?'

'I thought she was.'

'But she wasn't,' said Zorrita. 'She woke up, didn't she? And what did she do?'

458

'All right, she found my digital camera and started downloading the images I had on it. They included two shots of Marisa.'

'You must have been *very* angry when you found out. When you came across her in the act, caught her red-handed,' said Zorrita, not quite able to ease back on his relish. 'She was very fragile, your wife, wasn't she? The Médico Forense estimates her weight before the catastrophic blood loss as 47 kilos.'

'Look, we were in the kitchen, I just brushed her aside,' said Calderón. 'I didn't realize my own strength or her fragility. She fell awkwardly against the kitchen counter. It's made out of granite.'

'But that doesn't explain the fist mark on her abdomen, or the toe mark over her left kidney, or the amount of her hair we've found distributed around your apartment.'

Calderón sat back. His hands fell from the edge of the table. He was not a career criminal and he was finding resistance very hard work. The only time he could remember having to trump up such a quantity of lies was when he'd been a small boy.

'As I swept her aside I must have tapped her diaphragm. She hit the counter and came down on my foot.'

'The autopsy found a ruptured spleen and a bleeding kidney,' said Zorrita. 'I think it was less of a tap and more of a punch, wasn't it, Sr Calderón? The Médico Forense thinks from the shape of the bruise around her loin area and the darker red imprint of a toenail, that it was more of a kick with a bare foot than someone "falling" on to a foot, which would, of course, be flat on the floor.'

Silence.

'And all that took place on Tuesday morning?'

'Yes,' said Calderón.

'How long was that after your lover's little joke about solving the problem of your divorce?'

'Her joke had nothing to do with that.'

'All right, when was the next time you beat your wife?' asked Zorrita. 'Was it after you found out that your wife and lover had accidentally met in the Murillo Gardens?'

'How the fuck do you know that?' asked Calderón.

'I asked Marisa if she'd ever met your wife,' said Zorrita, 'and she started off by lying to me. Why did she do that, do you think?'

'I don't know.'

'She said she hadn't, but you know, I've been interviewing liars more than half my working life and after a while it's like dealing with children; you become so practised at reading the signs that their attempts become laughable. So why do you think she lied on your behalf?'

'On *my* behalf?' asked Calderón. 'She didn't do anything on my behalf.'

'Why didn't she want me to know that she had had this . . . vocal confrontation with your late wife?'

'I've no idea.'

'Because *she* was still angry about it, Sr Calderón, that's why,' said Zorrita. 'And if she was angry about being insulted by your wife, about being called a whore, in public, by your wife . . . I'm wondering how she made you feel about it . . . Well, she told me.'

'She *told* you?'

'Oh, she tried to protect you again, Sr Calderón. She

460

tried to make it sound like nothing. She kept repeating: "Esteban's not a violent man," that you were just "annoyed", but I think she also realized just how very, very angry you were. What did you do on the night that Marisa told you Inés had called her a whore?'

More silence from Calderón. He'd never found it so difficult to articulate. He was too stoked up with emotion to find the right reply.

'Was that the night you came home and pummelled your wife's breasts and whipped her with your belt so that the buckle cut into her buttocks and thighs?'

He'd come into this interview with a sense of resistance as dense and powerful as a reinforced concrete dam, and within half an hour of questioning all that was left were some cracked and frayed bean canes. And then they caved in. He saw himself in front of a state prosecutor, facing these same questions, and he realized the hopelessness of his situation.

'Yes,' he said, on automatic, unable to find even the schoolboy creativity to invent the ridiculous lie to obscure his brutality. There was nothing ambiguous about the welt of a belt and the gouge of its buckle.

'Why don't you talk me through what happened on the last night of your wife's life,' said Zorrita. 'Earlier we'd reached the moment when you'd just made love to Marisa on the balcony.'

Calderón's eyes found a point midway between himself and Zorrita, which he examined with the unnerving intensity of a man spiralling down to the darker regions of himself. He'd never had these things said to him before. He'd never had these things revealed to him under such emotional circumstances. He was stunned by his brutality and he couldn't understand where, in all his urbanity, it came from. He even tried to imagine himself dealing out these beatings to Inés, but they wouldn't come to him. He did not see himself like that. He did not see Esteban Calderón's fists raining down on his fine-boned wife. It *had* been him, there was no doubt about that. He saw himself before and after the act. He remembered the anger building up to the beatings and it subsiding afterwards. It struck him that he had been in the grip of a blind savagery, a violence so intense that it had no place in his civilized frame. A terrifying doubt began to crowd his chest and affect the motor reflex of his breathing, so that he had to concentrate: in, out, in, out. And it was there, in the lowest and darkest circle of his spiralling thoughts, the completely lightless zone of his soul, that he realized that he *could* have murdered her. Javier Falcón had told him once that there was no greater denial than that of a man who had murdered his wife. The thought terrified him into a state of profound concentration. He'd never looked with such microscopic detail into his mind before. He began to talk, but as if he was describing a film, scene by horrible scene.

'He was exhausted. He had been completely drained by the experiences of the day. He stumbled into the bedroom, collapsed on to the bed and passed out immediately. He was aware only of pain. He lashed out wildly with his foot. He woke up with no idea where he was. She told him he had to get up. It was past three o'clock. He had to go home. He couldn't wear the same clothes as he had yesterday and appear on television. She called a taxi. She took him down in the lift. He wanted to sleep on her shoulder in the street. The cab arrived and she spoke to the driver. He fell into the back seat and his head rolled back. He was only vaguely aware of movement and of light flashing behind his eyelids. The door opened. Hands pulled at him. He gave the driver his house keys. The driver opened the door to the building. He slapped on the light. They walked up the stairs together. The driver opened the apartment door. Two turns of the lock. The driver went back down the stairs. The hall light went out. He went into the apartment and saw light coming from the kitchen. He was annoyed. He didn't want to see her. He didn't want to have to explain . . . again. He moved towards the light . . .'

Calderón paused, because he was suddenly unsure of what he was going to see.

'His foot crossed the edge of the shadow and stepped into the light. He turned into the frame.'

Calderón was blinking at the tears in his eyes. He was so relieved to see her standing there at the sink in her nightdress. She turned when she heard his foot-fall. He was going to skirt the table and pull her to him and squeeze his love into her, but he couldn't move because when she turned she didn't open her arms to him, she didn't smile, her dark eyes did not glisten with joy . . . they opened wide with abject terror.

'And what happened?' asked Zorrita.

'What?' asked Calderón, as if coming to.

'You turned into the kitchen doorway and what did you do?' asked Zorrita.

'I don't know,' said Calderón, surprised to find his cheeks wet. He wiped them with the flat of his palms and brushed them down his trousers.

'It's not unusual for people to have blank moments about terrible things that they have done,' said Zorrita.

'Tell me what you saw when you turned into the doorway of the kitchen.'

'She was standing at the kitchen sink,' he said. 'I was so happy to see her.'

'Happy?' said Zorrita. 'I thought you were annoyed.'

'No,' he said, holding his head in his hands. 'No, it was . . . I was lying on the floor.'

'*You* were lying on the floor?'

'Yes. I woke up on the floor in the corridor and I went back to the kitchen light and it was then that I saw Inés lying on the floor,' he said. 'There was a terrible quantity of blood and it was very, very red.'

'But *how* did she end up lying on the floor?' asked Zorrita. 'One moment she was standing and the next she's lying on the floor in a pool of blood. What did you do to her?'

'I don't know that she *was* standing,' said Calderón, searching his mind for that image to see if it really existed.

'Let me tell you a few facts about your wife's murder, Sr Calderón. As you said, the cab driver opened the door of the apartment for you, with two turns of the key in the lock. That means the door had been double locked from the inside. Your wife was the only person in the apartment.'

'Ye-e-e-s,' said Calderón, concentrating on Zorrita's every syllable, hoping they would give him the vital clue that would unlock his memory.

'When the Médico Forense took your wife's body temperature down by the river it was 36.1°C. She was still warm. The ambient temperature last night was 29°C. That means your wife had just been killed. The autopsy revealed that your wife's skull had been smashed at the back, that there had been a devastating cerebral haemorrhage and two neck vertebrae had been shattered. Examination of the crime scene has revealed blood and hair on the black granite work surface and a further large quantity of blood on the floor next to your wife's head which also contained bone fragments and cerebral matter. The DNA samples taken from your apartment belong only to you and to your wife. The shirt that was taken from you down by the river was covered in your wife's blood. Your wife's body showed indications of your DNA on her face, neck and lower limbs. The scene in the kitchen of your apartment was consistent with someone who had picked Inés up by the shoulders or neck and thrown her down on the granite work surface. Is that what you did, Sr Calderón?'

'I only wanted to embrace her,' said Calderón, whose face had broken up into the ugliness of his inner turmoil. 'I just wanted to hold her close.'

32

The Taberna Coloniales was at the end of the Plaza Cristo de Burgos. There was something colonial about its green windows, long wooden bar and stone floor. It was well known for the excellence of its tapas and it was popular for its traditional interior and the seating outside on the pavement of the plaza. This was Angel and Manuela's local. Falcón didn't want Angel's journalistic nose anywhere near the police work around the destroyed apartment block, nor did he want to have to discuss anything sensitive in the glass cylinder of the *ABC* offices on the Isla de la Cartuja. Most important of all, he needed to be close to Angel's home so that there would be the least trouble possible for him to give Falcón what he wanted. This was why he was sitting outside the Taberna Coloniales under a calico umbrella, sipping a beer and biting into the chilled flesh of a fat green olive, waiting for Angel to appear.

He took a call from Pablo.

'The Americans have sent over the handwriting samples you asked for – the Arabic and English script belonging to Jack Hansen.'

'He looks more like a Tateb Hassani to me than a Jack Hansen,' said Falcón.

'What do you want us to do with the samples?'

'Ask your handwriting experts to make a comparison between Tateb Hassani's Arabic script and the notes attached to the drawings found in the fireproof box in the mosque. And compare the English script to the handwritten notes in the copies of the Koran found in the Peugeot Partner and Miguel Botín's apartment.'

'You think he was one of them?' asked Pablo. 'I don't get it.'

'Let's make the comparison first and the deductions afterwards,' said Falcón. 'And, by the way, the Imam's mobile phone records – we need to have a look at them. One of those numbers he called on Sunday morning belongs to the electrician.'

'I've spoken to Juan about that,' said Pablo. 'Gregorio's checked out all the numbers the Imam called on Sunday morning. The only one he couldn't account for was made to a phone registered in the name of a seventy-four-year-old woman living in Seville Este who has never been an electrician.'

'I'd like access to those records,' said Falcón.

'That's something else for you to talk to your old friend Flowers about,' said Pablo, and hung up.

Falcón sipped his beer and tried to persuade himself that he was calm, and that the present strategy was the right one. He'd taken Serrano and Baena away from their task of touring the building sites looking for the electricians, and had directed them to help Ferrera locate the hedge whose clippings had been dumped with the body. Ramírez and Pérez had photographs of Tateb Hassani and were walking the streets around the

Alfalfa trying to find anybody who recognized him. This meant that no one from the homicide squad was now working on anything directly linked to the Seville bombing. He wasn't worried about Elvira for the moment. The Comisario had his hands too full of public relations problems to be worried about the gamble Falcón was taking.

'For a man who's supposed to be running the largest criminal investigation in Seville's history, you're looking remarkably relaxed, Javier,' said Angel, taking a seat, ordering a beer.

'We have to present a calm exterior to a nervous population who need to believe that somebody has everything under control,' said Falcón.

'Does that mean that it isn't under control?' asked Angel.

'Comisario Elvira is doing a good job.'

'He might be, from the policeman's point of view,' said Angel. 'But he doesn't imbue the general public with confidence in his ability. He's a public relations disaster, Javier. What was he thinking of, asking that poor bastard . . . the judge . . .'

'Sergio del Rey.'

'Yes – him. Putting him on national television when the guy could barely have had time to read the files, let alone comprehend the emotional aspect of the case,' said Angel. 'The Comisario must know by now that television is not about the truth. Is he the kind of guy who watches reality TV and thinks that it *is* reality?'

'Don't be too hard on him, Angel. He's got a lot of excellent qualities that just don't happen to suit the televisual age.'

'Well, unfortunately, that's the age we're in now,'

said Angel. 'Now, Calderón, he was *the* man. He gave the TV what it craves: drama, humour, emotion and brilliant surface. He was a huge loss to your effort.'

'You said it: "brilliant surface". It wasn't so pretty underneath.'

'And how do you think you look now?' asked Angel. 'Remember the London bombings? What was the story that kept rolling out in the days after those attacks? The story that maintained the emotional pitch and focused the emotions? Not the victims. Not the terrorists. Not the bombs and the disruption. That was all part of it, but the big story was the mistaken shooting by plainclothes special policemen of that Brazilian guy, Jean Charles de Menezes.'

'And what's our big story?'

'That's your problem. It's the arrest, under suspicion of his wife's murder, of the Juez de Instrucción of the whole investigation. Have you seen the stuff coming out of the television about Calderón? Just listen . . .'

The tables around them had filled up and a crowd had gathered outside the open doors of the bar. They were all talking about Esteban Calderón. Did he do it? Didn't he do it?

'Not your investigation. Not the terrorist cells that might be active in Seville at the moment. Not even the little girl who survived the collapse of the building,' said Angel. 'It's all about Esteban Calderón. Tell Comisario Elvira that.'

'I have to say, Angel, that for a man who loves Seville more than almost anyone I know, you seem . . . buoyant.'

'It's terrible, isn't it? I am. I haven't felt as energized

in years. Manuela's infuriated. I think she preferred me when I was dying of boredom.'

'How is she?'

'Depressed. She thinks she's got to sell the house in El Puerto de Santa María. In fact she *is* selling it,' said Angel. 'She's lost her nerve. This whole idea of the Islamic "liberation" of Andalucía has taken hold in her mind. So now she's selling the gold mine to save the tin and copper mines.'

'There's no talking to her when she's like that,' said Falcón. 'So, why are you so buoyant, Angel?'

'If you're not watching the news very much you probably don't know that my little hobby is doing rather well.'

'You mean Fuerza Andalucía?' said Falcón. 'I saw Jesús Alarcón with Fernando Alanis on television a few hours ago.'

'Did you see the whole thing? It was sensational. After that programme Fuerza Andalucía picked up 14 per cent in the polls. Wildly inaccurate, I know. It's all emotional reaction, but that's 10 per cent more than we've ever polled before, and the Left are floundering.'

'When did you first meet Jesús Alarcón?' asked Falcón, genuinely curious.

'Years ago,' said Angel, 'and I didn't much care for him. He was a bit of a boring banker type and I was dismayed when he said he wanted to go into politics. I didn't think anybody would vote for him. He was a stiff in a suit. And as you know, these days it's not about your policies or your grasp of regional politics, it's all about how you come across. But I've got to know him better since he came down here and, I tell you, this relationship he's developed with Fernando

Alanis . . . it's gold dust. As a PR man, you just dream of something like that.'

'Was that the first time you met him – when you were doing PR work?'

'When I left politics I did a PR commission for Banco Omni.'

'That must have been nice work to walk into,' said Falcón.

'We Catholics stick together,' said Angel, winking. 'Actually, the Chief Executive Officer and I are old friends. We went to school, university, did our national service together. When I finished with those wankers in the Partido Popular, he knew that I wouldn't be able to just "retire", so he commissioned me and it led to other things. They were the bankers for a group in Barcelona and I did their fortieth anniversary PR for them; then there was an insurance group in Madrid, and a property company on the Costa del Sol. There was a business for me if I could have been bothered with it. But, you know, Javier, corporate PR, it's so . . . small. You're not going to change the world doing that shit.'

'You didn't change it in politics.'

'To tell you the truth, the PP was no different. It *was* like working for a huge corporation: play safe, toe the party line, everything happening by millimetres, no striding out to new horizons and changing the way people think and live.'

'Who wants change?' said Falcón. 'Most people hate change so much that we have to have wars and revolutions to bring it about.'

'But look at us now, Javier, talking like this in a bar,' said Angel. 'Why? Because we're in crisis. Our way of life is being threatened.'

'You said it yourself, Angel. Most people can't cope with it, so what *do* they talk about?'

'You're right. It's Esteban Calderón on everybody's lips,' said Angel. 'But at least it's not the usual trivia. It's tragedy. It's hubris bringing down the great man.'

'So what would you tell Comisario Elvira to do now?' asked Falcón.

'Aha! Is this what it's all about, Javier?' said Angel, smirking. 'You've brought me down here to get some free advice for your boss.'

'I want the PR man's take on the world.'

'You have to focus, and you have to focus on certainty. Because of the nature of the attack it's been difficult for you, but now you've finally got into the mosque it's time for you to reveal more and be specific. The evacuations of the schools and university buildings, what's that all about? People need a bone to chew on; uncertainty creates rumour, which does nothing to quell panic. Juez del Rey's mistake was that he hadn't taken the pulse of the city, so when he started spreading uncertainty again . . .'

'It was the interviewer's question that spread uncertainty,' said Falcón.

'That wasn't the way the viewers saw it.'

'Del Rey only found out afterwards that someone had leaked the Arabic script.'

'Del Rey should never have presented the truth of the situation: that there is still considerable confusion about what went on in that mosque. He should have pressed home the certainties. If, in the end, the truth happens to be something else, you just change your story. Your investigation lost a lot of its credibility when your spokesman was arrested for murder. The only chance of regaining that credibility lies in confirming the public's suspicions. The interviewer *knew* that the public would be in no mood to be told that there *might* be a homegrown element to this terrorist plot.'

'Elvira has trouble deciding when to use what kind of truth so that his investigation can get on with the business of finding out what actually happened,' said Falcón.

'Politics is great preparation for that,' said Angel.

'So you think Jesús Alarcón has got what it takes?'

'He's made a good start, but it's too early to say. It's what's going to happen six or seven months from now that's important,' said Angel. 'He's riding a big wave of public emotion now, but even the biggest waves end up as ripples on the beach.'

'He could always go back to the Banco Omni if it didn't work out.'

'They wouldn't have him,' said Angel. 'You don't *leave* the Banco Omni. Once they've given you a job, they take you into their confidence. If you leave them and become an outsider, that's where you remain.'

'So, Jesús is taking some risks.'

'Not really. He had a good introduction from my friend, who thinks very highly of him. He'll find him something else to do if it all comes to nothing.'

'Have I met this mysterious friend of yours?'

'Lucrecio Arenas? I don't know. Manuela's met him. He's not so mysterious now that he's retired.'

'You mean he was mysterious before?'

'Banco Omni is a private bank. It runs a hefty percentage of the Catholic Church's finances. It's a secretive organization. You won't even see any photographs of Banco Omni executives. I did a specific PR job for them, but I only got that job because of Lucrecio. I found out nothing about the organization, other than what I needed to know in order to perform my task,' said Angel. 'Why *are* we talking about Banco Omni?'

'Because Jesús Alarcón is the man of the moment,' said Falcón. 'After Esteban Calderón.'

'Ah, yes. You still haven't told me what you want to see me about,' said Angel.

'I'm sounding you out, Angel,' said Falcón, shrugging. 'I told Elvira about our conversation earlier today when you offered to help us, but he's wary. I want to be able to go back to him and make him feel better about employing your talents. He just needs to be pushed, that's all.'

'I'm prepared to help in a crisis,' said Angel. 'But I'm not looking for permanent work.'

'Elvira's problem is that he sees you as a journalist, and therefore the enemy,' said Falcón. 'If I can talk to him about your PR activity and the sort of clients you've represented, that will give him a different perspective.'

'I'll give advice but I won't be employed,' said Angel. 'Some might think there was a conflict of interest.'

'Just give me some other company names that you've worked for,' said Falcón. 'Who was it you represented for their fortieth anniversary?'

'Horizonte. The property company was called Mejorvista and the insurance group was Vigilancia,' said Angel. 'Don't promote me too much, Javier. I've got my work cut out steering Fuerza Andalucía through the media maze.'

'The only thing is that PR is a difficult concept to sell. Other people's press cuttings are meaningless. If I

474

could show Elvira the quality of the people you've worked for, that might help. Have you got shots of the people at Horizonte, or Banco Omni, or something from the Horizonte fortieth anniversary celebrations? You know, pictures of Angel Zarrías with senior executives. Elvira likes tangible things.'

'Of course, Javier, anything for you. Just don't over-sell me.'

'We're in crisis,' said Falcón. '*Both* our instructing judges have been discredited. We *have* to rebuild our image before it's too late. Elvira is a good policeman, and I don't want to see him fail just because he doesn't know how to play the media game.'

They went up to the apartment. Manuela wasn't there. It was a huge, four-bedroomed place, with two of the bedrooms used as offices. Angel walked to the wall of his study and pointed at a shot in the middle.

'That's the one you want,' he said, tapping a framed photograph in the centre of the wall. 'That's a rare shot of all the executives of Horizonte and Banco Omni in the same place. It was taken for the fortieth anniversary event. I've got a copy of it somewhere.'

Angel sat at his desk, opened a drawer and went through a stack of photographs. Falcón searched the shot for a likeness of the police artist's drawing of the man seen with Ricardo Gamero.

'Which one is Lucrecio Arenas?' asked Falcón. 'I don't see anybody I recognize here. If I'd met him, where would that have been?'

'He has a house in Seville, although he doesn't live in it for half the year. His wife can't stand the heat so they go and live in some palatial villa, built for them by Mejorvista, down in Marbella,' said Angel. 'You remember that big dinner I had in the Restaurante La Juderia last October? He was there.'

'I was away teaching a course at the police academy.'

Angel gave him the shot and pointed out Lucrecio Arenas, who was in the centre, while Angel was on the very edge of the two rows of men. Arenas had similarities to the police artist's drawing in that he was the right age, but there was no revelatory moment.

'Thanks for this,' said Falcón.

'Don't lose it,' said Angel, who put it in an envelope for him.

'What about this shot of you and King Juan Carlos,' said Falcón. 'Have you got a copy of that?'

They both laughed.

'The King doesn't need me to do his PR for him,' said Angel. 'He's a natural.'

'Are you getting anywhere, José Luis?' asked Falcón.

'I can't believe it, but we've drawn a total blank,' said Ramírez. 'If Tateb Hassani *was* staying with someone in this area, he didn't go for a coffee, he didn't eat a tapa, drink a beer, buy bread, go to the supermarket, get a newspaper – nothing. Nobody has seen this guy before, and he's got a face you don't forget.'

'Any news from Cristina and Emilio?'

'They've seen most of the big houses in the area and there are no box hedges. They've all got internal patios rather than gardens. There's the Convento de San Leandro and the Casa Pilatos, but that doesn't help us much.'

'I want you to find and check out another house. I don't have the address, but it belongs to someone called Lucrecio Arenas,' said Falcón. 'And I spoke to the CNI about the Imam's phone records. They've checked out the electrician's number already. It was a dead end.'

'Can we have a look at those records ourselves?'

'They've become classified documents,' said Falcón, and hung up.

He was on his way to see the security guard who'd finished his shift at the Archaeological Museum and gone home. It was a long drive out to his apartment in the northeast of the city. He took a call from Pablo.

'You're going to be pleased about this,' the CNI man said. 'Our handwriting expert has matched the Arabic script to the notes attached to the architect's drawings of the schools and the biology faculty. He's also matched Tateb Hassani's English script to the annotations in both copies of the Koran. What does this mean, Javier?'

'I'm not absolutely sure of its greater significance, but I'm confident you can tell your code breakers to stop looking for a key to crack the non-existent cipher in those copies of the Koran,' said Falcón. 'I think they were planted in the Peugeot Partner *and* Miguel Botín's apartment, specifically to confuse us.'

'And that's all you can say for the moment?'

'I'll be seeing you later at my house,' said Falcón. 'I'm hoping it will all be clearer by then.'

The lift to the security guard's apartment on the sixth floor was not working. Falcón was sweating as he rang the doorbell. The wife and kids were despatched to bedrooms and Falcón laid the photograph down on the dining-room table. His heart was beating tight and fast, willing the guard to find Lucrecio Arenas.

'Do you see the older man in this photograph?'

There were two rows of men, about thirty in all. The security guard had done this before. He took two pieces of paper and isolated each face from the rest of the shot and took a good look at it. He started on the left and worked his way across. He studied them carefully. Falcón couldn't bear the tension and looked out of the window. It took the guard some time. He knew it must be important for an Inspector Jefe to come all the way out to his apartment to show him this shot.

'That's him,' said the guard. 'I'm absolutely sure of it.'

Falcón's heart was thundering as he looked down. But the guard wasn't pointing at Lucrecio Arenas in the centre of the shot. He was tapping the face at the extreme right of the second row – and that face belonged to Angel Zarrías.

33

The sun was setting on the third day since the explosion. As Falcón drove back into the city his mind reached a static but profound level of concentration focused entirely on Angel Zarrías.

Back in the security guard's apartment he'd become quite angry. He'd torn the police sketch out of his pocket, smoothed it out on the dining-room table and asked the poor guy to show him the similarities. Falcón had been forced to admit a few things: that all old people looked the same, or invisible, to younger people; that Angel was 1.65m and only a little heavier than 75 kilos; that Angel had no facial hair and he did have a side parting and, even if he was a bit thin on top, he used all available hair to make it look as if he was still hanging on to it. Only when the security guard had talked him through the jaw line and nose did Falcón see Angel in the sketch, as an adult finally sees the outline of a face in a cloud, as pointed out by a frustrated child.

Ramírez met him in the car park outside the pre-school.

'We found Lucrecio Arenas's house,' said Ramírez. 'It was in the Plaza Mercenarias. I sent Cristina over there to take a look and it was all closed up. The neighbours say they don't spend much time there in the summer and there's no garden, only an internal patio. They didn't recognize Tateb Hassani either.'

They went into the classroom at the back where Juez del Rey and Comisario Elvira were waiting. Eight hours' sleep in three days was ruining Elvira. They sat down. They were all exhausted. Even del Rey, who should have been fresh, looked rumpled, as if he'd been jostled by a disgruntled crowd.

'Good news or bad?' asked Elvira.

'Both,' said Falcón. 'The good news is that I've identified the man seen speaking to Ricardo Gamero in the Archaeological Museum in the hours before he killed himself.'

'Name?'

'Angel Zarrías.'

Silence, as if they'd all seen someone sustain an ugly blow.

'He's your sister's partner, isn't he?' said Ramírez.

'How did you identify him?' asked Elvira.

Falcón briefed them on his conversation outside the Taberna Coloniales and how he'd extracted the Horizonte/Banco Omni executive photograph from Angel.

'But that's only part of the bad news,' said Falcón. 'The other part is that I'm not sure whether this gets us any further down the chain.'

'Meaning?'

'What have we found out that will help us apply pressure on Zarrías to reveal more?' said Ramírez.

'Exactly,' said Falcón. 'He was the last person to speak to Ricardo Gamero, but so what? He knew Gamero from church and that's the end of it. Why did he go to Zarrías and not his priest? His priest is dead. What did they talk about? Gamero was very upset. What about? Maybe Zarrías will give the same answer that Marco Barreda gave me. Perhaps Zarrías told Barreda to *tell* me that Gamero had been a closet gay. We don't know enough to be able to crack him open.'

'I can't believe that Ricardo Gamero would go to Angel Zarrías at that particular moment to discuss emotional problems,' said del Rey.

'You could show Zarrías the shot of Tateb Hassani and see what reaction you get,' said Elvira.

Neither Elvira nor del Rey had heard from Pablo, so Falcón told them about Tateb Hassani and how his handwriting matched that of the documents found in the fireproof box from the mosque and the notes found in the two copies of the Koran.

'And why did you ask for that comparison to be made in the first place?' asked Elvira.

'It went back to a question I asked my officers when we first discovered the dead body on the rubbish dump: Why kill a man and take such drastic steps to destroy his identity? You would only do that because knowledge of the victim's identity would lead investigators to people known to the victim, or because knowledge of his expertise might jeopardize a future operation. Tateb Hassani's identity revealed a number of things. His expertise, as a professor of Arabic Studies, meant that he could write Arabic and would have a sound knowledge of the Koran. He had also given maths classes in Granada during the summer months and therefore spoke and wrote Spanish. His profile was not that of an Islamic militant – he was an apostate, a sexual predator and a drinker of alcohol. Once he lost his job at Columbia University, which had cost him his New York apartment, he became so desperate for money that he'd taught maths privately in Columbus, Ohio, which was the home of I4IT, who own Horizonte, who in turn own Informáticalidad. Finally, I was not comfortable with the fact that the keys found in the Imam's apartment, which successfully opened the fireproof box from the mosque, had been discovered in the kitchen drawer and not in the Imam's desk with his other keys. This struck me as a plant by someone who had access to the Imam's apartment, but not his study when he wasn't there.'

'Who would have planted the keys?'

'Botín, under instructions from Gamero?' said Ramírez.

'At the beginning of this investigation Juan was telling us to keep an open mind and not to look at this attack historically, because there is no pattern in the way Islamic terrorists work. That's true. That's their style. Each attack comes out of the blue and there's always some new twist that teases greater terror into the mind of the West. Just think about the virtuosity of the attacks experienced so far.

'When I was driving back from the security guard's apartment, something that struck me about the Seville bombing was its *lack* of originality. Of course, that wasn't my first thought. My first thought was: these terrorists are prepared to attack residential property. But now I'm beginning to see that the Seville bomb refers back to some element in those previous attacks. The collapse of the apartment building reminded us of the Moscow apartment blocks coming down in 1999. The discovery of the Islamic sash, the hood and the Koran in the Peugeot Partner reminded us of the Koran tapes and detonators found in the Renault Kangoo outside the station at Alcalá de Henares. The use of Goma 2 Eco in the device planted in the mosque reminded us of the explosive used on 11th March. The threat to the two schools and the biology faculty was reminiscent of Beslan. It was as if the person who planned this operation was drawing inspiration from something in those previous attacks.'

'VOMIT,' said Ramírez. 'If there's anybody who knows everything there is to know about Islamic terrorist attacks, it's the author of that website.'

'And now that the security guard has pointed the finger at Angel Zarrías there's a logic to it. He's a journalist, but he's also a PR man. He knows how things work in the human mind,' said Falcón. 'I'm now asking myself: who leaked the Arabic script found in the fire-proof box to Canal Sur? Or rather, who didn't have to leak it, because it was already in their possession? And who planted the stories about the MILA? Who sent the Abdullah Azzam text to the *ABC* in Madrid from Seville?'

'How far do you think this goes?' said Elvira. 'If they planted the Korans, the hood and the sash, was it because they knew about the hexogen?'

'I don't think so,' said Falcón. 'I think the idea was conceived as just an attack against the mosque and the people in it. They were getting information from Miguel Botín, via Ricardo Gamero, that something was happening. The CGI had been frustrated in their first attempt to get a bugging order. Gamero found another way, or rather, another way was revealed to him by Zarrías, which was that the mosque could be put under surveillance by Informáticalidad's sales reps. Once it appeared that Hammad and Saoudi were making sinister preparations they decided to kill them, and anybody else unfortunate enough to be in the mosque at the time, before they could carry out the attack they were planning.

'The decision was made. The surveillance terminated. The apartment on Calle Los Romeros rented out again. Meanwhile the fake council inspectors went into the mosque, laid a small device that would blow the fuse box, which would give the electricians access. Miguel Botín was given the electrician's card and told to make it available to the Imam. It's quite possible that Botín wasn't part of the conspiracy and that he was told by Gamero that they had now been granted a bugging order and these electricians were going to position the microphone so that the CGI could carry out their surveillance. Botín was there to ensure that the Imam made the call to the right electricians. The Goma 2 Eco bomb was planted, along with the fireproof box. The design of the attack was to make it look like a bomb had gone off in the preparatory stage. Everybody would be killed and the ultimate, atrocious aim of the plot that was supposedly being planned would be found in the fireproof box.

'They knew that Hammad and Saoudi were up to no good, but what I don't believe they realized was just how powerful the explosive was that they were storing in the mosque. The detonation of 100 kilos of hexogen and the complete destruction of the apartment building and the damage to the pre-school were not part of the plan. And that was why Ricardo Gamero killed himself. Not just because his friend and source had been killed, but also because he felt responsible for all the deaths.'

'Well, that returns the logic to the scenario,' said Elvira. 'But first of all, I can't see Angel Zarrías as the sole perpetrator and mastermind of this conspiracy. And secondly, I don't know how the hell you set about proving any of it so that it can stand up in a court of law.'

'The problem is that, if this scenario is the correct one, I cannot go to Angel Zarrías and reveal my hand, because the only cards I've got are the fact that I know he was the last person to speak to Gamero, face to face, and the shock value of having identified Tateb Hassani.'

'You have to find the next link in the chain *after* Angel Zarrías,' said del Rey. 'He's a journalist and a PR man. What are his PR connections?'

'That's how I got to him in the first place,' said Falcón. 'I was sure that the people from Informáticalidad couldn't be operating on their own. I assumed they would be getting orders from their parent company. I looked at Horizonte, and that's where I came across their bankers: Banco Omni. And . . .'

'And?'

'Jesús Alarcón used to work for Banco Omni,' said Falcón, more things occurring to him. 'He was put forward as a political candidate by Angel Zarrías's old friend, the Chief Executive of Banco Omni, Lucrecio Arenas.'

'Political candidate for what?' asked del Rey.

'He's the new leader of Fuerza Andalucía.'

'But Fuerza Andalucía are nowhere in regional politics,' said Elvira. 'They poll 4 per cent of the vote, if they're lucky.'

'After Jesús Alarcón appeared with Fernando Alanis on television today they polled 14 per cent,' said Falcón. 'Zarrías was very excited about it. He calls the PR work he does for Fuerza Andalucía his hobby, but I think it's bigger than that. He's looking for a share of power with the Partido Popular because, for once in his political life, he wants to have the strength to change things. I think he's trying to manoeuvre Jesús Alarcón into a position where he can challenge for the leadership of the Partido Popular. I don't think I'm exaggerating when I say that he is to Jesús Alarcón what Karl Rove was to George Bush.'

'So who is the next link in the chain?' asked del Rey.

'Tateb Hassani was staying somewhere while he was being put to work and it was there that he was probably killed,' said Falcón. 'I had assumed it would be in a house near where he was dumped. The bins were in a cul-de-sac on a quiet street, and that implied knowledge. That knowledge, I realize, came from Zarrías, who lives nearby, on the Plaza Cristo de Burgos. I'm now thinking that the house where Tateb Hassani was probably staying was the headquarters of Fuerza Andalucía, which belongs to Eduardo Rivero on Calle Castelar.'

'Does it have a garden?' asked Ramírez. 'With a hedge?'

'There is some sort of formal garden between the front of the house, where Rivero has the office, and the back part, which is the family home. I went there once with Angel and Manuela for a party, but it was in the dark and I wasn't looking at hedges. What we need now is a sighting of Tateb Hassani going into that house, which will give us our next link in the chain.'

'What about Angel Zarrías?' asked Ramírez. 'Do you think it's worth putting him under twenty-four-hour surveillance?'

'I think it would be, especially as it might not be for long,' said Falcón. 'But there is something else which bothers me about all this, and that is the killing.'

'Tateb Hassani was poisoned with cyanide,' said Ramírez. 'It's not like stabbing, shooting, or strangling.'

'First of all, how did they get hold of cyanide?' asked Falcón. 'And then there was the disfigurement. The clean amputation of the hands. I'm thinking there must be a doctor or surgeon involved in all this.'

'And what about the bomb?' said Ramírez. 'It takes real criminal ruthlessness to do something like that.'

Falcón called Angel Zarrías to arrange a meeting with Comisario Elvira to talk about reviving the image of the investigative team. They'd agreed to profess an interest in Zarrías's PR talents. It would also bring Zarrías to them so that Serrano and Baena could start the first shift of the surveillance.

It was too risky for Falcón to be seen in Calle Castelar near Eduardo Rivero's house where he might be recognized. The work of placing Tateb Hassani in Rivero's household fell to Ferrera, Pérez and Ramírez.

Elvira, del Rey and Falcón waited in the pre-school for Angel to turn up.

'You're not happy, Javier,' said Elvira. 'Are you concerned about how this will affect your relationship with your sister?'

'No. That *does* concern me, but it's not that,' said Falcón. 'What I'm thinking about now is that, if my scenario proves to be the correct one, it still doesn't explain why Hammad and Saoudi brought 100 kilos of hexogen to Seville.'

'That's the CNI's job, not yours,' said Elvira.

'What scares me is that if you *did* want to bring Andalucía back into the Islamic fold, without an army or navy, then your best chance of achieving that would be with a Beslan-type siege,' said Falcón. 'I thought at the time that the Russian special forces probably started that firefight because Putin could see how impossible the situation was becoming. He had to act before the global media circus made it an intense, emotional focal point. Once that happened he could only see himself making concessions. Putin's reputation is built on strength and toughness. He couldn't allow a bunch of terrorists to make him look weak. So he met their ruthlessness with his own and more than three hundred people died. If a similar situation happened here, with children taken hostage just at the moment when they should be going on holiday, can you imagine the reaction in Spain, Europe and the world? Putin-style ruthlessness would not be acceptable.'

'Steps have been taken,' said Elvira. 'We can't go through all the schools in Andalucía in the same way that we've gone through the three buildings here in Seville, but we've told them to search their premises and we've got the local police involved, too.'

'You've also told us that you believe the idea of MILA involvement to be a media invention of Zarrías,' said del Rey. 'So we have no real idea what the Islamic terrorists' original intention was.'

'But why bring powerful explosive to Seville, the capital of Andalucía?' said Falcón. 'There's an unnerving brilliance to the idea of the MILA launching a ruthless attempt to bring Andalucía back into the Islamic fold. It's as if the fiction and the truth could easily meet. Have we had any results from the DNA sampling? Are we certain that Hammad and Saoudi died in the mosque? Do we know yet whether they deviated from their route between the safe house in Valmojado and Seville?'

'The forensics have been told to contact me as soon as they've had confirmation, but I doubt that will be today,' said Elvira. 'We haven't heard anything more from the Guardia Civil about the route of the Peugeot Partner. Don't try to overthink this situation, Javier. Just concentrate on *your* task.'

Angel Zarrías arrived at 9 p.m. Falcón made the introductions and left them to it. He went over to the forensics tent. They were working under lights on the bombsite, which was almost flat. The crane had gone, as had the diggers. Only one tipper was waiting to remove any further rubble. Falcón changed into a boiler suit and went into the tent, which was bright with halogen light. He found the chief of the forensics hovering over a vast array of rags, bits of shoe, plastic, strips of leather. He introduced himself again.

'I'm looking for anything that could be construed as an instruction for making and placing bombs,' said Falcón.

'Something more than what we've already found in the fireproof box?'

'Detail about the bomb making is what I'm after,' said Falcón. 'It might have been sewn into a jacket lining or in a wallet.'

'We've still got plenty of work to do to get into the mosque. We got to the fireproof box early, because it happened to have been blown upwards in the blast,' he said. 'We're working our way downwards now, but it's piece-by-piece work, with everything having to be documented as we go. Tomorrow morning will be the earliest that we'll get into the main body of the mosque.'

'I just wanted you to know that we're still looking for another piece in the jigsaw,' said Falcón. 'It could be in code, numbers or Arabic script.'

There were ten people working outside under the lights. It was similar to an archaeological dig, with a plan of the mosque under a reference grid on a table where each find was logged. The forensics were barely thirty centimetres below ground level. The stink of putrefaction was still heavy in the warm air. They worked in silence and low murmurs. It was hard, gruesome work. Falcón put a call through to Mark Flowers and asked for a meeting.

'Sure, where are you?'

'I'm at the bombsite now but I was thinking a good place to meet would be the apartment of Imam Abdelkrim Benaboura,' said Falcón. 'You know where that is, don't you, Mark?'

Flowers didn't respond to the sarcasm. Falcón walked to the Imam's apartment, which was in a block nearby, similar to the one that had been destroyed. There was a permanent police guard on the door. Falcón showed his ID and the guard said that he did not have the authority to allow him to enter.

'You know who I am?' said Falcón.

'Yes, Inspector Jefe, but you're not on my list.'

'Can I see your list?'

'Sorry, sir. That's classified.'

The guard's mobile rang and he took the call, listening intently.

'He's already here,' he said, and hung up.

He unlocked the door and let Falcón in.

The CNI men had not been exaggerating about the quantity of books in the apartment. The living and dining rooms were lined with books, and the bedroom floors were stacked with them. They covered all areas of human knowledge and were mostly in French and English, although there was a whole room given over to Arabic texts. The back room should have been the master bedroom but was the Imam's study, with just a single bed at one end and his desk at the other. The walls were covered in books. Falcón sat at the desk in a wooden swivel chair. He looked through the drawers, which were empty. He swivelled in the chair and reached for a book on the nearest shelf. It was called *Riemann's Zeta Function*. He put it back without troubling to open it.

'He'd read them all,' said Flowers, standing at the door. 'Pretty amazing to think of all this knowledge in one guy's head. We had a few people in Langley with this kind of reading behind them, but not many.'

'How long had you known him?' said Falcón. 'Assuming that he's dead.'

'I'm sure he's dead,' said Flowers. 'We met in Afghanistan in 1982. He was a kid then, but he was one of the few mujahedeen who spoke English, because, although he was born in Algeria, he went to school in Egypt. We were supplying them with weapons and tactics to fight the Russians. He appreciated what we did for them; helping to keep those atheistic communists out of the land of Allah. As you know, not many of the others did. Isn't there a saying about helping people being the quickest road to resentment?'

'And you kept in touch all this time?'

'There have been breaks, as you'd expect. I lost track of him in the 1990s and then we resumed contact in 2002. I dug him out on one of my foraging trips to Tunis. He never bought into the Taliban and all that Wahhabi stuff. As you probably gathered, he was a bright guy and he couldn't find an interpretation of any line of the Koran that approved of suicide bombing. He was one of them, but he saw things very clearly.'

'And you didn't think to tell one of your new spies, who was investigating –'

'Hey, look, Javier, you had the information from day one. Juan told you he didn't have clearance for his history and that the Americans had vouched for him on his visa application. What more do you want? His CV? Don't expect to be spoon-fed in this game,' said Flowers. 'I can't have it released into the public domain that I was running an Imam as a spy in a local mosque in Seville.'

'And that's why we didn't get in here,' said Falcón, 'and why we didn't get access to his phone records?'

'I had to make sure the place was clear of anything that might implicate him in CIA work. That meant going through all these books,' said Flowers. 'And I'm not irresponsible. I made sure the CNI checked out the electrician's number.'

'All right, I accept that. I should have been a bit more . . . aware,' said Falcón. 'Did Benaboura tell you about Hammad and Saoudi?'

'No, he didn't.'

'That must have hurt.'

'You don't understand the pressure on these people,' said Flowers. 'He gave me plenty of useful information, names, movements, all sorts of stuff, but he didn't tell me about Hammad and Saoudi because he couldn't.'

'You mean he couldn't risk telling you about them, and you then acting on the information, with the result that all fingers would be pointing at Abdelkrim Benaboura?'

'You're learning, Javier.'

'Did he know about Miguel Botín?'

'Benaboura was an experienced guy.'

'I see,' said Falcón, thinking that through. 'So he decided that Miguel Botín was an acceptable route for the information about Hammad and Saoudi to come out, which was why he used the electricians Botín put forward.'

'He read that situation very clearly. He understood why the fake council inspectors came in, he appreciated the fuse box blowing and the "right" electrician being put in his hand,' said Flowers. 'What he didn't expect was for the electricians to plant a bomb, as well as a microphone.'

'There was a microphone?'

'Of course, he had to find out where it was so that he could have his conversations there,' said Flowers. 'They put it in the plug socket in his office.'

'I wonder if that was in use and who was listening to it?' said Falcón. 'What did the CNI have to say about it?'

'It was supposed to be the CGI who planted it,' said Flowers. 'Botín was working for Gamero, who was with the CGI, and I never spoke to them about it because

I was told that there was a security problem in their ranks.'

'What about the extra socket Benaboura had installed in the storeroom?'

'That was probably a request from Hammad and Saoudi,' said Flowers. 'He never spoke to me about it.'

'So you didn't know about the hexogen either?'

'It would have all come out when Benaboura was ready for it to come out.'

'Did he pick up on the surveillance?'

'In the apartment across the street?' said Flowers. 'He was so amazed at how unprofessional it was he'd begun to think it wasn't surveillance.'

'Did you talk to somebody about that on his behalf?'

'I asked Juan and he said it wasn't anything to do with them and he nosed around the CGI for me and said they weren't involved either. I had a look in the apartment myself one evening and it was empty. No equipment. I didn't bother with it any more after that.'

'You're uncharacteristically allowing me to ask a lot of questions.'

'It's all old news.'

'You don't seem bothered by the fact that Botín's electricians put a bomb in the mosque.'

'Oh, I'm bothered, Javier. I'm very bothered by that. I've lost one of my best agents.'

'Do you buy the CNI's story?'

'That Botín was a double?' said Flowers. 'That the Islamic terrorists he was working for knew about Benaboura and wanted to get rid of him?'

'And Hammad and Saoudi.'

'That's bullshit,' said Flowers, bitterly. 'But I'm not

thinking about that now. It's *your* job to rummage in the past.'

'Now you're thinking: what were Hammad and Saoudi going to do with 100 kilos of hexogen in Seville?'

'The GICM are not interested in returning Andalucía to the Islamic fold,' said Flowers. 'Their priority is to make Morocco an Islamic state, under Sharia law, but they do hold the same feelings about the West as those people we call al-Qaeda.'

'Is it certain that Hammad and Saoudi were GICM?'

'They've worked for them before.'

'So what was the hexogen going to be used for?'

'And was there more of it elsewhere?' asked Flowers. 'Those are the big unanswerable questions. It was probably still in its raw form when it exploded. We can only hope for more clues when we get into the mosque.'

'What would have had to be done to it to make it usable?'

'Normally they'd have mixed it with some plastique so that it could be moulded. The best clue would be to find what they were going to pack it into. The hardware.'

'But if you wanted to destroy a building, you could just stick it all in a suitcase, put it in the boot of a car and drive it through the entrance?'

'That's correct.'

'Do you know what the CNI are working on?' asked Falcón, realizing now that his conversation with Flowers was no longer evolving.

'You'd have to ask them,' said Flowers. 'But my advice to you is to do what you're paid to do, Javier. Stick to the past.'

Falcón's mobile vibrated. It was Ramírez. He took the call in the kitchen, well away from Flowers.

'We can confirm a sighting of Tateb Hassani in Rivero's house,' said Ramírez. 'We weren't having any luck on the outside, but Cristina spotted a woman coming out of the house who happened to be the maid looking after Hassani's room. She first saw him on 29th May and last saw him on 2nd June. She didn't work weekends, none of the maids in the main house do. She's not absolutely certain, but she doesn't think he left the house the entire time he was there. He worked in the Fuerza Andalucía offices at the front of the building and took most of his meals over there.'

'What news about Angel Zarrías?'

'That's why I'm calling. He's just arrived at Rivero's house about five minutes after Jesús Alarcón turned up. They're all here. It must be a Fuerza Andalucía strategy meeting.'

'Tell Cristina she has to find someone who was working at Rivero's house on Saturday evening. There must have been some kind of dinner for Tateb Hassani, which means cooks, serving staff, those kinds of people.'

34

'I think we should get Eduardo Rivero on his own,' said Falcón, 'without any sense of support from Jesús Alarcón and Angel Zarrías. Tateb Hassani was in *his* house, as *his* guest, and he was murdered there in *his* offices. If we can break him first, I'm sure he'll give us the rest.'

'What about the transport?' said Elvira. 'Can we get our hands on the car that took the body from Rivero's house to dump it in those bins on Calle Boteros?'

'The only sighting we've had of that car has been by an elderly alcoholic who was looking down from a height of about ten metres at night. All we've got from him is that it was a dark estate,' said Falcón. 'Ramírez is round there now, with Pérez, trying to find a more reliable witness. We're also checking all the cars in Rivero's name, and his wife's, to see if any match the basic description.'

'And who's watching Rivero's house?'

'Serrano and Baena are keeping Angel Zarrías under twenty-four-hour surveillance. They won't leave until

497

he does,' said Falcón. 'What about a search warrant for Rivero's house?'

'I'm worried about that, Javier,' said Elvira. 'Rivero might not be the leader of an important party, but he is a huge figure in Seville society. He knows everybody. He has important friends in all walks of life, including the judiciary. The trump card you hold at the moment is surprise. He doesn't realize that you've identified Tateb Hassani and located him at his house in the days before his murder. If I apply for a search warrant I have to make the case and reveal everything to the judge. The vital advantage you have has more opportunities to leak.'

'You'd rather I tried to break him first?'

'There are risks either way.'

'They're having a meeting now and they'll probably have dinner afterwards,' said Falcón. 'Let's see what the next hours bring us and we'll confer before we make the final move.'

Falcón went back to his house to have something to eat and to think about the best way to get Eduardo Rivero to talk. Inspector Jefe Luis Zorrita called, wanting to talk to him about Inés's murder. Falcón told him that now was the only moment he could spare.

Encarnación had left him some fresh pork fillet. He made a salad and sliced up some potatoes and the meat. He smashed up some cloves of garlic, threw them into the frying pan with the pork fillet and chips. He dashed some cheap whisky on top and let it catch fire from the gas flame. He ate without thinking about the food and drank a glass of red rioja to loosen up his mind. Instead of thinking about

Rivero, he found his mind full of Inés again, and it was playing tricks on him. He couldn't quite believe that she was dead, despite having seen her lying by the river. She'd been here only . . . last night, or was it the night before?

It was stuffy in the kitchen and he took his glass of wine and sat on the rim of the fountain in the patio, under the heat, which was still sinking down the walls like a giant, invisible press. They'd made love in this fountain, he and Inés. Those were wild, exhilarating days: just the two of them in this colossal house, running naked around the gallery, down the steps, in and out of the cloisters. She had been so beautiful then, in that time when youth was still running riot. He, on the other hand, was already carrying his ball and chain, he just didn't know it, couldn't see it. It occurred to him that he'd probably driven her into the arms of Esteban Calderón, the man who would eventually kill her.

The doorbell rang. He let Zorrita in and sat him down in the patio with a beer. Falcón had just finished describing his marriage to Inés, her affair with Calderón, their separation and divorce when his mobile vibrated. He took it in his study, closed the patio door.

'We've had some luck with the car,' said Ramírez. 'There's a bar on Calle Boteros called Garlochi. Strange place. All decked out with pictures and effigies of the Virgin. The bar has a canopy over it like a float from Semana Santa. It's lit with candles, they burn incense and the house cocktail comes in a glass chalice and it's called "Sangre de Cristo".'

'Suitably decadent.'

'It's always been shut when we've checked the area before. The owner tells me he was closing up on Saturday night, or rather, early Sunday morning, when he saw the car turn into the cul-de-sac and reverse up to the bins. He described it just as Cristina's witness had, except that he got a good view of it when the car reversed out of the cul-de-sac. He recognized it as a Mercedes E500 because he wanted to buy one himself but couldn't afford it. He also looked for the registration because he thought the three guys were behaving suspiciously, but that was nearly a week ago. All he could remember was that it was a new type of number which began with 82 and he thought that the last letter was an M.'

'Does that help you?'

'Baena just called me to say that three other cars have now turned up at Rivero's house,' said Ramírez. 'We've checked the plates and they're owned by Lucrecio Arenas, César Benito and Agustín Cárdenas. We're running a search on those people . . .'

'Lucrecio Arenas introduced Jesús Alarcón to Fuerza Andalucía through Angel Zarrías,' said Falcón. 'I don't know anything about the other two.'

'Listen. Agustín Cárdenas's car is a black Mercedes Estate E500 and the registration is 8247 BHM.'

'That's our man,' said Falcón.

'I'll get back to you when I know more.'

Falcón went back to Zorrita, apologized. Zorrita waved it away. Falcón told him about the last time he'd seen Inés. How she'd unexpectedly turned up at his house on Tuesday night, swearing about her husband and his endless affairs.

'Did you like Esteban Calderón?' asked Zorrita.

'I used to. People were surprised. I only found out much later that he and Inés had been having an affair for the last part of our short married life,' said Falcón. 'I thought he was an intelligent, well-informed, cultured person and he probably still is. But he's also arrogant, ambitious, narcissistic, and a lot of other adjectives that I can't retrieve from my brain at the moment.'

'Interesting,' said Zorrita, 'because he asked me if you'd go and see him.'

'What for?' asked Falcón. 'He knows I can't talk about his case.'

'He said he wants to explain something to you.'

'I'm not sure that's a good idea.'

'It's up to you,' said Zorrita. 'It won't bother me.'

'Off the record,' said Falcón. 'Did he break down and confess?'

'Nearly,' said Zorrita. 'There was a breakdown, but not in the usual way. Rather than his conscience forcing out the truth, it was more as if he suddenly doubted himself. To start with he was all arrogance and determined resistance. He refused a lawyer, which meant I could be quite brutal with him about the way he'd abused his wife. I think he was unaware of the intensity of his rage, the savagery it unleashed and the damage he'd done to her. He was shocked by the autopsy details and that's when his certainty really wavered and he began to believe that he *could* have done it.

'He described arriving at his apartment as if he was telling me about a movie and there was some confusion about how the script played out. At first he said that he'd seen Inés standing by the sink, but then he

501

changed his mind. In the end, I think there were two Calderóns. The judge and this other person, who was locked up most of the time but would come out and take over.'

'Inés said he needed psychological help,' said Falcón, 'but I don't think she had something as serious as schizophrenia in mind.'

'Not clinical schizophrenia,' said Zorrita. 'There's a beast inside most of us, it just never gets to see the light of day. For whatever reason, Calderón's beast got out of the cage.'

'You're convinced he did it?'

'I'm certain there was nobody else involved, so the only question is whether it was premeditated or accidental,' said Zorrita. 'I don't think his lover stood to gain anything out of Inés's death. She didn't want to marry him. She's not the marrying kind. She admitted that they'd had a "joke" about "the bourgeois solution to a bourgeois institution" being murder, but I don't think it was her intention that he should go off and kill his wife. He'll try to make out it was accidental, although no court is going to like the sound of how he abused her beforehand.'

Zorrita finished his beer. Falcón walked him to the door. Ramírez called again. Zorrita walked off into the night with a wave.

'OK, César Benito is the Chief Executive of a construction company called Construcciones PLM S.A. He is on the board of directors of Horizonte, in charge of their property services division, which includes companies like Mejorvista and Playadoro. The other guy, Agustín Cárdenas, is a bit more interesting. He's a qualified surgeon who runs his own cosmetic surgery clinics in

502

Madrid, Barcelona and Seville. He is also on the board of Horizonte, in charge of their medical services division, which runs Quirúrgicalidad, Ecográficalidad and Optivisión.'

'It looks like a gathering of the conspiracy to plan their next move now that the first phase has been successfully completed,' said Falcón.

'But I'm not convinced that we've got the full picture,' said Ramírez. 'I can see Rivero, Zarrías, Alarcón and Cárdenas poisoning Hassani, and probably Cárdenas did the work on the corpse, but none of these guys fits the descriptions of any of the men in the Mercedes E500 who dumped the body.'

'And who planted the bomb, or gave orders for it to be planted?'

'There's a missing element,' said Ramírez. 'I can see the money and the power and a certain amount of ruthlessness to deal with Tateb Hassani. But how could you get somebody to do the work in the mosque and rely on them to keep their mouths shut?'

'The only way to find that out is to put them under pressure in the Jefatura,' said Falcón, hearing the doorbell. 'Give Elvira an update. I've got a meeting with the CNI here. And tell Cristina she *has* to get a sighting of Tateb Hassani, as late on Saturday evening as possible. It's important that we have that before we talk to Rivero.'

Pablo and Gregorio went straight to the computer. Gregorio set to work, booting up the computer and getting access to the CNI's encrypted site, through which they would 'chat' to Yacoub Diouri.

'We've arranged for you to talk to Yacoub at 23.00 hours every night, unless you agree not to beforehand.

That's 23.00 Spanish time, which is 21.00 Moroccan time,' said Pablo. 'Obviously you have to be on your own to do this, nobody even in the house with you. The way in which you recognize each other is that each time you make contact you will start with a paragraph of incidental chat in which you will include a phrase from this book –'

Pablo handed him a copy of *Tomorrow in the Battle Think on Me* by Javier Marías.

'On the first day he will choose a phrase from the opening paragraph of page one, and you will respond with a phrase from the closing paragraph of page one,' said Pablo. 'Once you've recognized each other you can talk freely.'

'What if he doesn't use the phrase?'

'The most important thing is that you do not remind him and you don't respond with any classified information. You include your introductory phrase in your opening paragraph and if he still doesn't rectify the situation you log off. You must then not communicate with him until we've checked out his status,' said Pablo. 'The other thing is: no printouts. We will have a record on our website, which you will not be able to access unless we are here with you.'

'I still don't understand how you know that Yacoub will be accepted so easily into the GICM,' said Falcón.

'We didn't say that,' said Pablo. 'We said that he would be accepted into the radical element of the mosque in Salé. You have to remember Yacoub's history; what his real father, Raúl Jiménez, did and how his surrogate father, Abdullah Diouri, retaliated. That did not happen in a bubble. The whole family knew about it. That is the source of a certain amount of sympathy with some of the more radical elements of Islam. Don't ask any more . . . let's just see whether Yacoub has made contact with the radical element in the mosque and, if he has, how quickly he'll be put in touch with the high command of the GICM.'

'So what is the purpose of my conversation with him?'

'At this stage, to let him know that you're here,' said Pablo. 'Ultimately, we want to find out what was supposed to happen here in Seville and whether they still have the capability to make it happen, but we might have to be satisfied with confirmation of the history at this stage.'

The communication started at 23.03. They made their introductions and Falcón asked his first question.

'How's your first day been back at school?'

'It's more like the first day as a new member of a club. Everybody's sizing me up, some are friendly, others suspicious and a few are unfriendly. It's like in any organization, I've come in at a certain level and been welcomed by my equals, but I'm despised as a usurper by those who thought they were becoming important. There's a hierarchy here. There has to be. It's an organization with a military wing. The striking difference is that the commander-in-chief is not a man, but Allah. No action by this group, or any of the others that they read about, is referred to without mention of the ultimate source of the commands. We're constantly reminded that we're involved in a Holy War. It is powerful and inspirational and I've come back feeling dazed. Home seems strange, or rather, extremely banal after a day spent with people so certain of their place and destiny in the will of Allah. I can see how powerfully this would work on a young mind. They're also clever at depersonalizing the enemy, who are rarely specific people – unless you count Tony Blair and George Bush – but rather the decadence and godlessness that has engulfed the West. I suppose it's easier to bomb decadence and godlessness than it is men, women and children.'

'Any talk about what happened in Seville on 6th June?'

'They talk about nothing else. The Spanish satellite news is avidly watched for more information, but it's not so easy to work out the extent of their involvement.'

'Any talk about Djamel Hammad and Smail Saoudi and what they were doing bringing 100 kilos of hexogen to Seville?'

'I'm not sure how much is speculation and how much is hard fact. You must understand that these people are not the GICM themselves. They support the actions of the GICM, and some members have been involved in their activities, but mainly on the home front. Don't think that I've walked off the street into a tent full of mujahedeen with AK-47s. At this stage, I can only tell you what has happened rather than what *will* happen, as that is only known by the GICM commanders, who, as far as I know, are not here.

'My friends tell me that Hammad and Saoudi have worked for a number of groups, not just the GICM. They fund themselves through cash-machine fraud. They were only involved in recce, logistics and documents. They were not bomb makers. The hexogen came from Iraq. It was extracted from an American ammunitions cache captured at the beginning of 2005. It went via Syria into Turkey, where it was repackaged as cheap washing powder and sent to Germany in containers, for sale to the immigrant Turkish community there. Nobody knows how it got to Spain. The total quantity sent to Germany in the washing powder consignment is believed to be around 300 kilos.'

'Any speculation about how they intended to use it?' asked Falcón.

'No. All they say is that everything in the Spanish press and news is total fabrication: Abdullah Azzam's text, the MILA, the intention to attack schools and the biology faculty and the idea of bringing Andalucía back into the Islamic fold. They want to bring Andalucía back into Islam, but not yet. Making Morocco an Islamic state with Sharia law is the priority and we talked about that, which is of no interest to you. The current strategy, as far as foreign operations are concerned, is not specific, although they are still very angry with the Danish and think they should be punished. They want to weaken the European Union economically by forcing huge expenditure on antiterrorist measures. They plan to attack financial centres in Northern Europe, namely London, Frankfurt, Paris and Milan, while conducting smaller campaigns in the tourist areas of the Mediterranean.'

'Ambitious.'

'There's a lot of big talk. As to their capability . . . who knows?'

'The hexogen in Seville doesn't seem to fit with their general strategy.'

'They say the hexogen exploding was nothing to do with them.'

'And how do they know that?'

'Because the "hardware" for making the bombs had not arrived,' wrote Yacoub. 'Given that Hammad and Saoudi were recce and logistics, I assume there were others who were due to arrive with the "hardware" – the containers, plastique, detonators and timers – from some other source.'

'How much of this do you believe?' asked Falcón.

'There is definitely something going on. There's a tension and uncertainty in the air. I can't be more specific than that. This is information that has come to me. I am not enquiring as yet. I haven't asked about operational cells in Spain, for instance. I can only gather from the way people talk that there are operators in the field doing something.'

Falcón's mobile vibrated on the desktop. He took the call from Ramírez while Pablo and Gregorio talked over his head.

'Cristina has found a domestic who saw Tateb Hassani on Saturday evening, before dinner. His name is Mario Gómez. He says that the dinner wasn't served but laid out as a buffet, but he saw Tateb Hassani, Eduardo Rivero and Angel Zarrías going up to the Fuerza Andalucía offices just before he left, which was around 9.45.'

'He didn't see anybody else?'

'He said no cars had arrived by the time he left.'

'I think that's going to be good enough,' said Falcón and hung up.

'Ask him if he's heard any names, anything that will

give us a clue as to a network operating over here,'
said Pablo.

Falcón typed out the question.

'They don't use names. Their knowledge of foreign
operations is vague. They are more informative about
the present state of Morocco than anything abroad.'

'Any foreigners?' asked Pablo. 'Afghans, Pakistanis,
Saudis . . .?'

Falcón tapped it out.

'One mention of some Afghans who came over
earlier this year, nothing else.'

'Context?'

'I couldn't say.'

'Where does the group meet?'

'It's in a private house in the medina in Rabat, but
I was brought here and I'm not sure I could find it
again.'

'Look for clues in your surroundings. Documents.
Books. Anything that might indicate research.'

'There's a library which I've been shown, but I
haven't spent any time there.'

'Get access and tell us what books they have.'

'I have been told/warned that there will be an initiation rite, which is designed to show my allegiance to
the group. Everybody has to go through this, whatever
your connections to the senior members may be. They
have assured me that it will not require violence.'

'Do they know about your friendship with me?'
asked Falcón.

'Of course they do, and that worries me. I know
how their minds work. They will make me show allegiance to them by forcing me to betray the confidence
of someone close to me.'

The 'chat' was over. Falcón sat back from the computer, a little shattered by the last exchange. The CNI men looked at him to see how he'd taken this new level of involvement.

'In case you're wondering,' said Falcón, 'I didn't like the sound of that.'

'We can't expect just to *receive* information in this game,' said Gregorio.

'I'm a senior policeman,' said Falcón. 'I can't compromise my position by giving out confidential information.'

'We don't know what he's going to be asked to do yet,' said Pablo.

'I didn't like the look of that word "betray",' said Falcón. 'That doesn't sound like they're going to be satisfied with my favourite colour, does it?'

Pablo shook his head at Gregorio.

'Anything else?' said Pablo.

'If they know about me, what's to say they don't know about the next step we've taken?' said Falcón. 'That I came over to make Yacoub one of our spies. He employs ten or fifteen people around his house. How do you know that he's "safe", that he's not going to be turned, and that they still think that I'm just a friend?'

'We have our own people on the inside,' said Pablo.

'Working for Yacoub?'

'We didn't just think this operation up last week,' said Gregorio. 'We have people working in his home, at his factory, and we've watched him on business trips. So have the British. He's been vetted down to his toenails. The only thing we didn't have, which nobody had, was access. And that's where you came in.'

'Don't think about it too much, Javier,' said Pablo.

'It's new territory and we'll take it one step at a time. If you feel there's something you can't do . . . then you can't do it. Nobody's going to force you.'

'I'm less worried about force than I am by coercion.'

35

That's what Flowers had said: 'You don't understand
the pressure on these people.' Alone, now, Falcón
gripped the arms of his chair in front of the dead
computer screen. He'd only had a glimpse of it, but
now he understood what Flowers had meant. He sat
in his comfortable house, in the heart of one of the
least violent cities in Europe and, yes, he had a
demanding job, but not one where he had to pretend
every day or cope with 'an initiation rite' that might
demand 'betrayal'. He didn't have to cohabit with the
minds of clear-sighted fanatics who saw God's purpose
in the murder of innocents, who, in fact, didn't see
them as innocents but as 'culpable by democracy', or
the product of 'decadence and godlessness', and therefore fair game. He might have to face a moral choice,
but not a life-or-death situation which could result in
harm done to Yacoub, his wife and children.

Yacoub knew 'how their minds worked', that they
would demand betrayal, because that would sever the
relationship. They weren't interested in the low-quality
information of a Sevillano detective. They wanted to

cut Yacoub off from a relationship that connected him to the outside world. Yacoub had been with the group for twenty-four hours and already they were setting about the imprisonment of his mind.

The mobile vibrating on the desktop made him start.

'Just to let you know,' said Ramírez, 'Arenas, Benito and Cárdenas have just left. Rivero, Zarrías and Alarcón are still there. Do we know what we're doing yet?'

'I have to call Elvira before we make a move,' said Falcón. 'What *I* want is for the two of us to go in there as soon as Rivero is alone and break him down so that he reveals *everybody* in the whole conspiracy, not just the bit players.'

'Do you know Eduardo Rivero?' asked Ramírez.

'I met him once at a party,' said Falcón. 'He's fantastically vain. Angel Zarrías has been trying to lever him out of the leadership of Fuerza Andalucía for years, but Rivero loved the status it conferred on him.'

'So how did Zarrías get him out?'

'No idea,' said Falcón. 'But Rivero is not a man to hand in his ego lightly.'

'It happened on the day of the bomb, didn't it?'

'That's when they announced it.'

'But it must have been coming for a while,' said Ramírez. 'Zarrías never mentioned anything to you about it?'

'Are you speaking with some inside knowledge, José Luis?'

'Some press guys I know were telling me there was talk of a sex scandal around Rivero,' said Ramírez. 'Under-age girls. They've lost interest since the bomb, but they were very suspicious of the handover to Jesús Alarcón.'

'So what's your proposed strategy, José Luis?' said Falcón. 'You sound as if you want to make yourself unpopular again?'

'I think I do. I've done a bit of work on Eduardo Rivero and I think that might be the way to make him feel uneasy,' said Ramírez. 'Lull him into a false sense of relief when we move away from the hint of scandal and then give him both barrels in the face with Tateb Hassani.'

'That *is* your style, José Luis.'

'He's the type who'll look down his nose at me,' said Ramírez. 'But because he knows you, and knows your sister is Zarrías's partner, he'll expect you to bring some dignity to the proceedings. He'll turn to you for help. I think he'll be devastated when you show him the shot of Tateb Hassani.'

'We hope.'

'Vain men are weak.'

Falcón called Comisario Elvira and gave him the update. He could almost smell the man's sweat trickling down the phone.

'Are you confident, Javier?' he asked, as if begging Falcón to give him some resolve.

'He's the weakest of the three, the most vulnerable,' said Falcón. 'If we can't break him, we'll struggle to break the others. We can make the evidence against him sound overwhelming.'

'Comisario Lobo thinks it's the best way.'

Falcón pocketed his mobile and a photograph of Tateb Hassani. He used his reflection in the glass doors to the patio to knot his tie. He shrugged into his jacket. He was conscious of his shoes on the marble flagstones of the patio as he made his way to his car. He drove

514

through the night. The silent, lamp-lit streets under the dark trees were almost empty. Ramírez called to tell him that Alarcón had left. Falcón told him to send everybody home except Serrano and Baena, who would follow Zarrías once he'd left.

It was a short drive to Rivero's house and there was parking in the square. He joined Ramírez on the street corner. Serrano and Baena were in an unmarked car opposite Rivero's house.

A taxi came up the street and turned round by Rivero's oak doors. The driver got out and rang the doorbell. Within a minute Angel Zarrías came out and got into the back of the cab, which pulled away. Serrano and Baena waited until it was nearly out of sight and then took off in pursuit.

Cristina Ferrera had taken a cab back to her apartment. She was so exhausted she forgot to ask the driver for a receipt. She got her keys out and headed for the entrance to her block. A man sitting on the steps up to the door made her wary. He held up his hands to show her he meant no harm.

'It's me, Fernando,' he said. 'I lost your number, but remembered the address. I came to take you up on your offer of a bed for the night. My daughter, Lourdes, came out of intensive care this evening. She's in a room now with my parents-in-law looking after her. I needed to get out.'

'Have you been waiting long?'

'Since the bomb I don't look at the time,' he said. 'So I don't know.'

They went up to her apartment on the fourth floor.

'You're tired,' he said. 'I'm sorry, I shouldn't have

515

come, but I've got nowhere else to go. I mean, nowhere that I'd feel comfortable.'

'It's all right,' she said. 'It's just another long day in a series of long days. I'm used to it.'

'Have you caught them yet?'

'We're close,' she said.

She put her bag on the table in the living room, took off her jacket and hung it on the back of the chair. She had a holster with a gun clipped to a belt around her waist.

'Are your kids asleep?' he asked, in a whisper.

'They sleep with my neighbour when I have to work late,' she said.

'I just wanted to see them sleeping, you know . . .' he said, and fluttered his hand, as if that explained his need for normality.

'They're not quite old enough to be left on their own all night,' she said, and went into the bedroom, unhooked the holster from her belt and put it in the top drawer of the chest. She pulled her blouse out of her waistband.

'Have you eaten?' she asked.

'Don't worry about me.'

'I'm putting a pizza in the microwave.'

Cristina opened some beers and laid the table. She remade the bed with clean sheets in one of the kids' rooms.

'Do your neighbours gossip?'

'Well, you're famous now, so they're bound to talk about you,' said Ferrera. 'They know I used to be a nun so they're not too concerned about my virtue.'

'You used to be a nun?'

'I told you,' she said. 'So what's it like?'

'What?'

'To be famous.'

'I don't understand it,' said Fernando. 'One moment I'm a labourer on a building site and the next I'm the voice of the people and it's nothing to do with *me*, but because *Lourdes* survived. Does that make any sense to you?'

'You've become a focus for what happened,' she said, taking the pizza out of the microwave. 'People don't want to listen to politicians, they want to listen to someone who's suffered. Tragedy gives you credibility.'

'There's no logic to it,' he said. 'I say the same things that I've always said in the bar where I go for coffee in the morning, and nobody listened to me then. Now I've got the whole of Spain hanging on my every word.'

'Well, that might change tomorrow,' said Ferrera.

'What might change?'

'Sorry, it's nothing. I can't talk about it. I shouldn't have said anything. Forget I even mentioned it. I'm too tired for this.'

Fernando's eyes narrowed over the slice of pizza halfway to his mouth.

'You're close,' said Fernando. 'That's what you said. Does that mean you know who they are, or you've actually caught them?'

'It means we're close,' she said, shrugging. 'I shouldn't have said it. It's police business. It slipped out because I was tired. I wasn't thinking properly.'

'Just tell me the name of the group,' said Fernando. 'They all have these crazy initials like MIEDO – Mártires Islámicos Enfrentados a la Dominación del Occidente.'

Islamic Martyrs facing up to Western Domination.

'You didn't listen.'

He frowned and replayed the dialogue.

'You mean they weren't terrorists?'

'They *were* terrorists, but not Islamic ones.'

Fernando shook his head in disbelief.

'I don't know how you can say that.'

Ferrera shrugged.

'I've read all the reports,' said Fernando. 'You found explosives in the back of their van, with the Koran and the Islamic sash and the black hood. They took the explosive into the mosque. The mosque exploded and . . .'

'That's all true.'

'Then I don't know what you're talking about.'

'That's why you've got to forget about it until it comes out in the news tomorrow.'

'Then why can't you tell me now?' he said. 'I'm not going anywhere.'

'Because suspects still have to be interrogated.'

'What suspects?'

'The people who are suspected of planning the bombing of the mosque.'

'You're just trying to confuse me now.'

'I'll tell you this if you promise me that that will be the end of it,' said Ferrera. 'I know it's important to you, but this is a police investigation and it's totally confidential information.'

'Tell me.'

'Promise me first.'

'I promise,' he said, waving it away with his hand.

'That sounds like a politician's promise.'

'That's what happens when you spend time with them. You learn too much, too quickly,' said Fernando. 'I promise you, Cristina.'

'There was another bomb that was planted in the mosque which, when it exploded, set off the very large quantity of hexogen which the Islamic terrorists were storing there. That's what destroyed your apartment building.'

'And you know who planted the bomb?'

'You promised me that that would be the end of it.'

'I know, but I just need to . . . I *have* to know.'

'That's what we're working on tonight.'

'You have to tell me who they are.'

'I can't. There's no discussion. It's not possible. If it came out, I'd lose my job.'

'They killed my wife and son.'

'And if they are responsible, they will face trial.'

Fernando opened up a pack of cigarettes.

'You'll have to go out on the balcony if you want to smoke.'

'Come and sit with me?'

'No more questions?'

'I promise. You're right. I can't do this to you.'

Falcón and Ramírez were ringing the bell as Zarrías's taxi turned out of Calle Castelar. Eduardo Rivero opened the door, expecting it to be Angel coming back for the notebook he'd forgotten. He was surprised to find two stone-faced policemen in the frame, presenting their ID cards. His face momentarily lost all definition, as if the muscles had been deprived of their neural drive. Geniality revived them.

'What can I do for you, gentlemen?' he asked, his white moustache doubling the size and warmth of his smile.

'We'd like to talk to you,' said Falcón.

'It's very late,' said Rivero, looking at his watch.

'It can't wait,' said Ramírez.

Rivero looked away from him with faint disgust.

'Have we met?' he asked Falcón. 'You seem familiar.'

'I came to a party here once, some years ago,' said Falcón. 'My sister is Angel Zarrías's partner.'

'Ah, yes, yes, yes, yes, yes . . . Javier Falcón. Of course,' said Rivero. 'Can I ask what you'd like to talk to me about at this time of the morning?'

'We're homicide detectives,' said Ramírez. 'We only ever talk to people at this hour of the morning about murder.'

'And you are?' said Rivero, his distaste even more undisguised.

'Inspector Ramírez,' he said. 'We've never met before, Sr Rivero. You'd have remembered it.'

'I can't think how I can help you.'

'We just want to ask some questions,' said Falcón. 'It shouldn't take too long.'

That eased the tension in the doorway. Rivero could see himself in bed within the hour. He let the door fall back and the two policemen stepped in.

'We'll go up to my office,' said Rivero, trying to reel in Ramírez, who'd gone straight through the arch to the internal courtyard and was brushing his large intrusive fingers over the rough head of the low hedge.

'What's this called?' he asked.

'Box hedge,' said Rivero. 'From the family Buxaceae. They use it in England to make mazes. Shall we go upstairs?'

'It looks as if it's just been clipped,' said Ramírez. 'When did that happen?'

'Probably last weekend, Inspector Ramírez,' said

Rivero, holding out his arm to herd him back into the fold. 'Let's go upstairs now, shall we?'

Ramírez snapped off a twig and twiddled it between thumb and forefinger. They went up to Rivero's office where he showed them chairs, before sinking into his own on the far side of the desk. He was irritated to find Ramírez examining the photographs on the wall: shots of Rivero, in politics and at play with the hierarchy of the Partido Popular, various members of the aristocracy, some bull breeders and a few local *toreros*.

'Are you looking for something, Inspector?' asked Rivero.

'You used to be the leader of Fuerza Andalucía until a few days ago,' said Ramírez. 'In fact, didn't you hand over the leadership on the morning of the explosion?'

'Well, it wasn't a sudden decision. It was something I'd been thinking about for a long time, but when something like that happens it opens up a new chapter in Seville politics, and it seemed to me that a new chapter needed new strength. Jesús Alarcón is the man to take the party forward. I think my decision has proved to be a very good one. We're polling more now than in the party's history.'

'I understood that you were very attached to the leadership,' said Ramírez, 'and that moves had been made before now to persuade you to hand over, but you'd refused. So what happened to make you think again?'

'I thought I'd just explained that.'

'Two senior members of your party left at the beginning of this year.'

'They had their reasons.'

'The newspapers reported that it was because they were fed up with your leadership.'

Silence. It always amazed Falcón how much Ramírez enjoyed making himself unpopular with 'important' people.

'I seem to remember that one of them even said that it would take a bomb to get you to give up the leadership and, I quote: "That would have the satisfying side effect of removing Don Eduardo from politics as well." That doesn't sound as if you were actively thinking about giving up your position, Sr Rivero.'

'The person who said that was expecting the leadership to be conferred on him. I didn't think he was a suitable candidate as he was only seven years younger than me. It was unfortunate that we fell out over the matter.'

'That's not what was written in the newspapers,' said Ramírez. 'They were reporting that these two senior members of your party were not pushing themselves forward but were, in fact, pushing for Jesús Alarcón to take over. What I was wondering was, what happened between then and now to bring about this sudden change of heart?'

'I'm quite flattered to find you so knowledgeable about my party,' said Rivero, who regained some strength by reminding himself that these men were homicide detectives and not from the sex crimes squad. 'But didn't you tell me you were here to talk about something else? It's late; perhaps we should press on.'

'Yes, of course,' said Ramírez. 'It was probably just malicious rumour anyway.'

Ramírez sat down, very pleased with himself. Rivero looked at him steadily over the rims of the gold specs he'd just put on. It was difficult to know what was burning inside him. Did he want to know what this rumour was, or would he prefer Ramírez just to shut the fuck up?

'We're looking for a missing person, Don Eduardo,' said Falcón.

Rivero's head whipped away from Ramírez to focus on Falcón.

'A missing person?' he said, and some relief crept into the corner of his face. 'I can't think of anybody I know who's gone missing, Inspector Jefe.'

'We're here because this man was last seen in your household by one of your maids,' said Falcón, who had spoken each word clearly and slowly so that he could watch the accumulation ease into Eduardo Rivero with the intrusiveness of a medical probe.

Rivero was a practised politician, but even he could not relax and animate himself through the progression of this sentence. Perhaps because it was a line that he'd dreaded hearing and had forced to the bleakest region of his mind.

'I'm not sure who you could be talking about,' said Rivero, clutching at the rope of hope, only to find frayed cotton threads.

'His name is Tateb Hassani, although in America he was known as Jack Hansen. He was a professor of Arabic Studies at Columbia University in New York,' said Falcón, who removed a photograph from his inside pocket and snapped it down in front of Rivero. 'I'm sure you'd recognize one of your own house guests, Don Eduardo.'

Rivero leaned forward and planted his elbows on the desk. He glanced down, stroked his chin and massaged his jowls with his thumb, over and over, whilst ransacking the furniture of his brain for the inspiration that would take him to the next moment.

'You're right,' said Rivero. 'Tateb Hassani was a guest in this house until last Saturday, when he left, and I haven't seen or heard of him since.'

'What time did he leave here on Saturday and how did he depart from these premises?' asked Falcón.

'I'm not sure when he left . . .'

'Was it daylight?'

'I wasn't here when he left,' said Rivero.

'When was the last time you saw him?'

'It was after lunch, probably four thirty. I said I was going to take a siesta. He said he would be leaving.'

'When did you wake from your siesta?'

'About six thirty.'

'And Tateb Hassani had already gone?'

'That is correct.'

'I'm sure your staff will be able to confirm that.'

Silence.

'When did you last see the cosmetic surgeon, Agustín Cárdenas?'

'He was here this evening . . . for dinner.'

'And before that?'

Silence, while monstrous abstractions boiled up, loomed, subsided and loomed again in Rivero's nauseated mind.

'He was here on Saturday evening, again for dinner.'

'How did he arrive for dinner?'

'In his car.'

'Can you describe that car?'

'It's a black Mercedes Estate E500. He'd just bought it last year.'

'Where did he park his car?'

'Inside the front doors, below the arch.'

'Did Agustín Cárdenas stay the night here?'

'Yes.'

'What time did he leave on Sunday?'

'At about eleven in the morning.'

'Were you aware of that car leaving your house at any time between Agustín Cárdenas's arrival and his departure on Sunday morning?'

'No,' said Rivero, the sweat careening down his spine.

'Who else was present at that dinner on Saturday night?'

Rivero cleared his throat. The water was getting deeper, winking at his chin.

'I'm not sure what this could possibly have to do with the disappearance of Tateb Hassani.'

'Because that was the night that Tateb Hassani was poisoned with cyanide, had his hands surgically removed, his face burnt off with acid and his scalp cut away from his skull,' said Falcón.

Rivero had to clench his buttocks against the sudden looseness of his bowels.

'But I've already told you that Tateb Hassani left here before dinner,' said Rivero. 'Maybe four hours before dinner.'

'And I'm sure that can be corroborated by the domestic servants on duty here at the time,' said Falcón.

'We're not accusing you of lying, Don Eduardo,' said Ramírez. 'But we must have a clear idea of what happened here, in this house, in the hope that it will explain what happened later.'

'What happened *later*?'

'Let's take it step by step,' said Falcón. 'Who attended the dinner, apart from yourself and Agustín Cárdenas?'

'That will shed no light on the disappearance of Tateb Hassani, because HE HAD ALREADY LEFT THIS HOUSE!' roared Rivero, hammering out the last six words with his fist on the desk.

'There's no need to upset yourself, Don Eduardo,' said Ramírez, leaning forward, full of false concern. 'Surely you can understand, given that a man was murdered and brutally dealt with, that the Inspector Jefe has to ask questions that may appear mystifying but which, we can assure you, will have a bearing on the case.'

'Let's go back a step,' said Falcón, to make it sound less unrelenting. 'Tell me who prepared Saturday's dinner and who served it.'

'It was prepared by the cook and it wasn't served. It was brought up to the room next door and laid out as a buffet.'

'Can we have those employees' names please?' said Falcón.

'They left straight afterwards and went home.'

'We'd still like their names and phone numbers,' said Falcón, and Ramírez handed over his notebook, which Rivero refused to accept.

'This is an infringement . . .'

'Tell us what happened after the dinner,' said Falcón. 'What time did it finish, who left and who stayed, and what did those who stayed do for the remainder of the night?'

'No, this is too much. I've told you everything that's relevant to the disappearance of Tateb Hassani. I've co-operated fully. All these other questions I consider to be outrageous intrusions into my private life and I see no reason why I should answer them.'

'Why was Tateb Hassani a house guest of yours for five days?'

'I told you, I'm not answering any more questions.'

'In that case, we must inform you that Tateb Hassani was suspected of terrorist offences, directly linked to the Seville bombing. His handwriting was on documents found in the destroyed mosque. You were therefore harbouring a terrorist, Don Eduardo. I think you know what that means regarding our investigation. So we would like you to accompany us down to the Jefatura and we will continue this interview under the terms of the antiterrorism –'

'Now, Inspector Jefe, let's not be too hasty,' said Rivero, blood draining from his face. 'You came here enquiring about the disappearance of Tateb Hassani. I have co-operated as best I can. Now you are changing the nature of your enquiry without giving me the opportunity to address the matter in this new light.'

'We didn't want to have to force your hand, Don Eduardo,' said Falcón. 'Let's go back to why you entertained Tateb Hassani as your house guest for five days . . .'

Rivero swallowed and braced himself against the desk for this next lap of the course.

'He was helping us to formulate our immigration policy. He, like us, did not believe that Africa and Europe were compatible, or that Islam and Christianity could cohabit in harmony. His particular insights into the Arabic mind were extremely helpful to us. And, of course, his name and stature added weight to our cause.'

'Despite the fact that he rarely visited his homeland,

527

had spent his entire adult life in the USA and that he had to leave Columbia University under the cloud of a sexual harassment case, which cost him his apartment and all his savings?' said Falcón.

'Despite that,' said Rivero. 'His insights were invaluable.'

'How much did Fuerza Andalucía pay him for this work?'

Rivero stared into the desk, terrified by this burgeoning demand for more and more improvisation. How was he ever going to remember any of it? Fatigue got a foothold in his viscera. He viciously shrugged it off. He had to hang on, like a fatally wounded man he had to keep talking, to overwhelm any desire he might have to give up. The flaws were developing inside him. His shell had been weakening from the moment that DVD had come anonymously into his possession and he'd had to view the hideousness of his indiscretions. The cracks had spread further when Angel had come to see him. He had listened, his white mane of hair gone wild and his face battered by excessive alcohol, as Angel had told him how he'd saved him. The rumour had been rife, like a wildfire consuming the tinder-dry undergrowth, gathering strength to leap up into an enormous conflagration. Angel had saved him, but it had come at a price. The time had come to step down or be destroyed.

That conversation with Angel had weakened him more than he knew. Over the days the flaws spread through him until every part of him was ruined. Every step now was a step down into the dark. Murder had come into his house and a desecration of the sanctity of the body. He could not think, after it had taken place, how such a thing could have happened to him in a matter of weeks. One moment brilliant and whole, the next corrupt, fractured, fissured beyond repair. He had to get a grip on himself. The centre must hold.

'You must remember what you had to pay for such invaluable advice,' said Falcón, who had been watching this immense struggle from the other side of the desk.

'It was 5,000,' said Rivero.

'Was that with a cheque?'

'No, cash.'

'You paid him with black money?'

'Even policemen know how this country works,' said Rivero, acidly.

'I must say, Don Eduardo, that I do admire your poise under these very stressful circumstances,' said Falcón. 'Had I been in your shoes and found out that the man I'd paid € 5,000 for his advice on immigration had also been involved in a terrorist plot to take over two schools and a university faculty, I would be in a state of shock. That this man should also have been responsible for writing out those appalling instructions to kill schoolchildren, one by one, until their demands had been met would devastate me, if I were you.'

'But then again, you are a politician,' said Ramírez, smiling.

Sweat was raking down his flanks, his stomach was embarking on a ferocious protest, his blood pressure was screaming in his ears, his heartbeat was so fast and tight that his breathing had shallowed, and his brain gasped for oxygen. And yet, he sat there, tapping the side of his nose, bracing himself against the desk.

'I have to say,' Rivero said, 'that I cannot begin to think what this means.'

'So, you had this dinner on Saturday night,' said Falcón. 'It wasn't served, but was laid out as a buffet. How many people attended that dinner? So far, we have yourself and Agustín Cárdenas, but you'd hardly go to the trouble of a buffet for just two people, would you?'

'Angel Zarrías was there as well,' said Rivero, smoothly, thinking, yes, they could have Angel, he should go down with them, the little fucker. 'I quite often have buffets on Saturday nights, so that the servants can go home and enjoy dinner with their families.'

'What time did Angel arrive?'

'He was here around 9.30, I think.'

'And Agustín Cárdenas?'

'About 10 p.m.'

'Did he arrive with anybody else?'

'No.'

'He was alone in the car?'

'Yes.'

'You're saying there were only three people for dinner?'

Rivero didn't care about the lying any more. It was all lies. He stared into his desk and let them fall from his tongue, like gold coins worn to a slippery smoothness.

'Yes. I quite often have a buffet and whoever turns up . . . turns up.'

Falcón glanced at Ramírez, who shrugged at him, nodded him in for the kill.

'Do you know one of your staff called Mario Gómez?'

'Of course.'

'It was he who laid out the buffet in the next room on that Saturday night.'

'That would be his job,' said Rivero.

'He told us that he'd served Tateb Hassani with at least one meal a day since he'd arrived in your house, up here in these rooms.'

'Possibly.'

'He knew who Tateb Hassani was, and he saw you accompanying him upstairs to dinner with Angel Zarrías at 9.45 on Saturday night. Some hours later Tateb Hassani was poisoned with cyanide, horribly disfigured and driven from here, in Agustín Cárdenas's car, to be dumped in a bin on Calle Boteros.'

Rivero clasped his hands, drove them between his slim thighs and sobbed with his head dropped on to his chest. Released at last.

36

'Great news,' said Elvira, sitting at his desk in his office in the Jefatura.

'Nearly great news,' said Falcón. 'We didn't manage to force Rivero into revealing the entire conspiracy. He only gave us two names. It's quite possible that we can charge the three of them, but only with the murder of Tateb Hassani and not the planning of the bombing of the mosque.'

'But now we can get a search warrant for Eduardo Rivero's house and the Fuerza Andalucía offices,' said Elvira. 'We must be able to squeeze something out of those two places.'

'But nothing in writing. You don't draw this sort of stuff up in the minutes of a Fuerza Andalucía meeting,' said Falcón. 'We have a tenuous link between Angel Zarrías and Ricardo Gamero, but no proof of what they discussed in the Archaeological Museum. We have no idea of the connection of any of these men to the people who actually planted the bomb. Both José Luis and I think that there is a missing element to the conspiracy.'

'A criminal element,' added Ramírez.

'We're sure that Lucrecio Arenas and César Benito are in some way involved, but we couldn't persuade Rivero to even give us their names,' said Falcón. 'They could be the "other half" of the conspiracy. Arenas put up Jesús Alarcón as a candidate for the leadership, so we assume that he is involved. But did Arenas and Benito make contact with the criminal element who planted the bomb? We're not sure we'll ever find out who, or what, that missing element was.'

'But you can put Rivero, Zarrías and Cárdenas under enormous pressure . . .'

'Except that they know, with the clarity of self-preservation, that all they have to do is keep their mouths shut and we'll only be able to pin murder on one of them, and conspiring to murder on all three, but nothing more,' said Falcón. 'And as for Lucrecio Arenas, Jesús Alarcón and César Benito, we have no chance. Ferrera worked hard just to get that final sighting of Tateb Hassani. Once those few remaining employees left, the house was empty, which means we'll have a job to place Arenas, Benito and Alarcón there . . . that is, assuming that they turned up for the killing.'

'And if I was them, I'd have kept well away from that,' said Ramírez.

'The link to the bomb conspiracy is Tateb Hassani,' said Elvira. 'Work on the suspects until they reveal why Hassani had to be killed. Once they've admitted –'

'If it was *my* life that depended on it,' said Ramírez, 'I'd just hold out.'

'I can't speak for Rivero and Cárdenas, but I know Angel Zarrías is very religious, with a deep faith –

however misguided it might be. I'm sure he'll even find it in himself to be absolved of all his sins,' said Falcón. 'Angel is urbane. He knows what's tolerable in modern Spanish society, as far as expressing religious views is concerned. But I don't think we're talking about a mentality that's any less fanatical than an Islamic jihadist's.'

'Rivero, Zarrías and Cárdenas are going to spend the night in the cells,' said Elvira. 'And we'll see what tomorrow brings. You both have to get some sleep. We'll have search warrants ready in the morning for all of their properties.'

'I'm going to have to give my sister at least half an hour of my time,' said Falcón. 'Her partner has just been dragged out of bed and arrested in the middle of the night. There's probably a hundred messages on my mobile already.'

Cristina Ferrera slammed back into consciousness with dead-bolt certainty and sat upright in her bed, faintly swaying, as if moored by guy ropes in a wind. She only came awake like this if her maternal instinct had received a high-voltage neural alarm call. Despite the depth of the sleep she'd just abandoned, her lucidity was instantaneous; she knew that her children were neither in the apartment, nor in danger, but that something was very wrong.

The street lighting showed that there was nobody in her room. She swung her legs out of bed and scanned the living room. Her handbag was no longer in the centre of the dining-room table. It had been moved to the corner. She toed the door open to the bedroom she'd made up for Fernando. The bed was empty. The pillow was dented, but the sheets had not been drawn back. She checked her watch. It was coming up to 4.30 a.m. Why would he have come here just to sleep for a few hours?

She turned the light on over the dining-room table and wrenched open the neck of her large handbag. Her notebook was on top of her purse. She slapped it on the table. Nothing was missing, not even the € 15 in cash. She sat down as their conversation came back to her: Fernando badgering her for news. Her eyes drifted from her handbag to her notebook. Her notes were personal. She always kept two columns; one for the facts, the other for her thoughts and observations. The latter was not always tethered to the former and sometimes verged on the creative. She turned the notebook over. One of her observations jumped out at her from the page. It was alongside the names of the people who'd been seen by Mario Gómez going up with Tateb Hassani to the 'last supper'. In her observation column she'd scribbled the only possible conclusion to all the enquiries she'd made: Fuerza Andalucía planted the bomb. No question mark. A bold statement, based on the facts she'd gathered.

It was suddenly cold in the room, as if the air conditioning had found another gear. She swallowed against the rise of adrenaline. She headed for the bedroom, with the backs of her thighs trembling below the oversized T-shirt she wore in bed. She slapped the light on and opened the drawer of her dresser where she kept a vast tangle of knickers and bras. Her hand roved the drawer, again and again. She ripped it out and turned it over. She ripped out the other drawer and did the same. She thought she was going to faint with the quantity of chemicals her body was injecting into her system. Her gun was no longer there.

This was too big for her to manage on her own. She was going to have to call her Inspector Jefe. She hit the speed-dial button, listened to the endless ringing tone and reminded herself to breathe. Falcón answered on the eighth ring. He'd been asleep for one and a half hours. She told him everything in three seconds flat. It went down the line like a massive file under compression software.

'You're going to have to tell me all that again, Cristina,' he said, 'and a little slower. Breathe. Close your eyes. Speak.'

This time it came out in a thirty-second stream.

'There's only one person from Fuerza Andalucía who Fernando knows who isn't currently in police custody and that's Jesús Alarcón,' said Falcón. 'I'll pick you up in ten minutes.'

'But he's going to kill him, Inspector Jefe,' said Ferrera. 'He's going to kill him with my gun. Shouldn't we . . .?'

'If we send a patrol car round there he might get spooked and do just that,' said Falcón. 'My guess is that Fernando is going to want to tell him something first. Punish him before he *tries* to kill him.'

'With a gun he doesn't have to try very hard.'

'The concept is easy, the reality takes a bit more,' said Falcón. 'Let's hope he woke you up as he left your apartment. If he's on foot he can't be too far ahead of us.'

Fernando squatted on his haunches next to some bins on the edge of the Parque María Luisa. Only his hands were in the light from the street lamps. He looked from

536

the dark at the blue metal of the small .38 revolver. He turned it over, surprised at its weight. He'd only ever held toy guns, made from aluminium. The real thing had the heft of a much bigger tool, condensed into pure efficiency and portability.

He emptied the bullets from the chambers of the revolver's cylinder and put them in his pocket. He clicked the cylinder back into place. He was good with his hands. He played around with the weapon, getting used to its weight and the simple, lethal mechanisms. When he was confident with it, he counted the bullets back into the chambers. He was ready. He stood and did what he'd seen people do in the movies. He tucked it into the waistband in the small of his back and pulled the Fuerza Andalucía polo shirt, given to him by Jesús Alarcón, over the top.

The wide Avenida that separated the park from the smart residential area of El Porvenir was empty. He knew where Jesús Alarcón lived because there'd been the offer of a room for as long as he wanted it. He hadn't accepted it because he didn't feel comfortable with their class differences.

He stood in front of the huge, sliding metal gate of the house. A silver Mercedes was parked in front of the garage. If Fernando had known that it was worth twice as much as his destroyed apartment it would have stoked his fury even more. As it was, the malignancy growing inside him was too big to contain. His rib cage creaked against his endlessly extending outrage at what Jesús Alarcón had done. Not just the bombing, but the purpose with which he'd set out to make Fernando, whose family he had personally been responsible for destroying, his close friend. It was treachery and betrayal on a scale to which only a politician could have been impervious. Jesús Alarcón, with all his authentic concern and genuine sympathy, had been playing him like a fish.

There was no traffic. The street in El Porvenir was empty. None of the people in these houses was ever up before dawn. Fernando called Alarcón on his mobile. It rang for some time and switched into the message service. He called Alarcón's house phone and looked up at the window he imagined would be the master bedroom. Jesús and Mónica in some gargantuan bed, beneath high-quality linen, dressed in silk pyjamas. A faint glow appeared behind the curtains. Alarcón answered groggily.

'Jesús, it's me, Fernando. I'm sorry to call you so early. I'm here. Outside. I've been out all night. They threw me out of the hospital. I had nowhere to go. I need to talk to you. Can you come down? I'm . . . I'm desperate.'

It was true. He was desperate. Desperate for revenge. He'd only ever heard tales of the monstrousness of this horrific emotion. He had not been prepared for the way it found every crevice of the body. His organs screamed for it. His bones howled with it. His joints ground with it. His blood seethed with it. It was so intolerable that he had to get it out of himself. He wanted stilts so that he could step over the gate, smash through the glass, reach into Alarcón's bed and pluck out his beautiful wife and throw her to the ground, break her bones, dash out her brains, tread his sharpened stilt into her heart and then see what Jesús Alarcón made of that. Yes, he wanted to be enormous, to drive his arm into Alarcón's home as if it was a doll's house.

He saw his hand ferreting around the bedrooms reaching for Alarcón's small children, who would run squealing from his snatching hand. He wanted Alarcón to see them crushed and laid out under little sheets in front of the house.

'I'm coming,' said Alarcón. 'No problem, Fernando.'

Had he known the hidden hunger behind the eyes staring through the bars of the gate, Jesús Alarcón would have stayed in his bed, called the police and begged for special forces.

A light came on outside the front of the house. The door opened. Alarcón, in a silk dressing gown, pointed the remote at the gate. Fernando flinched, as if being shot at. The gate rumbled back on its rails. Fernando slipped through the gap and walked quickly up to the house. Alarcón had already turned back to the front door, holding out an arm, which he expected to fit around Fernando's shoulders and welcome him into his home.

Moths swirled around the porch light, maddened by the prospect of a greater darkness, which never materialized. Alarcón was still too groggy to recognize the level of intent moving up on him. He was astonished to feel a fistful of his dressing-gown collar grabbed from behind and the front door reeling away from him as Fernando, with the hardened strength of a manual worker, swung him round. Alarcón lost his footing and fell to his knees. Fernando yanked him backwards and trapped his head between his thighs. He had the gun out of his waistband. Alarcón reached back, grabbing at Fernando's trousers and polo shirt. Fernando showed him the gun, poked the barrel into the socket of his eye so that Alarcón gasped with pain.

'You see that?' said Fernando. 'You see it, you little fucker?'

Alarcón was paralysed with fear. His voice, with his neck pulled taut, produced only a grunt. Fernando pushed the gun between Alarcón's lips, felt the barrel rattle across his teeth and sensed the steel mushing into the softness of his tongue.

'Feel it. Taste it. You know what it is now.'

He wrenched the gun out of his mouth, taking a chip of tooth with it. He jammed the barrel into the back of Alarcón's neck.

'Are you ready? Say your prayers, Jesús, because you're going to meet your namesake.'

Fernando pulled the trigger, the gun pressed hard against Alarcón's shaking neck. There was a dry click. A gasp from Alarcón and a stink rose up from behind him as he loosed his bowels into his pyjamas.

'That was for Gloria,' said Fernando. 'Now you know her fear.'

Fernando moved the gun round to Alarcón's temple, screwed it into the top of his sideburn so that Alarcón winced away from it. Another dry click and a sob from Alarcón.

'That was for my little Pedro,' said Fernando, coughing against the emotion rising in his throat. 'He didn't know fear. He was too young to know it. Too innocent. Now look at the gun, Jesús. You see the cylinder. Two empty chambers and four full ones. We're going upstairs now and you're going to watch me shoot your wife and two children, just so you know how it feels.'

'What are you doing, Fernando?' said Alarcón, finding his voice and his presence of mind, now that the rush of the initial onslaught was past. 'What the fuck are you doing?'

'You and your friends. You're all the same. There's no difference between you and any other politician. You're all liars, cheats and egomaniacs. I don't know how I fell for your stupid, fucking line. Jesús Alarcón, the man who will talk to you without cameras, without the photo opportunity, without his beautiful profile in mind.'

'What are you talking about, Fernando? What have I done? How have I lied and cheated?' said Alarcón, pleading.

'You killed my wife and child,' said Fernando. 'And then, because you needed me, you made me your friend.'

'How did I kill them?'

'I read it in the police notes. You were all in it. Rivero, Zarrías, Cárdenas. You planted the bomb in the mosque. You killed my wife and son. You killed all those people. And for what?'

'Fernando?'

He looked up. A different voice from beyond the gate. Female. Not in his head. The blood was simmering in his brain, bubbling and popping in such arterial rage that he'd become confused.

'Gloria?' he said.

'It's me, Cristina,' she said. 'I'm here with Inspector Jefe Falcón. We want you to put the gun down, Fernando. This is not how you resolve things. You've misunderstood . . .'

'No, no. That is not true. I have *finally* understood only too well. You listen. You listen to my "friend", Jesús Alarcón.'

Fernando knelt down by the side of Alarcón and whispered harshly in his ear.

'I am not going to shoot you or your family on one condition,' he said. 'The condition is that you must tell them the truth. They're the cops. They know what the truth is. You're going to tell them the truth for the first time with your gilded politician's lips. Tell them how you planted the bomb and you will live to see the rest of this day. If you don't, I will shoot you and, when you are dead, I will go inside and find Mónica and shoot her, too. Go on, tell them.'

Fernando stood up and prodded Alarcón in the neck with the gun. Alarcón cleared his throat.

'The truth,' said Fernando, 'or I'm sending you into the dark. Tell them.'

Alarcón crossed himself.

'He has asked me to tell you the truth about the bomb,' said Alarcón, his head hung on to his chest, his arms limp by his sides. 'If I fail to tell you the truth he says he will shoot me and then my wife. I can only tell you what I know, which may not be the whole truth, but only a part of it.'

Fernando stood back, arm straight. He rested the gun barrel on the crown of Alarcón's head.

'I had nothing to do with the planting of any bomb in that mosque, so help me God,' said Alarcón.

37

There was no gunshot. A force travelled from Alarcón's head, up the gun barrel, through Fernando's hand, arm and shoulder and into his mind. It made his upper body shudder so that the gun barrel drifted from its aim, and had to be retrained on to Alarcón's crown, not once or twice, but three times. His finger caressed the trigger with each retraining of the revolver. He blinked, took in huge gulps of air and looked down on the man, who a few moments ago had been the object of his deepest hatred. He couldn't do it. Alarcón's words had somehow drained all his resolve. It was the miracle cure for the malignancy of his revenge. He knew with absolute certainty that he had heard the truth.

At first light, with the sky turning from midnight blue to anil, Fernando dropped his arm and let it hang with the weight of the gun. Ferrera stepped forward and removed it from his slack grasp and holstered it. She moved him away from behind Alarcón, who fell forwards on to all fours.

'Take Fernando to the car,' said Falcón. 'Cuff him.'

Alarcón was dry retching and sobbing at the sudden

543

release of tension. Falcón got him to his feet and took him to where his wife was standing, wide-eyed, features rigid, by the front door. Falcón asked for the bathroom. The request brought Mónica Alarcón back to reality. She led Falcón and her husband upstairs to where the children were standing, one holding a fluffy tiger, the other a small blue blanket, uncomprehending of the adult drama. Mónica got the kids back into their bedroom. She joined Falcón in the bathroom where her husband was struggling to undo the buttons on his pyjamas. Falcón told her to strip her husband's clothes off and get him into the shower. He would wait downstairs in the kitchen.

Exhaustion leaned on Falcón like a big, stupid dog. He shut the front door and sat at the kitchen table, staring into the garden, with only one thought shuttling backwards and forwards through his mind. Jesús Alarcón was not part of the conspiracy. It looked as if he was their compliant and ignorant front man.

Mónica came back down to the kitchen and offered him a coffee. She was shaken, her hands trembled over the crockery. She had to ask him to work the espresso machine.

'Did he have a gun?' she asked. 'Did Fernando have a *gun*?'

'Your husband handled himself very well,' said Falcón, nodding.

'But Fernando and Jesús were getting on so well.'

'Fernando read something he shouldn't have done and misunderstood an observation as a fact,' said Falcón. 'Your husband's courage meant that it didn't end in tragedy.'

'We both admired Fernando so much for the way

in which he was managing his terrible loss,' she said. 'I had no idea he was so unstable.'

'He thought your husband had betrayed him, that he'd made him his friend to further his political career. And Fernando *is* unstable. Nobody can be called stable after losing their wife and son like that.'

Jesús appeared in the doorway. He'd lost the ashen look. He was shaved and dressed in a white shirt and black trousers. Falcón made him a coffee. Mónica went back upstairs to check on the children. They sat at the kitchen table.

'A lot has happened overnight,' said Falcón. 'Can you answer a few questions before we discuss that?'

Alarcón nodded, stirred sugar into his coffee.

'Can you tell me where you were on Saturday 3rd June?' asked Falcón.

'We were north of Madrid for the weekend,' said Alarcón. 'One of Mónica's friends got married. The wedding party was at a finca on the way up to El Escorial. We stayed there on Sunday and came back on the AVE train early on Monday morning.'

'Did you go to the Fuerza Andalucía offices in Eduardo Rivero's house during the week before that?'

'No, I didn't,' said Alarcón. 'On the advice of Angel Zarrías I was staying clear of Eduardo. Angel was still working on him to relinquish the leadership and he reckoned that for Eduardo to see the new young blade of the party around him might be construed as humiliation. So, I didn't see any of them, except Angel, who came here a couple of times to tell me how things were going.'

'When you say you didn't see any of them, who do you include in that?'

'Eduardo Rivero and the three main sponsors of the party, who are all my supporters: Lucrecio Arenas, César Benito and Agustín Cárdenas.'

'When did you last see Eduardo Rivero?'

'On the Tuesday morning, when he formally handed over the leadership.'

'And before that?'

'I think we had lunch around the 20th of May. I'd have to check my diary.'

'Have you ever seen this man before?' asked Falcón, looking at Alarcón as he pushed a photo of Tateb Hassani across the table. It was clear he didn't recognize the man.

'No,' he said.

'Have you ever heard mention of the name Tateb Hassani or Jack Hansen?'

'No.'

Falcón took the photograph back and turned it over and over in his hands.

'Has that man got anything to do with what Fernando was talking about?' asked Alarcón. 'He looks North African. That first name you mentioned . . .'

'He's originally a Moroccan who became a US citizen,' said Falcón. 'He's dead now. Murdered. Rivero, Zarrías and Cárdenas are under arrest on suspicion of his killing.'

'I'm confused, Inspector Jefe.'

'Don Eduardo told me a few hours ago that he paid Tateb Hassani a € 5,000 consultancy fee last week for his advice on the formulation of Fuerza Andalucía's immigration policy.'

'That's ridiculous. Our immigration policy has been in place for months. We started work on that last October when the EU opened the door to Turkey and all those African immigrants tried to jump the wire into Melilla. Fuerza Andalucía does not believe that a Muslim country, even with a secular government, can be compatible with Christian countries. Europeans have shown themselves to be consistently intolerant of other religions throughout history. We have no idea of the social consequences of introducing Turkey, whose membership will result in one fifth of the European Union population being Muslim.'

'You're not on the campaign trail now, Sr Alarcón,' said Falcón, holding up his hands against the avalanche of opinion.

'I'm sorry. It's automatic,' he said, shaking his head. 'But why are Rivero, Zarrías and Cárdenas accused of murdering a man who they'd just paid to help formulate policy? Why does Fernando think that Fuerza Andalucía is in some way responsible for planting a bomb in the mosque?'

'I'm going to give you an irrefutable fact and I want you to tell me what you construe from it,' said Falcón. 'You heard on the news that a fireproof box was found in the destroyed mosque, which included architect's drawings of two schools and the university biology faculty, with notes attached in Arabic script.'

'The ones giving the horrific instructions.'

'Those were written by Tateb Hassani.'

'So, he was a terrorist?'

Falcón waited, tapping the edges of the photograph, one after the other, on the table top, while the espresso machine fumed quietly in the corner. Alarcón frowned at the back of his hands as his brain worked through the permutations. Falcón gave him the other facts that were not in the public domain, as yet: Tateb Hassani's handwriting also matched that found in the two Korans, found in the Peugeot Partner and in Miguel Botín's apartment. He also told him about Ricardo Gamero's final meeting with Angel Zarrías and the CGI agent's subsequent suicide. Alarcón turned his hands over and looked at his palms, as if his political future was trickling away through his fingers.

'I don't know what to say.'

Falcón gave him a short life history of Tateb Hassani and asked him if that sounded like the profile of a dangerous Islamic radical.

'Why did they pay Hassani to make up documents that would indicate a planned terrorist attack when, as has been made clear by the discovery of traces of hexogen in the Peugeot Partner, Islamic terrorists were positioning material to carry out a bombing campaign?' asked Alarcón. 'It doesn't make sense.'

'The executive committee of Fuerza Andalucía did not know about the hexogen,' said Falcón, which opened up the story about the surveillance by Informáticalidad, the fake council inspectors, the electricians, and the planting of the secondary Goma 2 Eco device and the fireproof box.

Alarcón was stunned. He knew all the directors of Informáticalidad, whom he described as 'part of the set-up'. Only then did he finally understand how he'd been used.

'And I was positioned as the fresh face of Fuerza Andalucía, who, in the aftermath of the atrocity, would attract the anti-immigration vote, which would give us the necessary percentage to make ourselves the natural coalition partner of the Partido Popular for next year's parliamentary campaign,' said Alarcón.

The revelations drained what little energy remained in Alarcón and he sat back with his arms limp at his sides and contemplated the catastrophe in which he'd been unwittingly involved.

'I realize that this must be hard for you . . .' said Falcón.

'There are enormous implications, of course,' said Alarcón, with an odd mixture of dismay and relief spreading across his features. 'But I wasn't thinking of that. I was thinking that Fernando's madness has had the inadvertent side effect of allowing me to exonerate myself in front of the investigating Inspector Jefe.'

'Our range of interrogation techniques no longer includes mock executions,' said Falcón. 'But it has saved me a lot of time.'

'It wasn't what I had in mind for the extension of police powers in the handling of terrorists, either,' said Alarcón.

'You might have to work a little harder than that to get my vote,' said Falcón. 'How would you describe your relationship to Lucrecio Arenas?'

'I'm not exaggerating when I tell you that he's been like a father to me,' said Alarcón.

'How long have you known him?'

'Eleven years,' said Alarcón. 'In fact, I met him before that, when I was working for McKinsey's in South America, but we became close when I moved to Lehman Brothers and started working with Spanish industrialists and banks. Then he head-hunted me in 1997 and since then he's been a surrogate father . . . he's shaped my whole career. He's the one who has given me belief in myself. He's second in my life only to God.'

It was the response Falcón had expected.

549

'If you think *he* is involved in whatever this is, then think again. You don't know the man like I do,' said Alarcón. 'This is some local intrigue, cooked up by Zarrías and Rivero.'

'Rivero is finished. He was finished before this happened. He was walking with the fly-buzz of scandal about him,' said Falcón. 'I know Angel Zarrías. He's not a leader. He makes people into leaders, but he doesn't make things happen himself. What can *you* tell me about Agustín Cárdenas and César Benito?'

'I need another coffee,' said Alarcón.

'Here's an interesting link for you to think about,' said Falcón. 'Informáticalidad to Horizonte, to Banco Omni, to . . . I4IT?'

The coffee machine gurgled, trickled, hissed and steamed, while Alarcón hovered around it, blinking in this new point of view, matching it to his own bank of knowledge. Doubt threaded its way across his eyebrows. Falcón knew this wasn't going to be enough, but he didn't have anything more. If Rivero, Zarrías and Cárdenas didn't break down then Alarcón might be his only door into the conspiracy, but it was going to be a heavy door to open. He didn't know enough about Lucrecio Arenas to induce a sense of outrage in Alarcón at the way in which he'd been shamelessly exploited by his so-called 'father'.

'I know what you want from me,' said Alarcón, 'but I can't do it. I realize it's not fashionable to be loyal, especially in politics and business, but I can't help myself. Even suspecting these people would be like turning on my own family. I mean, they *are* my family. My father-in-law is one of these people . . .'

'That was why you were chosen,' said Falcón. 'You

are an extraordinary combination. I don't agree with your politics, but I can see that, for a start, you are very courageous and that your intentions towards Fernando were completely honourable. You're an intelligent and gifted man, but your vulnerability is in your professed loyalty. Powerful people *like* that in a person, because you have all the qualities that they don't, and you can be manipulated towards achieving their goals.'

'It's a marvellous world in which loyalty is perceived as a vulnerability,' said Alarcón. 'You must be a man made cynical by your work, Inspector Jefe.'

'I'm not cynical, Sr Alarcón, I've just come to realize that it's the nature of virtue to be predictable,' he said. 'It's always evil that leaves one gasping at its bold and inconceivable virtuosity.'

'I'll remember that.'

'Don't make me any more coffee,' said Falcón. 'I have to sleep. Perhaps we should talk again when you've had time to think about what I've told you and I've started working on Rivero, Zarrías and Cárdenas.'

Alarcón walked him to the front door.

'As far as I am concerned, I have no wish to see Fernando punished for what he did to me,' he said. 'My sense of loyalty also enables me to understand the profound effects of disloyalty and betrayal. You might have charges you wish to press against him, but I don't.'

'If this gets out to the press I'll have no option but to prosecute him,' said Falcón. 'He stole a police firearm and there's a good case for attempted murder.'

'I won't talk to the press. You have my word on it.'

'You've just saved the career of one of my best junior officers,' said Falcón, stepping off the porch.

He walked to the gate and turned back to Alarcón.

'I presume, after last night's meeting, that Lucrecio Arenas and César Benito are still in Seville,' he said. 'I would suggest a face-to-face meeting with one, or both, of them while the information I've just given you is still out of the public domain.'

'César won't be there. He'll be at the Holiday Inn in Madrid for a conference,' said Alarcón. 'Is seventy-two hours from inception to demise of a political future some kind of Spanish record?'

'The advantage you have at the moment is that you, personally, are clean. If you can retain that, you will always have a future. It's only once you join hands with corruption that you're finished,' said Falcón. 'Your old friend Eduardo Rivero could tell you that from the bottom of the well of his experience.'

Cristina Ferrera and Fernando were sitting in the back of Falcón's car. She'd cuffed his hands behind his back and he leaned forward with his head resting against the back of the front seat. Falcón thought that they'd been talking but were now exhausted. He turned to face them from the driver's seat.

'Sr Alarcón is not going to press charges and he won't talk to the newspapers about this incident,' he said. 'If I were to prosecute you I would lose one of my best officers, your daughter would lose her father and only parent and would have to be taken into care, or go to live with her grandparents. You would go to jail for at least ten years and Lourdes would never know you. Do you think that's a satisfactory outcome for a burst of uncontrollable rage, Fernando?'

Cristina Ferrera looked out of the window blinking

with relief. Fernando raised his head from the back of the passenger seat.

'And had your rage got the better of you, had your hatred been so dire that no reason could have appealed to it, and you'd actually killed Jesús Alarcón, then all the above would still be true, although your prison sentence would be longer, and you'd have had the death of an innocent man on your conscience,' said Falcón. 'How does that feel, in the dawn light of a new day?'

Fernando looked straight ahead, through the windscreen, down the street growing lighter by the moment.

He said nothing. There was nothing to say.

38

'You didn't make it to our appointment last night,' said Alicia Aguado.

'I was in no condition,' said Consuelo. 'I left you, went to the pharmacy with the prescription you'd given me, bought the drugs and didn't take them. I went back to my sister's house. I spent most of the day in her spare room. Some of the time I was crying so hard I couldn't breathe.'

'When was the last time you cried?'

'I don't think I ever have . . . not properly. Not with grief,' said Consuelo. 'I don't even remember crying as a child, apart from when I hurt myself. My mother said I was a silent baby. I don't think I was the crying type.'

'And how do you feel now?'

'Can't you tell?' said Consuelo, twitching her wrist under Aguado's fingers.

'Tell me.'

'It's not an easy state to describe,' said Consuelo. 'I don't want to sound like some mushy fool.'

'Mushy fool is a good start.'

554

'I feel better now than I have done for a long time,' said Consuelo. 'I can't say that I feel good, but that terrifying sense of impending hideousness has gone. And the strange sexual urges have gone.'

'So, you don't think you're going mad any more?' said Aguado.

'I'm not sure about that,' said Consuelo. 'I've lost all sense of equilibrium. I can't seem to have just one feeling, I'm both extremes at once. I feel empty *and* full, courageous and afraid, angry and placid, happy and yet grief-stricken. I can't find any middle ground.'

'You can't expect your mind to recover in twenty-four hours of crying,' said Aguado. 'Do you think you could describe what happened yesterday morning? You came to some sort of realization which completely felled you. I'd like you to talk about that.'

'I'm not sure I can remember how it came about,' said Consuelo. 'It's like the bomb going off in Seville. So much has happened that it already feels like ten years ago.'

'I'll tell you how it came about afterwards,' said Aguado. 'Concentrate on what happened. Describe it as best you can.'

'It started off like a pressure, as if there was a membrane stretched across my mind, like an opaque latex sheet, against which someone, or something, was pressing. It's happened to me before. It makes me feel queasy, as if I'm at that crossover point between being merry and drunk. When it's happened in the past I'd make it go away by doing something like rummaging in my handbag. The physical action would help to reassert reality, but I'd be left with the sensation of the imminence of something that had not come to pass.

The interesting thing was that I stopped getting these moments a few years ago.'

'Were they replaced by something else?'

'I didn't think so at the time. I was just glad to be rid of the sensation. But now I'm thinking that it was then that the sexual urges started,' said Consuelo. 'In the same way that the pressure started during a lull of brain activity, so the urges would come, sometimes in a meeting, or playing with the kids, or trying on a pair of shoes. It was disturbing to have no control over when they appeared, because they would be accompanied by graphic images which left me feeling disgusted with myself.'

'So what happened yesterday?' asked Aguado.

'The membrane came back,' said Consuelo, palms suddenly moist on the arms of the chair. 'There was the pressuré, but it was much greater and it seemed to be expanding at an incredible rate, so that I thought my head would burst. In fact, there *was* a sensation of bursting, or rather splitting, which was accompanied by that feeling you get in dreams of endlessly falling. I thought this is it. I'm finished. The monster's come up from the deep and I'm going to go mad.'

'But that didn't happen, did it?'

'No. There was no monster.'

'Was there anything?'

'There was just me. A lonely young woman in a rain-filled street, full of grief, guilt and despair. I didn't know what to do with myself.'

'When this happened, we were talking about someone you knew,' said Aguado. 'The Madrid art dealer.'

'Ah, yes, him. Did I tell you that he'd killed a man?'

'Yes, but you told me about it in a certain way.'

'I remember now,' said Consuelo. 'I told you about it as if his crime was greater than my own.'

'What does that mean?'

'That I believed that I had committed a crime?' said Consuelo, questioning. 'Except that I knew what I'd done. I had always faced up to the fact that I'd had the abortions, even the appalling way I'd raised the money for the first one.'

'Which had resulted in some confusion in your mind,' said Aguado. 'The graphic sexual images?'

'I don't understand.'

'This pain you mentioned when you watched your children sleeping, especially the youngest child – what do you think that was?'

Consuelo gulped, as the saliva thickened in her mouth and tears flooded her eyes and rolled down her face.

'You told me before that it was the love that was hurting,' said Aguado. 'Do you still think it was love?'

'No,' said Consuelo, after some long minutes. 'It was guilt at what I had done, and grief at what could have been.'

'Go back to that time when you were standing in the rain-filled street. I think you told me earlier that you were looking at some smart people coming out of an art gallery. Do you remember what you were thinking, before you decided that you wanted to be like them, that you wanted to "reinvent" yourself?'

There was a long silence. Aguado didn't move. She stared straight ahead with her unseeing eyes and felt the pulse beneath her fingers, like string untangling itself.

'Regret,' said Consuelo. 'I wished I hadn't done it, and when I saw those people coming out into the street I thought that they were not the sort of people to get themselves into this state. It was then that I decided I wanted to leave this pathetic, lonely, pitiful person on this wet street and go and be someone else.'

'So, although you've always "faced up" to what you'd done, there was also something missing. What was that?'

'The person who'd done it,' said Consuelo. 'Me.'

The search warrants for Eduardo Rivero's house, the premises of Fuerza Andalucía, Angel Zarrías's apartment and Agustín Cárdenas's residence were issued at 7.30 a.m. By 8.15 the forensics had moved in, the computer hard disks had been copied and evidence was being gathered and gradually shipped back to the Jefatura. Comisario Elvira, all six members of the homicide squad and three members of the CGI antiterrorism squad convened for a strategy meeting in the Jefatura at 8.45. The idea was that the nine-man interrogation team would interview the three suspects, with a few breaks, for a total of thirteen and a half hours. To prevent the suspects developing relationships or getting used to a certain style, every member of the team would interview each suspect for an hour and a half. While the first three interviewers worked the next wave would watch, and the third wave would rest or discuss developments. Lunch would be taken at 3 p.m. and there would be another tactical discussion. The next session would run from 4 p.m. to 10 p.m. and, if none of the suspects had cracked, there would be a break for dinner and a final ninety-minute session at midnight.

The point of the interviews was not to persuade the suspects to admit to the killing of Tateb Hassani, but to force them to reveal who had put Fuerza Andalucía in touch with him, why he was being employed, where the documents he'd prepared had been delivered, and who else had been at the dinner at which Tateb Hassani had been poisoned.

Exhaustion was the communal state. The meeting broke up with sighs, hands run through hair, jackets removed and shirt sleeves rolled up. It was agreed that Falcón would take Angel Zarrías first, Ramírez would handle Eduardo Rivero, and Barros would start on Agustín Cárdenas. Once they were told that the suspects were in the interview rooms they went downstairs.

Ferrera was due to follow Falcón interviewing Angel Zarrías. They stood in front of the glass viewing panel, looking at him. He was sitting at the table, wearing a long-sleeved white shirt, hands clasped, eyes fixed on the door. He seemed calm. Falcón began to feel too tired for this confrontation.

'You're going to find out that Angel Zarrías is a very charming man,' said Falcón. 'He especially likes women. I don't know him very well because he's the sort of man who keeps you at a distance with his charm. But there has to be a real person underneath that. There has to be the fanatic that wanted to make this conspiracy work. That's the man we want to get to, and once we've got to him we want to keep him there, exposed, for as long as possible.'

'And how are you going to do that?' said Ferrera. 'He's practically your brother-in-law.'

'I've learnt a few things from José Luis,' said Falcón,

nodding at Rivero's interview room, which Ramírez had just entered.

'Then I'll keep an eye on both of you,' said Ferrera.

Angel Zarrías's eyes flicked up as Falcón opened the door to the interview room. He smiled and stood up.

'I'm glad it's you, Javier,' he said. 'I'm so glad it's you. Have you spoken to Manuela?'

'I spoke to Manuela,' said Falcón, who sat down without turning on any of the recording equipment or following any of the normal introductory procedure. 'She's very angry.'

'Well, people react in different ways to having their partners arrested in the middle of the night on suspicion of murder,' said Zarrías. 'I can imagine some people might get angry. I don't know how I'd feel myself.'

'She wasn't angry about your arrest,' said Falcón.

'She was pretty fierce with your officers,' said Angel.

'It was after I'd spoken to her that she became . . . incandescent with rage,' said Falcón. 'I think that would be a fair description.'

'When did you speak to her?' he asked, unnerved, puzzled.

'At about two o'clock this morning,' said Falcón. 'She'd already left about fifty messages on my mobile by then.'

'Of course . . . she would.'

'As you know, she can be quite a daunting prospect when she's emotionally charged,' said Falcón. 'It wasn't possible for me to just say that you'd been arrested on suspicion of murder and leave it at that. She had to know who, where and why.'

'And what did you tell her?'

'I had to tell her by degrees because, of course, there

are legal implications, but I can assure you I only told her the truth.'

'What was this "truth" that you told her?'

'That is what *you* are supposed to tell *me*, Angel. You are the perpetrator and I am the interrogator, and between us there is a truth. The idea is that we negotiate our way to the heart of it, but it's not up to *me* to tell *you* what I think you've done. That's your job.'

Silence. Zarrías looked at the dead recording equipment. Falcón was pleased to see him confused. He leaned over, turned on the recorder and made the introductions.

'Why did you kill Tateb Hassani?' asked Falcón, sitting back.

'And what if I tell you that I didn't kill him?'

'If you like, for the purposes of this interview, we won't draw a distinction between murder and conspiring to murder,' said Falcón. 'Does that make it easier for you?'

'What if I tell you I had nothing to do with the murder of Tateb Hassani?'

'You've already been implicated, along with Agustín Cárdenas, by the host of Hassani's final and fatal dinner, Eduardo Rivero. You've also been identified as being present at the scene of the crime by an employee in his household,' said Falcón. 'So for you to say that you had *nothing* to do with Hassani's death would be a very difficult position to defend.'

Angel Zarrías looked deeply into Falcón's face. Falcón had been looked at like this before. His old technique, before his breakdown in 2001, was to meet it with the armour-plated stare. His new technique was to welcome them in, bring them to the lip of his deep well and dare them to look down. This was what he did to Angel Zarrías. But Angel wouldn't come. He looked hard but he never came to the edge. He backed off and glanced around the room.

'Let's not get bogged down in all the detail,' said Falcón. 'I'm not interested in who put the cyanide in what, or who was present when Agustín Cárdenas did his gruesome work. Although I *am* interested to know whose idea it was to sew Tateb Hassani into a shroud. Did you come up with any suitable Islamic orisons for him? Did you wash him before you sewed him up? It was a bit tricky for us to tell once we'd discovered him, bloated and stinking, with the shroud torn off, on the rubbish dump outside Seville. But I thought that was a nice touch of respect from one religion to another. Was that your idea?'

Angel Zarrías had pushed his chair back and, in his agitation, had started to pace the room.

'You're not talking to me already, Angel, and we've only just started.'

'What the hell do you expect me to say?'

'All right. I know. It's difficult. You've always been a good Catholic, a man of great religious faith. You even managed to get Manuela to go to Mass, and she *must* have loved you to do that,' said Falcón. 'Guilt is a debilitating state for a good man, such as yourself. Living in mortal sin must be petrifying but, equally, it's a daunting task to bring yourself to the confessional for the greatest of human crimes. I'm going to make this easier for you. Let's forget about Tateb Hassani for the time being and move on to something you're more comfortable with, that you should be able to talk about, that should loosen your vocal cords so that you will, eventually, be able to come back to the more demanding revelations.'

Angel Zarrías stopped in his tracks and faced Falcón. His shoulders slumped, his chest looked like a cathedral roof on the brink of collapse.

'Go on then, ask your question.'

'Where were you on Wednesday, 7th June between 1.30 p.m. and 3 p.m.?'

'I can't recall. I was probably having lunch.'

'Sit down and think about it,' said Falcón. 'This is the day *after* the explosion. You would have received a phone call from someone who was desperate. I'm sure you'd remember that: a fellow human being in distress who needed to speak to you.'

'You know who it is, so you tell me,' said Angel, who'd started his agitated walking again.

'SIT DOWN, ANGEL!' roared Falcón.

Zarrías had never heard Falcón shout before. He was shocked at the anger simmering beneath the placid surface. He swerved towards the chair, sat down and stared into the table with his hands clasped tight.

'You were seen and identified by a security guard,' said Falcón.

'I went to the Archaeological Museum and met a man called Ricardo Gamero.'

'Are you aware of what happened to Ricardo Gamero about half an hour after you spoke to him?'

'He committed suicide.'

'You were the last person to speak to him, face to face. What did you talk about?'

'He told me he had developed feelings for another man. He was very ashamed and distressed about it.'

'You're lying to me, Angel. Why should a committed

563

CGI agent leave his office during the most important antiterrorist investigation ever to happen in this city, to go and discuss his sexual angst with you?'

'You asked me a question and I replied,' said Zarrías, without taking his eyes off the table.

Falcón pummelled Zarrías with questions about Ricardo Gamero for three-quarters of an hour, but could not get him to budge from his story. He accused Zarrías of telling Marco Barreda from Informáticalidad to offer up the same lie. Zarrías didn't even give Falcón the satisfaction of a flicker of recognition at this new name. Falcón made a show of ordering Barreda to be brought down to the Jefatura for questioning. Zarrías hung on grimly, knowing that this was the difference between life and a living death.

It was well past 10 a.m. when Falcón returned to the murder of Tateb Hassani. Zarrías looked pale and sick from maintaining his wall of deceit. One eye was bloodshot and his lower lids were hanging down from his eyeballs to reveal raw, veined and shiny flesh.

'Let's talk about Tateb Hassani again,' said Falcón. 'An employee, Mario Gómez, saw you, Rivero and Hassani going upstairs to the Fuerza Andalucía offices in Rivero's house to dine on a buffet that he'd just laid out. The time was 9.45 p.m. Rivero has told us that Agustín Cárdenas arrived a little later and parked his car underneath the arch of the entrance. Tell me what happened in the time between you going up the stairs and Tateb Hassani's body being brought down to be loaded into Agustín Cárdenas's Mercedes E500.'

'We drank some chilled manzanilla, ate some olives. Agustín turned up a little after ten o'clock. We served ourselves from the buffet. Eduardo opened a special bottle of wine, one of his Vega Sicilias. We ate, we drank, we talked.'

'What time did Lucrecio Arenas and César Benito arrive?'

'They didn't. They weren't there.'

'Mario Gómez told us that there was enough food for eight people.'

'Eduardo has always been generous with his portions.'

'At what point did you administer the cyanide to Tateb Hassani?'

'You're not going to get me to incriminate myself,' said Angel. 'We'll leave that for the court to decide.'

'How was Tateb Hassani introduced to you?'

'We met at the Chamber of Commerce.'

'What did Tateb Hassani do for you?'

'He helped us formulate our immigration policy.'

'Jesús Alarcón says that was already in place months ago.'

'Tateb Hassani was very knowledgeable about North Africa. He'd read a lot of the UN reports about the mass assaults by illegal immigrants on the enclaves of Ceuta and Melilla. We were incorporating new ideas into our policy. We had no idea how well-timed his help would be in view of what happened on 6th June.'

Falcón announced the end of the interview and flicked off the recorder. It was more important now that he prepare Zarrías for the next interview. There was plenty of evidence of decrepitude in his face, but he had retreated into himself, concentrated his powers into a nucleus of defence. Falcón had only achieved some superficial damage. Now he had to make him vulnerable.

'I had to tell Manuela,' said Falcón. 'You know what she's like. I told her that you'd had to murder Tateb Hassani because he was the only element outside the conspiracy and, therefore, the only danger to it. If he was left alive it would render Fuerza Andalucía vulnerable. Manuela wasn't prepared to deal in those sorts of generalizations so I had to give her the detail; how you'd employed him and where evidence of his handwriting was found. She knows you, of course, Angel. She knows you very well. She hadn't quite realized how far your obsession had gone. She hadn't realized that you'd gone from being extreme to fanatical. And she admired you so much, Angel, you know that, don't you? You helped her a lot with your positive energy. You helped me, too. You saved my relationship with her, which was important to me. I believe that she could have forgiven you this misguided attempt to finally grab a workable power, even if she didn't hold with your extreme beliefs. She thought, at least, that you were honourable. But there was something that she could not forgive.'

At last Zarrías looked up, as if he'd just come to the surface of himself. The tired, bruised and sagging eyes were suddenly alive with interest. In that moment Falcón realized something he'd never quite been sure about: Angel loved Manuela. Falcón knew that his sister was attractive, plenty of people had told him that they found her funny and that she had a great zest for life, and he'd seen her affect men touchingly by playing the little girl as well as the grown woman. But Falcón knew her too well and it had always seemed unlikely to him that anybody not related to Manuela could love her absolutely, because she had too many faults and dislikeable traits constantly on display. Clearly, though, she'd given something to Angel that he'd missed from his previous marriage, because there was no mistaking his need to know why she hated him.

'I'm listening,' said Zarrías.

'She could not forgive the way you talked to her that morning, when you'd already planned for that bomb to explode and she hadn't sold her properties.'

39

Yacoub was in the library in the group's house in the medina when they came for him. With no warning there were suddenly four men around him. They put a black hood over his head and tied his hands behind him with plastic cuffs. Nobody said a word. They took him through the house and out into the street, where he was thrust into the footwell in the back of a car. Three men came in after him and rested their feet on his supine body. The car took off.

They drove for hours. It was uncomfortable in the footwell, but at least they were driving on tarmac. Yacoub controlled his fear by telling himself that this was part of the initiation rite. After several hours they came off the good road and began labouring up some rough track. It was hot. The car had no air conditioning. The windows were open. It must have been dusty, because he could smell it even inside his hood. They spent an hour dipping and diving on the rough track until the car came to a halt. There was the sound of a rifle mechanism, followed by an intense silence as if each face in the car were being searched. They were told to carry on.

The car continued for another fifteen minutes until it again came to a halt. Doors opened and Yacoub was dragged out, losing his barbouches. They ran him across some rocky ground so fast that he stumbled. They paid no attention to his lost footing and hauled him on. A door opened. He was taken across a beaten earth floor and down some steps. Another door. He was hurled against a wall. He dropped to the floor. The door shut. Footsteps retreated. No light came through the dense material of the hood. He listened hard and became aware of a sound, which did not seem to be in the same room. It was a human sound. It was coming from a man's throat, a gasping and groaning, as if he was in great pain. He called out to the man, but all that happened was that the voice fell silent, apart from a faint sobbing.

The sound of approaching feet kick-started Yacoub's heart. His mouth dried as the door opened. The room seemed to be full of people, all shouting and pushing him around. There was the sound of screaming from the next room and a man's voice, pleading. They picked Yacoub up bodily, held him face down, and took him back up the stairs, outside, across rough ground. They dropped him and stood back. Whoever had been downstairs in the cells was now out in the open with him, crying out in pain. A rifle mechanism clattered close to his ear. Yacoub's head was pulled up and the hood removed. He saw a man's feet, bloody and pulpy. His hair was grabbed from behind and his vision directed towards the man lying in front of him. A gunshot, loud and close. The man's head jolted and matter spurted from the other side. His bloody feet twitched. The hood was pulled back over Yacoub's head. The barrel of a gun was put to the back of his neck. His heart was thundering in his ears, eyes tight shut. The trigger clicked behind his head.

They picked him up again. They seemed gentler. They walked him away. There was no rush now. He was taken into a house and given a chair to sit on. They removed his plastic cuffs and black hood. Sweat cascaded down his neck and into the collar of his jellabah. A boy put his barbouches down by his feet. A glass of mint tea was poured for him. He was so disorientated that he could not even take in the faces of those around him before they left the room. He put his head down on the table top and gasped and wept.

After being inside the hood, his eyes were already accustomed to the darkness of the room. There was a single bed in the corner. One wall was covered with books. The windows were all shuttered. He sipped the tea. His heart rate eased back down to below the one hundred mark. His throat, which had been tight with hysteria, slackened. He went over to the books and studied the titles of each one. Most of them were about architecture or engineering: detailed tomes on buildings and machines. There were even some car manuals, thick manufacturer's plans for some four-wheel-drive vehicles. They were all in French, English or German. The only Arabic texts were eight volumes of poetry. He sat back down.

Two men came in and gave him a formal, but warm, welcome. One called himself Mohamed, the other Abu. A boy followed them, carrying a tray of tea, glasses and a plate of flat bread. The two men were both heavily bearded and each wore a dark brown burnous and army boots. They sat at the table. The boy poured the tea and left. Abu and Mohamed studied Yacoub very carefully.

'That is not normally part of our initiation procedure,' said Mohamed.

'A member of our council thought that you were a special case,' said Abu, 'because you have so many outside contacts.'

'He felt that you needed to be left in no doubt as to the punishment for treachery.'

'We did not agree with him,' said Abu. 'We did not think that anyone bearing the name of Abdullah Diouri would need such a demonstration.'

Yacoub acknowledged the honour accorded to his father. More tea was poured and sipped. The bread was broken and distributed.

'You had a visit from a friend of yours on Wednesday,' said Mohamed.

'Javier Falcón,' said Yacoub.

'What did he want to discuss with you?'

'He is the investigator of the Seville bombing,' said Yacoub.

'We know everything about him,' said Abu. 'We just want to know what you discussed.'

'The Spanish intelligence agency had asked him to approach me on their behalf,' said Yacoub. 'He wanted to know if I would be willing to be a source for them.'

'And what did you tell him?'

'I gave him the same answer that I'd given the Americans and the British when they'd made the same approaches,' said Yacoub, 'which is why I am here today.'

'Why is that?'

'In refusing all these people, who dishonoured me

by offering money for my services, I realized that it was time for me to take a stand. If I was certain that I did not want to be with them, then it should follow that my loyalties lay elsewhere. I had refused them because it would be the ultimate betrayal of everything my father stood for. And, if that was the case, then I should take a stand for what he believed in, against the decadence that he so despised. So when my friend left I went straight to the mosque in Salé and let it be known that I wanted to help in any way that I could.'

'Do you still consider Javier Falcón to be a friend?'

'Yes, I do. He was not acting for himself. I still consider him to be an honourable man.'

'We have been following the Seville bombing with interest,' said Mohamed. 'As you've probably realized, it has caused great disruption to one of our plans, which has demanded a lot of reorganization. We understand that some arrests were made last night. Three men are being held. They are all members of the political party Fuerza Andalucía, a party holding anti-Islamic views, which it wants to translate into regional policy. We have been watching them closely. They have recently elected a new leader, who we know little about. What we do know is that the three men they have arrested are being held on a charge of suspected murder. It is believed that they killed an apostate and traitor called Tateb Hassani. That is of no interest to us, nor are these three men, who we believe to be unimportant. We would like to know – and we think that your friend, Javier Falcón, will be able to help – who gave the orders for the mosque to be bombed?'

'If he knew that, then I am sure they would have been arrested.'

'We don't think so,' said Abu. 'We think that they are too powerful for your friend to be able to touch them.'

Falcón knew that his goading of Angel Zarrías would not help in any material way, but he hoped that it would cause some unseen structural damage, which might lead to a breakdown later on. Angel Zarrías had revealed himself, of course – how could he not? While he'd been squaring up to do battle with the corruptive powers of materialism and the ruthless energy of radical Islam, his partner, the woman he loved, was having a tantrum like some spoilt two-year-old, consumed by her pathetic needs and concerns. It represented to him all that was wrong with this modern existence that he'd grown to despise, which was how he justified employing equally corruptive powers and fanatical energy to bring the aimless world back to heel.

Falcón became quite concerned that the rage unleashed by his revelation of Manuela's comparative peevishness might result in a fatal embolism or lethal infarction. Angel's forty-five years of political frustration had finally erupted, producing spluttering admissions which indicated, beyond any doubt, his and Fuerza Andalucía's involvement in the conspiracy, but did nothing to help the investigation cross the divide into unknown areas.

By prior arrangement, Falcón was not going to be interviewing anybody between 10.30 and midday. He was going to attend the funeral of Inés Conde de Tejada.

573

He drove out to the San Fernando cemetery on the northern outskirts of the city. As he drew near he counted three television vans and seven camera crews.

Everybody from the Edificio de los Juzgados and the Palacio de Justicia was in attendance at the cemetery. Close to two hundred people were milling around the gates, most of them smoking. Falcón knew them all and it took him some time to work his way through the crowd to reach Inés's parents.

Neither of her parents was tall, but the death of their daughter had diminished them. They were dwarfed by its enormity and overwhelmed by the numbers of people around them. Falcón paid his respects and Inés's mother kissed him and held on to him so tightly it was as if he was her lifesaver in this sea of humanity. Her husband's handshake had nothing in it. His face was slack, his eyes rheumy. He'd aged ten years overnight. He spoke as if he didn't recognize Falcón. As he was about to leave, Inés's mother grabbed his arm and in a hoarse whisper said: 'She should have stayed with you, Javier', to which there was no answer.

Falcón joined the crowd walking up the tree-lined path to the family mausoleum. The camera crews were there, but they kept their distance. As the coffin was taken up the steps there was a great wailing from some of the women in the crowd. These occasions, especially with untimely deaths, were so emotionally lacerating that many of the men had their handkerchiefs out. When one elderly woman cried out, 'Inés, Inés,' as the coffin disappeared into the dark, the crowd seemed to convulse with grief.

The crowd dispersed after the short ceremony. Falcón

walked back to his car, head bowed and throat so constricted he couldn't respond to the few people who tried to stop him. Driving back alone was a relief, a great unknotting of strangled emotion. He arrived at the Jefatura and wept for a minute, with his forehead on the steering wheel, before pulling himself together for the next round of interviews.

By lunchtime they'd all discovered their fundamental problem. Not even Rivero, who was the weakest of the three, would give the interrogators the necessary link between Fuerza Andalucía and the bomb makers. Not one of them would even yield up the link to Informáticalidad, never mind to Lucrecio Arenas and César Benito.

In a conference between Elvira, del Rey and Falcón, in which they were trying to work out the most serious possible charges with which they could hold the three suspects, Elvira put forward the possibility that the link wasn't forthcoming because it didn't exist.

'They had to give Hassani's work to someone,' said del Rey.

'And I think we all believe now that the reason Ricardo Gamero killed himself was that the electrician's card, which would end up in the Imam's hands, via Botín, made him feel responsible,' said Falcón. 'Mark Flowers told me that the Imam was expecting more intrusive surveillance. In fact, he wanted the microphone planted in his office so that the CGI antiterrorist squad would find out about Hammad and Saoudi's plan. Obviously, none of them knew a bomb was going to be planted with that microphone. The point is that Gamero went back to the person who had given him the card, looking for an explanation. Who gave that card to Zarrías?'

'It's possible that Zarrías didn't know about the bomb either,' said Elvira. 'Perhaps he just thought this was an escalation of the surveillance carried out by Informáticalidad.'

'The person I would really like to see down here is Lucrecio Arenas,' said Falcón. 'He positioned his protégé, Jesús Alarcón, to take over the leadership from Rivero. He is a long-standing friend of Angel Zarrías and he has been involved with the Horizonte group, with whom Benito and Cárdenas are associated and who ultimately own Informáticalidad.'

'But unless these guys give him up, all you *can* do is talk to him,' said del Rey. 'You have no leverage. The only reason we've got this far is a lucky sighting of Tateb Hassani late on the Saturday night in Rivero's house, and Rivero's subsequent confusion and loss of nerve when you and Inspector Ramírez first spoke to him.'

Falcón was in the observation room for the next interviews, which started at four o'clock. At about five Gregorio appeared at his shoulder.

'Yacoub needs to talk,' he said.

'I thought we weren't due to "chat" until tonight.'

'In an emergency we've given Yacoub the possibility of making contact,' said Gregorio. 'It's to do with the initiation rite.'

'I haven't got the Javier Marías book with me.'

Gregorio produced a spare copy from his briefcase. They went up to Falcón's office and Gregorio prepared the computer.

'You might find there's more of a delay between each line of "chat" this time,' said Gregorio. 'We're using different encryption software and it's a bit slower.'

Gregorio gave up Falcón's seat and went over to the window. Falcón sat in front of the computer and exchanged introductions with Yacoub, who opened by saying he didn't have much time and gave a brief account of what had happened that morning. He wrote about the execution he'd witnessed, but wrote nothing of his own mock execution. Falcón reeled from the computer screen.

'This is out of control,' he said, and Gregorio read Yacoub's words over Falcón's shoulder.

'Steady him. Keep him calm,' said Gregorio. 'They're just warning him.'

Falcón started to type just as another paragraph came through from Yacoub.

'Important things in no particular order. 1) I was taken from the house in the medina at about 6.45 a.m. The journey was about three and a half hours long and then there was about forty minutes before I met the two men, who called themselves Mohamed and Abu. They told me they were following the Seville bombing very closely. 2) They said that the explosion had caused "great disruption to one of their plans which had demanded a lot of reorganization". 3) I was left in a room with books on one wall. The titles were all about architecture or engineering. There were also a number of manufacturer's car manuals for four-wheel-drive vehicles. 4) They knew about the arrest of three men from a political party called Fuerza Andalucía, who were suspected of murdering "an apostate and traitor" called Tateb Hassani. They also knew that this was in some way connected to the Seville bombing, but said that these men were "unimportant". 5) The information they want from you, Javier, is as follows: the identities of the men who were responsible for the planning of the bombing of the mosque in Seville. They know about the three arrests, and they believe that although you know who the real perpetrators are, they are too powerful for you to touch them.

'I don't expect you to reply immediately. I know you will have to talk to your people first. I need your answer as soon as possible. If I can give them this information I believe it will increase my standing with the council immeasurably.'

'That last bit I don't even have to think about,' said Falcón. 'I can't do it.'

'Just wait, Javier,' said Gregorio, but Falcón was already typing out his reply:

'Yacoub, it's completely impossible for me to give you that information. We have our suspicions, but absolutely no proof. I assume the leaders of this council are looking for revenge for the bombing of the mosque and that is not something I am prepared to have on my conscience.'

Falcón had to hold Gregorio back as he hit the send button. After about fifteen seconds the screen wavered and the CNI secure website disappeared to be replaced by the msn home page. Gregorio played about on the keyboard and tried to get back into the website, but there was no access. He made a call standing at the window.

'We've lost the connection,' he said.

After several minutes of listening and nodding he closed down the mobile.

'Trouble with the encryption software. They had to terminate the transmission as a precaution.'

'Did my last paragraph go through?'

'They said it did.'

'All the way through to Yacoub?'

'That I don't know yet,' said Gregorio. 'We'll reconvene at your house at 11 p.m. I'll have had a chance to discuss the meat of what Yacoub was saying and its implications with Juan and Pablo by then.'

40

On the way back down to the interview rooms Falcón ran into Elvira and del Rey in the corridor. They'd been looking for him. The forensics computer specialists had hacked into the Fuerza Andalucía hard disks. From the articles and photographs found on one of the computers they could tell that the user was compiling the raw material to be transformed into the web pages that would appear on the VOMIT website. From other material on the same hard disk, the user was evidently Angel Zarrías. Elvira seemed annoyed that this news didn't impress Falcón, whose mind was still reeling from the exchange with Yacoub.

'It's more leverage,' said Elvira. 'It places Zarrías and Fuerza Andalucía closer to the heart of the conspiracy.'

Falcón had no ready opinion about that.

'I'm not sure that it does,' said del Rey. 'It could be construed as a separate entity. Zarrías can defend it as a personal campaign. All he's done is use a Fuerza Andalucía computer to draft the articles, which he's downloaded on to a CD and given to some geek, to anonymously slap them up on the VOMIT website. I can't see the leverage we can extract from that.'

Falcón looked from one man to the other, still with no comment. Elvira took a call on his mobile. Falcón started to move away.

'That was Comisario Lobo,' said Elvira. 'The media pressure is at breaking point.'

'What has the media been told so far about these men being held?' asked Falcón, coming back down the corridor to Elvira.

'Suspicion of murder and conspiring to murder,' said Elvira.

'Has Tateb Hassani been named?'

'Not yet. Naming him would involve revealing too much about the nature of our enquiry at the moment,' said Elvira. 'We're still sensitive to the expectations of the people.'

'I'd better get back to work. I'm due to start on Eduardo Rivero in a few minutes,' said Falcón, looking at his watch. 'Tell me, have the forensics found any blood traces in the Fuerza Andalucía offices, yet? Especially in the bathroom?'

'I haven't heard anything on that,' said Elvira, moving off with del Rey.

All the interrogators were in the corridor outside the interview rooms. A paramedic in fluorescent green was talking to Ramírez, who caught sight of Falcón over his shoulder.

'Rivero's collapsed,' he said. 'He started gasping for air, getting disorientated, and then fell off his chair.'

Rivero was lying on the floor between two paramedics who were giving him oxygen.

'What's the problem?' asked Falcón.

'Heart arrhythmia and high blood pressure,' said the paramedic. 'We're going to take him to hospital, keep him under observation. His heart rate is up around 160 and completely irregular. If we don't bring it down there's a danger that the blood will pool and clot in the heart, and if a clot gets loose he might have a stroke.'

'Shit,' said Ramírez from the corridor. 'God knows how this is going to play out in the media. They'll tell the world we're running Abu Ghraib down here.'

All the interrogators thought that Rivero, of all the suspects, had been the least attached to the central conspiracy. He had only been important as the leader of the party and, given that the intention was to wrest that from him in order to install Jesús Alarcón, it would stand to reason that he would be kept the least informed. His collapse had occurred under persistent questioning from Inspector Jefe Ramón Barros about the real reason for his relinquishing of the leadership. The pressure of sticking to his story about old age, while the truth worked away at the flaws in his mind, had proved too much.

Just after 7 p.m. Marco Barreda, the Informáticalidad sales manager, was brought in. He'd been met at the airport having flown in from Barcelona. His mobile phone records were accessed but none of the numbers called corresponded to any of those owned by Angel Zarrías. Falcón made sure that Zarrías knew about Barreda's appearance in the Jefatura. Zarrías was unperturbed. Barreda was questioned for an hour and a half about his relationship with Ricardo Gamero. He didn't deviate from his original story. They released him at

8.30 p.m. and went back to Zarrías and lied to him about Barreda, saying he'd admitted that Gamero had said nothing about being in love with him and wasn't even a homosexual. Zarrías didn't buy any of it.

By 9 p.m. Falcón couldn't take any more. He went outside to breathe some fresh air, but found it hot and suffocating after the chill of the Jefatura. He drank a coffee in the café across the street. His mind was confused with too much going on between Yacoub and the interrogation of the three suspects. He drank some water to wash out the bitterness of the coffee, and Zorrita's words from last night came back to him.

In the Jefatura he went down to the cells where he asked the officer on duty if he could speak to Esteban Calderón, who was in the last cell, lying on his back, staring at the back of his hands held above him. The guard locked Falcón in. He took a stool and leaned back against the wall. Calderón sat up on his bunk.

'I didn't think you were going to come,' he said.

'I didn't think there was much point in coming,' said Falcón. 'I can't help you or discuss your case with you. I'm here out of curiosity only.'

'I've been thinking about denial,' said Calderón.

Falcón nodded.

'I know you've come across a lot of it in your work.'

'There's no greater guilt than that of a murderer,' said Falcón, 'and denial is the human mind's greatest defence.'

'Talk me through the process?' said Calderón. 'The theory's always different to the reality.'

'Only in the aftermath of a serious crime, such as murder, does the motive for taking such disastrous measures suddenly seem ridiculously disproportionate,'

583

said Falcón. 'So, to kill someone for, say, the paltry reason of jealousy seems like madness, an affront to the intellect. The easiest and quickest way to deal with the aberration is to deny it ever happened. Once that denial is in place, it doesn't take long for the mind to create its own version of events which the brain comes to believe with absolute certainty.'

'I'm trying to be as careful as I can,' said Calderón.

'Sometimes care is not enough to defeat a deep-seated desire,' said Falcón.

'That scares me, Javier,' said Calderón. 'I don't understand how the brain can be at the mercy of the mind. I don't understand how information, facts, things we've seen and heard can be so easily transformed, reordered and manipulated . . . by what? What is it? What is the mind?'

'Maybe it's not such a good idea to lie in a prison cell, torturing yourself with unanswerable questions,' said Falcón.

'There's nothing else to do,' said Calderón. 'I can't stop my brain from working. It asks me these questions.'

'Wish fulfilment is a powerful human need, on both a personal and a collective level.'

'I know, which is why I'm being so careful in examining myself,' said Calderón. 'I've started at the beginning and I've been admitting some difficult things.'

'I'm neither your confessor, nor your psychologist, Esteban.'

'But, apart from Inés, you are the person I have most wronged in my life.'

'You haven't wronged *me*, Esteban, and if you have I don't need to know.'

'But I need you to know.'

'I can't absolve you,' said Falcón. 'I'm not qualified for that.'

'I just need you to know the care with which I am conducting my self-examination.'

Falcón had to admit to himself that he was interested. He leaned back against the wall and shrugged. Calderón took some moments to prepare his words.

'I seduced Inés,' he said. 'I set out to seduce her, not because of her beauty, her intelligence or because of the woman she was. I set out to seduce her because of her relationship with you.'

'Me?'

'Not because of who you were, the son of the famous Francisco Falcón, which was what had made you interesting to Inés. It was more to do with . . . I don't know how to put this: your difference. You were not well liked in those days. Most people thought you cold and unapproachable, and therefore arrogant and patronizing. I saw something I didn't understand. So, the first way, the most natural way for *me* to understand you was to seduce your wife. What did this beautiful, much-admired woman see in you, that I didn't have myself? That's why I seduced her. And the irony of it was, she gave me no insight at all. But before I knew it, it was no longer just an affair as I'd intended; we became an open secret. She was always way ahead of me in public relations. She could manipulate people and situations with consummate ease. So, we became the golden couple and you were the cuckold, who people enjoyed laughing about behind your back. And I admit it now, Javier, just so that you know what I'm like: I enjoyed that situation because, although I didn't understand you, which made me feel weak, I had inadvertently got one up on you, and that made me feel strong.'

'Are you sure you want to tell me this?' said Falcón.

'The next item isn't so personal to you,' said Calderón, batting him down with his hands, as if Falcón was thinking of leaving. 'It's important that you know me for the . . . I was going to say "man" but I'm not sure that's appropriate now. Remember Maddy Krugman?'

'I didn't like her,' said Falcón. 'I thought she was sinister.'

'She's probably the most beautiful woman I never went to bed with.'

'You *didn't* sleep with her?'

'She wasn't interested in me,' said Calderón. 'Beauty – I mean, great beauty – for a woman is both her good fortune and her greatest curse. Everybody is attracted to them. It's difficult for normal people to understand that pressure. Everybody wants to please a beautiful woman. They spark something in everybody, not just men; and because the pressure is so constant, they have no idea who has good intentions, who they should choose. Of course, they recognize the poor, slack-jawed fools who drool on to their lapels, but then there are the others, the hundreds and thousands with money, charm, brilliance and charisma. Maddy liked you because you brushed aside her beauty . . .'

'I don't think that was true. I was as much affected by her beauty as everybody else.'

'But you didn't let it affect your vision, Javier. And Maddy saw that and liked it. She was obsessed with you,' said Calderón. 'Of course, I had to have her. She teased me. She played with me. I amused her. That was about it. And the worst of it was that we had to talk about you. I couldn't bear it. I think you knew that it was eating me up inside.'

Falcón nodded.

'So when we got into that final and fatal scenario with Maddy and her husband . . . I had to lie about it afterwards,' said Calderón. 'I perjured myself, because I couldn't bear your fearlessness. I couldn't stand the poise with which you handled that situation.'

'I can tell you that I didn't *feel* fearless.'

'Then I couldn't stand the way you overcame your fear and I was left sitting on the sofa, paralysed,' said Calderón.

'I've been trained for those situations. I've been in them before,' said Falcón. 'Your reaction was completely natural and understandable.'

'But it was not how I saw myself,' said Calderón.

'Then your standards are very high,' said Falcón.

'Inés was marvellous to me after the Maddy Krugman affair,' said Calderón. 'You couldn't have wished for a better reaction from a fiancée. I'd humiliated her by announcing our engagement and on the same day, I think it was, I ran off with Maddy Krugman. And yet she stuck by me. She picked up the pieces of my career and self-esteem and . . . I hated her for it.

'I stored up all her kindnesses to me and mixed them with my own bitterness into a rancorous stew of deep resentment. I punished her by having affairs. I even fucked her best friend during a weekend at Inés's parents' finca. And I didn't stop at affairs. I refused to look for a house. I made her sell her own apartment, but I wouldn't let her buy the sort of house she desperately wanted. I wouldn't let her change my apartment to suit her. When I started hitting her – and that was only four days ago – it was just the physical expression of what I'd been doing to her mentally for years. What made it worse was, that the more I abused her, the tighter she clung to me. Now there's a story of denial for you, Javier. Inés was a great prosecutor. She could persuade anybody. And she persuaded herself, totally.'

'You should have left her.'

'It was too late by then,' said Calderón. 'We were already locked in our fatal embrace. We couldn't bear to be together, we couldn't wrench ourselves apart.'

The key rattled in the door. The guard put his head in.

'Comisario Elvira wants to see you in his office. He said it's urgent.'

Falcón stood. Calderón raised himself with effort, as if he was stiff or under a great weight.

'One last thing, Javier. I know it will seem incredible after what I've just told you,' said Calderón, 'and I'm quite prepared to face the punishment handed down to me for her murder, because I deserve it. But I need *you* to know that I did not kill her. You might have spoken to that Inspector Jefe from Madrid, and he might have told you that I gave a very confused account of what happened that night. I *have* been in a fairly wild state . . .'

'So who did kill her?'

'I don't know. I don't know what their motive could have possibly been. I don't know anything, other than that *I* did not kill Inés.'

The Comisario was not alone in his office. His secretary nodded Falcón in. Pablo and Gregorio were there, along with the chief forensic pathologist. They all sat wherever they could except for the pathologist, who remained standing by the window. Elvira introduced him and asked him to give his report.

'The mosque is now empty of all rubble, detritus, clothes and body parts. We have conducted DNA testing on all body parts, fluids and blood that we've been able to find. That means we have tested every square centimetre of the available area in the mosque. We have all the results of these tests, except for the final two square metres closest to the entrance, which was the area containing the least DNA material and was the last batch to be sent off. We have been able to find matches to all DNA samples supplied by the families of all the men believed to have been in the mosque. We have also matched a DNA sample retrieved from the Imam's apartment with some in the mosque. However, we have been unable to match DNA samples taken from the Madrid apartment belonging to Djamal Hammad and Smail Saoudi with any found in the mosque. Our conclusion is that neither of those two men were in the mosque at the time of the explosion.'

41

Falcón woke up early, with renewed determination. Once the pathologist had left the night before, after his stunning revelation, they discussed what could possibly have happened to Hammad and Saoudi. Pablo updated Comisario Elvira on the intelligence they'd received from Yacoub, whose group believed that a total of 300 kilos of hexogen had been sent to Spain. The bomb disposal officer had thought, as a 'conservative' estimate, that 100 kilos of hexogen had exploded in El Cerezo on 6th June, which would leave between 150 and 200 kilos still at large. They all agreed that having secured the remaining hexogen, Hammad and Saoudi would have either gone to ground or left the country.

Elvira put a call through to the Guardia Civil about the route of the Peugeot Partner last seen at a service station outside Valdepeñas at 4 p.m. on Sunday, 4th June. There'd still been no sightings of the van on any of the main roads in the Seville, Cordoba and Granada triangle. There was now a huge operation underway, looking for sightings on the smaller routes, but it was an impossible task, given the anonymous quality of the vehicle and the fact that the journey was made nearly a week ago. Falcón sent Pérez and Ferrera back to El Cerezo to check with the residents that the Peugeot Partner had not been seen until the Monday morning of 5th June.

The meeting broke up with Elvira drafting a press release about Hammad and Saoudi and announcing the reinstatement of spot checks on vehicles coming into the city. This was to be aired on the TVE ten o'clock news and on Canal Sur. Gregorio had come back with Falcón to his house on Calle Bailén, where they made another unsuccessful attempt to reach Yacoub. They drafted a report about Hammad and Saoudi, including photographs, which Gregorio pasted into the clipboard of the CNI website to send to Yacoub later, in the hope that he could locate them in Morocco.

For one reason or another Falcón had not yet interviewed Agustín Cárdenas, and it had been decided that he would talk to him first thing in the morning while Ramírez tackled Zarrías for a second time. The rest of the squad would be up early to walk the streets around El Cerezo to see if they could get any confirmed sightings of Hammad and Saoudi either on Sunday evening/Monday morning, or after the explosion on Tuesday.

By 7.30 a.m. Falcón had called ahead to the Jefatura to make sure that Agustín Cárdenas would be waiting, ready to be interviewed as soon as he arrived. He stopped for a coffee and some toast on the way and was sitting in front of a still groggy Agustín Cárdenas by 7.50.

In his photograph, Agustín Cárdenas looked in his mid thirties, while his CV told Falcón he was forty-six years old. By this Saturday morning he'd found his way up into the mid fifties, which was somewhere he'd never been before.

'You're not looking good, Agustín,' said Falcón. 'You could do with a bit of nip and tuck yourself this morning.'

'I'm not a morning person,' he said.

'How long have you known César Benito?'

'About eight years.'

'How did you meet him?'

'I did some work on his wife and then he came to see me himself.'

'For some work?'

'I removed the bags under his eyes and tightened up his neck and jowls.'

'And he was happy?'

'He was so happy he got a mistress.'

'Were your clinics part of the Horizonte group at this stage?'

'No, César Benito thought that Horizonte should buy my business.'

'Which made you a lot of money,' said Falcón. 'Did they give you stock options in Horizonte?'

Cárdenas nodded.

'And being a part of the group meant that you had capital,' said Falcón.

'I expanded the business to nine clinics in Barcelona, Madrid, Seville, Nerja and another due to open in Valencia.'

'It's a shame that you've built up such a successful business and you're never going to see the fruits of your labour,' said Falcón. 'You're not protecting César Benito just because he's made you this fortune that you'll never enjoy?'

Cárdenas took a deep breath and stared at the table, thinking to himself.

'No,' said Falcón. 'It would have to be more than that, wouldn't it? There's your Hippocratic oath. César must have had quite a hold on you to be able to persuade you to not only poison Hassani at his last supper, but also to use your surgical skills to cut off the man's hands, burn away his face and scalp him. You didn't do all that for César just because he made you a rich man?'

More silence from Cárdenas. Something was eating away at him. Here was a man who'd done a lot of thinking and not much sleeping overnight.

'What can you offer me?' said Cárdenas, after some long minutes.

'In terms of a deal?' said Falcón. 'Nothing.'

Cárdenas nodded, rocked himself in his chair. Falcón knew what was working its way from Cárdenas's insides out: resentment.

'I can only give you César Benito,' said Cárdenas. 'He was the only person I had contact with.'

'We'll be happy with that,' said Falcón. 'What can you tell me?'

'One of the reasons I was not as wealthy as I should have been when I first met César was that I'd been a gambling addict for almost ten years,' said Cárdenas.

'Did César Benito know about that when he arranged for Horizonte to buy your cosmetic surgery clinics?'

'No, but he found out soon afterwards,' said Cárdenas. 'It was through him that I managed to get it under control.'

'And how did it get out of control again?'

'I went on a business trip with César down to the Costa del Sol in March. He took me gambling.'

'*He* did?'

Cárdenas nodded, looking at Falcón very steadily.

'That started me off again. But this time it was even worse. I was much better off than I had been the last time. My funds seemed to be limitless by comparison. By the beginning of May I owed over one million euros and I was having to sell things to make the interest payments on some of the loans I'd taken out.'

'And how did César find out?'

'I told him,' said Cárdenas. 'I'd had a visit from somebody I owed money to. They took me into the bathroom of my rented flat in Madrid and gave me the wet towel treatment. You know, you really think you're going to drown. They said they'd be back in four days' time. It scared me enough to go to César and ask for help. We met in his apartment in Barcelona. He was shocked by what I told him, but he also said that he understood. After three days of being completely terrified I was relieved. Then he told me how he could make this problem go away.'

'Are you a religious man, Sr Cárdenas?'

'Yes, our families go to church together.'

'How would you describe your relationship with César Benito?'

'He'd become a very close friend. That's why I went to see him.'

'When Benito told you that you would have to commit murder and gross disfigurement, surely you must have asked him for every detail of the conspiracy?'

'I did, but not on that occasion,' said Cárdenas. 'Once I realized what he was asking I decided on a safety strategy. The next time I met him was in my rented apartment in Madrid and I secretly recorded our entire conversation.'

'And where is that recording?'

'It's still in the apartment,' he said, writing down the address and telephone number. 'I taped it to the back of one of the kitchen drawers.'

When Lucrecio Arenas was at his villa in Marbella he liked to get up early, before the staff arrived, which on a Saturday was not before 9 a.m. Arenas put on a pair of swimming trunks, shrugged into his huge white bathrobe and slipped into a pair of sandals. On his way out of the house he picked up a large, thick, white towel and a pair of swimming goggles. He hated chlorine in his eyes and always liked to see clearly, even under-water. He walked down the sloping garden in the warm morning, pausing to take in the glorious view of the green hills and the blue of the Mediterranean, which at this time of day, before the heat haze had risen, was so intense that even his untouchable heart ached a little.

The pool had been built at the bottom of the garden, surrounded by a dense growth of oleander, bougainvillea and jasmine. His wife had insisted it be put down there because Lucrecio had wanted a 20-metre monster. They'd dynamited three hundred tons of rock out of the mountainside so that he could swim his daily kilo-metre in fifty lengths, rather than having the awful bore of turning just as he'd got into his stride. He reached the poolside and flung his towel on a lounger and let his bathrobe fall on top. He stepped out of his sandals and walked to the end of the pool. He fitted his goggles over his face and nestled the rubber into his eye sockets.

He raised his arms and through the rose-tinted lenses

of the goggles he saw something that looked like a postcard on the end of the diving board. He dropped his arms just as he felt two colossal thuds in his back, like sledgehammer blows but more penetrating. The third blow was to the neck and came down on him with the full weight of a cleaver. His legs would not support him and he collapsed messily into the water. The dense growth behind him rearranged itself. There was the sound of a small scooter starting up. The splendid day continued. The ice blue water in the swimming pool clouded red around the body. A speedboat nosed out into the blue morning, pursued by its white frothy wake.

The Holiday Inn on Plaza Carlos Triana Bertrán in Madrid was not one of César Benito's favourite hotels, but it had some advantages. It was close to the conference centre where he'd given a speech to Spain's leading constructors the night before. It was also near the Bernabeu Stadium and even when Real Madrid weren't playing he enjoyed being close to the beating heart of Spanish football. The hotel had a third advantage on this Saturday, which was that it was only twenty minutes to the airport and he had a flight to catch to Lisbon at 11 a.m. He'd asked for breakfast to be served in his suite as he hated looking at other people, who were not his family, early in the morning. The room service boy had just wheeled in the trolley and Benito was flicking through Saturday's *ABC* and chewing on a croissant when there was another knock at the door. It was so soon after the room service boy had left that he assumed it was him coming back for some reason. He didn't look through the spy hole. He wouldn't have seen anybody if he had.

He opened the door on to an empty corridor. His head was just coming forward to look out when the edge of a hand swung into him with rapid and lethal force, chopping across his Adam's apple and windpipe and making a loud cracking noise. He fell backwards into the room, spluttering flakes of croissant over the front of his bathrobe. His heels worked furrows into the carpet as he tried to draw air into his lungs. The door closed. Benito's feet slowed after a minute and then stopped working. There was a gargling rattle from his collapsed throat and his hands lost all grip. He didn't feel the fingers searching for a neck pulse or the light touch of the card placed on his chest.

The door of the hotel room reopened and closed with a *Do not disturb* sign swinging on the handle. The air conditioning breathed easily in the hush of the empty corridor, while unclaimed newspapers hung in plastic bags from other, indifferent, doors.

At 9.30 a.m. Falcón had taken a break from his interview with Agustín Cárdenas and called Ramírez out to give him the news of the recording Cárdenas had made, hoping it could be used to apply pressure on Angel Zarrías. Cárdenas was taken back down to the cells while Falcón went to his office to call Elvira to get the Madrid police to pick up the recording from Cárdenas's rented flat, while simultaneously arresting César Benito in the Holiday Inn.

It was Ferrera, calling him from a café on the Avenida de San Lázaro, who told him to look at the latest news on Canal Sur. Falcón ran through the Jefatura and burst into the communications room just in time to see a shot of Marbella disappear from the television screen, to be replaced by the newsreader who repeated the breaking news item: Lucrecio Arenas had been found by his maid floating face down in his swimming pool at 9.05 that morning. He had been shot three times in the back.

His mobile vibrated and he took the call from Elvira.

'I've just seen it,' he said. 'Lucrecio Arenas in his pool.'

'They got César Benito in his hotel in Madrid as well,' said Elvira. 'That's going to come through in the next few minutes.'

It took another five minutes for the Benito item to break. A TVE camera crew got to the Holiday Inn before Canal Sur reached Arenas's villa in Marbella. It took a further half an hour before their camera crew pushed a lens into the face of the maid, who'd only just recovered from the hysteria of finding her boss dead in the pool. The newsreaders jumped between the two dramas. Falcón called Ramírez out of the interview room to let him know, went back to his office and slumped in his chair, all the enthusiasm of the morning gone.

His first thoughts were that this was the end. It didn't matter what they found out now from Cárdenas and Zarrías, it was all immaterial. He stared at his reflection in the dead, grey computer screen and it started him thinking in a slightly less linear way about what had happened. He made some uncomfortable connections, which made him furious and then another idea came to him, which frightened him into calming down. He got the communications room to send a patrol car to Alarcón's house in El Porvenir. He called Jesús Alarcón. His wife, Mónica, answered the phone.

'You've heard the news,' he said.

'He can't speak to you now,' said Mónica. 'He's too upset. You know Lucrecio was like a father to him.'

'First thing: none of you are to go outside,' said Falcón. 'Lock all the doors and windows and go upstairs. Don't answer the door. I'm sending a patrol car round there now.'

Silence from Mónica.

'I'll tell you what it's about when I get there,' said Falcón. 'Did Jesús speak to Lucrecio Arenas yesterday?'

'Yes, they met.'

'I'm coming round now. Lock all the doors. Don't let anybody in.'

On the way to El Porvenir, Falcón called Elvira and asked for armed guards to protect Alarcón and his family. The request was granted immediately.

'There's more stuff coming out all the time,' said Elvira, 'but I can't talk about it on the phone. I'm coming in.'

'I'm on my way to see Alarcón,' said Falcón.

'Do we know where Alarcón was on the night of Tateb Hassani's murder?'

'He was at a wedding in Madrid.'

'So you think he's clean?'

'I know he's clean,' said Falcón. 'I've got a special insight.'

'Special insights, even *your* special insights, don't always look good in police reports,' said Elvira.

The street was empty of people and Falcón parked behind the patrol car, which was already outside the metal sliding gate of Alarcón's house. Mónica buzzed him in. Falcón had a good look around before he went through the front door, which he closed and triple locked. He went to the back of the house and checked all the doors and windows.

'We're just being careful,' said Falcón. 'We don't know who we're dealing with yet and we're not sure whether Jesús is on their list. So we're putting you under armed guard until we know.'

'He's in the kitchen,' she said, looking sick with fear.

She went upstairs to sit with the children.

Alarcón was sitting at the kitchen table with an untouched espresso in front of him. He had his arms stretched out on the table, fists clenched, staring into space. He only came out of his trance when Falcón broke into the frame of his vision and offered his condolences.

'I know he was important to you,' said Falcón.

Alarcón nodded. He didn't look as if he'd slept much. He made light knocking noises with his fists on the tabletop.

'Did you speak to Arenas yesterday?' asked Falcón.

Alarcón nodded.

'How did he react to the information I gave you?'

'Lucrecio had reached the point in his life and business career where he no longer had to bother with detail,' said Alarcón. 'He had people who did the detail. I shouldn't think he'd seen a bill for the last twenty-five years, or read a contract, or even been aware of the tonnage of paperwork involved in a modern merger or acquisition. His desk is always clean. It doesn't even have a phone on it since he discovered that the only people he wants to talk to are on his mobile. He never learnt how to use a computer.'

'What are you telling me, Jesús?' said Falcón, impatient now. 'That the services of Tateb Hassani and his consequent murder were "details" that did not concern Lucrecio Arenas?'

'I'm telling you that he's the sort of man who will

listen to the business news, with all its astonishing up-to-the-minute detail, even a channel like Bloomberg, which is right on top of its subject, and laugh,' said Alarcón. 'Then he'll tell you what's *really* happening, because he is talking to the people who are actually *making* it happen, and you realize that the so-called news is just a bit of detail that a journalist has either picked up or been given.'

'So what did you talk about?'

'We talked about power.'

'That doesn't sound as if it's going to help me.'

'No, but it has been an enormous help to me,' said Alarcón. 'I'll be resigning from the leadership of Fuerza Andalucía and returning to my business career. My statement to the media will take place at eleven o'clock this morning. There's nothing left, Javier. Fuerza Andalucía is over.'

'So, what did he tell you about power?'

'That all the things that matter to me about politics, such as people, health, education, religion . . . all these things are details, and none of it can happen without power.'

'I think I can grasp that.'

'There's a saying in business, that what happens in the USA takes about five years to start happening here,' said Alarcón. 'Lucrecio told me: look at the Bush administration and understand that you only achieve power in a democracy with an enormous sense of indebtedness.'

'You owe favours to all the people who've made it possible for you to reach high office,' said Falcón.

'You owe them so much that you begin to find that *their* needs are shaping *your* policies.'

Three armed police arrived as Falcón left. Falcón drove back to the Jefatura, amazed at his naivety in thinking that Jesús Alarcón would be able to get anything approaching an admission from an animal like Lucrecio Arenas.

Elvira was alone in his office, standing by the window, peering through the blinds as if he was expecting insurgents in the street. Without turning round he told Falcón that he was going to have to prepare for a major televised press conference whose time, as yet, had not been set.

'The CNI will be here in a minute,' he said. 'Did you get anything from Alarcón?'

'Nothing. He's resigning later this morning,' said Falcón. 'He had a very unappetizing lesson on the nature of power from his old master.'

'Who seems to have met his nemesis,' said Elvira. 'A card was found on the diving board of his swimming pool. An identical card was found on César Benito's body in his hotel room. Arabic script. A quote from the Koran about the enemies of God.'

Elvira finally turned round when he sensed something thunderous developing behind him.

'Are you all right, Javier?'

'No,' he said, gritting his teeth. 'I'm not all right.'

'You're angry?' said Elvira, surprised. 'It's very dismaying, but . . .'

'I've been betrayed,' he said. 'Those bastards from the CNI have betrayed me, and it's cost us the possibility of a resolution to this entire investigation.'

A knock on the open door. Pablo and Gregorio came in. Falcón wouldn't shake their hands, got up and went over to the window.

602

'So, what's going on here?' asked Elvira.

Pablo shrugged.

'I recruited a Moroccan friend of mine . . .' started Falcón, and Gregorio tried to interrupt by saying this was all top-secret CNI business and not for public consumption. Pablo told him to sit down and shut up.

'My Moroccan friend has infiltrated the group which positioned Hammad and Saoudi with the hexogen in Seville. The group demanded that he show his loyalty by passing an initiation rite. This required him to ask me who was behind the Fuerza Andalucía conspiracy. I refused to do this. At which point there was a very timely breakdown in communication – "a problem with new encryption software". Since then, I have not been able to contact my friend. I do not think that the deaths of César Benito and Lucrecio Arenas are unconnected with what happened. I believe that my refusal to help was intercepted and replaced with the information my friend required. The fact that these two men were found dead with quotations from the Koran on, or near, their bodies seems to indicate that revenge has successfully been taken.'

Elvira looked at the CNI men.

'Not true,' said Pablo. 'It proves nothing, but we can show you the transcripts. It's true that your refusal to help did *not* go through before the system failed, but we did not replace it with anything else. The encryption software problem has still not been solved and we are now thinking of going back to the original software so that we can at least make contact with your friend. On the subject of the deaths of Arenas and Benito: the detectives and forensics on the ground in Marbella and Madrid have independently told us that

603

they believe this to be the work of professional hitmen. They say that, whilst they have no record of any individual "hits" being taken out by Islamic jihadists, they do have records of professional hitmen using these methods.'

'Agustín Cárdenas had just given me César Benito,' said Falcón slowly.

'We know,' said Pablo. 'We spoke to Madrid. They've picked up the recording he mentioned in his interview with you.'

'You nailed him,' said Gregorio.

'For the murder of Tateb Hassani,' said Falcón. 'Don't you think the families of the people who died in El Cerezo deserve a bit more than that?'

'They might get it in court,' said Elvira.

'You said it yourself on Tuesday night,' said Pablo. 'Terrorist attacks are complicated things. You only have a *chance* at a resolution. At least in this one the perpetrators have all suffered.'

'Apart from the electrician who planted the Goma 2 Eco,' said Falcón. 'And, of course, the people who are so contemptuous of law and order that they will assassinate anybody who might make them vulnerable.'

'You have to be satisfied with what you've achieved,' said Pablo. 'You've prevented a dangerous group of Catholic fanatics from developing a power base in Andalucían politics. And in the process, through the actions of Hammad and Saoudi, we have uncovered an Islamic jihadist plot. Juan doesn't think that that is such a terrible outcome.'

'Which brings us back to the business in hand,' said Elvira. 'Hammad and Saoudi. Their faces have been all over the news and there's been a terrific response. Unfortunately, there have been sightings from all over Spain. They've been seen on the same day, at the same time, in La Coruña, Almeria, Barcelona and Cádiz.'

Elvira took a call on his mobile.

'Chasing Hammad and Saoudi is a waste of time,' said Pablo. 'It's been four days. They'll have done whatever needed to be done and got out. The only thing that will help us now is intelligence.'

Elvira came back into the conversation.

'That was the Guardia Civil. They've had a confirmed sighting of Hammad and Saoudi, early on Monday morning 5th June, on a stretch of country road near a village called El Saucejo, about twenty-five kilometres south of Osuna.'

'And how do we know this is a bona fide sighting?' asked Pablo.

'They were changing the back tyre, driver's side, on a white Peugeot Partner,' said Elvira.

42

'We thought we'd lost you back there,' said Pablo.

'*I* thought you'd lost me,' said Falcón.

'Are you still with us?'

'I'm tired, I'm shocked that my sister's partner is so deeply involved in this; I've been disturbed by what's happened to Yacoub and, because of these two assassinations, I've lost the possibility of a resolution to my investigation,' said Falcón. 'Maybe you're used to this in your world, but in mine it feels lurid.'

'I told Juan when we first came up with the idea of using you that we were expecting too much,' said Pablo. 'Operating in two worlds, the real and the clandestine, is the quickest way to paranoia.'

'Anyway, I'm out the other side now,' said Falcón. 'I think we should go to El Saucejo.'

'I can't,' said Pablo. 'Juan's just recalled me to Madrid. There's a lot of internet "chatter" and now there's been some movement as well. He can't spare me down here to help you . . .'

'So what are you going to do about Hammad and Saoudi, the other quantity of hexogen, the "hardware" that didn't arrive and the "disruption to a plan which has required a lot of reorganization"?' said Falcón. 'Isn't that what you'd call intelligence? Yacoub has been frightened half to death to get this stuff for you.'

'I don't know what you're expecting to find in El Saucejo,' said Pablo. 'Hammad and Saoudi sitting on some hexogen, helping people pack it into the "hardware" and carrying on with the plan? I don't think so.'

Falcón paced the room, chewing on his thumbnail.

'This hardware . . . that keeps getting referred to. It doesn't sound as if it's easily available, not something you go down to the shops and buy,' said Falcón. 'For some reason it sounds to me as if it's been custom made for a certain task.'

'It could be. Keep having ideas. Keep feeding them to Yacoub and see if he can come back with something relevant. That's all we can do.'

'You said the only thing that would make you sit up and get interested in our investigation was if we found that the Imam, or Hammad and Saoudi, were not in the mosque when it exploded,' said Falcón. 'And now you don't seem to give a damn.'

'Things have moved on. I've been recalled to Madrid. I'm being asked to look at other scenarios.'

'But don't you think it's significant that the original hexogen was brought to Seville, that there's additional hexogen out there, that Hammad and Saoudi are alive and well, and we know that there's an intention to attack?' said Falcón. 'Doesn't all that add up to . . . something?'

'Given the level of security around all major buildings, the announcement made last night of the reinstatement of spot checks and the police presence on

607

the streets, I think it unlikely that they'll launch anything in Seville.'

'That sounds like an official communiqué,' said Falcón.

'It is,' said Pablo. 'The truth is, we have no idea. On Tuesday afternoon they were checking all vehicles going in and out of Seville, by Wednesday evening they were doing spot checks because people were complaining about traffic jams, on Friday they stopped all checks because people were *still* complaining, now they've reinstated them and you'll see what happens. Life goes on, Javier.'

'That sounds as if you're saying that *we* shouldn't worry too much if the population are so unconcerned,' said Falcón. 'But they don't know what we know – that there's more hexogen, that there is an intention to attack, *and* there was a twenty-four-hour break in the spot checks on vehicles.'

'All that information is in Juan's hands, and he's called me back to Madrid because what is going on there is more "significant" than anything that could happen here,' said Pablo.

They went to El Saucejo: Gregorio and Falcón in the front and a bomb squad officer and his dog in the back with Felipe the forensic. In Osuna they were met by the Guardia Civil, who led them up to El Saucejo in their Nissan Patrol. They stopped in the village and picked up two men and continued in the direction of Campillos. The rolling hills around El Saucejo were either given over to endless olive trees or had been ploughed up to reveal dun-coloured earth, with chalk-white patches. The Nissan Patrol stopped outside a ruined house on the right-hand side of the road, which had a view over the shimmering verdigris of the olive trees up to some distant mountains. The entrance and a section of the verge on the opposite side of the road about twenty-five metres down towards El Saucejo had been taped off as a crime scene.

The Guardia Civil introduced the owner of the house and the man who'd spotted Hammad and Saoudi changing the rear tyre early on Monday morning. Felipe started work on the tyre tracks on the side of the road and confirmed that they matched those of the Peugeot Partner in the police compound. He then examined the tyre tracks going into and out of the courtyard to the left of the ruined house.

After half an hour Felipe was able to tell them that the Peugeot Partner had come from the direction of Campillos, which was to the east, entered the court-yard and then exited it sustaining a puncture, which was repaired twenty-five metres down the road.

Inside the courtyard the bomb squad officer released the dog, which ran around for a few minutes before sitting down under some secure roofing near the main house. The officer then made some tests on the dry, beaten earth under the roofing and confirmed that there were traces of hexogen.

The owner of the house said it hadn't been lived in for over thirty years because it was too isolated for most people and there was a problem with water. He'd rented it out to a Spaniard with a Madrileño accent for six months. There was no contract and the man had paid him 600, saying he just wanted to use it occa-sionally for storage. The man who'd spotted Hammad and Saoudi changing the tyre said he drove past the house every day and had never seen anybody using it. He hadn't even seen the Peugeot Partner coming out of the courtyard. It was already on the side of the road, with one of the guys changing the tyre.

'What's important,' said Falcón, 'is: did anybody see a car going into or out of this courtyard at any time since Tuesday morning?'

They shook their heads. Falcón drove back to El Saucejo. They talked to as many people as they could find in the village, but nobody had seen any vehicle using the ruined house. They left the problem with the Guardia Civil.

On the way back to Seville, Gregorio took a call from the CNI communications department, saying that they had reinstalled the old encryption software and the system was now up and running. They had made the Hammad and Saoudi file available to Yacoub, but he had not, as yet, picked it up.

By 2.30 p.m. they were back in the Jefatura, sitting in front of the computer. They saw immediately that Yacoub had now picked up the file. A prearranged signal email was sent to him and he came online.

'The men you know as Hammad and Saoudi are already back in North Africa,' wrote Yacoub. 'They have been here since Thursday morning. I only know this because there was much cheering and clapping when the satellite news announced that it was now known that the two men had not been in the mosque when it exploded.'

'We've found the place where they stored the remaining hexogen but have no idea when it was picked up or where it has gone.'

'It has not been talked about here.'

'The two men who were assassinated earlier today, Lucrecio Arenas and César Benito, were the answer to your initiation test. Their killings were made to look like the work of Islamic militants.'

'A denial has already been issued to Al-Jazeera.'

'Have you heard anything more about the "hardware" that was supposed to be made available for the original consignment of hexogen?'

'It has not been discussed.'

'Since yesterday there has been an increase in internet "chatter" and also some cell movement here in Spain. Can you comment?'

'There's nothing specific. There's a sense of excitement here and there's talk of one or more cells being activated, but it's nothing definite. Nothing I am told by the group who meet here in the house in the medina can be relied on.'

'Can you spend some time thinking about what you saw when you were taken out of Rabat to be given your initiation test? You mentioned the architectural and engineering books and some car manuals.'

'I'll think about it. I have to go now.'

After lunch Falcón arranged for Zarrías to be brought up to the interview room.

'I'm not going to record this,' said Falcón. 'Nothing we say to each other now will be used in a court of law.'

Zarrías said nothing, he just looked at the person who could have been his brother-in-law.

'My Inspector has already told you that Lucrecio Arenas was shot three times in the back,' said Falcón. 'The maid found him face down in the pool. Do you want the people who did that to Lucrecio to get away with it?'

'No,' said Zarrías, 'but I can't help you, Javier, because I don't know who he was involved with.'

'Why was César Benito important to this?' said Falcón. 'Do you think it was something to do with his construction company?'

Zarrías looked troubled, as if this question had brought something into the frame that he hadn't considered before.

'I don't think this was about money, Javier,' said Zarrías.

'On your part,' said Falcón. 'In a discussion between Lucrecio and Jesús yesterday your old friend told him that power in a democracy does not come without a great sense of indebtedness.'

Zarrías's head snapped back, as if he'd just been kicked in the face.

'Maybe you were working at cross purposes, Angel,' said Falcón. 'While you and Jesús were in it to make this world into what you consider to be a better place, Lucrecio and César just wanted pure power and the money that comes with it.'

Silence.

'It happened in the Crusades, why shouldn't it happen now?' said Falcón. 'While some were out there battling for Christendom, others just wanted to kill, pillage and conquer new territory.'

'I cannot believe that of Lucrecio.'

'Maybe I should get Jesús to come down here and he can talk you through *his* disappointment,' said Falcón. 'I didn't see it, but he told me he was going to resign at eleven this morning and resume his career in business. I've never seen a man's idealism so emphatically extinguished.'

Angel Zarrías shook his head in denial.

'Didn't you stop to think, Angel, about the nature of the forces you were joining?' asked Falcón. 'Was there not one moment, after you'd poisoned Tateb Hassani and you knew that Agustín Cárdenas was amputating his hands, burning off his face and scalping him, that you thought: "Are these the extremes to which one must go to achieve goodness in the world?" And if it didn't happen then, what about when you saw the shattered building and the four dead children under their school pinafores? Surely then you must have thought that you had inadvertently teamed yourself with something very dark?'

'If I did,' said Angel quietly, 'it was too late by then.'

The press conference took place at 18.00 in the Andalucían Parliament building. Falcón had prepared a statement on his investigation, which had been incorporated into the official press release, to be delivered by Comisario Elvira. Falcón and Juez del Rey were attending the conference, but only to answer any questions on which Elvira didn't have the specific information. They were told to keep their replies to an absolute minimum.

The conference lasted about an hour and was a subdued affair. Elvira had just reached the point where he was looking to wrap up the event when a journalist at the back stood up.

'A final question for Inspector Jefe Falcón,' he said. 'Are you satisfied with this result?'

A brief silence. A cautionary look from Elvira. A

woman leaned forward in the front row to get a good look at him.

'Experience tells me I might have to be,' said Falcón. 'It is the nature of all murder investigations that, the more time passes, the less chance there is that fresh discoveries will be made. However, I would like to tell the people of Seville that I, personally, am *not* satisfied with this outcome. With each act, terrorism reaches new depths of iniquity. Humanity now has to live in a world where people have been prepared to abuse a population's vulnerability to terrorism in order to gain power. I would have liked to have provided the ultimate resolution to this crime, which would have been to bring everyone, from the planners to the man who planted the device, to justice. We have only been partially successful, but, for me, the battle does not end with this press conference, and I want to assure all Sevillanos that I, and my squad, will do everything in our power to find all the perpetrators, wherever they may be, even if it takes me the rest of my career.'

From the end of the press conference until 10.30 p.m. Falcón was in the Jefatura, catching up on the monumental load of paperwork that had accumulated in the five days of investigation. He went home, took a shower and changed, and was ready for the evening transmission to Yacoub when Gregorio came round at 11 p.m.

Gregorio was nervous and excited.

'It's been confirmed, from several different sources, that three separate cells are on the move. A group left Valencia last night by car, a married couple left from Madrid, in a transit van, early this morning and another group left from Barcelona, some together, some alone, at various times between Friday lunchtime and early this morning. They all seem to be heading for Paris.'

'Let's see what Yacoub makes of it,' said Falcón.

They made contact and exchanged introductions.

'I have no time,' wrote Yacoub. 'I have to leave for Paris on the 11.30 flight and it will take me more than an hour to get to the airport.'

'Any reason?'

'None. They told me to book my usual hotel in the Marais and that I would receive my instructions once I arrived.'

Falcón asked about the three cells activated in Spain since Friday, all heading for Paris.

'I've heard nothing. I have no idea if my trip is connected.'

'What about the "hardware"?'

'Still nothing. Any more questions? I have to leave now.'

Gregorio shook his head.

'When you were taken to the GICM camp for your initiation, you wrote about a wall of books – the car manuals. Have you remembered anything about them? It seems a curious thing to have.'

'They were all four-wheel-drive vehicles. I remember a VW insignia and a Mercedes. The third book was for Range Rover and the last I had to check my memory of the insignia on the internet. It was Porsche. That's it. I will try to make contact from Paris.'

Gregorio got up to leave, as if he'd just wasted his time.

'Any thoughts on that?' asked Falcón.

'I'll talk to Juan and Pablo, see what they think.'

615

Gregorio let himself out. Falcón sat back in his chair. He didn't like this intelligence work. Suddenly everything was moving around him at an alarming pace, with great urgency, but in reaction to electronic nods and winks. He could see how people could go mad in this world, where reality came in the form of "information" from "sources", and agents were told to go to hotels and wait for "instructions". It was all too disembodied for his liking. He never thought he'd hear himself say it, but he preferred his world, where there was a corpse, pathology, forensics, evidence and face-to-face dialogue. It seemed to him that intelligence work demanded the same leap of faith as religious belief and, in that respect, he'd always found himself in a twilight world, where his belief in a form of spirituality couldn't quite extend itself to the recognition of an ultimate being.

The three notebooks he'd filled during the course of the investigation sat on his desk, next to a pile of paperwork he'd brought home with him. He took a sheet of paper from the printer and opened up the first notebook. The date was 5th June, the day he'd been called to view Tateb Hassani's corpse on the rubbish tip outside Seville. He saw that he'd semiconsciously written *El Rocío* next to the date. Perhaps there'd been something on the radio. It was always reported when the Virgen del Rocío had been successfully brought out of the church and paraded on Pentecost Monday. As he doodled out the shape of one of the painted wagons that was so typical of the pilgrimage, he realized how El Rocío had become almost as important an event to tourists as Semana Santa and the Feria. It had always drawn thousands from all over Andalucía, and they

616

had now been joined by hundreds of tourists, looking for another Sevillano experience. His brother, Paco, had even started providing horses and accommodation on his bull-breeding farm for an agency specializing in more luxurious forms of the pilgrimage, with magnificent tents, champagne dinners and flamenco every night. There were luxury versions of everything these days. There was probably a caviar version of the walk to Santiago de Compostela. Decadence had even got into the pilgrimage trade. Below the drawing of the wagon he wrote: *El Rocío. Tourists. Seville.*

More flipping through the random notes and jottings. When he did this he couldn't help but think of artists and writers with their notebooks. He loved it, in the great retrospective of an artist, when the museum showed the notebook sketches, which eventually became the great, and much recognized, painting.

A single line he'd written on the reverse side of a sheet of paper caught his eye: *drain the resources of the West through increased security measures, threaten economic stability by attacking tourist resorts in southern Europe and financial centres in the north: London, Paris, Frankfurt, Milan.* Who had said that? Was it Juan? Or perhaps it was something Yacoub had written?

There was a map of Spain on the wall next to his desk and he crabbed across to it on his chair. Was Seville the obvious place to bring explosives together to launch attacks on the tourist infrastructure of Andalucía? Granada was more central. The Costa del Sol was more accessible from Málaga. Then he remembered the 'hardware'. To create panic in a tourist resort needed nothing more than a pipe bomb packed with nuts, bolts and nails, so why go to the trouble of special hardware and procuring hexogen? Back to the desk. Another note: *hexogen – high brisance = explosive power, shattering effect*. Exactly. Hexogen had been chosen for its power. A small quantity did a lot of damage. And with that thought his mind slipped back to the important buildings of Andalucía: the regional parliament in Seville, the cathedrals in Seville and Cordoba, the Alhambra and Generalife in Granada. Pablo was right, it would be impossible to get a bomb anywhere near those places with the whole region on terrorist alert.

His computer told him it was midnight. He hadn't eaten. He wanted to be out and amongst people. Normally he would have relied on Laura to fill his Saturday night, but that was over now. He'd allowed himself that morbid thought and it led him back to Inés's funeral. Her parents, lost as children, in the sea of people. He snapped out of it and was walking aimlessly from his study to the patio when he remembered Consuelo's call. He hadn't expected her to be so thoughtful. She'd been the only person to call him about Inés. Not even Manuela had done that. He dug out his mobile. Was this a good time? He retrieved her number, punched the call button, let it ring twice and cut it off. It was Saturday night. She'd be in the restaurant, or with her children. Two or three images of their sexual encounters shot through his mind. They'd been so intense and satisfying. He had a rush of physical and chemical desire. He punched the call button again and before it even started ringing he could hear himself trying to smother his desire with inept small talk. He cut the line again. This was all too much for one week: he'd split up with a girlfriend, his ex-wife had been murdered and now he wanted to rekindle a love affair which had burnt out after a matter of days nearly four years ago. Consuelo had called him about Inés as a friend would. It was nothing more than that.

It was warm outside and there was life in the streets. Human beings were resilient creatures. He walked to El Arenal and found the Galician bar, which did wonderful octopus and served wine in white porcelain dishes. As he ate, he saw himself appear on the news, answering that last question put to him by the journalist at the press conference. They showed his answer in its entirety. The waiter recognized him and wouldn't take money for the food and instead sloshed more wine into his white porcelain dish.

Out in the street he was suddenly exhausted. The hours of adrenaline-filled work had caught up. He bought a *pringá* – a spicy, meat-filled roll – and ate it on the way home. He fell into bed and dreamed of Francisco Falcón, back in this house, knocking down a wall to reveal a secret chamber. It woke him in the intense dark of his bedroom, with his heart pounding in his ears. He knew that he would not sleep for at least two hours after that.

Downstairs he flicked through the endless satellite channels, looking for a movie, anything that would quieten down his brain activity. He knew why he was awake: he'd heard himself on the news making that promise to the people of Seville. He still had Hammad and Saoudi on his mind. The hexogen they'd stored in the ruined house outside El Saucejo. The great deal of 'reorganization' that 'the disruption' of the bomb had caused to the GICM's plan.

The TV screen was filled with the face-off between two colossal armies in some recent swords-and-sandals epic. He'd seen it before and it had made no lasting impression on him apart from the designer's vision of what the wooden horse would have looked like if the Greeks had built it, as he supposed they had, out of broken-up triremes. He had to wait for more than an hour for the horse to be given its roll-on part and, as he lay on the sofa, drifting along with the plot, he wondered at the power of myth. How an idea, even one with faulty wiring in the logic, could worm its way into the psyche of the Western world. Why *did* the Trojans drag the damn thing inside their city walls? Why, after all they'd been through, weren't they in the least bit suspicious?

Just as he'd reached the point of wondering whether there would ever be a generation of kids that didn't know about the wooden horse, the beast hove into view on the screen. The sight of it triggered something in his brain and all the random thoughts, notes and jottings of the past five days came together, jolting him off the sofa and into his study.

43

The Hotel Alfonso XIII was, in terms of size, probably Seville's grandest place to stay. It had been built to impress for the 1929 Expo and had a mock *mudejar* interior, with geometric tiles and Arabic arches, around a central patio. It was dark in the reception and the strong scent of the lilies in the huge flower arrangement struck a funereal note.

The manager arrived a few minutes after eight. Falcón had dragged him out of bed. He was shown into the office. The manager glanced at the police ID as if he saw them every day.

'I thought it was a heart attack,' he said. 'We get plenty of those.'

'No, nothing like that,' said Falcón.

'I know you. You're investigating the bomb,' said the manager. 'I saw you on the news. What can I do for you? We haven't got any Moroccan clients here.'

People saw the news, thought Falcón, but they only listened to what they wanted to hear.

'I don't know exactly what I'm looking for. It could be a block-booking for a minimum of four rooms made

621

by some foreign tourists, possibly French, maybe from Paris. The booking would have been made for El Rocío,' said Falcón. 'It could possibly be for more rooms, but the crucial thing is that they would have four-wheel-drive cars, driven down from Northern Europe rather than hired locally.'

The manager spent time at his keyboard, shaking his head as he entered variations on Falcón's data.

'Around the time of El Rocío I've got large tour groups in coaches,' he said. 'But there's nothing in the smaller block-bookings of between four and eight rooms.'

There were roadworks where the metro was being built outside the Hotel Alfonso XIII and Falcón decided that this was not the sort of place they'd stay in. He'd had a look at the Porsche Cayenne on the internet, and he reckoned that the owner of a car like that would be looking for exclusivity. Somehow the Alfonso XIII's grandeur made it passé. It was a conservative person's hotel.

He tried the Hotel Imperial. It was hidden away down a quiet street and overlooked the gardens of the Casa Pilatos. He had no luck there either. His epiphany of last night was beginning to take on the luridness of an early-morning idea that looked absurd in the cold light of day.

The first indication that his creative instincts hadn't gone completely awry was at a boutique hotel where the receptionist remembered a woman from London, calling in March, asking for four rooms before and after El Rocío with parking for four vehicles. The hotel had no parking and only two rooms for the dates she'd wanted. The woman had asked to hold those rooms for twenty-four hours to see if she could find another two elsewhere. The receptionist showed an email from a UK company, which had arrived after the call, from a woman called Mouna Chedadi making the booking on behalf of Amanda Turner. Falcón was certain that he'd found what he was looking for.

He started working his way through a list of local hotels, asking for a booking made by Amanda Turner. Thirty-five minutes later, he was sitting in the manager's office of the Hotel Las Casas de la Judería.

'She was lucky,' he said. 'A group had just cancelled ten minutes before she called and she got her four deluxe suites together.'

'What about their cars?' asked Falcón, giving him Mouna Chedadi's name to make the search through the hotel email database.

'They had four cars,' said the manager. 'And I see here, she was asking if they could leave them in the hotel while they went on the pilgrimage to El Rocío.'

'Did you let them?'

'The garage isn't big enough to hold four cars for people who aren't current clients of the hotel at that time of year. They were told that there were plenty of car parks in Seville where they could leave them.'

'Any idea what they did with their cars?'

The manager called the receptionist and asked her to bring in the hotel registration forms for the four rooms. She confirmed that the eight people had arrived in taxis from wherever they'd parked their cars.

'They stayed here on 31st May,' said the manager, 'and left the following day to go on the pilgrimage.

They came back on 5th June and left again on 8th June.'

'I remember they were going to Granada for a night,' said the receptionist.

'They came back here on 9th June and left . . . have they left yet?'

'They paid their bill last night and left at seven thirty this morning, when the garage opened.'

'So they *did* leave their cars here when they came back from Granada?' said Falcón. 'Do you know the models?'

'Only the registration numbers.'

'What do they give as their professions?'

'Fund managers, all four of them.'

'Did they leave any mobile phone numbers?'

Falcón asked for photocopies of the forms. He went outside and phoned Gregorio, gave him the four UK registration numbers and asked him to find which models they belonged to. Back in the hotel he asked to speak to the bar staff who'd been on duty the night before. He knew what English people were like.

The bar staff remembered the group. They tipped very well, like Americans rather than English people. The men drank beer and the women drank manzanilla, and then gin and tonics. None of the bar staff knew enough English to understand anything of their conversation. They remembered a man who'd had a short exchange with them and then left soon after and there was another couple, some other foreigners, who'd joined them for drinks. They'd all gone out for dinner afterwards.

The other couple were identified as Dutch, and were called down to reception. Falcón worked on identifying

624

the lone man who'd had a brief chat with the group before leaving. The bar staff said he looked Spanish and spoke with a Castellano, rather than Andaluz, accent. The receptionist remembered him and said that he'd paid his bill last night as well. She dug out his registration form. He'd given a Spanish name and ID card. He'd arrived on 6th June and had parked a car in the hotel garage as well. Falcón asked them to scan the ID and registration form, paste it into an email and send it to Gregorio.

The Dutchman appeared looking hungover. They'd had a big night out with the English, who they'd met on the pilgrimage to El Rocío. They hadn't got to bed until two in the morning and yet the English said they were leaving early.

'Did they say where they were going?'

'They just said they were going back to England.'

'What about their route?'

'They were staying in paradors, then going via Biarritz and the Loire to the Channel Tunnel. They all had to be back at work a week tomorrow.'

Falcón paced the patio, willing his mobile to start vibrating. Gregorio called back just before 10 a.m.

'First of all, that Spanish ID card was stolen last year and we haven't got a visual match for his face in any of our files. His car was a Mercedes and was hired in Jerez de la Frontera on Monday, 5th June in the afternoon, and it was returned at 9.15 this morning. I've told them not to touch the car until they hear from us. Are you going to tell me what this is about?'

'What about the car models of UK registrations?'

'They're coming through now,' said Gregorio, reading

them off. 'A VW Touareg, a Porsche Cayenne, a Mercedes M270 and a Range Rover.'

'You remember the car manuals Yacoub saw?'

'Let's meet in your office now. I can get secure phone lines there.'

Forty-five minutes later Falcón was still waiting in his office, making notes as the complications to the scenario multiplied in his mind. Gregorio called from Elvira's office and told him he'd set up a conference call with Juan and Pablo, who were in Madrid.

'The first thing I want to hear is the line of logic in all this,' said Juan. 'Gregorio's talked us through it, but I want to hear it from you, Javier.'

Falcón hesitated, thinking there were more important things to discuss than the workings of his brain.

'This is urgent,' said Juan, 'but we're not in a panic. These people are going to take their time travelling back and it's going to give *us* time to find out what we're up against. I've sent some people from the bomb squad to take a look at the Mercedes in the car-hire company down in Jerez. Let's get the information first and plan our action afterwards. Tell me, Javier.'

Falcón talked him through last night's thought processes, the transmission with Yacoub and the car manuals, the notes he'd looked over about El Rocío, the high brisance of hexogen, the idea of crippling the EU with attacks on tourist resorts and financial centres. Juan was irritable and interrupted frequently. When Falcón happened to mention seeing himself on television, Juan was sarcastic.

'We saw it here, too,' he said. 'Very *nice*, Javier. We don't allow ourselves to get too sentimental in the CNI.'

'People need hope, Juan,' said Pablo.

'They get enough bullshit rammed down their throats by politicians, without having to listen to the police version.'

'Let him talk,' said Gregorio, rolling his eyes at Falcón.

'I went to bed and woke up a few hours later. I watched a movie called *Troy*,' said Falcón, and added a little jibe for Juan. 'You know the story of Troy, Juan, don't you?'

Gregorio shook his hand, as if this was getting hot.

'The Greeks packed a wooden horse full of soldiers, left it outside the gates of Troy and faked a retreat. The Trojans pulled the horse inside and, in doing so, sealed their fate,' said Juan, at speed.

'The first thing that occurred to me was: how in this high-security age could Islamic terrorists get a bomb into a significant building in a major city's financial centre?'

'Ah!' said Pablo. 'You'd get the people who work in the city centre to take it in there for you.'

'And how would you do that?' asked Juan.

'You'd pack someone's car full of high explosive while they were unaware,' said Falcón. 'Tourists going to El Rocío stay in Seville before and after the event. The main celebration of the pilgrimage finished on 5th June. Hammad and Saoudi brought the hexogen to Seville on 6th June with the intention of packing it into "hardware" and fitting it into these people's cars, so that they would drive it back to the UK and into the heart of the City of London.'

'The first, and possibly the most important thing, about this scenario,' said Juan, reasserting his control

627

over the call, 'is that the terrorists have intelligence. The four guys who own these cars all work for the same company: Kraus, Maitland, Powers. They manage one of the City's largest hedge funds, specializing in Japan, China and Southeast Asia. The relevance of that is they are all wealthy men. They all live in big houses outside London, which means that they drive into work every day, and they don't get stuck in traffic because their work day starts at 3 a.m. and finishes at lunchtime. Their cars are guaranteed to be in the building in the heart of the City at rush hour. Their office is in a landmark building known as the Gherkin.'

'Where did you get all that information?' asked Falcón.

'MI5 and MI6 are already involved,' said Juan. 'They are now looking for various candidates who could have given the terrorists their intelligence.'

'What about this woman, Mouna Chedadi – the one who made the bookings for Amanda Turner?' asked Falcón.

'They're looking at her records now. She is not a known terrorist suspect. She lives in Braintree in Essex, just outside London. She's Muslim, but not particularly devout and definitely not radical,' said Juan. 'She's only been working for Amanda Turner's advertising agency since the beginning of March. She would, of course, have known everything about their holiday arrangements.'

'But possibly not very much about Amanda Turner's boyfriend and his colleagues working in the hedge fund,' said Pablo. 'Which means the terrorists probably have two or more sources of intelligence.'

'But we don't know who they are, so we cannot talk to anybody in any of the companies associated with these eight people,' said Juan.

'We've also consulted with the British, and they agree that we cannot talk to the people in the cars either,' said Pablo. 'Only a highly trained soldier would be capable of behaving normally whilst driving a car known to be packed with explosives.'

'Which brings us to the final problem,' said Juan. 'Because the "hardware" has been kept separate at all times from the high explosive and seems to be from different provenance, the British are concerned that the core of the hardware might contain something toxic, like nuclear waste. They are also assuming that the cars will be shepherded back to their destination. This means that the option of getting the people away from the cars is not a viable alternative.'

'You've got a call on line four, Juan,' said Pablo in Madrid.

'Hold on a moment,' said Juan. 'No talking while I'm gone. Wc all need to know everything that's said.'

Gregorio looked for an ashtray but it was a no-smoking office. He went into the corridor. Falcón stared into the carpet. One of the advantages of the clandestine world was that nothing cver achieved reality for these people. Were any of them to actually see Amanda Turner, sitting in the passenger seat of the Porsche Cayenne as it ripped past the Spanish countryside, it might be a different matter. As it was, she'd become an element in the video game.

Juan came back to the conference. Gregorio crushed his cigarette out.

'That was the bomb squad from Jerez de la Frontera,'

said Juan. 'They've found traces of a hexogen plastique mix in the boot of the rented Mercedes. They've also found two air holes drilled through from the boot into the back seat, and evidence of food and drink. It looks as if he drove into the hotel car park with the bombs and one or two technicians in the boot. They were left overnight to install the devices in the British tourists' vehicles.'

'I don't think we need any more confirmation than that,' said Pablo.

'But now we have to find these tourists,' said Juan, 'without creating a national police alert.'

'How long have they been on the move?'

'They left Seville just after 7.30 a.m.,' said Falcón. 'It's now 10.45. The Dutch couple said the British were heading north to spend a few nights in paradors.'

'The slow route would be via Mérida and Salamanca,' said Gregorio. 'The fast route via Cordoba, Valdepeñas and Madrid.'

'We should call the Paradors de España central office and find out where they made their bookings,' said Pablo. 'We can have a bomb squad waiting for them. They can disable the devices overnight and the tourists can continue on their way without knowing a thing.'

'That should give us their route, too,' said Gregorio.

'OK, we'll start with that,' said Juan. 'Any news from Yacoub?'

'Not yet,' said Gregorio.

'Am I needed for this?' asked Falcón.

'There's a military plane waiting for the two of you at Seville airport to bring you to Madrid,' said Juan. 'We'll meet in Barrajas in two hours' time.'

630

'I've still got a lot to do here,' said Falcón.

'I've spoken to Comisario Elvira.'

'Have you put anybody on Yacoub in Paris?' asked Gregorio.

'We've decided against it,' said Juan.

'And what about the three activated cells heading for Paris?' asked Falcón.

'They're looking more like decoys now,' said Pablo. 'The DGSE, French intelligence, have been alerted and they're following their progress.'

They closed down the conference call. Gregorio and Falcón drove straight to the airport.

'I don't understand why you're involving me in this,' said Falcón.

'It's the way Juan works. This was your idea. You follow it through to the end,' said Gregorio. 'He's annoyed that one of us didn't pick up on the piece of information that unlocked the scenario, but he always performs better when he has something to prove.'

'But it was pure luck that I picked up on an inconsequential bit of information.'

'That's what intelligence is all about,' said Gregorio. 'You put someone like Yacoub into a dangerous situation. Nobody has any idea what he's supposed to be looking for. We have a vision of a developing scenario, which he cannot see. He tells us what he can. It's up to us to translate it into something meaningful. You managed to do that. Juan is annoyed because he was left looking at the decoy but, then again, he couldn't afford to ignore it.'

'Are you worried about Yacoub being sent to Paris?' said Falcón. 'If he was part of the diversion, that would mean the GICM know, or at least suspect, he's spying for us.'

'That's why Juan is leaving him alone. He won't even tell the DGSE about him,' said Gregorio. 'If the GICM are looking at him they'll see someone completely clean. That's the beauty of what's happened. *They* put Yacoub into the position where he found the information, even though he didn't know what those car manuals represented. It means he hasn't had to expose himself in any way. When their operation breaks down, they won't be able to point the finger at him. Yacoub is in a perfect position for the next time.'

'Am I being stupid in asking why, if you know so much about the GICM, you don't just take it out?' asked Falcón.

'Because we need to take out the whole network with it,' said Gregorio.

They landed at Barrajas airport in Madrid at 1.15 on a hot afternoon, with the air crinkling above the tarmac. A car met the plane and took them to an office at one end of the terminal building where Juan and Pablo were waiting for them.

'We've had some developments here,' said Juan. 'The Parador central office has records of bookings in Zamora for tonight and Santillana del Mar for tomorrow night. Pablo called both hotels and found that the British cancelled their bookings four hours ago.'

'MI5 are trying to work out why they've changed their plans,' said Pablo. 'It could be a family matter. Two of the women are sisters. Or it could be work. The only problem is that they don't have anybody vetted on the inside of the hedge fund company. There hasn't been any seismic movement in the Far East markets. They're talking to City people now to see if there's talk of a buy-out, or a take-over.'

'Have you found the cars yet?' asked Falcón.

'If they cancelled four hours ago they were already well on their way, so we still have no idea whether they're heading north via Madrid or Salamanca.'

'What about the ferries?' asked Gregorio.

'We've checked both Bilbao/Portsmouth and Santander/Plymouth and they've made no bookings. Their Channel Tunnel booking still stands, with no alteration to the date,' said Pablo. 'That's the Interior Minster's line, Juan.'

Juan took the call, making notes. He slammed down the phone.

'British intelligence have now been in touch with French intelligence,' said Juan. 'Amanda Turner has just changed the Channel Tunnel bookings to Monday afternoon – tomorrow – so it looks as if they're driving to northern France non-stop. Neither the French Ministry of the Interior nor the British Home Office want those cars going through the Channel Tunnel. The French have said that they don't want those cars going through France. Their route north will take them close to nuclear reactors and through densely populated areas. The cars are on Spanish soil. We have areas of low population density. We're going to have to deal with it here. He's given us direct access to special forces.'

'It's about 550 kilometres from Seville to Madrid,' said Gregorio. 'It's 200 kilometres from Seville to Mérida. If they changed their plans four hours ago they could have still switched to the quicker route north, via Madrid.'

'So if they went to Madrid directly they should already be past us, but if they changed their route they should be around Madrid now.'

Pablo called the Guardia Civil and told them to watch the NI/E5 heading north to Burgos and the NII/E90 heading northeast to Zaragoza, emphasizing that they only wanted a report on the cars; there was to be no pursuit and definitely no general alert.

Juan and Gregorio went to the map of Spain and studied the two possible routes. Pablo contacted special forces and asked them to have two cars ready, a driver and two armed men in each unmarked vehicle.

At 14.00 the Guardia Civil called back with a sighting of the convoy on the Madrid/Zaragoza road, just outside Guadalajara. Pablo asked them to put motorbike police in all the service stations along the route and to report if the convoy left the road. He went back to special forces, gave them the route information and told them to watch out for the convoy's shepherd. Their two cars left Madrid at 14.05.

At 14.25 the Guardia Civil called to say the convoy had left the road at a service station at Kilometre 103. They had also noticed a silver VW Golf GTI, whose registration number had shown it to be a hire car from Seville, which had come off at the same time as the convoy. Two men had got out. Neither of them had gone into the service station. They were both leaning on the back of the Golf, one of them was making a phone call on a mobile.

While Pablo relayed that information to the special forces vehicles, Gregorio called the car-hire company in Seville. It was closed. Falcón called Ramírez and told him to get it open as soon as possible. Juan ordered a helicopter to be ready for immediate take-off. He gave the Interior Minister an update on the situation and told him that at some point they would have to close the mobile phone network down for an hour on the Madrid/Zaragoza road between Calatayud and Zaragoza.

'Special forces are going to have to take out the shepherd vehicle over one of the mountain passes,' he said. 'That way, if they're using mobile phone technology to detonate the devices, the network will be down and if they're using a direct signal there's less chance of a good connection.'

At 15.00 Ramírez called back from the car-hire company. Gregorio gave the registration number of the silver Golf GTI. The car-hire company gave them the ID card of the driver. Gregorio checked it on the computer. Stolen last week in Granada.

The helicopter tilted and rose up into the cloudless sky above Barrajas airport. Falcón hadn't wanted the privileged seat next to the pilot. It had been ten years since he'd been in a helicopter. He felt exposed to the elements and had an unnerving sensation of lightness of being.

They tracked the NII/E90 autopista from Madrid to Zaragoza and in less than an hour they were up above the mountains around Calatayud.

'We don't often get to see this,' said Juan, over the headphones. 'The denouement of an intelligence operation, I mean.'

Even now, as they raced towards the culmination

of months of work and days of intensity, it hardly felt real. Spain tore past under his feet and men somewhere below made their final preparations as the convoy of four-wheel-drive vehicles, full of real, live people, sped north unknowing and unconcerned at this vast and complicated mechanism moving into action behind them.

The pilot gave him binoculars and pointed down at the section of road where he watched as a silver Golf GTI was overtaken by a dark blue BMW. The BMW braked so sharply that puffs of smoke came out of the wheel arches. The Golf GTI slammed into the back of it, but the soldiers were out, their guns ready, arms jerking with the recoil. The helicopter swooped down on the scene. Two men were being dragged from the car; its windscreen was shattered, the front crumpled, steam pouring out from under the bonnet.

The helicopter hopped over to the other side of the mountain pass where the tourists' convoy had been pulled over on to the hard shoulder by other armed special forces travelling in a forward car. The helicopter turned and hovered as the four couples got out and ran away from their cars.

To see it all played out with no sound – or rather, too much sound from the thumping blades thrashing the air – added to the unreality. Falcón felt faint at the thought that this final operation had all happened as a result of his hunch. What if reality yielded no bombs in the vehicles and a Golf GTI with two injured innocent men? He must have been looking bewildered and lost, because Juan's voice came on in his head.

'We quite often think that,' he said. 'Did this really happen?'

The helicopter banked away from the distant city of Zaragoza, which bristled under the heat and a stagnant smog. The pilot muttered his position and direction as the brown, hard-baked mountains settled back into the late afternoon.

CODA

Falcón was sitting in the restaurant at the back of the bar in Casa Ricardo. It was almost four years to the day that he'd last been in this place and it had been no accident. He took a sip of his beer and ate an olive. He was just cooling off after the walk in the atrocious heat from his house.

There had been no time for anything in the last month. The paperwork had achieved surreal dimensions, from which he broke away to re-enter a world he'd expected to find changed. But the bomb had been like an epileptic fit. The city had suffered a terrible convulsion and there had been much concern for its future health, but as the days passed and there were no further outbreaks, life reverted to normal. It left a lesion. There were families with an unfillable space at the table. And others, who regularly summoned their courage to face another day at waist height to people they'd always looked in the eye. There were the forgotten hundreds who looked in the mirror every morning to shave around a scar, or smooth foundation on to a new blemish. But the one force greater than

638

the terrorist's power to disrupt was humanity's need to get back into a routine.

The debrief on the intelligence operation had lasted four days. Falcón had been relieved when four explosive devices had been found in the British four-wheel-drive vehicles. Each device was a small marvel of engineering, as each bomb's aluminium casing had been built to fit in the car as if it was an integral piece of the structure. Falcón couldn't help but think that the bombs were like terrorism itself, fitting so perfectly into society, its sinister element indistinguishable. His relief had been that they existed. They weren't a figment of his, or the intelligence world's, imagination. And there had been no 'dirty' element in the core as the British had feared.

Since returning from Madrid, Falcón had been working with Juez del Rey to bring the case against Rivero, Cárdenas and Zarrías to court although, since Rivero had suffered a stroke and been left unable to speak, it was really against the last two. The case was being prepared in another surreal dimension. Del Rey had decided to prosecute the two men for the murder of Tateb Hassani first because he wanted to proceed step by step towards proving their involvement in the greater conspiracy. What the public knew about Hassani was that he had written the horrific instructions attached to the plans of the schools and biology faculty. Somehow, through a collective blindness, these instructions had been separated from the fiction that the conspiracy had attempted to establish. The result was that large sections of the public thought of Cárdenas and Zarrías as folk heroes.

Yacoub had made contact on his return from Paris.

The GICM high command had given him no instructions. He thought that they suspected him and had therefore made no attempt to contact the CNI. He had wandered about in public places, afraid to stay in his hotel room in case there was a knock he couldn't bear to answer. He returned to Rabat. He attended the group's meetings in the house in the medina. There was no mention of the failed mission.

Calderón's case was due to be tried in September. Inspector Jefe Luis Zorrita and the instructing judge, Juan Romero, were convinced of his guilt. Their case was rock-solid. Falcón had not seen Calderón again, but had heard that he was resigned to his fate, which was to spend fifteen years in prison for the murder of his wife.

Manuela had been a worry to Falcón. He'd thought that the vacancy left by Angel's removal would leave her lonely and depressed, but he'd underestimated her. Once the horror, rage and despair at his crime had burnt out, she found a renewed vitality. All those lessons on positive energy from Angel had paid off. She did not sell the villa in Puerto de Santa María; the German buyer came back to her and she found a Swede to take the other Seville property. She also didn't lack for dinner invitations. People wanted to know everything about her life with Angel Zarrías.

There had been other positive developments in the aftermath to the bomb. Last Sunday, while sitting on a park bench in the shade of some trees in the Parque María Luisa, Falcón had found his eye drawn to a family group. The man was pushing a wheelchair occupied by a young girl and he was talking to a small blonde woman in a turquoise top and white skirt. Only when two kids sprinted up to join them did Falcón recognize that the children belonged to Cristina Ferrera, who put her arm around her son while her daughter reached over and helped the man push the wheelchair. It was only then that he realized that he was looking at Fernando Alanis.

Falcón had arrived too early in the Casa Ricardo. He finished his beer and asked the passing waiter to bring him a chilled manzanilla. The waiter came back with a bottle of La Guita and the menu. The dry sherry misted the glass as it trickled in. He fanned himself with the menu. He was on a different table to the one he'd been at four years ago. This one gave him the perfect view of the door, which drew his attention every time someone came in. He couldn't bear the teenage anxiety creeping up on him. At times like this his mind would gang up on him and he'd find himself thinking about the other thing that made him anxious: that promise he'd made to the people of Seville to find the ultimate perpetrators of the bombing. The sight of himself on the television in the Galician bar came back to him again and again, along with Juan's sarcastic comment. Had that been a crazy thing to do or, as Juan had said, just senti-mental? No, it hadn't been, he was sure of it. He had his ideas. He knew, when he had more time, where he was going to start looking.

It's always the way that, just as your mind engages elsewhere, the person you've been waiting for all this time arrives. She was over him before he knew it.

'The pensive Inspector Jefe,' she said.

His heart leapt in his chest, so that he sprang to his feet.

'As usual,' he said, 'you're looking beautiful, Consuelo.'

A Small Death in Lisbon

Robert Wilson

A Portuguese bank is founded on the back of Nazi wartime deals. Over half a century later a young girl is murdered in Lisbon.

1941. Klaus Felsen, SS officer, arrives in Lisbon and the strangest party in history, where Nazis and Allies, refugees and entrepreneurs, dance to the strains of opportunism and despair. Felsen's war takes him to the mountains of the north where a brutal battle is being fought for an element vital to Hitler's blitzkrieg. There he meets the man who makes the first turn of the wheel of greed and revenge which rolls through to the century's end.

Late 1990s, Lisbon. Inspector Zé Coelho is investigating the murder of a young girl. As he digs deeper, Zé overturns the dark soil of history and unearths old bones. The 1974 revolution has left injustices of the old fascist regime unresolved. But there's an older, greater injustice, for which this small death in Lisbon is horrific compensation, and in his final push for the truth, Zé must face the most chilling opposition.

'Compulsively readable, with the cop's quest burning its way through a narrative rich in history and intrigue, love and death'   *Literary Review*

ISBN: 978 0 00 732215 2

Printed by RR Donnelley at Glasgow, UK